The MX Book of New Sherlock Holmes Stories

Part XIX – 2020 Annual (1882-1890)

THE MX BOOK OF NEW
SHERLOCK HOLMES
STORIES
PART XIX
2020 ANNUAL
(1882-1890)
SOUTHAMPTON
STREET
359
EDITED
By
David
Marcum
OFFICES
TRADITIONAL HOLMES
ADVENTURES
COMPILED FOR THE
BENEFIT OF THE
RESTORATION OF
UNDERSHAW

First edition published in 2020

ISBN Hardback 978-1-78705-561-2
ISBN Paperback 978-1-78705-562-9
AUK ePub ISBN 978-1-78705-563-6
AUK PDF ISBN 978-1-78705-564-3

Published in the UK by
MX Publishing
335 Princess Park Manor, Royal Drive,
London, N11 3GX
www.mxpublishing.co.uk

David Marcum can be reached at:
thepapersofsherlockholmes@gmail.com

Cover design by Brian Belanger
www.belangerbooks.com and *www.redbubble.com/people/zhahadun*

CONTENTS

Forewords

Adventures

(Continued on the next page . . . .)

(Continued on the next page . . . .)

These additional adventures are contained in

Part XX: 2020 Annual (1891-1897)

The Sibling (*A Poem*) – Jacquelynn Morris
Blood and Gunpowder – Thomas A. Burns, Jr.
The Atelier of Death – Harry DeMaio
The Adventure of the Beauty Trap – Tracy Revels
A Case of Unfinished Business – Steven Philip Jones
The Case of the *S.S. Bokhara* – Mark Mower
The Adventure of the American Opera Singer – Deanna Baran
The Keadby Cross – David Marcum
The Adventure at Dead Man's Hole – Stephen Herczeg
The Elusive Mr. Chester – Arthur Hall
The Adventure of Old Black Duffel – Will Murray
The Blood-Spattered Bridge – Gayle Lange Puhl
The Tomorrow Man – S.F. Bennett
The Sweet Science of Bruising – Kevin P. Thornton
The Mystery of Sherlock Holmes – Christopher Todd
The Elusive Mr. Phillimore – Matthew J. Elliott
The Murders in the Maharajah's Railway Carriage – Charles Veley and Anna Elliott
The Ransomed Miracle – I.A. Watson
The Adventure of the Unkind Turn – Robert Perret
The Perplexing *X*'ing – Sonia Fetherston
The Case of the Short-Sighted Clown – Susan Knight

These additional adventures are contained in

Part XXI: 2020 Annual (1898-1923)

The Case of the Missing Rhyme (*A Poem*) – Joseph W. Svec III
The Problem of the St. Francis Parish Robbery – R.K. Radek
The Adventure of the Grand Vizier – Arthur Hall
The Mummy's Curse – DJ Tyrer
The Fractured Freemason of Fitzrovia – David L. Leal
The Bleeding Heart – Paula Hammond

(Continued on the next page . . . .)

These additional Sherlock Holmes adventures can be found in the previous volumes of

The MX Book of New Sherlock Holmes Stories

(Continued on the next page . . . .)

PART III: 1896-1929

PART IV – 2016 Annual

(Continued on the next page . . . .)

PART V – Christmas Adventures

(Continued on the next page . . . .)

PART VI – 2017 Annual

(Continued on the next page . . . .)

(Continued on the next page . . . .)

Part IX – 2018 Annual (1879-1895)

(Continued on the next page . . . .)

Part X – 2018 Annual (1896-1916)

Part XI: Some Untold Cases (1880-1891)

(Continued on the next page . . . .)

Part XII: Some Untold Cases (1894-1902)

PART XIII: 2019 Annual (1881-1890)

(Continued on the next page . . . .)

(Continued on the next page . . . .)

PART XV: 2019 Annual (1898-1917)

Part XVI – (1881-1890)

(Continued on the next page . . . .)

Part XVII – (1891-1898)

Part XVIII – (1899-1925)

(Continued on the next page . . . .)

The Tollington Ghost – Roger Silverwood
You Only Live Thrice – Robert Stapleton
The Adventure of the Fair Lad – Craig Janacek
The Adventure of the Voodoo Curse – Gareth Tilley
The Cassandra of Providence Place – Paul Hiscock
The Adventure of the House Abandoned – Arthur Hall
The Winterbourne Phantom – M.J. Elliott
The Murderous Mercedes – Harry DeMaio
The Solitary Violinist – Tom Turley
The Cunning Man – Kelvin I. Jones
The Adventure of Khamaat's Curse – Tracy J. Revels
The Adventure of the Weeping Mary – Matthew White
The Unnerved Estate Agent – David Marcum
Death in The House of the Black Madonna – Nick Cardillo
The Case of the Ivy-Covered Tomb – S.F. Bennett

The following contributions appear in this volume:
The MX Book of New Sherlock Holmes Stories
Part XIX – 2020 Annual (1882-1890)

The following contributions appear in the companion volumes:
The MX Book of New Sherlock Holmes Stories
Part XX – 2020 Annual (1891-1897)
Part XXI – 2020 Annual (1898-1923

Editor's Foreword
Not Just "Always 1895" – A Hero for *Now*
by David Marcum

In late 1887, Dr. John H. Watson finally accomplished what he'd been promising to do for years – to publish an account of the first case that he'd shared with Mr. Sherlock Holmes.

It had occurred back in early March 1881, when Watson had known Holmes for about nine weeks. They had first met a couple of months before that, in the laboratory of Barts Hospital on New Year's Day, a Saturday, after being introduced by a mutual acquaintance – simply because both had mentioned in this friend's hearing that they were in need of someone to split the cost of affordable lodgings.

The following day they examined the rooms at 221 Baker Street and, finding them acceptable, Watson moved his own possessions around that very night, with Holmes doing the same the next morning.

Watson's physical assets were limited. He'd only recently returned from Afghanistan, where he'd received a grievous and nearly fatal wound while serving at the Battle of Maiwand, only to further face the trials of enteric fever during his subsequent recovery. He states that after he and Holmes agreed to share the lodgings at 221b Baker Street, he was able to move his possessions from his hotel in a single night. Holmes's were a bit more extensive, consisting of several boxes and portmanteaus. No doubt these included materials for his scientific research, records of past cases, and his extensive commonplace books.

From early January to early March 1881, the two settled into a tolerable existence, mostly as adjacent strangers. Holmes turned twenty-seven a few days after they moved to Baker Street, and Watson was then around six months past his twenty-eighth birthday. However, in spite of this similarity in ages, they were vastly different individuals. Holmes, always brilliant, had been earning his bread and cheese as a consulting detective for a number of years, living in Montague Street by the British Museum while pursuing various studies to broaden and deepen his professional experience. Watson had trained as a doctor, and after receiving his degree in 1878, had eventually ended up in military service in India and Afghanistan, leading to his injuries and severance from the British Army.

In Baker Street, they each carried out their separate lives while trying not to bother the other. Watson was simply concerned with recovery, having neither the energy nor the inclination to do much more than stay around their rooms and wonder what his new flatmate was up to.

For Mr. Sherlock Holmes was something of a mystery to him. Watson, with nothing better to do, nowhere to go, and no other friends, began to try and learn more about this mysterious person. He wasn't very successful. In those early days, Holmes kept regular habits – early to bed, and gone before Watson rose in the morning. Holmes's trips away from Baker Street involved long walks through London, or to Barts. Some days he was energetic, and others found him lethargic, barely moving or speaking – just as he'd warned would happen when he and Watson first met and described themselves to one another.

Watson once made a list of Holmes's skills and limits, but after realizing that it wasn't really telling him anything, he threw it in frustration into the fire. He wanted to know more about this unusual person who seemed to be educating himself toward some specific but unknown goal, and who was visited by so many interesting people – for it wasn't long after they started sharing rooms that a curious collection of individuals began dropping by to consult with Holmes – although about what Watson didn't have a clue.

There was a young fashionably dressed girl, and an excited and grey-headed seedy visitor. And a slip-shod elderly woman. And an old white-haired gentleman and a railway porter. As Watson recalled, one of the visitors who came three or four times in a single week was a "*little sallow rat-faced, dark-eyed fellow*", introduced simply as "*Mr. Lestrade*". And every time that one of these callers arrived, Holmes would politely ask that Watson withdraw to his own bedroom so that he could use the sitting room as his "*place of business*" to see his "*clients*". And Watson would climb the stairs for a while to his room – which was probably good therapeutic exercise for him – and then return a little while later, never quite willing to simply ask Holmes just what his business actually was.

This changed on March 4th, 1881, when the two flatmates had a discussion about a magazine article, written by Holmes, regarding observation and deduction. Watson was inclined to dismiss it as "*ineffable twaddle*" . . . although it was true that Holmes had demonstrated his skills at their first meeting when he'd stated that Watson had been in Afghanistan – an action that puzzled the doctor greatly.

That morning, Holmes had revealed to Watson that he was something called a "*consulting detective*", so now Watson knew what and why Holmes did what he did – but he didn't really know anything at all. Not yet. Who can say what would have happened if this conversation had simply ended then and the two of them had gone about their normal daily business?

We are told that in a quantum universe, *all* possibilities exist. Schrödinger's cat is alive *and* dead. Every choice isn't an either/or proposition – rather, *both* happen . . . somehow. Somewhere there's a world where Holmes received a message from the police that morning of March 4th, 1881, in the midst of that conversation with Watson, and then he retrieved his hat and coat, departing to examine a murdered body on his own, while the invalid physician remained in the Baker Street sitting room, purposeless as he had been for the previous two months. Life in that universe continued along the same lines, with Holmes going out on his typical errands, and continuing to meet clients who came to obtain his armchair advice, while Watson continued to politely retreat upstairs. In a few months, Watson probably tired of this and sought another residence, while Holmes was likely making enough money from his consulting practice to no longer need anyone else to share expenses. After moving out, Watson might have continued to get better, or he might have slid into a life of profligacy and drunkenness. Holmes would certainly have continued to develop his skills, and to those that knew of him, he would have provided a great deal of help. But without anyone to make him known to a wider world, a lot less people would have known of him.

But in *our* universe, in the midst of their conversation about deduction and being a consulting detective, Holmes received the message from the police regarding a murder across the Thames in Lambeth, and instead of simply leaving, he curiously invited Watson to join him. Luckily we live in *that* universe where Holmes said, "*Get your hat.*"

"*You wish me to come?*" asked a surprised Watson.

"*Yes, if you have nothing better to do.*"

And so, after having been acquainted with Sherlock Holmes for sixty-three days, Watson finally actually *met* Sherlock Holmes – the *true* Holmes, and not just the random bits and pieces that he'd seen and tried to list over the previous couple of months – with just enough data jotted on a sheet to indicate that all the important questions were still unanswered. Finally, after seeing Holmes in action, Watson began to understand the *true* Holmes for the first time.

Of course this initial investigation was a success, and at the end Watson learned another thing – Holmes did this work for the sake of *the game*, and not for the public glory. Watson was amazed to see that the public records of the case gave credit for Holmes's work to the official force. Holmes didn't seem to care, but Watson felt otherwise. "*Your merits should be publicly recognized!*" he cried. "*You should publish an account of the case. If you won't, I will for you.*"

"*You may do what you like, Doctor,*" Holmes replied. One wonders if he knew what he'd actually allowed with that one simple statement, for Watson – doctor and stalwart friend – was also an incipient writer. He faithfully recorded the facts of this case, and so many others that followed.

"*I have all the facts in my journal,*" he told Holmes, "*and the public shall know them.*"

Which brings us back to late 1887, when Watson, with the assistance of a literary agent, Dr. (and later Sir) Arthur Conan Doyle, finally published his version of that first investigation, initially relating his own personal history prior to January 1st, 1881 (in less than four-hundred words), and then telling of his meeting with Holmes, the empty days of January and February 1881, and finally the events connected with the murder in that empty house in the Brixton Road. But between early 1881 and late 1887, when *A Study in Scarlet* (as Watson's narrative was titled) was published, Holmes was involved in hundreds – nay *thousands* – of other investigations, many of which were shared with Watson. The good doctor kept notes about these, as well as additionally recording what he could learn concerning other adventures that took place without him, and also those that had occurred before he and Holmes were introduced. And thank heavens that he did make notes about these, and then find time to write them up, because one way or another, they've been finding their way into print by various paths ever since for those of us who want to know what else Mr. Holmes did besides what we're told those wonderful and yet pitifully few sixty stories that make up the official Holmesian Canon.

Initially there was a contemporary immediacy about the Holmes tales. When Watson first published *A Study in Scarlet*, he was narrating circumstances that had occurred less than seven years earlier. His next published volume, *The Sign of the Four*, appeared in early 1890, approximately seventeen months after that case took place. In June 1891, less than two months after Holmes was presumed to have perished at the Reichenbach Falls, further revelations of Holmes's adventures began appearing in *The Strand Magazine*, itself having been in business only since January of that year. Again, these records of Holmes's investigations were relatively immediate. "The Red-Headed League", published in August 1891, begins with Watson explaining that "*I had called upon my friend, Mr. Sherlock Holmes, one day in the autumn of last year . . .*" Further internal evidence places this narrative in October 1890 – less than one year before Watson's version of what happened appeared in print.

Imagine the thrill of Londoners reading these stories and finding out the complete facts in relation to what they may have already known, but without comprehending the full truth. For instance, "The Speckled Band" was published in February 1892 – not quite ten years after the business that it related. Certainly many who lived in the area of Stoke Moran still recalled the mysterious death of Dr. Grimesby Roylott in April 1883, but here was where many of them discovered for the first time – by way of Watson – what *really* happened on that terrifying night.

From the beginning, Watson's motive for recording the facts related to Holmes's investigations was to tell the public of this heroic figure. Of course, Holmes wasn't one-dimensional – he had faults, and uncertainty, and failures. But without a doubt he was a *hero*, which is certainly one of the most important reasons that he is still so well-known today, in the 2020's, decades after his death. And yet we are a great distance now from when Watson was writing of contemporary investigations for people who were aware of them as "current events". As of this writing, the investigation that made up *A Study in Scarlet* took place over 139 years ago.

When certain noted and legendary Sherlockians such as Christopher Morley and Vincent Starrett began assisting in the care and protection and promotion of Holmes's legacy and reputation in the 1920's and 1930's, Holmes and Watson were still with us, and Watson was still, with the assistance that same literary agent, publishing new accounts of Holmes's cases – right up until 1927, although they were no longer contemporary by that point. The last time that Watson released a narrative close to when the action actually occurred was when "His Last Bow" appeared in October 1917, telling what Holmes and Watson had done at the beginning of The Great War in early August 1914. After that, between 1921 and 1927, he wrote and published a further twelve Canonical cases (later collected in *The Casebook of Sherlock Holmes*) that occurred between 1896 and 1907, with most of them grouped around the turn of the century. And from the first published Canonical effort in 1887, *A Study in Scarlet*, to the last in 1927, "The Adventure of Shoscombe Olde Place", Holmes was presented as the hero that he truly was.

Too often of late, it has become fashionable to try and redefine Holmes as someone broken – from small instances to having him be a full-on sociopathic murderer. No doubt this is due to the need of some individuals to tear down heroes rather than admire them – For how can they who are not heroic themselves ever make a connection with someone that is? Better to replace the hero with someone damaged and with whom they can identify than have someone provide an example. With these motivations, some have tried to drag Holmes a long way from the hero that we first met in the publications of the late 1800's. And this is a mistake.

This can be blamed to a certain degree on the nature of the world in which we now live. Lately I've been seeing Vincent Starrett's poem *221b* referenced by Sherlockians quite a bit more than I usually do – often with a whiff of desperation. It's very familiar to those in the Sherlockian community, as it's often recited at the close of various Holmes-related gatherings as something of a benediction before returning to the responsibilities of daily modern life. Perhaps, with its nod toward times past, it provides a comfort as the world seems to be moving in an increasingly speedy express line in the proverbial hell-bound basket.

For those who don't know Vincent Starrett's well-known work:

221b

Here dwell together still two men of note
Who never lived and so can never die:
How very near they seem, yet how remote
That age before the world went all awry.
But still the game's afoot for those with ears
Attuned to catch the distant view-halloo:
England is England yet, for all our fears –
Only those things the heart believes are true.

A yellow fog swirls past the window-pane
As night descends upon this fabled street:
A lonely hansom splashes through the rain,
The ghostly gas lamps fail at twenty feet.
Here, though the world explode, these two survive,
And it is always eighteen ninety-five.

The concluding line – *And it is always eighteen ninety-five* – is often referenced amongst Sherlockians as if there is something particularly special about *that* year. As I've written elsewhere, (in the editor's foreword to Parts XI and XII of *The MX Book of New Sherlock Holmes Stories,*)1895 is definitely of Holmesian interest, as it's a year that falls squarely during those years that Holmes was in practice in Baker Street – but it certainly wasn't his busiest or most famous year. Canonical cases that occurred then – although agreement amongst Holmesian Chronologicists is by its very nature an impossibility – include "Wisteria Lodge", "The Three Students", "The Solitary Cyclist", "Black Peter", and "The Bruce-Partington Plans". But 1894 was a year that Watson specifically mentioned (in "The Golden

Pince-Nez") when discussing just how busy Holmes had been then, with three massive manuscript volumes required to contain both his and Holmes's work. And if one is looking for those cases that are often more remembered as reader's favorites, then one must examine the 1880's for all of those beloved tales recorded in *The Adventures* and *The Memoirs*. (For example, the highly revered "The Speckled Band" took place way back in 1883, when Holmes was only twenty-nine years old.) All four of the longer published Canonical works, *A Study in Scarlet*, *The Sign of the Four*, *The Valley of Fear*, and perhaps the most famous, *The Hound of the Baskervilles*, occur chronologically a number of years before 1895 – the first in 1881, and the other three in 1888.

And yet, 1895 is still the representative year most mentioned by Sherlockians – where "*it is always eighteen ninety-five*" . . . .

Vincent Starrett wrote these lines in 1942. While I cannot place myself in his mind, I can – as the holder of a Liberal Arts degree that involved numerous hours in English and Literature classes, teasing out various (and often ridiculous) themes and interpretations and speculations from honored literary works, and then going one step beyond to manufacture extensive entangling constructs from the vaguest of gossamer threads of guesswork and pretentious projection simply to impress teachers who became weak and giddy from being fed that kind of thing – be tempted to speculate that Starrett was looking around at the complicated and dark world of 1942 and wishing for the "simpler" times of 1895. Starrett himself was nine years old in 1895, so looking back, it probably represented a period that seemed less complex, less dangerous, and less depressing than what he was reading about in the 1942 newspapers. (And it didn't hurt that, as a poet, he'd found a year that rhymed with "*survive*".)

In 1942, Starrett was fifty-six – just a year or so older than I am right now as I compose this essay. While our experiences were completely different – he was a Canadian born in the late 1800's who moved to Chicago as a small child, where he spent the rest of his life as a newspaper man, while I was born in the 1960's in the southern United States, where I still live and have ended up as a civil engineer – I can't help but think that there is some commonality among people of any historical period who reach a certain age and obtain any kind of earned wisdom. Thus, looking around now at the madness in today's world, I sense something of what Starrett felt when he expressed a wish for past days of the better and more innocent variety.

In 1942, Starrett must have thought that the world was falling apart. The Great Depression had started in 1929, and had continued throughout the 1930's – some say right up to the beginning of the World War in 1939, the event which forced the world economy to re-tool and get back to work for such a terrible reason. The war itself began in Europe in the fall of 1939 after a crazed period involving the unimaginable rise of vicious and evil nationalism across the world. While the war's initial spark might have started anywhere, in fact it was due to the actions of a diabolical madman, a seemingly unstoppable juggernaut of evil who had seized dictatorial power, inch by inch, in plain sight, and with the enthusiastic consent of both the ignorant cheering masses influenced by the dictator-controlled press and a group of equally evil, self-serving, and corrupt people within his own government who thought that they could control him, only to find that he was carrying out the Devil's own work with their assistance. How could such a thing happen?

1942 was the first full year that the United States had officially been involved in World War II, although support had been given to England and other allies for quite a while before then. The start of 1942 was just a few weeks after the events of Pearl Harbor, when America was suddenly in a race to bring its industrial machine to a war footing, and all over the country patriots rushed to volunteer for whatever service that they could provide. And sometime during this same year, as all around him America went to war, Starrett was prompted to write his famed poem, which is still referenced and recited at Sherlockian meetings across the U.S. – now seemingly more than ever.

But was 1895, particularly in Victorian England, really worthy of such idealization? Obviously not. 1895 was just seven years after the Ripper Murders, which had thrown London into a frenzy of panic while exposing the vast and disgusting gulf between haves and have-nots. It has been pointed out that The City in the center of London, which was probably the wealthiest place on the planet, was literally next door to the most vile and diseased part of London, where the Ripper rampaged amongst the poorest and most pathetic who existed in unimaginable conditions.

By 1895, England was still incredibly polarized in terms of politics and division of wealth. There was no diminishment of the fear of foreigners, and intolerance within the country took many other forms as well, as evidenced by the trial and imprisonment that year of Oscar Wilde. Additionally, the British were certainly aware of equally unpleasant conditions across the Channel, such as the ongoing miscarriage of justice against Alfred Dreyfus.

But as Starrett rightfully pointed out, there were two men of note living at 221b Baker Street during that time: One a detective, the other a doctor. Both were men of their times, but also enlightened and committed to seeking justice – which wasn't always defined by the actual law. As

Holmes remarked to Watson during a notable trip that they took to the Continent in late April and early May 1891:

> *I think that I may go so far as to say, Watson, that I have not lived wholly in vain. If my record were closed tonight I could still survey it with equanimity. The air of London is the sweeter for my presence. In over a thousand cases I am not aware that I have ever used my powers upon the wrong side.*

There are many casual Sherlockians who try to pigeon-hole Holmes and Watson into a specific era, while forgetting that they lived lives encompassing multiple decades. Both were born in the 1850's and lived well into the Twentieth Century. They saw the best and worst of those times – the continuing rise of industrialization and the various quality-of-life improvements that such could provide (for some), the increasing influence of Britain and its Empire upon the rest of the world, and advances in science with their theoretical benefits for mankind. But each of these had their substantial drawbacks, such as population displacement and the increased divisions between wealth and labor caused by new more efficient manufacturing methods, and the inevitable evils of greedy colonialism that went hand-in-hand with empire-building, and the losses of feeling toward humanity as cold science sometimes became the be-all and end-all goal of those in responsible positions.

Is it any wonder, then, that knowing Holmes and Watson were working on the side of *right* in 1895 – and for several decades on either side of that as well – that Vincent Starrett looked back from 1942 and a world at war and wished for what seemed to be a simpler time? And is it any wonder that we do the same now from our own snarled and grim days? For Watson wanted to let us know about a *hero* when he first published in the 1880's, and Vincent Starrett needed to *remind us* of that hero in the dark days of World War II. It's no mystery that, in today's inundation of daily spiraling disasters, we need to know about him too.

We live in an age of immediately available and constant information, which is forcing us to evolve as a species – whether we want to or not. I recently heard of a study that showed that the use of electronic maps through various online sources actually causes a part of the brain that affects one's sense of direction to atrophy – Why bother to try and keep track of where you are, or how to get from here to there, if you can simply look it up on your phone? Likewise, we don't have to memorize things anymore – We can simply look up a state capitol or a recipe. It's sad that human beings, who developed *reading* as a way to store information outside of our heads, have now reached the point where we store so much information that way (because there *is* so much information) that if we had to, it might be impossible to go back to the way things used to be.

While we used to have time to process information, we now have immediate news (as well as immediate opinions from countless scads of yapping heads to interpret it for us), and we can binge every episode of a television show, one episode after another, without ever going away and thinking about each separate piece and examining it this way and that to ponder and appreciate the development or the inherent puzzles. In the midst of this, our current world, there are people – some, but not all – that yearn for the simpler times. Maybe not 1895, but certainly a step back from the madness of today. And this can be found in the adventures of Mr. Sherlock Holmes.

Some are happy with the original sixty tales of The Canon. Others want more. I fall squarely in the latter camp. And while I complain about the crazed frenzy of the modern world, I can't argue that today's technology has allowed for more of Watson's narratives to be newly discovered than ever before.

When Watson first started publishing, *A Study in Scarlet* and *The Sign of the Four* appeared without much fanfare. It was only in mid-1891, when his efforts were placed in *The Strand*, that excitement spread. Over the next four decades, Holmes's adventures appeared at a very irregular rate. There were two-dozen in the initial *Strand* run from 1891 to 1893, and then nothing from Watson's pen (by way of the literary agent) until *The Hound of the Baskervilles* was serialized in 1901 and 1902. In September 1903, further short stories appeared in *The Strand*, beginning with "The Empty House", with thirty-two short stories and one novel appearing between then and 1927. And for those wishing to know more about Mr. Holmes, the pickings were slim – the Canonical stories appeared at a very uneven pace. Those seven collected in *His Last Bow* were published between 1908 and 1917, *The Valley of Fear* was serialized in 1914 and 1915, and the twelve in *The Casebook* between 1921 and 1927.

There were some other bits available for those who wanted more Holmes during these times, but not much. The countless parodies that appeared through these decades, as collected by such able scholars as Bill Peschel in his *223B Casebook Series*, don't really count as actual cases. A true early extra-Canonical story was William Gillette's 1899 play, *Sherlock Holmes*. Others were few and far between. In 1920, Vincent Starrett discovered "The Unique Hamlet", which he wisely brought forth years before his scholarly work *The Private Life of Sherlock Holmes* (1933) – showing that his skills at setting priorities are a shining example to us all.

In 1930, Edith Meiser brought Holmes to radio, correctly recognizing that the detective's cases were perfectly suited to that medium. But after several years of repeated adaptations of The Canon, she began to pull other tales form Watson's records, including an account of The Giant Rat of Sumatra, and another called "The Hindoo in the Wicker Basket" (broadcast January 7th, 1932). These narratives from beyond The Canon, both by Meiser, and later by Leslie Charteris, Denis Green, and Anthony Boucher, helped pave the way for easier acceptance of cases that didn't have to be presented by first crossing the literary agent's desk. But there were still far too few of them.

Through the 1930's and 1940's, extra-Canonical Holmes stories appeared in films starring actors such as Arthur Wontner, Basil Rathbone, and Reginald Owen. In 1948, the world was shocked to learn of a new Holmes story, apparently found in the literary agent's files, thus giving it some kind of supposed extra legitimacy. This story, "The Case of the Man Who Was Wanted", was actually determined to have been brought forth around the turn of the Twentieth Century by a man named Arthur Whitaker. The excitement that this one new story caused shows just how hungry the world was, even then, for new Holmes adventures.

In 1952 and 1953, twelve newly discovered chronicles, later collected as *The Exploits of Sherlock Holmes* (1954) were published in *Life* and *Collier's* magazines. These, as presented by the literary agent's son Adrian Conan Doyle and famed mystery author John Dickson Carr, were very authentic – although received with caustic hostility at the time in the Sherlockian community because of the well-earned animus directed toward Adrian by his past greed-directed actions in trying to "own" Sherlock Holmes.

In 1954-1955, the world was blessed with thirty-nine half-hour episodes – only a handful of which were based on Canonical tales – of the television show *Sherlock Holmes*, starring Ronald Howard. As is often the case with film presentations of Holmes and Watson, one must look past poor screen-writing or abysmal casting to see the Watsonian Truths underneath – but for 1950's television, and following those years when Watson's reputation was so terribly damaged by Nigel Bruce's portrayal, these are actually very good Holmes stories.

Scattered through the years were occasional stand-alone stories that kept the Holmes-fires burning. There were several films and early television broadcasts that presented new adaptations of Canonical stories. In 1965, something new arrived on the scene with the premiere of *A Study in Terror*, the first time that one of Holmes's many encounters with Jack the Ripper, a massively complex case from 1888, was widely revealed to the public. And then for the most part, except for the occasional appearance of a new and random Holmes short story, there was nothing until 1974, when Nicholas Meyer's *The Seven-Per-Cent Solution* was published, igniting a Sherlockian fire that has only grown ever since.

Meyer made people aware that Watson's manuscripts were out there – in attics and old trunks and stacks of family papers – just waiting to be found and presented to a public starving for more about Sherlock Holmes. Meyer found a few more, including his most-excellent 1895 exploit, *The West End Horror* (1976). In that same period, John Gardner uncovered some of Moriarty's journals – not those of the Professor, but instead his younger brother. In 1976, Nicholas Utechin and Austin Mitchelson discovered *The Earthquake Machine* and *Hellbirds.* Sean M. Wright and Michael P. Hodel found one of Mycroft Holmes's early investigations, *Enter the Lion* (1979).

Through the 1980's and 1990's, the flow of newly discovered Watsonian adventures continued, growing a little each year. Interest was fueled by the Granada television show (1984-1994), in spite of its steadily declining quality. (Sadly, except for a few stand-alone Holmes films, there have been no ongoing series about Sherlock Holmes on British or American television whatsoever since the end of the Granada series.) In the 2000's, the rise of the internet and the opportunities that it presented allowed for the dam to burst, and a very welcome surge of discovered Holmes history began to appear in the form of hundreds of online-stories, as well as books that could be prepared and sold without the strangling baggage that had been associated for so long with the publishing industry. A new paradigm washed away the old, where before a Holmes story might sit in limbo for a year or more before being published – if it were to be published at all. Now one of Watson's works could be found and brought to the public nearly immediately. And for someone like me, who has collected literally thousands of Watson's narratives for over forty years, the amount of Sherlock Holmes stories in the world was finally on the right track to being correct. But it isn't there yet, because truly *there can never be enough tales about the* true *Sherlock Holmes*.

And why? Because Holmes is a *hero*, and we need him now more than ever. As we're assailed by corruption, ignorance, intolerance, and pure evil at the highest levels – criminals and perverts and cheats and traitors of Biblical proportions – we need an essential example of someone who *thinks* and seeks knowledge instead of relying on superstition and ignorance and hunches and prejudice. We need someone who doesn't see facts as hoaxes, and someone who searches for the honorable path to justice, and not ways to subvert it. We need someone who *helps* rather than *destroys*, because of completely self-centered narcissistic greed, or simply for the warped and deviant joy of chaos. And like Vincent Starrett – who looked around in 1942 thinking that "*though the world explode*" and wished for a simpler time – we too need someplace where, though imperfect, we can look for inspiration – not finding Holmes as a broken criminal, the way that some now try to present him, but rather as the true heroic figure whom Watson wanted to honor in the 1880's, and whom Starrett wanted to remind us about in the dark depths of the early 1940's.

We may look back on Holmes where "*it is always eighteen-ninety-five*" – or several decades on either side of that – but in fact the *true* Holmes is a hero for *all* ages, and never more necessary now, and in as many stories about him as we can find.

* * * * *

As always when one of these sets is finished, I want to first thank with all my heart my incredible wonderful wife of nearly thirty-two years (as of this writing,) Rebecca, and our amazing son and my friend, Dan. I love you both, and you are everything to me!

Also, I can't ever express enough gratitude for all of the contributors who have donated their time and royalties to this ongoing project. I'm constantly amazed at the incredible stories that you send, and I'm so glad to have gotten to know all of you through this process. It's an undeniable fact that Sherlock Holmes authors are the *best* people!

The contributors of these stories have donated their royalties for this project to support the Stepping Stones School for special needs children, located at Undershaw, one of Sir Arthur Conan Doyle's former homes. As of this writing, these MX anthologies have raised over $60,000 for the school, and of even more importance, they have helped raise awareness about the school all over the world. These books are making a real difference to the school, and the participation of both contributors and purchasers is most appreciated.

Next is that group that exchanges emails with me when we have the time – and time is a valuable commodity for all of us these days! I don't get to write as often as I'd like, but I really enjoy catching up when we get the chance: Derrick Belanger, Bob Byrne, Mark Mower, Denis Smith, Tom Turley, Dan Victor, and Marcia Wilson.

There is a group of special people who have stepped up and supported this and a number of other projects over and over again with a lot of contributions. They are the best and I can't express how valued they are: Larry Albert, Hugh Ashton, Derrick Belanger, Deanna Baran, S.F. Bennett, Andrew Bryant, Thomas Burns, Nick Cardillo, Craig Stephen Copland, Matthew Elliott, David Friend, Tim Gambrell, Jayantika Ganguly, Paul Gilbert, Dick Gillman, Arthur Hall, Stephen Herczeg, Mike

Hogan, Craig Janacek, Steven Philip Jones, Michael Mallory, Mark Mower, Will Murray, Robert Perret, Tracy Revels, Roger Riccard, Geri Schear, Brenda Seabrooke, Shane Simmons, Robert Stapleton, Subbu Subramanian, Tim Symonds, Kevin Thornton, Charles Veley and Anna Elliott, Peter Coe Verbica, I.A. Watson, and Marcy Wilson.

I also want to thank the following:

- John Lescroart – While many know John as the best-selling author of the Dismas Hardy books (as well as a number of others also set in the Hardy Universe), I first encountered him by way of his novels relating adventures of young Nero Wolfe (although not quite under that name) during World War I – *Son of Holmes* (1986) and *Rasputin's Revenge* (1987). Holmes is very much a part of these books, and I later discovered that John had also written his own version of "The Giant Rat of Sumatra". It was only natural that I would ask him to write a foreword for these books, and he very graciously wrote a really good one. I've been a fan of his works – both Holmes-related and the highly-recommended chronicles of Dismas Hardy – for a very long time, and it's my personal thrill that he's a part of these volumes. Many thanks!
- Roger Johnson – I'm so grateful that I know Roger. His Sherlockian knowledge is exceptional, as is the work that he does to further the cause of The Master. But even more than that, both Roger and his wonderful wife, Jean Upton, are simply the finest kind of people, and I'm very lucky to know them – even though I don't get to see them nearly as often as I'd like! In so many ways, Roger, I can't thank you enough, and I can't imagine these books without you.
- Steve Emecz: I had the great good fortune to communicate with Steve way back in 2013, when I was interested in placing my previously first-published book with MX, the fast-rising superstar of the Sherlockian publishing world. It was an amazing life-changing event for me, and ever since, Steve has been one of the most positive and supportive people I've known, letting me explore various Sherlockian projects and opening up my own personal possibilities in ways that otherwise would

have never been possible. Thank you Steve for every opportunity!

- Brian Belanger – In January 2020, I was able to attend – for the first time – the Holmes Birthday Celebration in New York. I met a number of wonderful people there in person after getting to know them through emails over the last several years, and I was especially glad to meet Brian, one of the nicest and most talented of people. He's amazingly great to work with, and once again I thank him for another incredible contribution.

And last but certainly *not* least, **Sir Arthur Conan Doyle**: Author, doctor, adventurer, and the Founder of the Sherlockian Feast. Present in spirit, and honored by all of us here.

As always, this collection has been a labor of love by both the participants and myself. As I've explained before, once again everyone did their sincerest best to produce an anthology that truly represents why Holmes and Watson have been so popular for so long. These are just more tiny threads woven into the ongoing Great Holmes Tapestry, continuing to grow and grow, for there can *never* be enough stories about the man whom Watson described as "*the best and wisest . . . whom I have ever known.*"

David Marcum
March 4th, 2020
The 139th Anniversary of
Holmes telling Watson to
"Get your hat."

Questions, comments, or story submissions
may be addressed to David Marcum at

thepapersofsherlockholmes@gmail.com

Foreword
by John Lescroart

Ironically enough, Sherlock Holmes entered my life as a respite from literature. At the time, I was majoring in English at UC Berkeley, with an emphasis on *The Continental Novel In Translation*, immersed in the works of Tolstoy, Dostoevsky, Stendahl, Goethe, Flaubert, Camus, Thomas Mann, and many others of the all-time literary greats.

The problem was that they may have been superb stylists, but they were often not exactly easy to read. So, for example, I would have just spent five hours and three-hundred-and-fifty pages getting to the point in *Anna Karenina* where somebody's long-lost aunt dies (Not really, but you get the idea), and I found that I couldn't force myself to read another word of this high literature. Of course, in those days, I had neither a television set nor a computer – entertainment at my apartment came only in the form of more reading.

Fortunately, I had somewhere and somehow acquired the two-volume set of William S. Baring-Gould's *Annotated Sherlock Holmes*, and one day in the midst of my required reading of another of the classics, I couldn't take it anymore and, in despair, I reached over to my bookshelf to see what Dr. Arthur Conan Doyle was up to with this Sherlock Holmes fellow.

The answer was: Plenty.

I'd of course heard of Holmes, who after all is perhaps the most well-known fictional character in human history. But the discovery for which I was completely unprepared was the sheer accessibility of these stories. They were in many ways the polar opposite of the books I'd been laboring through. They were, in fact, eminently readable and plot driven – and yet there was an elegance and approachability in the writing itself that, in my opinion, stood up to the best of what my continental novels had to offer.

Beyond the "English Major" stuff, though, from the very first words of the very first book, *A Study In Scarlet*, Holmes (and Watson) come alive not just as interesting characters, but as fully realized human beings, imbued with depth, great intelligence, irony, humor, bravery, and sensitivity. These are wonderful people we come to know and yes, even to love. We want to spend more time with them, hang out with them, and be part of their lives, which are so familiar and yet so unique and remarkable.

Hence, this volume of new and original Sherlock Holmes stories.

One would be tempted to think that enough had already been written about Holmes and Watson and the world they inhabit. Surely, with Conan

Doyle's original sixty stories, with literally hundreds of pastiches published over the past century and more, the trove of Holmesiana must be close to exhausted.

But this is the miracle of Sherlock Holmes. It is not so.

Sherlock's appeal is so universal, Watson's language is so identifiable, the mysteries they encounter speak to all ages and to the human condition, that it is small wonder that writers, like the talented contributors to this latest volume, continue to be driven to visit and revisit Holmes and Watson, and to add their narrative voices to The Canon as nothing less than a universal tribute to the original.

Holmes comes fully alive again in these stories and, indeed, from the evidence presented herein, he will never die.

Enjoy.

John Lescroart
May 2019

"What Could Be Better For the Purpose?"[1]

by Roger Johnson

Arthur Conan Doyle was generally tolerant when his work was parodied. In his reminiscences *Memories and Adventures*, he cheerfully quotes in full "The Adventure of the Two Collaborators", a short and very funny spoof written in 1893 by his friend J.M. Barrie.[2]

He was less amenable to more serious imitations. The French author Maurice Leblanc appropriated Holmes as the only detective worthy to challenge the famous *gentleman-cambrioleur*, Arsène Lupin, but Conan Doyle understandably took exception, and the name was changed to "Herlock Sholmès" – or in some English editions "Holmlock Shears". On a lower literary level, Sherlock Holmes quickly became a hero in the European pulp magazines, where he was given a young assistant named Harry Taxon in place of Dr. Watson. From 1907, innumerable stories appeared on the bookstalls in Germany, France, Denmark, Spain, Poland, and even Croatia. Russia developed its own more intelligent and better written series. None had the approval of Conan Doyle – but he could be generous in his rejection. Consider "The Case of the Man Who Was Wanted".

After Conan Doyle's death in 1930, the family made no proper effort to examine his papers. It wasn't until 1942 that Hesketh Pearson, researching what was intended as *the* authorised biography, discovered among them the typescript of an unpublished Sherlock Holmes story. In 1948, "The Case of the Man Who Was Wanted" was published in *Cosmopolitan*, but upon its British publication the following January the Conan Doyles received a letter from a retired architect named Arthur Whitaker, claiming that he had written the story in 1910 and sent it to Sir Arthur, who had given him ten guineas for the rights to the plot. And despite furious denials and threats of legal action from Sir Arthur's sons, Denis and Adrian, Whitaker easily proved his claim, as he had kept his carbon copy of the typescript and the letter from Conan Doyle. "The Case of the Man Who Was Wanted" is not at all a bad story, written in a fair imitation of the Watson style.

The Conan Doyle brothers' almost fanatical opposition to imitations of their father's work had been demonstrated in 1944, when Ellery Queen's anthology *The Misadventures of Sherlock Holmes* was published in America. That outstanding collection of parody and pastiche – which includes stories by Anthony Boucher, Agatha Christie, S.C. Roberts, Vincent Starrett, and Mark Twain – was short-lived. Denis and Adrian detested the tongue-in-cheek scholarship of the Sherlock Holmes societies, and jealously guarded their legal rights in his characters. After two printings, *The Misadventures of Sherlock Holmes* was withdrawn from circulation.

Ironically, the major contribution to Sherlock Holmes pastiche came in the early 1950's with a series of twelve stories by Adrian Conan Doyle himself, six of them written in collaboration with John Dickson Carr. They appeared in book form in 1954 as *The Exploits of Sherlock Holmes*, and despite the dismissive comment of Edgar W. Smith, head of the Baker Street Irregulars, that they should be called "Sherlock Holmes Exploited", they are about as close to the real thing as any writer has got.

Denis and Adrian's sister Jean outlived them both and achieved far more in her life, becoming head of the Women's Royal Air Force (the first Director to have risen through the ranks), and ADC to the Queen. Her relationship with Holmesian enthusiasts was gracious, courteous, and supportive. As an Honorary Member of The Sherlock Holmes Society of London, she happily attended the Annual Dinners and even took part in pilgrimages to Switzerland. In 1991, she became the first woman to be admitted to the Baker Street Irregulars *with all rights and privileges*. Her investiture, most appropriately, was "A Certain Gracious Lady".

Dame Jean was never entirely happy with Holmesian pastiche, believing that authors should create their own characters. It's a simplistic view of a rather complex phenomenon, but understandable. Now, of course, the afterlives of Holmes, Watson, and the rest have become vastly more complex since the expiry of the original copyrights, everywhere except the United States, in 2000. (Under the USA's unique copyright law, some stories were never protected there, while a few of the late ones will not enter the public domain until the mid-2020s – which has made the situation even more complicated.)

Nevertheless, I fancy that Dame Jean would be pleased with the success of this remarkable series of books. The contents are evidence of worldwide affection and admiration for her father's work, undiminished ninety years after his death. And she would surely approve of the reason for the books' creation and publication: To help support the regeneration – you might say the *rejuvenescence* – of The House That Conan Doyle Built.

Roger Johnson, BSI, ASH
Editor: *The Sherlock Holmes Journal*
January 2020

NOTES

1 – From *The Sign of the Four*, Chapter XII.
2 – Thanks to *Arthur Conan Doyle: A Life in Letters*, edited by Jon Lellenberg, Daniel Stashower and Charles Foley, we know that Barrie was also responsible for the equally neat "My Evening with Sherlock Holmes", published anonymously in 1892.

An Ongoing Legacy for Sherlock Holmes
by Steve Emecz

Undershaw
Circa 1900

The MX Book of New Sherlock Holmes Stories has now raised over $60,000 for Stepping Stones School for children with learning disabilities and is by far the largest Sherlock Holmes collection in the world – by several measures, stories, authors, pages and positive reviews from the critics. *Publishers Weekly* has been reviewing since Volume VI and we have had a record thirteen straight great reviews. Here are some of their best comments:

> *"This is more catnip for fans of stories faithful to Conan Doyle's originals"* (Part XIII)

> *"This is an essential volume for Sherlock Holmes fans"* (Part XI)

"The imagination of the contributors in coming up with variations on the volume's theme is matched by their ingenious resolutions" (Part VIII)

MX Publishing is a social enterprise – all the staff, including me, are volunteers with day jobs. The collection would not be possible without the creator and editor, David Marcum, who is rightly cited multiple times by *Publishers Weekly* and others as probably the most accomplished Sherlockian editor ever.

In addition to Stepping Stones School, our main program that we support is the Happy Life Children's Home in Kenya. My wife Sharon and I are on our way in December for our seventh Christmas in a row at Happy Life. It's a wonderful project that has saved the lives of over 600 babies. You can read all about the project in the second edition of the book *The Happy Life Story.*

Our support of both of these projects is possible through the publishing of Sherlock Holmes books, which we have now been doing for a decade.

You can find out more information
about the Stepping Stones School at:

www.steppingstones.org.uk

and Happy Life at:

www.happylifechildrenshomes.com

You can find out more about MX Publishing
and reach out to us through our website at:

www.mxpublishing.com

Steve Emecz
August 2019
Twitter: *@steveemecz*
LinkedIn: *https://www.linkedin.com/in/emecz/*

The Doyle Room at Stepping Stones, Undershaw

Partially funded through royalties from
The MX Book of New Sherlock Holmes Stories

A Word From Stepping Stones

by Lizzie Butler

Undershaw
September 9, 2016
Grand Opening of the Stepping Stones School
(Photograph courtesy of Roger Johnson)

Undershaw continues to develop during this new era as Stepping Stones School. The school is going through a very exciting time of change in 2020, with our student cohort at full capacity of ninety-five students across both our lower school and upper school sites, making daily life here at Undershaw rewarding, exciting and busy.

We really appreciate the support and donations received from MX Publishing and we look forward to another successful year as we fulfil the wants and needs of our students and their families.

"I didn't want to get up in the morning and go to school but now I love school. Everyone accepts each other and we're like a family, we trust, look after and understand each other, I think that's very special. This is now my happy place, where I can be who I am."

– Stepping Stones Student, 2019

Best wishes,

Lizzy Butler
Fundraising Manager, *Stepping Stones,* Undershaw
February 2020

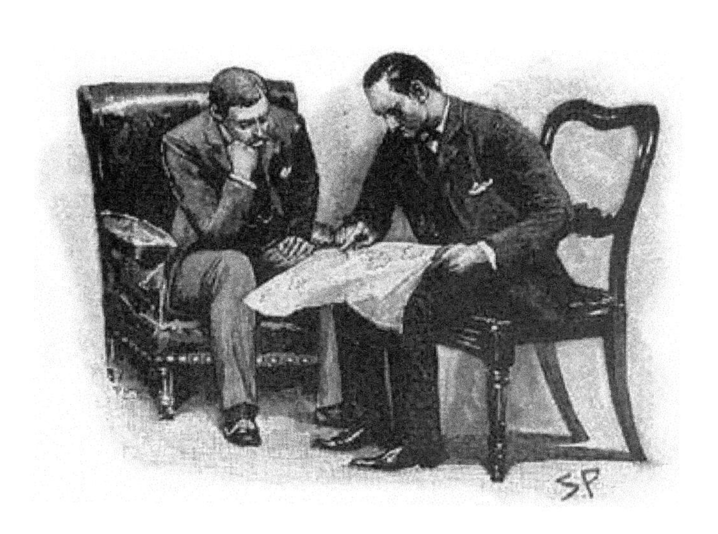

Sherlock Holmes (1854-1957) was born in Yorkshire, England, on 6 January, 1854. In the mid-1870's, he moved to 24 Montague Street, London, where he established himself as the world's first Consulting Detective. After meeting Dr. John H. Watson in early 1881, he and Watson moved to rooms at 221b Baker Street, where his reputation as the world's greatest detective grew for several decades. He was presumed to have died battling noted criminal Professor James Moriarty on 4 May, 1891, but he returned to London on 5 April, 1894, resuming his consulting practice in Baker Street. Retiring to the Sussex coast near Beachy Head in October 1903, he continued to be associated in various private and government investigations while giving the impression of being a reclusive apiarist. He was very involved in the events encompassing World War I, and to a lesser degree those of World War II. He passed away peacefully upon the cliffs above his Sussex home on his 103rd birthday, 6 January, 1957.

Dr. John Hamish Watson (1852-1929) was born in Stranraer, Scotland on 7 August, 1852. In 1878, he took his Doctor of Medicine Degree from the University of London, and later joined the army as a surgeon. Wounded at the Battle of Maiwand in Afghanistan (27 July, 1880), he returned to London late that same year. On New Year's Day, 1881, he was introduced to Sherlock Holmes in the chemical laboratory at Barts. Agreeing to share rooms with Holmes in Baker Street, Watson became invaluable to Holmes's consulting detective practice. Watson was married and widowed three times, and from the late 1880's onward, in addition to his participation in Holmes's investigations and his medical practice, he chronicled Holmes's adventures, with the assistance of his literary agent, Sir Arthur Conan Doyle, in a series of popular narratives, most of which were first published in *The Strand* magazine. Watson's later years were spent preparing a vast number of his notes of Holmes's cases for future publication. Following a final important investigation with Holmes, Watson contracted pneumonia and passed away on 24 July, 1929.

Photos of Sherlock Holmes and Dr. John H. Watson courtesy of Roger Johnson

The MX Book of New Sherlock Holmes Stories Part XIX: Part XIX – 2020 Annual (1882-1890)

Holmes's Prayer
by Christopher James

Grant me an undisturbed room,
cigar ash, and a singular detail.
Grant me an adversary
who believes he is better than he is.
Grant me clear sight
through the problem.
Grant me coffee for my pot,
my briar pipe and a pound
of strong tobacco.
Grant me a match, so it can
throw its friendly light.
Grant me Watson in a moment
when he is not taken
by his practice, his club or his wife.
Grant me a sudden gleaming
in the dark; the moment
I see the truth behind the lie.
Grant me a case that cannot
be solved, until it is.

A Case of Paternity
by Matthew White

In writing up these narratives of the adventures that I have been privileged to share with my friend, Mr. Sherlock Holmes, with the intent to lay them before the public, I have occasionally been obligated to overlook many which would be of interest to the reader, and which ably demonstrated the methods by which my friend achieved his remarkable results. Regrettably, the details of such cases were often of such a sensitive nature that to even hint at them would constitute a grave breach of trust. The case I am about to relate could not possibly have been made public at the time without doing an injustice to the parties concerned. Now, however, due to the death of the last principal actor in the drama, there is no longer any reason why, after making discrete alterations in the matter of names and places, the events themselves may not be told.

It was in March of 1882, in the early days of my association with Sherlock Holmes, that I returned one morning to our Baker Street lodgings after spending the early part of the morning at Charing Cross Hospital, comforting an old comrade from my service in Afghanistan whose wounds had taken a slow but terrible toll on his health. My heart was quite heavy, therefore, when I opened the door to our sitting room to find Holmes in conversation with a visitor. He was a respectable but nervous-looking man, no older than thirty, I should say, dressed all in black, with red hair and an upturned mustache. He sat on the sofa cradling a parcel in his hands.

"Ah, Watson, do come in," said Holmes, beckoning me to my accustomed chair by the fire. "I hoped you would be back in time. Mr. Dougherty," he said, addressing his visitor, "this is my friend and colleague Doctor Watson, of whom I told you. You may speak before him as freely as before myself. Watson, allow me to introduce Mr. Patrick Dougherty."

"How do you do, sir?" I greeted the visitor. "I hope you will excuse me, but I do not quite feel myself at the moment. I shall go to my room and – "

"Oh pooh-pooh, Doctor," Holmes interrupted. "I would not do without you for all the world! Please, do sit down here, there's a good man."

I have seldom turned down my friend's requests for help, but I was sorely tempted at that moment, being in a black mood and having no heart for mysteries or investigations. I had even less desire to argue in front of a guest, however, and so I seated myself and endeavored to show no trace of my irritation.

"Mr. Dougherty was just going to tell me about himself," said Holmes. "You will perceive immediately, of course, that he is unmarried, a vegetarian, is fond of dogs, and has a charitable soul. He is in mourning (you have my sincere condolences), and has recently been granted a position of great responsibility at his firm – I should say three weeks ago. Allow me to congratulate you."

At the conclusion of Holmes's statement, our visitor's face had assumed such a comical aspect of slack-jawed wonder that even in my cheerless mood I was forced to cover my mouth in order to stifle laughter.

"It is all perfectly true, Mr. Holmes," Mr. Dougherty said at length. "I suppose it's plain enough to see that I'm in mourning, though how you knew the rest I cannot guess."

My friend smiled. "It is no great mystery. That you are a bachelor who is fond of dogs may be seen not only by your bare ring finger but also – if you will forgive me for saying so – by the state of your trousers."

"My trousers?"

"A visible amount of dog hair has accumulated on the lower part of your trouser legs. No woman who cares for her husband would possibly allow him to leave the house before those trousers were brushed."

"Holmes," I warned, "perhaps you are – "

"Being insensitive?" Holmes interrupted. "The thought had occurred to me, but I think I am safe in saying, sir, that it is not a wife that you are mourning."

"No indeed. How did you – "

"That you are a vegetarian can be inferred from the bill which I see protruding from your waistcoat pocket. It is, if I am not mistaken, from a vegetarian restaurant which recently opened in the Strand. Your coat is rumpled and stained in several places where street Arabs pulled at it – so much in fact, that it seems you tolerated them rather than shooing them away, and in all probability left the encounter with fewer coins in your pocket. I can infer, therefore, that you are unusually open-handed. You have a sentimental nature, sir, which does you credit. I would hardly expect a sentimental man to have removed his wedding ring so soon after the passing of his wife."

"And my new position?" Mr. Dougherty asked eagerly.

"Your shoes, watch chain, waistcoat, gloves, and hat are all quite new, but professional rather than fashionable. Your cuffs are also new, but your cuff links, though highly polished, have seen some use. Your position in the word has clearly gone up, but the state of your coat and trousers show that you are not used to being so careful of your wardrobe."

Our visitor clapped. "Very good, very good! You interest me a great deal, Mr. Holmes. I have indeed been promoted to the position of head clerk at the Birmingham branch of Cox and Company. But this is beside the question."

"Pray tell me how we can assist you, Mr. Dougherty," said my friend.

"My mother passed away last week," he began.

"I'm so sorry to hear that," I interjected.

"Thank you, Doctor Watson. Something you should understand about me, gentlemen, is that I was raised by my mother. I never knew my father, or anything about him. I do not even know his Christian name."

"My word," I muttered.

"Watson, please be good enough to devote your full attention to the narrative at hand. Pray continue, Mr. Dougherty."

"My mother and I lived with her brother, Mr. Norbert Wallis, and as he had no children of his own, he saw to it that I had a good education and every advantage which it was in his power to provide. My childhood was not an unhappy one, Mr. Holmes, and because my uncle served as a kind of surrogate father, I was lucky enough not to feel my own father's absence. The same could not be said for my mother. She suffered from occasional bouts of melancholy and, as I grew older, I had an intuition that it was because of my father. But try as I might, I never could get her to tell me anything at all about him. Apart from my mother's sadness, which affected me deeply, I was also, as you can imagine, intensely curious about him – what sort of man he was, what he did, where he was from, what his people were like. Not a word would she tell me."

"Could your uncle not answer your questions?"

"He felt bound by my mother's wishes on the matter and said that if she wouldn't speak of my father, it wasn't for him to do so either."

"That is interesting," said Holmes, who was leaning back in his armchair, eyes closed, with his fingertips steepled beneath his chin.

"The mystery must have been unbearable," I said sympathetically.

"It did seem so, Doctor Watson, and yet I had no choice but to bear it. Painful as it was, I resigned myself to the possibility that I would never know anything about my father."

"But that has changed," said Holmes, "since your mother's death."

"Quite so, Mr. Holmes. I was the executor of her estate, and among her personal belongings I found a number of objects which I had never seen before, but which I believe with all my heart belonged to my father – or had to do with him."

"May I?" asked Holmes. Mr. Dougherty relinquished the parcel to my friend, who then sat down at our table and carefully laid its contents in a row before him.

"A watch, a cigarette case, and a photograph of three men standing outside of a building, beside a low stone wall. These objects are indeed a treasure trove of information."

"I hoped you might find them so, sir," said Mr. Dougherty. "The man on the right is my uncle. I do not know the others."

Holmes nodded and examined the photograph under the light.

"I have heard of you, Mr. Holmes," continued our visitor, "and of your reputation for solving mysteries that seem impenetrable to others. I cannot help feeling that you are the last hope I shall ever have of knowing the truth about my father. Please sir, say that you will help me."

Holmes stared at the objects on the table for some moments before answering. At last he spoke.

"Mr. Dougherty, you have brought me a most absorbing problem, I should be happy to assist you to the best of my ability. Where does your uncle live?"

"His house is just outside Birmingham," said Mr. Dougherty, as he tore a page out of his notebook and wrote the address for us. "I also live in Birmingham, at a different address."

"To the best of your knowledge, has your family always resided there?"

"My mother never mentioned living anywhere else."

"That is of the utmost importance. Good morning, Mr. Dougherty. You may rest assured, I will inform you of any developments without unnecessary delay."

Mr. Dougherty rose and took his hat and stick. "Thank you both," he said. "You give me hope, Mr. Holmes."

"Do not hope for too much, Mr. Dougherty. I am not a miracle worker."

"Nonetheless, I feel that I am in good hands. Good morning gentlemen."

"It is certainly very strange," I remarked once our visitor had left.

"It is not unheard-of that a woman should wish to hide the truth of a shameful liaison," said Holmes, as he puffed thoughtfully at his pipe. "But that is not the motive in this case. While she might have borne the child out of wedlock and taken the name Dougherty to indicate a fictitious and deceased husband, I don't believe that to be what happened here."

"How can you be sure?"

"An unmarried woman's name would naturally be the same as her brother's," Holmes replied. "Her name, and her son's, was Dougherty, not Wallis. We can assume, therefore, that our client's parents were married and there can be no question of an illicit *affaire de coeur* or a child born out of wedlock. Furthermore," Holmes gestured to the objects upon the table, “if the father’s identity were a source of shame, she would not have kept these mementos. No, he was someone she cared about – someone she wanted to remember.”

“But why would she refuse to tell her son about his own father, if she loved the man so?”

“I am very much mistaken if the answer to that question does not provide the solution to our mystery. For the moment, let us concentrate our attention upon the articles before us, for they will provide us with our first clues. Would you be kind enough to retrieve my lens?”

Once I had taken the lens from Holmes’s desk and passed it to him, he began a minute and systematic examination of the objects, during which he continually muttered to himself, punctuated by the occasional “A-ha!” or appreciative whistle. He turned the watch in his hands, examining every angle under the powerful magnifying lens. After similarly inspecting the cigarette case, he opened it and shook some fine particles onto the table, which he studied closely. Last of all he scanned the photograph, passing the lens over each figure before examining the back.

“The late Mrs. Dougherty’s choice of mementos has proven very convenient for us,” said Holmes. “I have remarked to you before, Watson, that everyday personal effects invariably bear the marks of their owner’s individuality, and here we have two to work with.”

“What do you deduce, then?” I asked. Holmes laughed.

“Look them over for yourself first, my good fellow. I would not wish to bias your judgment.” He held out the lens toward me. I accepted it and bent down over the table in order to gain a better view of my subjects.

“Neither the watch nor the case have been polished for some time,” I said.

“Very good, Watson. You are scintillating this morning. What else?”

“The cigarette case is monogrammed with the initials *T.D.* I should take the *D* to stand for *Dougherty*.”

“And?”

“I do not doubt you saw much which was invisible to me,” said I, feeling quite foolish.

“Not at all, but I deduced a little more.”

“What then?”

“Let us begin with the watch. A man’s character is always revealed by a close examination of his watch. You will observe that it is of superior quality. These scratches were made by someone attempting to open the watch. When we open the watch, we see that the delicate inner workings are scratched as well. These scratches clearly were made by someone repairing the watch using inferior tools. A gentleman who can afford such a fine watch would surely entrust it to a competent watchmaker if he could afford to do so. If we judge by the degree of wear, these pawnbroker's marks on the inner cover were made during the same period. It is also obvious by the way the numbers are scratched out that he was able to redeem the pledge. So already we have learned something about our man: He was well-to-do, but fell on hard times. Subsequently, his fortunes changed again and he became prosperous, or at the very least was no longer poor."

"I see."

"That is not all. Those scratches are worn down, and now quite difficult to see unless one is looking for them. But take the lens and look closely at these scratches around the keyhole. They are newer, and the newest ones, which you can tell apart by how they cut through older scratches, were done much more violently. Inference: As time went on, it became harder for him to hold the watch steady in order to wind it. I fear the owner of this watch suffered some terrible decline in his physical health."

"Remarkable, Holmes."

"Quite elementary," he answered, but his slight smile told me that my admiration pleased him. "Now, let us turn our attention to this cigarette case. You will observe at once that it is of more modest craftsmanship than the watch. Its outer surface is stained in several places by acid. This fellow worked in a laboratory."

"He was a chemist, then?"

"That is a strong possibility, but there are others. Observe that the spring inside is broken. But our man was quite resourceful. He attached a thin band of cloth to the inside to hold the cigarettes in place.

"I recognize this cloth, Holmes," said I. "It is sometimes used by surgeons to dress wounds."

"Very good, Watson!" my friend exclaimed. "You are getting better all the time. If we couple this detail with the knowledge our man worked with chemicals, we can safely conclude that – "

"Holmes, these articles belonged to a fellow medico!"

"I have no doubt that you are right," said my friend as he packed more shag into his pipe. "Dougherty *pere* was a doctor. So you see, by simple logic and deduction we have, without leaving this room, made significant progress. We now know that our man, who is almost certainly one of the three men in this photograph, was a doctor who spent some years on the verge of poverty before his circumstances changed and he was able to live, if not in prosperity, then at least in comfort – very probably, because he obtained a position at a hospital, where he would have access to a laboratory. He met a woman, they fell in love and had a son. Then, as we have seen, his health began to deteriorate, and the doctor disappeared from the family's life, seemingly without a trace."

"Perhaps he fell to drink or some other noxious influence," I conjectured. "Perhaps he found his wife and child too burdensome. There may even have been another woman."

"It wouldn't do to taint our facts with conjecture. However, we now have an ample set of data with which to start our investigation. I trust you would not be adverse to a trip to Birmingham?"

"By no means."

"Well, then let us pack. There is a train which leaves in an hour, if I am not mistaken. Do not forget your toothbrush, for it is just possible we shall have to stay the night."

An hour later found us settling comfortable into our carriage. As the train began to move, Holmes took the photograph from his pocket and handed it to me.

"Have a look, Watson. Are there any details which commend themselves to your attention?"

"I see nothing more than I saw earlier."

"Take a close look at the man in the middle. Does he not look familiar?"

"Well, yes, I suppose. Do you mean that you believe him to be Mr. Dougherty's father?"

"I am quite certain of it. Note the ears, the distinctive brow ridge, the down-turned edges of the mouth. The bridge of the nose and the square chin are also very similar to our client's. It's a pity that we don't know the identity of the man on the left."

"Surely that is immaterial, if we know these two are the father and uncle."

"Never discount the value of any fact in a case such as this. There is no telling what information may be useful."

We arrived in Birmingham in the early evening and made our way past the swarming mass of humanity upon the platform. When we reached the street outside the station, Holmes waved his stick in the air and a four-wheeler pulled up beside us, driven by old whiskered fellow in a long brown coat and bowler. He climbed down with some difficulty, for he was lame in one leg, and helped us with our baggage.

"Can you recommend a good hotel, cabby?" asked Sherlock Holmes.

"The Warwick House is close, sir."

"Very good. The Warwick House then, if you please."

We stepped into the cab and the driver whipped up the horses. We rattled down the Birmingham streets, which became less crowded as we got further from the station. In no more than fifteen minutes, we turned down a cobbled street and our four-wheeler stopped in front of an unremarkable, modest-looking house.

"Here you are, gentlemen," said our genial cabby as he helped us again with our bags. "It may not be Buckingham Palace, but them that own it are good, honest folk, and they keep a clean house."

"I'm sure it will do," said Holmes. "Tell me, have you been driving in this city long, Mr. – ?"

"Davies is my name sir, and I've been cabbing in Birmingham for nigh twelve year now. Before that, I was a police constable, sir, but I had to take a different line on account of my bad knee."

"Then you know the city well?"

"There's no one knows it better."

"Do you recognize this building?" Holmes retrieved the photograph Mr. Dougherty had left with us and held it before the cabby's eyes. Davies looked thoughtfully at it for a moment before speaking.

"It reminds me of a few places, sir."

"Could you find these places?"

"Without a doubt, sir."

"Excellent, Mr. Davies! I am Mr. Holmes and this is Doctor Watson. If you would be kind enough to meet us here at nine o'clock tomorrow morning and take us around Birmingham, you will be well compensated for your time."

"I should be happy to be of service."

"That's settled then," said Holmes. He drew out a sovereign and offered it to the cabby.

"That's more'n your fare, Mr. Holmes."

"Consider it an advance then. Good evening, Mr. Davies. Remember, nine o'clock!"

Warwick House proved to be, as Davies had said, a pleasant and charming little hotel. Holmes and I were given two rooms close together. After dinner, Holmes retired immediately to his chamber while I sat for a while smoking with the landlord and another guest. Before long I had difficulty keeping my eyes open, and so excused myself, making my way to my own room.

On the following morning I rose rather later than I'd intended, so that by the time I had finished my toilet, breakfast was already cold and Holmes had left on an errand. At ten-minutes-to-nine he was still absent, and I became nervous, for I didn't know what I would do if I were forced to carry out the investigation alone. I was saved, however, by Holmes's timely reappearance at exactly nine o'clock. He pulled up in a hansom at the very moment that Mr. Davies's four-wheeler came rattling down the street.

"Where in the deuce have you been?" I asked him. "I thought I might have to go on without you."

"You really ought to have more faith, my dear fellow. If you must know, I have been assembling a list of the names and addresses of hospitals and dispensaries in Birmingham that were operating during the time Doctor Dougherty would have been practicing."

He brandished a folded sheet of paper as evidence.

"Do you suppose that the building in the photograph is on that list?"

"I shall be very surprised if it is not," he said. "Hulloa there, Davies! Do you need to see the photograph again before you set off?"

"I remember it well enough, Mr. Holmes."

"Then let's not waste any more time. Come, Watson."

Before long we were rattling down one of the main thoroughfares of Birmingham. It was my first time in the city, and so I felt myself to be entirely in the hands of our cabby, whom I hoped was as capable as he was confident.

After twenty minutes and many turnings, we pulled up in front of a low brick building set a little back from the road and surrounded by a stone wall similar to the one in the photograph. Holmes put his head out of the window to regard it.

"No, this is wrong," he declared after only a second or two. "Move on, Mr. Davies."

Our next four stops proceeded in much the same manner, and by noon I was sore from the constant bumping and rattling of the cab, as well as ravenously hungry. I was on the point of asking Holmes if he would like to stop for something to eat, but thought better of it. My friend was in the habit of forgoing food for days at a time when he was absorbed by a case, and I knew that he was now like a beagle which has caught a scent and will stop at nothing until it has run down its quarry.

As I was thinking on these things, we pulled up at our fifth stop and Holmes gave a cry of triumph.

"Yes, I am sure this is it. Come, Watson, up and out! Wait for us here, Davies."

The building in front of us could be none other than the very one which was visible in Mr. Dougherty's photograph. A sign above the door proclaimed it to be the Chesterfield-Wallis Hospital for the Poor. I confess to being somewhat taken aback by the state of the hospital's interior. The building was obviously a very old one, and ill-suited to use as a hospital. Despite obvious signs that the staff did their best to keep it clean, there was a persistent scent of decay such as always lingers in old buildings. As we walked down the hall, I observed that much of the equipment was aged, if not positively obsolete. Moaning came intermittently from the rooms which we passed, and now and again I heard a demoniac howling from the deeper parts of the building. A gentleman in doctor's attire approached us and asked our business.

"My name is Sherlock Holmes, and this is my associate Doctor Watson, late of the Army Medical Department. May I ask, sir, what kind of patients you treat here?"

"Most of our patients suffer from those maladies all too common to the poorest classes. Rheumatism, phossy jaw, syphilis – "

"I see. We would like, if you please, to consult the employment records of this establishment."

"May I ask why you wish to do so?" the doctor asked with some suspicion. At that moment I was struck by sudden inspiration.

"I know it must seem most irregular," said I, "but you see, I am looking for a dear friend of mine, a fellow who served with me as an army surgeon. I fear some misadventure has befallen him, for his correspondence ceased suddenly some time ago, but I am sure he once told me that he worked here. As a brother medico and a former comrade in arms, I feel somewhat responsible for him, and I would desperately like to discover anything I can about what has happened to him."

I could see that the doctor was sympathetic to my story, and I confess that I felt some guilt for deceiving him so.

"I suppose you are looking for his address, relations, things of that nature?"

"Quite," I answered.

"Well," said he, "you were right to say that it is irregular, but I cannot see that any harm will come of it. I must ask you not to mention that it was I that let you see the records."

To this we readily agreed. The doctor showed us down the hall and, pulling a key from his pocket, opened a door, and led us into a small room full of cabinets.

"This is where the hospital's records are kept," he said. "It is the strict policy of the hospital that this room must remain locked, but I have many patients to see to, and cannot spare the time to wait while you look. I shall be back around in ten minutes."

"Thank you very much, that will do," said I, and the doctor left the room, closing the door behind him.

"Very well done, Watson!" Holmes said in hushed tones. "I never can get your limits."

I was quite flattered to hear my companion say so, but the hopeful mood was not to last, for it seemed quite certain that no doctor by the name of Dougherty had ever been employed at the hospital. Holmes glowered sullenly as we walked back to the cab and passed the cabby his list.

"Davies, I would like to visit each of these places, one after the other."

The sky was growing dark, and we were no closer to the solution of the mystery when the four-wheeler deposited us back at Warwick House. Davies stammered his thanks when Holmes gave him a princely sum indeed for a cabby's services, but my friend was absorbed in his own thoughts and said nothing. I thanked Davies for his time and followed Holmes into the hotel to discover that he had retreated immediately to his room. I followed upstairs and knocked at the door.

"Come in, Watson."

I found Holmes sitting in an armchair lighting his pipe, knees drawn up to his chin, eyelids half-closed, wearing an expression which told me that beneath his calm, almost-sleepy exterior, his active mind was working to penetrate the mystery which had occupied our day. Not wishing to interrupt his thoughts, I sat down on the edge of the bed and waited for him to speak.

"I have missed something," he said at last, and stabbed his temple with the stem of his pipe.

"I cannot see what you could have overlooked," I replied, attempting to console him.

"Nevertheless, there is something," he snarled.

"You must not be so hard on yourself, my dear fellow," I said. Holmes removed the photograph from his pocket and stared at it.

"It cannot be a coincidence," he said. "I was warm at that hospital Watson, I know it."

"The records were quite conclusive," I said. "Dougherty could not have worked there."

"Yes, they were quite conclusive on that point. Nonetheless, it is still the most promising lead we have. Well, we can do nothing more today, Watson. I must think."

"Will you not have dinner?"

"I cannot spare the energy for digestion just now," he answered. "But by all means, go yourself. I will see you in the morning."

The next day, I found that my friend's spirits had improved, for he now seemed to believe that the solution to the mystery was nearly at hand.

"I have formed a theory which accounts for all the facts," he said at the breakfast table. He himself ate nothing, but I rather over-indulged on the landlady's excellent fare.

"Let me hear it," I said.

"Not just yet, Watson, not just yet. I must still put it to the test. But if I'm right, I have been as blind as a beetle."

Twenty minutes later we were in a hansom bound for the Chesterfield-Wallis Hospital. When the cab came to a stop, Holmes leaped out and strode energetically toward the door, leaving me to pay the cabby. I entered a moment later to find him in conversation with a doctor.

"Who's been on staff longest? Why that'd be the head doctor himself, Doctor Delapore," he told Holmes.

"I see. And is Doctor Delapore in today?"

"He is sir, but he's very busy."

"I am sure he is. Please give him my card, and tell him myself and Doctor Watson would like only a brief moment of his time."

"I will, sir."

We waited for nearly an hour before a grey-haired man in a leather apron and a pair of silver pince-nez approached us. At his appearance, Holmes's eyes brightened with excitement.

"I am Doctor Delapore. I am sorry for the wait, gentlemen, but we are hard put it today."

"We understand completely," I assured him. "I am a doctor, myself."

"Indeed?" he said. "What can I do for you gentlemen?"

"Only this," said Holmes, producing the photograph. "Would you be kind enough to tell me if you recognize any of the men in this photograph?"

Doctor Delapore took the photograph and regarded it for a moment.

"Why yes, of course! There I am, on the left. My word, this must have been taken almost thirty years ago. Where did you get this?"

"Do you recognize anyone else?" Holmes pressed.

"The man on the right is Norbert Wallis. He has always been our most generous benefactor."

"Thank you very much for your assistance, Doctor," said Holmes, taking back the photograph. "Might I trouble you for one more thing?"

"I'm afraid I am very pressed for time."

"Very good. We would be most grateful for a chance to peruse your patient records."

"We do not ordinarily grant the public access to patient records."

"I have reason to believe a patient of mine passed through here," I interjected, "under an assumed name. He is in very bad condition and it is of the utmost importance that I gain access to his complete medical records."

Doctor Delapore wavered for a moment before agreeing. "Very well. I shall have a nurse show you to the records room."

"Thank you very much," I said. The doctor summoned a nurse and provided her with the key. She guided us back to the little room we had visited the day before. With a determined air, Holmes opened the cabinet used to store patient files and rummaged through it.

"You recognized the name, of course?" he said in an offhand manner while he searched the cabinet.

"Which name?"

"Norbert Wallis."

"It sounds familiar. Why, isn't he – ? "

"Yes, Watson. Our client's uncle."

Suddenly Holmes have a cry of exaltation and held up a record with the name *Theodore Dougherty* written at the top.

"Here is our Doctor Dougherty! Died in 1861 of syphilis."

"My word!"

"Take a look at these notes, Doctor, and give me your professional opinion."

I took the papers and looked them over.

"Good heavens, Holmes. I've never seen a case of syphilis this extreme. It is horrifying."

"My thoughts, exactly, Watson. I think that it's time we visited Mr. Norbert Wallis."

Mr. Wallis lived in a rather stately house just outside the city, separated from the road by a large garden and a gravel drive which led up to the front door. We alighted from our cab and Holmes marched to the door, full of purpose, and rang the bell.

The butler showed us in and Holmes took out a page out of his notebook and wrote a short message before depositing the paper, together with our cards, on the butler's tray.

"We will wait here," Holmes told him, and the butler gave a curt bow of his head and turned down the hall. A moment later he reappeared and ushered us into a large study with full bookcases on every available inch of wall. At the far end of the room was a heavy wooden desk, behind which stood an older, red-faced gentleman with grey side whiskers. He was heavily built with broad shoulders, and had the look of a man possessed of great physical strength despite his advanced age. Upon the desk was a riding crop which he tapped nervously with his fingers.

"Mr. Norbert Wallis, I presume," said Sherlock Holmes, affecting a gracious bow. "I am Sherlock Holmes, and this is my friend – "

"I saw your card," said Mr. Wallis tersely. "I don't know who you are Mr. Holmes, or what you think you know about my late brother-in-law, but you had better have a good reason for being here. If it's money you want, sir, then by God you'll have none!"

The man's face had turned even redder now, and his tone was one of barely suppressed rage.

"I assure you, Mr. Wallis," my friend replied calmly, "that our intentions are strictly honorable."

"We will see about that! Well, if it isn't money you want, then why are you here?"

"I am here on behalf of Mr. Patrick Dougherty."

Mr. Wallis's face froze in an expression of perplexity.

"Patrick? What on earth do you mean, on his behalf?"

"Mr. Dougherty has retained my services in order to discover the identity of his father."

"He wanted you to find out about Theodore?"

"I fear it was his belief that, given the reticence of his relations, outside help was the only option left to him."

The redness in Mr. Wallis's face had dissipated. His defiance had melted into sorrow, and he sank into the chair behind the desk.

"Then your note was true, and you really do know all. What will you do?"

"As I told you, Mr. Dougherty commissioned me to find out the truth about his father. This I have done. You need not fear that your family secret will be exposed to the world."

"How on earth did you learn of it?"

"If you will permit me to sit, I'll tell you what I have discovered, and you may feel free to correct me if I go astray."

Mr. Wallis nodded his assent and Holmes and I seated ourselves in the two chairs which stood beside the desk. My friend lit a cigarette and held it airily in his long, thin fingers.

"When your nephew came to see me," Holmes began, "he told me about the extraordinary secrecy surrounding Theodore Dougherty – his life, death, even his very name. He also brought three objects to me for examination: A watch and cigarette case, and a photograph, believed to be his father's. These objects told me much about the man to whom they had belonged. Your unfortunate brother-in-law was a doctor, but not a rich one. He fell in love with a woman, your sister, and they had a son. Then some time later, his fortunes plummeted and never rose again. This much I could read in the watch and the cigarette case, which also furnished me with his initials: *T.D.*

"But how to find this Doctor T. D.? The photograph led me to a hospital which treats, among other unfortunate persons, sufferers of syphilis. I was disappointed when an examination of the hospital's records revealed that no Doctor Dougherty had ever been employed there. So said every hospital in the city. I was convinced, however, that the photograph could not be a coincidence. We returned there and spoke to the head doctor, a man named Delapore. Perhaps you recall the name?"

Our host nodded.

"I showed him the photograph," said Holmes, "and asked him if he recognized any of the men in it. I expected him to recognize this man here, whom I believe I may safely say, due to the physical resemblance to my client, was Doctor Dougherty. Instead, he recognized you.

"At that moment, all the pieces fell into place. I asked to see the patient records, and found Theodore Dougherty. My case was complete. Doctor Dougherty was syphilitic – hence the decline in his fortunes and degeneration of his physical health indicated by his possessions. You, Mr. Wallis, arranged to have him put quietly into one of the hospitals that benefits from your considerable philanthropic gifts. You and your sister resolved never to tell my client about his father."

"You amaze me, sir," said Wallis. "You are absolutely correct in every particular. But it was not I who wished to hide the truth from Patrick. It was his mother. She made me promise never to tell him, and I must keep my word sir – surely I must keep my word, especially to my own flesh and blood."

"Then perhaps you would be kind enough to tell me the whole story from the beginning?" said Holmes.

"I can hardly refuse," answered Wallis. "For I can see there is no use in attempting to conceal the truth from you, and if, as you say, you are acting for my nephew, then it is only right that you should know all."

"I inherited a successful business from my father, and, being so blessed, wished to bless the world in return. I gave money where I thought it might be useful to the impoverished and unfortunate. I was introduced, through a mutual acquaintance, to Theodore Dougherty, who was at that time a young doctor working at a voluntary hospital in a very poor part of the city. I could see that was a remarkable man possessed not only of great integrity and strong character, but also of remarkable talent, and so I arranged for him to have a position at a small specialist hospital for the destitute to which I had given considerable sums of money. I was not the only one who saw his quality, for I soon became aware that my sister, Rosalyn, had fallen quite in love with him. Our father was dead, so Doctor Dougherty asked for my permission to marry Rosalyn, and I was overjoyed, for I could not have wished for a better husband for her."

"He wasn't a very rich man," remarked Holmes.

"Nor was my father, sir, when he began his business. Fortunes change, Mr. Holmes, but not strength of character."

Holmes nodded and indicated for our host to continue.

"For a long time, their lives were exceedingly happy. Then, sometime after Patrick was born, Theodore contracted syphilis through exposure to a patient's fluids. The disease progressed astonishingly rapidly, and in five years he was at the most extreme stage. I used my influence to have him cared for discretely. Within a year of being committed to their care, he was dead.

"It broke my poor sister's heart. She was absolutely devoted to him, and he in turn showed her as much love and tenderness as ever a man showed a woman. His condition was a terrible blow to her. When it ruined his mind and corrupted his body, it was more than she could bear. That is one reason, I believe, why she hid the truth from her son: She simply could not bear to speak of it. The other reason was shame. I need hardly explain that, I think."

"But he contracted the disease in the course of his duty as a doctor," I said. "Surely there is no shame in that. On the contrary, I should call him a hero who sacrificed his life for his fellow man."

"You have a compassionate heart, Doctor Watson," Wallis said. "But not everyone does. Too many people in this world are fond of ignorant gossip, and delight in pronouncing judgment on matters of which they know nothing." There was bitterness in the older man's voice.

"She feared disgrace not only for himself, but for her son," he continued. "Patrick was still very young when Theodore became ill, and she believed that he would have no memory of the ordeal to trouble him later in life, and so it proved. But he was always clever and determined, even as a child. I should have known he would one day discover the truth. I suppose that you will tell him all that I have told you."

"Mr. Wallis," Holmes said, "don't you think it would be better if you were the one to tell him?"

"I made a solemn promise, Mr. Holmes."

"Your sister is dead, Mr. Wallis, and the truth cannot harm her anymore. Think of Patrick. You are the only family he has left. If I go to him and tell him what you have hidden for so long, he will never trust you to be truthful with him. If he hears the truth from your lips, he will love you for it. Surely that would be better."

For a long moment Wallis sat in thought with his broad shoulders bent and his brow furrowed.

"I cannot deny that you are right, Mr. Holmes. I will tell him."

"I suggest you send for him at once then, and with your permission, we will wait here with you."

Of the long conversation that took place between Holmes, myself, Wallis, and Patrick Dougherty, little need be said. Truthfully, Holmes and I said very little, for Wallis, having determined to tell his nephew the truth, made good on his word.

"I knew," said our client after his uncle had finished, "that he must be dead, though part of me hoped against hope that he was still alive. I spent years imagining terrible stories about what might have happened, but the reality is worse than any of them. How horrible! How senseless!"

I could see that young Dougherty was fighting back tears, and I searched in my mind for comforting words, though I knew nothing I could ever say would have the power to lift the burden of grief from his shoulders.

"I should not say 'senseless'," said Holmes unexpectedly. "On the contrary – your father, by his death, gave more meaning to his life than most men ever do."

"I'm not sure that I understand you, Mr. Holmes," said Dougherty.

"Your father was a very selfless person, Mr. Dougherty, with great generosity of spirit – traits which, it is clear, he passed to you as well. Indeed, some might argue," Holmes said, with a glace toward me, "that he sacrificed himself for the sick and impoverished whom it was his self-appointed mission to assist. Surely that is a father of whom any son could be proud."

I could see that my friend's words had an effect on Dougherty, for he sat up straight and smiled.

"You are right, Mr. Holmes. Thank you – and you, Doctor Watson – for all that you have done."

"For what you've done for us both," said Wallis. "How can we repay you?"

"You are very kind," said Sherlock Holmes, in his easy, genial way, "but I have done no more than my duty to my client. My professional fees are all the thanks I shall require."

That afternoon found us aboard the train to London with a carriage to ourselves. Holmes sat with his legs outstretched, his pipe between his lips, dreamily blowing rings of blue smoke, while I occupied myself with a little novel that I had brought with me. Suddenly Holmes stirred.

"It is just as well," he said, "that we are sworn to secrecy on this case, for I am sure it will come to represent the most embarrassing failure of my career."

"Failure? But you solved the mystery. Not only that, but you helped to restore a broken trust between two close relatives. Surely you have succeeded beyond expectations!"

"It was not a failure of results, but a failure of reasoning, which is worse. I knew Theodore Dougherty had been ill, I knew that our client's uncle's name was Wallis, but when I happened upon a hospital with the man's name on the door, a hospital both men were photographed in front of, a hospital which treated syphilitics, I failed to realize the significance of those facts in relation to each other. I really have done remarkably badly."

"I cannot agree with you. You are too hard on yourself, as I've said."

"Nevertheless, it was certainly the most interesting case since the Drebber murder, and it really has been very instructive."

"I'm glad you think so," I said. "We should celebrate. Dinner at Simpson's, perhaps?"

"The very thing, Watson. The very thing."

The Raspberry Tart
by Roger Riccard

NOTE: Due to the conservative values of the times, Dr. Watson had a hand-written note clipped to this story which read: "*The following case contains some delicate explanations of medical conditions which may not be suitable for publication, yet their presence is essential to the story. I must consult with Dr. Doyle and the publisher as to how best to convey this aspect in the least offensive way.*" – R.R.

Chapter I

It was early in our association, late in the spring of 1882 if I recall correctly, when a client came to call upon my flatmate, the consulting detective, Sherlock Holmes. It was shortly after noon when he arrived our lodgings at 221b Baker Street. He was a well-dressed gentleman whom I would put in his mid-forties. Clean-shaven and of average build, he stood about five-foot-nine, with the demeanor of a man who could command a room with no need to resort to physical size.

He identified himself as Donald Ellington. Holmes introduced me as his "trusted colleague", which gave me no small amount of pride. Once we sat down, my friend proceeded to address our guest in the manner with which I had begun to become accustomed.

"Tell me, Mr. Ellington, what brings a banker from Cox and Company to privately consult with me in my rooms rather than at your office in Charing Cross Road? Is there a problem at the bank, such that you wish to avoid publicity, or is this of a more personal nature?"

Ellington was taken aback. He leaned away from Holmes with such consternation on his face that I thought he might flee the room. After a few seconds, he took a deep breath to settle himself and replied, "It is not bank business, sir. But how could you possibly know what I am and where I work?"

"I will tell you only if you promise not to say 'How simple!'" said the detective.

Our guest agreed and Holmes explained. "You are a well-dressed gentleman, more so than a clerk. You have a bearing of command about you which is common to managers in business offices. Your shirt-front indicates some minor wear from leaning against your desk, as you frequently do in order to process paperwork. But neither your hand nor shirt cuff reveal any ink stains from significant amounts of writing. Thus, you are performing tasks limited to reading and signing documents, common managerial duties of a banker.

"Your shoes, which are shined and brushed regularly, as evidenced by the condition of the leather, have received an unfortunate layer of dust on them this morning. It is not the common dust of dirt, such as one might receive from a walk in the park or in one's yard. It is, rather, concrete dust that is currently in abundance as city construction workers are tearing up the street for repairs along Charing Cross Road in front of Cox and Company. It has clung to your shoes and lower trouser legs.

"Finally, the time of your arrival coincides with the amount of time it would take a cab to travel from your office to our humble abode at this time of day, when many are out and about seeking their noon meal."

Ellington replied, "Your explanation does seem simple, (Holmes scowled), but it is obviously the result of an observant and intelligent man whose gifts are far beyond those of the average citizen. I am gratified that this is so, for I need such a man who can use these talents, along with cunning and cleverness, to assist me in a family matter."

Appeased by the continuation of the banker's statement and acknowledgement of his skills, Holmes replied, "Then tell me, sir, what is your issue and what do you require of me?"

Ellington leaned forward, elbows on knees and hands folded. He spoke in low tones, almost as if he were afraid of being overheard, "I am a widower, Mr. Holmes, with only one son to carry on the family name. It's my son, Jasper, of whom I wish to speak. He has fallen head over heels in love with a tart who works as an actress at the Criterion Theatre named Judith Morrow. She is not of our class, but he doesn't care. He is blinded by her beauty as most young men are, including myself at that age. I understand his dalliance, for she is a pretty little thing, with raspberry red hair and a well-rounded figure. But he is talking marriage and I cannot allow such a union. If his mother were still alive, I believe she could talk sense to him. He was always closer to her. However, he has inherited my stubbornness and seems to have developed a rebellious streak since attending university."

Holmes replied with a bit of a frown, "What steps have you taken thus far? Have you met the young lady?"

"No, I only went to the theatre one evening, without my son's knowledge, so I could see her for myself. She's a decent actress, but then, she's an *actress*! It will never do!"

"I see," said Holmes. "What have you told your son?"

The banker shook his head in frustration, "I've tried reasoning with him, bribing him, and even threatening to send him to another school on the Continent. But he just says he would run away with her before allowing anything to separate them."

Holmes crossed his arms. "He seems quite determined. What would you have me do?"

Ellington sat up straight and responded, "I need you to look into her background. She is older than he, by two or three years I would guess. There could well have been a previous marriage, or at least other lovers. I need you to prove she is not the sweet young maiden that he idolizes – that she's just a raspberry tart that may satisfy his sweet tooth, but not sustain him for the life that his station allows him."

My companion sat back in his chair, tapping his fingers on the arm of it as he stared at our visitor. I was expecting him to inform Ellington that he did not deal with such cases and to take his business elsewhere. Instead, he stood and replied, "I shall look into it. I assume you do not wish me to communicate with you at the bank. What is your home address?"

Ellington stood also and handed him a card, which Holmes took, glanced at. Then he turned his back to retreat to his chemistry table, saying over his shoulder, "I shall have something for you in the next few days. Until then, do not threaten your son further, or you may precipitate the very action you fear. Will he be at the theatre tonight?"

"No, I've sent him over to Liverpool on a business errand. He won't be back until day after tomorrow at the earliest."

"Very well. Good day."

Our client seemed a bit miffed at this abrupt dismissal. Thus, I walked him to the door and assured him that Holmes was already turning over ideas in his mind. After he nodded and left, I turned back to my friend and enquired, "What are you doing, Holmes? I've never seen you take a case like this before. It is surely beneath you, and certainly no great exercise for your mind to puzzle over."

"You are correct on the first point, Watson. I would normally have dismissed such a client out of hand. There is something deeper here and, as I have no other case at the moment, I am intrigued enough to investigate further."

"What do you suspect by, 'something deeper'?"

"Donald Ellington is more than a concerned father," answered the detective. "He is an accomplished liar, and that makes me want to find the real truth of this matter.

Chapter II

"Really? What was he lying about?" I asked.

"That is what I am determined to discover, Doctor, for it is a lie of omission. He is holding something back, and it weighs significantly upon him. In the meantime, I suggest that you take in the show at the Criterion tonight and see how good an actress this Miss Morrow is."

"What will you be doing?" I asked.

"I, or rather, William Scott [1], veteran actor, shall arrive early and wander about backstage to learn what I can about the young lady."

"I did not realize your acting reputation was known beyond Henry Irving's troupe." [2]

"Actors go where the work is, Doctor. I have also worked for the Sasanoff Company and others. I know the stage door attendant, as well as the stage manager at the Criterion. I'll have no problem gaining access."

That evening I enjoyed dinner at the restaurant within the Criterion Theatre building, a structure that was less than a decade old. It brought back the memory of my meeting my friend, Stamford, just a year-and-a-half before at the Criterion Bar and the discussion that led him to introduce me to Sherlock Holmes. [3] The facility had been designed by the famous architect, Thomas Verity, and included a large restaurant, dining rooms, ballroom, and galleried concert hall. I was only able to obtain a ticket in the upper gallery, for it was a popular show and nearly sold out. Fortunately, I had brought my opera glasses with me and was able to follow the performance of Miss Judith Morrow quite well.

Ellington had not exaggerated her beauty. She had a very pretty and expressive face with high cheekbones and a dazzling smile. Her figure was well-rounded with an ample bosom yet trim waist. The most striking feature of her appearance was her luxurious hair. It was long and full and fell in waves nearly to her waist. Its color was a deep red, such as I had rarely seen. It was much like the hue of the well-ripened raspberries I had enjoyed with dinner just before the performance. That alone made her stand out among the women of the cast, even though she was not the leading lady.

I noted that she moved with grace and athleticism and was of excellent voice. From this distance there wasn't much else that I could glean about her. I did note that several men in the audience near the stage, especially those near to her age, seemed quite taken with her and were especially enthusiastic with their applause when the cast took their curtain call.

I made my way backstage afterward, with the assistance of Holmes (as William Scott) vouching for me. The usual chaos of a theatre during a performance had subsided. There was merely the storing of props and scenery and performers, now out of costume and makeup, bidding each other "Good night", or drifting off in cliques to some nearby pub. I was standing with Holmes when Miss Morrow's dressing room door opened. My friend had decided that would be his cue to leave and wait outside where he could catch a cab and be ready to follow her. I would exit behind her, attempting to get as close a look at her as I could for signs of any medical condition she might have, or with whom she might consort.

Once out the door however, she was inundated by a group of hopeful admirers. The crowd of young men forced her to stop and I nearly ran into her from behind. The pushing and shoving was getting out of hand. The stage door guard couldn't contain so many. Finally, I stepped around beside her and took her arm, using my cane to push through the chaos. I called out, "Please, I'm a doctor! You must let us pass!"

That gained us enough of a pathway to make it to the street and a nearby cab. I helped her inside and reached to close the door so she could depart, but she stopped me and asked, "Are you really a doctor, sir?"

"Dr. John Watson, at your service, Miss Morrow," I replied, still attempting to close the door so she could be off before the crowd changed its mind and came after her.

"Would you please come with me?" she implored. "I have need of a doctor at home."

The crowd was starting to suspect that something was up and began making its way toward us. I made the decision to jump in and join her as she called out an address to the driver. It might not make Holmes happy to have given away my identity, but my Hippocratic Oath comes first.

As we rode along, I enquired as to what health condition I might be treating. She replied, "It's my mother, Doctor. She's been suffering pains in her breast, and our local doctor says there's nothing to be done. I may be grasping at straws, but I'm hoping you can find something to give her some relief besides the laudanum that he's prescribed."

I sympathized with her, for she seemed sincerely grieved over her mother. "I'll certainly see her, but I don't have my medical bag. It will have to be a cursory examination."

She put her delicate hand on my forearm and gazed upon me with golden brown eyes, "Whatever you can do, sir, 'twill be of some comfort, I'm sure."

Weaving our way westward for about three miles, we disembarked in Chelsea on a street called Mulberry Walk. She led me to a first-floor apartment. Her mother was in bed asleep. It was late, being about an hour after Miss Morrow's show had ended, and I whispered to her, "I hate to disturb such a peaceful repose. Perhaps I should come back in the morning."

"Oh, it's quite all right, Doctor. She always wants me to wake her when I get home so she can hear how the show went. She was an actress herself and it's still in her blood."

I waited out in the hallway so as not to startle the woman as her daughter gently woke her.

"Mum, I'm home," she spoke softly, as she laid a hand on her mother's shoulder.

The bed-ridden lady, who I would have put in her late forties, slowly opened her eyes and smiled in recognition of her child as I ducked back out of sight.

"Judy, my sweet," she said, as she reached up and stroked her daughter's hair. "How was the show? How were your curtain calls?"

"Everything went perfect, Mum. It was a grand audience."

"Very good, very good," she replied, as her hand collapsed back onto the bed.

"Mum, I've brought a man with me who was at the show. He's a doctor. I'd like you to let him see you."

"Oh, dear, not like this! My hair! I've no makeup on. No, no child. Have him come back tomorrow."

"Mum please. He's here now. He was very kind to me after the show. He saved me from a crowd of would-be courters. When he said he was a doctor, I implored him to come see you. It will only take a few minutes.

She looked back in my direction through the open door where I was just out of her mother's sight and nodded for me to come. Hesitantly I stuck my head around the corner and waved, "Good evening, madam. I'm Dr. Watson. I don't wish to disturb you, but your daughter is quite persistent."

She looked at me, gave a little "Hmmf!" and then back up at her daughter's eyes. "Stubborn you mean. Very well, Dr. Watson. You may come in."

I stepped into the room. Miss Morrow vacated her seat so that I could sit at her mother's bedside. The elder woman was quite attractive for her age. I could see where her daughter received her looks – even the same raspberry red hair, though shorter and slightly greyed at the temples, adorned her crown. She pushed herself up into a sitting position and looked me over. "A bit young for a doctor, aren't you? How old are you, boy?"

"I'm twenty-nine, madam. May I take your pulse please?"

She gave me her wrist and continued her questions, "At what hospitals have you worked?"

"I am currently working part-time at St. Bartholomew's. Prior to that I was attached to Her Majesty's Fifth Northumberland Fusiliers in Afghanistan."

"An Army doctor! Have you any experience at all with female patients?"

"Part of my duties were to help treat the local populace. I've delivered children, dealt with infections, and . . . other female problems. At Barts, my duties include both genders and all ages . . . . Your pulse could be stronger. What symptoms are you experiencing?"

"Judy didn't tell you?"

Her daughter spoke up, "I didn't want to prejudice his opinion, Mum. Let him determine for himself, if it's true."

I turned to the girl, "You know what's wrong?" I said, almost accusingly.

The mother grabbed my elbow and turned me back toward her. "We know what other doctors have said. Judy just won't accept it."

I nodded, then continued, "As I explained to your daughter, I was there to enjoy the show. I don't have my medical bag with me, so this examination will depend largely upon your answering questions."

"You saw the show? Wasn't she marvelous?"

I smiled, "She was indeed very fine. In some ways she outshone the leading lady."

"That's my baby! She'll be a great star, just you wait and see. She's already better than I ever was."

"Oh, Mum, that's not true."

"Yes, it is, and don't you ever doubt it, young lady!"

"If I may, Mrs. Morrow," I interrupted. "Please tell me what your symptoms are."

The mother took a deep breath, which made her give a slight wince, then answered. "A few months ago I began to get a rash on my right breast. I thought it was just prickly heat, but then I began to get a slight discharge that was yellowish in color. I thought it may have been some form of jaundice, so I went to see a doctor and he found lumps on my breast. Well, I had had those before and they usually went away after my time of the month. This time they have not. The doctor wants to perform some new procedure invented in Russia, but I do not wish to be anyone's guinea pig."

Needless to say, this concerned me greatly, for she had symptoms of cancer. I asked her, "Does he want to do a biopsy?"

"Yes, that's what he called it. He wants me to see a Dr. William Talmadge at Charing Cross Hospital. Says he's some sort of specialist."

I nodded, gravely, "It's not a new procedure, madam. It's been around for nearly eight-hundred years in the Middle East. [4] I saw one performed while I was over there. They don't call it that though. A Frenchman [5] gave the name to the procedure just a few years ago, after learning of Russian doctors practicing the technique.

"If your doctor is recommending this, you really must consider it. From the symptoms you've described, there's a chance that you have a cancer. If that proves to be the case, delaying treatment could be fatal. Talmadge has a good reputation. I'd certainly recommend him as well"

"Just what would he do to me, Dr. Watson?"

Her concern was evident now that I had confirmed my colleague's diagnosis and I attempted to be a gentle as I could with the truth. "He will use a syringe to extract material from inside the lump so that he may examine it under a microscope. He will do some tests to determine if cancer cells are present. I presume your doctor has already tested the discharge from your nipple?"

"Yes, that's what made him suggest this new test," she replied. Then she reached out and took my wrist in her hand, "Tell me the truth, Doctor. Do I really have a cancer?"

"Without the biopsy, it is difficult to be sure. Unfortunately, by the time devastating symptoms present themselves, it is often too late. That's why I strongly recommend you get this done immediately."

She pulled her arm back and folded her hands together in her lap as she looked down. With her head bowed, she quietly asked, "If I do have it, can anything be done?"

I sat up a little straighter, looked back at her daughter and then to her. "I'm afraid there is no cure. If it hasn't spread too far it could be removed surgically. If it is advanced, your doctor can give you something to help with the pain, but there is no treatment."

She looked to the ceiling, almost as if in supplication to God. I could not let that statement hang in the air so I continued, "Remember, Mrs. Morrow, nothing has been determined yet. There could be multiple causes for your symptoms. Even if it is cancer, you may have caught it in time. You mustn't give up hope. Let Dr. Talmadge do the tests and let's see where you stand."

She patted my forearm again and said, "Thank you, Doctor. I will consider your advice. I'm feeling very tired and I'm afraid I must bid you good night."

I stood, bowed to her, and left the room in the company of Judith. As we walked through the flat, I noted a table with what appeared to be family portraits. I stopped to take a closer look at the man in the photos, next to a much younger version of her mother and asked, "Is this your father?"

"Yes, Thomas Morrow. He passed on two years ago. If he were only alive, I'm sure he could have convinced mother to see a doctor months ago."

"I am sorry," I said with genuine feeling. This girl hardly seemed like the tart that Ellington had described. "He appears to be fairly young. How did he die, if I may ask?"

She folded one arm across her breast and held her other hand to her mouth. I immediately regretted my enquiry as it was obviously painful to her. She bore up though and answered, "Lung cancer, Doctor. Which is why I am so afraid for mum. She lived through it with him and I am not sure she would allow herself to go through with that much suffering on her own."

I placed my hand on her arm in a gesture meant to comfort, but before I could offer my condolences she fell sobbing into my arms. Embarrassed and unsure what to do, I held her lightly and patted her back. Anything I could say would sound like a platitude. However, all I could think of was to keep her chin up and take things one day at a time until we knew for certain her mother's condition. I offered her my handkerchief as she withdrew from our embrace. She dabbed her eyes and handed it back.

"I'm sorry, Doctor. My emotions tend to run on the surface after a show and I couldn't hold back any more. Please forgive me."

"Nothing to forgive, Miss Morrow, I assure you. Anyone in your position has a right to a few tears."

She smiled, "Thank you, Dr. Watson. I shall see that Mum takes your advice."

We walked to the door, opened it, and stepped out onto the stoop. She asked a question, "If we should need you again, where can we contact you?"

My Baker Street address immediately popped to mind. Then I realized that Holmes may not wish to chance her showing up there and running into him or our client. Therefore, I answered, "A message can always reach me through Barts Hospital. I'm usually there or making rounds of patient's homes."

"When you're not at the theatre," she challenged.

"A rare occurrence, I assure you." Thinking on Holmes and our mission I asked one more question. "Do you have anyone who can assist you? A beau of your own perhaps?"

A coquettish smile crossed her lovely face. "I do have a young man in my life, Dr. Watson, although we haven't reached a stage in our relationship where I have introduced him to mother in her current condition. Jasper is out of town for a few days. That's why I was so glad you came to my rescue tonight. You were a Godsend, sir."

She leaned over, kissed my cheek, and said, "Goodnight."

I reached up and touched my cheek, "A lucky man, your Jasper. Does your mother approve of this fellow?"

She held the door as she leaned her raspberry tresses against the frame with a dreamy look in her eye. "She only knows what I have told her of 'my Jasper'. He is such a gentleman, I cannot imagine she would not love him on sight."

I smiled at her until she closed the door, then turned to the street wondering how difficult it would be to find a cab at that hour, which was now approaching midnight.

I needn't have worried. I hadn't walked more than fifty feet when a hansom rattled up and Holmes bid me to get in.

Chapter III

I settled myself in beside the detective, who ordered the driver to Baker Street while I arranged traveling rugs over my legs against the night's chill. Once settled, he questioned me. "You seem to have ingrained yourself with Miss Morrow, Watson. Is she that fickle a lover?"

I returned his jibe with indignation, "Certainly not! She was merely overwrought with emotion." I went on to explain the circumstances regarding her mother and that she considered Jasper Ellington the "man in her life".

Holmes stroked his chin and asked, "You say that she resembles her mother. How closely?"

I thought back to the woman I met and tried to compare her to her daughter. "I would say that at her daughter's age they would have been enough alike to be sisters, but not twins. The eyes, nose, and cheekbones are similar, but the mouth is slightly different. The daughter's lips are fuller. I couldn't see Miss Morrow's ears, as you recall her hair covered them. The hair is the exact same color and, I would wager, completely natural."

"How young was Miss Morrow in the picture with her mother and father?"

"I did not pry so deeply, Holmes," I admonished. "I had just relayed the news that her mother may have a terminal disease. It was hardly the time for socializing."

"I realize that, Watson, but for my own curiosity, how young was she in these family photographs?"

I tried to picture the photos on the table and could only recall one of her at a fairly young age with her parents, "I would say she was about age three."

Holmes sat back and nodded to himself. He didn't speak another word. When we arrived at Baker Street, he suggested that I go to bed, as he was "going to smoke a pipe or two" while he considered the facts at hand thus far.

The next morning, I awoke to an empty flat, Holmes having left quite early according to our landlady, Mrs. Hudson. "Oh, he was off like a shot this morning, Doctor. No breakfast, not even coffee. Can I get you anything?"

"Coffee and toast with jam, if convenient. I have rounds at Barts."

Thus fortified, I went about my morning duties at the hospital. I couldn't help thinking about Mrs. Morrow's condition. I consulted a colleague about my initial findings. He concurred my diagnosis, limited as the conditions were, was likely accurate. He also assured me Dr. Talmadge was one of the best oncologists in London. If anything could be done, he was the man for it.

Somewhat reassured, I finished my rounds and was back at Baker Street by three o'clock. Holmes had returned and was reading over one of his indexes. "Ah, Watson! Just the man I need. Are you free this evening?"

"I have no plans. Is this for your case?"

"*Our* case, dear boy. You are playing an integral part. I find it essential that you introduce me to Miss Morrow . . . as *William Scott*, of course."

"Of course," I replied, sarcastically, as if I understood his methods.

"Patience, dear Doctor. I have been poring over files at newspaper offices all day. I have ascertained just who Miss Morrow's mother is."

"How does that help your case for Ellington?"

"A case may turn on the slightest bit of information. One must learn as much as possible about suspects, victims, and even clients, if one is to arrive at the truth and a successful resolution."

"You consider Mrs. Morrow a suspect?" I asked with some indignation.

Holmes shook his head, "Our *client* considers her daughter a suspect. I believe the relationship between mother and daughter could prove revealing. Based upon your observations, colored as they may be by your gentlemanly manners and inherent capacity to see the good in people, there may be a factor helpful to our case. It may not be likely, but it must be eliminated. Then I can re-direct my thoughts and hypotheses, if need be."

We decided that I would introduce him to Miss Morrow that evening backstage. I advised him that a confrontational meeting with her mother should not take place late at night after the show, when she would be at her weakest. He, surprisingly, concurred. He suggested that we seek permission for him to visit the next day.

That evening, after the show, Miss Morrow was in her dressing room. I knocked and when she said, "Come in."

I opened the door. "Miss Morrow, good evening."

She turned and smiled with recognition, "Why, Dr. Watson! Good evening. So you managed to tear yourself away from your patients for a second performance. Should I be flattered, or is there someone else attracting the attention of a handsome man like you?"

I felt a flush begin to climb my neck, because I *was* attracted to her. I subdued my natural desire however and replied, "Your charms and beauty are worth twice the price of admission, my dear, although I know you are spoken for. I am not some masher with dubious intent. I wished to check with you about your mother, and also to introduce my friend here, Mr. William Scott. He is an actor and believes that he may know her."

Holmes bowed in his most courteous fashion as he took her extended hand, "A pleasure, Miss Morrow. The doctor and I share a flat. He happened to mention that he escorted you home last night and met your mother. When he described her as having the same lovely raspberry red hair as yourself, I wondered if she might be Edith Morningstar, with whom I worked in Henry Irving's production of *Hamlet* back in '74."

Her face lit up with a broad smile, "Why, yes, Mr. Scott. She was the understudy for the role of Gertrude. She rarely got to play the part and was primarily relegated to background scenes. I thought that she was outstanding whenever I got to watch from the wings."

"I knew it!" cried Holmes/Scott, excitedly. "I played Rosencrantz in that same production! We never had scenes together, but your mother's beauty made her a standout, just like you are now."

Miss Morrow bowed her head in that coquettish fashion of hers and batted her eyes, "Why, thank you, sir. Are you in anything now?"

Holmes/Scott shook his head, "Sadly, no. I've been visiting some of my old haunts like the Criterion here, attempting to learn of anything new I might get in on. However, the Doctor, in spite of being the soul of discretion, let enough slip that I believed your mother to be ill. I was wondering if I might pay a call to give her my good wishes?"

"I think that she would like that. Unfortunately, thanks to you, Doctor," she said, nodding my direction, "she has allowed herself to be admitted to Charing Cross Hospital for the tests that Dr. Talmadge has recommended. I expect she will be there for a few days."

Holmes allowed himself a measure of disappointment. I knew this was not convenient to his plans and he probably felt it keener than he let on. "Oh, no, Miss. I do hope it is nothing too serious!"

He turned to me, "Perhaps, Watson, you could drop in and see if she would be up to a visit from a fellow thespian?"

"I'll do what I can – with your permission, of course, Miss Morrow?"

The actress smiled – such an enchanting sight – and replied, "I think that would be just the thing to lift her spirits. If it's all right with her doctor then, by all means, please do, Mr. Scott."

We offered to escort her through the crowd outside to a cab and she gladly accepted. This time, however, she pulled her hair back, piled it on top of her head, covering it with a fashionable hat which had a veil to hide her face. Holmes seemed to take an intense interest in this and I made a mental note to ask him about it later.

Once she was safely off, Holmes and I retired to Baker Street. I asked him about his close scrutiny when she pulled her hair back.

"Just a small detail that may help complete the picture, Watson. A more revealing portrait of the lady's features may or may not assist our investigation. I will know more after I've met the mother. Can you get me into Charing Cross tomorrow, preferably in the afternoon, when her daughter will be performing in the matinée?"

"I don't see a problem," I responded. "I know several doctors who work at both there and Barts. I should be able to get you in to see her, as long as her doctor allows visitors."

"Excellent. Then I propose a good night's sleep and a hearty breakfast. I intend to call on Mr. Ellington at home tomorrow and see if I can meet Jasper."

"I was under the impression that he didn't want his son to know of your investigation."

"And he shan't. I shall be in disguise and pretend to drop in on bank business. I need to see the young man for myself."

An early morning telegram informed Ellington of Holmes's intentions. The banker's reply suggested he drop in at noon, while father and son were dining. Holmes later relayed to me what occurred.

He arrived as scheduled and was shown to the dining room by the butler. The senior Ellington stood and greeted him warmly, as though he was a valued client. He then introduced his son. Jasper stood and shook Holmes's hand cordially. He suggested to his father that he leave them to their business, as he wished to run some errands. The father frowned, knowing he was likely on his way to see his young lady in her matinée performance. Reluctantly he allowed the boy to go. He and Holmes carried on their charade and walked to the study to discuss business. Once settled and the boy was gone, our client questioned the detective. "What have you found, Mr. Holmes? Is she the little tart that I suspect?"

Holmes, notorious for not revealing his thoughts too soon, put Ellington off, "My investigation is on-going, sir. Thus far, the young lady has proven loyal to your son in his absence, in spite of temptations put into her path. At present, she is more concerned about her mother's health than any intrigue you suspect."

"Her mother?" responded the banker, with some surprise. "I would have assumed her to be an orphan." He paused a moment in thought, then continued, "What self-respecting parent allows their daughter to enter the theatrical profession?"

"Life circumstances summon strange dictations to our paths, Mr. Ellington. Some choices are not ours to make. Others come from the heart and cannot be ignored. I suggest you consider your own choices of your youth and contemplate where you might have gone had you taken another path that presented itself."

Ellington seemed taken aback by the remark. Seizing the silence, Holmes arose, bid his client "Good day," and promised a full report soon.

By one-thirty Holmes had doffed his disguise. He retrieved me from Baker Street to journey on to Charing Cross Hospital. I was able to gain permission from Dr. Talmadge to see the lady. The cancer specialist also thanked me for my efforts in recommending seeking his opinion of Mrs. Morrow's condition. We were shown to her room and I introduced my companion as *William Scott*.

She held out her hand and Holmes took it gently as he sat in a chair by her bedside, "Good afternoon, Miss Morningstar. I don't expect you to remember me, but we were in Irving's *Hamlet* together, some eight years ago."

She peered closely at him and finally nodded in recognition, "Of course, Willy Scott. How could I forget those steely grey eyes? Rosencrantz, wasn't it?"

"I am flattered at your memory, madam," said Holmes in all earnestness. "When the doctor mentioned his encounter with your daughter and described that delightful red hair, I knew it must have come from you. I am sorry to see you in these circumstances. Is there anything I can do for you?"

"Oh, that's very kind of you, Willy, but I'm afraid it's all in the doctor's hands now . . . and God's, of course."

Holmes nodded, "I understand. I hear that you lost your husband a few years ago. I don't wish to be indelicate, but if there is anything I can do financially, I have access to funds that may be put at your disposal."

"Oh, Willy, that's kind of you, but why would you even think of me in such a fashion? Our camaraderie was so brief and so long ago."

Holmes/Scott smiled, and I believed that he now spoke from the heart, "I never told you what an inspiration you were to me, Miss Morningstar. To see you carry on in that understudy role, so close and yet so far from realizing your goal to be the leading lady, kept me going in my darkest hours when I thought of giving up the stage. If I can repay you for that, I would be honored."

"You are still acting, Willy?"

Holmes actually gave a little chuckle, "Nothing Shakespearean. However, I have played some significant roles these last few years."

She smiled and replied, "Good for you! As to finances, I have some small income from my late husband's investments and Judy brings home a fair amount. Thank you for your kindness!"

During this last statement, Dr. Talmadge had rejoined us. He suggested Mrs. Morrow needed her rest. We bid her "Goodbye," walking out with the doctor.

"I couldn't help but overhear that last statement, gentlemen," Talmadge said. "So far her test results are not good, and any treatment option is going to be more expensive than I believe she realizes. If you can obtain funds for her, it will be of significant assistance."

Holmes nodded, "Understood, Doctor. I believe I have a source that should cover her bills. I will let you know."

Holes insisted on sending me back to Baker Street on my own, as he had, "a little side stop to make".

Chapter IV

When Holmes arrived back at our flat to join me for the supper that Mrs. Hudson had laid out, I queried him on his errand. He merely stated it was additional confirmation of his deductions. He would reveal all at the proper time. He only needed to discern how to approach the matter. He dug in heartily to his meal, which told me the case was solved in his mind. He could therefore afford the minor distraction of digestion.

When we finished our supper, we took up our chairs by the fireplace with brandy and cigars. I was full of curiosity about the case. However, knowing Holmes's flare for the dramatic exposé of facts in his own good time, I settled down with a medical journal. He took up an evening paper as he sat across from me in his chair. After several minutes, he suddenly folded the paper and tossed it onto the lamp table next to him.

"Very well, Watson, I cannot stand to see you suffer so, and your opinion may be of value to me."

I looked up from my journal at this interruption to my thoughts and replied, "Whatever are you talking about?"

"Your curiosity over this case is practically filling the room with its aura, Doctor. You haven't turned a page for over four minutes, your foot is twitching like a dancer before a performance, and your eyes have been glazed over in thought. Let me tell you what I now know and my plan for its revelation. Perhaps, with your more emotional approach to life, you may have an option that I haven't considered."

Flabbergasted by his deduction of my mood, I set the magazine aside and gave him my full attention. What he had to tell me was both surprising and disturbing. When I pressed him for proof, he waved my question aside and merely said, "Later, Doctor. Let me present you with the options I have considered for revelation."

After he explained his considerations and the pros-and-cons of each, I made some few observations, but agreed that his chosen course of action seemed the most prudent. He suggested, tomorrow being Sunday, that we should exercise that option in the afternoon. He enquired if I would be amenable to accompanying him. I insisted that he could not keep me away, as my presence might be needed. He seemed pleased by my reaction. Thus he stepped out to send off a telegram to Mr. Ellington, advising him of his need to join us in a meeting that would resolve his son's situation.

The following afternoon, Ellington's carriage arrived at our door. It was a modest brougham pulled by a neat pair of bays – certainly not ostentatious, yet still a symbol of moderate means. We met him at our front door and Holmes informed him of our need to travel elsewhere. When he told the driver where to go, it caught our client off-guard and he questioned Holmes's temerity.

"I assure you, Mr. Ellington, the person we are going to meet is essential to the resolution of your case."

Within twenty minutes, we were entering the room of Judith Morrow's mother at Charing Cross Hospital. Holmes had sent word ahead to Talmadge to have her expect visitors. He was reluctant, due to her delicate state. When Holmes explained the matter, he agreed. Thus, the lady was ready for our visit, but not necessarily our client.

When we walked in, Holmes greeted her with an assuring warmth I had only seen on rare occasions as he sat next to her, "Mrs. Morrow, I see you are feeling a bit better. There is more color to your cheeks."

She nodded in agreement, but then she saw our client. She could not take her eyes off him, as her color began to drain. Holmes bowed his head, "I see you have noted our companion. I must make a confession to you, madam. When you knew me, *William Scott* was my stage name. I am really Sherlock Holmes. My current profession is as a private consulting detective. This gentleman is my client, whom I believe you once knew."

He turned to the banker and said, "Mr. Ellington, this is the widow, Mrs. Thomas Morrow – formerly the actress, Edith Morningstar. She is Judith's mother."

Turning back to the woman sitting up in her bed, he solemnly stated, "Mr. Ellington is Jasper's father."

Her hand flew to her mouth as she whispered, "No, no! It cannot be! Please tell me there's a mistake! Dr. Watson, this can't be true!"

I came closer and confirmed, "I'm afraid so." I looked back at Ellington. He was frozen in shock with his mouth open and hands gripping tightly onto his bowler's brim. I beckoned him forward so he could take the seat that Holmes had vacated.

He slowly sat as she stared at him in disbelief. Finally, he found his voice, "Edith, I . . . I . . . I cannot believe it is really you!"

She reached up and touched his cheek with the back of her hand as she stared into his eyes, "Donald, oh my poor Donald."

"What happened to you?" he asked in quiet desperation. "You just disappeared without a trace. I searched for you for weeks. I was desperate to find you. First, I was worried, then I became angry that you had deserted me. Months went by and finally my parents convinced me to move on with my life."

"I will tell you my story, Donald, but first tell me, is it true? Are you really Jasper's father?"

"You've met Jasper?"

"Not yet, but he is all that my Judith can talk about. She is sure they were meant to be together. She says she feels a connection to him stronger than anyone she's ever met. Now I know why."

The banker kept staring at her, slowly shaking his head, "I can't believe she's your daughter. When I saw her perform, and the color of her hair, it reminded me of you and how you deserted me. It made me fear for him and what he may be getting into. That's why I was so against it. Now I understand how he fell in love with her, just as I did with you."

She took his hands in both of hers, "Donald, you must listen to me. They cannot be together. We must put a stop to it."

"What? What's wrong? They could have what you and I were denied." He pulled his hands back and suddenly was wary, "Would you have her do to him what you did to me?"

She put her face into her hands as tears began to flow. "Donald, you don't understand – *Judith is your daughter!*"

Holmes and I discreetly retreated to the hallway, though as a doctor I felt obliged to stay close by, should this conversation trigger an adverse physical reaction. I overheard enough to confirm what Holmes had told me the night before. When Miss Morningstar found she was with child, she knew that Ellington's parents would never permit him to marry her. She left without a word and went away to an institution where she could have the child in secret. Determined not to give her baby girl over to an orphanage, she returned to the stage in Liverpool. There she met and married Thomas Morrow, a theatre manager, who adopted the baby Judith as his own. They never told the child that Morrow was not her real father. The years went by and she later caught on with Irving at the Lyceum in London. As Judith grew, she took up the family business and her talent was now bringing her significant roles, allowing her to make a living and take care of her mother on a decent income.

Dr. Talmadge arrived shortly and we took our leave after explaining the delicacy, though not the details, of the conversation taking place within. He confided to me that Mrs. Morrow's tests indicated advanced breast cancer. She would only have a few months at best.

Holmes and I took a cab back to Baker Street in silence at this news. Upon arrival, we ensconced ourselves in front of the fire with full glasses of whisky. I don't know about my friend, but I contemplated the tragedy of happiness lost when artificial class distinction overruled matters of the heart.

Our melancholia was interrupted about an hour later by the arrival of a message from Ellington. My companion was staring into the fire when I answered the door and accepted the note. When I told him it was from our client he said, "I've no taste for more depressing news, Watson. You read it."

I tore it open and read as follows:

> *Mr. Sherlock Holmes,*
>
> *Your services shall no longer be required. Please remit your bill at your convenience. Edith and I have agreed to tell our children the truth. I have also pledged to pay her medical bills and move her and Judith into my home, where she can have a full-time nurse. I have also promised to care for Judith as the daughter I never knew for the rest of her life.*
>
> *Your servant, sir,*
> *Donald Ellington*

"Well, it's good to see Ellington has a heart under his banker's brain," I noted. Refilling my whisky, I asked Holmes, "Just how did you come to your conclusions? Where did you go yesterday?"

Seemingly relieved to have something else to occupy his mind, my companion put down his drink and reached for his pipe instead. Once he had it going, he replied, "You recall, Watson, from the very first I was suspicious of our client's motives. There were physical signs – twitches, the movement of his eyes, and his tone of voice – that led me to believe he was holding something back. I especially noted the way he said the word 'tart'. It wasn't delivered merely with the derision of someone speaking of a lower class. There was a vehemence there that told of a deeper story. This intrigued me and thus I took up the case.

"Your initial episode with Miss Morrow painted a far different picture of the lady than we had been told. It also provided me with seeds of information that needed to be nurtured. Once I met both Jasper and Judith and was able to observe their physical characteristics, I knew that I had to obtain more information to confirm my theory. While Miss Morrow was performing and her mother in hospital, I left you to stop by their home. I confess to putting my lock-picks into practice, Doctor. After I'd examined pictures of Thomas Morrow, I was convinced my deductions were accurate. I confirmed there were no baby pictures of Judith with Morrow. That, and my observation of her mouth and ears, which you noted were unlike her mother's, further supported my deductions. Hers are nothing like Morrow's, but they are very similar to Ellington's, and identical to Jasper's. I believe it was the physical characteristics they shared that attracted them to each other in the first place. It is much like the attraction that first cousins experience – only more so with two children who share a parent."

"Why didn't you tell Ellington all this before meeting with Mrs. Morrow?" I enquired.

Holmes shrugged, "I admit, it was a gamble, especially in exposing Mrs. Morrow to whatever reaction he might have. However, I believed that he needed to hear the truth from her own lips. As a paid consultant, he could have disbelieved or ignored me. I felt morally bound to force him to confront his past and remember the feelings he once experienced, so as to better understand his son's dilemma."

"How curious," I observed, "that he should achieve his goal of ending the romance between his son and the 'raspberry tart', as he called her, and instead end up with a daughter instead of a daughter-in-law."

My friend replied, "His class prejudices led him to confront his own indiscretions, Watson. Now, he is forced to face the consequences at a price he never dreamed of. I believe it is the Buddhists, or possibly Hindus, who have a concept for it called '*karma*'."

"I am well aware of that term," I answered. "When I served in Afghanistan, I heard it often. '*What we put into the universe will come back to us*.' Much like the Bible says, '*That which you sow, you shall also reap.*'"

Holmes took up his glass and raised it to me. “Let us hope, dear Doctor, that the deeds you and I sow will return a more kindly crop than that of our client.”

NOTES

1 – Holmes stage name, based on his real name, *William Sherlock Scott Holmes*.
2 – In his latter university years and early career, Holmes supplemented his income as an actor with the troupe of Henry Irving at the Lyceum Theatre. Irving was one of the most famous English actors of the Victorian era and was the first actor to be awarded a knighthood. Holmes is also known to have worked with the lesser known Sasanoff Company.
3 – See *A Study in Scarlet* for details of this meeting.
4 – The Arab physician Abulcasis (1015-1107) developed early diagnostic biopsies using needles to puncture goiters and then examining the extracted material.
5 – Ernest Besnier, Dermatologist, in 1879.

The Mystery of the Elusive Bard

by Kevin P. Thornton

"Watson, I am expecting a visitor later this morning, and he promises to bring with him a puzzle worthy of our time and my effort. If you would be kind enough, I'd like you to stay and listen to what he has to say."

"I'd be delighted to," I said, and I was telling the truth. There was some small irresponsible part of me that found it easy to rearrange my life so as to make myself available for an investigative consultation by Sherlock Holmes. Even in those early days of our shared accommodation and nascent friendship, I couldn't help but be fascinated by the ways in which his mind, so superior to all others that I had ever encountered, enabled him to see what others could not. He alone, it seemed, could solve the unsolvable and create the most miraculous of conclusions from the most mundane of events. Thus if he called I came running, or rather walking, into the sitting room we shared, fascinated by the man and grateful to be afforded a seat to view his great games, as he sometimes described his adventures. Little did I know how close he would come, in this instance, to failing.

I was ready and waiting when Mrs. Hudson showed the gentleman to our door, and at first glance, he seemed ready to disappoint my heady expectations. Jeremiah Knox was a man of medium height, weight, and age. He had the look to me of someone that could pass unnoticed on the street, and I half-expected him to disappear into a dark corner of the room. I was discouraged as to the possibilities of adventure emanating from the man. Holmes, as always, saw more to him than most.

"Do you think that you'll see out this slight downturn in your book business?" Holmes inquired. He was holding Knox's presented card but hadn't yet looked at it. He did so, his smile thin and brief, then handed it to me as if to affirm his conclusions.

Mister Knox was amused. "I had heard of your trickery, Mister Holmes, and I am impressed. Clearly you deciphered my occupation before reading my card. How, pray tell?"

"It is several small things, none of which is trickery," said Holmes. "Printers' ink has a distinct smell which is still with you, regardless of the windy day outside. Such an odour indicates one of only half-a-dozen trades, thus narrowing my focus. Your introductory card is of a particular quality rarely seen – or in this case felt – outside royal circles. A printer would have the pride to display his best wares in such a manner. As regards the kind of printing, you have the peculiar callouses on your right thumb and fingers that are caused by extensive stitching work. Sailors have them, as do seamstresses. In your case, a bookbinder. That you are still doing some binding yourself shows that business is not as brisk as you would wish. Yet you are well-dressed – keeping up appearances to show that your publishing house is still viable and has been successful in the recent past. Gathered together, all these little signs point towards my conclusion."

"And you are absolutely correct. We are suffering a tail-off in business after some recent misfortunes, and that is half the reason why I am here to seek your help."

Holmes motioned to a chair and Knox sat down as he began his tale.

"Knox Publishing has been in the very lucrative business of popular poetry for the last fifty years. The company was started by my grandfather, and I am the third generation to run it. We are not considered literary enough for the grand publishers of inner London, as we publish what people *wish* to read, not what we *think* they should. Because of this, we make money – well most of the time at least – and every now and then we will have a success that will ensure our finances for several years." He mentioned several poets of whom I'd heard. Holmes clearly had not, and Knox noted this.

"You are no lover of verse, Mister Holmes?"

"I have no opinion, save it has never helped me to solve a case."

'The writers that I mentioned are all rich men because they write what people want to read. Every now and then, such populist writing crosses into the world of the literati – the current poet laureate is a notable example – and the publishing world heaves a sigh of relief. Such writers create trends and sales that sustain us all."

"You are not Lord Tennyson's publisher."

"No, more's the pity. I am here about another poet that we missed. Three years ago, a retired sailor living in Devon self-published some poetry that he had written. Unlike most of the bawdy verse that comes from men of such ilk, the work of Edgar Gateshead, for that is his name, was earthy yet elegant. Simple enough for the common man, his poetry exploded on the literary scene as well. We tried to publish him after we had seen an early copy of one of his pamphlets, but he had some uncommonly good advice, and his family, chiefly his daughter Jemima, took control of his output and published it all directly themselves, to great success"

"So far," said Holmes, "I fail to see why you need me. Please reach your point quickly, Mister Knox."

“In addition to my work as a bookseller, I represent an association of publishing companies who, on occasion, have a little book festival and give out an award to writers of literary estimation. It was decided to award Edgar Gateshead with our latest honour at an appropriate time.”

“A-ha!” said Holmes. “He is missing, is he not? You can’t find your poet, and your literary festival will founder without the guest of honour. Why not have the local constabulary assist you, or give the prize to another?”

“It is not that simple. While we look forward to the event, we have some scruples, and wish to honour the man and his work.” Holmes looked doubtful but kept his opinion to himself.

“We have tried to do enlist the authorities, to no avail. In addition, we have twice sent representatives to the village of Crooklebank, for that is where he lives. It is a small place, numbering but sixty souls, and the whole community is sustained by the success of their most famous son. His books are published there, the local tavern has been renamed ‘The Poet’s Corner’, and there is even a shop selling mementos along with signed copies of his volumes of poetry, which are published with some frequency and to tremendous acclaim and sales. There is in this village everything that a great poet could need or wish for, except for one thing: The poet himself. On both visits, we were told that we had just missed him, or he’d gone to London, or he was writing and not to be disturbed. His home is surrounded by a tall wall which almost makes the house seem like a prison, and despite presenting ourselves at the front gate, we weren’t permitted entrance. It has been most frustrating, Mister Holmes. It’s most important that we invite him to our festival, which is why I beg of you . . . .” He stopped then, silenced by Holmes’s imperious finger.

“Let us be quite clear here, Mister Knox. You want me to find a man who does not wish to be found so that you can exploit his fame financially. You need him to make a success of your literary festival so that you can sell more books, and you ask me to do this sordid thing for you. Is that right?”

Knox hung his head in shame. “When you put it that way, you make me seem crass and money-grabbing. My apologies, Mister Holmes. I did not mean to insult you so.”

“I’ll take the case,” said Holmes.

“I beg your pardon?”

“I’ll take your case, Mister Knox. Despite your reasons for coming to me, there is more to this than meets the eye. Where is Crooklebank?”

“It is just outside the port of Bideford, on the west Devon coast.”

"Then Watson and I shall travel there on the morning train. You mentioned that Gateshead has had continued and frequent success. Has the quality of his poetry remained where it once was?"

"In many ways it has improved," said Knox. "It's hard to define how long a poet should take to create his work, but Gateshead is most industrious and seems to be getting better the more he publishes. His earlier work was swarthy, with the words of a Jack Tar interspersed with the gentleness of an Elizabethan. As his work has progressed, so too has his style. The hint of bawdy sea shanty has made way for stanzas of extraordinary beauty and gentleness. It is part of his success, I suppose, and one reason for his popularity. That such a man – a sailor, fighter, and carouser – could be capable of such beauty gives hope to us all, does it not?"

"I am not convinced," said Holmes, "of the beauty of his work, and I suspect we will find a baser reason for his skill and his sales. You say you have been there. Is there a local resident who has some knowledge of poetry? Such a man may prove valuable in our investigations, for I will leave nothing to chance in uncovering the secret behind his work."

"There is one young man whom we found valuable when we visited. His ability to analyse rhythm and meter is quite exemplary. He has just finished his schooling at the United Services College and awaits his ship to India, where he is to work as a newspaperman." He wrote a name down on the back of a card and gave it to Holmes. "There is one notable inn in Crooklebank, home to the aforementioned tavern. I shall arrange for him to speak with you there."

Early the next morning we set off for Devon. It would be a journey of some hours, and although I had questions to ask of Holmes as to why he had taken the case, I already knew it would be a waste of my breath. As always, he would keep his own council. He surprised me, then, by explaining his actions.

We were alone in the carriage and not yet thirty minutes into the journey when he said, "You are surprised that I took the case. Maybe you are even a little disappointed that I decided to do so for no nobler reason than a healthy remittance once I solve it, hmm?"

"I'm sure that you have your reasons," I said, and Holmes laughed once, a short sharp *Ha!* that startled me.

"My dear Watson, you must never play a card game that requires you to bluff. Your honesty compels you to register your emotions, and it is only politeness that prevents you from saying what you really feel."

"I am indeed puzzled. Why *did* you take this case?"

“I’ll tell you: I know nothing about *poetry*, but I know a thing or two about *talent*, and one of the first steps towards any talented performance, be it detection, medicine, or indeed poetry, is the accrual of such skills needed, mostly through learning and experience. I took this case because it has some puzzles that go contrary to the way I have taught myself to think. I wish to either confirm my views or disprove them.”

“Assuming,” I said, “that you solve it.” I wish I could have bitten back my words because Holmes raised a subtle but incredulous eyebrow to me and said no more for the rest of the journey.

Crooklebank was nestled in a vale on a tributary of the Torridge River, which flowed into the port of Bideford. It was a pretty little village of some twenty houses and a small high street which housed the inn, not far from the main road into the harbour town. Holmes and I took a walk around the town and went into the shop. Holmes purchased all six volumes of Gateshead’s verse and then said, “Do let us take a turn by the manor. It is the only house of substance in the village and, judging by its walls, it’s the home of the great Gateshead, as Knox described it. Maybe we’ll be invited in and all will be resolved. Failing which, I shall return to the hotel to meet Knox’s young poet master. Would you then, Watson, put yourself out and about among the parish, asking how you could meet Mister Gateshead. There is no need for subtlety. I’m interested in the reactions you get from the locals.”

There was nothing to see at the manor house, save a large stout locked gate the same height as the wall, ten feet tall within an inch.

“It seems as if it is a prison,” I said. “The walls are designed to keep people within.”

“That is a way of looking at it,” said Holmes, and I took some satisfaction from what I thought was his approbation. “Such walls are as useful for keeping people out as in, and for protecting secrets.”

“I see no means of calling on the house,” I said. “I assume that we’ll need to at some point.”

“There is an easy way to do so,” said Holmes. “When the time comes, we shall be allowed entry.” He refused to explain anymore to me. I’d already discovered this vexing habit he had of keeping his cards close to his chest. In these early days, I thought it to be showmanship, making as much of his artistry and rationalizations as possible. Later, I came to realize that although he could be theatrical for a cause, dressing up as a beggar or masquerading so as to hide in plain sight while on a case, he never did so for effect. His reticence to explain himself was often a means to give himself every opportunity to gather all the relevant facts. When he started, he was the world’s first and only consulting detective, and he was aware that the footsteps he created often led into new and uncharted territory – hence his caution. He felt the need to prove that his methods worked.

Later that evening we dined together. Afterwards, we took our cigars out onto the road outside the inn and strolled up and down. Although it was a small village, many of the locals ate in the inn that night, so there was occasional traffic as people meandered home. If such dining out was common practice, it indicated a level of prosperity rarely found in the countryside, and I said as much to Holmes.

"Indeed, the people of this town have done well from the Gateshead publishing phenomenon. Did you get to talk to any of the villagers?"

"I did. There was a construction man repairing a wall who seemed delighted to stop and tarry for a moment. He was appreciative of the largesse of Crooklebank's most successful son, and said that he's never had so much work. I also spoke to the local policeman, a soldier home for the weekend from his unit, and a man out-and-about on his penny-farthing. All were delighted at how well the village is doing, and none seem to question that it has all come about through the most unlikely of poetic endeavours. It was as if they are supported by the goose that laid golden eggs without pondering the means of the egg-laying. I also found out that the village is indeed lucky to have become the centre of all this poetic activity. It was quite by chance that Gateshead settled here. His wife died while he was at sea, and he bought a small cottage here to give his daughter a home."

"But why here?" said Holmes.

"I'll wager because it was so cheap and it was all that he could afford at the time," I said. "Gateshead was a bit of a rummy, and whatever spare money he had went on the drink. This village was dying, the manor had been empty for years, with the farmlands owned by outsiders. Gateshead bought here because it was a bargain, and it was quite by chance that he started printing out his poetry. The house he bought was once owned by the editor of a now defunct local newspaper. The rumour is that he got the man's printing press up and running. He started out by giving away his poetry to anyone who would buy him a drink. It was our friend Knox who heard about it and offered to publish him, but he chose to do everything by himself. His success allowed him to buy the manor, and he has barely been seen since by anyone outside the local villagers. There is a sister at the manor, Julie Rowe, along with her husband, a retired doctor. No one knows whether she helps keep the house or run the business. And there is Jemima Gateshead, now nineteen so I'm told, who seems to be her father's spokesman"

"And no one sees the Father?"

“The villagers all claim to see him every now and again, and they all talk about his robust health and his shyness.”

“Fascinating,” said Holmes. “I have also talked to some of the people of the village. There are two men staying in the hotel who have been ranching in America. They heard of the prosperity here and have returned home to take up their old homes and find work. Both of them used the same phrase that you mentioned – that Mister Gateshead is often seen around the village and is in robust health.”

“It is as if they are following a script. There seems to be a keenness to keep outsiders unaware of the true nature of Mister Gateshead’s health. What if he is ill, Holmes – or dead?”

“A possibility that crossed my mind. To that end, I have engaged Knox’s poetry student to give me an opinion on Gateshead’s writings. He promised to study through the night and report to us in the morning. Though only sixteen years of age, he is of course familiar with the work, but I’ve tasked him with some specificities that may throw some light on the mystery of Edgar Gateshead.”

“Is that not a monumental task for one so young who has barely finished school?” I asked.

“He is both young and strong, Watson, and most anxious to earn the fee that I offered him. He sails next week for India, and I think he has found the expenses of his first summer out of school difficult. Let us meet again in the morning where we shall break our fast with our scholar and see what he says.”

“I did what you wished, Mister Holmes. I haven’t yet had time to aggregate all my studies into a formal report, but I shall do so, if you desire, immediately we are done here.”

“Tell us your impressions, young Sire, based on the parameters I set you.”

“If, as you said, you thought that these six volumes of Gateshead’s poetry were written by more than one person, I’m afraid I must disillusion you. The style and use of language shows a clear progression of one writer becoming more experienced, and better at his craft. Volume Three is a better collection than Volume Two, and each subsequent volume shows improvement and further maturity. If you were to predict the future, I would say this is a poet not yet in his prime.”

“Why would you ask such a question?” I said.

“Because I know nothing of the creation of poetry, and I wondered if this was some grand con game.”

“If you thought that, Mister Holmes,” said our scholar, “then you do indeed know little about poetry. It is not something that could be parsed piecemeal from obscurity. For such a con to be successful, Gateshead would need a source of brilliant unknown verse, and that is highly unlikely."

"So it hasn't been concocted by a team of trained writers scribbling away in secret?" said Holmes.

"To what purpose, Mister Holmes? However it was written, it is still good – some may say great – work. The readers will not care how many origins there are to the work, only that it is original. And I've never heard of such a thing. Volumes of work can be increased in the industrial world by the application of more resources. It cannot happen in the creating of original art."

"And you have answered my question in a way that allows me to follow the only other logical conclusion about Gateshead. I had thought that he kept hidden because if he were allowed to be in public, it would be obvious that he couldn't have written this poetry. He is after all a sailor, and his first volume of work attests to this in some way. Did Knox not tell us it was coarser than his subsequent writings? He has grown and changed, become more refined."

"If that was the impression either Knox or I gave you," said the young man, "then I apologize. It is not what I think. I am of the opinion that the first volume was written to seem as if it was of the sea, as there is some shanty feel to the early stanzas. It is almost done in homage, but I don't think this poet grew out of that style as much so much as reverted to his original. If there is a false note to be struck in his six volumes of work, it is in the first. Volume One rings slightly more hollow than the subsequent five."

"But how can such a man write such elegant poetry?" I asked. "He was a sailor, not an educated man."

"Maybe," said Holmes, "he was a man who spent much of his time at sea bettering himself. It is unlikely, but not beyond the realms of possibility, and would explain his talent. There is a philosophy that I have lived by in my quest for knowledge: One must continue to learn so the minutes of experience become hours, and the hours become days. At the heart of expertise, however, is to fill each unforgiving minute with sixty seconds of work done."

"I say," said the young man. "If that is your line, it is a jolly good one."

"If it was mine, it is now yours," said Holmes. "You are sailing soon, are you not?"

"I am. My parents are in Lahore and have secured me a position as the assistant editor of the local newspaper, *The Civil and Military Gazette*.

I hope to be a writer – poetry at first, and then books. A start in journalism is an excellent way to learn my trade."

"Good luck, young man," said Holmes. "If you are half as good at writing poetry as you are at analyzing it, then I think you'll do well in your chosen career, Mister Kipling."

"Please," he said, shaking our hands. "Call me Rudyard,"

After he had left, I said to Holmes, "How does his analysis help you."

"Patience, Watson. Once we've finished here, we shall find a way to beard the bard in his own den, and then all will be revealed.

The little shop next to the inn was more than just a treasury of poetry and souvenirs. It had a back section that held groceries and some local wares, enough to supply the needs of the residents of the village.

"The proprietor is the innkeeper's wife," Holmes said. "In a village such as this, relying as it does on the patronage of the manor, I believe we have found our means of ingress to the poet and his family without having to suffer the indignity of climbing a ten-foot wall. Let us be about sending a message."

The shop was quiet when we walked in. There were two women behind the counter, and they had the look of a mother and daughter. Holmes addressed the elder one. "What time do you deliver supplies to the big house?"

"We leave in thirty minutes sir, but I'm charged not to disturb them with matters of the outside world. The Gateshead family is very insular."

"Indeed," said my companion. "When you go this morning, you may tell them that Sherlock Holmes and John Watson will be waiting to be given entry at the main gates. Failure to do so will cause us to return with a force from the local constabulary to investigate the fate of the poet Edgar Gateshead." He handed her his visiting card, the one that stated his occupation. "Take that with you. It will convince them as to how serious our intentions are."

We left the store and Holmes began to amble along the street towards the manor. I followed beside him, and less than two minutes later we saw the delivery cart leave the back of the inn and proceed down a parallel lane to the delivery entrance of the manor.

"They shall be waiting for us," said Holmes, and they were.

Doctor George Rowe, husband of Julie Rowe *née* Gateshead, was waiting at the gate with a key on a chain jangling in his hand, magnifying his nervous disposition. For a man who had spent his life as a medical practitioner, presumably projecting confidence while treating the ill, he seemed a man on the verge of tears, and he scurried up the pathway, expecting us to keep up while trying to distance himself from us. He compared favourably with the white rabbit in Lewis Carroll's book and I said as much to Holmes.

"Who?" he said, and I was once again reminded of the specificity of his knowledge. Although Doctor Rowe was a man in his retirement and his wife, the older sister of Edgar Gateshead, a woman in her early fifties, both of them deferred to the youngest member of their group. I had to remind myself that Jemima Gateshead was not yet twenty. In appearance she was severely dressed, as if she clothed herself with authority and asperity.

"We have permitted you entrance to our abode only to prevent you from spreading false stories, Mister Holmes. My father is not dead, and we will defend him with the finest legal minds in the country."

"Or," said Holmes, "you will make us an offer to go away, for that is indeed your *modus operandi*, is it not? You control your surrounds with the largesse that comes of your publications. This was a dead village three years ago, and now everyone is doing well, and they would have it no other way. In return, they protect you from the outside and your big secret. All the poetry, and the image of the sailor who writes such striking verse, are publications that are in his name, though not from his pen. Is that not so, Miss Gateshead?"

Holmes had clearly hit the mark. Jemima Gateshead stood silently, fuming. I think she was at that moment torn between brazen defiance or upping the ante. Holmes saved her from her quandary.

"We are not here to ruin your business. Indeed, I admire much of what you have done here. The villagers are happy, the world of poetry is a better place, and you have secured a lifestyle far beyond what your father could actually provide to you. But we came here because a group of benevolent publishers wish to make an award to the poet. Even if they go away mollified, someone else will take their place. The story of the wandering sailor coming home to write such lyrical work is one that captures the imagination, but the real story, the tale of the young prodigy who credited her father with her own poems, may even be a better one."

"He knows all," said her Aunt Elizabeth. "What can we do?" She turned to her husband for comfort, but he had already sat down.

"There was nothing ethically wrong with what we did," said the doctor. "We have broken no laws."

"You would do well to explain yourself," I said, prepared to take umbrage on behalf of the entire medical profession.

"No," said Jemima. "It was my idea. Therefore, the blame is mine and mine alone. Gentlemen, please follow me." She led us to the back of the manor, to a room that was half-bedroom and half-hospital. There was a nurse in attendance, but I'd wager her job was not a difficult one. Her patient, Edgar Gateshead, lay on the bed, staring unseeingly at the ceiling. I moved closer to examine him.

"He had a debilitating seizure," said his daughter, "and he has been like that for nearly three years." Gateshead appeared unmoving but well-treated, and I could find no fault with her tale.

She returned to the front room and we followed behind.

"Leave us please, Aunt Elizabeth and Uncle George. I would talk to Mister Holmes and his friend alone."

They left and Jemima Gateshead smiled briefly. "They are good people. They have been of some solace to me, and my Uncle has arranged all manner of medical visitation from experts, to no avail." She paused in her thoughts, wondering how much to say. Honesty won out. "You understand now why it is a big secret? We can't publish poetry from a man who cannot write – maybe cannot even think."

"Why did you do so in the first place?" I asked.

Jemima sat down in the chair vacated by her uncle. "It all just happened so suddenly," she said. "When my mother died and my father came home to take care of me, it became obvious that he was unable to do so. I was fifteen, and I persuaded him to allow me to control his finances, such as they were. We rented a cottage here in the village. It came with a printing press. More importantly, it came with a neighbour who had worked the press, which mattered little at the time until my father chanced upon some of my scribblings."

"He recognized your talent," I said.

"He recognized my facility with words, and he saw in my poems the means to make money. He was well read, and he told me what every teacher I have ever had had already said to me – that I was extraordinarily gifted with words. It is a talent I've had since I could first read and write. There are some that would call me a prodigy. My father, for all he tried to be a good man, saw only a means to buy his next drink. 'Come' he said, 'we have your skill and the means to print them. What other writer has her own press?' It seemed a jolly jape at first, so I wrote some ditties in a style that would seem more in common with his experiences. We ran them off, my father started trading them in the inn, and he found some interest from travellers, so we printed a batch and took them into town."

"You must have been delighted at your success," said Holmes.

"I was surprised," said Jemima. "It is one thing to be told of your talent, but another to have tangible proof in the bank. That was when it happened. I gave my father some money to go and celebrate, and he, from the reports I had from the innkeeper, overdid things and collapsed on the floor. He has not moved unaided since then."

Jemima Gateshead was wringing her hands together as if to twist her fingers off.

"Imagine that," she said. "I had already planned a gradual transition. The next volume was to be a joint effort with less of 'his' work and more of my own. But his volume sold so well I couldn't risk losing that income. We could afford to look after him in comfort as long as the poems, under his name, kept selling well, but I dare not risk telling the truth, lest my vanity cause our sales to plummet."

"And so the untruths became bald-faced lies," said Holmes, "which needed to be perpetuated to protect your secret."

"You have seen my father," she said, "I beg you, do not risk our way of life. I must protect him. It was I who caused this harm to him."

"No," I said. "Your father most likely had many years of alcohol excess under his belt. This was likely to happen eventually. You have no burden of guilt here." I could see she wanted to believe me. Whether she ever would or not I didn't know.

"I will not give up your secret," said Holmes, "but someone eventually will. My advice, if you ever sought it, would be to talk to someone like my client, Jeremiah Knox. His family has been in publishing in three generations and he is aware of the quality of your work. If anyone can ensure a smooth poetic transition from Edgar to Jemima Gateshead, it will be him, or someone of his ilk."

"Thank you," she said. "I will do so. You have allowed me the opportunity to extricate myself from this veil of lies, and I shall take full advantage of it."

Two hours later we were on the train bound for home. "This was not a case that I thought you would take on," I said. "There was no dastardly crime, no evil genius doing something despicable. I know you better than to think you did it for the fee. So why did you decide to investigate?"

"There is something about the mystery of genius that eludes me, Watson. Not the genius of a mathematician who has spent years studying theorems and has the knowledge to take his field a step further. Not the master composer who uses his eighty-eight keys and creates a new a song that has never before existed. These talents I understand. They are those of a master craftsman, and I know how their minds work because in my own field I am one of them. As they studied scales and librettos or angles and tables, so I studied crime and criminals."

He paused, choosing his words carefully. They were those of a realistic man, one who was fully aware of his own talents and beginning to be aware of his failings.

"Thus, I presumed to know the sacrifice that genius demands and the hard work that is involved. When Knox presented to us the story of a sailor who wrote sublime poetry without the requisite honing of his skills, I smelt a rat. I tried to be open-minded, but we came down here because I thought I would find a simple scam involving wordsmiths putting readable verses together to cheat the public in some way."

I wanted to interject some encouragement at this point, but I didn't want to interrupt him.

"I have found out that the public will buy what it wants, and it doesn't matter if they think it was written by a dipsomaniac sailor or his polymath daughter. I have discovered, through the lessons from our schoolboy Kipling, that good writing cannot be faked, and I have had to acknowledge to myself that not all genius is grasped through hard work. It has been a lesson, Watson, and a surprise that some genius can be innate. There is no logic to it. Nevertheless, it exists.

"You hired young Kipling because of your own lack of knowledge about poetry?"

"More than that. My ignorance of the creative spark is almost absolute. I needed an expert to help me see the unseen. It has also overturned my theories about experience and the time taken to gather it. Our poet is barely nineteen and has published six successful collections in the last three years, and I nearly dismissed the facts as unlikely, even impossible. It took a sixteen-year-old boy to look at her work and quantify it for me. I very nearly drew conclusions based on my own prejudices, which were predicated on the assumption that all things empirical and measurable were superior. I nearly came to the wrong conclusion."

He must have seen the surprise on my face. "I said *nearly*, Watson. It didn't actually happen."

"Mozart composed a minuet when he was five," I said. "Pascal was doing whatever mathematicians do at age nine." Holmes looked surprised at my comment "I had a lecturer who taught us these things: To prevent hubris, he said – something from which all young doctors suffer. He was trying to show us that the human mind is a mystery almost beyond our capacity to understand."

"That is something that doesn't sit well with me."

"You can understand the mind of Charles Dodgson the Oxford mathematician, but not Lewis Carroll, the writer of nonsense verse?"

Holmes looked at me as if I had lost track of the conversation. "How do those two men even begin to compare?" he asked.

I hadn't the heart to tell him.

The Man in the Maroon Suit
by Chris Chan

"That sounds delicious to me, Watson. I shall also order the mulligatawny soup and curried lamb at dinner tonight."

"Capital!" I said with a smile. Immediately, my muscles stiffened, as I realized that my friend had performed one of his noted performances where he had managed to read my mind without my speaking a word.

I resolved not to give him the satisfaction this time of asking him how he'd managed to follow my thought processes. Holmes sat in his chair, staring at me with an amused smile on his lips, pressing his fingertips together, until I finally broke my silence. I thought that I'd managed to hold out for at least ten minutes, but a glance at the clock told me I'd only stayed quiet for twenty seconds.

"How did you do it?" he and I said simultaneously.

My friend allowed himself a little chuckle and replied, "Quite simple. I noticed you rubbing your stomach a minute ago, a sure sign that your gastric juices are informing you that your body needs sustenance sooner rather than later. We have, of course, already made reservations at Wilton's at seven-thirty tonight. You are a frequent patron of that establishment – I believe that you've eaten there no fewer than seven times in the past two months. Therefore, you ought to be familiar with their menu and have determined which dishes rank as your favorites."

Holmes paused, either to take a breath or for dramatic effect. I suppose he was only silent for a couple of seconds, but I am embarrassed to say that my impatience got the better of me, and I found myself asking rather louder than I had any right to, "But how did you know what I wished to order?"

"Quite simple, Watson. I notice you running your hand over the wound caused by the Jezail bullet. You were not wincing, as you do when your war injury causes you pain. Therefore, you were reminiscing, which causes you to unconsciously touch your scarred limb. You developed a fondness for curries and other southern Asian foods during your time in Afghanistan. I next saw you looking down on the right lapel of your suit and examining it between thumb and forefinger. Three weeks ago you permanently stained your tan suit when you dribbled mulligatawny – one of your favorite starters – on your right lapel. I therefore calculated that you were determined to partake of a beloved food, but this time you would take special care to protect your clothing from spills. As for the lamb curry, I suspected that you would continue to dine upon foods of southern Asian origin, and then I saw your gaze light upon the fleecy quilt that Mrs. Hudson crocheted for you last Christmas. Soft, white, and woolly, I daresay it made you think of a sheep. I tie the threads together, and I concluded that you had developed a craving for lamb curry. Simple, of course."

"Of course," I replied, not meaning to include sarcasm or asperity in my tone, but realizing that I might have inserted a touch of those unpleasant attributes into my voice inadvertently. Holmes, thankfully, displayed no offense over how I enunciated my words.

Later that evening, Holmes and I were enjoying our meals at Wilton's. I had carefully draped a large napkin over the front of my clothing in order to preserve my suit from being damaged. I had recently lost rather more money than I care to admit in a card game, and my budget for sartorial matters was completely wiped out for the foreseeable future. My current wardrobe would have to last me for some time, and I was grateful to Holmes for treating me to dinner that night.

I had just carefully and neatly deposited the final spoonful of mulligatawny into my mouth when a young man wearing a perfectly pressed suit and sporting a shock of dark curly hair that probably hadn't been combed in weeks rushed forward to our table, carrying a chair. He set it down with a heavy thud between Holmes and myself and turned to us both with a desperate look on his face.

"Mr. Holmes, Dr. Watson. My name is Ernest Townshore. Please forgive me for interrupting your dinner like this, but I'm in a terrible state, and I didn't know what to do. I was walking down the street trying to make heads or tails of my situation, and when I looked through the window and saw the two of you eating, it was like kismet to me. I know that I should have made an appointment to see you both at your lodgings at Baker Street, but I think that if I have to wait to talk to you, I might explode."

If I didn't know Holmes as well as I do, I would have sworn that the slight upward twitching of his lips was amusement rather than polite annoyance. "Very well, Mr. Townshore," Holmes said. "I wouldn't like it on my conscience that my desire to have a pleasant, quiet meal with my friend inadvertently led to a case of spontaneous human combustion. Please tell me what's bothering you. And if I may make a suggestion, there is no need to include every single detail. A general sense of your predicament will be sufficient for my investigative needs at present. You will, of course, not mind if we continue to dine while you tell us your problem," Holmes added as the waiter cleared away our soup bowls and replaced them with our lamb curries.

"Yes, of course." Townshore gulped and tugged at his collar. "The problem, you see, is the man in the maroon suit."

"I beg your pardon?" I asked, my fork unconsciously suspended in the air. "A maroon suit? I don't believe that I've ever seen anybody wearing clothing of that color before."

"Nor have I, Doctor, but he's taken over the gallery."

"Do you know this man's name?" I queried.

"Well . . . no. You see, he's not a real person, as far as I know. He's a little man wearing a maroon suit and tie. And sometimes a maroon top hat. Not always. I forgot to mention that. I've never seen him before, but over the past three days he's been popping up in most of the pictures in the Sternhull Gallery."

"Popping up in pictures?" I was thoroughly confused. "Is he an actual human being?"

"Well, I don't know if he's a true-to-life representation of a real person, but I don't think I've ever seen him in the flesh myself. I've only seen the little pictures of him that have been added into the paintings."

A glint danced in Holmes's eyes, and I knew at once that he had developed an interest in our unexpected dinner guest's problem. "Some vandal is taking a brush and paint and adding a human figure to the artwork at the gallery?"

"Precisely!" Townshore produced a small brown paper parcel from under his coat. "Please, take a look!"

Holmes took another bite of curry before picking up the parcel gingerly, weighing it in his right hand for a couple of seconds, and then untying the string and neatly unwrapping the brown paper. He examined it for a few moments and then set it down on the table.

"Not a particularly distinguished work," he finally pronounced. "It's a simple pastoral scene. The kind of art one sees on chocolate boxes."

I leaned over and examined the painting. It was a depiction of a small brown cottage in a green field, with several trees along the sides. A little man wearing a maroon suit and hat was leaning against the wall of the cottage. It was rather skillfully done, and if I hadn't known that the figure wasn't supposed to be there, I would never have guessed that the maroon suit man wasn't supposed to be a part of the painting. Personally, I didn't see anything very wrong – or for that matter very right – about it, but I have never declared myself to be an art connoisseur. "Who painted this?" I asked.

Townshore gulped. "I did."

Holmes's face betrayed no embarrassment or contrition for his blunt assessment of Townshore's work. "I can understand your distress at seeing your work vandalized, Mr. Townshore. Do you have other pictures at the Sternhull Gallery?"

"Yes. Seven of them. And all of them have had that man in the maroon suit added to them."

"How many pictures does the Sternhull Gallery hold in all?"

"I haven't counted. At an estimate, I'd say around two-hundred."

"Have all of those pictures been altered?"

"No. Only about sixty-five of them."

Holmes put down his fork and shot Townshore a piercing glare. "You didn't count them? Why didn't you take the time to acclimate yourself to the details of the situation before coming to me?"

Townshore squirmed and had the decency to look shamefaced. "I thought that you could take stock of the situation more effectively than I could."

Holmes's face demonstrated that he could see the justice in this remark, but despite his lingering annoyance, he was still clearly intrigued by this unusual problem. "Are all of the other pictures of the men in the maroon suit the same size?"

"Roughly, yes. Some are a bit bigger or smaller, so the figure's proportionately sized to fit into each picture. None are more than a few inches tall, and it's not always a complete man. In some cases, it's just the top half of him sticking out from behind a tree, or just his face and maroon top hat looking in the window. In one, he's swimming – fully clothed – in a pond, in another he's sitting on a rock or talking with people who were already in the painting."

"Do you recognize his face?" I asked.

"No. I've never seen the man before in my life."

Holmes resumed the questioning. "Have there been any threats to the gallery? Any attempts at vandalism?"

"None that I know of."

"Are the paintings permanently defaced?"

"Well, as far as I can tell, all of the images of the maroon suit man are in oil-based paint. I suppose that it could be cleaned off by a skilled restorer, but it would take time and probably would cost quite a bit. As I said, the images are all quite small. It would probably be a lot easier for the artists who painted the pictures to simply paint over the man. That's what I plan to do."

"Hmm. Have you spoken to any of the other artists about their defaced work?"

"No. It's only by pure chance that I even found out about the damage. I visited the gallery an hour ago to meet with the owner, Mr. Bradnick. He had a payment for me after one of my paintings sold a few days ago. The gallery was closed today, so no one had been there for almost twenty-four hours. Plenty of time for some miscreant to have painted those little men. Anyway, I met Mr. Bradnick at the door, he let me in, and we discovered the vandalism together. I rather lost my grip on things, and before I knew it, I was here."

Holmes ran the tip of his finger gently over the painted man in the maroon suit. "How long do you think it would take for a skilled artist to paint one of these men?"

"It's a bit crude. Not very true to life. I suppose that if I were going for speed rather than detail, I could paint one in three or four minutes. No more than five. Less if I fell into the rhythm of reproducing the figure."

"Hmm." The calculations flashed across Holmes's eyes. "With about sixty-five paintings, at three to five minutes per figure, it would take between three-and-a-quarter hours to just under five-and-a-half hours to complete the project. And the gallery was empty was a full day. Plenty of time. And it would take several hours for the figures to dry. This one has no trace of dampness, so whoever painted it didn't do the job too recently." He paused. "How many people would know that the gallery would be empty today?"

"Everyone. It's always closed on Mondays."

"And no one was supposed to be there at all?"

"Well, Mr. Bradnick sometimes stops by on a Monday for one reason or another. I made the appointment with him to pick up my payment around lunchtime today. I've no idea who else might have known about it. I certainly didn't tell anybody."

"No security guard?"

"I don't believe so, no."

"No cleaning staff?"

"Oh . . . ." Townshore closed his eyes and thought for a few moments. "There is a charwoman who comes by a few times a week to dust and mop the floors. I don't know her very well, but I am aware that Mr. Bradnick trusts her completely. He gave her a key to the gallery, and she comes by when she has a spare evening to do her work. Perhaps she does come in on Mondays. It would make sense. But you don't think that she would do something like this, do you?"

Holmes lifted his shoulders a fraction of an inch. "I don't have nearly enough information to draw any conclusions. I do contend that one would need to be a fairly proficient artist in order to paint so many figures so quickly."

"I wonder, Holmes, is it possible that the vandal sought to paint the man in every single picture, but he ran out of time?"

"That's one of many possibilities, Watson. I shall have a better idea of the motive when I examine the gallery."

Townshore looked elated. "Then you'll help me?"

"I shall. After I finish my meal, of course. My curry is getting cold. Mr. Townshore, if you wish to order some for yourself, I highly recommend it. I have no intention on rushing as I eat, and you look as if you could use some sustenance in order to regain your composure. Also, I have an eye on a bit of bread-and-butter pudding for after."

Holmes firmly informed Townshore that any further talk of the man in the maroon suit could wait until we arrived at the gallery. Townshore took Holmes's advice and ordered some dinner, and over the next half-hour the conversation centered around Holmes's musings on the career and legacy of his great-uncle, the French artist Vernet.

Once we'd all finished our generous servings of pudding, we started on our walk to the gallery. Holmes peppered Townshore with a handful of additional questions regarding the details of the damage, though our new acquaintance's memory was not nearly as helpful as Holmes wished. Eventually we reached the gallery, where three men were standing in the entryway. Townshore identified the eldest, a stocky man with a large, gleaming forehead, as Mr. Bradnick. A wispy man with a trace of cropped rusty hair was introduced to us as the artist Auguste Pilston, and the tall, strongly built fellow with a light brown mane that fell past his shoulders was the successful painter, Marcus Hallard.

It took mere seconds to make the proper introductions, and the moment after Holmes mentioned that he had been asked to investigate the vandalism, Bradnick burst into a rage that made me fear that he would fall into an apoplectic fit. My remonstrations to convince him to calm himself down met with no success whatsoever.

"Calm down! Like hell I'll calm down!" Bradnick's face was now approaching the color of a beet, and he began pounding his walking stick against the floor with such vehemence that I was sure that either the cane or the tiles would crack, but I wasn't sure which would be damaged first. "This is a deliberate attack on my life and legacy! I've devoted my entire career to finding the best and most beautiful works of art that London's painters have to offer, and decades of building up a reputation, I'm going to be a laughing-stock! No artist is going to want his pictures to be displayed in my gallery if there's a chance that they're going to be defaced. I just know the connoisseurs are going to amble into my gallery and crack snide remarks like "This portrait's nice, but do you have any with a man in a maroon suit on them?" My business is ruined! And now that I've finally got some top-drawer talent displaying their work here . . . ."

"Thank you so much for your kind words," Hallard replied lazily. "And you needn't worry about my continued willingness to work with you. So far, I haven't suffered in any way. My work remains unharmed."

"I wish that I could say the same," Pilston sighed. "All five of my paintings have that ridiculous little fellow prancing about in the background. They're ruined!"

Hallard laughed, but there was an unpleasant undertone. "I don't know if 'ruined' is the right word to use, my dear Auguste. That would imply your little efforts had any artistic value whatsoever. I rather think that the presence of the little man has made your work much more charming, if not actually any better, really."

Pilston turned scarlet and jerked his arm back, closing his fingers into a fist.

"None of that," Holmes said sharply, as he placed his hand over Pilston's fist. "This isn't the time for violence. Right now, if you want to do some good, I suggest that you answer all of my questions about this vandalism."

"What are you doing here?" Pilston asked. That is actually a bowdlerized version of his question. The original query was marked by a couple of profane terms that would not be accepted by my readership, so I have taken the initiative to delete them.

"As you heard just a few seconds ago, I am Sherlock Holmes, and I am a detective. If you would be so kind as to give me a tour of this gallery and point out the damage, it would be my pleasure to assist in finding the person responsible."

Pilston quivered and looked as if he was much too furious to provide any help, but Bradnick leapt forward, pushed Pilston to one side with a red, beefy hand, and offered his other hand to Holmes. "Sir, it's a pleasure to finally meet you. I've been following your activities for some time, and I'd be honored if you would please condescend to use your enormous talents on this little problem. I know it's not a murder or a bank robbery or an affair of state – I'm afraid you might see this as something of no more interest than a nasty little scribbling on a public lavatory wall – but to me, this gallery is hallowed ground. You must excuse my tantrum a moment ago. I have a notoriously short fuse. Always have, and probably always will. Your name didn't sink in for a while, but when I finally realized who you were, I thanked my lucky stars, because you're just the man I need to figure out who performed this little joke."

Holmes smiled. "Thank you, sir. I'm glad to see that you have calmed down and are approaching this matter in a much more constructive way."

Hallard laughed again. I didn't like his laugh at all. It sounded as if it came from a man who treated the rest of humanity with contempt, and his eyes were cold and joyless. "I didn't want to point out that you were indulging in an awful tizzy of hyperbole a few minutes ago, but if you'd only take a moment to observe exactly which pictures were damaged, you'd realize that there's nothing very much to get upset over, is there? After all, it's only the cheap pictures that are vandalized. The valuable art – the work by talented fellows like myself – that's all untouched. None of it is damaged in the slightest. But the dreck – the work by the artists that you only give a place as a favor in order to give them a chance at finding an audience for their tawdry little attempts at creation – those are the pictures where the maroon man has made his appearances. Grissold's appalling landscapes. Frug's lifeless panoramas. And Pilston's . . . . Well, I'm not sure what word you'd apply to his wastes of perfectly good paint, other than 'garbage'."

Pilston swore again and lunged at Hallard, who seemed highly amused by the attack. Hallard performed a little backwards shuffle and pivoted on his left heel, and Pilston couldn't correct his balance in time, so he fell forward in a painful-looking somersault. I stepped forward in an attempt to perform my duties as a medical professional, but before I could examine Pilston, he waved me away, raised himself up, whipped out his handkerchief, and began wiping away dust that was invisible to my eyes, muttering vulgarities under his breath all the while.

Holmes observed Pilston with a look that might have been a glare of contempt or a gaze of repressed amusement, I couldn't tell which. Once Pilston had dusted off his entire body, Holmes took a deep breath and asked Bradnick, "Sir, would you like me to investigate the damage to the pictures in your gallery?"

Bradnick was not the sort of man to limit himself to two words when he had the ability to use hundreds, and after a few minutes of ranting and politely yet loudly asking for help, Holmes finally cut him off and announced his acceptance of the case. "I should like to interview each of you shortly, but for the moment I shall need to examine the entire gallery. I trust that you can all be reasonably quiet long enough for me to concentrate and make the necessary observations?"

Pilston pocketed his handkerchief in a failed attempt to appear dignified. "Mr. Holmes, I'll be delighted to help you, but I shall not stand around in silence, wasting my time. I believe that I'll go out and purchase an evening newspaper. I'll return shortly."

Hallard made a half-hearted attempt to suppress a yawn. "I am rather peckish. There's a baked-potato cart down the street. Would anybody else care for one?" As there were no takers, Hallard shrugged and ambled out the door.

Bradnick's face was still unnaturally mottled. "I'll be going to my office and pouring myself a very stiff drink." As he walked away, Holmes withdrew his powerful magnifying lens from his coat pocket and began a circuit of the gallery, examining each portrait in turn, whether or not it had a little man in a maroon suit in it, though he paid particularly close attention to each image of the unusually-dressed man. I followed Holmes around and, though I possessed no item to aid in my examination, I scrutinized each picture to the best of my ability. Luckily, Townshore's estimates were high, and there were only one hundred forty-two pictures in the gallery, and just fifty-one of them had the maroon-suited man added to them.

Our examination of the gallery lasted just under an hour, though none of the three men who had left had returned yet. Townshore had perched himself on a windowsill near the entryway and had spent the entire time nibbling away at his fingernails. Holmes didn't seem to be in any hurry to speak to the other gentlemen. After looking over the last painting, which featured the maroon suit man performing what appeared to be an awkward dance, Holmes leaned against the wall and started tapping his lens against his palm as he stared up at the ceiling. I stood there quietly and watched the gears of his mind turn for a while. After several minutes, I regret to say that my impatience got the better of me, and I interrupted his reverie to prompt him to share his thoughts.

"I was thinking . . . about fairy tales."

His answer stupefied me. The thought of Holmes reflecting on Cinderella and Sleeping Beauty seemed painfully out of character. My friend noticed my amazement, and with no shortage of amusement in his face, elaborated on his comment.

"Are you familiar with the story of 'Ali Baba and the Forty Thieves' from *The Arabian Nights*? Or Hans Christian Andersen's 'The Tinder Box'?"

"I'm fairly sure that I read them as a child, but adulthood has wiped them from my memory."

"Both of them contain the same plot point. In 'Ali Baba and the Forty Thieves', a clever family servant notices that someone has marked the door of their house with a piece of chalk, so she takes some chalk and places an identical mark on every other front door on the street. In 'The Tinder Box', a dog with enormous eyes performs exactly the same trick to save his master."

"And what do clever servants and big-eyed dogs have to do with this defaced gallery, Holmes?"

"My dear fellow, consider this possibility. Only one of these little men in maroon serves a purpose. The others are merely decoys."

"I don't follow you."

"Have you noticed what all of the vandalized pictures have in common, Watson? Aside from the nature of the addition, what quality connects the paintings that had the maroon man added, and which were left undamaged?"

I reflected for a moment. "Only the oil paintings had the little maroon man added. None of the watercolors were altered."

"True. But there are only thirteen watercolors in the gallery. All the rest are oils, and there are many oil paintings that were not harmed."

I thought for a little while, trying to find a link in the subject matters. Eventually, I conceded defeat.

"You're focusing on the pictures themselves, Watson. Look at the little cards tacked to the side of each picture."

I took a quick walk around the gallery, and midway through my review, I realized something notable. "Only the cheapest pictures have been vandalized!"

Holmes chuckled. "Precisely, my dear fellow. All of the damaged pictures have been created by the same seven artists, and – " He lowered his voice so that Townshore couldn't hear him. " – they are the least talented of the artists displayed at the gallery. None of their pictures are priced at more than twenty pounds, and most of them are worth even less. And none of these works are likely to rise in value, either. Of course, I do not profess to be an expert in art, but I feel fairly confident that the artistic merit of the damaged paintings is of fairly low quality. In contrast, the paintings that remained untouched are being valued, at minimum, a hundred pounds apiece, and many of them are fetching a price of several times that. The creators of those paintings are, to my untrained eye, far more worthy of the higher price than their more amateurish peers. About a dozen of them are quite valuable. Those have real historical value, and are worth well over a thousand pounds.

"Do you think that the vandal was afraid he'd get caught, and didn't want to get billed for damaging the priciest works?"

"I think that the motive has a touch more nobility than that, Watson. Consider this. The vandal didn't want to damage a work of genuine art. He couldn't bear to deface something created by someone with genuine talent."

"You're being as clear as mulligatawny soup, Holmes."

"Let's take a look at some of Hallard's paintings. Whatever personality defects the fellow may have, even his harshest critics can concede that he can paint. There's genuine warmth in those portraits – they have a real glow that makes them seem almost lifelike. No hack can create that sort of effect. It takes real talent. The pictures are fetching prices from five- to seven-hundred pounds apiece, and though I would never pay that much myself, even if I had that kind of money to fritter away, I still concede that the gallery is justified in asking such a price."

"I'd disagree, but I don't want to start an argument."

"That's very generous of you, Watson. Now, take a good look at the pictures created by Pilston. What do you think of them?"

I leaned forward and examined the price. "This picture of a picnic is going for fifteen pounds. I wouldn't give five for it." I paused, then added, "I'm really not sure if that little man in maroon actually adds to the painting or damages it." The maroon man was sitting next to a lady in a blue dress, eating a sandwich.

"Indeed, Watson. Compare the man in the maroon suit to the others at the picnic. Does anything strike your eye?"

I pondered for a while, and then surrendered. "Sorry, Holmes. I'm don't have any idea."

My friend looked regretful. "We'll leave it there for a bit, then. Take a look at this other picture by Pilston. This one, with three deer in a field."

I shrugged. "Twenty pounds. Still overpriced, but I do like it much more than the picnic one." The maroon suit man was petting the largest of the deer.

"What is your critique of the artwork?"

"Nothing special, I'd say."

"I would be the first to note that much of the painting – the grass, the shrubs, the clouds in the sky . . . all of those are fairly pedestrian. Clumsy work, really. But observe the eyes of the deer, Watson. Don't you see the spark of life in them? And that little tree off to the right. Do you see the skill that went into that to give it a three-dimensional effect?"

After Holmes pointed it out, I could see it. "But what does that mean?"

"It means that Pilston's work is rather like that cartoon in *Punch* about the curate's egg – parts of it are excellent! Mr. Pilston does have a flair for painting, but for the lion's share of the picture, he is willing to content himself with producing flat and uninspired work."

"A bit harsh, Holmes."

"Not so, Watson, just stating a fact. Mr. Pilston has talent, yet he chooses to paint pictures as if he's a first-year student at a disreputable art school. These are pictures painted by a man who isn't putting very much effort into his compositions."

I thought for a few moments of my time as a schoolboy, and how one of the more brilliant fellows of my acquaintance consistently scored just enough points on his exams to pass, even though he could have earned a place at the top of the class if he had only tried. When I'd asked him about his marks not reflecting his potential, he'd laughingly explained that school was boring, and as the eldest son of a prominent peer of the realm his future was assured, even if he was illiterate. He proclaimed that his time would be far better spent exploring topics of real interest to him, although he never explained to me what he considered more intriguing than school. Upon further reflection, the comparison didn't appear to be a particularly apt one, since my classmate was a privileged young man, and Pilston was a man who was probably trying to make a living off his art, so it would be in his interest to create the best pictures possible.

I voiced my thoughts to Holmes, who smiled and replied, "Quite right, Watson. Now, how would you judge the images of the man in the maroon suit?"

"On an artistic level? Nothing very notable. A bit crude – rather more of a cartoon than a realistic representation of a person."

"True, the artwork is rough, but notice the form and style of the brushwork. Though unrefined, it shows a familiarity with human anatomy, not like the completely untrained, who reduce the form of the body to a compilation of shapeless blobs."

"The artist was probably in a rush."

"I concede your point, but the argument I am advancing is the fact that no matter how much a skilled artist tries to hide his talent, he can never truly produce work at the same level as a rank amateur. So now we have two collections of works that reflect suppressed talent. I cannot expect you to draw the same conclusions that I did, due to the fact that you lacked a magnifying lens of your own, but after a careful examination of the brushstroke patterns used to create the maroon suit man and Pilston's paintings, I would wager my violin that they were created by the same man."

"Pilston is the vandal? But why would he damage his own paintings?"

"From the lack of effort he put into them, it's obvious that he doesn't care about them very much."

"But what would be the purpose of this entire charade?"

"The answer comes from observing everything, old chap. You thought that I was only examining the pictures, didn't you? You really ought to have known better, my friend. You know my methods. I examined the walls and floor as well and found . . . ." Here Holmes crossed the room and pointed at a pair of small dark ovals on the wainscoting. "These."

I scrutinized them. "I can't be certain without that test of yours, but could they be blood?"

"I'm fairly certain of that. There are other, tinier droplets here – " He pointed. "And there. And there. Given the lighting, they're easy to miss."

"But what does this mean? Was someone injured?"

"One can only hope it was something so simple and comparatively harmless." Holmes's mouth twitched upward into a wry smile. "I dare say that if you choose to write an account of this adventure, the odds of your recording my covering myself in glory are far outweighed by the probability that in less than a minute, I shall humiliate myself so badly that I shall have no choice but to abandon detecting forever and take up bee-farming in the countryside."

"Heaven forbid, Holmes. But what are you thinking?"

"Watson, the droplets on the wall suggest that some unfortunate person was killed here. From the angle and shape of the blood, I would suspect a stabbing. It's my belief that after the murder, some blood spattered on one of the paintings, most likely this one here. Now, after the killer hid the body and wiped away as much of the blood as he could find, he came back and realized that he had to cover up the bloodstain on the picture. He couldn't wash it off the oil paint, so he came up with the idea to cover it with something – a man in a maroon suit. The problem was, the image would draw a great deal of attention, so the killer realized that the best way to disguise his vandalism would be to paint similar figures on as many other paintings as he could."

"This 'he' to whom you refer – Would that be Pilston?"

"I am. If you observed, his jacket pocket contained a little case, the kind artists use to carry brushes and some tubes of oils, so we know he would have paint handy."

"But who did he kill? And why?"

"You'll notice that he only damaged the cheap, poorer quality paintings. When I scrutinized the pictures, I discovered that several paintings, the older ones costing over a thousand pounds, had brush strokes that matched some of Pilston's paintings."

"Forgery? Pilston replaced the valuable paintings with his own copies?"

"Precisely. And his victim walked in on him in the act, and the poor woman died simply because she was in the wrong place at the wrong time."

"Who is this woman?"

"The charwoman, of course. Pilston came in during the night to make his latest switch. She saw what she was doing, and he stabbed her with his pocketknife. You can tell that the gallery hasn't been cleaned in a few days. The rest of the cover-up occurred as I said."

"What did he do with the body?"

"I can't say for certain before further examination. He must have found a hiding place nearby, hid the unfortunate lady, and I suspect he's spent most of the past hour trying to move the corpse. In any case,

Townshore hasn't left that windowsill, I can hear Bradnick and the sound of clinking glass in his office, and you can see Hallard sitting on the wall out that window there, munching on a baked potato and reading a newspaper. As far as I can tell, Pilston is nowhere to be found – "

Holmes's voice faded away as a couple of police officers appeared in the window, with a handcuffed Pilston in tow. Holmes let them inside, greeted them, and asked, "I presume you caught Mr. Pilston attempting to dispose of a woman's body?"

One policeman's eyes widened. "Yes. How did you know?"

Holmes summarized his conclusions, and surprisingly, Pilston chimed in every few moments to confirm what Holmes had deduced. If being amazingly right based on scanty evidence was feeding his ego, he did a remarkable job of disguising his self-satisfaction. Pilston, for his part, was being a remarkably good sport about his capture, and he accepted his fate with more grace than I'd ever seen before or since.

"Just one more question," Holmes asked Pilston as the police led the criminal away. "Why on earth did you choose to paint that little man in a maroon suit?"

Pilston shrugged his shoulders. "I had a limited amount of paint with me, and not many colors. I just so happened to have a lot of maroon paint, so it seemed like a sensible idea at the time to make that the color of the suit."

The Scholar of Silchester Court
by Nick Cardillo

In glancing over the notes which I have kept of my time with Mr. Sherlock Holmes, I am always awed by the detective's ability to remain ever the rationalist, ever the cold, calculating machine who never once let the follies of the unexplained weigh upon him. To a man of lesser stuff than my companion, he might have been led astray, influenced by the unexplained and seemingly unexplainable, and ultimately come up with a solution which simply had no accord in the real world. In times of reflection, I wonder if I had never met Holmes and, if I were on my own in some of the situations which we found ourselves, if my resolve too should have been diminished.

As I flip through the pages of my notebooks, several such cases immediately present themselves as fine examples of Holmes's maxim that the world was big enough for us – that no ghosts need apply. There was, of course, the affair of Robert Ferguson and his son, the infamous tale on the Cornish Coast, and I should be remiss if I did not put down mention of the Baskerville family. All of these cases I have deemed appropriate for the reading public at large to read, but there were many, many instances in which my friend stared the impossible in the face and denounced it. Matters such as the curious case of the absent headmaster and the incredible affair of the lady in the jade kimono naturally present themselves, as do the unusual circumstances surrounding Mr. Larkin, the scholar of Silchester Court.

It was in the early days of my acquaintance with Sherlock Holmes, a chilly autumn morning on the brink of winter. It was a quiet morning as Holmes and I busied ourselves with the routine, I seated by the fire with the first edition of *The Times*, while Holmes sat before his chemical apparatus making detailed notes in the margins of one of his innumerable reference volumes. We were in silence like this for nearly an hour before I heard Holmes's voice cut through the quiet which had enveloped us.

"You have decided against a brisk stroll, then, Watson?"

I cast a glance over to my friend who was peering down the lens of a microscope. "I beg your pardon?"

Without lifting his gaze from his specimen, Holmes continued. "You had intimated some time ago that you were keen on a walk about town. I believe you even asked me if I were interested in accompanying you, but you know my distaste for exercise for the sake of exercise alone. If you had handled me a foil and instructed me to duel you here in our very rooms, I should have been more keen for I would, at least, be grooming my swordsmanship skills. But I digress.

"Nonetheless, on account of the rain you have foregone this desire – our boots, however, remaining unvarnished and uncleaned in the event that when the rain dissipates you should lace them up anew and head off on your sojourn. We have had a stretch of four clear days now, and this morning you put your boots out to be cleaned, suggesting to me that you have no wishes of strutting about any more lest you scuff them entirely."

"Your train of reasoning is exact in every regard," I replied. "And it is so simple."

Holmes lifted his eyes from the microscope and stared at me from across the room. "Everything, when explained away, is rendered absurdly simple. It is the presentation of a conclusion without the initial inference linked up to it that produces such an astonishing affect."

Holmes stood from the stool before his workbench and thrust his hands deep into the pockets of his tattered, mouse-colored dressing gown, which bore many stains and marks from years of arrant cigarette ash and chemical experimentation. He plucked up his preferred pipe from the mantelpiece and applied a match to the bowl. "The world in which we live," he continued as he began to pace up and down before the fire, "is actually a simple one. Despite what Hamlet may have told Horatio, there is not more on heaven and earth than can be dreamed of, studied, and calculated. Much like the work of the actor or the conjurer, it is the work of the ingenious criminal to suggest that there is more than what our eyes see or our ears hear. As a detective, I have trained myself to peer beyond the veil which obscures and complicates the truth."

I cast aside the paper and stood to gather up my own pipe from where I had laid it on the breakfast table. As I began to lazily fill it, I cast a glance out the window and perceived the figure of a man pacing back and forth on the pavement before our door.

"I say, Holmes, I rather think that you have a client."

We both moved to the bow window and cast a glance into the street below. Indeed, there was a man, dressed in a rather shabby tweed suit, who moved with trepidatious steps across the causeway, stopping every so often to cast an imploring glance up at our windows and then continue traversing his stunted path.

Holmes suddenly threw open the window and called down into the street.

"Sir! If you seek my assistance, I do invite you in. If you touch the bell there, my landlady shall be more than inclined to show you up."

Then refastening the window, my friend turned to me with a smug smile.

"I do hope that that shall help the poor fellow to make up his mind," he declared. A moment later, the bell was ringing from below and soon the man himself was in our sitting room. As I looked at him now, I became keenly aware of his learned features, and he seemed to contemplate both Holmes and me through the eyes of an intellectual. There was, however, a queer sense of anxiety that hung over the man. He clasped his hands together as he stepped into our room, the thumb of one driving into the palm of the other.

"Mr. Sherlock Holmes," he said in a tentative voice, thin and reedy.

"I am Mr. Holmes," my friend replied, 'and this is my colleague, Dr. Watson. Please, have a seat, Mr. – "

"Larkin," our visitor said, slowly lowering himself into the chair proffered for our guest, "Augustus Larkin."

Holmes slid into his own chair before the fire and pulled on his pipe. "Larkin," he said contemplatively. "No relation to the scholar, surely?"

"Yes," Larkin said. "Sylvester Larkin was my father. An academic of the classics, Mr. Holmes. But you seem already familiar with his work."

"Your father's treatise on the role of Salarino in *The Merchant of Venice* is an invaluable research to any actor – or historian, for that matter." Holmes pointed with the stem of his pipe. "I perceive ink upon your own fingers, Mr. Larkin. Have you followed your father's footsteps into academia?"

"Indeed, I have," Larkin replied, "but I fear that I have not had such successes as my father. I have had a few minor speaking engagements, but my academic works have not been met with as much praise as my late father's. The works of a folklorist seldom do, I am afraid."

"Folklore?" I asked. "That is your area of study?"

"Yes," Larkin answered. "English folklore has always been an area of intense interest for me. Even as a boy when my father would read to me the classics, and pry apart the words of *Macbeth*, I didn't much care for the literary intricacies over which he obsessed. I simply wanted to know more about the witches. I endeavored to learn much more, and in time I did. I have been fortunate enough to publish a few papers in esteemed journals, but the works haven't been able to keep me afloat. I have had to take on several jobs in order to make ends meet. However, of late, I find myself driven completely to distraction, unable to concentrate upon anything."

"What is worrying you so, Mr. Larkin? It doesn't take a detective to tell that you are clearly perturbed."

Larkin drew in a deep breath. "Would you think me mad, Mr. Holmes, if I told you that for the past three weeks, I have been able to predict the future?"

For an instant, it felt as if all the air had been sucked out of the room. The silence which had descended over Holmes and me that morning had returned, only with even greater weight.

"I do not even need to hear your answer to know what it is," Larkin said. "Surely, the notion of predicting the future is absurd. Yet, I cannot deny what has been happening to me, gentlemen. I wake from my sleep feeling not refreshed, but more drained, for I hear the voices from another world, and they warn me of the things that are to come."

"Perhaps," said Holmes, leaning back in his seat, "you had best start your tale from the beginning. Omit nothing, no matter how insignificant you may think it."

Holmes closed his eyes and pressed his palms together under his chin in his usual stance of contemplation. I reached for my notebook and began to take notes as Larkin started to speak.

"I suppose the only place to begin is with the place itself: Silchester Court. I cannot imagine that you have heard the name, Mr. Holmes, let alone the history that is connected up to it, so allow me to elucidate for a moment. Silchester Court is, today, a cheap tenement in Soho. It is mostly inhabited by some of this city's less fortunate residents. Conditions are hardly ideal, but it is a haven for those of us at low water. For me, the place comes with something of greater interest: History. You see, centuries ago, Silchester Court was the seat of the Silchesters, a wealthy banking family in the seventeenth century. The patriarch of the clan was Elias Silchester who, it was believed from contemporaries, was capable of communicating with the dead. Some of Silchester's more envious business rivals accused him of being a fraud, yet he maintained his clairvoyance to the end. In his own diary, Silchester wrote significantly of his relationship with the dead."

"His own diary?" I asked. "You have had access to such a document?"

"Indeed, Doctor," Larkin replied. "I spend most of my days in the archives room of one of the larger universities. They have many of Silchester's original documents, including his journals. They are of particular interest to me because Silchester writes of the voices that he heard from beyond the grave. And it was in his final diary entry that he admitted that it was the voices which drove him to . . . murder."

"Murder?"

"Yes," Larkin said. He pulled the delicate *pince-nez* from his nose and massaged the bridge. "You see, the Silchester home never passed onto successive generations for, one night in the year 1666, Silchester murdered his wife and three children with a hatchet. He then turned the weapon upon himself. His last diary entry, written only moments before the bloody deed was carried out, was an admittance to what was to come and a claim that it was the voices from the grave that told him to do it."

Larkin returned the *pince-nez* to his nose and clasped his hands again. "It was pure coincidence that I soon found myself living in Silchester Court, you understand. I simply called around at the place after studying the original Silchester documents and discovered that there were rooms to let. In need of cheap accommodations, I moved in immediately. I wish to God that I never did. It was quite ordinary in the beginning. I spent my days at the university and my nights writing and researching. I have hopes of completing a paper on the Silchester tragedy, but I fear that I shall lose my reason before it is completed. Or worse, I fear that I may lose my life. You see, Mr. Holmes, I have begun to hear the same voices that Elias Silchester heard over two-hundred years ago."

"When did you first hear these voices?" Holmes asked without opening his eyes.

"Three weeks ago, almost to the day," Larkin replied. "Soft, dull whispering at first. I took them to be the voices of my neighbors. But I realized quite suddenly that that is an impossibility. I live on a corner of the building so there is only one room to my right, and that is unoccupied. The whispering continued off and on, yet I could not place it. And then I began to predict things. These are not mental visions, you must understand. I do not conjure up pictures of what is to come. I cannot foresee whether tomorrow shall bring with it sun or rain, but I get feelings at the oddest of times. Feelings as if I knew that something was going to happen. A messenger arrived a few days ago at precisely 10:20 in the evening. He knocked on my door mistaking me for a tenant upstairs, but after I sent him on his way, I realized quite suddenly that I knew he would be there at that exact time.

"These are the sort of odd events that have been happening to me of late, Mr. Holmes, and they are occurring with greater frequency. I cannot explain them, other than to say that I am hearing the same voices heard by Elias Silchester…the same voices that drove him to kill."

Sherlock Holmes opened his eyes at length. "Your perturbation is not unfounded, Mr. Larkin, and I should say that I have never had a case quite like yours before."

"Then you do believe – "

"I have not taken leave of my senses, Mr. Larkin," Holmes retorted, holding up a protesting hand. "In fact, I was just saying to Dr. Watson this morning that our world is built entirely upon cogent facts, not the follies and fantasies of ghosts and bogies. Nevertheless, I admit to feeling unease at your situation too. Perhaps you can answer for me a few questions. Are you well acquainted with the other tenants of Silchester Court?"

"We have a casual familiarity – little more than that."

"And you are the most recent tenant of the building?"

"A brother and sister moved into the rooms above me only a few days after I did, but I have spoken to them little."

"Perhaps you can tell me of this messenger, the man whose presence you predicted. Had you seen him about in the building ever before?"

"Never. He was a complete stranger to me."

"And you to him? I mean, Mr. Larkin, did he seem quite surprised when you answered his call at your door?"

Larkin considered. "I should say that he was."

Holmes tapped a finger to his thin, pursed lips. "I should make a note of that in particular, Watson," he said with a glance in my direction. Then, rising from seat, Holmes began to move about the room, busying himself once more at his chemical workbench.

"Do you have nothing more for Mr. Larkin," I asked at length.

"I should imagine that there is not much more that I can do for him now," Holmes replied. "Indeed, his case – while wholly unique – is actually a simple one."

"Then what is going on at Silchester Court?" Larkin cried, jumping up from his seat. "Am I in great danger?"

"By no means," Holmes said. "I cannot confirm my suspicions until I make a visit to Silchester Court. However, I wouldn't worry any longer, Mr. Larkin. But please do feel free to keep me abreast of any curious developments. Dr. Watson will show you out."

I was taken aback by Holmes's odd behavior towards Larkin but after I assured the anxious academic that all would be right soon enough, I returned to the sitting room to confront my friend on the matter. Holmes had returned to his paraphilia, scrutinizing the contents of a beaker with unwavering keenness, as though he hadn't moved from that spot or fixed his eyes upon any other subject in hours.

"Holmes," I declared upon entering the room, "I must admit that you treated Mr. Larkin rudely. The poor man was frightened out of his wits, and you did not give him ample time or attention. You insist that you have already solved the case, and yet your refuse to enlighten him or me."

Holmes returned the beaker to the workbench. "Mr. Larkin's case illustrates the very philosophy to which I referred this morning, my dear fellow," Holmes amiably responded. "On the surface, his tale is a confounding one. Voices from the dead. Premonitions of the future. Murders from two centuries ago. And yet, even without moving from my chair, I was able to come up with at least six cogent explanations with the facts provided to us. You, my dear Watson, have allowed yourself to be led astray by the multiple veils which have shrouded you from the truth."

"And the truth is?" I asked.

Holmes raised an index. "Ah, you shall have me divulging my theories before it is time. If you recall, I never suggested that I was finished outright with the case. It is by no means solved. I cannot solve it until I have paid a visit to Mr. Larkin at Silchester Hall, and from there eliminated various theories from the six possible solutions. Until then, I can do nothing."

I sighed. "And when shall you visit Mr. Larkin at Silchester Court?"

"Tomorrow? Day after tomorrow? I am presently engaged on a bit of work for Scotland Yard. The chemical solution in that beaker is of the utmost importance and I am waiting the results from my work of this morning. It is an exceedingly complex business, Watson. Mr. Larkin's, by comparison, could not be more simple."

It could not be more simple, I thought to myself, for the rest of the day. I lounged about Baker Street in relative silence as Holmes contemplated his work as though he were a natural-born chemist. We supped early and, after losing myself in the pages of one of my preferred adventure novels all evening, I retired early, Holmes still up and about as I headed off to bed. I found sleep hard to come by, however, as the problem of Mr. Augustus Larkin still hung over me. What did Holmes know that I did not? What had he gained from Larkin's interview that had escaped my notice? I knew Holmes well enough by now to understand that he had a notorious habit of keeping things to himself, a practice which I fully begrudged.

It was early the next morning that I rose, washed, and dressed, and hurried downstairs to breakfast. The room smelt of stale tobacco smoke. Holmes had evidently been up late, but he was very much asleep as I tucked in, and still when the morning post was delivered and placed upon the breakfast table. It was another quarter-of-an-hour before he rose and joined me. As he poured himself a cup of coffee, his long dexterous fingers sifted through the newly-arrived correspondence. His eyes fell upon a telegram of particular interest.

"From Augustus Larkin," he said as he tore open the envelope. I watched as Holmes read the message within and he suddenly blanched. "I fear that we shall have to go to Silchester Court sooner than I anticipated."

He tossed the telegram across to me. It read:

The voices spoke again last night. Someone is going to die. –

I didn't know what to anticipate before we set out for Silchester Court that brisk morning, but the building which we drew up to was a hideous marvel. It was clear that at one time the tall, stone dwelling had been the seat of aristocracy. However, now it seemed as if time had decayed the whole thing. The stone façade was crumbling, with great portions exposed to the elements. Great splotches of black mold clung to the exterior, and seemed to be slowly spreading like outstretched tendrils intent on grasping onto and swallowing what was left of the building whole. In defiance, the structure almost looked as if it were trying to grow, its centuries-long design dissolving and melding into the stonework edifices that lined the street to such an extent that for a moment I knew not where Silchester Court ended the others began.

Sherlock Holmes, however, didn't seem to notice any of this. Instead, by the time that I had paid our fare and joined him, he had bustled out of our hansom and was rapping upon the door with the head of his stick. His knock was answered by a dowdy, ugly older woman who wore a tattered bonnet atop a head of frizzy, greying hair, and who dried her hands upon a dirty rag.

"What?" she growled. "What do you want?"

"Mr. Larkin," Holmes said.

In response the woman gestured with her pointed elbow. "Number 11," she said. "Third floor."

Holmes brushed past her and stepped into the building, which was no more luxurious within than it was without. We were seemingly accosted by a rickety-looking staircase which bore down on us and proved to be our only method of further ingress. We mounted the steps with trepidation, listening to them creak and cry out with each new step. We climbed until we came to the door marked "*11*". Holmes knocked and it was answered immediately by Mr. Augustus Larkin. He drew us into his room and closed the door harshly behind us.

Larkin's rooms were surprisingly spacious, but had been ravaged by the hands of time, just as the rest of the building had been. The walls were cracked and shabby, the floors worn, warped, and in places showing severe signs of wood rot. There was a stove tucked away in the corner of the room, and on the opposite wall was a bed. In the center of the room was a desk overflowing with Larkin's research materials, and before this desk stood the man himself. We had clearly interrupted him in the middle of his toilet, for he looked even more slovenly and distressed than he'd the previous morning when he had called upon us. He was still anxiously wringing his hands, pacing the room in ever-shrinking concentric circles as he spoke.

"Oh, Mr. Holmes, it was dreadful. Positively dreadful. I awoke this morning with the most intense fear. An overwhelming dread for which I simply could not account. I rose and crossed to my washstand and was in the process of splashing some tepid water on my face to calm my nerves when I felt the same strange feeling that has come over me before. And I heard the voices echoing in my head. They said, 'Tomorrow night he will be dead, and at last everything shall be complete.'"

Larkin seemed on the brink of tears. "I don't know what it means, Mr. Holmes! Who is this man who is to die? Who are these voices that foretell this man's death? I simply know no longer!"

Holmes retorted, "Calm yourself, Mr. Larkin. All shall be set to right."

Yet the academic seemed not to hear my friend. "I was doing some reading last night. I discovered that this room – *my* room – was Elias Silchester's own room! It was in this very room that he awoke that fateful night, wrote a few lines in his diary, and then closed it forever before he went through the house and . . . ."

"Mr. Larkin," I interjected, "if you ask me, you are giving yourself nightmares reading this ghoulish material at night. I myself would never read a penny dreadful before going to bed, else I shouldn't sleep a wink."

"But I have an iron constitution, Dr. Watson," Larkin replied. "I have never suffered from nightmares before. And certainly never like this."

Holmes, meanwhile, was pacing the room. "You are indeed the last room on this floor," he said. "And you say that the room next door is vacant?"

"Yes," Larkin replied. "I tell you, Mr. Holmes, that I've considered more than once moving rooms. This one is surely cursed. Perhaps I could escape from all these terrible voices and awful premonitions if I laid my head somewhere else."

Holmes rocked back and forth on his feet, gently undulating from heel to toe. "Please do not purchase the room next to this one, Mr. Larkin."

"Why? Why should I not try to save myself from all of this?"

"Because, Mr. Larkin," Holmes replied. "I should like to buy it."

"You!" I cried. "Holmes, why on earth should you wish to buy a room here?"

"Baker Street is all well and good to rest my head at nights, Watson, and to entertain clients, but in my line, I do find myself requiring more than one base of operations in the city. A room here in Silchester Court would do admirably.

"And what is more," he added, "if I purchase a room here in Silchester Court, then I can lend it to you for no charge at all this evening, Mr. Larkin."

"Then you will let me escape this place?"

"Yes," answered Holmes, "provided you allow Dr. Watson and me the use of it this evening."

"You can have it!" Larkin cried. "I want nothing to do with it at all."

Holmes smiled a wry grin. "And you can do me another favor, Mr. Larkin. I am exceedingly interested in reading the diary of Elias Silchester. Would you take me to the archive room this afternoon so that I read up on it myself?"

The academic replied in the affirmative and asked for a few moments to prepare himself. We stepped out into the hall.

"You really don't want a room here do you, Holmes?" I asked.

"Nonsense, Watson," my friend replied. "I have no need for lodgings in Silchester Court. But I do want the use of Mr. Larkin's room this evening – that shall, I think, prove quite instructive – and I figured I should spare the poor man any further anguish. Now that we have a few minutes to ourselves, I should like to continue my investigation on the floor above."

On the next floor, Holmes paced back and forth about the hall for a few moments. Then, eyeing one of the doors in particular, he approached and knocked politely. His call was answered by a dark-haired young woman. She was simply dressed, and her response to Holmes's intrusion into her life was answered with forthrightness which bordered on brusqueness.

"May I help you?" she asked.

"Yes, madam," Holmes replied. "I'm a prospective tenant in this building, and I was hoping that my solicitor and I – " Holmes gestured wide to me behind him. " – could have a look about your flat? You know, to see if it's dissimilar to the room I've got my eye on below. You hear such tales, you know, madam, of unscrupulous landlords who will entice you with a fine, fine dwelling, only for the actual residence to be something far, far less decorous."

"I am afraid sir," the woman replied, "that I am quite occupied at the moment and cannot spare you any of my time."

She attempted to close the door on my friend, but he stuck his foot into the jamb. "But, madam," he said, "surely you have sympathy for a concerned buyer in your heart. I merely wish to have a look 'round. I shan't be but a moment."

"Sorry, sir," she retorted and closed the door in Holmes's face. He spun around, an odd smile upon his face. Then, silencing me with a look, he gestured that we return to meet with Larkin.

"What could you have possibly gained from that?" I inquired as Holmes and I retraced our steps down the stairs.

"I learned precisely what I wanted to know, my dear Watson," Holmes answered. "Ah, and here is Mr. Larkin too. Our timing could not have been better. I think, Watson, that I shall be dull company for much of the day. Let us meet at Baker Street, where I shall hopefully bear the fruits of today's labor."

The three of us quit the building, only to run into the landlady on the ground floor, fool-heartedly scrubbing at a spot of mold on the wall which was surely as immoveable as a mountain. Holmes stopped the woman in her task and presented himself as a prospective tenant. Claiming to have a full months' rent on his person, he said he was most interested in the vacant room next to Larkin's. He dropped a bag of coins into the woman's palm and she stared into it as if hypnotized.

"Perhaps," Holmes said, "you can be of aid to my friends and I in one other matter. You see, madam, I am something of an amateur photographer and I would be most interested in setting up a dark room in this building. I trust there is a cellar?"

"Aye, there is," the woman replied. "No one goes down there. On account of the stories, I suppose."

"Stories?" I asked. "What kind of stories?"

The woman shrugged her shoulders. "Ghost stories, I'd expect."

We separated as Holmes suggested, and he returned elated early that evening just as the sun was sinking beneath the horizon, throwing long shadows about our rooms and bathing us both in shades of muted orange and red. It was the perfect setting for our somber meal and, after we finished, Holmes pushed his chair back and stretched himself out before he reached for his pipe.

"The diary of Elias Silchester could not have been more fascinating," he began. "It was truly a remarkable study, especially to a student of crime like me. I confess that before yesterday, I hadn't heard the name Silchester before, nor had I known of the remarkable tragedy which befell him and his family."

"Remarkable indeed," I said. "The senseless, brutal murder of four people – an entire household. It curdles the blood."

"There I am afraid that you are incorrect," Holmes replied, pulling on his pipe. "I do not deny that the affair does curdle the blood, but the murder of four innocent people did not constitute the eradication of an entire household. There was a fifth member of Silchester Court there that evening whose name, it seems, is lost to the pages of history entirely. That of Silchester's cousin, a name called Lewis Grayale. His presence in our narrative sheds new light upon the entire business and all but confirms many of the suspicions that I had regarding this case."

"I confess that I am entirely lost."

From his breast pocket, Holmes withdrew a sheet of paper. "That," he said, "is a transcription of the last diary entry of Elias Silchester before the murder of his family and his suicide. It is copied word for word from his journal which Mr. Larkin and I studied all of the day. Read it and tell me if anything strikes you as significant."

I took up the sheet and read what Holmes had copied:

> *January 9:*
>
> *I fear that I cannot abide the voices any longer. They have become louder and more persistent of late. No longer are they simply the hushed whispers of the world beyond. These are the full-throated shouts of malignant beings, and they have but one instruction for me: To kill. To kill. To kill. They say that I shall never be free if I do not kill and I fear that they are right. If I wish to silence these blasted demons and return them to whatever pit from whence they have crawled, then I must do as they wish.*
>
> *I do not do what I do out of malice or out of lust (as I am sure my enemies shall suggest in the days to come). I simply do what I must do to save myself and save my soul. Surely once I have left this earth, I can find peace, at last separated from the voices that are damned to whisper in my ears and drive me to do what I do. Peace. That is all that a man could want. Peace. This is my only way to get it.*
>
> *The hatchet blade is sharp and shined. It shall serve its purpose well.*

It was bone-chilling stuff, and I handed the sheet back to Holmes with a tremor agitating my fingers.

"Do you not find it suggestive?"

"I find it repulsive," I said. "It is undoubtedly a full confession of guilt."

"Tut, tut, Watson," Sherlock Holmes said. "Have I not taught you that there is nothing more deceptive than an obvious fact? Does this diary entry reveal to you nothing more than a desperate man's last moments on earth?"

I reconsidered what I had just read. “The voices,” I said at length. “Silchester says that they got louder in the end.”

Holmes struck the tabletop with an open palm. “Excellent, Watson. We shall make you a first-rate detective yet. You have picked up on the mot pertinent piece of information in the entire diary.”

“Are you saying that someone – perhaps this Grayale man – was the one speaking to Silchester? That he lured Silchester in murdering his entire family?”

“That is precisely what I am suggesting, and I believe that much the same is happening to our unfortunate Mr. Larkin.”

“How? Both Silchester and Larkin were alone in their rooms. Their rooms are on the corner of the building. No one could possibly speak to them from the third-story window without floating in the air like some phantasm. And I know you well enough, Holmes, to understand that you reject that possibility outright. Granted, this Grayale character may have been speaking to Silchester through the wall on the opposite side of the room, but we know that to be impossible in Larkin’s case, as the room is unoccupied. Someone may have stolen in there at nights, but what with the way the whole building creaks, it would be near impossible for someone to stealthily move about without Larkin knowing. And what’s more, I cannot see any reason to drive a poor, down-on-his-luck academic mad.”

“You fail to grasp the magnitude of this case,” Holmes replied. “In doing so, you have managed to isolate nearly every point of importance, and yet failed to interpret them as you should. What you have failed to grasp, Watson, is that Mr. Augustus Larkin is but a tangential element in this case. He was never the point of focus.”

“I am afraid that I do not understand.”

Holmes stood and began to make a circuit about the room, as was his habit when in the depths of oration.

“Over two-hundred years ago,” he began, “Mr. Lewis Grayale conjured up a devious method of murder. He would masquerade as the spirit voices that he knew his cousin, Elias, would listen, and use them to influence Elias Silchester into murdering his entire family and then himself. Then, no doubt with no family left to claim the substantial estate that was would remain following Silchester’s death, Grayale could claim it and abscond with it. No wonder then that Silchester Court fell into such ruin and disrepair with no one occupying the seat who would maintain it.

“Now, two centuries on, history is repeating itself, but merely by happenstance. Mr. Larkin has quite unwittingly stumbled into the midst of a plot which is no doubt just as devious as the one perpetrated by Lewis Grayale in the seventeenth century.”

"But what is going on?" I cried. "Who is perpetrating this scheme, and what exactly do they wish to accomplish?"

Holmes pulled a photograph from his voluminous collection. "Did you by chance recognize the face of the young woman who answered the door today at Silchester Court?"

"I must admit that I did not. Should I?"

"If you paid a little less attention to cricket scores and more time to the society pages of *The Times*, then perhaps you might have."

Holmes picked up a news-sheet and dropped it onto the table. Staring up at me was a detailed sketch of three persons, two men and a woman. Seated in the middle was a distinguished-looking, white-bearded man. On either side, standing over him, were two young people, the woman undoubtedly the same that we had seen earlier in the day. My eyes moved to the article.

Financial Tycoon at Death's Door?

I stared at the bold headline then my eyes fell upon the newsprint written beneath:

> *Reports remain unsubstantiated, but it is believed that financial tycoon G.J. Petty, the business magnet formerly of Kansas, USA, is in poor health. His recent absences from share-holders' meetings have worried many close to the Petty family, though his son, Arthur, insists that there is nothing with which to be concerned. Though he admits that his father has been battling frequent bouts of fatigue, he insists that the patriarch of the Petty family is hale and healthy.*
>
> *Arthur Petty, our readers may well recall, recently married Catherine O'Martin, formerly of Baltimore, Maryland, and daughter of the noted American senator, Thaddeus Martin. The wedding was the talk of English aristocracy last May when the couple was united at Petty's country estate in Kent.*

"Do you not smell deviltry?" Holmes asked.

"Are you suggesting that this O'Martin woman, Petty's daughter-in-law, is conspiring to murder him?"

Holmes returned to his chair. "It is the perfect scheme, Watson: Catherine O'Martin takes up residence at Silchester Court, a crumbling tenement building in Soho, where it is certain that she shall go unrecognized. The locale is an odd one, but it wasn't chosen at random.

Though records were hard to come by, I established that Lewis Grayale, after fleeing England, escaped to the new world. The Petty family are descendants of Lewis Grayale – distant relations of the Silchester family – and therefore still have legal claim over Silchester Court in London. From there, Catherine O'Martin established a base of operations where she can conduct her illicit business, notably the importation of deadly poisons with which she may slowly poison her father-in-law, masking his wasting away as another battle of fatigue. I have no doubt that the messenger who arrived in the night and who mistook Larkin's room for hers is her co-conspirator.

"But this business goes deeper still. You recall exactly who is living above Larkin's room, do you not, Watson?"

"He said a brother and a sister." The truth dawned on me at once. "You do not mean to suggest that Petty's son is involved too! That they are masquerading as a brother and sister and are conspiring together to murder Petty?"

"The man sits upon a fortune which would drive you or me to distraction," Holmes intoned. "Surely it's a sum that could cause any man or woman to commit desperate acts. Tonight, we must catch them in the act and bring their scheme to an end. We don't have much time. You recall what Larkin heard the voices say: 'Tomorrow night he will be dead.'"

Suddenly Holmes sprung into action. He had jumped up from his seat and was reaching for his hat and coat. "Do be so good as to drop a bulls-eye lantern into your pocket, Watson. We shall be in need of it tonight."

As we readied ourselves, I turned to my friend and asked, "I must know: What did you hope to see in Catherine O'Martin's room this afternoon?"

"I saw exactly what I wanted to see," Holmes replied. "I wanted to see if her room was the same as Larkin's. It was not. Larkin has a stove."

It was just past eight, but the city was already wrapped in the fog of night when we returned to Silchester Court. By dark, the dwelling took on an even more menacing aspect, a great, dark mass which looked down upon us as we approached. Holmes rapped upon the door and was greeted by the same woman who had answered his call earlier in the day.

Holmes tipped his hat to the woman who let her well-paying newest tenant past without a word and started up the creaky steps, gesturing for me to follow. Once we had reached the top, he knocked upon Larkin's door. The academic answered it in a frenzy.

"Calm yourself, Mr. Larkin," Holmes hissed. "Your ordeal is nearly over. I have gained access into room Number 10. If you don't mind roughing it for a few hours, I imagine that I can return you to the safety of your own bed in a few hours' time."

"Safety? Safety? I cannot think of a more dangerous place in the whole world than that god-forsaken room," Larkin said.

"I think that I shall be able to disprove that, sir," Holmes said. Then, sending the man on his way, he stepped inside Larkin's room and closed the door after me.

"I don't think that we shall need to wait long," he said as he took a seat. "Make yourself as comfortable as possible, Watson, but keep your wits about you. I suspect that soon you will witness something which, on the face of it, cannot be reconciled with the settled order of nature."

So we waited. From time to time I consulted my watch as I watched the minutes crawl by. It was gone 10:30 when I first thought I heard something. I looked to Holmes and saw his ears perk up as though he were a dog on the scent. He stood from his seat and gestured for me to follow him across the room. I approached apprehensively, stopping just before the low stove that was wedged into the corner of the room. It struck me suddenly that the sounds I heard were emanating from the stove itself. They sounded garbled and distant, inhuman almost, as though the natural intonations of the human voice had been distorted by the shrill sound of a hand playing the glasses. However, as I concentrated, I could make out the words being spoken:

"He arrives tonight. 11:15. It will be the last shipment. Then, I will return home and administer the final dose. We return by the servant stairs as if nothing has happened."

In that instant, everything seemed to fall into place. I felt Holmes's iron grip upon my forearm.

"Now, Watson!" he said. "Grab the bulls-eye and follow me!"

I scooped up the lantern from where I had placed it upon Larkin's desk and followed Holmes into the dark passageway. We were met with impenetrable, inky blackness, and I groped with the flaps upon the light as we made our way blindly towards the staircase. Holmes took each one with great care so as to not emit any sound as we descended. Once we had arrived on the ground floor, he hastened his steps towards the rear of the building, no doubt in search of the entranceway to the cellar. We found the door in due course and wrenching it open, we descended, I rushing after my friend. I heard the sound of commotion below and when I reached the landing at the bottom, I found Holmes poised before both the man I knew to be Arthur Petty and the woman that was his wife, with his cane at the ready in defense.

Two hours later, Holmes and I were once more ensconced within the familiar environs of Baker Street. I was nursing a glass of brandy before the fire, while Holmes packed his pipe with his strong shag tobacco. Our attention was focused on our guest, Mr. Augustus Larkin, who, for the first time since we had made his acquaintance, didn't look quite so perturbed.

"From the beginning I asserted that this case was a simple one," Holmes began, striking a match and easing back in his chair. "Rejecting an otherworldly explanation for the voices that you heard, Mr. Larkin, and from the position of your room in the building, I knew that they must have originated from somewhere in Silchester Court. It became, then, a matter of divining where they came from in the building and what they meant. I combated numerous theories, but the pieces of the puzzle began to fall into place when we visited there this morning.

"I noted the singular fact that you were staying in what was at one time Elias Silchester's own room. Your room, then, would undoubtedly be different from nearly every other chamber in the building, belonging as it did to the master of the house. I was proven right in this regard when I saw that you had what appeared to be a stove. However, the room above yours, belonging to Mr. Arthur Petty and his wife, did not. Coupling this fact with the knowledge that Silchester Court was at one time a single house, I came to the conclusion that what appeared to be a stove in your room, Mr. Larkin, was in fact a small fireplace. It therefore required a heat source from elsewhere, which suggested that there was some means of transporting the heat from one part of the building to the other, a system of heating pipes with their origin in the basement.

"In this way, I developed a theory which explained how Elias Silchester's cousin, Lewis Grayale, was able to convince his cousin that the spirits voices were speaking to him, and how you were hearing voices of your own. Grayale, hiding in the cellar, would merely have to speak into the fireplace in the cellar and his voice would carry up through the ducts and into Silchester's room. Grayale plotted the murder of Silchester's family and, with the residue of the estate to claim, he disappeared entirely.

"Curiously, Mr. Larkin, the voices that you heard were also tied to murder, but these voices weren't intentional. Arthur Petty and his wife, fearful that they might be overheard by someone in their own room, took to conferring in the cellar by night. Unbeknownst to them, their voices too travelled up through the pipes and into your room. As you slept, you became an unwilling eavesdropping on their schemes and, in the morning, would awake with memories and knowledge you didn't know you had."

Holmes laid aside his pipe. "As usual," he said, "the truth proves to be simplicity itself. And with a little rational cognition not only have we uncovered the truth of your case, Mr. Larkin, but brought to a close an affair which has remained open for over two centuries. And now that your case has been finished, I have but one for suggestion for you."

"What is that, Mr. Holmes?"

"Get yourself some well-deserved sleep."

The Adventure of the Changed Man
by MJH Simmonds

Chapter I

It was the first Friday of September, in the year 1884. We had spent the summer engaged in several notable cases, and I was hoping for a brief period of calm reflection. This was partly for the good of my health, but also to allow me to commit to paper our most recent adventures while the memories were still fresh. The days were already beginning to shorten. However, I still harboured slim hopes of convincing Holmes to join me in taking a short holiday before the weather inevitably turned for the worse – preferably somewhere by the coast.

I had risen at eight and was enjoying my breakfast alone, Holmes having spent the previous evening happily engaged in a long and complex chemical experiment. He had continued working long after I had bid him farewell and left for my bed, and I was actually a little surprised not to find him still hard at work this morning, surrounded by his scientific equipment.

Just as I was finishing my toast and pouring a second cup of coffee, Holmes joined me at the table in a terribly dishevelled state. Normally, seeing his wild hair and distressed attire I would be concerned, but knowing that he had spent the night in front of his test tubes and gas burners, I barely raised an eyebrow.

"Good morning. Having trouble sleeping off the effects of yesterday's fumes?" I asked, with little sincerity.

"I am close to a major breakthrough, Watson," Holmes explained, smoothing down his hair and straightening his dressing gown. "Assuming that the solutions I have left simmering do not combust in the next hour or so, of course," he added, pouring himself a coffee.

"In the next hour or so?" I asked, incredulously. "Do you mean that they could have burst into flames at any time during the night? When completely unattended?"

"Oh, don't worry. I was fairly certain that they would not, and so – "

However, Holmes did not finish his explanation, as he was interrupted by a loud fizzing sound, followed by a muffled bang. We turned towards his workspace in the corner of the room, just in time to witness a large plume of flame leaping from a test tube clamped above a small gas burner.

"Fairly certain?" I asked.

Holmes sighed and rose to deal with the minor conflagration. I took a sip of coffee and a glance at the newspaper. He returned after a few minutes looking rather deflated.

"I'm sure you'll crack it," I said. "After all, it very nearly made it to your deadline," I said, as comfortingly as I could manage in the circumstances, knowing full well that any excessive encouragement might lead to further dangerous and pungent chemical experiments.

"Sadly not, Doctor. I fear that I've reached the end of this particular avenue of scientific investigation," Holmes replied, wiping a hand, greatly stained with unknown chemicals, across his damp, furrowed brow.

"Sorry to hear that, but if it's any consolation, I read here that the first volume of Trollope's autobiography is set to be serialised later this month." I pointed to the relevant column on the front page of my newspaper.

"First volume? Yes, I suppose that is reasonable. However, I have always maintained that, by definition, it is impossible to finish writing an autobiography."

"Really?" I asked. "Why would that be?"

"Because one cannot write about the end of one's life. Is an autobiography not a history of the writer's *entire* life?"

"Semantics, Holmes. We need to find you a case."

The morning dragged on. I tried to relax with the paper and a pipe, while Holmes attempted to salvage what he could from the fire. Every so often a small blackened item would fly by on its way towards the front door, as Holmes judged it damaged beyond repair.

"But what is this?" he announced. "I hear a telegram arriving." It was now well into the afternoon.

I had heard nothing to indicate such, but within a few seconds we heard the tinkle of the front doorbell and shortly afterwards the sound of the boy climbing the stairs to our apartment. Holmes opened the door just as the delivery lad had his hand raised to knock. Holmes snatched the message from the surprised boy, replaced it with a coin, and shooed him away.

"'*Vespasian's. Come now*'," Holmes read aloud. "Well, what do you make of that?"

"I take it that the message is from Lestrade," I replied with a smile, "so Vespasian is more likely to be the restaurant in the City rather than the Roman Emperor himself."

"Yes, of course, but should we attend? Lestrade has provided no details." I sensed that Holmes was testing me.

"Yes," I replied, with certainty. "I think that the lack of detail actually implies urgency. It may be that the case is too complex to be explained via the short message form of a telegram. That would explain the extreme brevity and also the direct order."

"I would add only that friend Lestrade is obliged to work within an extremely tight budget, but otherwise perfect, Watson. We must hasten to the City at once."

Chapter II

We took an open cab and enjoyed the ride in the late summer sunshine. The four-mile journey passed quickly, the usually distracting sounds and smells of London diluted by the warm sun on our faces. The cab pulled up outside Vespasian's, its large wooden-framed windows glistening and reflecting the bright sunlight. The gaily painted restaurant, with its hanging baskets of cascading flowers, appeared a most unlikely setting for criminal activity.

A pair of uniformed policemen guarded the entrance, but Holmes ignored them and walked directly inside. His air of authority was such that they never even turned to confront him. The restaurant was unoccupied, save for a group of three men standing in front of one of the many wooden tables. A chair had been upturned, and beyond this we could just make out the shape of a body, lying face down on the floor. The man in the centre was small and wiry. He wore a checked woolen suit and bowler hat. On either side of him loomed larger men in uniform. Inspector Lestrade turned to face us.

"Ah, welcome, gentlemen. Good of you to join us. What we have here is – " He began but was cut off mid-sentence.

"Dear Inspector, it is, as always, a pleasure to see you." Holmes smiled, raising his hat in welcome. "Would you please forgive my interruption and indulge me a little? Let me see what I can observe," he added, sweeping a hand across the scene before him, "before you explain what you know of the affair. Let me first create my own unbiased interpretation of what has occurred

"I suppose that would be acceptable," replied Lestrade, attempting to retain his authority.

Holmes glided towards the table. I followed a couple of steps behind. The men before us moved aside and we saw fully for the first time. The man had been dining alone. Only one place had been set. On the table was a plate of half-eaten food – a pasta dish, rich in tomatoes by the look of it.

An unused knife sat to the right of the plate. The fork had fallen to the floor and lay close to the body. An open bottle of red wine stood next to a small vase of flowers. The accompanying wine glass lay on its side just to the right of the plate, a funnel-shaped, blood-red stain had spread away across the white tablecloth.

Holmes examined the table and everything on it in minute detail, taking out his glass to gain an even closer view. Then, instead of moving to inspect the body as I would have expected, he turned and started to look closely at the chair, lying on its side. It appeared to me to be a perfectly standard chair, rather rustic for my tastes with its wicker seat, but just the thing one might find in any Mediterranean restaurant. Holmes paused, frowned, and then finally turned his attention to the body.

"Well, well, Watson. You had better take a look at this. It is rather more your field than mine."

Holmes stood and allowed me through. I knelt down and saw the victim's face, his head turned to the left. I was for a moment taken aback. He was dark red and hideously bloated. A thin trickle of blood left a trail from the right side of his mouth, down towards the floor. I looked at his hands. They were also ruddy and swollen, the fingers curled tightly into fists.

"I cannot be certain until I examine the body in a morgue, but I would bet a month's pension that this man has been poisoned. And what is more, I have pretty good idea what poison has been used here."

"Excellent," Holmes replied. "Do continue." He was now walking around the table, closely examining the floor.

"From the look of this poor man, I would conclude that he was killed by the venom of the Indian Cloaked Viper, one of that continent's most deadly snakes. The signs are unmistakable: Dark red skin, horribly swollen face, hands, and probably feet. The poison has to enter the bloodstream directly – if ingested it has no effect – but once exposed to this terrible venom, death is certain and occurs within a minute."

"That sounds truly terrible, Doctor," said Lestrade, a slightly anxious look on his face. "I take it that there is no chance one of these vipers could be here, perhaps escaped from a private collection?"

"I wouldn't think so," I replied.

Holmes laughed from behind us. His examinations had spread to the far limits of the restaurant. "Fear not, Inspector. The snake from which this venom originated is far away from here. This man was murdered. The method of delivery of said poison is what I've been seeking." He then squatted down, produced a pair of tweezers from within his coat, and carefully picked up something from the floor. He held this to the light before moving carefully to the closest table and placing the object onto a napkin. He then folded this carefully, several times, and placed it back upon the table.

"Within that serviette is a truly deadly object," Holmes finally announced. "Treat it with extreme caution, Lestrade."

"What on earth is it?" I asked.

"It is a simple pin, but it has likely been coated with the venom of the snake that you so accurately identified, Doctor. How much poison remains I cannot tell, but the slightest prick or graze could still prove fatal. It must be examined and then destroyed."

"You said murder, Mr. Holmes," said Lestrade. "That certainly seems more than likely, given what we see before us, but how was the victim poisoned here when this pin of yours was discovered over there, some ten yards away from the body?"

"I have several theories on that issue, but one seems the most probable. By the way, have you identified the victim? A City banker, and a successful one, by the look of his suit and shoes. However, there are also other more unusual details."

"The owner of the restaurant has identified him as one Josiah Bancroft, a director at Boutte's and Company," Lestrade confirmed, reading from his pocket notebook. "A City banker, right enough, but that's not really much of a deduction, given where we are."

"Boutte's," I repeated, quietly. "One of the oldest banks in London – solid, traditional, and conservative in their dealings. This will certainly shake them up. It must be the biggest scandal in their entire history."

"Not quite, Doctor," corrected Lestrade. "You haven't yet heard the complete story here."

Holmes leapt up from his examination of the body and rounded on Lestrade. "Explain please. From the tone of your voice, I believe that something singular has occurred."

"More singular than a City banker being poisoned in an Italian restaurant, in London, with the venom of an Indian snake?" I muttered, expectantly. "I can't wait to hear this,"

"Watson, please listen rather than utter superfluous comments," admonished Holmes. "Please continue, Lestrade."

"At twelve o'clock, Mr. Bancroft here left his office on Lombard Street. He passed the doorman, who wished him a good afternoon. Less than ten minutes later, Bancroft returned, stating that he had forgotten his newspaper. After a further fifteen to twenty minutes, Bancroft left again."

"So far, nothing particularly unusual, I have to say," I commented.

"Except, Doctor, that this time when he left, he was carrying one-hundred-thousand pounds worth of bonds and stocks," declared Lestrade.

"He stole them?" I asked, incredulously. "How did he manage to take them without anyone noticing?"

"It seems that he had easy access to the company's safes – he was a senior director after all. To answer the second part of your question, he *was* noticed. Two clerks witnessed him taking the items from a safe, a safe that he, himself, had ordered them to open. The clerks did exactly as they were told, for he was by far their senior and they obeyed without question. It was only after Bancroft had left that a senior manager noticed that the safe was open and inquired into what had happened. The manager raised the alarm and the police were called. We soon learned from the doorman that Bancroft usually dined here at Vespasian's. We never believed for a moment that he would be here, but we sent a man anyway. Expecting him to have fled, I sent men to watch all the nearby stations and search all of the trains leaving the city."

"And then you received the news that your man was indeed here and had died right in front of the other diners and staff." Holmes added. "I take it that the stolen bonds and stocks were not found on the body?"

"You're quite right," replied Lestrade. "They aren't here or anywhere on the premises. We have searched thoroughly."

"Admirable," said Holmes, "but pointless. I don't believe the stolen items were ever here."

"Not here? Then where are they? If he had passed them on to someone else, then why on earth would he then come here to eat? He must have known that the alarm would have been raised, sooner or later, and if he had passed them on already, then why was he killed?" Lestrade's agitation was growing, his face becoming red and rather flustered.

"He might have been killed to prevent him from exposing the final recipient of the bonds and stocks," I suggested. "Perhaps he was blackmailed into committing the crime. That might explain why he came here after passing on the items – he was simply waiting for his inevitable arrest. Or possibly he couldn't live with what he'd done and took his own life? He pricked himself with the poison and in his death throes the pin was thrown to the far side of the room."

"Why, Watson, you're full of ideas today," replied Holmes. "These are all good questions and theories which must be investigated. There is, perhaps, another possibility, but we must make further inquiries before we come to any conclusions. Lestrade, I suggest that you examine the blackmail theory. Watson and I will investigate independently, if you have no objections."

"None at all, gentlemen. In fact, I have already raised the possibility of blackmail with my men and they have begun inquiries in that direction," Lestrade replied, happy that he appeared to be on the right track.

"One more question, Inspector. At what time did Bancroft sit down for lunch?" asked Holmes.

"They say he dined here alone regularly and arrived at about his usual time. They aren't exactly sure to the minute, but say that he was usually here by half-past-twelve. Apparently, he always seated himself at his regular table.

"I've already sent constables to both the bank and to the address which he used to settle the monthly account he held here," added the proud policeman, tapping at his open notebook. "I shall be paying them a visit them myself, in due course."

"I suggest we meet up back at Baker Street at seven tonight, Lestrade. Mrs. Hudson would be happy to lay an extra place for supper," Holmes stated, before raising his hat and bidding the inspector farewell.

I followed Holmes out of the restaurant and back into the bright sunlight.

Chapter III

"Well, where do we start?" I asked, blinking as my eyes adjusted to the sun.

"We need to interview three people – the two clerks, of course, but most importantly, the doorman. Lestrade will, hopefully, provide us with information on his background and life outside the bank."

We strolled the short distance back to Lombard Street. Apart from a single constable standing outside the large but open doors, the bank looked just the same as any other. Holmes nodded towards the constable who touched the brim of his helmet in salute and we entered. We enquired into the location of the doorman and were told he was currently being interviewed by senior managers of the bank. Rather than wait for him to be free, Holmes decided to talk to the two clerks who had witnessed the actual robbery.

The men were both young, in their early twenties, and a sorry sight they were. They were pale and clearly terrified of what might happen to them. Dismissal at this stage of their careers would be a blow from which it would be nearly impossible to recover. Holmes tried to put them at ease, promising to talk to senior management on their behalf on the understanding that they reveal all that they knew.

This seemed to help settle their nerves, and they proceeded to give a detailed and extensive account of what had happened. They didn't know Bancroft well – he rarely visited this part of the bank. He had wandered in, looked around, and then approached the safes. They had obeyed his orders without question. He hadn't asked them to close the safe once he removed its contents, and that was what had eventually alerted a nearby manager that something was amiss. When they had finished their account, Holmes asked one of them to provide Bancroft's address. Then he thanked them and we headed for the offices where the doorman was giving his testimony to his superiors.

"That was interesting," I said. "However, despite all of the added detail, I can think of nothing they said that adds anything of substance to what we already knew."

"Possibly, but we have, at least, confirmation of Bancroft's exact actions when he returned to the bank. I believe that this case hasn't yet given up all of its secrets," Holmes added, enigmatically.

We didn't have to wait long to interview the doorman. The managers allowed us to swap places – they left the office and we replaced them. It was a small room and the doorman sat before a mahogany partner's desk. He looked tired and agitated. Another round of interrogation was not what he wanted.

"Sir, I must apologise for having to question you again upon this matter," began Holmes, sitting himself behind the desk. "I'll try to keep this as brief as possible. How long have known Mr. Bancroft?"

"More than ten years sir," the doorman sighed. He was a wiry man of at least fifty. His hair was grey but still thick underneath his dark cap. He had bright blue eyes and, beneath them, a large bulbous nose. His mouth was small and barely moved as he spoke. "He was here when I started."

"And you would say that you know him fairly well? That you would recognise him anywhere, in any circumstances?"

"It isn't for me to say that I knew him, sir," replied the doorman, "but I would recognise him, of course, no matter how many times he changed this or that, or grew that beard of his."

"And, pray, tell me, when did he first start to effect these little, changes?" Holmes asked carefully.

"Oh, about six months back, I suppose. First the red waistcoat, then the beard. Finally, he took to wearing tinted lenses in his spectacles. He told me the first two were for a wager, but the rest he never chose to explain."

"Thank you." Holmes dismissed the doorman. "That has been most helpful."

We left the bank and walked through the City. The late afternoon sun shone on the white stone and columns of the buildings to either side of us, giving a brief glimpse of how ancient Greece might once have looked. We found a cab at the top of the street and set off back to Baker Street.

"What made you ask the doorman about changes in Bancroft's appearance?" I asked as we headed towards Holborn.

"Did you not notice how he was attired?" Holmes replied, with evident disappointment.

"At the time I was rather more concerned with the cause of death, to be honest," I admitted.

"In this instance you can be forgiven, but you have missed vital clues that might help solve this case."

"Whatever do you mean? Kindly explain what I missed."

"I feel it would be better to show you. We must take a slight detour." Holmes tapped his cane on the back of the driver's bench.

"Take us to Mayfair," ordered Holmes. "Berkeley Square."

Chapter IV

After twenty minutes or so, we entered the grand square, its opulent mansions overlooking the smart gardens, generously left open to the public. We pulled up in front of a typical house, three imposing storeys faced with handsome white stone. Tall London plane trees in the central gardens cast long fingers of shadow over the building's anaemic face.

"According to the good inspector's notebook," Holmes announced, "here lived the late Mr. Bancroft." He hopped out of the cab, instructed the driver to wait for our return, and swept up the steps to the large black front door. Then he rapped loudly upon the forbidding portal and at length it opened a crack. A pair of beady little eyes peered out of the dark. Holmes introduced us and explained that we were assisting Scotland Yard in their inquiries. The man acknowledged that he'd already learned of Bancroft's death from the police.

The door swung open and we were beckoned inside. For the first time, I could see who had allowed us entry. Bancroft's man, who introduced himself as Suffolk, was a small, nervous-looking fellow. No more than five-feet-four in height, Holmes towered over him like some ravenous raptor. The man's small, brown, piggy eyes were deep set and sat above a round nose which itself appeared to be balanced upon a thick but narrow moustache.

"Mr Suffolk, I can see from your countenance that you are upset by the terrible news regarding Mr. Bancroft. May we firstly both offer you our condolences on your master's sad demise," began Holmes. "We are allied to, but not a part of, the official inquiry, who no doubt will be along shortly to debase the scene in their traditional clumsy manner. We're here to briefly examine certain aspects of Mr Bancroft's residence. Please allow us to work unobstructed and I guarantee we will be gone in just a few minutes."

This seemed to put Suffolk a little more at ease.

"But first," continued Holmes, "I wish to ask you a few perfectly simple questions. I hope that is acceptable?"

"Yes, well, I suppose so," mumbled Suffolk, now caught off guard.

"How long have you been in Mr. Bancroft's service?"

"Just over six months, sir, but before that I was employed by the Du Villepain family, just across the Square. I have worked here in Berkeley for nearly fifteen years." The small man stuck out his chest with obvious pride.

"Very good. Now, pray tell, did Mr. Bancroft's changes of habit and appearance begin before, or after, you started here?"

Suffolk looked surprised. "However did you know about that? Well, I suppose you are detectives, after all."

He moved towards the front study and asked us to follow. He approached the mantel above an empty fire and pointed to a framed photograph. It showed the head and shoulders of a serious looking man. He was clean-shaven with balding grey hair. He wore a dark waistcoat and black jacket. After a few seconds, I realised at whom I was looking.

"That is Bancroft? He looks little like man that we saw this morning," I declared. "We must be dealing with an imposter. That would explain everything, surely. The poison was deliberately chosen to disfigure and therefore disguise the victim's face."

"So you did observe something of the victim," said Holmes. "Well done, Watson. However, I'm certain that the man we saw this morning and the man in this photograph are one and the same."

"But the man we saw had a thick beard and his head was hairless. He was also rather more extravagantly attired. I saw a burgundy waistcoat, and his jacket was dark blue I think."

"Green, actually. A pair of spectacles was lying near the body, with tinted lenses." Holmes then addressed the butler.

"Now, Suffolk, I believe you were about to reveal to us exactly when Mr. Bancroft began to dress in this flamboyant manner?"

"Not long after I started," began Suffolk, "he began to grow his beard. Nothing unusual in that – I didn't give it a moment's thought. Then he shaved his head – not to my tastes but, again, I thought nothing of it. After that, he started to wear the burgundy waistcoat. I did comment upon it once – I actually thought it added a splash of much-needed colour to his otherwise monochrome wardrobe. He seemed to take this as the compliment I had intended, and he smiled in response but said nothing. About three weeks ago, he got himself that green jacket, along with a top hat that was at least twelve inches high, light grey with a blue band."

"Did his behaviour change in any other way over this period?" I asked. "Did he show signs of stress or fatigue? I am a medical doctor.

Please feel free to share any details with us, however personal they may be. After all, we're trying to catch the man who killed him."

"That's the funny thing. Apart from the clothes, hats, and a few odd scarves and canes, he was exactly the same man. His character was unchanged. He was generally a quiet man, traditional in all other aspects of his life – meticulous and always polite and professional."

"So you have no idea from whom or where he may have been influenced into sporting such unusual attire?" sighed Holmes, with little optimism.

"Far from it, gentlemen," Suffolk replied. "I know exactly where he picked up these new habits."

Holmes, for once, looked genuinely surprised. "Then tell us – quickly, man."

"Mr. Bancroft is a member of the City of London Club. I do not need to tell you how exclusive an organisation that is, and where one must be in society to attain, as he had, life membership. He visited after work most days, often taking his evening meals there with friends. However, this all changed shortly after I began to work here. It seems he had met a new acquaintance who had recommended to him an alternative club, one of a rather different character."

"How different?" I asked.

"Well, for a start, he began to stay out until the early hours of the morning. Then he was out nearly every night, returning only on Sunday mornings. Then he would take to his bed, from where he would not move again until he rose the next day for work. The beard appeared shortly afterwards, followed regularly by an additional eccentricity of one sort or another."

"What is the name of this new friend?" asked Holmes.

"He never told me," replied Suffolk, rather sheepishly.

"And do you know the name of this club and where it is located?"

"I'm not really certain, sir," Suffolk replied. "He simply referred to it as 'my new club', although I did once overhear him instruct a cab driver to take him to Brewer Street in Soho. I wish that I could give your more information, but as I said, he was always a very private man."

"Brewer Street sounds about right," I agreed. "There are some pretty disreputable clubs in the side streets and alleyways there. Or so I have been told," I quickly added.

"Watson, you need not be embarrassed. I know that some of your earthier military comrades favour a more exciting night-time experience," replied Holmes with just a glimmer of a smile. "I take it that Bancroft was a bachelor." Holmes diplomatically changed the subject. "I see no sign of a wife or family."

"Indeed sir. He is – or was – a very quiet man. In my six months or so here, I cannot remember him entertaining a single guest."

"And yet he frequented a club of dubious repute with a mystery friend," I commented.

"Oh, one more thing, gentlemen," announced Suffolk. "How could I forget? One evening, not long after Mr. Bancroft had started visiting this new club, he was picked up by a cab – one in which there was already a passenger."

"Excellent," exclaimed Holmes. "Can you describe him?"

"It was dark, so I didn't see him clearly," admitted Suffolk, his head dropping.

"Please tell us what you did see. Anything that you can remember could well be vital to our investigation," Holmes insisted.

"Let me see. He was young, no more than five-and-twenty years of age. He wore a long dark coat. I could see nothing else of his dress. He sported a short-brimmed hat and – wait a minute – Yes, he removed this at one point to brush his hair back from his eyes. Dark and long at the front it was. Then he replaced his hat and sat back into the shadows inside the cab. That is all I saw. I am sorry. The master deserved better." Suffolk's face was dark with regret.

"On the contrary, Suffolk," Holmes countered. "You have provided us with excellent testimony which has been of the greatest value. I sincerely believe that we will identify Bancroft's killer. I thank you for your cooperation and bid you farewell."

Chapter V

We climbed into our waiting cab and set off on the short final leg of our journey back to Baker Street.

"Did you really divine anything useful from that visit?" I asked.

"Of course," Holmes replied curtly, "I wouldn't have claimed otherwise."

"A single man, probably a lonely man, finally discovers worldly pleasures in a disreputable club in London. He is led astray by a devious criminal, who somehow convinces, or forces, him to rob the bank for which he works in a position of absolute trust. After the robbery, he meets with these associates to share the haul, but here he is done away with, severing all links of the plotters to the crime." I sat back, rather pleased with my reasoning.

"That, my dear fellow, is an excellent hypothesis," Holmes replied. "It is well-reasoned and completely believable. The fact that it is incorrect shouldn't completely take away from its otherwise unimpeachable credentials."

"I'm not sure whether to thank you or strike you," I grumbled, half-heartedly.

"Oh Doctor, don't be disheartened. I believe you to be more than halfway there. The remainder simply waits to be discovered or confirmed. I'm sorry, but we won't be home for long. A short supper, and then we must head out again – this time to Soho and an evening spent examining the underbelly of London's gentlemen's entertainment."

Chapter VI

After a light supper of cold cuts and toast, we left Baker Street and headed for Soho. The journey was short, a trot along Oxford Street then right into Regent Street. We left the cab and began our search at the southern end of Brewer Street. Feeling confident that this was more my area of expertise than Holmes, I decided to list which clubs I felt were most likely to be Bancroft's "new club".

"West's, The Blue Lotus, and Liberty's are where I would start, Holmes. All three are lively, bohemian, and popular among those with loose morals and large purses."

"Too popular, too legitimate and too public. In that order," replied Holmes as we strolled along the cobbled street. "We are looking for a smaller, more intimate venue, one whose rules and traditions are rather more . . . *singular*."

"Once again, I think that you already know exactly where you're going," I sighed. "Just name the club and let us be on our way."

"I have an idea of which it may be. As you have correctly determined, I've had dealings with several of the lesser known establishments in this area. Have I not told you of the incident at Freddie's? Or the vanishing room at the Fifteen Club?"

"You know full well that you have not," I replied, with more than a hint of frustration.

"Well, remind me, one day, when we have more time. However, we are in the here-and-now. Do you recall what the doorman said when I asked him about Bancroft's changed appearance?"

"He said he would still recognise him anywhere," I began, but then I remembered. "He also told us that Bancroft had said that it was part of a wager!"

"And I know of only one club where debts can be settled in such a way. The party which is owed the debt can set a challenge, or forfeit, often known as a 'dare', which the debtor must perform, regardless of how it might appear to those around him or the world at large."

"How singular. So the poor man had to do whatever he was told. That, or pay off the debt, I presume. Which makes me wonder: Bancroft was a wealthy man. Surely he could afford to pay off whatever debts he'd accumulated at a London club."

"I believe that he could do just that, with considerable ease," Holmes agreed. "We are dealing with something a little different here. I am almost certain that Bancroft completed these forfeits, not by necessity, but by choice."

"He enjoyed them? Yes, well, I suppose I can understand that. A man used to a black-and-white, regulated world is suddenly freed from his bland shackles. He begins to enjoy these little 'dares' – a change of facial hair, a brighter wardrobe – hardly an unbearable forfeit."

"But one serious question remains," Holmes added. "Why would someone who is owed money be satisfied with such a simple forfeit?"

"There must be more to it, something connected with the robbery," I replied. "I can see that a relationship has been built between Bancroft and his new friend, but surely this wouldn't have been enough to convince him to rob his own bank? Even as a forfeit, this would be too much for Bancroft to consider."

"I agree, the jump from wearing unusual clothes to robbing a City bank is too far," Holmes agreed. "We are not seeing things here from the correct perspective. A-ha! Here is where we might find some answers."

To our left was a dark alleyway. I peered into the gloom but could see nothing to indicate the presence of a club, or indeed a functioning business of any kind.

"Are you sure? I know of no club or tavern here."

Holmes ignored me and headed off into the darkness. I followed blindly, hoping that I wouldn't be swallowed up by some gaping hole in the ground. Holmes stopped opposite a dark doorway of an equally dark building. He knocked upon the door with his cane. After a short pause, a bright crack of light appeared as a hatch in the door was opened an inch.

"Who is there?" demanded a gruff voice.

"Mr. Sherlock Holmes and Dr. Watson," answered Holmes, confidently.

The hatch closed, we heard the sound of scraping metal, and finally the heavy door opened to reveal a large man in a dark suit.

"In you go, sir. But, please, this time promise me you will try not to injure quite so many of our guests," he pleaded as we shuffled past.

"What on earth?" I asked, incredulously

"Ancient history," grinned Holmes, "Simply an old case – it matters not. The country involved has recently ceased to exist, so all is now forgotten."

I opened my mouth to protest, but it was snapped shut by the sight that now lay before us. I had expected a small, dingy drinking den, but I gazed upon a large open space – two-dozen tables set in a room of exquisite good taste, somehow both contemporary and traditional. Classical statues stood between modernist paintings. Bright Persian carpets and coloured glass chandeliers gave the place an unworldly atmosphere. Bohemian patrons sat at tables with exotic companions – men and women from around the world, all resplendent in extravagant dress and colourful headwear.

"What is this place?" I whispered.

"This is the New World Club, Watson. It is the most nonconformist, fashionable, and exclusive club in London."

"Then why have I never heard of it?" I asked.

"Because you are, clearly, none of those things," replied Holmes.

"Oh, I see," I sighed.

"Oh, do buck up, Watson. What you are is steadfast, honourable, and loyal – all qualities that you will *not* find in abundance here tonight."

Before I could respond, Holmes headed off towards the bar, a long counter which lined one side of the room. I quickly followed, still taking in the unusual decor and clientele. The front of the bar was ornately carved in dark mahogany. The countertop was black marble with contrasting white veining. On the wall were fixed long shelves, filled with bottles of all shapes, sizes, and colours. I thought I had acquired a decent knowledge of liquor over the years, but I struggled to identify even a fraction of what lay before me.

"Two brandies," requested Holmes. "House Number Fifteen."

The young barman leaned back and, with a practised hand, picked out a dark bottle with hardly a glance. He poured large measures into two glasses.

"Put these on my friend Bancroft's account, if you will," ordered Holmes, casually.

"Certainly sir. I believe Mr. Bancroft has yet to arrive this evening," he added.

Holmes nodded, and picked up the glasses. "We will seat ourselves, thank you."

We found an empty table on the far side of the club. In front of us was a small stage, a dark burgundy curtain hiding whatever lay beyond.

"Well, I can't say that I approve of you charging our drinks to the poor victim's account," I admonished.

"My dear friend, I was merely testing two hypotheses. Firstly, that Bancroft was in the habit of buying drinks for others, even those who were complete strangers to him. Did you not see? The barman didn't even raise an eyebrow at my request."

"And secondly?" I asked.

"That news of his death has yet to reach here. If the staff here are unaware of today's events, then we can be fairly sure that, unless they were directly involved, no one else here knows of Bancroft's death either."

Holmes picked up his glass, tilted it towards me in a small toast, and drained it in a single gulp. He then waved his hand and in less than half-a-minute we were joined by a waitress.

"Two more House Fifteen brandies," he requested.

"Be careful, old chap. You will be sozzled at this rate."

Holmes ignored me and waited for the waitress to return.

"Thank you," he said graciously as she placed the drinks before us. "We are old friends of Bancroft, meeting him here for the first time. I hear he has a new friend, a young man. Can you tell us anything about him?"

The waitress looked troubled, "I'm sorry, sir, but I cannot talk about the members." She was in her mid-twenties, with long, dark hair worn in a single plait. Her face was pale, but her bright blue eyes still shone, even in the half-light of the club.

Holmes leaned closer and, with such speed that it could hardly be observed, slipped a sovereign into the black leather purse that hung from her waist. The waitress thought for a moment and bent over.

"Make that two and I might know something of what you ask."

Holmes slipped her the second coin.

"I can see that you aren't really friends of Mr. Bancroft. I don't think that you are police – they would never flash the gold – but maybe you can help him anyway. He has fallen foul of a terrible influence. The young man of which you speak calls himself Mr. Charlton Watlock. He seems to have some sort of hold over Mr. Bancroft."

"You are very observant, Miss – ?"

"Ruth," replied the waitress. "Ruth Brooks."

"We are, as you say, not the official police, but we do have Mr. Bancroft's interests at heart. Please tell us all that you know.

"They started coming to the club some six months back. Bancroft had clearly never been to such a place before and was quite the fish out of water. Watlock plied him with drink until he relaxed, then persuaded him to play cards and other games. Bancroft, being a complete beginner, lost badly. This didn't seem to trouble Bancroft – he had more than enough money with him to pay for his losses – but Watlock suggested an alternative. The club, you see, has an unusual rule. Those who owe money have the right to ask their creditors for a forfeit to perform in lieu of their debt."

I nodded in agreement. This certainly seemed to confirm what we had heard from the doorman of the bank.

"And so began Bancroft's long list of forfeits," said Holmes.

"The losses were not large, so the forfeits were not harsh. Most were quite comical – wear a funny hat, grow a beard, that sort of thing. But after a while, Mr. Bancroft seemed to tire a little of these games and once again offered to pay for his losses in the more traditional way. It was Watlock who insisted he continue with the forfeits, right up to last week when Bancroft finally declared that he no longer wished to perform in such a way. He would honour the forfeits to which he had agreed up to that point, but made it very clear that he would accept no more. That was the last time he visited the club, as far as I know."

"This Charlton Watlock – can you describe him?" inquired Holmes. "I trust that he isn't here tonight."

"No, I haven't seen him here for a few days. He is quite young, perhaps middle twenties, with dark hair in a long fringe. He is always smartly dressed in the latest fashion. I thought, perhaps, that he was a sportsman as he always wears soft-soled athletic shoes, but there is something very dark about him – maybe it is his eyes. They're deep set and always so black."

"I take it that Watlock is a member of the club?" asked Holmes.

"Yes, he must be. Otherwise he wouldn't have been able to bring Mr. Bancroft in as a guest."

"Thank you, Miss Brooks. I believe you may have provided me with the perspective in this case that I was previously lacking." Holmes slipped another coin into the waitress' leather purse.

Once she had left, Holmes turned to me, anger and frustration creasing his face.

"Watson, I have been stupid! Unforgivably so. How could I have not seen it?"

"Calm down, Holmes. What do you mean? What should you have seen?"

"Everything!" he hissed. "It was right before me and I saw nothing. Our only hope now is to be found in the club's membership lists. We must have access to these, immediately."

"That won't be easy," I warned. "Clubs guard their members' personal details very closely. Their reputation would be ruined if anyone learned of these being shared or even viewed by an outside agency. Maybe if we return with Lestrade?"

"No, I have a better plan. If we can convince the manager that the scandal that will surely follow, once the news of Bancroft's murder and membership becomes public, could be mitigated, then maybe he will let us see Watlock's particulars."

Holmes was quite correct. Once he had convinced the manager that a scandal would expose the club to exactly the kind of public scrutiny that it so obsessively avoided, he agreed to Holmes's request to see Watlock's details. In turn, Holmes promised to do everything that he could to see that the club received as small a mention as possible in the affair.

Holmes was handed the membership book in the manager's office. He quickly turned the pages until he arrived at Watlock's entry. His face darkened. Without a word, he stood up and turned to leave the room.

"Whatever is the matter?" I asked.

I peered at the open book and found the relevant entry. It was simply a name and an address.

Charlton Watlock
221b Baker Street, London

Chapter VII

By the time I caught up with Holmes, he was already outside the club and climbing into a cab. I tried to follow him, but he raised a hand to stop me. "I need to make some inquiries which would best succeed alone. Please return to Baker Street and await my return. Or better still, return to the club, find that waitress, and make sure she really has told us all that she knows."

"What on earth is going on? How did he have our address? Who is he?"

"With every passing minute, we will only drift further away from the truth. All that I can safely say, for now, is that there is no Mr. Charlton Watlock, nor has there ever been. The name is both an insult and a challenge. You can also be certain that he knows exactly who we are and has known right from the start. I believe that our paths have crossed before."

Holmes rapped on the cab roof to alert the driver that he was ready to depart.

"Wait a minute! What insult?" I asked, thoroughly confused.

"Charlatan, Watson!" he exclaimed, as the black cab pulled away.

"Charlatan?" I shouted, rather caught off guard. "Me?"

"Me also, Watson. The pair of us."

I could only just hear his reply as the cab trundled away into the evening gloom. I sighed, turned around, and walked back towards the unmarked entrance to the club. I thought about what Holmes had said – "Charlatan, Watson!" – and then suddenly I saw what he had meant.

"Oh, Watson, you fool," I muttered to myself. "*Charlton Watlock*" was simply a compression of a grubby little insult: "*Charlatans – Watson and Sherlock Holmes*". Clearly, our tormentor held us in utter contempt.

I then realised that this was what Holmes must have meant when he talked about him already having knowledge of us. If our paths had indeed already crossed, then Holmes must have, at least, previously thwarted a scheme of his, if not actually capturing the villain. This would explain his deep animosity towards us. The fellow wanted to best us, certainly, but it seemed just as important to him that we, along with everyone else, knew that it was he who had triumphed. It was almost a kind of flattery, I decided, trying to be optimistic. The man had certainly gone to a lot of trouble to try to humiliate Holmes and me. With an added spring in my step, I knocked heavily upon the club door and re-entered the surreal world that lay beyond.

I headed straight for the bar and the barman we had first approached.

"Excuse me, could I trouble you for a scotch and," I asked, slipping a sovereign across the table, "some information please?"

The barman poured a measure, put the coin in the till, and pocketed the change. "Ask away, sir," he said.

"Where can I find Ruth?" I asked, "I can't seem to see her here," I added, peering around the multi-coloured half-lit room.

"Ruth who? Was she with anyone I might know?" The barman continued wiping and polishing glasses as he spoke.

"Brooks. Ruth Brooks," I insisted. "She is a waitress here, I was just speaking with her not half-an-hour ago."

"Nobody here of that name, sir. Sorry."

I momentarily lost my temper, "Do you want me to return with Inspector Lestrade of Scotland Yard?" I snapped. "Would you prefer to answer his questions rather than mine?"

"Please calm yourself, sir. I meant no offence, but I swear I have no idea who this Ruth Brooks is – ask anyone here."

The young man looked genuinely surprised. I took a deep breath and tried to calm my nerves by taking a sip of the whisky.

"You're saying that there is no waitress here of that name," I said, grinding my teeth. I then described the girl in as much detail as I could remember.

"No sir, I don't know who you were speaking to, but she wasn't one of the waitresses that works here."

I tried to think what Holmes might do – certainly not leave with his head spinning, as I felt compelled to. I took another, larger sip of the scotch.

"I take it that you know Charlton Watlock?" I asked, finding a more reassuring line of questioning.

"Yes. He is a real character and popular with the other members, even if he isn't the most generous of tippers, if you know what I mean." The barman replied, less than subtly requesting further inducement.

I sighed and passed over another coin, "Make the whisky a single malt this time," I indicated to the glass before me. "This one tasted like you distilled it from Thames river water."

The barman smiled and replaced the foul liquid with a much more pleasant dram.

"Did he have a regular female companion, one who might have looked similar to the young lady that I described?" I asked.

"Well, no. Or maybe . . . ." the young man trailed off. "He was quite often accompanied by a young lady, but she had blond hair and never wore a plait."

"Do you happen to know her name or occupation?"

"I think her name was Bonnie – I'm not sure. But I do know that she was an actress."

"An actress?" I sighed. It was almost too obvious.

"Yes, in a small theatre. She also told the girls here that she does the makeup and hair too, I think she was looking to make an extra bob or two from the waitresses."

Chapter VIII

I found a cab and set off back to Baker Street. The two brandies, along with the whisky, had given me quite a headache. I was grateful that I managed to sleep lightly for most of the journey.

I trudged tiredly up the stairs and into the apartment. All was dark, and there was no sign of Holmes. I decided that I could achieve nothing more by waiting up for him and so headed off to bed.

I was awakened the next morning by bright sunshine streaming through the gap where I had failed to properly close the curtains. I checked my watch. It was just past seven and I, having failed to eat the previous evening, was now ravenous.

I entered the sitting room to see Holmes already sitting at the table, sipping a cup of fresh coffee. Around him was spread a magnificent breakfast of toast, eggs, bacon, and jars of Mrs. Hudson's homemade preserves. Without saying a word, I sat down and began to eat, savouring the feast yet again provided by our oft-times saviour.

Once I had finished, I sat back with my coffee and waited for Holmes to finally break his silence. As, after a while, he seemed disinclined to do so, I thought that I should recount the events of yesterday evening after he had departed the club.

"Well done!" said Holmes, much to my surprise. "Another small, but significant, piece of the puzzle, and one that confirms what I already suspected. I believe I now have the complete solution to this affair."

"Solution? Surely we are nowhere near to catching those responsible. In fact, I'm not entirely sure that we even know who is responsible for these crimes," I stressed.

"The true identities of all those involved are now known to me and, shortly, I will be sharing this information with Scotland Yard. In fact, I believe I hear the footsteps of friend Lestrade upon the stair carpet even as we speak."

"Well, I shall look forward to hearing what you have to say. Shall we remove to more comfortable seating? I feel a good bowl or two might be necessary to aid my understanding of these events."

Lestrade bid us good morning and we were all soon sitting comfortably, Holmes with his stygian black clay, Lestrade with one of Holmes's *Hoyo de Monterrey*'s, and I with my trusty brown Rhodesian briar.

"I can't see much being changed in my report, truth be told," began Lestrade. "Bancroft robbed his own bank and was done away with by his accomplice, identity unknown. You did well with the murder scene, I'll grant you, but that hasn't brought us any closer to apprehending the killers."

"You may well be right, for now," replied Holmes, much to the inspector's surprise.

"I thought this was the point where you pluck the suspects from thin air," replied Lestrade, sounding disappointed.

"Let me tell you what I do know, Inspector," began Holmes. "Bancroft did not steal anything from anywhere, that is for certain. The robbery was carried out by someone else altogether, and the subsequent murder was committed by his accomplice.

"We must start with what we learned at the murder scene," Holmes continued, seemingly oblivious to our open-mouthed expressions. "Bancroft had left the bank at twelve and arrived at the restaurant sometime around twelve-thirty. He sat down and, soon afterwards, was dead, poisoned by a pin dipped in snake venom which was placed in the seat of his chair. He was found to be wearing all manner of unusual attire that he had been sporting as the result of losing various wagers at a club that he had recently been frequenting.

"Does not anything about this strike you as being unusual?" he asked, impatiently.

"Well, yes," I admitted. "Everything. But surely the point of all of those wagers was to encourage Bancroft towards the villain's ultimate goal – persuading him to rob his own bank."

"Actually," interrupted Lestrade, "I had begun to wonder whether Bancroft thought of this 'robbery' as being simply just another wager. Perhaps he planned to return the stolen stocks and bonds once he had proved to his associate that he had completed his forfeit."

"Yes, Inspector," I agreed. "That would explain just about everything, wouldn't it? The poor fellow was poisoned at this meeting and the stolen items taken by his killer. Surely you cannot seriously believe that anyone else could have stolen the securities?"

"I believe it because it is true," said Holmes. "Think, gentlemen. There are several ways to make a man commit a crime – blackmail, physical threats, or good, old-fashioned financial inducement, to name but three. But have you ever heard of anyone acting so completely out of character, and against every fibre of their professional and moral code, for the completion of a wager? No, Bancroft would never act in this way, certainly not for a bet. In any case, we know that he had grown weary of these games and was on the verge of ending his association with the villain."

"We only have the word of an imposter for this," I contested, "one whom we are now certain is in league with this 'Watlock' fellow." I told him of the events at the club the previous night.

"It's becoming clear," said Holmes, "that one of the ambitions of this whole scheme appears to be to my personal humiliation. As such, this fake waitress had nothing to lose by telling us the truth. I believe every word that she said. It was all part of Watlock's plan to show us exactly how clever he had been and how easily he bested us."

"So then, assuming that what you say is indeed the case, who exactly did carry out the robbery?" asked Lestrade, with some frustration.

"Watlock himself, of course," revealed Holmes. "He knew that he could never convince Bancroft to actually steal from his own bank, so it had to be someone else. Whom else could he trust to perform the deed and hand over the ill-gotten gains, once the deed was done? No, he had to rob the bank himself. His first thought would have been to impersonate Bancroft, but he soon realised that no disguise or make-up expert could transform him into even a passable impersonation of the dour, soberly-dressed banker.

"He then had a moment of inspiration. If he couldn't make himself appear as Bancroft, then maybe he could alter Bancroft's appearance into a form that was simpler to replicate. He formed the idea that he would befriend the banker and introduce to him a world of pleasure and indulgence, one which he had never previously imagined. He would then be able to manipulate him into acting against his previous pedestrian character. He knew he couldn't make him commit an actual crime, but he could persuade him to change his appearance, initially in subtle ways. By the time Bancroft began to show signs of beginning to tire of this new lifestyle, Watlock had achieved his aim and was ready to strike."

"Bancroft's appearance had now changed to such an extent that he was almost unrecognisable from the man that he had been before. However, those who had contact with him on a daily basis had seen these changes occur gradually over several months and so were not overly alarmed."

"Such as those at the bank," I asked, seeking clarification. "The doorman and the staff you mean?"

"Along with those who worked at the restaurant, of course," confirmed Holmes, before continuing. "Watlock then employed his associate, the actress and make-up artist, in creating a disguise that would be convincing enough to fool the doorman at the bank. Remember, it only needed to be successful once, and only for fifteen to twenty minutes. He would, obviously, have visited the bank previously with his new friend on some pretence or other over the previous six months – probably several times. He would have learned the layout of the offices, the location of the safes, and at what times they were open and most vulnerable. Whether he had stolen or copied Bancroft's keys is still to be determined. Either way, he knew how to gain access to the safes.

"Think about it," Holmes stressed. "How easy would it now be to impersonate Bancroft? The new, bright clothing and the beard, all designed to hide Bancroft's genuine, recognisable features. The shaven head was easy to replicate, either with simple razor or rubber stage skullcap – aided, of course, by our phony waitress-*cum*-theatre make-up artist. The most ingenious part of the disguise was, however, the tinted glasses. Our eyes say so much about us. They are, by far, the hardest facial feature to camouflage. Unlike Bancroft, Watlock has very distinctive dark eyes that he needed to conceal. I know this," Holmes stated, enigmatically, "because we have seen those eyes before

"My word, Mr. Holmes," gasped Lestrade. "That is brilliant. He couldn't impersonate Bancroft as he was, so instead, he changed Bancroft's appearance into one that he could convincingly mimic. Incredible."

"Yes, Inspector, we are dealing with a master manipulator and a ruthless killer. He formulated this scheme to earn both a fortune and a victory over me."

"But who on earth is he?" I begged. "You say we have encountered him before."

"My dear Watson, do you believe that every unsolved crime in London is perpetrated by a different villain?"

"Well, no, of course not," I grumbled, "However, I see no way to connect this most unique of crimes to any of those committed by a particular person – or group, if a gang might be involved."

"Wait a moment, Doctor," Lestrade interjected. "I think that I might know what Mr. Holmes is getting at here."

Holmes smiled encouragingly and let the inspector continue.

"I think we are looking for a very specific individual: Educated, imaginative, even flamboyant, but also ruthless, vicious, and terribly cruel. He was able to charm a stuffy, professional banker into performing all sorts of madcap antics, and then slay him in a most terrible and unnecessarily gruesome manner."

"He certainly has a taste for both the theatre and the macabre," agreed Holmes, releasing a cloud of dark pungent smoke before him.

"We should be looking for cases both violent and *outré*," concluded Lestrade.

"Do you mean something like that jewellery business in Chelsea, earlier in the year? Galton – Samuel Galton – Wasn't that his name?" I asked. "The fake theft itself was extremely cleverly planned. However, it wasn't until we had fully investigated the matter that we discovered that the robbery was only a small part of a much larger conspiracy involving some pretty unpleasant murders."

"Ah, yes, I recall the case. Hang on though," replied Lestrade, waving his cigar with such fervour that a full inch of ash flew off towards the fireplace. "Wasn't he the young man that ran off to America? But he never reached shore. We heard that he was lost at sea. Everyone assumed that he fell – or jumped – overboard."

"No, Inspector, he is very much alive and seeking vengeance, along with the fortune that we forever denied him."

"So how did he fake his disappearance from his transatlantic voyage?" I asked.

"When I left you at the New World club, I made some inquiries. I had recognised Galton from the description and contacted the shipping line on which he had booked his transit. The captain had noticed nothing unusual, but he put me in contact with the ship's purser. He, in turn, recalled an unusual incident where a crew uniform had gone missing, only to mysteriously reappear a few hours later in exactly the place from where it had vanished. This confirmed to me exactly how Galton had managed to disappear and convince the authorities that he was lost overboard, down into the infinite dark blue of the deep ocean."

"Very poetic, but how did Galton leave the boat without being seen?" I demanded.

"Remarkably simply. He boarded the ship as himself, stole the uniform, went to his cabin, changed his clothing for that of a crew member, and disembarked. After all, who would pay any attention to a crewman leaving the ship? To tidy up any loose ends, he then had an associate, who was genuinely bound for America, board the ship and replace the stolen uniform. When the ship reached the States, it would appear that Galton had vanished into thin air."

There was a long pause as we took in all of this new information. Lestrade took a long draw on his Havana and released a plume of blue-grey smoke. The sweet-and-spicy mix of the smoke from the handmade cigar wrapped itself around us and made me reluctant to suck upon my own tobacco, at least for a moment.

"So he is now gone, is he not?" Lestrade asked, the preceding silence making his words sound louder than he had intended.

"He is gone," confirmed Holmes, quietly. "He has a new fortune – he can go wherever he pleases. I suspect that he will venture abroad, the Continent most likely, where he will spend a year or so before returning to commit a new crime."

"Do you think that he'll return?" I asked. "Even if he did, he now has a huge fortune. Why would he need to return to crime?"

"To beat us and mock us again," replied Lestrade, before Holmes could answer. "This Galton character does not simply wish to acquire wealth. He also needs to show the world just how clever he is, as he not only bests the police but also defeats even you, Mr. Holmes. I believe that he has a mania, and it isn't just simple greed. The money will not satisfy him for long. I agree with Mr. Holmes – he'll be back.

"So we just sit and wait for him to return?" I huffed. "That doesn't sound very satisfactory to me."

"Calm yourself, Watson," Holmes retorted, sternly. "The inspector is watching the docks and railway stations. We have good descriptions – we may yet be lucky."

"You don't really believe that," I grumbled. "The disappointment is written all over your face. And in any case, I haven't forgotten that his accomplice is an expert at makeup and disguise. They won't be stopped."

"Now that you mention this so-called waitress, I can, at least, give you some information on that score. Her stage name was Bonnie Waters,"

Lestrade read the name from his leather-bound notebook. "Her real name was Mary Quinn, a small-time actress and makeup girl. No previous criminal record, which came as a great surprise to me, knowing what probably occurred at the restaurant."

"Agreed, Inspector," said Holmes, darkly. "Galton must have a very strong hold over her, indeed, to have persuaded her to act for him in such heinous way."

"Wait, I don't quite understand. What did she do?" I asked.

"If Galton really was the one who stole the stocks and bonds from Boutte's, then he couldn't have been the murderer at the restaurant," explained Lestrade. "He would have to have been waiting outside the bank for Bancroft to leave before he could commence his scheme. All this time, Bancroft would have been walking, completely unaware, towards his usual table at Vespasian's. There is no way that Galton could have robbed the bank and then caught him up over such short a distance."

"Which means that Quinn, the actress, must have been responsible for disposing of Bancroft!" I said.

"Yes, I believe it was she that laid the trap for poor Bancroft," Holmes confirmed. "Knowing his habit of lunching at Vespasian's, Galton had devised a terrible scheme to do away with the banker, once the theft had been successfully accomplished."

"Quinn entered the restaurant the moment it opened, when it was still free of other patrons. She sat at the least visible table and ordered something simple – a coffee or similar. While the waiter was away preparing her drink, she moved swiftly to Bancroft's favourite table and placed the deadly venomous pin into the top of the wicker seat, upon which he would shortly sit. Then she waited."

"Bancroft arrived and at some point, pricked himself upon this evil object. His death throes would have been dramatic. I believe that Quinn used the panic and confusion that ensued as cover for an attempt to recover the evil device. She may even have worn a waitress uniform under her coat to help disguise herself. As we know, she failed to recover the pin, only managing to kick it to the edge of the room. Having seen the effect of the venom at first hand, perhaps she decided that she daren't risk picking it up after all."

"Well, it sounds like these two were made for each other," I declared. "Both evil to their dark cores."

"At least until he tires of her," replied Holmes, unexpectedly. "I do not see Galton operating with a partner for long. I fear that Miss Quinn may not long enjoy the fruit of her wicked labours."

We talked some more, and it was well into the afternoon before Lestrade bade us farewell. Holmes returned to his chemical corner and I to my writing. After twenty minutes, I hadn't written a single word.

"Holmes, this case troubles me," I said to my friend. "I accept that Galton has got away – for now – but have we learned anything from this turgid affair?"

There was a pause before Holmes finally spoke.

"Habits, Watson. By our habits we are known, and by our habits we can be undone."

The Adventure of the Tea-Stained Diamonds
by Craig Stephen Copland

He was not much more than a child. I estimated his age at fourteen. He was a handsome boy, with the raven-black hair and deeply tanned skin color that marks a person who came from the lands under the Raj. His young body was beginning to show the signs of an emerging well-made sportsman. From his place, lying on his back on the pavement, his dark-brown eyes stared up at the morning sky . . . lifeless.

Behind his head was a pool of blood, now darkened and congealed.

"Was he one of yours, Mr. Holmes?" demanded Inspector Lestrade. "One of your, whatever you call them, *Irresponsibles*?"

"Yes, Inspector. He was one of my Irregulars."

"What was his name?"

"The other lads called him *Sahib.* He had no other name."

"What in heaven's name did you have him doing that ended up with his getting shot in the head?"

"He was engaged in surveillance," said Holmes.

"Of what?"

"Related to the recent robbery in Hatton Garden."

"Hatton Garden? We have not called you in to help on that. Who did? The shop owner?"

"No."

"Then who?"

"No one."

Lestrade paused his questions and glared at Holmes. "Mr. Holmes, that is beyond belief! You decided to poke your nose into a case for the sole reason to show off how clever you are and show up Scotland Yard. That's what you did, right?"

I looked at the face of my unusual friend. He had paled and seemed to be biting his lip to restrain any overt emotion.

"The case presented some interesting aspects which I thought to be challenging."

"Well now, isn't that just splendid? You want to strut your cleverness and let all of London see your superiority to the police, and what do you have to show for it? A dead child."

Holmes made no reply. Lestrade continued.

"And you have no idea where we can contact his family?"

"Most of the boys do not live with their families. They are street urchins."

"Let me enlighten you, Mr. Sherlock Holmes: Every one of your boys has a mother somewhere, and when one of them is murdered whilst working for Mr. Sherlock Holmes, the police have to find her and tell her."

"If I can assist you in that matter, I shall do so."

"No, Mr. Holmes, you cannot. But I will tell you what you can do. You can stop sending children out in the night and having them turn up dead in the morning. And here's something else you can do. You can drop everything you are doing and report to Scotland Yard whatever you have learned about that robbery. And do not expect a farthing from us for doing so."

Lestrade turned abruptly from us and motioned to the ambulance workers to lift the boy's body into their wagon. Two constables came forward with a bucket of water and a scrub brush and did their best to remove the blood from the pavement.

Holmes did not move. He stood frozen in place until the police had departed, and the gaggle of curious onlookers dispersed. Then he turned to me, his face was ashen. "When you looked at the body, was it clear what had happened?"

"It was. He had been shot in the back of his head by a revolver held against his skull."

"He must have seen something."

We had been standing on the pavement of Hart Street, adjacent to the square, and we hailed a cab to take us back to Baker Street. Holmes was silent as we made our way through Fitzrovia and up to Marylebone Road. As it was early in the morning, the traffic was light and pedestrians few. The newsboys were out, and the posters carried the headline: *£1,000 Diamonds Stolen from Hatton Garden. No Signs of thieves!* The brazen robbery of several days earlier was being talked about everywhere. Lacking much clear evidence, the police had hypothesized that sometime during the night of Saturday, 22 August, 1885, an agile robber had scaled the back wall of a building in Hatton Garden, north of Cross Street, skillfully opened a section of the roof, descended into the shop of a select jeweler, and collected a sack of uncut diamonds. He then must have covered his tracks and escaped back through the roof. There were no witnesses, and Scotland Yard seemed to be utterly befuddled.

Holmes reasoned that if a particular method worked for a thief once, he might try it again. So he had dispatched his Irregulars to spend the warm summer nights spread out across the rooftops of both sides of Hatton

Garden, from Clerkenwell Road to Grenville Street. All except one had returned with nothing to report.

On arriving at Baker Street, Holmes got out of the cab and blew a few blasts on his whistle. Moments later, a small collection of street urchins had gathered around him, listened to whatever he had to say to them, and scampered off.

"I told them," he said, as we climbed the stairs to 221b, "to bring Wiggins to me. I have to learn about this boy, this *Sahib*."

Within ten minutes, a tall, scrawny boy with a dirty face, appeared. He touched his forelock and gave a small bow to Holmes, exuding an air of superior insolence.

"You sent for me, Mr. Holmes, sir."

Holmes told him about the death of the boy they called Sahib. The face of the Captain of the Irregulars changed from unsavory to shock, to pain. Tears appeared in his eyes.

"Oh, Mr. Holmes, I am sorry. It was my fault. I should never have let him join your force, sir. He did not belong. He wasn't one of us. He knew nothing about living by his wits, sir."

"Who was he, and where did he come from?"

"He showed up at the end of June and said that his Summer Half-term had ended, and that he wanted to join Sherlock Holmes's Irregulars."

"His term? He attended a school?"

"He did, Mr. Holmes, sir. That's why we called him *Sahib.* He was Indian, sir, but he was a right proper little toff, he was, sir."

"What school?"

"He said it was something like *eating,* sir."

"And he came and lived on the street with you and the rest of the boys all summer?"

"Well, yes and no, Mr. Holmes, sir. Just during the week, sir. On Sundays, he had to go home for dinner with his gran, and then on Monday morning, he would come back, all cleaned up and such, sir."

"Where did he live? Do you know? And what was his true name?"

"Somewhere past Hyde Park, sir, where all the toff families live. His name was something like *taming,* like what they do to horses, Mr. Holmes, sir."

"Where was he stationed last night?"

"It was for two nights, sir. At the corner of Clerkenwell and Hatton Garden, sir. North end of the street. The south-east corner. There was a dozen of us, Mr. Holmes, sir. We had one of us on every third roof so we could cover the entire street for you, sir."

Holmes gave his young captain a shilling, dismissed him, and slowly collapsed into his armchair.

"I shall send a note to Lestrade. *Tamang* is a common name of well-to-do Indian families who have homes in Belgravia. That should be enough to go on to find his family. Perhaps, Watson, you could do that for me. Would you mind?"

He looked and sounded low, and I readily agreed to his request. As I was leaving the room to find a local page boy, I watched him lean forward in his chair and bury his head in his hands.

It was approaching ten o'clock in the morning, and the streets were now alive with people and vehicles. Whilst I was out in Baker Street, a newsboy was shouting the most recent headline: "*Second robbery in Hatton Garden! Second diamond robbery! Thieves get away with a fortune in diamonds and jewels!*"

I purchased a copy, ran back up the stairs, and thrust it in front of Holmes. He looked up, scanned the headline, and stood up.

"It says that the second shop to be robbed was at the intersection of Clerkenwell and Hatton Garden. That is beyond coincidence. If you can spare the time, Watson, would you mind accompanying me there?"

Two police wagons were already standing at the curb beside the intersection. Constables guarded the front doors of several of the shops, not permitting customers to enter. The shop facing Hatton Garden bore signage showing that it belonged to *Simon Shapiro – Gold and Diamonds.* Beside it was a small café offering kosher lunches. Facing Clerkenwell Road, the nearest shop bore the address of *Hyram Maxim – Useful Household Devices*, and the one beside it was a small bank offering currency exchange at good rates.

Holmes approached a constable who appeared to be in charge of the brigade and identified himself.

"Right, Mr. Holmes. We were expecting you. The inspector told us that you had better show up, and if you didn't, we were to go and fetch you and tell you to get to work."

"Did he? Well, now I am here. Could you tell me, sir, what happened last night?"

"There's no mystery, Mr. Holmes. The two skylights were still open this morning. Some acrobatic fellow comes up out of the shop of the inventor fellow on Clerkenwell, and being a bit of a billy-goat, he works his way across to the neighbor's roof – that would be the roof of the diamond shop – opens the skylight, and lets himself down. Whilst inside he removes a whole sack of fine jewelry and then he climbs back up and across the roof and over into the other skylight and must have hidden inside that shop until the owner comes along this morning and opens the door, and he waits until the owner isn't looking and lets himself out and Bob's your uncle."

The constable opened the door of the diamond merchant's shop and let us in. The interior was modest, bordering on dull. Rows of display cases filled the room, most with glass that was cleaned and polished. None of those near the front of the store had been disturbed. Two in the back corner had their tops open and were empty.

In addition to two constables, I counted five people in the store, all of whom appeared to be from the same family. Behind the counter, an elderly man with a kippah on his head and a prayer shawl draped over his shoulders, sat in a chair. Quietly, he rocked back and forth, and when he leaned back, I could see that his lips were moving slowly and silently.

Of the remaining four, three were men and one a young woman. Two of the men were young, not more than twenty-five. The older was middle-aged and, judging from the obvious family resemblance, it appeared that he was the father of one of the young men and the young woman. All three of the younger people were tall, slender, and attractive, and dressed in a fashionable way as one might expect of salespeople in a shop that caters to Londoners of significant wealth.

Holmes walked over to the elderly man and dropped to one knee beside him. Laying a hand on the old fellow's shoulder, he spoke to him quietly.

"Mr. Simon Shapiro. My name is Sherlock Holmes. I am terribly sorry for what has happened to you, but I give you my word: I will work without ceasing until I catch whoever did this to you and, Lord willing, return your missing property."

The old man stopped rocking, opened his eyes, and looked at Holmes.

"*Adank,*" he said, and closed his eyes and returned to his prayers.

"Thank you, sir," said the middle-aged man to Holmes. "I am Lemuel Shapiro. That was very kind of you. My father opened this business forty years ago when he came to England from Leipzig. He has built a good business and is trusted by all who have dealt with him. This is the first time anything like this has happened, and he is very distressed."

"And understandably so," said Holmes. "Forgive me for asking, but is your business insured against this type of loss?"

"In part. But what was stolen was from our most expensive cases, and we do not yet know the exact value. It was well over three-thousand pounds. It is far beyond the limit of our insurance."

"I'm sorry to have to ask blunt questions, but why were those pieces not securely locked away?"

"They were, Mr. Holmes. These display cases have been specially made. They have strong metal plates that close to cover the glass and are secured to the floor. The locks are the best that can be provided by Chubb. Whoever picked the locks was a highly skilled thief. You can see for yourself."

Holmes took a cursory look at the open cases and then turned back to Lemuel Shapiro.

"Will your shop stay open?"

"Yes, it will. Such wealth as our family once had is gone, but my father built his business once. He will do it again. This time my son and daughter and nephew and I will be there to help. If God grants my father another decade on the earth, he will again see his business prosper and his family secure, and he can die in peace."

"May God grant your family that blessing," said Holmes. "With your permission, Mr. Shapiro, I shall inspect the premises and then take myself up to your roof."

Holmes took his glass from his pocket and began a methodical inspection of the shop, taking time to note the scratches on the locks and on the woodwork beside them. He posed several questions to the son and daughter, Saul and Malka, and to the nephew, Helmut.

The son and daughter had grown up in the business. The nephew had moved to London recently from Leipzig and was learning the trade of the diamond merchant. All of them seemed utterly despondent and worried about their beloved grandfather, but they could offer no insight concerning the theft.

From the ground floor, we ascended the stairs to the third floor, and then up a ladder to the skylight.

As soon as we were on the roof, Holmes walked over to the central chimney at the south-east corner of the building.

"This unfortunate boy, Sahib," he said, "must have hidden behind this chimney and watched as the neighbor's skylight opened. He would have observed the thief climb up from the neighbor's side, cross over to this building, open the Shapiro glass, and descend."

"And come back," I said, "soon after with a sack of jewels. But then he must have spotted Sahib and decided that he could not leave any witnesses alive. His first robbery went off like clockwork, but this one went off the rails. Something like that, eh, Holmes?"

"No, my dear Watson, not like that. Not at all."

He then turned and started back to the skylight.

"Holmes, aren't you going to look in the other shop – the neighbor's?"

"Why would I want to do that?" he said and climbed back onto the ladder leading into the diamond merchant's. "The way across to his portion of the roof is treacherous."

For a few minutes whilst we were examining the premises where the second theft had taken place, Holmes's spirits seemed to lighten, but once up on the roof and observing where young Sahib must have been hiding, he lapsed back into despondency. His mood didn't improve on the drive back across London to Baker Street, and it was a half-hour after we returned to our parlor that I finally poured two glasses of brandy and held one in front of him.

"Holmes," I said, "you are my friend, and I sympathize with your sorrow over Sahib. But if you want me to help, you must tell me what you observed."

He rolled his eyes up at me and sighed. "Oh, very well then, what do you want to know? I should have thought that everything was obvious."

"To you, perhaps, but not to me. I could see nothing other than what the constable explained, and we know about Sahib. A skilled thief pulled off two robberies, and during the second one, he saw the boy watching him and killed him."

"There were two thieves. The first was a skilled professional. He will have to wait for a few days until we confront the second, the amateur imitator, and return the jewels to the old man."

"How do you know there were two?"

"Elementary, my friend. A skilled thief does not advertise his methods. In the first robbery, the police are not at all certain how he gained access to the shop. They are theorizing that he came through the roof, as they see no other possible way. In the Shapiro case, the thief flaunted his method, leaving the skylights wide open – a sure sign of an amateur."

"But he picked those Chubb locks, and you acknowledged that they are the best available."

"How do you know he picked them?"

"From the scratches. You saw them. I saw you looking at them."

"Honestly, Watson. Any thief who is sufficiently skilled to pick one of those locks is not so clumsy as to leave scratches on the lock and the wood up to an inch away. They were deliberately put there by one not particularly bright man to deceive a similar man into believing that the locks were picked."

I did not appreciate the underlying thought behind his comment, but was more concerned with the logic that I was obviously missing.

"But he knew what to take. He ignored the standard pieces and went straight for the expensive ones."

"Another mark of someone who doesn't know what he's doing."

"What?"

"Please, Watson. Let me put it simply, and perhaps it will help you understand. If I were to hold up two paintings in front of you, one by Stubbs and one by El Greco, could you tell them apart?"

"Of course, I could."

"Brilliant. If I were to hold up two paintings both by El Greco in front of an expert, Mr. John Ruskin, for example, could he tell me if one was a true piece by the artist, and one a skilled forgery?"

"Certainly. He is an expert in European painting. He could detect those small inconsistencies that tell one artist from another."

"Very good, Watson. There is some hope for you yet. It is the same with cut diamonds and fine gold mountings. There is a small group of master craftsmen throughout Europe, and one or two in America, who can cut and mount diamonds in pieces of jewelry that sell for hundreds of pounds. They all know each other. They all have distinct styles, just as a painter does, and they can identify one of their esteemed colleague's pieces in a minute. The sole means of selling jewelry of that price and quality is through the store of a master jeweler who has an impeccable reputation, and no respected store would touch such stolen goods. They would run for the police."

I pondered that one, and then a light went off in my brain.

"A-ha! So that is why the smart thief knew to take nothing but uncut diamonds."

"Precisely."

"But if thief number two was such a dumb ox, how did he get the cases open?"

"With a key."

"A key? One of the family? No. That seems highly unlikely. They are as thick as – " I stopped what I was about to say as my metaphor did not seem particularly appropriate.

"Who it was and how they obtained a key is still unknown. Possibly a member of the family, possibly not. It is too early to hypothesize. I will, however, devote my full attention to finding out, as the same person must have killed the boy. Now, if you will excuse me, I have work to do."

He departed from Baker Street, and I did not see him until the following morning. At seven o'clock, when I came down from my bedroom, he was already at the breakfast table. He stretched out his long arm as I approached, handing me the morning's newspaper.

"On page three," was all he said,

I sat down, opened to that page, and read the item about Sahib:

Boy from Belgravia Murdered in Bloomsbury

Scotland Yard reports that a student from Eton College was found shot in the head beside Bloomsbury Square. The victim has been identified as Master Rajiv Tamang, of the Tamang family of Lowndes Place in Belgravia. No reason was given for his tragic death, nor what he was doing so far from his home in the middle of the night.

"It is a terrible loss," said Inspector G. Lestrade, "and our thoughts and prayers go out to his family. We were even sadder when we learned that the boy's father, Mr. Parijat Tamang, the respected owner of the Royal Tea Company of Darjeeling, passed away this spring. It has been a very hard year for this wonderful Christian family."

We expect that Inspector Lestrade and his capable team at Scotland Yard will leave no stone unturned as they seek to bring the perpetrator of this horrendous crime to justice.

The funeral for young Rajiv will take place at 11:00 a.m. on Monday, 31 August, at St. Mary's, Bourne Street. Visiting the family to express condolences is scheduled for Sunday afternoon from two through six o'clock in the church hall.

I placed the newspaper back on the table. "What a devastating year for them. I hope the mother has other family members to support her."

"They are Indian," said Holmes. "Their families are all very close and strong. In some ways, that is good. It also means that many people were close to both the father and the boy, and the pain will be felt all the more."

"Will you go to the funeral?"

"To the visitation, yes. I cannot escape that obligation. However, as I was the one who sent the boy to his death, I fear my presence at the funeral would be a distraction. Might I impose on you, my friend, to accompany me on Sunday afternoon?"

"You know I will do that."

"I do indeed . . . and I thank you."

The summer of '85 was drawing to a close. The final Saturday of August opened with a warm and sunny morning that brought families out to London's great parks to enjoy a final picnic on the lawns, or to the shops of Oxford and Regent Streets to buy all those new clothes and shoes that children and youth need in order to return to their schools.

I took myself out for a walk from Paddington down to Hyde Park and along the Serpentine, where I stopped, sat on a bench, and read for a glorious hour. Perhaps it was the novel that I was reading that brought on an attack of conscience, but it struck me that I should try to drag Holmes out of his tobacco-infested study and force some fresh air upon him. With that purpose in mind, I walked back through Marble Arch and over to Baker Street. I was feeling positively chipper as I strode north and stopped to buy a newspaper from the newsagent at the corner of Marylebone. I looked up and down the rack of his offerings, trying to decide which version of the events of the day to read. My eye stopped, and then my heart stopped when I saw the front page of *The Evening Star*. The headline read:

Amateur Detective Uses Child as Bait. Child is Murdered

I ripped the paper off the rack and read the story. It named Sherlock Holmes as the one who had sent the young Etonian, Master Rajiv Tamang, out at night to spy on criminals. The boy had been shot in the head whilst undertaking his mission. "*This amateur detective*" the article opined, "*surely has blood on his hands*." It quoted Inspector Lestrade as saying, "*Mr. Holmes has some excellent abilities as a detective, but what he did with this boy was unconscionable. Scotland Yard has many trained officers who are capable of carrying out professional surveillance. We would never send a boy to do a man's job*."

My soul groaned, and I plodded the rest of the way to 221b.

"I have seen it," said Holmes when I came in.

"That was beastly of Lestrade," I said.

"No, Watson, it was honest and fair of him, even if hard. The boy was killed on my assignment. There is nothing I can do about that. If you have come to try to cheer me up, please do not bother."

"Are you still going to go to the visitation tomorrow?"

"I have to. It would be despicably cowardly of me not to. I have no expectation of you, my friend. Feel free not to join me. I, for one, would not want to be seen on the streets with me and would rather do anything than accompany me to the child's casket."

"Don't be silly, Holmes. We will leave at two."

When I had secured a cab, Holmes was waiting. He climbed inside, his face set like a flint to endure the afternoon. He was silent until we were a block from the church.

"If the mother and the aunts call me every vile name in the book, Watson, do not seek to defend me. If the cousins and uncles beat me black and blue, do not stop them. I deserve whatever punishment they administer. But I do thank you, my friend, for standing by me. There is no doubt in my mind that you are the only man on earth now willing to do so."

I do not recall in the years since I had met him that I'd ever seen him so despondent. I tried to think of something to say to lighten his mood, but no words came.

The church hall was busy with people, primarily members of London's Indian community who had departed the land of the Raj to live in the land of the Empress. Some, those of the Hindu faith, were dressed in spotless white, the Christians in black. No one seemed to recognize us, for which I was grateful. We joined a long queue of people standing in line to express their sympathy to the family. An older man, Sahib's grandfather, I assumed, was the first family member to receive the visitors. Beside him was an attractive middle-aged woman in a dark sari. Even with her coffee-colored complexion, one could see her reddened eyes.

"Good afternoon, Mrs. Tamang," I said, "I am Dr. John Watson, and this is my friend and colleague, Mr. Sherlock Holmes and – "

That was a far as I got. The woman lit up like a sunrise and gasped. "Oh, Mr. Holmes, oh, I am so glad you could come. We were all hoping you would so that we could thank you in person for what you did for our poor Rajiv. His time working for you, his last two months on this earth, was such a joyful time for him. We miss him so, but he died a happy boy. We shall always be grateful."

I stared at this woman and then turned around and looked at Holmes. He had a look of complete confusion on his face and mumbled a few incoherent words of thanks.

The woman turned and looked down the line of family members and in a rather loud voice, announced, "This is Mr. Sherlock Holmes."

Five Indian men in formal suits and five women in dark saris looked up and smiled at him.

"Oh, Mr. Holmes," continued the mother. "Goodness gracious, please do not leave before we have an opportunity to talk. I must greet all these people behind you in the line, else I would keep you here for an hour and talk about Rajiv."

Then she looked down the line to a man who was of the age of a university student.

"Bimal, son, you will leave the line and talk to Mr. Holmes. Thank you, son."

The young man, who looked remarkably like the dead boy that I had seen lying on the pavement just a few days before, stepped out and greeted us.

"Please, Mr. Holmes, Dr. Watson, come. Some tea and some sweets?"

Holmes looked at me, and I back at him.

"It is so very good to meet you," the young man said to us. "My brother was so very, very sad when my father died just after Christmas. The school sent us notes that he was failing his tests and that he had dropped off of the cricket team. He was overcome with brain fever. We did not know what to do for him. When he came home at the end of term, my mother was desperate. He would have been moping and crying in his room all summer long if it had not been for you and your Irregulars."

Holmes had recovered his wits enough to ask, "How did you know about me?"

"Oh, Mr. Holmes, sir, we are Indians. We know things. One Indian man hears about you, and he tells his wife, and she then tells twenty or thirty of her dearest and closest friends, other wives, and soon everyone from India living in London has heard about you. My mother heard these stories, and she said a prayer, and she believes that the Good Lord told her to take Rajiv up to Baker Street and ask if he could join your Irregulars. This was a very very strange idea. No boy from India, especially an Etonian, should be seen with urchins, but he was so terribly sad, and Mother was desperate. Rajiv, too, was very hesitant, but he went with her because he is a good boy, and he found one of your lads, Captain Wiggins he called him, and asked if he could be an Irregular for the summer. He said yes, bless him, and next thing we knew, the black cloud that had been over my brother's head vanished, and it was as if his soul was on fire. Every time he came home, we could not get him to stop talking. It was, 'I did this for Mr. Holmes,' or 'I did that for Captain Wiggins.' He stayed out all night at times and slept with his friends along the banks of the Thames. Oh, he had such adventures. It was the finest summer of his life. We miss him terribly, but it has been a very great blessing to us that his last days before going up to Heaven were so filled with happiness. He was thrilled to work for you, Mr. Holmes."

Sherlock Holmes was nonplussed. The look of utter bewilderment had not left his face – nor mine, for that matter.

"You are very kind," he said to Bimal. "I'm sure you saw what was said about my responsibility for your brother's death in the newspaper yesterday, and I have come – "

"Oh, Mr. Holmes, sir. Come, come now. We know that no one can believe what they read in the newspaper. In India, if they print the date correctly without lying, we think that the editor has had an attack of conscience. Oh no, Mr. Holmes, we all knew straight away that you and the Irregulars had nothing whatsoever, nothing at all to do with my brother's death."

"If I did not, then who did?"

Now a troubled looked came over the young man's face. "You do not know? Rajiv said nothing?"

"No. Other than seeing him with the other boys, we never spoke directly."

"Oh, dear me. We all thought by the way he spoke about you that he and you were confidants. Oh my, that was how much he adored you, Mr. Holmes. I am sorry. We should have understood."

"It is I who does not understand," said Holmes. "Tell me, who then was responsible for Rajiv's death if it was not connected to his surveillance in Hatton Garden?"

He was about to respond when the level of chatter in the room suddenly dropped. I looked around to see what had demanded everyone's attention. Three people stood in the doorway. One was a tall, young Indian woman, clad in an elegant black sari. Behind her were two enormous Lascars. The men waited by the door as the woman, with every eye in the room on her, came forward to speak to the mother. I could not hear what was said, but the reception was perfunctory and obviously cold. The woman now walked directly toward us. She was strikingly beautiful and appeared to be utterly and completely poised and confident.

When she arrived at the spot where we had been chatting with Bimal, she nodded briefly to Holmes and me.

"Forgive me for interrupting, gentlemen," she said, sounding entirely sure of herself. Then she turned to our companion. "Bimal, I am so very sorry."

"Thank you, Anna," the young man replied. "It was very brave of you to come."

"I had to. I wanted you to know – "

"It is all right, Anna. I know."

"Thank you, Bimal. I pray God that this has ended. I will see you on Broad Street. Until then."

"Until then, Anna. Godspeed."

Every eye in the room then followed the woman as she departed. Once she was gone from sight, the conversation started up again and people carried on as if nothing had happened.

I knew that both Holmes and I wanted to shout: *What was that all about?* But it was apparent that we were not going to find out. Bimal turned back to Holmes.

"Regarding your last question, Mr. Holmes, I am very, very sorry, but I cannot say. If you do not know, then I beg you, please do not ask. It is a very private family matter. We thought, from the way Rajiv talked about you, that he had confided in you. Now I see that we were mistaken. But it is not for you or anyone beyond the family to know. Now, if you will excuse me, sir, there are other members of my family who would like to meet you and express their gratitude."

He turned and called out to the other couples who had now finished their time in the receiving line. They came over to us, and one by one expressed their thanks to Holmes for the abundance of thrills and happiness he had brought to the all-too-short life of their cousin, or nephew, or whatever relationship fit the particular relative.

As they were shaking Holmes's hand or graciously bowing to him, Mrs. Tamang came over and joined them.

"Mr. Holmes, I have brought something with me from Rajiv. I was hoping and praying that you would come this afternoon, so I could give it to you. Rajiv would have wanted me to."

"Yes, Madam, that is very thoughtful of you."

She handed Holmes a thick envelope.

"On the night before he died," she said, "Rajiv came back to the house at two o'clock in the morning. He had run all the way across London from Clerkenwell. I was startled to hear him come in and thought he would be exhausted, but he was on fire. He kept saying that he had such an exciting night and that he had to write his report for Mr. Sherlock Holmes. I made him some cocoa, and he went up to his room and wrote for an hour. I told him that he had to go to bed but he insisted that he had to return to his post and complete his shift, and so I walked out with him and we found a cab to take him back. That was the last I saw of my son. This is his report to you, Mr. Holmes. It is the last thing he ever wrote, and he wanted to hand it to you in person, but as he is no longer with us here on earth, I am doing it for him. I think he is up in heaven looking down and thanking me."

"Thank you," said Holmes. "I expect it is well written in fine, polished prose."

To my surprise, she laughed. Many of the people in the room turned and looked at her in wonder.

"Oh, I am sorry. I should not laugh. I fear you will find that my son had a very active imagination. You will have some work to do to separate the fact from the fiction. He loved to read and write, but he had a future as a novelist, not a judge."

"My dear friend," said Holmes, looking at me, "writes in exactly the same way. I will read Rajiv's work and treasure it."

In the cab on the way home, Holmes was a different man. The intense gloom had departed and he was as close as he ever came to cheerful.

"Watson," he said, "I now have two cases to solve, which will double my workload, but I feel as if an enormous burden has been lifted from me.

I might even be persuaded to waste what little savings I have and treat the two of us to dinner at Simpson's. What do you say, old chap?"

"Are you not wanting to spend the evening reading the report that Rajiv, formerly Sahib, sent you?"

"Oh, yes, yes, of course. But that should not take long and is likely of no consequence now that it appears his death was not related to his work as an Irregular. As soon as we get home, you can read it aloud to me whilst I pour the brandy. How about that?"

As soon as we were back up in 221b, Holmes gave me Rajiv's report, and I settled back in my customary armchair as he attended to the decanter and glasses on the sideboard.

"He appears," I said, "to have written in a hurry, but still with a good neat hand. Are you listening, Holmes? Here is what he wrote:

> *It was a dark and stormy night. The rain fell in torrents, except at occasional intervals, when it was checked by a violent gust of wind which swept up the streets (for it is in London that our scene lies), rattling along the house-tops, and fiercely agitating the scanty flame of the lamps that struggled against the darkness. Through one of the obscurest quarters of London, and among haunts little loved by the gentlemen of the police, a brave boy, evidently of the higher orders, an Etonian, climbed his way up the treacherous bricks and downpipes of the building – the very building in which some horrific, murderous crime might take place that very evening . . . on his watch.*

"He wrote that?" asked Holmes.

"His mother did say that he had an active imagination and a habit of borrowing. Let me continue."

> *He found his hiding place, a desolate niche behind a tall, black chimney, and drew his greatcoat around him as he shivered in the elements.*

"It was August," said Holmes. "The moon and stars were lovely that night."

"Holmes, please . . . ."

> *In the distance, he heard the great bells of St. Paul's ringing out the hours of the night. Eleven, then twelve. He was dog-tired, but this was a critical mission. The future of the*

Empire was in the balance. As a spy planted behind enemy lines, he knew that he must avoid capture at all costs, and if he were to be discovered . . . no, he could not think about that.

A few seconds after midnight, in the depths of the night, he heard it. First, it was only a few faint thumps, but then a low groan, and then a creaking sound. It sent shivers up and down his young spine. The sound was coming from his left but there was nothing there. Was it a ghoul? A spirit sent by the evil lord of the enemy? Then he saw it. A skylight was moving, slowly, slowly upward. The moonlight danced off the glass.

"The storm had cleared?" said Holmes. "How convenient."
"Holmes, enough."

The skylight continued its arc until it was fully extended, and then a pale hand emerged from the abyss below. At first, the courageous boy thought the hand was floating, detached from any human form, like the fingers of Nebuchadnezzar's feast –

"Wasn't it Belshazzar's?"
"Yes, Holmes, it was. I doubt that it matters."

Behind the pale, ghostly hand came an arm, hidden in the pitch darkness, and then a body, a long, lean body. Spider-like, it crept out of the abyss below the skylight until it was standing on the roof. For a few seconds, it peered out over the rooftops of London, contemplating its evil plot. Then it started to move. With inhuman skill, it clawed across the opening, working its way to the roof of the adjacent building on the brave boy's right. Once there, it knelt down and slowly, deliberately, lifted the skylight of that roof and, like a ghostly ghoul, descended.

The boy was fighting the terror in his soul. Should he run now and report to his Captain? No. He would remain at his post. The ghoul would reappear. He knew it in his heart. An hour passed, then another. He heard the great bells of St. Paul's ring out twice. He summoned his courage and stayed at his post. A few fearful minutes later, he heard the sound again. First, the specter of the hand, then the arm, and once again the long, lithe spider-like body slithered out of the skylight to his right. It stood, again looking out over the great metropolis of London as if savoring its success. Underneath its arm, a portfolio case was tucked.

What was in it? No doubt the plans for the attack the defenders of the faith would launch against the evil enemy at dawn. The human arachnid scampered back across the divide between the buildings, returned to the skylight on the boy's left from which it had first emerged, and disappeared back into its hole. Now the boy must act. Now, before it was too late. He worked his way back down the loose downpipe – any misstep would send him tumbling to the pavement far below. But he had to get back to his camp, write his report, and submit it to his captain, knowing that he, in turn, would take it to the noble Emperor. He had done his duty.

"That's it," I said. "Quite that budding young novelist, wouldn't you agree, Holmes?"

He did not reply. He took the report from my hands and read it through again.

"Get your hat and stick, Watson. And your service revolver. Come, now, please."

There was an urgent tone in his voice, and I hurried to my room to get my gun. By the time I returned to our sitting room, he was already on his way down the stairs. I caught up to him on the pavement of Baker Street when he was shouting for a cab.

"Spitalfields!" he shouted to the driver.

"Who lives there?"

"The spider."

The cab rattled and bumped along Marylebone, then Euston, then Pentonville. He refused to say anything else until we were working our way south on City Road, and I demanded that he explain what we were doing.

"Did you not listen to what you were reading?"

"Of course I listened. What did I miss?"

"Where was he hiding?"

"Behind the chimney."

"You were up on that roof. In what corner was the chimney?"

"The . . . the south-east."

"There were two skylights. Which one did the thief climb out of?"

"He said it was the one on his left, and he scampered over to the building on the right."

"Precisely. Now, please, Watson, do try to think."

I was confused, but I forced myself to concentrate and remember my visit to the roof. I put myself mentally behind the chimney and imagined looking to my left to the skylight –

"He came out of the wrong building!"

"Excellent, Watson. The police assumed that the thief had been hiding inside the neighbor's shop, climbed out, crossed over, and descended into the old man's diamond store. As I should have expected, the police got it backward. He came from the jewelry shop and robbed the neighbor."

"But what about the jewels that were taken."

"A blind. I expect that we shall recover them soon."

Once we reached the Spitalfields Market, Holmes shouted an address on Brick Lane to the driver. The cab stopped in front of one of those large terrace houses that had been divided into rooms for the refugees, primary those of the Hebrew faith, who had been moving from the Continent to London over the past few decades. I followed him up the steps and into the small vestibule.

"Who lives here?" I asked.

"Helmut Shapiro."

"The nephew?"

"Is there another Helmut Shapiro? His suite of rooms is on the third floor. Have your revolver out when I knock. If he is in, we will rush past and into his suite. You will keep him at bay whilst I search the premises."

"What if he is not there?"

"I shall pick the lock, and then I will search."

There was no response to our knock on the door. Holmes gave me his hat and stick to hold whilst he dropped to his knees, and, holding the tools of the locksmith in each hand, he opened the door in a matter of seconds. He stood up, smiling, smugly.

"Compared to the locks his grandfather had on the jewel cases, this was child's play. Come. We need to find a sack of precious jewelry and a file folder with pages of technical drawings."

"Of what?"

"The secret plans of his neighbor's invention."

"Of what?"

"The Maxim gun."

Once inside, it took Holmes no more than a minute. Both the cloth sack with the fortune in perfectly cut and polished diamonds, beautifully set in gold, and the file were in the top drawer of a small desk. Holmes tossed me the sack, put the file under his arm, and turned toward the door. As he did, we heard footsteps coming up the stairs. Holmes motioned me to move back into the hallway where we could not be seen.

The footsteps stopped outside the door, and we heard the key enter the lock. It was followed by a loud cry as it had become apparent that the door was unlocked. It crashed open and a tall, young man rushed in. He immediately ran to his desk and threw open the top drawer. Then he froze, staring at the empty drawer. Then came a long, low groan of agony as the fellow leaned on the desk and then collapsed into the chair beside it.

"How much," said Holmes, quite loudly, "did Kaiser Bill offer for these?"

Helmut Shapiro jerked around and stared at the two of us. I had my revolver out and pointing directly at him.

"Young man," I said, "do not move, or I will have to shoot you."

Terror and panic were written across his face. His hands were trembling. "You . . . you!" he sputtered. "You have to give those back to me."

"So, you can deliver them to the German generals in Berlin?" said Holmes. "I am afraid not."

"No, no. Not the plans. The jewels. Please, I beg you. You cannot take them."

"I have no use for them. I will take them directly to Scotland Yard."

The young fellow groaned, and I could see tears in his eyes.

"Please, I was going to put them back in their cases tonight. I would never steal from my family. It will kill my grandfather if he learns that I stole from him. I don't want them. I never wanted them. Please, let me return them."

"They were a ruse?"

"Yes, that's all. I swear. I have to put them back."

"And you used them to make it appear as if a thief had come from Mr. Maxim's shop and into yours. And when the police then sealed off his shop, it allowed you to come and go for two more nights to complete your work of copying the plans."

The miserable fellow looked up at Holmes and uttered a feeble, "Yes. Please, keep the plans. I failed. But let me put the jewels back. They do not have to know it was me. Then you can arrest me, put me in prison, or just shoot me."

"We have no interest in shooting you, Mr. Shapiro. But you must tell us why you would do something so foolish? Why risk your family? Your future?"

He looked up at Holmes and then sat up straight and glared at him.

"Do you know, Mr. Holmes, what a Maxim gun is?"

"Yes, of course, I do."

"Do you know what the much-improved model, the Maxim-Vickers, can do? No? Well, let me tell you. It can fire off nearly one-thousand rounds in sixty seconds. Mr. Holmes, I am a loyal citizen of Germany. If any country were to go to war against Germany, my countrymen would be cut to ribbons. Whatever happens, the English have got the Maxim gun, and we have not. Would your English generals hesitate to use such a weapon against us? *Nein.* Not for one second would they do that. I was not paid a single Mark to copy the plans. I have acted for the protection of my homeland."

"The agents of the Kaiser approached you?"

"Yes. They knew about the new gun. They learned that my grandfather's shop was the neighbor to Hiram Maxim. They came and asked me if I would go to England to help him and, when the opportunity arose, copy the plans. The idea of using the jewels for a ruse was mine. It almost worked. How did you know?"

"One of my Irregulars, a courageous boy if I do say, was stationed on the roof. He watched you and reported."

"Working for you? I read about that in the newspaper. The boy who was murdered?"

"Yes. And if you are revealed as the thief, I am quite sure that Scotland Yard will immediately arrest you and charge you with his murder."

"But . . . but I did not do it! I would never murder a child. What sort of monster would do something like that? You cannot let them arrest me for such a crime. It would bring shame to my entire family, here and in Leipzig. It would be so much worse than even being a jewel thief."

"It would take some time, but you would be exonerated eventually, and then sent to prison for the theft."

"That would destroy my family. My grandfather would die of humiliation. I cannot let that happen. Do whatever you want to me, Mr. Holmes, but do not destroy my family."

"You might have thought of such consequences before you agreed to be the Kaiser's spy."

"I thought that I would succeed. I was sure that I would succeed."

Holmes said nothing and closed his eyes. Helmut Shapiro looked at him and then at me. I gestured for him to be patient.

Holmes opened his eyes. "Is your grandfather's shop still open at this hour?"

"Today is Saturday. It is closed all day."

"Excellent. Pack your bags. Pack up everything you have in these rooms. You have ten minutes. We shall return the jewels and then you will leave England. And do not even think about returning. Move. Now."

Fifteen minutes later, Helmut Shapiro, Holmes, and I were in a cab that took us from Brick Road back to Hatton Garden. We stopped at the intersection of Clerkenwell and descended.

"Open the door," said Holmes, "and then give me your key."

The young thief did as ordered.

"Now open the cases from which you took the jewels and give me those keys."

"Let me put them back," said Helmut. "They were all in order. I will put them back the way they were."

As Holmes and I stood over him, he put all the stolen pieces back in the case. Holmes closed it and locked it. We departed the shop, and Holmes locked the door.

"If you take a cab straight away to St. Pancras, you can catch the Southeastern to Dover in time for the night crossing to Calais. Goodbye, young man. I expect that I shall never see you again."

Helmut vanished into the first cab to come by.

"Holmes," I said. "Surely you aren't going to let him get away with what he did."

"I will file a report with the German Embassy exposing his failures and excoriating him. The Kaiser's men will be waiting for him when he returns."

"That could be harsh, but appropriate."

"I agree. Now then, my friend: Simpson's will still be open."

Holmes managed to relax and enjoy our dinner, but by the time the dessert course was served he was off again.

"The second jewel theft has now been solved. Whoever killed the boy is still at large. Finding him and bringing him to justice comes next. I will start tomorrow to devote my attention to that. Somebody knows something."

"Tomorrow is Sunday, Holmes. You are entitled not to work on the Sabbath."

He leaned back and lit his pipe. "My ox has fallen into a pit. Please finish your dessert. I have work to do."

I saw nothing of Holmes the following day, nor during the day on the Monday. He arrived back on Baker Street that evening and seemed chipper enough as he consumed what had once been a hot supper.

"Speak up, man," I said to him. "Where have you been? What have you learned?"

"I have spent all day in The City, mostly at the Stock Exchange. What do you know about Darjeeling tea companies, Watson?"

"Not much at all. There's Royal Darjeeling Tea and Empire Darjeeling Tea, and that's all I know."

"Well then, would you like to hear a story?"

"As long as you keep to scientific reason and avoid being sensational, pray, go ahead."

In between mouthfuls, he recounted a tale.

"Once upon a time, well, to be more specific, in the 1840's, a fellow named Archibald Campbell – "

"I know who he was," I interrupted. "My *confrère*. He was an army surgeon."

"The very one. He started planting tea in the hills of Darjeeling, quite successfully. A decade later, the British land agents, in their infinite wisdom, granted large tracts of land to some Indian farmers to plant tea gardens. Of course, being British, they gave the best plots to Anglo-Indians, respected Christian families. But not wanting to appear discriminatory, they gave equal shares to those families who were Roman Catholic and to those who adhered to the Church of England. One of the Anglican families was the Tamangs."

"I now know that name as well."

"As do I. They received grants for gardens south of the townsite and became singularly successful. A Catholic family by the name of Gurung received plots north of the town. They became equally successful."

"Go on," I said, refraining from reminding him that it is impossible to be both singular and equal.

"The two families became first intense and subsequently fierce rivals. In 1867, something happened, some tragic event that ended with one of the family members from the Gurungs being killed. No one was arrested or charged, but the finger of blame was pointed at a young man, one of the Tamangs. A month later, that man was found behind a restaurant in Darjeeling with his throat cut. Since that day, they have fought their version of the Wars of the Roses with a revenge killing after revenge killing."

"But they are in England now. Surely that type of barbaric behavior can be stopped."

"No, it cannot. Ten years ago, both families realized that the profits from tea were made not in the growing and processing, but in the packaging, distributing, and selling. Those latter processes take place in England and abroad, not in the hill country of India. Both families moved their headquarters here from India and have become even more successful and much wealthier. Every year or so, a member is murdered or disappears and is assumed to have been done in. No one expected that a child, the boy, would be targeted, but he was. The hatred and obsession with vengeance has not abated."

"Can you find who killed Rajiv?"

"Possibly, but even if I do, it will not end the killing. I have to break the cycle."

"How?"

"I do not yet know, but I will find a way. Providence, it would seem, has landed me in the midst of this, and I have no choice but to succeed. And for today, my friend, that is the end of my story."

"No, Holmes, it is not."

"What do you mean?"

I went over to the stack of newspapers that had arrived that day and extracted the pink one, *The Financial Times.*

"First page. Lower right," I said.

Tea Mogul Dies in his Sleep

> *The City learned this morning of the death last night, apparently from natural causes, of Mr. Prashant Gurung, the Managing Director of the Empire Tea Company. Further details have not yet been released by the family, but the reaction on the London Stock Exchange was immediate. It came as a surprise only to those not familiar with the world tea industry that the share price of Empire Tea rose by one-pound-six upon the trading floor's hearing the news. The reason, of course, is that traders all know that control of the vast company now passes to Miss Anna Gurung, the younger sister of Mr. Prashant.*
>
> *Although she is still a student at Somerville College, Oxford, it is suspected that she has been the true genius behind the company for the past two years. Mr. Gurung has led the company with a steady hand since assuming control six years ago after his father died, but he has been far from imaginative and has been criticized by some as highly risk-averse. Miss Anna Gurung is said to be the opposite. Further details on this story, sad for the family but with a silver lining for shareholders, will be made available by this newspaper as they become known.*

Holmes shook his head. "That did not take long."

"Poison?"

"Quite probable."

Throughout the entire month of September, Holmes came and went from 221b and chatted amiably about the weather, the Labouchere Amendment, the Blackpool tramway, and whatever else came to his mind. He had not taken on any new cases, or at least none that he deigned to speak about with me, although he did seem to be spending an unusual amount of time out on Baker Street conversing with his beloved Irregulars. All that changed on the first of October.

"The Michaelmas term begins next week, does it not?" he asked.

"Yes, why?"

"Might you be free to join me for a brief visit to Oxford?"

"When?"

"This weekend. You are not booked with patients, are you?"

Early on the morning of Saturday, 3 October, we caught the train from Marylebone to Oxford. By nine in the morning, we were sitting in the cozy front room of the Randolph Hotel, enjoying tea and scones.

"Are they both here?" I asked Holmes.

"Bimal is meeting us in front of the King's Arms in half-an-hour."

"Is he aware of your plan?"

"Not a clue."

"And Anna?"

"Even less."

"And you are sure it will work?"

"Not at all. But if I do not do something, another half-dozen or more good people will be dead within the next three years."

We walked the several blocks from the hotel past Balliol and Trinity to the pub. It was serving breakfast to those students who had arrived two days before the official start of classes. The air was electric with the sense of anticipation that accompanies any opening weekend of a new school year. Students and professors alike were pedaling carelessly along the streets, their robes flowing out behind them. Young men were greeting friends they hadn't seen since the end of Trinity. A much smaller number of young women from Somerville and Lady Margaret were poking into the shops and trying to ignore the clumsy efforts of the male students to impress them.

We waited outside the pub, and on the stroke of nine-thirty Master Bimal Tamang came walking across the intersection of Broad and Parks.

"I received your message, Mr. Holmes. You said it was imperative that we meet. Would you mind telling me what this is all about?"

"Please, Mr. Tamang, come inside and sit down. I assure you that it is of pressing importance and cannot be postponed. Please, sir. Follow me."

Holmes spoke with a tone of authority, and the exceptionally wealthy managing director of an exceptionally large firm followed him. Holmes walked to a table in the back where a young woman was sitting and poring over several books of ledgers. Miss Anna Gurung – the young woman who had spoken with Bimal at Rajiv's funeral – looked up when Holmes was standing beside her. She appeared shocked and not a little offended.

"You will have to excuse my lack of etiquette in not apprising you of this meeting, Miss Gurung, but it will not take long and I promise that it is in your best interest. Mr. Tamang, kindly be seated."

The young fellow sat slowly and hesitantly. He looked over at the young woman and shrugged.

"Anna, I have no idea – "

"Then I shall explain," said Holmes. "For the past month, I have been gathering data on your families and your firms. The barbaric cycle of revenge murders that has gone on now for twenty years has to come to an end. If it does not, then the information I have assembled indicates that it will not only continue but is bound to escalate beginning this fall. The two of you now control your respective firms. You have the power to make it stop. I ask that you listen to my recommendation. If you choose to reject it, we shall part company. Will you agree to that?"

"Mr. Holmes," said Anna, "I know who you are, and I do not question your good intentions. However, I am not at all comfortable with your aggressive demands. You are being rude, and I do not like this at all."

"I did not expect you would, Miss Gurung. Nevertheless, please listen for just one minute. I will read off a list of five names and I simply ask that you tell me if you know who these people are."

Without waiting for an answer, Holmes unfolded a piece of paper and began to read.

"Dibya Gurung, Bulu Gurung, Jamling Gurung, Amar Gurung, and Tripti Gurung. Do you know these men?"

"Of course, I know them. They are my uncles and cousins."

"And Bimal, do you know these men? Dinesh Tamang, Binay Tamang, Navneet Tamang, and Raju Tamang."

"Yes. They are my uncles and cousins. What is the meaning of this?"

"My surveillance of your homes, offices, and factories over the past month has revealed that these five names of the Tamang family are on a list within the Gurung family as targets for being killed in the next round of revenge murders. The names on the list I read to you, Miss Gurung, came from the homes, offices, and factories of the Tamang family, and have been decided upon for the same purpose."

"Mr. Holmes," said Anna, "this is an outrage. Surely you do not expect me to believe that. How could you possibly know what was being talked about within our walls? Either you prove what you are saying now or leave."

"Over the past month, you have hired twenty-four of either my fine army of Irregular boys or their sisters. They have worked for you as chambermaids, office boys, scullery maids, assistant grooms, gardeners' peons, housekeepers, nursemaids, pages, and houseboys. You consented to hire these young workers because they agreed to work for you for a wage well below the going rate. They did so because I supplemented their income to a level above the market as well as providing them with clean clothes and soap. They have kept their eyes and ears open and have reported faithfully to me concerning all aspects of your personal and corporate lives. I assure you, the list of names targeted for death is accurate."

"You . . . you have been spying on us," sputtered Bimal, turning red with anger. "Get out of here!"

"I will, but before I do, I omitted one name from each list. Would you like to know?"

"Fine," said Anna, loud enough for most of the pub to hear. "Tell us and be gone."

Holmes looked first at Bimal and then at Anna.

"Yours. Both of you."

For the average Englishman, it is difficult to know when a man or woman from India is turning pale with fear, given their darker complexion. But widening of the eyes and involuntary dropping of the lower jaw are usually good indicators. These changes happened in the faces of both of the young people sitting at the table. Holmes continued.

"I have done nothing over the past month but study your situation. I can see only one way to bring this senseless cycle to an immediate end. It requires, however, a radical solution."

He paused.

"Go on," said Anna, speaking just above a whisper.

"You must agree to merge the two firms and announce the same straight away."

Both of them looked stunned. Holmes started to say more, but Bimal held his hand up.

"Please, Mr. Holmes. This is between Anna and me." And then the two of them just sat and looked at each other, their intense gaze into each other's eyes interrupted by the occasional small nod. Anna spoke first.

"The share value would jump immediately by at least twenty percent."

"Maybe twenty-five by the end of October."

"We could organize an additional share offering in November. The new shares could be floated at three-pounds-six. Would that work?"

"We could offer two lakh of new shares," said Bimal.

"Three, as long as they have limited voting rights. That would bring in over one million pounds in capital."

"We could use that to buy the Marybong and Pussimbing gardens in the East."

"And the Happy Valley and Rungneet gardens in the West," said Anna. "The administrative staff could be combined and reduced by a third. The factories reduced by half, and 1886 could be the most profitable year yet."

Bimal nodded his agreement. "If you would not mind taking care of all of the importing, packaging, distribution, and sales here, on the Continent, and in America, I could look after the property management, production, and processing."

"That would be good. Your drying ovens are newer than ours. We will close our plant and use yours," said Anna. "What about the packaging plants?"

"Yours are better. Should we eliminate one of the brands and just have either Empire or Royal?"

"No, no. Keep both. One can be put on sale one month and the other the next. The tea is the same, and the English think that they are connoisseurs and like to fight over their favorite even if there is no difference."

"What about America?" said Bimal.

"We just put the dust off the floor into their tea bags. What do you do?"

"The same. Even one hundred years later, they are likely to throw it into the Boston harbor."

"Anything else come to mind?" asked Anna.

"Not now. The details we can work out later."

The two of them reached across the table and shook hands. Then they turned to Holmes.

"We have an agreement, Mr. Holmes," said Bimal. "Anna and I will announce our engagement tomorrow, and we will be married before Christmas."

Now it was Holmes's turn, and mine, to be shocked beyond belief.

"What? No, no, no, no!" he sputtered back. "No. I am not suggesting that the two of you get married, only that you merge the firms."

Now it was their turn, young though they were, to look at Holmes as if he were marginally above the level of imbecile.

"Mr. Holmes," said Anna in a highly condescending tone. "We are Indian. A firm is a fiction. The only thing that matters is family. Firms and companies are created to limit a family's liability. Bimal and I each have controlling shares of our family's assets. *We* are the firms. There is one way and one way only for your suggestion to work, and that is for us to marry."

Here, I felt compelled to intercede.

"But surely, you . . . you should . . . you will want to get to know each other and fall in love before you think about marriage."

"Dr. Watson," said Bimal. "Since the dawn of time, a man and a woman have married based on the mutual benefit they will bring to their families and their villages. It has only been in the past century in England, America, and Europe that people have become so foolish that they decide to base the fundamental unit of society on something so fickle, so inconsistent as *romantic love*. India has retained its common sense. Marriages are decided by families and, if all goes well, as it usually does, you build a life together and fall in love along the way."

"Now look, the two of you. I am going to speak to you as a medical doctor. Marriages need more than sensible business arrangements. What about your families? Will they be happy with this . . . this merger?"

"My dear Doctor," said Anna, "whether we like it or not, we are now the heads of our families. We pay respect to all of our elders, but we own by far the majority of shares in the family enterprises. We do not need to seek permission. We give it to ourselves."

"Fine," I said. "All well and good. Now, I do not wish to be indelicate or embarrass anyone, but good marriages also need a generous amount of physical affection. Are you sure that the two of you are compatible in that regard?"

Now it was my turn to be embarrassed. The two of them gazed at each other and ran their eyes up and down each other's torsos.

"Doctor," said Anna, "'there will be no worries in that department."

On Monday, 12 October, in the year of our Lord, 1885, the announcement of the merger of the two tea companies, to be known henceforth as the Royal and Empire Tea Company Limited, appeared in the financial sections of all of England's newspapers. The announcement of the engagement of Miss Anna Gurung and Mr. Bimal Tamang appeared the same day in the social pages. The shares of both companies increased in value by thirty percent.

The wedding was scheduled for mid-December, at the end of the Michaelmas term. It would be a stellar event.

There were no more murders. It became known that any employee who did not demonstrate complete loyalty to the new company and its owners was in danger of having his path of promotion blocked and his Christmas bonus denied. Those whom Holmes strongly suspected of having been involved in past murders were either sacked or transferred to an insignificant company warehouse in New Jersey.

On the day after the wedding, Holmes and I sat by the hearth in 221b, still feeling overfed by the wedding meal and passably satisfied by the way this case had concluded.

As we sat there, he handed me a note. It was from Lestrade at Scotland Yard and informed Holmes that the thief from the very first robbery in Hatton Garden still hadn't been apprehended and asking if the Yard might contract for the services of Mr. Sherlock Holmes to assist them in their quest.

"What do you think, Watson?" he asked. "Should I take it on?"

NOTES

The story was inspired by the report of the safe deposit robbery in Hatton Garden that took place in April 2015.

(See *https://en.wikipedia.org/wiki/Hatton_Garden_safe_deposit_burglary*.)

Six British chaps, senior citizens all of them, spent Easter Weekend drilling into a vault in Hatton Garden and made off with an estimated *£200*-million in gold, diamonds, and jewelry.

On reading about the robbery, I learned that during the 1880's, Sir Hyram Maxim had a small factory at the corner of Hatton Garden and Clerkenwell Road. It was there that he invented the Maxim gun, the first fully automatic machine gun. It was subsequently improved as the Maxim-Vickers model and became the incomparable weapon of British Imperialism. Variations of its design were used by all sides during the First World War.

Dr. Archibald Campbell, an army surgeon in the Indian Army, first planted tea seeds in Darjeeling in the 1840's. The results were highly successful and many tea gardens opened in the years following. Darjeeling tea is still among the most prized of all the tea of the worlds. I had the opportunity to visit Darjeeling and Kalimpong several times during the 1980's and returned to Canada bearing numerous packages of tea that were given to me by friends there.

One of my friends in India described the twenty-five million Anglo-Indians, of which he was a member, as "an everlasting monument to the adultery of the British Raj". Many of them now live in London, other parts of the UK, and all over the earth.

The Indigo Impossibility
by Will Murray

It was a beastly night in London.

A driving rain lashed the city, smothering the gas lamps and hammering the roofs of home and hotel alike.

The ride from Paddington to 221b Baker Street was an exercise in misery. Raindrops pummeled me as I sat alone in the hansom cab as it jounced through the nearly deserted streets, for the hour was late and sensible people had long before claimed their beds.

I shivered in my waterproof and wondered how the cabman could stave off a cold, riding about in such inclement weather.

Presently, with a scraping of wheels against curbing, we drew up to the apartments of Sherlock Holmes and myself. I steeled myself before alighting and rushed to the front door, clutching my Gladstone bag.

I have been on holiday in Northumberland, but now I was home. It was the third of May in the year 1886.

After he deposited my luggage at the doorstep, I paid the driver and used my house key to enter, immediately doffing my soaked waterproof. It lacked but a quarter-hour to midnight.

The mellow light coming from the first-floor window was a surprise, so I was not taken aback when I found Sherlock Holmes seated in his most comfortable chair, puffing on a briar and staring off into space. He might have been a wizard attempting to divine the swirls of tobacco smoke that climbed to the plaster ceiling. Certainly his eyes were dreamy, and his aquiline face possessed an aesthetic cast.

Despite my having trooped loudly up the stairs, Holmes took no notice of me when I entered the sitting-room.

"Well, good evening, Holmes," I said by way of greeting.

My friend snapped out of his dreamy reverie, and his sharp eyes came into focus in his hawk-like face. Rather than welcoming me home, Holmes asked, "Have you been reading about the sensation in Essex County?"

"I have not."

"In Thundersley. They are calling it 'The Indigo Impossibility'."

"And what may I inquire is meant by *it?*"

"Why, the Impossibility, of course. It is really rather extraordinary, Watson. Had I not expected you tonight, I would have already arrived in Thundersley to investigate the matter."

Dropping wearily into a chair opposite Holmes, I sighed. "Having come all this way in a beastly rain, I fear I have no appetite for immediate trouble."

"The morning will do," Holmes said thinly.

"You presume to assume that I am free to follow you into the heart of this impossibility."

"The Impossibility is not an event, but a thing. And I presume nothing, my dear Watson. I invite you to accompany me – if you are so inclined," he added in a voice as thin as the smoke emerging from it.

"What is this impossibility?" I asked wearily, for I had no energy for my friend's investigative enthusiasms on this rain-soaked evening. I would have sought my bed forthwith, but common courtesy forebode such rudeness.

"It is a hitherto-unknown creature that should not exist, yet it does. Worse for the rustic inhabitants of Thundersley, Watson, it slays. And in the most savage manner."

"I fear I still do not comprehend the nature of this impossibility," I admitted.

"Nor do I," returned Holmes. "And that is the intriguing aspect of the matter. All that is known is that the creature is a deep indigo color and that it walks upon two legs, leaving foot tracks like great horned talons, of which it possess three in number."

"A creature, is it? That *is* intriguing."

"A creature undiscovered by modern naturalists, it seems. One sufficiently formidable to disembowel a man with a single stroke of its claws."

Now I feared that I would never get my proper rest, for Holmes had captured my complete interest.

"I should like to read these newspaper accounts."

Gesturing with this pipe stem to a stack of London newspapers, Holmes murmured, "Help yourself, my good fellow."

Naturally, I selected *The Times* to begin with.

Surprisingly, the account was sensational in its details, if staid in the telling. Over several days, a creature standing almost as tall as the average man had been spied in a grove that in pagan times had been dedicated to the thunder god, Thunor, whom we today call Thor. This was in Thundersley, specifically at a place called Thundersley Great Common. The unknown creature stood upright, and was never clearly seen, except that its hide was an amazing indigo hue, unknown in any animal dwelling in the British Isles.

On the third day after it was first encountered, a man named Andrew Carrick had been discovered in the vicinity of this village, disemboweled in the most grisly manner. Leading away from the corpse were the bloody tracks of a creature possessing three sharp talons. It was evident that one of the massive talons had raked the man's stomach open with a slash that disgorged its organic contents.

"I have ranged from London to Afghanistan," I remarked as I put down the paper. "I have never heard of such a creature."

"Surely not."

"I beg your pardon?"

"Have you never read of the dinosaurs?"

"You full well know that I have," I snapped with a bit of impatience that I could barely control. "But such creatures are believed to be long extinct."

"Yet something like a dinosaur eviscerated Andrew Carrick. And the manner in which he was slain fits up with no creature known in the present day."

"Are you stating boldly that a dinosaur is loose in Essex?"

"It is difficult to imagine such a thing," admitted Holmes. "For if there is one dinosaur, there must be others. Biological organisms do not exist in isolation. For there to be one, there must be at least two others, a male and female parent, and these perforce, should have living antecedents, if not other offspring."

"Now you stretch my credulity to the breaking point, Holmes. I cannot imagine such a large and distinctly garish creature to be populating a wood so close to London."

"Nor can I," Holmes allowed. "Neither can the authorities. That is why the newspapers have dubbed it an Impossibility."

"Have you been called into the matter?"

"Not as yet. No doubt this will eventually be the case. But I choose not to await the inevitable call. I propose to train to Thundersley in the morning in order to take the measure of this monster, as it were. If you care to accompany me, I would be pleased to have you. But if you cannot, I understand. Fully."

"I had planned to resume my medical duties after a day of recuperation from my trip."

"You can recuperate in Thundersley as well as in London."

"If that is your way of insisting that I accompany you, I will consider it."

"Tut-tut, Watson. I insist upon nothing. I am merely offering you an intriguing opportunity. I might add that your medical skills and insight would be useful."

"A veterinarian might be more suitable to your needs," I retorted abruptly, for my eyes were growing intolerably heavy of lid, and a warm comforter appealed to me more than strong food and drink at this late hour.

"I will sleep upon it," I said, standing up.

"I will wake you at six in the a.m., then," said Holmes dryly.

"By Jove! That allows me only five hours of sleep. I do not think that I can do it."

"Would seven suit you, then?"

"If I am awake at that hour," I said firmly, "I will so inform you. Now if you will be good enough to excuse me, I am late to bed."

"Until tomorrow," said Holmes, tilting his head back and resuming his study of the swirling smoke that his briar produced. The focus went out of his eyes and his face became a mask, like a study of an American Indian communing with his wiser ancestors.

As I sought much-needed sleep, I reflected that Sherlock Holmes did not have to worry about awakening in time to catch a morning train. I did not expect him to do anything other than sit in the chair and apply his tremendous mental powers to the problem of the impossible indigo creature which had seized his vibrant imagination.

I do not clearly recall the morning train ride to Thundersley, for I slept through much of it.

Upon our arrival, I awoke with a start, peered about and was momentarily taken aback to find myself aboard a moving train.

"Did you sleep well?" asked Holmes.

"My word!" I muttered. "I don't clearly recall leaving my bed."

"You were rather logy at the time," observed Holmes. "In fact, you commenced drowsing directly upon our departing Fenchurch Street Station."

"Ah, yes. It is coming back to me. But I feel as if I am in a foggy dream."

"Here is Benfleet Station. Come, come. Let us hope that we aren't disembarking upon a nightmare," suggested Holmes ominously.

We exited the car and sought a hansom cab among the few loitering at the station.

As we stepped aboard a waiting cab, the driver took Holmes's bag and remarked, "What ho! This is rather heavy."

"Mind that you do not drop it, driver," Holmes told the man. Addressing me, he added, "I have come fully prepared. I also took the liberty of dropping your old service revolver into your bag. We may need both before our tour is over."

"Given the frightful descriptions of this Indigo Impossibility," I returned, "I would more describe our day's calendar as in the manner of the hunt."

"Yes, I suppose that it is. But a hunt for what?"

The driver urged his steed onward and we were soon clicking along the hilly vista and up the slope of Bread and Cheese Hill toward the village centre. The cool air was sweet with the scent of heather, which grew profusely hereabouts. A pungent sea breeze drifted in from the estuary to the south.

Apparently feeling deprived of suitable companionship over my slumberous disposition, Sherlock Holmes opened up a lively conversation.

"Watson, tell me what you know of the taxonomic order of *Dinosauria*?"

"The term means 'great lizard', of course. But I believe that you are the expert here, Holmes. I would rather you discourse upon the subject, my brain being in a bit of a morning fog."

"The term was first proposed by the anatomist Sir Richard Owen in 1841," he said. "You may remember that the discovery of the earliest fossil bones was the occasion of great controversy, which raged for years. Prior to Owen, unusual bones that could not be classified were often mistaken for things that they were not. Back in 1802, certain curious fossil tracks unearthed in South Hadley, Massachusetts were thought to be the remnants of a gigantic raven dating back to the time of Noah's ark, and possibly the very same one released from that improbable vessel of legend, which, as you will recall, friend Watson, never returned. It was not, of course. The Arabian Roc was another mythical creature believed to have deposited their dry bones here and there. In central China, the natives grind up what they believe to be dragon bones into medicinal powders. They are mistaken, of course. All were fossil ossifications of various dinosaurs."

"As I recall," I asserted, "some years elapsed before these mysterious bones were recognized as those of lizards of tremendous size and unimaginable configuration."

"You have very nearly correct. But it was Sir Richard who determined that they were neither avian nor saurian, but belonged to an entirely new group of animals he dubbed *Dinosauria*. Despite his sound determinations, there are those still who dispute his findings."

As we rattled along, I hugged my ulster closer to me. Mercifully, it wasn't raining, but the morning was coolish. I didn't mind this very much, remembering the inclement night before. I glanced warily towards the clouds, and they didn't promise rain, but neither did they deny the possibility.

Turning to Holmes, I inquired, "What species of dinosaur do you suppose this Indigo Impossibility to be?"

"I haven't arrived at any preliminary determination. Perhaps, once I discover its foot marks or other spoor, I will have sufficient data to posit possibilities. For the moment, I prefer not to jump to conclusions, sound or otherwise."

"A wise course of action, no doubt."

"I will point out that among the dinosaurs known to have lived in the British Isles in prehistoric times, the meagre descriptions of the Indigo Impossibility fit none of them."

"Yet you don't refuse outright to accept the possibility of a survival from an older age abroad in Thundersley?" I pressed.

"For many reasons, I think it improbable."

"The dinosaur theory is therefore all but ruled out, then?"

"I rule nothing out!" snapped Holmes. "We stand barely on the threshold of our investigation. Our minds must remain open and unbounded by such second-hand facts that come our way."

We soon arrived at Thundersley, where we sought the local constable, a bluff fellow was named Hume. We caught him as he was stepping out of his official preserves, presumably to make his morning rounds.

Directly, Holmes stepped up and introduced us.

"Welcome to our little hamlet, Mr. Sherlock Holmes," greeted the constable. "I imagine scientific curiosity brings you to our modest village, but you are welcome to contribute to the hunt."

"A hunt, is it?"

"Yes. Some of our more substantial citizens have been combing the heathland with their shotguns without result. We are about to embark upon another day's search. To a man we are determined to bag the beast."

"I see," mused Holmes. "As to why I am here, this Indigo Impossibility of yours presents a tantalizing mystery, and, as you may have read in your local newspaper, I can scarcely resist investigating such a phenomenon."

"Understandable. And your admirable skills may be of some use. Did you bring a pistol of some sort?"

Setting down his Gladstone, Holmes opened it up and produced a remarkable sight, a four-barreled pistol resembling a top-break shotgun, but of abbreviated barrel length.

"Good Lord!" Constable Hume expostulated. "I have never seen the like of it!"

"But I have," I interjected. "It is a howdah pistol. In India, it is employed to hunt tigers from the backs of elephants, the hunter riding in the howdah basket. Hence the unusual nomenclature."

“This particular weapon is formally known as a Lancaster pistol,” supplied Holmes, breaking it open and inserting four .410-calibre shotgun shells. He snapped the breech shut with a satisfactory sound, locking it in place.

Hume laughed out loud. “The very thing to bring down this blue blast of horror, as I call it. Well, come along now. We must begin our business.”

A group of local men had gathered. Stern of expression, each one brandished a shotgun of his own. No other weapon was in evidence.

“All expected are present?” asked Hume, searching their serious faces. “Hubbard? Smith? Very good. We shall set out for the heathland.”

Off we went. It was not a long walk through the cool morning air along Common Lane, west to the Great Common. Sherlock Holmes and I were introduced as curious Londoners, and the stolid citizens questioned us no further. Holmes has thought that his announced presence would be a distraction to the work at hand, and Hume had agreed.

During the march, Sherlock Holmes pressed the man on many particulars.

“I have given to understand that the victim was eviscerated.”

“Virtually disemboweled. The creature that attacked him had ripped Carrick from sternum down to his groin, and in such a way as to spill the bloody contents of his guts.”

“You are a plain-speaking man, I see.”

“No use beating about the bush. It was a savage attack. And nothing that has ever been known to live in Essex could have done it.”

“What has been seen of the creature?”

“Very little. A flash of blue here and there. The thing runs like a streak of lightning. There is some scarlet to it, apparently about its long neck. The eyes are said to be staring and hideous. Russet is their color. A dark-brown comb or crest sits upon the crown of its skull. Understand that this devil has only been seen by moonlight. Where it lairs during the day has not yet been ascertained, but we believe it sleeps at night. It is our hope to ambush it successfully.”

“Do you imagine it to be a dinosaur in truth?” asked Holmes.

“I cannot imagine it to be otherwise,” returned the man gruffly. “As I said, nothing like it has been seen in Essex before.”

“Where do you suppose it has come from?”

“I care not to know. I am only concerned with where I am going to send it. And that is to its lasting demise.”

“Has no thought been given to its capture?” pressed Holmes. “If it were truly a living dinosaur, I daresay it would be worth a pretty penny to the London Zoo, or a scientific institute such as the British Museum.”

Hume shook his heavy head. “No quantity of coin would tempt a Thundersley man to risk his life against such a terror. You haven’t seen the body of Andrew Carrick. It was a grisly thing to behold. A maddened bull could not have gored a man so thoroughly. It was necessary for the county coroner to pack young Carrick’s innards back into his stomach cavity and sew up the lot prior to burial.”

“I am sorry that I missed the sight,” murmured Holmes laconically.

“Be grateful that you were spared it. I wish I could wipe it from my brain, but no such cloth has ever been woven that would accomplish that merciful miracle.”

“I’m no connoisseur of morbidity, Constable,” Holmes hastened to add. “I venture to say that I might have gleaned a great deal from an examination of the fatal wound.”

“It’s too late for that. Andrew Carrick lies under the clay, God rest him.”

We soon came to the heathland. It was a fairy land, a natural wonder, a heather expanse quite unexpected, given the marshy nature of Essex County. Oak predominated, but I spied birch, aspen, and other sturdy trees.

“I have read up on your heath,” remarked Holmes as we paused to survey our wild surroundings. “It is unusual in Essex, is it not?”

“This has always been a wild and untamed spot, going back to the earliest days of Thundersley, when pagan rites to the Norse god, Thor, were practiced in these parts.”

We examined our weapons. Setting ourselves, we plunged in, tramping through bracken and bramble.

Holmes looked about with his keen eye. “I see plants that are not common to Essex County, the lesser spearwort among them.”

“Oh, true enough,” said Hume. “But they have always been present here.”

The further we marched, the more varied the terrain became. It was a heathery glory. The ground beneath our feet was composed of dry peat. Bronze dragonflies flitted about. We came to a pleasant dell and paused to survey our immediate environment.

Roots of gorse and heather lay about the ground in pleasant islands. I spied fire weal, peewit, and the purple-flowered milkwort. I imagine during warmer days, the area would be humming with wild bees. A solitary Heath Fritillary butterfly flitted by.

The luxury of unchecked growth surrounding us caused me to remark, “I can almost imagine that much of England looked like this back in the days before mankind arrived.”

Holmes laughed. "Watson, it was nothing like this. Far, far wilder than you can imagine were the plants and trees of those ancient days. These sedges and heather are tame by comparison."

We pushed on, towards the still waters of a pond.

I enjoyed the fresh smell of heather honey, but I confess that my nerves were becoming as tight as springs.

As we marched along, Holmes abruptly stopped and cast his glance downward.

"Hmm. What is this?" he muttered.

Clutching his shotgun more resolutely, Hume demanded, "Have you come across one of its foul tracks?"

"Alas, no," replied Holmes, stooping to pluck a flower. He lifted it up in order to examine the plant. "But I confess that I did not immediately recognize it."

"What is it?" I asked.

"Trillium – extraordinarily rare in these parts."

Constable Hume grunted, "If you pause to study every unusual plant encountered along the way, I fear that we will make slow progress – if any progress at all."

Dropping the specimen into his Gladstone, Holmes took up his impressive howdah pistol once more and we continued on, soon coming to a marshy spot of high grasses and sedges.

We had scarcely reached the edge of a still pool when we heard a tramping through the brush, and every man swung his shotgun barrel in that direction.

At first, we could only spy a disturbance amid the brush. Dragonflies fled the area, as if stampeded. We grew keenly expectant.

"Steady, men," warned Hume. "Do not fire until you know that the beast stands where your shot will fly."

Holmes inserted, "I would advise forbearance. For those noises suggest the tramp of a man."

It was fortunate that Holmes offered that possibility, for very quickly the dense thicket parted and out stepped a burly man attired for shooting game. He wore an old hunting coat, cords, Hessian boots, his square head topped by a green cap. He toted a double-barreled fowling piece of vintage manufacture.

Doubtless the blundering fellow would have been riddled with shot had Holmes not cautioned the agitated hunting party to hold their fire.

"What is this?" shouted Hume. "Is that you, Carrick?"

"Who do ye think it is?" demanded Carrick, all but snarling his words. His accent was Scottish. An Aberdeen man, I should judge.

"Step out and let us see you in full," called Hume.

The individual crashed into view and soon joined us. I am known for my nut-brown coloring, acquired in my military adventures, but this man was several shades darker than a state to which I could ever aspire. His eyes held a rather severe squint.

"Are you hunting the blue beast as well?" Hume asked.

"Why would I do otherwise?" the other flung back hotly. "Did it not destroy my only son?"

"No offense to you, Angus Carrick," Hume said firmly. "But if I had lost a son, I would not risk making my wife a widow hunting this blue beast all by yourself. Come join our hunting party."

"I prefer to do my own dirty work."

"And I would prefer not to witness another autopsy such as I did the other day. Do not be stubborn. There is safety in numbers."

Scarcely mollified, the burly fellow changed the subject. "I thought that I spied a flash of blue to the northwest. And towards the northwest I am bound. You may accompany me if you care to. But mistake me not. This is my hunt."

With that, he stormed off.

With a curt gesture of his chin, Constable Hume invited us to follow.

Holmes hurried up to the burly man, and engaged him in conversation. I joined them.

"Mr. Carrick. My condolences on the untimely passing of your son. Andrew. My name is Sherlock Holmes. You have perhaps heard of me?"

"I have. What is your business here?"

"It is my pleasure to solve unusual mysteries. This is only the latest in a long string of them. May I ask you some questions?"

"If ye do so intelligently."

If Holmes was stung by this gruff barb, he didn't display it in any outward manner. Calmly, he asked, "Have you lived around here all your life?"

"Much of it. What is that to you?"

"You have a very outdoorsy look about you. The way your eyes squint reminds me of outdoorsmen encountered all around the world."

"I have tramped the globe, if that is what you are getting at."

"Have you ever been to South America?"

"No."

"North America then?"

"Many times. As well as Asia and Australia. What of it?"

"I do not take you for a seaman."

"By profession, I am nothing of the kind."

"Might I inquire what it is you do for a living?"

"I am a promoter. The circus is my game. Presently, I am between connections."

"A circus man! How marvelous! I must hear more."

"Another time, Mr. Holmes. Your questions are tiring my patience. I am intent upon one thing and one thing only. Revenge."

"Understandable," returned Holmes. "You have a very determined air about you."

"Aye."

"One last question, Carrick. Have you any thoughts as to the nature of this blue beast?"

"Only the most murderous of thoughts, Mr. Holmes. Only the most murderous of thoughts."

"I see," murmured Holmes. With that, we fell back and rejoined the others.

I could tell by the alteration of his expression, and the curtain of thought that fell over the mask that was his face, that he had gleaned more than what his conversation would reveal to an ordinary ear.

I was tempted to pry into his innermost thoughts, but I knew that it would do a little good. Something was stirring in his agile brain, and I knew that if I left it alone, it would soon hatch into something marvelous, so I bit my tongue for the nonce.

Presently, I heard an odd sound emanating from the near distance. Low, intermittent, it reminded me of the grunting of a pig, but there was also a snorting equine quality that baffled me.

Abruptly, Mr. Angus Carrick broke into a dead run, trampling the gorse as he ran.

"He has spied something!" exclaimed Holmes, picking up his own pace.

For all his burly bulk, Angus Carrick ran like a demon and was soon smashing through the piney woods and lost from sight.

All of us raced after him. Our fingers close to our triggers. We were a resolute lot, and I was amazed at the absence of exclamations or curses as we charged ahead. This was earnest business.

Out of the range of our sight, Carrick blundered about, and then one after the other we heard him discharge the barrels of his shotgun.

"Damn ye!" he cried. "Damn ye to the everlasting regions beneath my feet!"

When we caught up with him, Carrick was breaking his shotgun open and attempting to insert fresh cartridges into the smoking breach.

"What did you see, Carrick?" demanded Holmes.

"The blue beastie himself," said the man hotly. "I think I winged him, but I'm not certain. He tore into the brush like a locomotive."

Snapping his weapon back into proper order, Carrick resumed his charge.

There came the sound of a splash. We raced towards it.

Breaking through the brush and into a clearing, we came upon another pond. But its surface was not still. Something was swimming across it, towards the opposite side. Its color was striking. A deep indigo. I could see slashes of scarlet edging its long, sinuous neck. But other than that, I could make out very little of the creature, which appeared to be emitting noises reminiscent of a very large bullfrog.

Emerging on the other side, it plunged into the close-lying brush, vanishing from our view.

We stood there, at the edge of the pond, watching the underbrush twitch and squirm as the azure fugitive worked its way through. The speed of the creature was astonishing. A horse couldn't gallop so swiftly. A locomotive alone would exceed its speedy progress.

Before we could get ourselves organized to resume our chase, the underbrush ceased its uncanny animation and the trail appear to have gone momentarily cold.

Turning to Holmes, I demanded, "What do you make of it? Surely with your fund of natural knowledge, you recognized the creature."

"It was all but submerged. The back of the head told me nothing. Nor did the shape of its hunched back. It lacked scale or feather, and its smooth hide suggested nothing in my present understanding."

"But the color, man. Surely, the color of its skin meant something to you!"

Holmes shook his head. "Alas, Watson, I know of no living creature possessing a hide of deep blue."

I was staggered by this frank confession, which suggested that we were hunting a survivor from the dawn of time.

"Shall we resume our hunt, gentlemen?" asked Constable Hume, coming up behind us.

We did so wordlessly. Breaking into two groups, we made opposite circles of the pond whose troubled surface was only now returning to its customary placidity.

Once more, Angus Carrick pushed ahead of us as if determined to be the one to rout the beast.

I regret to say that our investigations led us nowhere. We discovered a trace of blood here and there. Other than the fact it was very red and soon petered out, our progress was disappointing.

Holmes made a special study of the creature's foot marks. Since it had been moving rapidly, they were not distinct, merely choppy gouges in the peat. A few were bloody, but not excessively so.

Constable Hume observed them also and, after examining several specimens, he said, “I can only say that I imagine a dragon might leave such tracks.”

He looked to Sherlock Holmes.

“I would not disagree with you, Constable,” replied Holmes. “These are remarkable tracks. In size, as well is in configuration. It is plain that the thing has three large talons, and these natural daggers were what opened up the belly of poor Andrew Carrick.”

We continued to hunt for many hours, but all efforts were fruitless.

The setting of the sun combined with a lack of proper nourishment eventually forced us to reconsider our increasingly precarious position.

“Presently it will become dark,” advised Constable Hume. “This is no place to be after the sun goes down. We must return to our hearths. Tomorrow is another day. Perhaps it will be a brighter one.”

Sherlock Holmes didn’t contradict the man. Tucking his howdah pistol into his Gladstone, he closed it up.

Hume turned to the burly Scot. “What of you, Mr. Carrick? Will you call it a night?”

“I will call it what I will. But only when I am done. There is yet some wee light left.”

“True. But is a long and labored walk back to town. And much of it will be in utter darkness.”

“I know these woods like the back of my hand. Do not lecture me. If ye see me again, I will have the head of the beastie clutched in my fist. Having wounded it, I am of no mind to leave it to recover its strength.”

Hume said, “I will not make you return against your will, Angus Carrick. But I beg you to consider your poor grieving wife above all other considerations.”

“It is for the sake of my poor grieving wife that I intend to destroy the creature,” Carrick said gruffly. “A good night to you all.”

This last was uttered with such poor grace that no one cared to argue further.

As one, we turned about and started the tiresome trek back to Thundersley parish.

It was dark when we reached the little hamlet. Parting from Hume and the others, we sought the comfort of supper in the town’s lodging house, where Holmes and I ate in studied silence.

During our rustic but satisfying meal, Holmes’s grey eyes were reflective. He didn’t avail himself of his old briar pipe, but I could tell that his mind was fixed upon the problem at hand. So deep in thought was he that I might as well have been dining alone in the next town adjacent.

Only once did Holmes break his silence. And that was to remark, as if to himself, "Angus Carrick is a very troubled fellow."

This point was so obvious that I didn't undertake to add any observation of my own. I went on with my eating and Holmes did the same. We concluded our meal in a silence that was without strain, for I understood my dear friend's eccentricities. When his brain was awhirl like a great cogitation machine, there was no point in disturbing its recondite mental machinations.

Ultimately, he broke his reverie.

"The so-called 'Indigo Impossibility'," Holmes pronounced with clipped conviction, "is not native to these parts. Of that, I am now convinced."

"Pray tell me your reasoning," I invited.

"If the creature were native to the great heathland, there would have been other encounters down through the years. Other examples of a supporting population. Bodies of expired specimens. Weird bones. Mysterious disappearances. We have had none of these events. Therefore, the creature is not native to Essex. Indeed, not native to England. Ergo, it was transported from some other land to this remote spot."

"But from where?"

"'For what purpose' rings more important to my ear. For if we understand that point, we shall understand all."

That was as far as Holmes would take the matter.

We retired early, the day having been long and full of exertion. I slept soundly, but I cannot speak for Holmes. I've known the great detective to expend all of his physical energy by day and remain awake the entire night, his ever-active brain refusing the siren call to rest.

After a charming breakfast, I knocked on Holmes's door to no avail, only to learn from the innkeeper that he had departed earlier to seek Constable Hume.

I found the two men on the green and joined them there.

Turning at my approach, Holmes said, "Just in the nick, Watson! We are going to visit Mr. Angus Carrick at his home."

"Has there been news of his success?"

"None of which I am aware," replied Holmes. "But I am keen to speak with him."

We walked. There was a morning mist but it was burning off. The day promised to be sunny, a prospect that filled me with relief. It had had quite enough of rain.

"Mr. Holmes," remarked Constable Hume. "I am eager to see you go about your work. Your methods fascinate me."

"They are but the disciplined power of observation. The ordinary man isn't very observant, and much eludes him."

"I fancy I notice more than most," said the constable cheerily.

"Then this will be a test of your ability," remarked Holmes.

"But not a contest, for I fear I would be the loser."

"I am confident of it," I chimed in. "My friend is nothing short of a miracle man."

The domicile of Angus Carrick was a homey little cottage a little bit away from the general run of dwellings. We walked through an overgrown patch in order to reach it.

Speaking to the constable, Holmes asked abruptly, "Did you notice it?"

"Notice what?"

"I thought not," said Holmes. But he declined to further illuminate the man's curiosity.

We came at last of the front door and Holmes stepped aside while the constable did the honors of rapping with the worn brass knocker.

I noticed several chicken coops on either side of the cottage, and it was evident that the Carricks raised poultry and no doubt enjoyed a plentiful supply of eggs year round. There was a large shed for tools, and a great deal of litter of the natural sort. A barrel brimming with rubbish stood off a bit, out of which protruded what I took to be a discarded bed pillow.

Presently a careworn woman of about forty-five years in age opened the door and smiled with great difficulty.

"Good morning, Constable Hume," she said. "If you're after Mr. Carrick, he came home very late, slept fitfully, and departed with the dawn."

"Back to the heathland?"

"No. Angus told me that he had followed the blue beast of such horror out of the Great Common. Its foot tracks led east to the greater fastness of West Wood, he said."

"I see. Mrs. Carrick, may I present the esteemed Mr. Sherlock Holmes of London, and his associate, Dr. John Watson. May we come in to further to discuss the present emergency?"

There was a moment's hesitation, but at last the woman threw open the door and stepped aside that we made might enter.

The interior was presentable enough, I suppose. It was also rather eccentric. I noticed that upon the walls were bills ballyhooing various circuses with whom Mr. Carrick had been attached. I wouldn't have them on an interior wall of my house, but each man to his own tastes.

Sherlock Holmes addressed the woman in a tone of voice that was deeply respectful.

"First of all, Mrs. Carrick, may I express my condolences upon the death of your late son, Andrew? I can only imagine the grief that now sits upon your shoulders."

"You are very kind, Mr. Holmes. But my grief is compounded by my fear that my headstrong husband will follow my son to his sad fate."

"Rest assured that it is my firm intention that nothing of the sort will transpire," said Holmes. "I had hoped to speak with your husband, but in his absence, a word with you will suffice."

"I have nothing to tell you that Constable Hume couldn't have already divulged," the woman said rather quickly.

"One never knows about these things," Holmes said gently. "I noticed, Mrs. Carrick, that a good deal of trillium grows around this property."

"I am surprised that you can name the flower, Mr. Holmes. My husband brought them back from the Carolinas. He likes to plant exotic blooms. Speaking for myself, good English blossoms are more appealing."

"Thank you for confirming my suspicions."

The woman's hand rose to her breast with a start. "Suspicions?"

"Yes, for I also noticed trillium plants growing wild in the Common. Recognizing that they were not native to England, I wondered how they could have come to take root here. You have satisfied my curiosity. You see, I count botany among my main and varied interests."

The tense-fingered hand fell to her apron and Mrs. Carrick looked visibly relieved.

"Oh, I see. Of course. No doubt some of the seeds have traveled, for we have had these plants for several years now."

Holmes resumed speaking, "I have had the pleasure of meeting Mr. Angus Carrick on the hunt, as it were. He tells me that he is a promoter connected to the circus business."

"Yes. That is true, as far as it goes."

"Oh? Does it go any further than that?"

"Mr. Carrick is more than a promoter. He is fond of securing 'exotics', he calls them cut, for the circus. He is especially interested in stage magic, for he has grown tired of tripping about the world and bringing back the exotic and the unusual. He fancies himself a magician in the style of the late Robert-Houdin."

"I see. Where was he last, insofar as his global endeavors took him?"

"I see no harm in telling you, Mr. Holmes. He has been to Australia and New Guinea and such places. Of course, I did not accompany him. I had a young Andrew to raise. Now, I fear that I have been relieved of that pleasant duty."

"Regrettably so," murmured Holmes.

There was a moment in which Mrs. Carrick used her apron to dab fresh tears from the corners of her tired eyes. We observed this in respectful silence.

During this interview, both Holmes and Constable Hume were casting their glances about the sitting room. I had noticed that Mrs. Carrick hadn't invited us to sit down. This permitted Holmes to shift about, under what I took to be the pretense of reading the various circus bills.

His crafty gaze went to an adjacent room, which I perceived to be a modest study. From it came the twittering of a bird.

"I see you have a caged bird."

"Several of them. More of Mr. Carrick's exotics. These came from the United States."

"I do not immediately recognized the specimen. May I study them at close range?"

Here, Mrs. Carrick seemed to grow pale. I couldn't imagine why. It was an innocent enough request.

Gathering herself together, she nodded dutifully and then added, "Of course. I regret that I cannot name the species, only that it is American in origin. These specimens were captured in the Carolinas."

"Thank you, Mrs. Carrick."

Holmes strode into the room, and if he glanced at anything else, I didn't perceive it. He went directly to the caged birds and studied them from several angles.

They were tiny, twittering things, hopping around from perch to perch, with the usual nervousness of the avian species. Some were brown, but the majority was a deep blue. The cage was quite large, of wicker construction, and altogether its inhabitants numbered seven.

In the doorway behind me, Constable Hume exclaimed, "My word!"

"What is it?" I demanded.

Turning, Holmes laid one finger over his thin lips and said, "I agree that these are remarkable specimens. I shall have to look it up their classification when we return to London."

Gesturing for us to return to the sitting room, Sherlock Holmes asked Mrs. Carrick, "I imagine that Mr. Carrick hasn't been sleeping well of late."

"He has not, nor have I. We toss and turn endlessly, so much so that Mr. Carrick asked me to dispose of our feather pillows, which I directly did. He presented me with a fresh pair. But they haven't aided our slumber. Nor did I expect that they would."

"Could you tell me how young Andrew met his untimely demise?"

"Angus and Andrew had gone hunting, during which time they became separated. The terrible thing transpired during that regrettable interval. My husband has been beside himself since that awful day."

"As one naturally would," mused Holmes.

His gaze shot to the bedroom door, but it was shut. I could tell by the look upon his firm features that if he could, he would have investigated that room too. I couldn't imagine why it held any fascination for him.

Once more addressing Mrs. Carrick, he said, "Again, please accept our sincere condolences, but we must be going. Give Mr. Carrick our sincere compliments and let him know we will we look forward to speaking with him at his earliest opportunity."

"Oh, I do not think it wise, Mr. Holmes, for Angus is in a foul temper and it will not pass until he has avenged our son. You must understand that even at his best, Angus can be difficult. His uncertain occupation in the ever-changing tastes of the general public forces him to struggle to keep up with the times."

"I can well imagine," said Holmes. "But please convey our sentiments to him. Thank you, and good day."

The door closed behind us and Holmes murmured in an undertone, "Do not speak until we are out of earshot."

We passed the grassy patch where the trillium grew wild and free, its reddish flowers surrounded by broad green leaves. Not until the patch was behind us did anyone speak.

"I was on the point of bursting!" cried Constable Hume when he felt it safe to do so. "Did you notice the color of that bird?"

"I could hardly fail to do so," said Holmes dryly.

"It was indigo," I stated, only then understanding the significance of it all.

"Oh yes!" Hume gasped. "Virtually the same shade as the Impossibility! I know that it must mean something. But I cannot imagine what."

Holmes did not enlighten us on that point. Instead, he said, "I would have liked to have examined the bed pillows that were discarded."

"For what reason?" I asked, thinking it an irrelevant point.

"To determine their color," supplied Holmes.

"What would that mean?" I asked.

"If they prove as black as a raven's wing, it would explain why indigo buntings were kept in the Carrick family birdcage."

"Buntings, you say?" said Hume.

"Yes, a bird of the cardinal family whose range stretches from Canada to South America, although Asia boasts certain species. Like the trillium, one would never find a wild specimen in in Britain. The male bunting boasts indigo feathers, while the female is brown. Taken altogether, I believe I have a clear understanding of recent events, as bizarre as they might have seemed until the present moment."

Turning to Constable Hume, he added, "What would you say to an excursion into the wilds of West Wood?"

"To find the Impossibility?"

"Or Angus Carrick. In order to test my little theory, either would suffice."

"Your theory baffles me, Mr. Holmes. I do not connect any of it, except for the coincidence of the indigo bunting and the Indigo Impossibility."

"I think the word 'coincidence' is misused, Constable. It is nothing of the sort. But let us locate Carrick."

We didn't have to go far to find Angus Carrick. He had returned from the wood, but not of his own volition.

A horse-drawn dray cart rattled into the little village, and became the occasion of a great uproar.

For there in the back of the cart lay Carrick, bleeding profusely.

We rushed over to the spot where farmer pulled up, calling out to the constable.

"It's Carrick!" he showed hoarsely. "The Impossibility got him."

"He is dead?" demanded Holmes.

"He may wish that he were, but he still breathes."

We reached the back of the dray, and Holmes thrust aside the flannel blanket that covered Angus Carrick.

A gory mess was uncovered. Fortunately, the great claws had raked across Carrick's chest and not his belly. The wound was not mortally deep. Only glimpses of ribs were disclosed. The blow must have been a glancing one.

Hume cursed and called for the village doctor. I replaced the blanket and attempted to compress the worst wound, but I feared that it did little good.

Directing his attention upon the man's face, Holmes asked, "Carrick, do you understand my words?"

Without lifting his head, the fellow managed to nod.

"What befell you?"

With pained expression, Angus Carrick spoke. His words were thick and halting.

"The beastie hopped six feet in the air from behind bushes and came down on me . . . Managed to discharge both barrels. Do not know if I hit it . . . only that it tore off into the bracken. I crawled for my very life until I came to a farm house . . . ."

The effort appeared to be too much for Angus Carrick. His eyes rolled up in his head and he turned his face to the side of the cart.

I placed a hand over the man's heart. I could feel it pounding. His wrist pulse was thready, however.

"Not dead. But rather far gone," I stated. Lacking my medical bag, there was little that I could do for the poor fellow – otherwise I would have administered a sedative. Carrick's torn clothes were ill-suited for use as makeshift bandages, being dirty and unsanitary.

The village physician soon arrived. Inasmuch as he had the advantage over me with his little black bag, I stepped aside to permit him to make an examination, offering professional observations illuminated by my days as an army surgeon in India and Afghanistan, which he found helpful.

"We will take the poor fellow to my office and I will do what I can for him," he swiftly decided. "But no promises can I make."

"I will be happy to assist you," I offered. "I am Dr. John Watson of London."

"And I am Dr. Drake. Your assistance would be very welcome."

We left Holmes and Constable Hume and drove the man to the surgery, where we did what we could for him. This took the better part of the morning.

Alas, Carrick did not speak again. It was necessary to sedate him before sewing up his hideous wounds.

Freed of my immediate medical responsibilities, I found Holmes and the constable just as they were concluding a shared luncheon.

"Carrick may live, or he may not," I informed them. "Has Mrs. Carrick been notified?"

"Belatedly," replied Hume. "No doubt she is now on her way to see him."

Holmes spoke up. "With your kind permission and official indulgence, Constable Hume, I would like to take advantage of Mrs. Carrick's absence and search the Carrick premises. Let assure you that this will be for the sole purpose of solving the mystery."

Hume hesitated only briefly. "This must be done under my supervision."

"That is satisfactory. I welcome your company. Watson, I'm going to ask you to remain here, since the emergency is far from passed."

"Agreed."

And so they departed. I should like to have accompanied them, but I assumed that I would be of no value whatsoever, and three intruders would be one too many.

I took a late lunch at the lodging house. When I returned to my room, I discovered that Holmes had reclaimed his quarters, for the door was ajar.

"What is that?" I asked, poking my head in.

"This is a feather pillow I have borrowed from the Carrick residence."

"Heavens, Holmes! You have stolen the grieving woman's pillow from her very bed?"

"No, Watson. Please shut the door. I left it open because I was expecting you. This is one of the two pillows that were lately disposed of. I found it among the trash that hadn't yet been burned, having spied it earlier. Two perfectly good pillows lying amid the household rubbish appeared to be out of the ordinary for such a frugal family."

With a pocket knife, Holmes commenced cutting the pillowcase open. It appeared to be a handmade affair, such as if Mrs. Carrick had sewn the casing herself, which I imagined she had.

Taking hold of the parted seam, Holmes ripped it open with his strong fingers.

Out spilled the most amazing profusion of long black bristly quills I ever could have imagined. Holmes took one up and passed it to me. Then availed himself of another.

"Just as I thought, just as I thought," he murmured.

I examined the plume in my hand. It was exceedingly long. I couldn't imagine what manner of creature had produced it. But it was very black, and quite coarse to the touch.

"Do you recognize this feather?" I asked of Holmes.

"Not from direct experience. But it has confirmed my growing suspicions."

"It has flummoxed my own expectations. What is this dreadful affair all about?"

"Humbug, Watson. It is all about a clever sort of humbug."

"This feather feels quite solid between my fingers."

Standing up, Sherlock Holmes said, "Fetch your pistol, and I will bring my howdah gun. We are going to eradicate the blue beast, and finally put an end these outrages."

"If you insist," I returned. "But I still cannot imagine what manner of creature can jump six feet into the air, swim across a pond, and slash open two grown men with such savage ferocity."

"I admit that this is beyond my personal experience. Let us see if we cannot run the beast to earth and prove conclusively what I now believe to be the identity of the Indigo Impossibility."

We reached West Wood by hiring a hansom cab. At the verge of the ancient woodland, Holmes dismissed the driver with these words, "Kindly inform Constable Hume that Dr. Watson and I have gone into these words to hunt the Indigo Impossibility. If we do not return by evening, he must undertake a search for our bodies."

The cab man gasped. "Are you quite sure of this, sir?"

"I do not intend to fail," replied Holmes, removing the cumbersome howdah a gun from his Gladstone bag.

As the cab rattled off, he turned to me and asked, "Are you quite prepared, Watson?"

"Since I do not know what it is that I am hunting, I do not know how to know how to answer that question. But I'm game to follow you into this mystery."

Holmes uttered a pleased laugh.

"Watson, you are as true as steel. Come, let us seek the phantasm."

We entered gingerly, walking close together, our weapons in hand. As we penetrated the wild wood with its hornbeam and hawthorn trees shading bluebells and yellow cow-wheat, Holmes began explaining himself, a thing contrary to his usual habit. I imagine the possibility of falling victim to the creature we hunted compelled my friend to reveal his thinking prematurely.

"I must confess, my dear Watson, that I was almost entirely without substantial clues in the beginning. You may recall that I was a trifle short with you at one point."

"I didn't take it personally," I assured him.

"I couldn't dismiss the theory of a dinosaur as entirely impossible. That is to say, that an extinct creature might conceivably survive in our modern era. But neither did it seem very plausible for reasons that I've previously stated. If there is one survival, there must be others. There were none that I could discern. Thundersley doesn't have a history of savage animal attacks or mysterious disappearances of men or livestock. Therefore, this couldn't be a native creature."

He paused to study the ground, evidently for foot tracks. None were visible to me.

We pressed on. The light was good, but as we moved into the density of the forest, the intertwining boughs and leaves began to cut into the streaming sunlight, creating a dim shade.

I noticed many interesting plants, but nothing that I hadn't seen before. Bluebell and wood spurge appeared to be plentiful. Still, this was an ancient wood and there was no telling what might be found in its deeper regions.

"Mrs. Carrick had spoken of her husband visiting the Carolinas, Australia, and New Guinea," resumed Holmes. "These seemingly unconnected places, combined with the indigo buntings kept in a cage, created in my mind a sudden and surprising the web of associations. Until that point, I confess that I was groping rather blindly for clarity of thought."

"So you suspect Angus Carrick of something?"

"Surely you noticed that Mrs. Carrick was excessively nervous during our discussion."

"She was overwrought. Understandably so."

"Oh true, Watson. But the guilty often betray themselves in their attempts to conceal the truth. No doubt are familiar with the stage magician's art of misdirection?"

"I am."

"The clever magician points to his closed fist with his opposite hand so you do not see what the pointing hand is doing. That is the art. Both hands are inside. Your attention is directed towards only one. Thus you miss the cunning pass of the pointing hand, which palms or produces minor wonders.

"Is Mrs. Carrick guilty of something nefarious?"

"Only of having knowledge she wishes to conceal for the sake of her family," responded Holmes. "For Angus Carrick is the truly culpable one."

"Of what, pray tell?"

"Of causing the death of his only son, Andrew," replied Holmes. "Investigation may or may not show that he imported something into this country that he should not have. That remains to be seen. As you are doubtless aware, we are not far from the Thames estuary, where cargo may be unloaded and brought by dray cart into Thundersley."

Holmes paused, searching the demi-shadows between the trees. He was listening, but if he heard something, I failed to achieve his keenness of ear.

He continued on. A rudimentary footpath wound through the woods and we remained on it, where we would not break twigs or crush underbrush noisily beneath our feet. Here and there stood the stools of felled trees.

"The vivid blue of the indigo bunting," Holmes resumed, "struck me like a flash of illumination. My thoughts had been stuck on the curious blue hide, like a gullible man staring at the magician's closed fist, and what sort of animal it might be. Suddenly, what was obscure became plainly obvious."

"Speaking for myself, it does not."

"No, Watson, but to one possessing my fund of knowledge, I found myself staring at the point on the map where longitude met latitude. For whilst observation is of supreme importance, without underlying knowledge, the obvious remains obscure."

We crept along. Holmes fell back into his thoughtful silence. At length, he broke it.

"Do you remember Sir Richard Owen's remarkable fossil discovery, which he called *Dinornis robustus*?"

"Yes. It was an extinct bird also known as the 'Giant Moa', native to New Zealand. A flightless creature that stands, or should I say, stood seven feet tall before it was hunted to extinction by Maori tribesmen. My word, Holmes!" I exclaimed suddenly, "are we hunting a living moa?"

Holmes's clipped reply surprised me. "No, we are not. I merely remind you of this creature so you are not unduly astonished when we locate the Indigo Impossibility, for we will need our full wits to defeat it."

Holmes fell silent again. I confess that I remained baffled. I didn't know where my friend was attempting to lead me, either mentally or physically.

Holmes stopped dead still and was listening. My own ears told me something was moving some distance to the west.

"I think we are drawing close to the thing," said Holmes in a hush.

"And what thing is that?"

"The creature that Carrick imported from New Guinea, or possibly Australia, which he kept in a cage large enough to encompass its size. I suspect the cage was concealed in the shed that stood some distance from the Carrick cottage. No doubt it was difficult to manage due to do it size and natural ferocity. Somehow it escaped and, lacking its a natural coating of black feathers, became even more agitated due to the cold and inclement weather, foraging for food as best as it could. But after having crossed the Pacific Ocean, it was in no temper to be recaptured. Thus when Angus Carrick and his son went hunting it, tragedy struck."

I felt as if my brain were being placed on a carousel while shown a kaleidoscope of images that came too fast for me to make sense of them in their totality.

"Holmes," I said in exasperation, "I am bedazzled by a mental procession of indigo birds, large black feathers, and misplaced trillium. Kindly enlighten me."

"I suspect the trillium was something that it like to eat. But that is only surmise."

Sherlock Holmes seemed at the point of clarifying matters when he raised his free hand for me to come to a halt. He had stopped in his tracks, his grey gaze penetrating into the deeper recesses of the ancient forest.

I could hear the thing moving. A succession of measured footsteps like nothing I had ever before heard. This was not the racing sound of the Indigo Impossibility as we encountered it in the Common. This creature was stalking, walking with caution, and, I feared, quite aware of our presence. A low sound came. I could barely hear it. But it suggested a brutish animal with a hoarse voice, akin to a bullfrog.

"Watson," whispered Holmes carefully. "Kindly turn about and keep a watch on our southwestern approach. I will study the northwest prospect."

I obliged. The noise of peculiar footfalls continued to be heard, a fearfully disquieting sound. I felt as if I were the prey to something I could not see, only hear. Glancing back at my friend, I noted that Holmes stood in an attitude of great nervous tension. He swung the impressive howdah gun about, prepared to unleash a fiery blast at whatever was so carefully circling us.

Turning my attention back to the southwest, I caught a momentary streak of blue moving through the greenery, along with a glimpse of a single russet orb. I did not hesitate. Lifting my Adams service revolver, I fired at the flash of color.

A scream was heard, or perhaps I should term it a screech. And out of the brush lunged an ungainly thing that ran towards me like a raucous banshee, grunting and huffing with rage.

It neared five feet tall, the greater part of it indigo. Fierce russet eyes glared hatefully as it came on, head lowered, its high crest thrusting forward in the manner of a ram. My eyes went to its feet. Terrible talons churned up clods of dirt as it closed with us.

That was all I saw. I felt myself being knocked aside and I wondered if the thing had leapt atop me with such blinding speed that I did not perceive it.

But no, it was Sherlock Holmes. Thrusting me out of the way, he brought up his howdah gun and fired three barrels in rapid succession.

The sound was deafening. The thing's horrid screaming died when the momentum of its leap was foiled by the cloud of shot riddling its oblate body, causing it to crash backwards and slide several feet before piling up to a stop.

Gathering my wits, I struggled to my feet.

Sherlock Holmes had already raced to the side of the creature, evidently dead, although the powerful claws still twitched in their death throes. Its neck had been severed, with the result that the staring head lay separated from the body. Reddish wattles clung to the long neck, which was mottled by its brilliant life fluid. The beaked mouth was short and bird-like.

In general, it reminded me of an ostrich, but without a coat of feathers. The indigo hide was smooth and hairless, the talons grey and distressingly massive. There was a dark crest of horn running lengthwise over its scalp.

One glassy orb glared upward in death-stilled rage. I judged that the pathetic shredded remains would weigh nearly nine stone in life.

"What is it?" I demanded in a hushed voice.

"You will recall the giant moa," stated Holmes. "This is another example of a *ratite*, a large flightless bird native to Australasia. In this case, unlike the moa, this beast is not extinct. Naturalists consider this bizarre blue beast among the most dangerous birds living. It is known as a *cassowary*."

"I have never heard of such a creature."

"But I have," said Holmes, nudging the head with the tip of his shoe tip. "And that is why my observation of the indigo bunting proved illuminating. Recall Mrs. Carrick stating that her husband had begun to show an interest in stage magic. To her, this was an idle comment, intended to steer the conversation away from the truth. But to my ear, it was tantamount to a revelation."

Moving about the wretched tangle of the cruelly-perforated body, Holmes felt and grasped one of the scaly feet. The creature was three-toed. Its outer claws were formidable, their span as large as a man's shirt front. What lay between them was staggering.

"Here you see what accounted for the grievous wounds inflicted upon two men," he said grimly.

"I see it clearly," I said. For the center claw was longer and sharper in appearance than its mates, a fearsome dagger of a nail. Dried blood had darkened it.

Standing up, Holmes continued, "I don't know the precise timing of events, but I would imagine that Mr. Carrick had brought home a number of indigo buntings from the Carolinas in previous years. They naturally reproduced in captivity, sustaining their tiny population through the ensuing years. On his most recent excursion to New Guinea, Carrick happened upon the cassowary, a large flightless bird possessing a striking indigo hide under its bristling black feathers. Thinking with the imagination of a magician, Carrick was struck by a novel idea. What if he could create an illusion for an audience where it seemed as if he could transform a tiny indigo bunting into a ferocious cassowary? What a sensation that would be to a jaded audience! Or perhaps he contemplated the reverse – transforming a fierce caged cassowary into a harmless little bunting. It does not matter. During the course of his practicing for the stage, Carrick lost control of his rare specimen. Tragedy resulted. The rest you know."

"Why, it sounds preposterous!"

"I will not gainsay your good opinion, Watson. But all the pieces appear to fit. Carrick plucked the black feathers from his prize, and not wishing to squander the rare plumes, had his wife sew them into two pillowcases. After the loss of poor Andrew Carrick, sleeping on them became intolerable. Therefore, they were hastily discarded. You see how the unlikely strands fit together. Improbable as they are, a clear pattern is apparent."

Holmes stood, frowning. I imagined that he was contemplating the tragedy of the Carrick family. But he surprised me by saying, "I should have thought to bring a rabbit pouch. I would like to show Constable Hume the head. Well, he will just have to take our word for it, won't he?"

"I imagine that Hume will be relieved, immensely so."

"No doubt he will, Watson. No doubt he will."

Our business done, we reversed course for Thundersley proper. As we walked along, serenaded by the drumming of the elusive great spotted woodpecker, Holmes turned to me and asked, "Watson, I'm surprised that you have never heard of the terrible cassowary bird."

"Why should I?"

"Did you not spend a measure of your younger years in Australia?"

"True."

"Yet you never heard of *causarius casuarius*, which is native to that distant continent?"

"I was rather young, and have only pleasant memories of Australia. That frightful fowl is not among them."

"A pity. But for your lack of experience, you might well have identified the Indigo Impossibility before I did."

"While conceivable, I doubt that I could have solved the mystery in its totality. Only you are capable of such mercurial reasoning."

Sherlock Holmes smiled in his usual restrained manner. "On that point, my dear Watson, we are in perfect accord."

The Case of the Emerald Knife-Throwers

by Ian Ableson

It will likely come as no surprise, dear readers, if I should tell that Sherlock Holmes and I rarely had the opportunity to attend the circus. Many of our investigations into Holmes's various cases through the years took place at the times one would traditionally attend a circus performance – that is to say, evenings and weekends – and as such our awareness of the circus was typically limited to an increase in the number of cabs taking eager attendees to the outskirts of London. While the constabulary typically prevented the traditional processional parades from clogging the streets of London, the mere presence of a circus could still throw a spanner into a city that found itself in possession of enough variables already.

And yet, one fine summer evening a knock on the door took us into the world of the circus not for the sake of our entertainment, but for one of those fascinating cases whose solution was much more interesting than it first appeared. Mrs. Hudson ushered up to our apartment a gentleman somewhat past middle age, but who held himself in a proud and erect manner despite his advancing years. His hair was cut neatly in the manner of a respectable military man, and he wore a red coat reminiscent of those often see on British military officers in full dress. We made our introductions, and he introduced himself as a Captain Clifford Cordell.

"Well," said Holmes when all were seated. "While it's certainly a pleasure to make your acquaintance, sir, and I am eager to see what business you bring to me this evening, I must admit I am rather hesitant to address you by the title that you've given us. Your coat is a shade of red too dark to be the red of the British Army. Your haircut, while neat, seems to me a little too ostentatious to be acceptable for a ranking military man. Furthermore, the campaign medals on your breast, while quite eye-catching in design and especially provocative in coloration, do not call to mind any military campaign from at least the last fifty years or so. But then, my friend Dr. Watson here was once a military man. It is possible that he sees something I do not that would confirm the honorific. What say you, Watson? Is our client here an army man?

"I should think not," I agreed. "For all the reasons you that you have named, and one more piece of information that you may not yet have. Our client's name and visage appeared this morning on several flyers that I observed throughout the city on my morning walk, as the face of the manager and ringleader of Captain Cordell's Emerald Circus."

Holmes laughed aloud. "There we have it then. A stage name. Forgive me, Mr. Cordell, if I drop your invented title in our coming conversation."

"By God, you are good," said Cordell, a reluctant smile breaking out on his face after the surprise had passed from it. "Rest assured, Mr. Holmes, that I had no intention of maintaining the title during our conversation. It is, as you surmised, a stage name – although the first and last names are true, for I was blessed by my parents with an alliterative name worthy of showmanship. I believe it was Lord George Sanger who was responsible for the practice of ringleaders taking on invented titles to give their presence a little more grandeur during their performances. All of the incongruities you just named are entirely accurate, but not for reasons of laziness or poor costume design – in truth, I have no wish to anger any actual military men by appropriating their honors without earning them."

"Your prudence does you credit," said Holmes with a small smile playing at his lips. "Pray, tell us why a ringleader has come seeking a detective."

"I am glad that your reputation does you justice, Mr. Holmes, for I come to you with a case that both baffles and – to some greater or lesser degree – frightens me. While I can't say for certain whether any true crimes have been committed, I'm afraid my own theatrical way of thinking and some of the evidence surrounding the incident has caused me to fear the worst.

"My circus is not the largest, Mr. Holmes, but it has always done well enough for me to consider myself successful in the entertainment industry. We have enough memorable acts that much of our audience is happy to return next season when they see our flyer, and we have managed enough variety to keep our show from growing stale through the years. However, without a doubt one of our most noteworthy acts would have to be the Popkin Twins, Robert and Elizabeth, our brother-and-sister knife-throwing duo from Belfast. Their precision, their synchronicity, their sense of stage presence – all absolutely astonishing, gentlemen. They joined my crew nearly ten years ago, at the age of sixteen, and in the ten years that I've had them, they've consistently been one of the highlights of my circus. And in addition to their talents, they are cordial nearly to a fault, and overall delights to have in my company. I have no children myself, but if I did, I could only hope that they would turn into such wonderful young people as the Popkin Twins.

"Now, I have a very strict policy regarding the people of my company. It likely won't surprise you to learn that many of my performers have checkered pasts. While the theatrical arts have managed to mostly escape the stigma of centuries past, the circus is still an appealing option for people who have a combination of talent and a history that they would rather avoid. As such, I make a point of never questioning my performers about the mysteries of their past – if they wish to leave their mistakes behind them, then I'm willing to accept that so long as it doesn't disrupt the harmony of my circus. And so I have done the same for the Irish knife-throwers. They joined my company at a young age, as I have already mentioned, but this is not terribly unusual for performers. Given their disposition and their incredible talent and pleasant demeanors, I have never felt inclined to pry into their lives before joining my company, and they have never offered the information of their own accord. I know next to nothing about their past lives save for the names they've given me, and it has occurred to me many times that even those may not be the names they were born with.

"About one month ago to this day, I hired a quartet of temporary stagehands to help us with the busy travel season. Among them was a man named Burt Wyman. A quiet man, perhaps in his mid-thirties, but competent at every task assigned to him. To tell the truth, I was so impressed by his work that I never interfered with him, preferring to let him work off his own intuition. That is, until a moment yesterday, when I stumbled across what appeared to be a vicious argument between him and the Popkin Twins. When I entered the room, I was fair astonished at the tableau before me.

"Robert had grasped Burt's collar and used it to force the man's face close to his, and he was hissing words that I could not understand into the stagehand's ear. Elizabeth, meanwhile, stood but a shoulder's width away from her brother, and her countenance stood in such a stark difference to her normal demeanor that I fear I will have difficulty ever forgetting it. Across her face there was written such an expression of quiet fury that I nearly physically recoiled at the sight. Never in my life have I heard either of the Popkin Twins so much as raise their voice to another soul, save in jest or while in the thralls of some game of chance or cards, and yet here they stood with Mr. Wyman at their mercy, wrath etched into their every muscle.

"When I entered the room a silence befell the trio, and Robert slowly released Mr. Wyman's coat. When I tried to question them about their dispute, all three assured me that it had been an insignificant matter regarding the arrangement of the targets during the Twins' act. While I didn't believe their words for a moment, I decided to let the matter rest and wrote it off as one of the inevitable conflicts that result from the close proximity of so many artist's souls. Perhaps, I thought, Mr. Wyman made an unwelcome pass at Elizabeth, and Robert had responded a little more harshly than intended.

"Such were my thoughts until this morning, when I learned that Burt Wyman had disappeared without a trace. He spoke not a word to anyone else. He left no note or indication that he would leave. I may have simply written him off as a deserter, as occasionally happens with temporary workers, save for a few details that have left me concerned about his fate. The first of these, of course, is the altercation with the Popkin Twins, which came to mind immediately when the stage manager reported his disappearance. The second is the strength of Mr. Wyman's character – he was a quiet man, yes, but a more diligent and intelligent stagehand I couldn't have asked for. If he hadn't disappeared, I imagine I would have asked him to stay on year-round by the end of the month. That sort of man doesn't just disappear without warning. Thirdly, his spare set of boots were still next to his bed, and what sort of temporary worker leaves good boots behind? Fourthly, and perhaps most suspiciously, the stagehands are paid tomorrow. In all of my years in this line of work, never have I heard of a man disappearing two days before payday, for nearly all will manage to stick it out until they have a little extra money.

"All of these pieces of evidence speak to me of foul play, gentlemen, but none of them lay the blame at the feet of the knife-throwers. However, there is one additional piece of information that ties Mr. Wyman's disappearance to the Popkin Twins too inextricably for even me to ignore."

At this, Cordell handed Holmes a small, cloth-wrapped bundle that he took from his coat pocket. Holmes unwrapped the package with the utmost care. Sitting in the cloth was a handsome throwing knife, perhaps six inches long, with three bands of striped green rock laid into the handle at equal intervals, giving the knife a pleasant dark green appearance when held up to the light.

"I found that knife under Mr. Wyman's pillow yesterday evening while searching for a note that might explain his disappearance. When the Popkin Twins first joined my circus, they brought fourteen identical knives with them. It was, in fact, those knives, and the lovely way that the green catches the sunlight as they twirl, that inspired the emerald theme that my circus holds to this day.

"Hmm," said Holmes as he subjected the knife to his own meticulous examinations. "While I'm sure this is a revelation that you've already had in the past ten years, Mr. Cordell, I feel obligated to point out that the green stone on this handle is not emerald, but instead appears to be well-polished malachite."

"Correct again, Mr. Holmes. I've taken some small liberties with the name. 'The Malachite Circus' just doesn't roll off the tongue quite so well.

And besides, few audience members are ever allowed to examine the set pieces quite as closely as you. Now, as I mentioned, the Popkin Twins arrived with those knives, and as is my policy I've never asked them were they may have obtained them. At first, I thought that perhaps Mr. Wyman had stolen a knife, but when I went to confront the Popkin Twins this morning, I chanced upon them practicing their act in the yard. They threw fourteen knives, one after another, at the target. They joined this circus with fourteen identical knives, Mr. Holmes, and fourteen knives they've always had. And yet in your hand lies a *fifteenth*, apparently in the possession of the vanished Mr. Wyman."

Holmes turned the knife over in his hands several times. "A fascinating tale. Tell me, Mr. Cordell, where might we find your circus?"

Later that afternoon, Holmes and I took a cab to the outskirts of the city to the site of Captain Cordell's Emerald Circus. We went in the guise of potential investors in Mr. Cordell's business, which we hoped would allow us to ask questions of his performers with minimal suspicion. Cordell met us outside of his largest tent and greeted us warmly with firm handshakes.

"Thank you for coming so quickly, gentlemen. Let me show you inside. I will introduce you to the members of my company that we discussed earlier."

I won't describe every aspect of the tent's interior here, but suffice to say that I was suitably impressed by the décor. Upon entering the tent, my most immediate thought was that the world had suddenly gone green. Each strip of the canvas material that made up the tent was a different shade of green, ranging from the deep greens of the ocean to lighter grass-like shades. Performers and workers of all sorts rushed around the tent, each of them focused on their own tasks, each of them (as Captain Cordell assured us in our invented position as investors) absolutely essential to the resulting performance this evening. As we walked around the tent's interior, Cordell kept a running narration of the effects being prepared all around us. Several workmen prepared packets of unfamiliar powder, which Cordell told us would be applied to the surrounding torches at a particularly climactic point in the performance and turn every flame in the tent a mysterious green color.

"No doubt a remarkable effect," said Holmes amiably. "A copper compound?"

"Spot on again, Mr. Holmes! Copper sulfate. Devilishly difficult to get ahold of, but it does not do to underestimate the importance of good lighting's effects on the audience's mood. Ah, here we are. Mr. Hall, Mr. Webb, allow me the self-indulgence of showing you one of our premiere acts. All the way from sunny Belfast, these two fine young folk are the best knife-throwers I've ever known. Gentlemen, allow me to introduce the illustrious Popkin Twins!"

This proclamation, said by our host with noteworthy aplomb and much extraneous gesturing, was met by the twins with an undeniably hostile icy silence. Both stared daggers at Holmes and myself, anger barely contained in their expressions. They resembled each other in the way that only twins could – both with sharp facial features and piercing green eyes beneath high, arching eyebrows, all topped with a mop of fiery red hair that stood in eye-catching contrast to their matching emerald outfits.

To his credit as a showman, Captain Cordell recovered impressively quickly from the unexpected antagonism of his performers. "Ah. Come along, my friends. It would seem that the Twins have already entered the focused mindset necessary for their performances. Far be it from any of us to disturb their meditations."

As soon as we were out of earshot, Cordell turned back to us, speaking softly, his face full of worry. "That, gentlemen, was unusual in the extreme. I have introduced the Popkin Twins to many an investor and personal friend, and every soul has been greeted warmly and given an impressive demonstration of their talents. It would seem that I made the right choice in coming to you this morning, for something is supremely wrong."

"Yes," said Holmes. He seemed thoughtful. "For such personable individuals as you've described them to greet strangers so coldly seems unusual indeed. I would very much like to see Mr. Wyman's sleeping quarters now, if you so please."

"To call them sleeping quarters may be applying a degree of loftiness to the rooms that doesn't necessarily apply," said Cordell. "Mr. Wyman slept in the stagehands' tent with his fellows, with little in the manner of personal effects. But follow me nevertheless – perhaps your more experienced eye will catch the key to this mystery that I have missed."

"Such is my calling," said Holmes with a small smile. "After you, Mr. Cordell."

The search of Mr. Wyman's bed proved mostly fruitless. Only one personal effect remained to show that the man had ever been there – the pair of boots Cordell had mentioned which, although of abnormally large size, provided no other immediately useful information about the man. The day had grown late, and Holmes and I were discussing our return to 221b Baker Street, when Cordell invited us to stay and attend the evening's show as his personal guests. Somewhat to my surprise, Holmes agreed immediately.

Only an hour remained until the performance, during which Holmes and I observed the rest of the setup procedures. I found the process fascinating, and truthfully more than a little hypnotic – performers, stagehands, managers, and the like all moved in perfect synchronicity, speaking only in curt, one-word questions and answers. Every person was in their place, every cog in the great theatrical wheel spinning with the sort of efficiency that only constant repetition can provide.

Holmes, I sensed, was far less captivated by the preparations than I. He seemed to be waiting impatiently for something in particular, his eyes darting this way and that as he watched the room. Whatever he was waiting for apparently didn't come to pass, however, and we were soon ushered to our seats by an attendant as the crowds outside streamed into the tent, murmurs and laughter filling the space as they readied themselves for the evening's entertainment.

Overall, I would say I quite enjoyed the show, or at least that of it which I saw. Captain Cordell was a commendably charismatic ringmaster, able to command the attention of the crowd with the ease of a true showman, and the acts themselves were suitably impressive as well. Indeed, my only objection with the show was the constant analysis from my companion. While I do appreciate Holmes' exceptional analytical abilities, I will admit that I privately felt I would be enjoying the show much more without his explanations of every illusion and feat of athleticism. I will not transcribe his whispered remarks here – as I said, I enjoyed the performance, and have no desire to ruin the experience for future circusgoers – but I feel confident that I can leave the gist of such remarks to my readers' imaginations.

I had nearly forgotten why we were at the tent in the first place and had just about trained myself to ignore the stream of commentary to my right, when his sudden exclamation jerked me out of my circus-induced reverie.

"There they are. Come, Watson. It's time that we excused ourselves." I had just enough time to see the fiery red hair of the Popkin Twins take center stage before he hurried us both from our seats and then out of the show tent entirely. We crossed quickly into the nearby ring of tents that housed performers and stagehands, our earlier tour from Cordell allowing us to pass easily amongst the few people who remained in the area, all of whom recognized us from our afternoon visit and greeted us cordially.

The Popkin Twins were prominent enough members of the circus to have earned their own private tent, a privilege that Cordell had informed us he made certain to grant to his senior performers. It was this tent to which Holmes purposefully strode, with me trailing behind him. We waited until we were certain that our entry would go unnoticed by those around us and slipped quietly inside.

Despite the honor bestowed upon them by having their own tent, it appeared that the Popkin Twins kept few possessions with which to fill it. Two beds, separated by a simple divider, several scattered chests that must have contained the majority of their personal belongings, a half-size mirror hanging from a coat stand, and a few other minor pieces of furniture and personal effects were scattered through the tent. All of it appeared to be small, lightweight, and easy to break down so as to facilitate a life of constant travel. A large, simple black mat, kept in place by a series of holes on the tent's walls, served as the floor. The overall structure was supported by three poles – two smaller poles to the left and right and one larger pole in the center.

Holmes had stopped me before I'd gone more than perhaps a yard into the tent, and he seemed to be squinting at the black mat in disappointment.

"I'd hoped that the floor might conserve some signs of the entrants – footprints, mud, or the like – but either this particular material holds no such impressions or the Twins are fastidious in their cleaning. Come, Watson – I don't wish to spend too much time here, but having seen Mr. Wyman's quarters, I feel that it would be quite remiss of us not to examine the Twins' tent as well."

We searched the room as quietly and efficiently as possible. While I will never claim to possess even a fraction of Holmes's talent for observation and investigation, I like to think that my time spent with him has given me at least something of an edge over the average London medical professional. I was examining one of the small chests when I saw something curious enough that I felt it warranted calling Holmes over.

A long, thin spoke of metal was stuck in the chest's lock. Experimental pulls from each of us proved insufficient to free it from its prison, and we soon stopped the attempt.

"Well!" said Holmes, something of a smile on his face, "It would seem that someone wished to get a look at the Twins' belongings without their permission. Although it's far too early to jump to any conclusions, I think that we can safely place Mr. Wyman very high on the list of suspected burglars. If you don't mind, Watson, I would like to examine the lock-pick a little more closely."

I continued to search the room as he looked over the lock-pick with his magnifying glass, but it seemed that my luck had run out, as I found nothing more that added any significance to the case. Holmes, on the other hand, called me over perhaps a minute after I'd restarted the search, pointing with excitement to a spot in the tent's wall just above the chest with the stuck lock-pick.

"Look, Watson! That's no popped seam. Something tore the canvas here by force."

"Perhaps it tore during travel?"

"Perhaps. But the nights have been cool of late, and Cordell's circus has been in town for a few days. If the tear occurred during travel, why wasn't it repaired before the tent was erected? It looks to be a clean slice, much of the sort that might be caused by a blade. And . . . Ah, what's this?" He grabbed something from behind the chest, a small clump of paper that, when unfolded, revealed a strange diagram.

When assembling my notes for this story, I had initially believed this particular piece of evidence to have long since disappeared into Holmes's stacks of files, but to my astonishment, I found the sketch among my own notes, and can only assume that even at the time I realized that I would want to reproduce the image for a future publication. It's a very simple diagram, and I'll present it below:

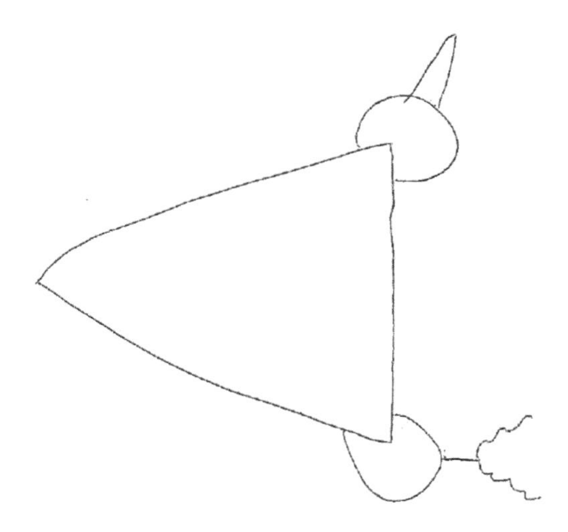

I couldn't make heads or tails of it, but Holmes was completely engrossed. He looked at the diagram, looked at the lock-pick, looked at the hole, and laughed very suddenly.

"Come, Watson," he said. "We are no longer needed here. Let us take a cab back to Baker Street. We can only hope Mr. Cordell will forgive our sudden departure. I'll need to make one or two inquiries in the morning, but if all goes well, I believe that we can have all of this settled by tomorrow evening."

By the time I'd roused myself the next morning, I found Holmes already pacing around the sitting room. He'd said nothing more about the case after we'd returned, nor did he seem to be giving any great consideration to the matter. As far as I knew, the only action that he'd taken was to summon one of his Baker Street Irregulars to deliver a note, though he didn't tell me what the note entailed. When there was finally a ring of the bell at around nine-thirty, Holmes greeted and ushered our surprise guest into the apartment with great cheer.

"Watson, it is my pleasure to introduce to you my colleague, Mr. Arnold Pearce. Mr. Pearce is a London-based private investigator much like me. I have high hopes that he'll be able to shed some light on this most confounding case in which we find ourselves embroiled."

"And I shall do everything in my power to ensure that these hopes don't go unfulfilled," Pearce rumbled. He was a tall man with a short brown beard and good-natured countenance, the corners of his eyes wrinkled from laughter. His voice was deep but not loud, in the manner of a man who'd learned long ago that he needn't speak with any great volume to make himself heard. "Your friend has referred nearly half-a-dozen cases to me in the past year alone, Dr. Watson, and has lent me advice more often than I can count."

"London is a large, complex organism," said Holmes lightly. "Plenty of room for more than one private investigator."

"So it would seem. Yet I fail to see what sort of aid you wish me to lend to you, Mr. Holmes. Your letter provided me with very few details apart from your summons."

"All in good time, Mr. Pearce. I hope that you'll forgive the vagueness of my letter, and I hope you will allow me to maintain the mystery for just a few minutes more. As Watson knows, my penchant for theatricality is one of my few true indulgences. Rest assured, however, that I am confident that there is knowledge you possess which will greatly help me bring this particular case to a close. Watson, would you be so kind as to order a cab that will take us to our client? I would like to take this opportunity to catch up with Mr. Pearce."

Holmes and Pearce spoke nearly without halting for the entirety of the cab ride, with Holmes taking a special interest in Pearce's most recent cases. He quizzed the man incessantly about clients, time periods, and the specifics of his deductions. I had the sense that Mr. Pearce was quite enjoying himself, and he spoke proudly of his success with a few tricky cases during the past winter. As it was, neither of the men had so much as glanced out the window by the time the cab stopped and we emerged to the sight of circus tents.

The moment he saw the bustling circus before us, Mr. Pearce stopped, halfway out of the cab, his face frozen in an unreadable expression. "Ah. Mr. Holmes, I believe I now understand the meaning of your summons."

"I'd hoped you might. You have my sincerest apologies for any deception, Mr. Pearce, but I felt that bringing you here was the only way to be sure."

Before Pearce had a chance to respond, we were hailed by a familiar voice, which swiftly morphed into a cry of astonishment. Captain Cordell rushed over to our cab, his face slack in shock.

"Mr. Wyman! By God, man, it's good to see you well! But where have you been? And how on earth did Mr. Holmes find you?"

"Captain Cordell," said Pearce grimly, "I apologize for disappearing so suddenly, and I fear it's only the first of many apologies that I owe you. If you will lead us to your office, I will share my story with all of you."

We gathered in Cordell's office – which was, of course, only another small tent, containing nothing but a desk, a few chairs, and a handful of other amenities – to hear Pearce's story. Holmes, Cordell, and I were seated, while Pearce stood, his agitation and eagerness clear in the way he fiddled with his sleeves as he spoke. "Allow me to preface my story, gentlemen, by admitting that I myself do not yet have all of the details of the saga, and much of what I do possess comes secondhand from written correspondence. Nevertheless, I'll share that which I know with you. In early spring I was contacted by the young Viscount Middleton, of Cork County in Ireland. As it happens, I spent some time in Cork County around eight years ago, and while I was there, I developed a robust friendship with the Viscount's older cousin, who referred him to me for this case, for the viscount wished to employ an England-based detective rather than sending one here from Ireland.

"The young viscount – whose name is Alan Brodrick – had only just gained his title upon the unexpected death of his father in March of this year, and he took me into his trust upon his cousin's recommendation. In his letter he beseeched me to accept a handsome commission to search for his younger siblings. They were twins, a man and a woman, both of whom had fled Middleton over a decade previously.

"The young viscount confided in me that his father, the previous viscount, had been a cruel, hard man – never in the realm of politics, where he was shrewd enough to avoid any behavior that might gain him enemies – but in his family life he was a poor husband and a poorer father, and his behavior worsened upon the death of his wife, the children's' mother. Nowhere was this cruelty more evident than in his treatment of his younger son and daughter, Patrick and Bridget. Despite Alan's attempts to protect them, or at least to keep them out of his father's thoughts, by their fifteenth years the situation had grown inhospitable enough that the twins were entertaining serious thoughts of fleeing their home. Alan himself overheard their discussions several times, often enough to learn the outlines of their plan, but admits that in his own relative youth he assumed all such discussions to be mere hypotheticals, wishful thinking from children who yearned for a different life.

"Not until their disappearance did he realize how serious their plans had become. They'd taken very little, all things told – a handful of personal belongings and a set of twenty malachite throwing knives from the family's collections that had been purchased by their mother. It seems that she was something of an eccentric and had been a performer herself in her youth, and she encouraged Patrick and Bridget to practice all sorts of unusual skills. I can confirm myself that their abilities with the knives is incredible, and they've been hard at work with them since the time they could barely walk.

"Alan's father flew into a rage at the twin's disappearance, and he hired a veritable army of private investigators to find them. He assumed they'd stolen the knives as a source of funding for their incoming travel expenses, and as such he instructed the investigators to search for any merchant who may have purchased a malachite knife within the past few days. He was partially correct – six of the knives were repurchased from merchants and dockhands in southern Cork County, enough to determine that the twins had sold them in order to gain passage to England. Upon expanding the search to England, however, the trail ran cold, and they found not one knife anywhere in England. Alan's father, it seemed, never considered that the twins might use the knives as a source of employment rather than immediate material gain, and his instructions to the investigators were therefore consistently misleading. Although he would hire a new investigator every few years to try and pick up the trail, none of them ever found the Brodrick Twins.

"Alan, however, was much more attuned to his siblings' dispositions than their loveless father and had a suspicion that they had become performers in England. However, he never attempted any sort of investigation himself out of fear of his father's retribution towards either the twins or himself should he prove successful. The moment their father had passed, however, and his retribution was no longer a concern, he sent a message to me. I received a very different set of instructions than any previous investigator: Look for a pair of twin knife-throwing performers, possibly using malachite knives, of about twenty-five years of age, with red hair and a possible Irish accent.

"He sent me one of the six recovered knives for comparison, and a copy of their family crest as well – it seems a few personal objects that the twins took with them bore the crest, and he hoped they may still have some of those items with them – but apart from that, he could offer little other information. And finally, he implored me to try and perform the task as quietly as possible, and not to make my employer known, for if I should become absolutely certain that I'd found them, he wished to come in person and implore them to return, rather than relying on an intermediary.

"Thankfully for me, there are not so many twin knife-throwers in England as to make the job infeasible, although to my considerable surprise there were enough to give me one false start before landing on the so-called "Popkin Twins". They seemed like exceedingly likely candidates for the long-lost Brodricks. I joined the circus as a stagehand to make my investigations easier as I set out to confirm their identity before I contacted the young Viscount again. This took somewhat much longer than I intended.

"Although they were the proper age, the right nationality, and as skilled as their brother had implied, I wouldn't allow myself to consider the case solved until I was able to compare their knives to the one that I had in my possession. But the Twins are not inclined to show their knives to a brand new stagehand, for they are extremely careful with them – as they must be, in the performing world, to have kept them in such good condition for nearly a decade – and it wasn't until I'd been working for the circus for the better part of a month that Bridget trusted me enough to show me one of the knives up close.

"Unfortunately, it seems I was careless, and somehow the twins determined my true purpose. Examining the knife confirmed my suspicions immediately, of course, and I promptly smiled at the pair, called them by their true names, and told them they were wanted at home, despite my employer's instructions to stay quiet about my task. Sadly, I didn't anticipate their reaction. Once they recovered from their shock, their expressions twisted into fury. Patrick grabbed my collar and angrily told me they would never return home, for the circus was their family now. I have no doubt they would have threatened me for my silence had you, Mr. Cordell, not chosen that moment to walk in.

"I knew at that point that I had to leave the circus that very evening, but I still stubbornly wished to find something to send to Alan Brodrick as proof that I had done my best to satisfy the terms of my employment. I slipped into their tent in an attempt to find something bearing the family crest – perhaps one of the personal items that Alan had mentioned – but was interrupted in my attempt.

"The twins' reaction was rather violent when they found me in their tent, searching for the family crest that I mentioned. Patrick threw a knife so near to me that I swear another inch would have cost me my nose, and it tore a hole straight through the tent. My nerves are as hardened as any good London detective, by I must say I was fairly rattled by the experience. I left in something of a hurry. It never occurred to me the concern my disappearance might cause you, good sir, but I wasn't in the right state of mind to formally tender my resignation."

"Goodness," said Cordell. "It all seems so difficult to believe. To think that I've been unintentionally harboring Irish nobility for the past ten years is a difficult concept to accept."

Before anyone could respond the flap to the tent shuffled, and to our great united astonishment the Popkin Twins walked through the opening. Pearce let out a shout of alarm and leapt backwards, but the male twin, Patrick – for I shall refer to them by their given names for the rest of this narrative – held up a hand in a placating gesture.

"Peace, sir! Rest assured that my sister and I no longer hold any of the same ill intent towards you that we did two nights ago. We made an incorrect assumption, without which this whole matter would have been cleared up much more quickly."

"We apologize for eavesdropping," said Bridget, "but when we spotted you leading Mr. Wyman into the tent, we felt we had to know the content of your discussion. Tent flaps, I'm afraid, are not nearly so soundproof as solid doors." She turned to speak directly to Pearce. "Good sir, we owe you even more apology for our behavior yesterday. But as it happens you possess a piece of information that my brother and I were missing until mere moments ago – namely, that our father is dead and our brother Alan has inherited his title. When we heard our birth names from your lips, we assumed that our father had finally tracked us down. In our own fear we wished to scare you away from pursuing us any further. Knowing that you are in the employ of our brother, however, and not our father, changes our situation entirely. We will be happy to accompany you back to the city proper, and from there perhaps you can help us arrange passage back to Middleton."

She turned to Holmes and I and bowed low, her brother following suit shortly afterwards. "We owe you an apology as well, Mr. Holmes. We heard the good captain say your name before he introduced you to us, and we recognized it as the name of a prominent London detective, for we have kept track of such things out of a sense of caution. We assumed you to be in our father's employ as well." She turned now to Cordell, and her expression softened. "Thank you for everything you've done for us, Captain, but it seems our past has finally caught up to us. Should you ever come to Ireland, you will have a home in Middleton for as long as you desire it."

Cordell laughed merrily, leapt to his feet, and clapped Robert and Elizabeth on the shoulder. "Then to Ireland I shall have to come one day, if only to see the pair of you dressed in all your noble finery! Well done, Mr. Holmes. This is about the best conclusion I could have asked for, save only one detail – it seems your investigation has cost me my best act!"

Holmes smiled. "My apologies, Captain. Perhaps we can find you some runaway noble Welsh acrobats before your next show."

It wasn't until later that evening, as Holmes and I took the cab back to Baker Street, that I learned of the reasoning behind his deductions.

"The first curiosity," he said to me, "was, of course, the knives themselves. By Mr. Cordell's description, the two of them were nearly penniless when they joined his circus, and yet they had fourteen rather valuable throwing knives on them. They had to be inherited – a thief would have sold them long before, or else been hesitant to reveal their presence for fear of retribution. Secondly, we had their mysterious past. This, combined with the aforementioned knives, put me in mind of a pair of wealthy young folk fleeing their homes, a thought that proved to be correct. The stark differences in behavior that they showed seemed, to me, to be most likely the result of some aspect of their past lives come back to haunt them. It's a reaction we've seen before, Watson, more than once, although not all such stories turned out as well as this one did. The nature of Mr. Wyman, however, I initially had completely wrong. Until we investigated the twins' tent, I guessed him to be a simple thief or blackmailer trying to take advantage of the past that he'd somehow discovered.

"The hole in the tent from the thrown knife made it clear enough that he'd been discovered in his investigations, but it was the piece of paper, dropped by Mr. Pearce in fear at the twins' hostility as he tried to pick the chest's lock, that held the key to this particular case. The strange diagram was his rough outline of the family crest, for he likely wished to keep the original safe and hidden. Look," he said, pulling the paper from his pocket and smoothing it out for my examination. "The upside-down triangle is an approximation of an inverted shield, the rightmost circle a stag's head with antlers, and the leftmost a bird's head. Had Mr. Wyman been a thief he would have cared little about the family crest, and had he hopes for blackmail he would have no need of it, for simply saying the twins' real names to their faces likely would have sufficed."

"Goodness," said I, squinting at the diagram. "It would seem Mr. Pearce is not much of an artist."

"I'm sure the symbols were clear to him. But it was only their similarity to notes that I myself have made in the past that allowed me to identify their purpose."

"But how on earth did you manage to identify Arnold Pearce as the detective in question?"

"For this deduction we must turn once again to the paper. Look at the embossing on the bottom corner of the page – exceptionally high-quality paper to have any sort of embossing, another hint that our Mr. Wyman was no common thief – it reads "*Hooper and Sons*". A very small firm that distributes only to a handful of paper sellers throughout London, which pointed to a London-based detective. And finally, we have the boots that Pearce left behind in his haste. I'm sure you noticed, as I did, that they are exceptionally large boots, for an exceptionally tall man, and they are of a style that I've noted Pearce to wear frequently.

"Once I had the basics of the matter set in my mind, I confirmed my theory on the cab ride over. You may have noticed that when I asked him to tell me about his recent cases, the most recent that he mentioned took place this past winter, as this case has taken all of his time since then. This I find somewhat heartening – it seems that even though his loyalty to his employer prevented him from telling me about this case at first, he still had the decency not to invent false cases to explain away the time."

"Or perhaps he's merely intelligent enough not to make the attempt," I said bluntly. "I myself gave up lying to you years ago."

Holmes laughed, and we passed the rest of the cab ride in a comfortable silence.

A Game of Skittles
by Thomas A. Turley

In the summer of 1886, I returned to London from a two-year sojourn in America, having regained a brother and wooed the beautiful young woman who was soon to be my wife. [1] I found the city in an uproar over what my readers may remember as "The Great Home Rule Debate". The aged Liberal Prime Minister, Mr. Gladstone, had split the country – not to mention his own party – over a bill to extend self-government to Ireland. Both the Radicals, led by Mr. Chamberlain, and the Whigs, led by Lord Hartington, had deserted Gladstone and combined with the Tories to defeat the measure. Instead of resigning, "The Grand Old Man" had asked Her Majesty to dissolve Parliament. Now, politicians of all parties had begun to stump the country, for everyone realised that the coming election would decide the issue, with the future of the United Kingdom in the balance.

Needless to say, all this public furor was of no more than marginal concern to Mr. Sherlock Holmes. Although his political knowledge was less "feeble" than I had once described it, his interest in political affairs was variable at best. I had not, at this time, met his brother Mycroft, who secretly kept him apprised of matters related to foreign affairs and national security. While Holmes held a degree of veneration for the Queen, he had nothing but contempt for politicians, whom he lumped with gypsies, peddlers, and card sharks as plagues upon the commonweal.

Our relations since my return from San Francisco had become a bit ambiguous. My friend had cordially, if uneffusively, welcomed me back to Baker Street, absent-mindedly acknowledging my repayment of his loan that had financed my voyage to America. But the news that I was soon to marry seemed to nettle him, and the congratulations he extended were perfunctory at best. Such reserve led me to question (as on occasion I had done before) Sherlock Holmes's true attitude concerning women. He treated most of them, including clients, with an impersonal courtesy, and while he could be affable enough to individuals (our landlady being one example), taken collectively he was wary and distrustful of the sex. In the years of our acquaintance, I had never known my friend to demonstrate, or even reminisce about, any romantic attraction to a woman. (The reader must recall that in that far-off decade, we both were of an age when such attractions were the rule. I noted, however, that when I showed him a pocket-watch portrait of my lovely Constance, there came a glint of something close to envy in his eyes.)

Naturally, it was not a matter we discussed, nor was it the only barrier to picking up the threads of our interrupted friendship. During those days, I was frequently away from Baker Street, overseeing renovation of the newly-purchased house in Kensington that would also serve my practice. Holmes was often absent on unknown errands of his own. Consequently, we saw relatively little of each other and, when we were together, my fellow-lodger seemed preoccupied with chemical experiments or unmelodious improvisations on his violin. To my disappointment, he said nothing of any cases he might have on hand and did not invite me to resume our old detective partnership. All in all, it was not the homecoming I had once envisioned. There were moments in that summer – as when I had received a letter from dear Constance or my brother Henry – that I actually regretted leaving San Francisco.

On an afternoon in mid-July, I returned to find Sherlock Holmes ensconced on the settee in our sitting-room, still in his dressing-gown and browsing through the morning's mail. He responded to my greeting by waving the missive he had been perusing.

"It appears, Doctor, that since our reunion I have risen in society. This letter enjoins me to entertain a duchess!"

"Indeed?" I marvelled dutifully. "Which one?"

"Manchester. With typical aristocratic arrogance, she has not requested an appointment, but simply announced the time of her arrival, in – " He spared a glance at the clock upon the mantel. " – Good heavens! A quarter-of-an-hour!" He fled into his bedroom to make himself presentable, while I leafed through the morning *Standard*. "What can you tell me of this lady, Watson?" Holmes called through the door. "Her note contained no indication as to what it is she wants."

"As to that, Holmes, I haven't a clue, but surely you must have heard of her. She is probably the most famous non-royal duchess in the British Isles!"

"Ha!" he chuckled, "I can always count upon your childish fascination with 'The Great'." My friend, now fully dressed, reentered and began to clear up the clutter of his earlier *ennui*. "Would you mind ringing for the landlady?" Holmes gestured towards the remnants of his luncheon and offered me a cigarette when I had touched the bell. "Now, Doctor," he continued, after Mrs. Hudson had performed her task and gone, "we should just have time for your summation before Her Grace arrives."

"I don't know what you're expecting," I grumbled, taking my seat beside the hearth. "My only sources are club gossip and the same newspapers that you read yourself."

"Yes, but while I scour the agony columns and the news of crime, you swoon over the comings-and-goings of the idle rich. Proceed!"

"Well, from what I've gathered, Louise von Alten was a storied beauty in her day, even though that day is long behind her. She came from Hanover, as a mere countess, in the early 'Fifties and married the heir to the Duke of Manchester. After he succeeded to the title, she was appointed Mistress of the Robes. Her salon attracted all the leading politicians of the day, and she soon acquired an almost unrivalled position in society. However, the Manchesters fell from Her Majesty's favour after they joined the 'Marlborough House Set'. As you're aware, Holmes, the Prince of Wales and his coterie are reputed to be 'fast'."

My friend, whose opinion of the Prince had suffered from an unfortunate encounter, merely grunted in disgust as I went on.

"The intriguing thing is that Lord Hartington, the leader of the Whigs, is likewise a member of that set. My old friend, Colonel Hayter – whose social connexions rise far above my own – has hinted that Her Grace and Hartington have long shared more interests than cards and horses. Among 'The Great' (as you refer to them), it is known that she has been his mistress since the middle 'Sixties. With relatively few exceptions, that fact has not gained wider currency. Their public conduct is impeccable, of course."

"Of course," sneered the detective. "And what does the *Duke* of Manchester say to this arrangement?"

"Very little, it appears. He is an amiable eccentric and a political nonentity, elderly now and content with his unfaithful wife's affection. She has, after all, given him five children."

"Most of whom," Holmes snorted, "we may presume to be his own! Watson, I must admit that on some subjects you are a veritable fount of information. I suppose you had better stay to meet the Duchess." With a touch of asperity, he added, "Who knows, after you are married, when such an opportunity is likely to arise again?"

By now, we were aware of voices on the stairs below. One was our good landlady's. The other was rather guttural, with a marked Germanic accent. Having surmounted the top step, Mrs. Hudson opened our door and announced with satisfaction:

"Her Grace, the Duchess of Manchester."

"Thank you, my dear," that lady nodded. "No, tea will not be needed." She smiled graciously before she turned to us, while a look of relief passed across Holmes's face. We rose and bowed, my friend waving the Duchess to the now-pristine settee. I took the basket chair adjacent to his favourite seat.

When she raised the veil beneath her flowered hat, it was apparent that although the bloom of youth had left her (she was then in her mid-fifties), Louise von Alten's beauty had not altogether faded with the years.

Her small but prominent blue eyes cast back and forth between us before settling on my companion.

"Mr. Sherlock Holmes?"

"I am, Your Grace."

"And this gentleman?" The look she gave me was less cordial. "My mission, Mr. Holmes, is extremely delicate, and I had expected to consult you privately."

I began to rise, but Holmes placed a forestalling hand upon my arm. "My friend, Dr. John Watson, is occasionally good enough to assist me with my cases. He is an old campaigner who fought for the Queen at Maiwand. You may safely trust him with any private information you confide to me."

"As you wish," the Duchess sniffed, no doubt unused to contradiction. "I have come to you, gentlemen, on behalf of an eminent statesman, who is a long-time friend of both my husband and myself. He is also, in my estimation, the only man who can save this country from disunion. My friend is entirely unaware that I am here. For that reason – and for others that will soon be clear to you – I must require you both to promise that nothing I am about to tell you will ever leave this room."

I complied at once, but Holmes smiled wryly. "Your Grace, I cannot possibly make such a promise before beginning an investigation. Who knows where it may lead? Am I to deprive Your Grace, and your imperilled statesman, of all the other sources of assistance that may be at my disposal?"

"If you refer to the police, Mr. Holmes, I do not wish for them to be involved."

"Obviously, or you would not have come to me. It would save us all a considerable amount of time, Your Grace, if you would simply explain the problem that besets Lord Hartington."

The Duchess blanched. "I have said nothing of Lord Hartington. Why should you draw such an impertinent conclusion?"

'Oh, spare me, madam," my friend sighed. "Presumably, you are aware of any small deductive powers I possess. The ducal houses of Montagu and Cavendish share the same exalted stratum of society. [2] Your own political and social connexions with the leading Liberal statesmen are well known. And who but the Marquess of Hartington – the former leader of his party – has the following and reputation needed to displace Mr. Gladstone and (as you so dramatically express it) 'save this country from disunion'?"

Her Grace and I both stared at Holmes in some surprise. My look was tinged with irritation, for it was evident that my friend knew a great deal more about current political affairs, and the personalities involved, than he had chosen to reveal to me. The Duchess, however, was regarding the detective with a new respect.

"Very well," she replied briskly. "I shall abandon obfuscation and impart to you the facts. Many years ago – well before he had seriously entered the political arena – Lord Hartington contracted an alliance with a young woman of low morals and far beneath his station. He was hardly the first young man of his class to do so, and it is unlikely he will be the last. As most often happens in such cases, the affair soon ran its course, and the girl was pensioned off and moved on to fresh endeavours. Lord Hartington resumed the political career that has carried him to the brink of the Premiership – that *would*, in fact, have given him that office had not that . . . had not Mr. Gladstone made his sudden and unprecedented return."

"The Midlothian Campaign," [3] Holmes nodded, before adding idly, "Lord Hartington has never married, I believe?"

"No, sir, he has not – though why you consider that fact relevant I have no idea."

"A passing thought, Your Grace, no more. Please continue."

"I shall now come to the point. This past Thursday, Lord Hartington received an anonymous letter at Devonshire House. It contained a photograph purporting to depict His Lordship's illegitimate son. Judging by the young man's appearance, he is of an age to have been spawned soon after the Marquess ended the affair of which I spoke."

The detective emitted a low whistle. "Do you have the letter, Duchess?"

"Alas, Lord Hartington destroyed it." Overriding my friend's howl of dismay, Her Grace continued, "I *have* brought you the photograph." Before handing it over, she was challenged by a meaning look from Holmes.

"Yet, you say Lord Hartington is 'entirely unaware' that you are here?"

"I volunteered to investigate the matter on Hartington's behalf. He is unaware of your involvement. Do you propose to interrogate me, Mr. Holmes?"

"No, madam, I do not." My friend groaned wearily, rubbing his brow as though it pained him. He glanced perfunctorily at the photograph. "I should like to keep this, if I may. Does the boy bear any resemblance to His Lordship?"

"I am sure I cannot say."

"Let us return, then, to the letter. Aside from its obvious intent to blackmail, what were the specifics?"

"They were quite explicit. Should he speak publicly again against Home Rule, should his dissident Liberals join the Tories in a Unionist coalition, or should he accept the office of Prime Minister, Lord Hartington was threatened with immediate exposure."

"Strangely political demands to come from a disgruntled doxy, Watson!" Preferring not to emphasise my unwanted presence, I remained silent as Holmes added, "Did the letter appear to have been written in an educated hand?"

"I did not see the letter, Mr. Holmes, but Hartington told me it was written in block letters."

"The usual procedure," the detective sighed. "I take it there was no overt demand for money?"

"None."

"Then it seems evident, Your Grace, that this blackmail scheme did not originate with Lord Hartington's long-ago *inamorata*. Even should she be involved, hers is not the guiding hand. Has His Lordship any thoughts as to whose the guiding hand may be?"

"If so, he has not confided them to me. Hartington has his enemies, of course, like any man of wealth and power. My own opinion, Mr. Holmes, is that the Irish are behind it. They have the most to lose if Gladstone goes and Home Rule is defeated, and I have never believed Parnell's denials that he was involved in Phoenix Park. The one point in his favour, I suppose, is that the gentleman lives in something of a 'glass house' where matters of this kind are concerned." [4]

"Ah, Your Grace," Holmes chided, "you must not tell tales out of school."

"Quite so." For the first time in the interview, they exchanged a smile, and I was conscious – once again – of my position as the dullard in the classroom.

"Well, Duchess, I believe we need detain you but a little longer. Tell me what you can, please, of the young woman with whom Lord Hartington conducted his affair."

"Her name, I understand, is Catherine Walters." With an expression of distaste, our client rummaged briefly in her reticule. "Here is her place of residence."

My friend took the proffered note with an expectant look, but Her Grace seemed to regard the matter as concluded. Only Holmes's raised hand prevented her from rising.

"Essential though these details may be," he said, "a bit more information would be helpful. This is a very fashionable address in Mayfair. I take it, then, that Miss Walters is still the beneficiary of Lord Hartington's munificence?"

"His, and no doubt that of others," the Duchess said disdainfully. "I expect she is of an age to have retired from her profession, although it is said that broad-minded gentlemen still attend her Sunday teas. Hartington, I assure you, is not one of them."

"Do you know how they met, and when?"

"Oh, that is an old story, though you are too young to have heard it. When I first came to London, Mr. Holmes, young women of a certain type would ride their horses in Hyde Park, looking to ensnare equestrian gentlemen of wealth and prominence – who, I must admit, were often there for the same purpose."

"The 'pretty horse-breakers'!" I involuntarily chortled, recalling a memory from my army days. "Their photographs used to adorn the walls of our mess in India. Colonel Hayter would talk of them for nights on end, especially of one called 'Skittles'."

With horror, I realised that I had said these words aloud. "Behold!" the Duchess cried. "The Sphinx holds forth, and not in riddles. Yes, Doctor, the girl we are speaking of is the same 'Skittles'. Legend has it that her career began in a Liverpool skittles-alley."

"Charming, but irrelevant," my friend intervened. "Do let us keep upon the subject. During its continuation, was this liaison well-known?"

"Unfortunately, yes. After Hartington imprudently took the girl to Derby Day, their affair became public knowledge. In consequence, the Marquess acquired a rather vulgar nickname for a time."

"'Harty-Tarty'," I recalled, before Her Grace's scowl returned the Sphinx to silence.

She went on to tell us that Lord Hartington, fearing that his father would learn of the romance, embarked upon a tour of America during that nation's Civil War. Unreconciled to her abandonment, Skittles followed him. They reunited briefly in New York before he sent her home. "It was there, I suspect, that she became with child – if such an event in fact occurred."

"Did they meet after Hartington returned to England?"

"Twice more, I believe, but according to His Lordship, not since 1863."

"That is a useful fact," said Holmes, writing a note upon his cuff. "And what became of his discarded mistress?"

"She left for Paris, presumably to whelp her offspring there. Later on (so I am told), she maintained a profitable alliance with Napoleon III's financial minister. Not until the Second Empire fell did she regress to London. My informants say that Skittles has lived more-or-less respectably for the past fifteen years. No doubt the income from her youthful exploits will see the woman comfortably through her declining years."

My friend chuckled appreciatively at this acerbic verdict. "And in all this time, there has been no sign of any son in residence?"

"None of which I am aware. Naturally, my enquiries are quite recent and are by no means comprehensive."

"Then let me see what I can add to them, Your Grace." Sherlock Holmes rose to indicate that the interview was at an end. "I shall initiate my own enquiries and communicate my findings within the next few days. Until then, you will please inform me promptly of any new developments."

"I shall. Remember, Mr. Holmes: This is not simply a matter of saving one man from his folly." Holding my friend's eye, the Duchess turned upon him the full force of her imperious will. "What is at stake – as Hartington himself expressed it – is no less than 'the maintenance of this great Empire' – "

" – 'to unite as one man for the maintenance of this great Empire'," I found myself reciting, "'to hand it down to our successors compact and complete.' Stirring words, Your Grace, to any man who ever served the Empire and our Queen."

"Yes, Doctor," smiled the Duchess. "Once the Marquess is fully roused to action, no man in the kingdom can speak with greater power. When that speech carried the vote against Home Rule in April, Harry Chaplin told me that its author soon would be 'Prime Minister for certain'. You *must* save his reputation, Mr. Holmes. Too much depends upon it for Hartington's political future to be lost."

My friend returned no answer to this plea, but he nodded gravely before he showed our client to the door.

After Her Grace had departed, Holmes decreed the afternoon too far advanced to accomplish anything useful on the case. Instead, we sat and smoked, conversing amiably as we had not done for quite some time. The detective admitted his surprise at finding the Duchess of Manchester to be "a formidable woman". He opined that in the present state of politics, she might well succeed in her ambition to make Hartington Prime Minister. This remark offered me an opportunity to question my friend regarding the surprising political insight he had shown.

"Why did you ask *me* about the Duchess, Holmes? It was apparent that you knew much more about both her and Hartington than I do."

"My apologies, Doctor," he replied. "I have sources, when I choose to utilise them, that are far more highly placed than Colonel Hayter's. No doubt it was after consulting those sources that the Duchess came to us. Nevertheless, I often find it expedient to test the political knowledge and opinions of ‘the man on the street’. You are perfectly fitted to represent that class, although in this instance you were better-informed than I expected.”

I could but swallow my exasperation. “I never get your limits, Holmes.”

“Nor I yours, Watson. But it is satisfying, is it not, to discover that even now we can surprise each other?”

It would be several years before I learned that my friend’s political knowledge came largely from his brother Mycroft. We ended, on that summer evening, by sharing a fine meal at Simpson’s, the first such occasion since my return from America.

When I came down to breakfast the next morning, Sherlock Holmes was not in evidence. He had, however, left a letter and a shilling on the table, instructing me to give them to a member of the Baker Street Irregulars who would soon appear. Just as I was finishing my kippers, the bell pealed from the street, and I heard a scandalised cry from Mrs. Hudson before a particularly small and dirty street Arab burst into our sitting-room. I did not recognise this specimen, who introduced himself as “Marcum, sir!” No doubt Holmes had recruited him during my absence overseas. I entrusted the boy with both coin and missive, observing that the latter was destined for a street in Mayfair. Young Marcum took off at a gallop.

“Really, Doctor!” protested our good landlady, having all but been bowled over on the stairs. “Duchesses one day and street urchins the next! I don’t know what I’m to do with Mr. Holmes.”

“At least, Mrs. Hudson,” I replied consolingly, “you cannot say your lodger lacks an entertaining clientèle!” The look she gave me sent me dashing for the street as well.

The remainder of my morning was occupied at my new house in Kensington, where I had arranged to meet the painters. As was typical of Railey’s minions, they were late, so it was early afternoon before I returned to Baker Street. I found the detective stalking about restlessly as he awaited my arrival.

“Ah, Watson! I was afraid you would be late. I am expecting another visitor at two o’clock – one whom I am sure will be of interest to you.”

I asked my friend where he had been that morning.

“Conferring with one of my associates in Whitehall, who will be of some assistance in this business. Ah, there’s the bell.”

After the requisite delay, Mrs. Hudson announced, with evident approval, our latest visitor: “Miss Catherine Walters.”

As Holmes had prophesied, it was with great interest that I gazed upon the famous “Skittles”. By then in her late forties, she might easily have passed for thirty-five. The tawny hair that framed her perfect profile remained untouched by grey, and her clear blue eyes retained a childlike innocence. The slender figure, which had been clothed in skin-tight riding habits in the photographs that I recalled, was now attired more modestly, although in the very height of fashion. She gave Holmes a smile of greeting that would have reduced most men to stammers. The detective merely nodded civilly and gestured towards my armchair. There Skittles perched demurely, while he took his own seat across the hearth from her and I collapsed into the basket chair beside him.

After introducing me, Holmes informed our visitor, "I have here a photograph, Miss Walters, that I desire you to examine." Taking the picture of her supposed son from his coat pocket, he passed it to her and silently awaited her response.

A look of surprise passed across the lovely face, and Skittles raised her eyes to my friend in some confusion. "Here, now, Mr. Holmes," she demanded, her accent bearing traces of her origin in Liverpool. "Where did you get this?"

"That, madam, is for me to know, if you do not know already. Do you recognise the youth?"

She studied the photograph again, nodded, and said to Holmes decidedly, "It looks exactly like my son Emile, but much older than when I saw him last."

My friend sat back in his armchair with a sigh of evident relief. "Thankfully, then, we can dispense with any pretended ignorance or plain denials. I feel sure that my next question will not be unexpected. Who is the young man's father?"

Skittles gave him a look in which pride and irony were intermixed. "If you've ever seen the gent, Mister Detective, you can answer that one for yourself. Emile's Lord Hartington's, of course. Couldn't be anybody else's!"

"You're quite sure of that?" Holmes queried, with sufficient gravity to make his meaning clear. "My sources tell me that you were in company with an Irish squireen at the time you travelled to the United States."

For the first time, our visitor seemed impressed by the detective. "Now, how did you know *that?* You mean Beauclerk? He meant no more to me than a ticket to New York. Even whores have standards, Mr. Holmes!" Her amusement fading, Skittles looked directly at my friend and told him quietly, "When I met Cav [5] in America in '62, and he got me in the family way, I hadn't been with anyone else recently enough to matter."

"And yet," Holmes murmured, "you named your son 'Emile'."

"What the hell was I supposed to name him?" Skittles thundered, "'Harty-Tarty'?"

To his credit, my friend laughed heartily, and the atmosphere inside our sitting-room became a trifle warmer. "Well, Miss Walters," he proposed, "why not tell us the whole story? What became of Emile afterwards?"

Now it was the courtesan who lay back in her chair and sighed. "It's a long time since I talked of this," she said reluctantly. "Why is it any of *your* business?"

"My business," replied Holmes severely, "is to protect the alleged father of your son from being blackmailed. If you wish to clear yourself of involvement in that crime, I advise you to be frank with us."

"There's naught 'alleged' about it, ducky, and I'm not part of any blackmail!" For a brief interval, Skittles sat gathering her thoughts. Then we heard her story. Before she left New York that long-ago November, Hartington had told her firmly that he could never marry her. "Oh, he'll have his duchess in the end," our visitor sighed, "but it won't be some skittles-alley girl from Liverpool!" By the time she learned "a bun was in the oven," Skittles' condition was too far advanced for her to stay in London. After selling the fine house that Hartington had given her, she fled to Paris and had her baby in a convent run for disgraced girls. [6] "Disgraced girls, indeed! Even at three-and-twenty, Mr. Holmes, it was a long time since I'd been a 'disgraced girl'!"

Indeed, Skittles had shown remarkable resilience. For a while, she "took up with a young poet" [7], but his fiancée's father found us out and sent him home. So I made my way to the French court, and I did *very* well there. Conquered Paris on me back, just like I'd conquered London!"

"What of the child?" I interjected, and received an approving nod from Holmes. For the first time, the beautiful courtesan looked my way and dimpled.

"*Hello*, dearie. I was starting to wonder if the cat had got your tongue! You needn't worry about my sweet Emile," she added. "The nuns took good care of him till he grew up a bit. Then they found a nice family for him in the country."

In reply to further enquiries, Skittles recounted that she had supported her son on the £400 *per annum* she received from Hartington, besides additional funds from "other gentlemen". She had resided in Paris "until the bleeding war brought down the Empire", after which she had returned to London. She had not seen her son since then. "Never even told him who his mother was," she ended sadly.

Holmes, who had endured this long recital with impatience, said, "Very well, Miss Walters. I see no need for us to trace your subsequent career. Aside from the Parisian nuns and Emile's guardians, who else knows you have a son by Hartington?"

"Well, I didn't send out birth announcements!" Skittles scoffed. "Couldn't very well print it in *The Times*. Let's see, now. . . ." She sat pondering a moment, then assured us brightly, "The only one I told, on *this* side of the Channel, was old Gladstone."

Sherlock Holmes was thunderstruck. After we exchanged a look of consternation, he asked her carefully, "You told the Prime Minister that you'd borne a son to the most senior of his Cabinet colleagues?"

"Oh, no!" our visitor hastily amended. "I didn't tell him it was *Cav's!* That would have been *most* indiscreet," she added primly. "I only told him that I'd had a child."

My friend eyed Skittles with suspicion. "What led you to make this revelation?"

"How was it, Miss Walters," I tactfully amended, "that you and Mr. Gladstone came to discuss the matter?"

"Why, he came to visit me last year!" Skittles announced gaily. "Attended my salon one Sunday, then came back later on his own. No, not for *that,"* she coyly chided me, "although I could see the old goat would have loved to. When I let him measure me waist, his hands were positively *twitching!* [8] But all he asked of me was to become one of his 'rescue projects'."

Noting our blank looks, she asked in wonderment, "You've never heard about old Gladstone's rescue projects?" It was evident from my friend's face that he had not. "What kind of a detective *are* you?" Skittles queried saucily.

Holmes sprang from his chair as though stung by a wasp. I saw him feel inside a pocket for his pipe and glance longingly at his tobacco in the Persian slipper. Denied that release, he stalked to the bow window and glared down upon the street. After perhaps a quarter-of-a-minute, he turned back to our visitor with a disarming smile.

"Very good, Miss Walters! I admit that on this subject you have me at a disadvantage. *Please*," he added, waving magnanimously as he resumed his seat. "Enlighten us!"

The enlightenment she provided was burdensome to hear, although delivered quite offhandedly. If Skittles was to be believed, the Prime Minister of Great Britain had, since his days at university, regularly consorted with streetwalkers – not, it seemed, for the expected purpose, but ostensibly to undertake the reclamation of their souls. He would, at night and in secret, walk the streets of Westminster and meet the fallen women as they plied their trade, seeking to return them to the path of virtue. On occasion, Mr. Gladstone would visit the prostitutes in their abodes, or take promising penitents home to meet his wife ("She must be barmier than *he* is!"), who would then retrain them in domestic work.

Some had even served as maids at Hawarden, the Gladstones' Welsh estate.

Morally laudable – if politically dangerous – though this activity might be, Skittles, from her courtesan's perspective, found the Prime Minister's motives to be suspect. "One of my *other* friends," she told us, "says His Holiness won't bother with a girl unless she's pretty. [9] You don't see him out saving those poor slags in Stepney or Whitechapel!"

Challenged by Holmes as to her information's source, Skittles again flummoxed the detective by insisting it had come from "The Grand Old Man" himself. During one visit, Mr. Gladstone had confessed to performing "strange and humbling acts" after his nightly expeditions. "He told me that after meeting with a pretty whore, he'd go home and flog himself to stave off 'lustful thoughts'. Silly old bugger! Never told *that* to Mrs. G, I'll warrant!" [10]

It was at this stage that my friend's thirst for data was overwhelmed by his disgust. Recalling Skittles to the attempt to blackmail Hartington, he subjected her to a stern interrogation, but with purely negative results. She denied giving her son's photograph to the Prime Minister. Her own most recent picture of Emile had been taken at age nine. Moreover, she disclaimed any interest in destroying her old lover's political career. "Why would I," the courtesan reminded us, "when he's giving me a house and an allowance? It would be killing the goose that lays the golden eggs!" [11]

In the end, Holmes acknowledged the good sense of her objections. Rather frostily, he thanked Skittles for her cooperation, asking whether she was willing to sign a memorandum of the interview should one be needed. (I naturally had taken careful notes.) Our visitor readily agreed, indignantly rejecting any compensation. Nonetheless, she added, "I do have one condition, gentlemen."

Her condition met, the courtesan departed, but not before she paused to stroke my cheek. "You're *delicious,* ducky!" she informed me. "But your friend over there – " She turned to smile mockingly at Sherlock Holmes. " – needs to find himself a girl!"

After Skittles left us, Holmes and I engaged in a quarrel that threatened to undo our budding rapprochement. It began innocently enough. When Mrs. Hudson brought our tea, she risked a hopeful comment about our "lovely client". The detective's reply left her unsatisfied, but after she withdrew, he admitted his gratification at the bizarre but useful information our "client" had revealed. When I expressed doubt that the Prime Minister (whose private morals I had assumed to be beyond reproach) would stoop to blackmail, my friend shook his head impatiently.

"He is the obvious culprit, Watson. Who else stands to gain if Hartington is ruined? After Phoenix Park, even blackmail would not convert him to the Irish cause. [12] Hence, the Duchess's suspicions are unfounded. I am satisfied that Miss Walters is not colluding in the plot. The nature of the blackmailer's demands excludes a common prostitute."

"Hardly common, Holmes! Surely, even you must be a little moved by an encounter with a famous courtesan."

"Must I?" he answered irritably. "Some men, weary of the refinement required of ladies in polite society, may find Miss Walter's lack of inhibition quite enticing. I do not. My ideal woman, Watson, would possess not only beauty, but character and breeding, as well as an intelligence more suited to my own. She would not be, like our recent visitor, a debauched, wilful, aging child!"

"Perhaps you would prefer a more youthful edition of the Duchess of Manchester?" I warily suggested.

"By no means. What is the difference, Doctor," he demanded, refusing a slice of Bakewell Tart, "between the most beautiful *demimondaine* in London and a bedraggled East End streetwalker? Or between a streetwalker and a woman of society who commits adultery to further her social and political ambitions? It is purely a matter of degree."

"That is most unjust to the Duchess, Holmes, and even to Skittles," I replied. "I had not realised until this day that you were such a prig!"

He merely shrugged. "Is it priggish to regard such matters realistically? The sexual urge is common to us all, but must it always be romanticised?"

By now, I was in doubt as to the postulate before his query, at least as it applied to Holmes. "I am disappointed, Watson," he continued loftily, "to find you condoning prostitution. As a doctor, you are surely aware of the danger it presents to public health. Such moral laxity bodes ill for your marriage to Miss Constance."

"Of course I do not condone prostitution! But neither do I condemn the unfortunates who practice it – or far less so than a pious hypocrite like Gladstone, who derives vicarious pleasure from these woman while purporting to reform them. And I'll thank you, Holmes, to leave 'Miss Constance' out of this!"

Fortunately for the endangered future of our friendship, we were interrupted at that moment by a knock upon the door. It was Inspector Gregson, seeking help from the detective on a case. In the prevailing atmosphere, I decided not to stay, so it was not a case that lies within the confines of my tin dispatch box. I spent the evening at my club.

For the next two days, Sherlock Holmes and I once more came and went from Baker Street with little reference to each other. When our paths did cross, he said nothing of having fulfilled his promise to the Duchess, nor of any efforts to foil the designs of Mr. Gladstone. Meanwhile, it was apparent from the newspapers that the elections were going heavily against the Gladstonian remnant of the Liberal party. Speculation was rife as to whether "The Grand Old Man" would resign without meeting the new Parliament and – if so – whether the Liberal Unionists would join the Tories in a coalition, which might result in Her Majesty inviting Lord Hartington to form a government.

At last, late in the morning of July 24th, I returned to our rooms determined to remain in ignorance no longer. "What of the Hartington case, Holmes?" I demanded as I closed the hallway door behind me.

"That business?" he replied, keeping his eyes upon the beakers of chemicals before him. "It was successfully concluded. If you wish to remain at home this afternoon, you may be a witness to its *denouement*."

This overture – if overture it was – led to our mutual apologies, after which I asked Holmes to be apprised of the details. For the sake of greater clarity, I shall approximate below my friend's recounting of the story.

"As you can hardly be aware, Doctor, there is a department in Whitehall whose sole charge is to collect, analyse, and correlate information on a wide array of seemingly unrelated subjects. Much of the data they acquire pertains to foreign affairs or military matters, although it must be said that in planning imperial defence, we lag far behind the Continental powers. [13] Certain issues of domestic policy also fall within their ken. Of special interest are the private, as well as public, lives of those you and I have referred to as 'The Great' – the most prominent individuals in political, diplomatic, military, naval, and even social circles. Given the importance of the posts they hold, their personal activities – even the most confidential ones – become questions of national security.

"Due to his relative youth, my contact is still a junior member of this strange cabal, but his talents are such that he will rise eventually to its highest level. It was to him, therefore, that I went for confirmation of the lurid tales Miss Walters told us. And to my dismay, Watson, I found that her primary charge against the Prime Minister was verified. It is well known to this obscure branch of government that Mr. Gladstone has associated with prostitutes for many years, even though his commerce with them appears to be as innocent of 'sin' – or at least the sin of fornication – as our informant stated. As for his 'strange and humbling acts' of flagellation, which I felt obligated to report, they were news to my gentleman from Whitehall. Yet, I blush to say that he was not surprised. Such peculiarities are evidently more widespread among 'The Great' than I had realised.

"Of course, my more important task was to stop the blackmail of Lord Hartington. Here, too, my acquaintance provided information of great value. It was already known that Skittles has a son. Her high, if irregular, connexions in the court of France made her a person of interest long ago. Due to the birth's timing, it was surmised, though never proven, that Hartington had been the father. Apparently, His Lordship was never told – which, I must admit, raises my opinion of Miss Walters. To my contact's knowledge, no attempt has been made to find the boy, although the Prime Minister is easily in a position to undertake the search. Despite the security risks imposed by his own conduct, his access to intelligence resources is virtually unlimited.

"Considering all this, my colleague and I agreed that a direct approach to the problem was the most expedient. He requested a personal interview with the Prime Minister, and such is the prestige of the men he represents that we were quickly granted one. We saw Mr. Gladstone yesterday at four o'clock in Downing Street.

"It was a strange meeting, Watson. 'The Grand Old Man' received us in his private office, where the curtains were already drawn. He sat alone, almost in darkness. Not quite alone, indeed, for a large black cat lay curled amid the papers on his desk. Puss regarded us less distrustfully than did the Prime Minister. My Whitehall friend had warned me that Mr. Gladstone was an embittered man since returning from Hawarden, indulging in acrimonious correspondence with those he holds responsible for the government's defeat. [14] The light from his desk lamp cast a glow around him as he glared at us like a tattered old eagle brought to bay. Seeing Gladstone thus, it was not difficult for me to credit that his vindictiveness might extend to blackmail.

"The Prime Minister's mood was not improved when my colleague laid our knowledge of the facts before him. Yet, his unimpeachable honesty, as well as his unshakable belief in his own righteousness, led him to acknowledge those facts freely.

"'After all, gentlemen,' he patiently explained, 'our fallen sister has lain with some of the most prominent leaders of this country, including one exalted personage whom I am not at liberty to name! The same may be said of her French associations. It is only natural that her activities should come under scrutiny from men charged with maintaining the safety of this kingdom.'

"'As one of those so charged, Prime Minister,' my gentleman from Whitehall noted, "I can assure you that Miss Walters never engaged in espionage while she was in France, either against this kingdom or upon its behalf.'

"'Ah, sir, but how much is *your* assurance worth?' Mr. Gladstone answered snidely. 'Fortunately, I have spoken of the matter with your seniors. You are, in fact, correct. Of espionage Miss Walters is as innocent as the driven snow. But I have visited the little sinner! When I learned last year that she had birthed a child, I felt it my duty – both for the security of the country and the welfare of her soul – to discover who her bastard's father was.'

"'And when his father proved to the leading opponent of Home Rule?' I queried, if only to contribute to the conversation.

"Mr. Gladstone chortled gleefully. 'When I saw that photograph, gentlemen, I was delighted! It could be no one else! The Lord had delivered Hartington into mine hands! Is it not marvellous how the Almighty turns even sin to His own purposes? The Pharaoh of the Whigs must now free the Israelites – that is to say, the Irish – or be cast down.'

"'And how did you proceed, Prime Minister?' I encouraged him respectfully.

"'Well, Mr. Holmes, after we lost the Home Rule vote in April, I secretly had the young man brought from France and informed him of his parentage. I fear it took both threats and bribes to ensure his cooperation, but the Lord has many weapons in His arsenal! Thankfully, Hartington's young progeny seems even more slow-witted than his sire. He also speaks very little English. I soon saw that I had naught to fear from him.'

"'There is a thing I do not understand,' I pondered. 'The public has known for many years of Lord Hartington's love affair with Skittles. Yet his reputation is undamaged – is, indeed, enhanced – by that youthful indiscretion. Those in high places, including the Queen, are also aware of his longstanding liaison with a certain duchess. How could you be sure that the revelation of a natural child would suffice to ruin him?'

"Gladstone met this objection cheerfully. 'Oh, I couldn't, sir, if you speak only of the public. But all I really have to do is to discredit "Harty-Tarty" with the Queen. Her Majesty may prefer him to myself as leader of her government, but she has never taken kindly to his private conduct. In view of the current crisis in political affairs, she could hardly ask a man known to have fathered his whore's bastard to create a ministry. If nothing else, dear Skittles has given me a means of balancing the scales should Mr. Parnell's lamentable adultery ever become public knowledge.'

"It was at this point, Watson, that my associate intervened to prick the bubble of Mr. Gladstone's insufferable complacency. 'And what, Prime Minister,' he asked sternly, 'of your own private conduct?'

"The old hypocrite turned to him in what seemed genuine surprise. 'My conduct, sir? To what conduct do you refer?'

"'The conduct that has led you, throughout your political career – and, so I am told, even earlier – to walk the streets of London and solicit fallen women of a far lower order than Miss Walters. You have visited their rooms. You have even taken them into your own home. Suppose *those* private indiscretions should become public knowledge? Or even become known to your political opponents?'

"Mr. Gladstone's equanimity was only slightly ruffled under this assault. 'Indeed, gentlemen, working to reclaim our fallen sisters is a calling to which the Almighty led me early on. Since our blessed union, my dear wife has encouraged and assisted me in these endeavours. We guide unfortunate women back to a more-Godly path, and we have had remarkable successes! Why, one of our protégés is celebrated nowadays as an evangelist! Another (he could not repress a snigger) had her portrait painted as *Beatrice.*' [15]

"'Oh, I suppose,' he airily admitted, 'that I would suffer some embarrassment if my work was widely known, but I can assure you that my Liberal colleagues have long been aware of it. In fact (here his eyes took on a rheumy gleam), they have recently entreated me to desist in my good works, lest our Conservative opponents – as you two seem to threaten – set spies upon me and report my "indiscretions" to the Queen! In consequence, the Lord has allowed me to postpone my task of reclamation. Until Home Rule is passed, I shall not walk London's streets again.' The Prime Minister gazed upon us with benign contempt, stroking the feline that lay purring in his lap. 'Given that decision, gentlemen,' he added smilingly, 'it seems to me that you have no cards left to play!'

"However, Mr. Gladstone had underestimated my ally from Whitehall. 'One card more, Prime Minister,' he answered softly. 'Those of us who work behind the scenes are aware that your moral ascendancy over the present Cabinet remains unchallenged. But what, sir, becomes of that ascendancy when your colleagues learn that the leader of their party (a man they have venerated as the pillar of virtue he so oft proclaims himself to be) is, instead, *a common blackmailer* who whips himself after consorting with streetwalkers, in order to resist a vice most men outgrow as schoolboys? Your continued leadership, it seems to *me*, sir, would then become not only untenable but ludicrous!'

"The 'Grand Old Man' turned crimson and leapt from his chair, as the black cat fled in indignation. 'What spies have *you* set upon me, sir?' he hissed to my companion. 'No man knows of my life-long struggle against sin who has not read my private diaries!'

"Both of us regarded him impassively as he slowly sat again, and from that moment it was a simple matter to conclude a settlement of the affair. Perhaps because he was so shocked, our host seemed not to realise that Skittles' revelations had led to his defeat. In obedience to our demand, Mr. Gladstone provided the address of the young man in the photograph. We promised, in return, not to inform Lord Hartington that his long-time political leader had set out to blackmail him. That promise, Watson, we faithfully have kept. Sadly for Prime Minister, however, he forgot to ask us not to tell the Duchess!"

After we laughed merrily at his account's conclusion, I said to Sherlock Holmes that one day I should like to meet his contact in Whitehall.

"One day, Doctor, perhaps you shall. But now I must appeal to Mrs. Hudson, for we are to entertain more visitors this afternoon. A lady and two gentlemen."

"The Duchess is returning?" I surmised.

"No, I was referring to Miss Walters." He seemed a bit abashed at having done so.

""Then one of the gentlemen is, I presume, her son?"

"Quite so, and the other is his father. That, you recall, was the bargain Miss Walters made with us. You know, Watson," he added in a sudden inspiration, "I really think that on this occasion we might ask Mrs. Hudson to serve tea."

And so events transpired. Skittles arrived first, shortly followed by a tall, fair-haired, youth who shyly greeted us in French. Our landlady had kindly lent her downstairs parlour for their joyous reunion, and there we left them to talk privately for half-an-hour before Lord Hartington arrived.

I looked forward to meeting the Whig magnate, whose political reputation, until the recent crisis, had undeniably been mixed. "The serious son of a respectable duke," as one opponent sneeringly described him, the Marquess's habitual lethargy led to comparisons to a boa constrictor or Rip Van Winkle. [16] Yet, because it was still impossible (as one wag noted) to form a Cabinet without peers in it, Hartington had held office for over twenty years and even, during Gladstone's brief retirement, served as Liberal leader. Obviously, the wealth he would inherit could explain Skittles' attraction to the man, but so shrewd an observer as the Duchess of Manchester had also seen more in the young Marquess than ostensibly was there. Eventually, she had found her faith rewarded. After the Prime Minister's sudden conversion to Home Rule, Lord Hartington had opposed the measure, both in the House and in the country, with an energy and power few people had believed him to possess. More than that of any other speaker, his oratory had been responsible for bringing Mr. Gladstone's latest crusade down.

His Lordship's visit to 221b Baker Street, however, began inauspiciously. We heard Mrs. Hudson calling worriedly from the staircase, "Not *that* way, sir. It's the door behind you, to the left." That door opened to reveal a tall, bearded aristocrat of middle age, who stared as though uncertain how he had arrived there. Barring a pendulous lower lip and an air of slightly vacant boredom, he was still a handsome man. My friend stepped forward and introduced the two of us, but the Marquess seemed singularly unimpressed. Ambling to the fireplace, he lit a cigar and mumbled incoherently behind it, "What's all this, then, gentlemen?"

A timid knock sounded on the hallway door, and Holmes smiled faintly as he turned to open it. When Hartington saw the person standing there, his entire demeanour altered. From that moment, I doubt he was aware that Sherlock Holmes and I were in the room.

"Hullo, Skitsy."

"*Hello,* Cav!" With a little squeal of happiness, she rushed and threw herself into his arms, and we saw, if only for an instant, the girl she once had been.

The Marquess guffawed and kissed her soundly. "So, little Skitz, you did not join a convent, after all? I told you that one should never suit you."

"No, Cav, but I did spend a few weeks there all the same. Do you remember the last time I came to Matlock, while you were at Chatsworth visiting the Duke?"

"Indeed. I came to your hotel, but in the end you would not see me."

"No, for by then it was too late to hide the truth. I feared you would decide you had to tell your father. So I hid myself in a nunnery in Paris, and it was there that I left our son."

She turned towards the young man who had entered silently behind her, and who now bashfully stepped forward into view. His Lordship stared for a long moment before moving to examine him.

"Humph. . . ." he rumbled, reaching to turn the boy's face this way and that. "Yes, he has the Cavendishes' Habsburg lip, poor lad, and something of my sleepiness about him. Well, well! So what Gladstone's letter said was true. How curious."

"Oh, Cav," cried Skittles, "you must not believe that I had anything to do with *that*. I knew nothing at all of the old *roué*'s letter! And I did not know our boy had come to England until the day before you knew yourself."

Lord Hartington patted her arm gently. "Don't fret, dear girl, it doesn't matter." Smiling quizzically behind his beard, he turned back to his irregular descendent and said gruffly, "Hullo, youngster."

"*Bonjour, Papa,*" young Emile stammered. "My English . . . is not good."

"That's alright, my boy. No use in a lot of blather. Now, then, Skitsy," the Marquess assured Emile's mother, "I should like to help you with this fellow. We must extend your allowance to cover his expenses."

"Oh, no, Cav," replied Skittles stoutly. "You are generous enough the way it is, and Emile and I have other means. Our son has prospects of his own, don't you, Emile?"

"*Oui, Maman.*"

"Very well, lad, but should the need arise you must not hesitate to ask me." Fondly, he smiled again at Skittles. "*You* never did in the old days, you know!"

"Things have changed now," his former mistress answered primly.

"Indeed they have." Lord Hartington shook his head, perhaps recalling happy times. "Well, dear Skitz," he sighed, "I must be off. The old man has resigned at last, and Salisbury has asked me to head a coalition ministry. I must go and let him know that I cannot accept, although I should have liked to." Stifling a massive yawn, he tossed his cigar into the hearth. "What a deuced bore!"

"Am I not to see you now and then, Cav?"

"No, little girl, it would not do. I have responsibilities to certain people now, you know, who were not there when we were young."

"Oh, I know about *her!*" Skittles pouted prettily. Nevertheless, she smiled at her old lover, kissing him sweetly in farewell.

His Lordship shook Emile's hand. "So long, my boy. I doubt that we shall meet again, but I shall follow your doings with great interest, and you have my blessing, now and always. I never thought that I should have a son, you know," he added softly, and I was surprised to see a tear upon the hairy cheek.

After giving his "pretty horsebreaker" one last embrace, the Marquess of Hartington nodded absently to us and took his leave, off to decline the office – but fulfill the role – his Duchess had ordained for him.

"Now, *there* was a real lady!" Mrs. Hudson noted happily when Skittles and her son had gone. "I must congratulate you, Mr. Holmes, on attracting a better class of clients lately. Except that boorish fellow with the beard," she grumbled as she removed the tea service. "I can't imagine *he'll* amount to much!"

It soon became evident that our landlady was both right and wrong in her prediction. "Holmes," I called a few days later, while my friend was dressing in his bedroom, "let me read you this article from the *Pall Mall Gazette*: '*Lord Salisbury,*' it begins, '*is to be in office, but Lord Hartington is to be in power. By externally supporting, instead of joining, the Conservatives, his Liberal Unionists control the balance in the House and maintain the Unionist alliance. Yet, their independent stance still holds out the prospect of Liberal reunion, whenever Mr. Gladstone surrenders to the disabilities of age.'* [17] To me, such an outcome seems eminently satisfactory for all concerned – except, perhaps, one lady."

"No doubt," admitted the detective, "but I foresee some danger in denying Ireland's aspirations. Should Great Britain become involved in war with a Continental power, we may find another enemy at our own backs. If that war comes, Watson, we may live to rue the day that Mr. Gladstone failed in his attempt to free the Irish. [18] Meanwhile," he added philosophically, "one can only hope that the Duchess is not *too* disappointed."

Her Grace soon reassured my friend upon this point. A week later, there arrived at our lodgings a handsome case that bore the ducal arms of Manchester. Inside it lay a diamond stickpin, beside a note of thanks addressed to Holmes. In later years, after two inconvenient peers had belatedly removed themselves, the formidable lady married the new Duke of Devonshire and began her long-awaited reign over society as "The Double Duchess." Her reign outlasted King Edward's by a year. Skittles – remarkably, perhaps – is still living as I write. [19]

Following this case, I noticed that Sherlock Holmes began to exhibit a more tolerant and, on occasion, even appreciative view of the fair sex. It would not be long, of course, until the detective met "The Woman" who fulfilled his ideal and soon eclipsed all others in his eyes. Yet, it seemed to me that the essential change had come the year before. [20] Shortly after we had bade farewell to Skittles, my friend approached me, with some diffidence, to ask whether he might serve as best man in my wedding. Later, when my first marriage brought only loneliness and tragedy, Holmes reacted with both sympathy and a new understanding, ensuring not only that our once-endangered friendship would survive, but that it would deepen and endure for the remainder of our lives.

NOTES

1. Watson told of his time in America during 1884-1886 in "A Ghost from Christmas Past". This story was published in *The MX Book of New Sherlock Holmes Stories – Part VII: Eliminate the Impossible*, edited by David Marcum (London: MX Publishing, 2017), pp. 130-152. It later appeared, paired with an interpretive painting by artist Nune Asatryan, in *The Art of Sherlock Holmes: West Palm Beach Edition,* curated by Phil Growick (London: MX Publishing, 2019), pp. 196-211.
2. Montagu is the family name of the Dukes of Manchester and Cavendish, the family name of the Dukes of Devonshire. Spencer Compton Cavendish (1833-1908), later Eighth Duke, was known at this time by his courtesy title, Marquess of Hartington. Ostensibly a commoner while his father was alive, Hartington was eligible to sit in the House of Commons. It was from that location that he conducted the most important phase of his political career.
3. After the Liberals' defeat in 1874, Gladstone professed to withdraw as party leader. Lord Hartington assumed that duty in the House of Commons, and Lord Granville in the Lords. However, such was "The Grand Old Man's" popularity with "middle-class Liberal opinion" that even in retirement his shadow loomed ominously over his colleagues at Westminster. "*Gladstone had only to speak and the country would listen and respond.*" Invited to stand for the Scottish constituency of Midlothian in 1879, he launched "*a string of speeches against Disraeli's government [that] galvanized the country.*" This sudden resurgence rendered Hartington's position untenable as party leader, for Gladstone refused to accept a subordinate office in 1880 when the Liberals returned to power. Reluctantly, therefore, the Marquess declined Queen Victoria's offer to form a government. Her Majesty was left with a Prime Minister whom she despised, and Lord Hartington (whose lack of political ambition has been overstated) with what a less phlegmatic man would have regarded as a grievance. See Henry Vane's *Affair of State: A Biography of the 8th Duke and Duchess of Devonshire* (London: Peter Owen Publishers, 2004), pp. 109-130.
4. In May of 1882, during a period of more than usual unrest in Ireland, Prime Minister Gladstone sent Lord Frederick Cavendish (Hartington's younger brother and his own nephew by marriage) to serve as Chief Secretary to the new Viceroy, Lord Spencer. On the evening he arrived in Dublin, Lord Frederick was stabbed to death, along with his undersecretary, Thomas Burke, by Irish terrorists in Phoenix Park. The leader of the Irish Parliamentary party, Charles Stewart Parnell (just out of prison after agreeing with the government to curb agrarian violence in return for reform) was horrified and repudiated the murderers. As the Duchess's "glass house" remark indicates, Parnell's own vulnerability in sexual matters made him an unlikely blackmailer. When his long-time affair with the married Kitty O'Shea was finally revealed in 1890, Gladstone quickly disavowed his Irish ally, and the cause of Home Rule was significantly damaged.

5. Before his father succeeded to the dukedom, Spencer Compton Cavendish's title was Lord Cavendish. Instead of Hartington, he was usually called "Cav" or "Cavendish" within the family, the same name Skittles calls him here.
6. Although Watson does not specify the convent, it was most likely the Refuge Sainte Anne, founded in 1854 by Victoire-Thérèse Chupin (the "*Bonne Mère*"). By the time of Skittles' residence, it was located in the Parisian suburb of Clichy de Garenne and overseen by the Dominican Order. For more information on this Refuge, see Ann Dring Daughtry's Ph.D. dissertation, "Convent Refuges for Disgraced Girls and Women in Nineteenth-Century France" (University of Adelaide, 1991), available online at: *https://digital.library.adelaide.edu.au/dspace/bitstream/2440/19593/1/01front.pdf.*
7. The diplomat and poet Wilfrid Scawen Blunt (1840-1922). Skittles' account of their affair is verified in Maggie McNeill's blog "The Honest Courtesan" (April 18, 2013) at: *https://maggiemcneill.wordpress.com/2013/04/18/skittles/*
8. According to *The Times* (December 24, 2006), the Prime Minister visited Skittles in May 1885, although they may first have met at an earlier time. On this occasion, "*Gladstone marvelled at the smallness of her waist and then, according to her account, tested the size 'by manual measurement'.*" The meeting is confirmed in other sources cited in this story. *https://www.staylace.com/gallery/gallery05/index_personages.html*
9. An apparent reference to Henry Labouchère (1831-1912), English journalist, diplomat, Radical politician, and gadfly, who noticed that "*Gladstone manages to combine his missionary meddling with a keen appreciation of a pretty face. He has never been known to rescue any of our East End whores. . . .*" See Anne Isba's *Gladstone and Women* (London: Hambledon Continuum, 2006), p. 115.
10. In fact, it was to avoid the vice of masturbation that Gladstone flogged himself. Lest the reader conclude that Watson is indulging in pornography, the eventual publication of Gladstone's private diaries confirmed Skittles' tale. For an analysis of his forty-year crusade to redeem prostitutes and master his own passions, see Chapter 6 (pp. 99-121) of Isba, cited above.
11. To quote Labouchère again, he believed that Skittles "*must be the only whore in history to retain her heart intact*" (Vane, *Affair of State*, p. 58), at least until numerous successors had theirs encased in gold. Her discretion was so appreciated by the Cavendish family that the Ninth Duke of Devonshire continued her allowance even after his predecessor (Skittles' "Cav") died in 1908. Skittles retained her house in South Street, Mayfair until her own death in 1920.
12. In fact, Hartington supported significant concessions to Ireland, short of Home Rule. They included local self-government through county councils, a tax-funded buyout of the landed classes to enable Irish peasants to purchase their own land, and (at least by 1887) sub-national assemblies in both Dublin and Belfast. His objection to Gladstone's 1886 Home Rule bill was that it

would have handed Ireland over to a united Irish Parliament under Parnell, with no protection for Ulster's Protestant minority or the safeguard of Irish representation at Westminster. Had Gladstone resigned after his bill's defeat, or had Hartington later accepted leadership of a Unionist coalition, one historian believes he might have become "the man who solved the Irish problem." See Vane, pp. 165-166, and Barry Howard Rosen, "The Political Influence of the Eighth Duke of Devonshire in the 1880s" (Ph.D. dissertation, University of South Carolina, 1974), pp. 292ff.

13. At a later stage in his career, Lord Hartington played a role in helping the British Empire to catch up. The Hartington Commission (1888-1890) laid the foundation for the unified system of imperial defense that emerged before the First World War. Although not all of his commission's recommendations were immediately implemented, Hartington (by then Duke of Devonshire) chaired a cabinet committee in Lord Salisbury's third administration that served – albeit inefficiently – as a precursor of the modern Ministry of Defence. The editor's Ph.D. dissertation, "Chairman of an Aulic Council: The Eighth Duke of Devonshire and British Imperial Defence, 1895-1903" (Thomas A. Turley, Vanderbilt University, 1985) dealt with this arcane topic.
14. Even the Prime Minister's daughter worried that the publication of these letters in the press would give "'*the whole world (and no wonder) a mistaken impression' of her father's mental condition . . . . '[E]ach was dashed off without reflection, in the heat of the moment'.*" Philip Magnus, *Gladstone: A Biography* (New York: E.P. Dutton & Co., Inc., 1964), pp. 359-360.
15. Gladstone speaks of Laura (Bell) Thistlethwayte and Marian Summerhayes, whom he met in the 1850's and 1860's. See Isba, pp. 112-114, as well as Mrs. Thistlethwayte's *Wikipedia* entry, for the details. The artist who painted Miss Summerhayes as Beatrice was the Scottish Pre-Raphaelite William Dyce.
16. Joseph Chamberlain, Hartington's Radical rival, made the "serious son" and "Rip Van Winkle" quips a year before joining him in leaving Gladstone's Liberal government in 1886. The Conservative gadfly Lord Randolph Churchill compared the Marquess to a boa.
17. Beyond the astute first line quoted, Watson evidently paraphrased *The Gazette*'s issue of July 26, 1886. In his letter to Salisbury of July 24, Hartington explained his reasons for declining the Premiership. First, he recognized that any coalition "*resting mainly on the support of 320 Conservatives*" would be regarded as a Conservative administration in all but name. Moreover, Salisbury's refusal to include Chamberlain in a Hartington ministry might persuade the Radical wing of the Liberal Unionists to revert to Gladstone, thus endangering the Unionist majority. The Marquess persisted in his refusal even when pressed again to become Prime Minister after Randolph Churchill's resignation. Negotiations to reunite the Liberal party failed in 1887. Only in 1895, after Gladstone had retired for good with the defeat of his second Home Rule bill, did Devonshire, Chamberlain, and other Liberal Unionists join Lord Salisbury's

third administration. Besides the sources already cited, see Patrick Jackson's *The Last of the Whigs: A Political Biography of Lord Hartington, Later Eighth Duke of Devonshire* (1833-1908) (London and Toronto: Associated University Presses, Inc., 1994), pp. 246-248.

18. Holmes's prescience was sadly accurate, as shown by the 1916 Easter Rising, two years after Home Rule had been passed, but shelved for the duration of the First World War.
19. Dr. Watson's comment dates this story as written before Skittles' death on August 4, 1920.
20. The Canon dates "A Scandal in Bohemia" as occurring in March 1888. However, as Watson would admit in a tale that he wrote in 1928 that it actually took place almost a year earlier. Nor was Irene Adler's faithless king Bohemian! Here, the Doctor evidently recalled the true year of Holmes and Adler's meeting, not the subterfuge he had concocted for "Bohemia." His replacement for that story, "A Scandal in Serbia," appears in *The MX Book of New Sherlock Holmes Stories, Part VI: 2017 Annual*, edited by David Marcum (London: MX Publishing, 2017), pp. 545-572.

The Gordon Square Discovery
by David Marcum

Many of Sherlock Holmes's investigations were handled quickly, but that never made them any less interesting to the student of his methods. Today I was reminded of this after reading in the newspaper of the untimely passing of someone who was peripherally associated with one of his past cases. This led me to reminisce about those days before my marriage when I was still residing in Baker Street, and I was moved to pull down my journal for that year. However, rather than immediately refreshing my memory concerning that specific series of events, I found myself lingering over recollections of this-and-that other previous adventure, glad that I had made such extensive notes when I had the opportunity.

Turning the pages, I recalled the vivid dilemma related to the disquieting observations of the funeral mute, and Holmes's quick thinking which had saved an old woman from an unhealthy marriage. And then there was the curious narrative of the four-fingered Methodist, which featured so widely in the press of the time. Holmes's demonstration of the charlatan's Bible and what was hidden in it had been a sensation – and both objects ended up going straight into Scotland Yard's unofficial Black Museum.

Each of these were solved within hours of being brought to Holmes's attention. Another, that related to the mystery associated with Lord St. Simon's marriage, was started and finished within one rainy October afternoon and evening, and that case led to a second investigation that (for the most part) also took little more than a day – although with more tragic results.

It had been after nine o'clock the previous night that Holmes had returned from his investigations into the missing wife of Lord St. Simon. His efforts had proceeded quite quickly. Holmes's involvement began in mid-afternoon when the nobleman had arrived to seek my friend's help in relation to the mystery that had been upon everyone's lips for the previous week. That day I had remained indoors, as heavy rains were being thrown against the window and the strong winds were occasionally finding their way down our chimney. I see from reviewing my journal that I was suffering particularly from my Afghan wound, in spite of it having occurred over half-a-decade earlier.

Holmes, however, had been quite active, as he had six or eight matters on hand at the time. His preferred to let some of them cook slowly, so to speak, while others progressed at a naturally accelerated pace. He had made mention that one such was complete, involving a curious furniture van associated with Grosvenor Square, and that he would be ready soon to reveal the true facts to the authorities. From this, our conversation moved to a letter that he'd received that morning from Lord St. Simon, regarding his new bride, the former Hattie Doran, American heiress, who had vanished during their wedding breakfast on the past Wednesday. Now a full week later, suspecting foul play and disgusted with the failed efforts of the official police, the groom requested – nay, *required* – an appointment with the private consulting detective.

Lord St. Simon arrived at four o'clock and told his story within a few minutes. The small marriage had gone off as planned. Later, during the wedding breakfast at the bride's father's home near Lancaster Gate, the new bride, following some conversation with her maid, had walked across the street into Hyde Park and vanished. She had last been seen then in the company of one of St. Simon's former female acquaintances, Flora Miller, who was now being held by the police, but it was uncertain as to whether the woman was actually involved in the bride's disappearance. Upon questioning, the nobleman could only add that his new wife had been in good spirits until immediately after the ceremony, when she suddenly seemed distracted. In fact, a change had come over her as she was leaving the church, when she curiously dropped her bouquet, which was then retrieved for her by a man in a nearby pew, apparently one of the many loiterers who turn up to watch strangers' weddings and funerals as a form of entertainment.

After Lord St. Simon's departure, we were joined almost immediately by Inspector Lestrade, in a pea-jacket as a concession to the terrible weather outside. He had been investigating the case with the idea that the bride, somehow lured from the wedding breakfast, had been murdered. He exhibited a wedding dress and appurtenances that had been found by a park-keeper, floating in the Serpentine, whose upper end was near the bride's father's house. Inside one of the dress pockets was a card-case that identified the owner as the missing Hattie Doran, along with a note stating "*You will see me when all is ready. Come at once. F. H. M.*" on one side and "*Oct. 4th, rooms 8s., breakfast 2s. 6d., cocktail 1s., lunch 2s. 6d., glass sherry, 8d.*" on the other. Lestrade felt that the initials added further evidence against the woman in custody, Flora Miller, but Holmes seemed to find great interest in the note for other unexplained reasons, to Lestrade's vexation. My friend was amused at some of the official policeman's notions, while Lestrade – who hadn't yet learned to trust

Holmes in those days quite as much as he would in later years – left thinking that Holmes was on the wrong track. After the inspector's withdrawal, his evidence bundled under his arm, Holmes also departed around five o'clock, and I didn't see him again until after nine.

However, those four hours did have a bit of excitement when, less than an hour later, a caterer arrived, laying out a meal fit for a nobleman, if not a king. Cold woodcock, and a pheasant. A *pâté de foie gras* pie – never my favorite – along with a grouping of bottles that seemed to be of very dear vintage indeed. Mrs. Hudson had followed the confectioner's man up the stairs, alternating between curiosity and a few comments of her own about sensible cooking being good enough for anyone. Then they were both gone, and I had several hours to fill, attempting to read both the newspapers and a recently acquired novel, but finding instead my thoughts returning again and again to Lord St. Simon's problem, and Holmes's seeming understanding of the solution based simply upon hearing the specifics of the events. (Additionally, the pervasive scent of the food was an ongoing distraction.)

At nine o'clock Holmes returned, looking approvingly at the little supper and seemingly happy to have arrived before the guests that he'd invited while he was out. I commented that he must have done so nearly first thing, as the food had arrived within an hour of his departure. He waved a hand dismissively, stating vaguely that the solution had been obvious to him before he left, and that his efforts since then had simply been to verify a few specifics – such as where to offer his invitation. I was about to ask who else would be joining us when Lord St. Simon arrived, sinking into the same chair that he'd occupied just a few hours earlier and bemoaning his misfortune in a most un-Lord-like manner. Apparently he had received a message from Holmes relating the solution to the problem – although I myself was still in the dark.

Yet all was soon revealed when there was a ring at the bell, and within a few moments a man and woman entered our modest sitting room.

Introduced as Mr. and Mrs. Francis Hay Moulton – the *F.H.M.* of the note found in the abandoned wedding dress – it became quickly apparent from the lady's solicitation as to Lord St. Simon's welfare that this was his missing bride, the American girl that he had met and married after traveling to the United States earlier that year. She was beautiful, in a rather coarse way. Clearly she had spent a great deal of her formative years out-of-doors, and she moved with a confident power that indicated she'd had no hesitation at helping her father with the physical labor that had been required as he made his fortunes in the gold field. She offered her hand to me in a forthright and modern American way, and I was surprised to find that her grip was strong and her palm rough, and covered with not-a-few callosities.

Moulton seemed just as toughened as his wife, although he was shorter than her, and wiry. He had a sharp face and darting eyes, looking quickly from person to person. He was clean-shaven and burned by the sun – quite unusual to see during a rainy October in London.

Mrs. Moulton quickly explained that two years before, long before she'd ever heard of Lord St. Simon, she had impulsively married the man at her side, but had later believed that he'd died after reading in the newspaper that he'd been killed in an Indian attack while on a prospecting trip. In fact, Moulton hadn't died, but instead had been grievously wounded. When he was finally able to return to civilization, it was as a rich man, but only to learn that his new wife of only a few days, believing herself to be a widow, had since agreed to marry a British nobleman. She and her father had come to England the previous summer, and Moulton had followed. Uncertain as to his wife's feelings after his prolonged absence, he didn't immediately reveal that he was still alive, but rather sat in the pew at her wedding. She had seen him and was momentarily startled, dropping her bouquet. Moulton retrieved it for her and slipped a note inside. Afterwards, she had abandoned Lord St. Simon during the wedding breakfast, walking into Hyde Park. She had been momentarily approached by Flora Miller then, the woman currently under arrest, but they'd only had the briefest of conversations before Miss Doran had joined Moulton, her true husband and love.

After tracking them down, Holmes had arranged the little supper in the hopes that hurt feelings could be mended, but Lord St. Simon was having none of it, instead preferring to depart immediately, with no wish to celebrate the reunion of the apparently happy couple. And who could blame him? He walked out with all the dignity that he could muster, leaving Holmes and me to share the meal with the Moultons.

It was quite interesting, especially hearing of Moulton's adventures in the American West. Holmes and I had travelled there in days past, both separately and then later when involved in various investigations, so some of what was related to us wasn't unknown. Moulton finished up one of his anecdotes and took a sip of wine. He had maintained a certain reserve throughout the evening. His wife, however, had treated the little gathering as something of a celebration. She clearly felt that the revelations were liberating, and she made free use of the contents of the various bottles.

Early on it was apparent that she was becoming rather inebriated, and Holmes had stopped offering to refill our glasses. However, that was meaningless to an American heiress raised in the rough western gold fields. She simply stood and opened the next bottle for herself, and proceeded to finish it on her own over the next hour or so as the rest of us declined.

It was after some comment related to one of Holmes's past cases that she said, "Of course, we've had own little mystery as well."

Moulton frowned and made as if to speak, but Holmes leaned forward and said, "What sort of mystery?"

Moulton waved his hand dismissively at what she'd said, a look of irritation on his face. His wife, seeing his expression, frowned slightly, and then, in what seemed to be typical willfulness, continued to pursue the matter. "The letters," she prompted. "Tell him about the letters."

Moulton's lips tightened. "It's nothing. Hattie, you're drunk."

She turned up her glass and finished what was left before reaching out to the bottle beside her. Finding it empty, she said, "I suppose that I know what is and isn't *nothing*." Then she looked at Holmes. "There was a problem at the hotel. After I walked out on Robert and joined Frank, we went to his house in Gordon Square, but after a day or so, I felt like the walls were closing in, so we went to the Metropole, where Frank had stayed when he first came to London. At first we had no reason to complain, but we returned from an outing one night to find that our room had been searched, and some of Frank's papers were missing."

"What sort of papers?" asked Holmes. I kept my eye on Moulton, who was poised as if he might spring to his feet to silence his wife. And yet, he did nothing except watch her intently.

"A few letters," she continued. "Nothing important, but Frank dearly hated to lose them. It was obvious that his case had been tampered with. I saw it as soon as we came back. We called for the manager, and he agreed with me completely, but Frank begged that he keep from involving the police."

Holmes turned to Moulton. "Is that true? You didn't summon the authorities?"

The American's mouth was tight. "Of course. As much as I hated my letters being stolen, Hattie and I didn't exactly want to come to the attention of the officials. Instead, we packed up and moved back yesterday morning to the house that I'd already leased in Gordon Square – where you tracked us earlier today. Since then, I've been considering what to do about getting my letters back, as I don't trust the hotel's efforts." He took another sip of wine and set the empty glass on the table.

"But Frank," said his wife, with a rather vindictive smile on her face, as if she had found a way to frustrate him. I had to question the future success of this marriage if it was already so important for her to score points off of her husband so soon. "Maybe it's luck that Mr. Holmes came knocking on our door. He can help us now, and after all, we don't have to be cagey anymore about who we are." She looked at Holmes. "Would you look into this for us? I'd be very grateful if you could retrieve Frank's letters." Then her eyes darted toward Moulton again to see his reaction.

Her husband's face darkened and he started to speak – he clearly didn't like the idea. I could see that the letters themselves had ceased to be important. Instead, they and Holmes's involvement were being used to see who would have leverage in the marriage. I doubted that this couple would remain happy for very long.

Holmes was certainly aware of this, observing what I had seen, but he apparently found no need to soothe these troubled waters. He nodded. "I'll be happy to look into it," he said, "but more information will be useful. Was anything else taken? Any other papers? Or jewelry or other valuables?"

"No," said Mrs. Moulton. "Only the letters."

Holmes looked toward Frank Moulton. "Do you have any idea why the letters would have caused any special interest?"

"None," he growled. "They're simply routine correspondence. There is no need to pursue this."

"Did the hotel manager have any explanation?" asked Holmes, ignoring the man's objections. "Any suspicions as to how your room was entered, or who could have been responsible?"

Moulton looked at his wife. "It did seem as if the manager had an idea about that. Hattie noticed it."

She nodded. "He called in his assistant, and they whispered for a minute. The assistant said something about 'Vernham' being on duty earlier that afternoon, and the manager nodded as if that made some kind of sense to him – as if they'd expected something like this to happen, and now here it was."

"And did they summon this Vernham to be questioned?" asked Holmes.

"He'd apparently already gone for the day," replied Moulton, somewhat surly, but relaxing a bit now that his resistance to Holmes's involvement had been overcome. "They assured me – us – that they would follow up, and that they would send Vernham a message immediately."

"And what happened? Did he respond?"

"We asked late that night, and there hadn't been an answer. He isn't due back to work until tomorrow, so the manager said that nothing more could be done until he could be questioned. I asked why they hadn't sent someone to his house, but they acted as if that weren't possible. Then I wanted his address so that I could go around and see him myself, but they wouldn't give it to me.

"At that point, I became disgusted with their handling of the situation, and that's when I decided to decamp back to Gordon Square. I sent a message around to the hotel this morning, asking if there were any developments, but they were vague – just that they still hadn't heard from Vernham. Then you came knocking at our door, so I haven't had a chance to see if anything else has happened."

Moulton leaned forward. "What Hattie said – about you investigating . . . There isn't any need. You understand? It's just some missing letters. I'll take care of it."

Beside him, his wife started to speak, but Moulton had had enough. He stood and turned quickly toward her, moving with the foot-work of a nimble bare-knuckle fighter. She started, leaning back in her chair, and with a suddenly sober – and rather wary – expression on her face. She seemed to understand that she was dangerously close to pushing her husband too far.

I stood, intending to prevent the American from further threatening the woman. I was already worried for her during the rest of the evening after they left our presence. Holmes rose smoothly to his feet, taking a step forward to diffuse the situation. "I understand, Mr. Moulton. I'm sure that the hotel staff will resolve the situation. And now, I wish you both a very good evening. I understand that the weather will be clearing tonight, so tomorrow should be a more pleasant day for all of us."

Moulton looked over his shoulder, as if for a short period he'd forgotten where he was, or that Holmes and I were there. For a moment, he and his wife had shared a look that conveyed volumes.

But soon after that they departed, with the couple considerably and curiously more tense than they had been upon arriving to face Lord St. Simon. After they were gone, I expressed my concern to Holmes, and he nodded in agreement. Then I asked if he wanted something else to drink, and he opted for a small whisky. I joined him, feeling the need to cleanse my palate from the rather unpleasant couple.

We sat for a while, and Holmes spent the first few minutes explaining to me how he had traced them, based on the writing on the back of the piece of paper found in the card case. The prices shown had clearly been from an expensive hotel which turned out to be the Hotel Metropole in Northumberland Avenue, which Holmes had found after just a few tries. He had learned at the front desk that they'd recently moved back to their rented lodgings at 226 Gordon Square in Bloomsbury, and it was there that he'd gone and convinced them that it would be better to tell the truth about what had happened to the unfortunate bridegroom.

Recalling Lord St. Simon's departure after he heard their story, I remarked, "His conduct was certainly not very gracious."

"Ah, Watson, perhaps you would not be very gracious either, if, after all the trouble of wooing and wedding, you found yourself deprived in an instant of wife and of fortune. I think that we may judge Lord St. Simon very mercifully and thank our stars that we are never likely to find ourselves in the same position." He set aside his pipe and said, "Draw your chair up and hand me my violin, for the only problem we have still to solve is how to while away these bleak autumnal evenings."

He played for a while, something mournful to fit the rainy night, reflective of the turn which the evening had taken, and perhaps as well the sad ending for Lord St. Simon's hopes of marriage and dowry. Then he allowed the instrument to fall silent. I could see that a thought had occurred to him. "It doesn't quite ring true," he said in response to my query.

"What?"

"Something about Mr. Moulton's reaction."

"They are two strong-willed people who barely know one another, and haven't seen each other in years – after an impulsive and secret mining-camp wedding. He didn't like it when she asserted her own ideas about asking you to look for the letters."

"No, that isn't it. I mean his reaction towards the hotel."

I frowned. "I would be upset if I found that my possessions had been searched and looted while supposedly safely secured in my room at a noted hotel."

"And yet, why depart? Why not stay there, where you could more easily harass the management to investigate the matter?"

"He felt that they could no longer be trusted."

"Possibly. But if he was worried about protecting whatever else he has that might be of value, he could have found a way to lock it up in a better way than simply leaving it in his room – placing it in the Metropole's safe, for instance, or even by making a temporary arrangement at a local bank. No, there's something about these letters that goes beyond a man simply being angry that he was victimized in this way. And then there's the question of the Gordon Square house."

"What do you mean?"

"They were supposed to be in hiding. Gordon Square was a better choice than a busy hotel. As you know, the Square consists of rows of rather standard houses surrounding the park, north of the University. There's nothing special about them – why not remain there? Yet they returned to the Hotel Metropole soon after their reunion – even as all of London speculated as to the woman's mysterious disappearance and her current whereabouts. She had become quite well-known in recent weeks as interest in the wedding of a British Lord to an American heiress reached a fever peak in the press. Her image has appeared in a number of journals. Surely there was the danger that she would be recognized."

I laughed. "Clearly you aren't taking into account the persuasive ways of a woman. And incidentally, as I recall, you asked me to brief you this morning before St. Simon's arrival, claiming that you knew nothing about the matter, and stating that you only read the criminal news and the agony columns. It seems that you knew enough after all to be aware of the capitol's rising interest in Hattie Doran."

He smiled in return. "Perhaps I did have somewhat more knowledge of the affair then I let on – although I didn't pay too much attention as the weeks leading to the wedding went by, little realizing that we would be peripherally involved. In any case, my point is that a great many people *did* know about Hattie Doran, and what she looked like, and later about her disappearance. The papers have maintained speculation as to her fate at a frenzied level for nearly a week now – and yet, I repeat that Moulton had no hesitation at returning with this notable woman to a very public hotel for several days – dining and shopping with her, and generally doing the opposite of hiding until they could arrange to leave the country. Only when his supposedly unimportant letters were taken did they move, the very next day, back to Gordon Square. Before his letters were taken, he apparently had no concerns about traipsing all over London with his noteworthy bride. Yet this afternoon when I knocked on the Gordon Square door, he answered with a pistol in his hand."

I raised an eyebrow. "Indeed."

"I simply put it down at the time to him being an American from the same rough life where his wife originated. As we learned, that was true – they had met in the same mining camp where Mrs. Moulton was residing with her father. I could see from the second that Moulton opened the door that he was a toughened American. Of course you noticed that he was armed tonight as well?"

I had to confess that I had not observed it.

"It was a small weapon, but effective nonetheless. Now possibly, but not very likely, he came here with a gun because he feared some sort of violent reaction from Lord St. Simon, although I doubt it. He would have sized him up as being no threat. He was already nervous when he answered the door in Gordon Square this afternoon, but he was comfortable and confident when he arrived our sitting room tonight. Clearly he was worried about something out there, and not what he'd find in here – including a jilted bridegroom. I wonder if he's gone about armed since his arrival in London. From what I was able to ascertain, he didn't seem to show any fear *before* his letters were stolen . . . ."

His musings trailed off, and I could only assume that he was considering what might be in those supposedly innocent letters. Seeing that he intended to think – and likely smoke – for a goodly portion of the rest of the night, I wished him well and went upstairs to my room, hoping that both the weather and the pain from my old Army wound would be more agreeable in the morning.

The new day promised to be much different than the previous one, when we had been beset by the equinoctial autumn gales. The sky was a brilliant blue, and there was a decided coolness to the air, encouraging one to feel both brisk and vital. I found that despite the change in the weather, the pain from the Jezail fragment still resting in my shoulder, a constant souvenir of my time in Afghanistan, remained in evidence, although greatly lessened.

I descended from my bedroom to find that Holmes had already started his breakfast. He nodded in my direction without speaking, his attention focused on one of the morning newspapers. This silent companionship lasted until he he rose, remarking "Your shoulder is still bothering you, I see."

It was no great deduction upon his part, as he'd observed these symptoms many times before. I had long ago given up trying to hide my pain, when it occurred, behind some sort of false pride. He had no doubt noticed that I reached for the salt and pepper in the awkward manner that presented itself when the ache returned. I was frankly grateful when he indicated that he planned to carry out his initial investigation of Moulton's problem on his own.

After his departure, I hauled the accumulated morning newspapers to my chair before the fire and settled in to see what was new in the world. The events were singularly uninteresting, which I suppose was good news for the masses as a whole, although there were certainly the usual tragedies and injustices occurring on an individual scale. I lost interest rather quickly and tried to immerse myself in a novel by a Scottish author of my acquaintance, loosely based on one of Holmes's former investigations, but I found myself becoming somewhat irate at certain liberties that had been taken. For the hundredth time, I vowed that one day I would make use of the voluminous journal entries that I regularly recorded of my friend's investigations and work them into some sort of material worthy of publication. With that in mind, I rose and resettled myself at my desk, moving aside the fossilized jawbone of some ancient lizard that had been used to kill a blackmailer and proceeding to polish my notes related to several of Holmes's more noteworthy inquiries.

Mrs. Hudson checked on me quite a few times, and I was surprised in the early afternoon when she asked about any preferences that I might have for lunch, having been unaware of how quickly that time was passing. After that question was determined and then the meal subsequently consumed, I continued at my labors, vaguely aware as the afternoon passed that my shoulder had finally started to feel better once again.

I was just finishing up my account of the events concerning the hideous visitant to the grounds of Deddington Castle when I heard the front door open, followed by Holmes's spry steps as he climbed to the sitting room. I was surprised to see that the day was fading away, and that it was later than I'd realized.

The door opened and he glanced toward me as he entered. "Ah, Watson – feeling better, I see. Are you game for a bit of burglary?" Then, before I could answer, he stepped to the shelves containing his scrapbooks, where he spent several minutes checking through various volumes while I made ready for departure.

And so it was that half-an-hour later we found ourselves settled at a table at Naples in Charlotte Street, an Italian restaurant that I'd discovered a year or so earlier. Holmes had eschewed bringing some of his more elaborate burglary tools, instead relying on the comprehensive lock-picking set that he usually carried with him. While eating our dinner, and waiting for a certain amount of time to pass until our excursion could be carried out with some degree of discretion, Holmes recounted the events of his day, sometimes waving a piece of bread like a baton as he cheerfully went, step-by-step, through his gradual understanding of the situation.

"Naturally enough," he explained, "I began by sending several wires to make certain of our ground. Then I ended up back at the front desk of the Hotel Metropole, where I implied that I was acting as Moulton's agent and the reason for my questions. As you know, there are one or two managers there who still recall the little service that I performed for them back in '83, when the Countess of Grantham, apparently suffering from some sort of emotional crisis related to her fortieth birthday the previous year, had placed herself in such a position as to utterly destroy her reputation. The Metropole management was quite grateful then, and to this day as well, and they had no hesitation in providing me with Mr. Abel Vernham's home address – in spite of their reluctance to do the same for Mr. Moulton.

"Their account of the theft of the letters was similar to that of Moulton's, although they did provide a bit of additional information. It seems that Vernham was already being watched after a few similar incidents where the shadows of suspicion had tilted his way – minor thefts occurred in rooms that were generally connected with him. He is one of the under-managers at the hotel, assigned to several floors, and on at least a half-dozen past occasions since his employment began just four months ago, other small items have gone missing – odds-and-ends that have personal associations to the victims.

"There has been no evidence to specifically point to Vernham, but he has been on the premises – and in fact on the very floors – when each minor theft occurred. And his antecedents have given the hotel managers some pause, as at one time long ago – and they only discovered this after he was hired, based on some hints that he dropped in conversations with some of the maids – he was an *actor.*"

I smiled. "Scandalous."

"Exactly. And while we both know that being an actor in one's past does not automatically make one a criminal – for instance, it did me no harm! – it does still have a great deal of social stigma in certain quarters. The knowledge that Vernham had such experience in his past put him on thin ice – but that's not to say that in this case he was unfairly suspected. The evidence against him as shared by the managers is convincing, and he probably has been stealing. As I had arrived a bit too early this morning, I was prepared to wait and discuss the matter when Mr. Vernham joined us. Yet nine o'clock, when he was supposed to begin work, came and passed without his appearance. The managers were alternately irate and concerned, and it was then that they gave me his address, with the assurance that they would take no action until the heard from me, and that they would put Mr. Moulton off if he happened to arrive asking questions – in case leaving the matter in my hands wasn't enough for him after all."

He paused to take a sip of wine and continued. "Vernham's address is in Pocock Street, across the river in Southwark near Nelson Square. I hied myself in that direction to find that he actually lived just around the corner, in first-floor rooms above some stables, reached by a way of a poorly-kept mews. A word with his neighbors gave me to understand that he was at home, and that there was no landlord on the premises. I needed to convince him to speak with me – and I assumed that, if Vernham had chosen to abandon his job this very morning, coincidentally around the same time that the letters went missing, I wouldn't necessarily be welcomed. And I was right. At first he didn't answer the door at all, although I was aware from some slight sounds within the apartment that he was at home. Then, foregoing any attempt at deception, I identified myself and stated that I was there in regard to Mr. Moulton's missing letters. The resulting silence from that revelation was so emphatic that I began to fear that I'd made a mistake in not simply prevaricating. Then, after worrying that perhaps he'd skittered out through a back entrance, I heard the door unlock. Almost immediately a hand urgently gestured for me to enter the darkened rooms.

"There was a noticeable odor of neglect about the place, some of which was certainly from the various articles of unwashed clothing scattered around the floor. The room was dim, with the curtain pulled across the only window, and the only light coming from the fireplace and a feeble gas fixture above the mantel. Vernham – for it was he – pushed the door shut behind me and then stood watching, awaiting my further explanation. He's about thirty years of age, lean and striking in a theatrical way, with high prominent cheekbones that throw shadows across his thin mouth. One can see the stage training in him by the way he stands, but unfortunately he also showed obvious signs of an incipient and detrimental opium addiction. All-in-all, he has the appearance of a skittish animal that would as soon bolt as remain, although I didn't know where he should have run this morning if the decision had been made to do so. Most important, the man was in fear.

"Normally an awkward silence is a useful tool for a man asking questions, but I could see that in this case, I would have to give way first. 'The managers of the hotel suspect that you stole the letters from Mr. Moulton's room,' I opened. He nodded noncommittally but didn't reply. 'When you didn't show up this morning,' I added, 'it rather sealed that belief.' Still no response. 'What made taking the letters worthy of such trouble, above other choices?' Then, in a flash of insight, I asked, 'Who hired you to retrieve them?'

"With that, his expressionless features devolved into something like a rueful sneer. 'I've heard of you, Mr. Sherlock Holmes. I thought that you knew everything. Well, you don't know what I've gotten myself into.'

"Here was something new, then. I had suspected that there was more to Moulton's letters than we had been told – why else should the man change his place of residence, and answer his door with a gun? But I seemed to have peeked under the very edge of something much more substantial. Affecting to have a bit more omniscience than was entirely true, I carefully replied, 'You've read the letters, then?'

"Of course I had no idea what was in them, but I gave the impression that I did. He nodded in reply. 'And I wish that I hadn't.' Then he frowned, as if just realizing that he'd made a mistake. 'Did Esher send you?'

"The name was familiar, but I shook my head in reply. 'The hotel is concerned,' I prevaricated. 'Too many guests have reported thefts lately. They've had their eyes on you.' I named off several of the items that had been taken, as based on what I'd been told an hour earlier. Vernham simply listened until I mentioned an insignificant ruby ring. Then he angrily reacted. 'I didn't take that! You can bet that one of the old lady's brats snagged that one, and is blaming the hotel!'

"'But you took the other things?' He nodded grudgingly. 'Those were all objects of demonstrable value," I continued, "but without enough worth to lead to police involvement. They might very well have been misplaced by the owners. Why change your method and take letters instead?'

"He shook his head as if I were a slow pupil. 'Esher! He forced me to. He told me just what to look for – he described the envelopes, and where they would be hidden in Moulton's luggage. He said that they would be in a secret pocket in the lining of the man's travel case. But he also wanted me to find something else, some other papers about Moulton's past, and they weren't there."

"'To be clear,' I asked, 'are we talking about Jack Esher, the swindler?'

"'Jack Esher the killer, you mean.'

"'I thought that he fled to America two years ago.'

"'He did, but he's been back for a week or so – at least that's what he said. He followed this Moulton – they came over on the same ship, but Moulton never realized it.'

"'And how did Esher convince you to help him?'

"'I knew him from . . . from before he left in such a hurry. He knows some things about me. When he followed Moulton to London, and to the hotel, he saw me working there. After that, he couldn't wait to have me nick those papers for him.'

"'Then why are you so frightened? Surely all that you needed to do was deliver the letters that you found, and report to him that the others weren't there. Then you simply had to return to work and brazen it out.'

"'You don't understand!' he snarled. 'I read the letters, and stupidly mentioned to Esher that I did it. Now *he* knows that *I* know!'

"'And what is it that you saw?' I asked.

"At this point he suddenly became cagy. 'Why should I tell you, Mr. Sherlock Holmes? How will you help me out of this mess?'

"'I'm not even sure about the extent of what this mess is,' I replied honestly, 'but if you feel that you need some sort of protection – '

"'I do,' he said. 'I certainly do need that.'

"So the long-and-short of it, Watson, was that I helped him get away from his meagre lodgings and into a place of safety that I maintain elsewhere in the city – one of my little hidey-holes where I keep disguises and other materials that I might need in the course of my work. I hated to let him know about it, and I told him that it belonged to an actor friend. Being a former actor himself, I think that he believed me, seeing the various items of clothing and the theatrical make-up on the mirrored table that is the main object of furniture in the place. After he was settled there, he told me the rest of his story.

"It seems that the letters that he was to retrieve were not – as you probably have realized by now – the innocent personal missives that Mr. Moulton tried to lead us to believe. In fact, they are a series of introductions promising substantial funds from a group of American criminals to be delivered to Bill Wayman of Bennett Street."

My eyes widened. "Bill Wayman, who has been making a serious play to replace Professor Moriarty's organization with his own?"

"The same. He doesn't have a chance, of course, but it's been useful for us to let him continue unhindered, as every resource that the Professor is forced to direct toward holding Wayman in check is one that he can't exert somewhere else."

"And if I recall correctly," I said, "Jack Esher was – at one time, at least – one of the Professor's lieutenants."

"Something like that," replied Holmes. "The Professor's chain of command isn't exactly laid out along military lines, but that description fits close enough."

I leaned back as the implications washed over me. "So Moulton has something for Wayman which will give him an advantage – a promise of American criminal support – and Moriarty's man contracted with Vernham to steal it before it could be delivered."

"That is how I read it as well," replied Holmes. "Somehow they became aware of the letters, even in America, but were unable to retrieve them while they were in transit.

"Well," I said, "why interfere? Let them settle it however they wish. As you said, everything that Wayman is allowed to accomplish for now diminishes Moriarty to some degree. Why not let Moulton complete his mission, so that Wayman can divert Moriarty's resources to an even greater extent?"

"It isn't that easy now. You forget, the letters have already been stolen and placed into Esher's hands, and surely Moriarty has them now. To get them back would be nearly impossible, even if we wished to do so. They're usefulness for Wayman is finished. And in any case, Wayman has been effective up to now because he functions at the same continuing level of success today as yesterday, and as he will tomorrow. To allow him a nourishing connection with American criminal resources would perhaps make him more powerful than would be healthy at present. There's always been the understanding that when Moriarty is ready, he'll kill Wayman and absorb his organization. If Wayman is allowed to expand his influence, he'll simply built a bigger resource for Moriarty to eventually control."

"And of interest from all of this is that Moulton is likely a criminal as well, and wasn't just delivering these documents as a favor for a friend?"

"Oh, it's quite certain. Vernham indicated that the other papers that he was supposed to locate contain evidence of Moulton's own crimes, which Esher – working for Moriarty – wishes to use as a way to control Moulton. Having these documents in his own possession could allow Esher to force Moulton into Moriarty's service. As I mentioned, I took a moment this morning to send a few wires – all of them to some of my American acquaintances. You may be interested to learn that there is no record of an American named Francis Hay Moulton."

"But surely – " I began, and then checked myself. "To enter the country, he would have needed legitimate papers."

"Precisely, Watson. And someone that I know with a great deal of influence within the Foreign Office quickly checked the records of recent arrivals from America, confirming that no one named *Francis Hay Moulton* has entered the country, but one *Francis Harris Mason* did – a man of the same approximate age and description as our recent acquaintance, arriving ten days ago through Liverpool."

"*F.H.M.*" I said. "Still, traveling under another name is not evidence of a crime, or of a deep connection with a known criminal organization."

"This is true, but it turns out that Francis Mason, or 'Frank' as he's known in America and to his wife, has a long history of mayhem to his credit – theft, assault, fraud, and the odd murder or two when it was to his benefit."

"He sounds like a rough character – and too smart to have spoken with you at all."

"I puzzled over that as well. I unexpectedly intruded into their lives yesterday evening, having traced them from the Hotel Metropole to the Gordon Square house. They really had no choice but to visit Baker Street and let the matter with Lord St. Simon play out. For all they knew, I had the Gordon Square lodgings under observation in case they tried to escape, and might have complicated things much worse than they already were."

I took a sip of wine. "But again I have to ask, what is the purpose of your – *our* – continued involvement? Moriarty has the letters, and they are now as good as gone. This seems to be some sort of scuffle between two rival gangs, and any damage that they do to one another only benefits the greater good."

"Except that disrupting their plans is always good practice as well. Moriarty gaining some sort of ascendance over Mason – or Moulton, as I will continue to call him – is likely much worse than simply letting Wayman have access to American financial resources. The Professor would love to expand his influence to both the Continent and the

Americas, and having the documents relating to Moulton's guilt would let him convince the American to change his allegiance, so to speak, from Wayman's team to that of the Professor. Then the Professor can make the American connections himself. And if nothing else, Mrs. Moulton needs to understand what sort of man that she has married, and be able to correct the problem, before it goes any further."

"And how will this bit of burglary that you promised do that?"

"I propose to find the papers relating to Moulton's guilty past, the ones that Vernham could not, and see him brought to justice."

"And what is your plan? Are we simply going to slide into their rooms – even as he guards them with his gun – and lurk behind curtains or the furniture until they go to sleep?"

"I have it on good authority that they are attending the theatre tonight."

"And how did you obtain that information."

"They told me so when I called upon them this afternoon."

I took a moment to ponder that before asking simply, "Why do that?"

"I visited on the pretext of being in the neighborhood on other business, making sure that they had arrived home safely last night, *etcetera.* I believe that Moulton was suspicious, but I didn't care. I was interested to observe that his wife is becoming impatient with being kept inside. I dropped a hint or two about some of the local theatrical productions which interested her greatly – the result of which is that they will be attending tonight's performance at the Haymarket, while you and I slip into the house in Gordon Square and search at our leisure."

I had a premonition – correct, as it turned out – that things wouldn't progress quite that smoothly, but I held my tongue as we paid our bill and found a hansom to carry us to Bloomsbury. We had the cabbie drop us at the corner of Gower and Keppel Streets, and then walked through the dark night until we entered Russell Square. Turning north, we paused on the steps of Christ's Church in Woburn Square, where Holmes raised his hand twice in a curious chopping motion. Within half-a-minute, a lad appeared from the darkness. It was Arthur Belling, one of his Irregulars.

"Something different from what you said to expect, Mr. Holmes," he said. "The lady left at the time you said she would, but there was no man with her, and she hired a growler. The driver helped her load a small trunk that was just inside the building. The lights to the rooms that you said to watch are still lit."

"Did you see which way they went?"

"To the south. Thad jumped on the back – he'll get word to us where they're going."

Holmes frowned and glanced at me. "I fear that I have been hoodwinked, Watson. This way!"

Leaving Arthur where we had found him, Holmes led me back down to the pavement, and so on along the eastern side of Gordon Square, and then straight to Number 226. Stepping off the street through the unlocked front door, he pounded up the stairs to the first floor, while I followed gamely behind. He reached a door as I stepped off the stairs and raised his fist to knock. Before he could do so, however, he sniffed, and then shifted his hand to push against the door. It opened, having not been entirely closed. He looked toward me. "Gun smoke – do you smell it?"

I did. As I took another step closer, his expression changed at whatever it was that he saw through the open door.

"Deviltry, Watson," he muttered, and then stepped inside.

From the doorway, I saw him approach the body of a man – Moulton – lying on the floor, his head lying in a thickening puddle of blood. The man's eyes were glazed in death, and his features were distorted, a result of the blackened wound on his left temple. A gun was tossed carelessly onto the floor at his side.

Holmes muttered to himself to a moment. "There is no attempt to fabricate a suicide," he finally said. "Moulton was right-handed – he wouldn't have fired into his left temple, and in any case, the gun is lying by his right hand." He leaned down over the weapon. "This appears to be the same gun that he had when I called up on the two of them yesterday evening." He stood and looked at me. "It would seem as if his wife somehow gained possession of it – probably without his knowledge, as there is no sign of a struggle – and she was likely able to approach him without arousing his suspicions. She killed him and then departed – probably for good, as she took a trunk."

He then turned and spent five minutes or so comprehensively searching the rooms, while I placed myself near the door, in case anyone should arrive with uncomfortable questions. I was struck by how solid the building seemed to be, and how silent as well. I couldn't hear anything from the neighboring flats – which was possibly why none of them seemed to have heard the sound of a gunshot.

Holmes returned and stood beside me. "She hasn't taken all of her possessions, but enough to indicate that she doesn't intend to return. And there is no sign of the documents related to the events in Moulton's past."

He raised a hand and rubbed his brow. "I have seriously erred, Watson. Something that I did today during my visit alerted them – alerted *her* – that I knew more than I was sharing. I thought that Moulton was the villain, but it seems that there was more than one viper in these rooms."

"You don't know that for certain," I said. "Perhaps Moulton was a brute, something that she never realized during the short time that they were previously married in the United States. We saw indications of it last night. Possibly he did something just today that drove her to kill him, entirely unrelated to the tale that you shared regarding Moriarty and Wayman."

"Possibly," he said. "But I can see from examining the rooms that her departure was efficient and organized. There was no panic here, no desperate attempt to flee from an emotional murder that came as the result of some sudden abuse. And the papers are missing . . . ."

There isn't much more to tell. One of Holmes's Irregulars, Thad Warren, passed the word to us that Hattie Doran Moulton's cab had deposited her at Victoria Station, where she had purchased a ticket and then entered one of carriages for the boat train to France. However, by the time the police could wire ahead and intercept it, she'd vanished from her compartment, abandoning her trunk in the process, long before reaching the coast. Holmes personally undertook to interview the lady's father, Aloysius Doran, still in England following her supposed wedding to Lord St. Simon. He had remained through the following week instead of returning to America, seemingly awaiting news concerning her disappearance. He claimed, as he always had, that he hadn't known where his daughter went after fleeing the wedding breakfast, and that she wouldn't have told him what she'd planned in any case, knowing his objections to her relationship with Francis Moulton. And yet, Holmes was certain after questioning the man that he had actually known all along where his daughter was during the week after the wedding, and more importantly, that he knew where she was now as well.

"I'm convinced that the old rascal helped arrange for her escape from the train," he said with great irritation a few evening later. We were sitting by the fireplace in Baker Street, Holmes with his pipe in hand. Old Doran had vexed him, and as Holmes cast more nets and obtained more information, it was clear that the American was a much more dangerous figure than we had first credited, based on the little that we'd previously heard of him.

"No great surprise there," I said. "A man like him who made a fortune in the western mines is surely ruthless and brutal."

"Exactly," said Holmes. "Just the kind of man who could parlay some sort of successful connection with Professor Moriarty, to their mutual benefit."

"You believe that is what's happening, then?"

"There is every indication of it. He hasn't been sitting idle during his visit to London. I've learned that he made several visits to Moriarty's Russell Square residence during the week that his daughter was missing."

"Then we have a rough idea of what is happening."

"But do we *really* know anything, Watson? It seems that these waters are even deeper and darker than we realized. Was Hattie Doran simply an innocent who found out the truth about her recently reunited husband? Or was there some newly threatened violence that prompted her to kill him? In either case, what made her choose to flee, rather than count on her father's money and influence to save her? Why walk away from her entire life – and in so effective and successful a manner? It might be easy for someone like her to do so – after all, she was ready a week ago to abandon Lord St. Simon and the security that life with him offered. Was she the woman that we saw the other night, talking too much while drunk and needling her new husband, or was she really pulling the strings all along?"

He set his pipe aside. "Thinking Moulton dead two years ago, did she then manipulate poor Lord St. Simon in search of a title, an entry-way into British society, only to abandon him when something better came along – a return to whatever life that she'd initially planned alongside a man with an extensive criminal history? I begin to think that the reappearance of the actual husband, while initially quite unfortunate for our saddened nobleman, was a rather lucky thing for him after all. The question now is where has she gone to ground – and why? Does it have something to do with her father's seeming association with the Professor? She and Moulton had already planned to go to France when I first visited them. Were they both taking direction even then from Moriarty? Is she still following that path laid out for her by the Professor, leaving behind her dead husband, her fortune, and even her identity? A striking woman like her cannot hide forever. Even under Moriarty's protection, if that's where she has taken herself, she must eventually be discovered."

And she was, but not until Holmes had a much greater understanding of the criminal enterprise which he faced, and only after the Professor had made one trip – only a little, little trip – which was more than he could afford when Holmes was so close upon him. From that starting point, Holmes wove his net around Moriarty, and all the little fish that encircled him as well. The final whereabouts of Hattie Doran, as I continued to call her, was one of the many mysteries that were cleared up to a small degree when Holmes's papers were examined in those dark days of May 1891, soon after he was believed to have perished at the Reichenbach Falls. I was with Inspector Patterson when he pulled the documents needed to convict Moriarty's gang from pigeonhole *M* – done up just as Holmes had described in a blue envelope and inscribed "*Moriarty*". Among them was a sheet telling how to find Hattie Doran, along with a long list of the crimes, some capital offenses, that she had committed since vanishing years before following the murder of her husband.

Holmes's notes were extensive, showing that he had found her just a few months after her disappearance. Rather than stay in that confining life of luxury, which she had apparently despised as her father attempted to marry her into the world of higher society, she had instead gone to work willingly for Moriarty's organization, a path that gave her some sort of satisfaction as she lived the dangerous life of an adventuress – and that eventually led her to the rope.

Holmes had gotten word of her activities in Monte Carlo, had set a watch in place, and then kept his eye upon her from that moment on, waiting. Sadly he wasn't around to see her arrest and conviction, as by that point he was using his presumed death to travel the world under the name "Sigerson" (among many others) while carrying out the nation's secret business under the direction of his brother.

I was allowed to speak with Hattie Doran in her cell the day before her execution, but she refused to answer any of my questions. She seemed to believe, even then, that somehow either her father's money or her association with the Professor's shattered organization would save her – the look of mocking and confident amusement at her plight was there in her eyes, and she made no effort to hide it. I understand that she became more frantic as the day progressed, and that she had to be sedated during the night as the hour of her execution approached. And yet, she took the truth of her relationship with Moulton with her, as well as whatever it was that had motivated her to kill him on that October night, just a day after our convivial little supper in Baker Street, sometime between the hour that Holmes had visited their apartment and when we later returned to burgle it.

I was at Newgate Prison the next morning when Hattie Doran was hanged, and I bore the brunt of the hatred meant for both me and Holmes as I tried to ignore the glare of her father. His blistering gaze was upon me instead of watching his daughter, even as the flooring beneath her feet gave away and we both heard her muffled and abruptly silenced gasp. He made it clear as I turned to go that he would never forgive, and he would never forget.

The Tattooed Rose
by Dick Gillman

It was the receipt of a somewhat urgent telegram, towards the end of June, 1887, that began the case that I have recorded as that of "The Tattooed Rose". I was staying in Baker Street, and Holmes and I had settled back after a delicious luncheon of lamb chops served with new potatoes from the island of Jersey, Savoy cabbage, and a generous splash of mint sauce. It was as Mrs. Hudson was clearing away our plates that she suddenly paused and thrust her hand into the commodious pocket of her apron, saying, "I'm very sorry, Mr. Holmes. This came for you some ten minutes ago and I forgot all about it!"

Holmes smiled as she passed the telegram to him. Running his finger beneath the gummed flap of the envelope, he replied, "It's of no consequence, Mrs. Hudson. Whomever is in need of my services will, no doubt, allow me some little time to consider their request."

Gathering up her tray, Mrs. Hudson nodded in thanks and made her way from the sitting room. I looked towards my friend who was now frowning as he idly waved the telegram before him. "What is it?" I enquired, eager to know its contents.

Holmes sat back, deep in thought. "It's from Lestrade. It seems that he would like us to immediately join him at an address in St. James's Street, and hopes that we have not yet eaten!"

I considered this for a moment before realising the import of it. "If we are required to have a strong stomach, I may well change into more suitable attire!"

Holmes laughed. "Come, Watson, I cannot believe that there will be blood-letting on that grand a scale! Let us be off!" Rising from his chair, he swiftly gathered his coat, hat, and cane and was off down the stairs. I trailed in his wake and, by the time I had reached the pavement, Holmes was beckoning me, somewhat enthusiastically, to step up into the waiting cab that he had hailed.

As we travelled, Holmes passed the telegram to me, but I found that there was nothing further to what Holmes had recounted except for the number for the address. "St. James's Street – that's adjacent to Jermyn Street from where I purchase my shirts, Holmes."

Holmes nodded. "Yes, it's a place that houses some of the finest tailors in London, and its clients run all the way up to the Royal family."

He chuckled. "I can imagine that Lestrade is somewhat uneasy in such a venue!"

After but a few short minutes, our cab pulled up a little before the junction with Jermyn Street. On tossing the cabbie a shilling, we dismounted and proceeded to peer at the intentionally diminutive numbers above the shop fronts. We continued our hunt until we found a discrete doorway, set back from the pavement, and which was now completely filled by a large constable.

The constable saluted smartly and stepped out from the doorway and stood to one side, saying, "Good afternoon, Mr. Holmes, Dr. Watson. The inspector is inside, sir, just on the right."

Holmes raised his cane, nodded, and stepped inside the passageway that was now revealed to us. On hearing our entry, a lean torso, topped with the pinched features of Inspector Lestrade, appeared from a doorway ahead of us. "Ah, there you are, Mr. Holmes. Doctor. In here, if you please. It isn't a pretty sight though!"

As we entered the room, my hand went to my mouth. Before us was the plump, sagging body of a grey-haired, middle-aged man, almost naked, and bound to a chair at the wrists, chest, and feet. A gag had been roughly placed in his mouth. With one glance I could see he had been badly beaten and, from the lurid blistering on his arms and chest, scalded. "Good Lord, Lestrade! Who is this?"

Lestrade drew himself up to his full height, replying, "This is – or was – Percival Small. I had dealings with him some ten years ago when he was a fence for many of the local villains. However, he then seemed to mend his ways and I hadn't seen hide nor hair of him until today."

We stood and considered this for a moment whilst Lestrade reached into his overcoat pocket and took out his notebook. Licking his thumb, he proceeded to riffle through a few pages before continuing. "He was found by an elderly lady, a cleaner that does these offices. The door was open, and when she saw Percy here, she ran out into the street and screamed the place down." Lestrade made a sweeping gesture with his free hand and informed us, "We found the place just as you see it, Mr. Holmes. Help yourself."

Holmes approached the body and began to examine it most thoroughly. Taking his lens from his pocket, he studied the wounds, and then the area around the corpse. "This man has a wound to the back of his head which probably incapacitated him. He has clearly been brutally tortured, Lestrade, before a curious, final knife wound to his back, piercing his heart. The knots and the rope are common enough, and the kettle that was used for the boiling water to scald Mr. Small is now quite cold, as is the grate." Holmes paused, asking, "Would you allow us to examine the room further, Inspector?"

Lestrade nodded whilst continuing to scribble down the details he had just gleaned from Holmes's examination. "Yes, Mr. Holmes. It's clear to me that Percy had annoyed somebody. My money is on revenge, but I'll leave you to it and get back to the Yard. Let me know if you find anything."

Holmes nodded and seemed relieved that Lestrade was now out of his way. I looked around me, finding it difficult to tear my eyes from the poor creature before us. The man had, as Holmes had remarked, been savagely tortured. As I walked around the slumped figure, I noted that the slightly curved, angry gash in his back would, at least, have ended his torment.

I frowned as I looked about me. The business carried out in this small office remaining something of a mystery. To one side, beneath a double-burnered gas light, was what I observed to be an examination table that wouldn't have been out of place in my own surgery. However, on the walls were posters with elaborate patterns drawn upon them and bold, cursive, letters of the alphabet. Beside the table was a stool and a shelf that contained bottles of coloured liquid, and some kind of brass, mechanical contraption containing a large, coiled spring and a jointed arm.

Holmes, I saw, was steadily working his way round the room and had paused at a small desk at the rear. As I watched, I observed him pick up an open ledger and then bring it nearer to the single window of the premises for better light.

"It seems, Watson, that whomever did this was after information and, indeed, found what he needed here." Holmes pointed to the ledger. "This has been opened to a date some three months ago. You can see were the torturer's blood-stained finger moved through the pages to this particular one – but why? What is it about this page and date that is so special? Is it the details of a particular client that he sought?"

As I heard the word "client", I was further confused and still struggling to understand the nature of this man's business. "What did Small do here, Holmes?" I asked.

Holmes face was grim. "It would appear that the late Mr. Small was a tattoo artist, hence his 'pattern book' of designs on the wall and that mechanical needle affair. I noticed that Small himself had several tattoos, some of them quite crude and – by their design – seemingly obtained overseas."

On hearing this, I moved back to the device I had observed and examined it more closely. It seemed to be a brass chassis upon which was mounted a spring-driven mechanism of the type that one might find inside a grandfather clock. However, the mechanism didn't drive clock hands.

Rather, it powered a reciprocating needle which seemed to have a reservoir attached, presumably for tattoo ink.

Holmes, I saw, was now busily noting down the names of the clients from the bloodied page of the ledger. Having done this, his attention turned to a closed door at the back of the office. After a minute or so of searching, Holmes called out to me. "Watson, what significance does the date *31st January, 1873* have for you?"

I pursed my lips as I thought. "I must confess that I cannot bring anything of import to mind. Is that date of particular importance?"

Holmes appeared carrying a small, flat, wooden crate which was lined with newspaper, yellowed with age. He frowned, saying, "There is a small storeroom to the rear where I found this. By examining the nails, I would suggest that this crate has been opened within the last six months. The head of each nail is rusted but the body of the nail is barely marked – and, intriguingly, the crate contains pages from a newspaper that is some fourteen years old."

Thinking about this, I proposed, "So, by the date of the paper, you believe that the content was placed in the crate on or around that date, but was *not* removed by the killer."

Holmes held his finger to his lips before uttering, "Quite so. Whatever was contained within it has long gone, although there is evidence, within the storeroom, that it was searched most diligently."

I pondered this for a moment. "Then the killer, on finding the crate empty, sought to extract information from Small."

Holmes's expression was cold as he nodded. "Yes, I believe so, but what was inside the crate and what information might Small's clients hold? I fear that the killer's interest could now turn towards them." I frowned, as this was something that I hadn't even considered.

Taking out his glass once more, Holmes painstakingly examined the interior of the crate. At one point he stopped and took from his jacket pocket a small brown envelope. Taking out his pen knife, he carefully scraped at something on the crate, catching whatever the sample was in the envelope before sealing it. This he placed carefully back in his pocket and, I noted, a single page of the yellowed newspaper also.

With nothing further to be found and with one final, hawkish sweep of the room, Holmes made his way back to St. James's Street. With a swift nod to the constable, he then held his cane aloft to attract the attention of an approaching cab driver.

Once back at Baker Street, Holmes wasted no time in setting up his brass microscope. Clearing the dining table with a single sweep of his arm, he took the instrument from its mahogany case and pointed its mirror towards our window onto Baker Street. Taking a glass slide, he gently tapped out the sample he'd gathered onto its glass surface. Focusing the device, Holmes examined the contents of the envelope before sitting back and then gazing at some far distant point.

Rising from the dining table, he thrust his hand into his jacket pocket and removed the yellowed sheet of newspaper before moving to his leather armchair. On seeing that the microscope was now free, I took the opportunity to examine Holmes's find. Refocusing the device, I was surprised to see that the particles on the slide glinted slightly and were a yellowish colour.

"Gold!" I cried but then, on looking again, I could see that some of the flakes of material had a whitish background and I realised that it might only be gold paint that had caught my eye. I looked across at Holmes who was clearly amused by my outburst. I wagged my finger at him and frowned. "Do not dare say it, for I am aware of the saying – and my folly!"

Holmes laughed. "I would not presume. So, if not gold, then *gilt*! The white material adhering to it I take to be an undercoat of gesso." Holmes paused whilst he filled his briar. "Tell me, Watson, what gilt-covered item, might you imagine, would be stored in a slim wooden crate of the size that we found today?"

I thought for a moment. "Well, certainly not a clock, but a flat object – a picture frame."

"Excellent – but perhaps not *just* a picture frame." At this he rose and then passed me the yellowed newspaper page from the crate. Carefully, I flattened it with my palm and began to scan its contents. It was, I saw, a page from *The Times*, dated the 3rd of February, 1873. Nothing seemed at all relevant on the first side, but as I turned it over, I blinked as I read "*Lord Ashburton's Art Collection Ravaged by Fire*."

I gave Holmes a quizzical look, asking, "Is this article relating to the fire at Bath House of some relevance?"

My friend drew strongly upon his pipe. "I believe it may be. From what I've read, many important works of great value were consumed in the blaze in the drawing room. As you can see, it's reported that as few as three survived the flames." Holmes paused before rising from his chair and then removing a large tome, relating to famous works of art, from his library. After a minute or so he returned to his chair, in great thought.

He took his pipe from his mouth and then proceeded to wag the stem in my direction, saying, "One of the paintings that was thought to have survived was a painting in the Flemish style by Pieter de Hooch, entitled '*A Woman with a Dish of Roasted Apples*'. Reading in a later paragraph from *The Times*, it is then reported that it did *not* survive, but had been destroyed in the flames."

I frowned, asking, "How can such a mistake have been made?"

Holmes pursed his lips. "In the confusion and the aftermath of such a fire, it is possible that a member of the household staff was confused. Perhaps the surviving canvases had been blackened by smoke damage." He then paused, his eyes now aflame. "But if I were to tell you that the de Hooch painting measured just barely eighteen inches by twenty-four inches – "

My eyes opened wide. "The . . . the crate, and the gilt paint!"

Holmes nodded slowly. "Indeed. Given that Percy Small was a fellow known to be a fence for stolen goods, he may well have been given the painting for safe-keeping. Such a valuable and recognisable painting would have to 'disappear' for some years before being offered for sale."

I pursed my lips as I heard this. "Surely nobody would openly buy it, knowing that once on display it would be instantly recognized."

My friend again wagged his pipe. "Ah, but some collectors would not have it openly on display. They would be content simply to posses the painting and keep it in their own very private collection."

I considered this for a moment, asking, "Why do you think that Small was the subject of such barbarous treatment?"

Holmes inclined his head and blew out a single, slender stream of smoke before replying. "I cannot be certain, but Lestrade noted that Small hadn't attracted the attention of the police for some years. Perhaps once he had possession of the picture, he deliberately vanished, taking a new persona . . . and the picture."

I observed Holmes as he built upon his proposal. "On opening the crate some months before his death, he may well have decided to sell the contents. Clearly, this was against the wishes of the 'owner' and, when tracked down and confronted, Small was reluctant to reveal its new location." Holmes then frowned, pausing before adding, quietly, "Perhaps, then, one of the clients on the bloodied ledger page was the buyer."

On saying this, Holmes took from his pocket his notebook. Opening it to the page where he had recorded the list of Small's clients, he raised an eyebrow as he considered it. "You know, Watson, the art of the tattoo is ancient to Japan and also to several primitive tribes worldwide. However, in Europe it is common to believe it to be simply the province of sailors and those that exhibit their tattoos in circus sideshows."

I nodded. "Indeed, that isn't entirely the case. Many of the most senior officers in my regiment had their arms and chest emblazoned with symbols of the Empire and our victories. It has become quite the fashion for the nobility to be tattooed also."

Holmes nodded, saying, "Quite so. There are some venerable names in this list, but there are some that I find quite improbable. For example, there are three ladies listed, one beneath the other, who, it appears, have paid a guinea for a single rose tattoo on their left shoulder blade."

I smiled. "Perhaps, then, I may have superior knowledge in this matter. You would be greatly surprised by the number of ladies who have availed themselves of tattoos." At this, Holmes turned towards me in great interest. "In my professional capacity, I am obliged to sometimes to examine my patients '*in toto*'. Although bound by confidentiality, I can assure you that whilst the flesh that is visible may be white and pristine, that which is concealed, for the sake of modesty, might well be adorned with a veritable plethora of tattoos. Flowers, songbirds, swags, and fine lacework are often elegantly depicted."

Holmes frowned, clearly unaware of this affectation. "You surprise me, Watson. So the presence of these three ladies in the ledger is nothing out of the ordinary?"

I smiled as I slowly shook my head. "Indeed not. Acquiring a tattoo is no longer solely the preserve of the male of the species." I was curious, asking, "Are these three ladies particularly notable in society?"

Holmes raised an eyebrow as he answered, "I would not know, for I particularly avoid reading the society pages in any broadsheet, as you are well aware. Let me see, Mrs. Louisa Heath of Bromley, Miss Abigail Carter of West Ruislip, and, finally, Lady Amelia Lawson of Bloomsbury. Do you recognise any of the names?"

I pressed my lips together as I turned the names over in my mind. "There is only one that I recall. It may be that Mrs. Heath is the wife of Major John Heath, a brother officer. I seem to remember that he married at the beginning of the year and he has a house in Bromley."

Holmes nodded slowly and we smoked throughout the evening, saying little more.

It was the next day, after breakfast, as I sat at ease with my newspaper that an item leapt off the page. I sat upright as I read, "'*Dreadful fall in Bromley robs officer of his young wife*'." Reading on, I could only gasp, calling out, "Holmes – read this!"

He stepped to my side, took the broadsheet from my hand, and read it aloud:

> *Mrs. Louisa Heath was discovered yesterday at the foot of the stairs in the home she shared with her husband, Major John Heath. The Major had returned home in the late afternoon to find his wife collapsed and unconscious on the bottom step with a most grievous head wound. Although medical attention was immediately sought, Mrs. Heath was pronounced dead at*

the scene. A post mortem *is to be carried out this afternoon at the mortuary of Beckenham Cemetery, London Road.*

On reading this, Holmes threw down the paper, rushed towards the coat-stand, and then down the stairs. I blinked but then rose from my chair as quickly as I could manage to follow my friend out into Baker Street.

It was only as my friend hurried me inside the cab and had shouted "Beckenham Cemetery" to the cabbie that I had an inkling where we were heading. As we travelled swiftly along, I turned to Holmes, asking, "Do you believe this to be coincidence, or is there more? Might Mrs. Heath have bought the painting?"

Holmes's face darkened. "A man is tortured and then killed. A woman named in a bloodied ledger at the scene dies the following day – Coincidence? Only as a moth is drawn to a lit candle." Having said this, he sat back in the cab, closed his eyes and would say no more until we arrived at Beckenham cemetery.

Leaving the cab, we tossed the cabbie a half-crown and, on asking him to wait, we made our way through the black-painted, iron gates towards the cemetery buildings. The mortuary stood to one-side, just before the triple archway that connected the cemetery's twin chapels.

Holmes knocked firmly upon the oak door and within moments, a mortuary assistant stood before us. Holmes touched his hat and reached for his card case before offering a single card to the fellow. "I would be obliged if you could give that to the doctor who is to perform the *post mortem*."

The assistant glanced at the card and then disappeared from view. After perhaps a minute, a gentleman of middle years, wearing a sturdy apron, appeared before us. "Mr. Holmes? I am indeed pleased to meet you, sir. I'm Doctor John Grayling. How might I be of some assistance?"

Holmes reached out his hand, saying, "A pleasure, Doctor. We're assisting Inspector Lestrade of Scotland Yard with a most delicate case which may touch upon the lady who lies within. I would be most obliged if you might allow me to examine the body with my colleague, Doctor John Watson, before you commence."

Grayling frowned for a moment before nodding agreement, and adding, "Watson . . . from Barts?" I nodded and Grayling smiled in return.

On entering the mortuary, I found myself within a narrow building, starkly painted with white limewash. High windows on both sides of the building gave some natural light and this was augmented by double-mantled gas lights. To one side was a single, glazed, ceramic mortuary slab, upon which the body of a woman was laid, covered to the shoulders by a drab, mortuary sheet.

Grayling led us to her, saying, "A dreadful thing to happen, Mr. Holmes. Indeed, I feel as though I am just going through the motions to confirm the obvious cause of death after the fall." With a smile, he added, "Please, spend a few minutes for the inspector before I commence."

I looked towards Holmes. He was now surveying the somewhat battered and bruised face of Louisa Heath. As I watched, my friend inclined his head slightly, a clear signal that he wanted me by his side. Gently holding her neck, Holmes established that it wasn't broken, but then paused to examine an area beneath her lower jaw. I saw his face cloud, and he then proceeded to examine her arms and fingers before turning the body on its side to reveal the back of the head. Again, I saw him stiffen before taking out his glass and examining, most closely, the tattooed rose on her shoulder.

Grayling seemed intrigued as he saw Holmes reach for his notebook and then copy, exactly, the detail of the tattoo. "Perhaps this is something of a novelty for you, Mr. Holmes? I'm sure that Watson will confirm that it is quite the fashion these days for ladies to acquire such a tattoo."

I nodded, but was greatly concerned by the serious expression on Holmes's face as he gently turned the body to lie flat once more. "Thank you for your patience, Doctor Grayling. I am indeed grateful. Might I trouble you to show me the clothes that Mrs. Heath was wearing? It might help me to understand how she fell."

Grayling smiled and pointed, saying, "Of course. They're arranged in the corner." Holmes nodded and moved to the neat pile of garments he had indicated. I was surprised when Holmes examined both the neck and the fastenings of the dress that had been worn and then went on to examine the hem in some detail.

Seeming satisfied, Holmes touched his hat to Grayling as he announced, "Come along. Watson. We have a cab waiting!"

With a nod to Grayling, I hurried after my friend as he strode at speed up the gravelled driveway towards the waiting cab. Climbing aboard, I was struck by Holmes's demeanour and asked, "What is it?"

He pressed his lips together before replying, "This was no accident. The woman was clearly murdered. Grayling will see what he expects to see and no more and, as a result, accidental death will be pronounced."

On hearing this, my eyes opened wide. "You . . . you have evidence to support this?"

Holmes sat back and would say no more. It wasn't until we were once more back in Baker Street and had sought some relaxation in a pipe of tobacco that Holmes continued his observations at the mortuary.

Drawing strongly on his favourite briar, he turned slightly towards me, asking, "Tell me, Watson. If you were to trip and fall forwards, what would be your instinctive response?"

I thought for a moment, playing out such a scenario in my head. "Well, as I fell, I would throw out my arms in an attempt to prevent my head from striking the floor."

Holmes nodded. "As would we all, Watson, but Louisa Heath's hands and arms showed no sign of abrasion or bruising. Beneath her copious hair, at the base of the skull I discovered a depression, evidence of a severe blow. A blow, that I would argue, was *not* consistent with a fall." Holmes paused. "But not only that. Beneath the jaw were pressure marks, from strong fingers where her head had been gripped before being smashed against a hard object, perhaps the staircase or the wall of the house."

I could barely believe what I was hearing, spluttering, "But why? Why was she killed? Had she indeed bought the painting?"

Holmes sat back and didn't answer for perhaps half-a-minute. "You will recall that I examined her clothes. There was no evidence on the hem of her dress that she may have tripped, but the fastening at the back had been roughly torn and was blood-stained. I don't believe that this occurred as a result of the fall."

It took me a moment to realise the import of what he was implying. "You . . . you mean she was violated?"

Holmes wagged his finger, saying, most strongly, "No! My initial theory was that Small had sold the picture to one of the clients listed on the ledger page. I believe now that this is not the case."

From his jacket pocket, he withdrew his notebook and turned to the page where he'd copied the detail of the tattoo. Passing the notebook to me, he added, "The murderer, I believe, wanted to have sight of this."

I looked at the detailed drawing and was startled to see that, hidden within the design, were a series of letters. Beneath the sketch, Holmes had copied them: "*L & P B – E*". My mind was a fog and, in puzzlement, I asked, "I recognise the image of the tattoo, but what is the significance of the letters?"

"Let us imagine, that I had received an item of great value which I wished to keep out of harm's way, safe and secure, and not residing in my own premises. Where might I find such a place?"

I frowned. "Well, if not in a safe in my office then, perhaps in a bank . . . ." My voice trailed away as I realised what I was saying. "A safety deposit box!" I cried.

Holmes smiled thinly. "Quite so. And which financial institution has the initials *L.* and *P. B.*? I can think of but one."

I wracked my brains before recalling, "The London and Provincial Bank." I then frowned, remembering the final character. "What of the final letter '*E*'? What is its significance?"

Holmes took his pipe from his mouth. "It is the Mayfair branch of this particular bank that is the repository for the most precious items of the rich – famous and, indeed, infamous. I had occasion to visit the strong room during a particular case, some years ago. It was, indeed, an impressive vault."

Holmes paused, half-closing his eyes. "The strong room is quite vast. So that the numbering of the strong boxes doesn't become too unwieldy, the walls of the vault are given the cardinal points of the compass. Hence the '*E*' indicates that a strongbox is located on the East wall."

Whilst I was intrigued by this, I was still confused as to where Holmes had obtained his data. On seeing my confusion, Holmes smiled. "Remember, Watson, that Small was something of an artist. History is littered with art that has hidden symbolism and, indeed, hidden symbols. How easy it was for Small to hide, within the curves of the rose petals, the initials we have discovered – especially as the rose was hidden from not only others, but, by its location, from the lady herself!"

Holmes now sprang from his chair and scribbled on a telegram pad. "I must alert Lestrade, as well as the next ladies on the list, that they are in great danger, as they may have the key to locating the safety deposit box. You and I must travel to the address in Bloomsbury to meet with Lady Amelia Lawson. I will advise her of our visit." With that, he scribbled a further telegram before stepping into his bedroom.

Glancing at one of our recently delivered newspapers caused me to call "Holmes!" at the top of my voice. On hearing my cry, my friend returned quickly from his bedroom. "Here, read this!" I said as I thrust the paper towards him.

Taking it from me, Holmes devoured the content. His face was ashen as he returned the paper to me. "We are too late for Miss Carter, Watson, and must make haste to protect Lady Lawson. But I must see Miss Carter's tattoo!" Quickly, he dashed off another telegram before pulling on the bell rope to summon Mrs. Hudson.

Within moments, he had gathered his hat and cane and gone down the stairs, handing the telegram that he'd written to Mrs. Hudson before pushing past her. I followed my friend towards Baker Street.

Breathless, I climbed aboard the cab as Holmes shouted out an address in Bloomsbury and then hammered on the roof of the cab with his cane.

With a jolt, we were off. Holmes, I could see, was plainly disturbed by what he'd read and was drumming his fingers on the armrest of the cab.

I determined to engage and distract him by asking, "To whom was the last telegram sent?"

Holmes turned, his eyes aflame. "To Lestrade. I must have sight of the tattoo. Scotland Yard has taken to employing a most excellent photographer, a Mr. Bamford, who is, I have noticed, most particular in recording the details of crimes and their victims. I've asked Lestrade to send the photographs of Miss Carter to Baker Street. Our sole task now is to protect Lady Lawson and, I believe that I've determined a way to do so by giving the killer what he desires."

On hearing this, my eyes opened wide and I sat forward in my seat, somewhat in alarm. "How might this be achieved, and do you believe it ethical to aid a murderer?"

Holmes turned and gave me a hard look. "Yes, if it means saving the life of an innocent and, at the same time, providing us with the opportunity to catch the fellow. However, it must be done with great subtlety so that the murderer suspects nothing, or he will escape justice and flee."

He sat back, saying, "I think it's you that has provided the germ for this deception, Watson. It was your revelation that ladies of quality are adorning themselves with tattoos that has set my course. What if Lady Lawson was to reveal, publicly, by way of a photograph, that she had been tattooed? Whilst some older ladies might be shocked, some other younger ladies might, indeed, feel some relief that their 'secret' was now fashionable and not so secret. Indeed, it might spur on other ladies in society to follow suit!"

I pursed my lips and blew out my breath. This was a most daring suggestion and yet, I deemed it to have great merit. I realised that by publicly revealing the tattoo, Lady Lawson would be kept safe. The killer would gain the information with no risk to her Ladyship, and in a way that appeared guileless, so public that there could be no hint of a trap.

I nodded slowly. "That is inspired. The only problem that might arise would be the willingness of Lady Lawson, herself, to be party to it, and finding an outlet so public that the killer would see the photograph."

Holmes frowned. "Yes, it must be done, and quickly! This fellow has struck within a day of killing his previous victim. I must have Lady Lawson's assistance, and also that of some of her tattooed friends!"

As Holmes said this, the cab drew to a halt beside the kerb. We had stopped in front of a large detached Victorian mansion of buff-and-red brick. Holmes tossed the cabbie a florin and with a crack of his whip, he was on his way. Passing through the decorative iron gates, we approached the imposing dwelling. A porchway stood to one side against a square, red-brick edged bay containing four tall windows, mirrored by a similar arrangement on the first floor. Reaching the porchway, Holmes leant forward and pulled upon the brass knob to sound the doorbell.

Within a minute, a liveried footman opened the door and bowed before us. Holmes took a card from his case and, after a single glance, the footman bowed again, saying, “This way, gentlemen, Her Ladyship is expecting you.” A waiting maid took our hats and canes and we were then led, by the footman, into a grand reception room.

The room was elegant, part-panelled and with exposed beams with carved motifs in the modern “Arts and Crafts” style. Rising from a winged floral-patterned chair, an equally elegant young lady of, I would imagine, thirty years, strode towards us, holding out her hand.

Holmes took it, but before he could introduce himself, Lady Lawson began, “Mr. Holmes, I am intrigued by your telegram, but I’m puzzled that you think that I might be in some danger. Please, do sit down.” At this, she turned and began to walk back to her chair. As I moved forward, I noticed a large photograph in a silver frame, in keeping with the décor of the room, that portrayed Lady Lawson, Louisa Heath, and a third lady whom I presumed to be Abigail Carter. I touched Holmes’s sleeve and briefly pointed. Holmes nodded in reply.

Once seated, Holmes began. “My colleague, Doctor John Watson. I couldn’t help but notice your photograph on the sideboard, Lady Lawson. I know Mrs. Heath, but who is the other lady?”

Lady Lawson smiled. “Abigail Carter. We were all at school together, Louisa, Abigail, and I – but why do you ask?”

Holmes immediately became more serious. “I see that you haven’t yet heard the news. It is most painful for me to tell you that your two friends have passed away, Lady Lawson. Louisa Heath is presumed, by the authorities, to have had a fatal fall at her home and Abigail Carter was attacked yesterday evening. However, it is my belief that both of these ladies were killed by the same man.”

All colour had drained from the face of Lady Lawson. Her hand went to her mouth and her body wavered in her chair. I rose and rushed to her side, exclaiming, “Brandy, Holmes!”

Holmes found a decanter and only after I had administered a good measure of the fiery spirit did some colour return to her face. Satisfied, I moved back to my chair. Lady Lawson’s voice stumbled as she shook her head and then looked towards Holmes, asking, “Why – why, Mr. Holmes? Whatever could have been the motive?”

Holmes pursed his lips. “It is a secret that all three of you, unwittingly, shared. Together, you visited the office of a gentleman in St. James’s Street who tattooed a rose on the left shoulder of each of you. In doing so, the tattooist hid a cryptic code within the tattoo, a code which gives the location of, and the way to retrieve, a priceless item that was stolen some years ago."

On hearing this, I noticed Lady Lawson raise the brandy once more to her lips before she dared to ask, "And I hold the third part of this code? Then, gentlemen, let us see what it reveals."

Turning to me, Lady Lawson asked, "Doctor Watson, would you be so kind as to help me with the fastening of my gown?"

I rose and moved forward, noticing that Holmes, chivalrously, had turned his back on his hostess whilst I went to her assistance. The gown, I discovered, was held by a single button at the nape of her neck and then a small line of buttons to mid-shoulder. I unfastened just sufficient so that the shoulder of the gown could be folded to one side to reveal the tattoo.

Nodding her thanks to me, she held the front of the gown against her chest with the palm of her hand whilst she looked over her shoulder towards my friend who still had his back turned to her. "There are times, Mr. Holmes, when modesty must give way to the greater good. Please, examine the tattoo and tell me what you find."

Holmes briefly turned and I inclined my head in a gesture to beckon him to approach. Taking his glass from his jacket pocket, he leaned forwards and peered at the tattoo. Returning his glass and then taking out his notebook, he jotted something before nodding to me. I then re-fastened the gown and we returned to our seats.

Lady Lawson was now quite business-like as she asked, "Well, what secret have I been the bearer of?"

Holmes replied, "Within the rose are hidden the numbers *1952*. These numbers are, I believe, the combination to open a safety deposit box in a bank vault in Mayfair – and your life depends on making these numbers available to public gaze."

I saw Lady Lawson frown, clearly, she wanted to know more, asking, "How might this be achieved?"

Holmes moved forward in his chair. "My friend, Doctor Watson, tells me that it is now the height of fashion for ladies to obtain an unobtrusive – nay, hidden – tattoo. In order to protect you, I need you to make the fact that you have this tattoo *very* public. Indeed, I would wish to emblazon it, as a photograph, in all the society pages of the major newspapers."

At this, a wry smile passed across Lady Lawson's face.

Holmes continued, "Not only that, but in order to remove suspicion, I need several of the fashionable ladies in your circle to be named and reveal their tattoos. It is to be seen as the 'coming out', if you will, of the tattooed ladies of fashionable London."

I could see that Lady Lawson was delighted with the idea, but then her face clouded. "I am grateful for your concern regarding my safety, Mr.

Holmes, but my compliance is weighed down by my feelings for my two friends . . . This person must be caught."

Holmes nodded slowly. "By your action, you will not only ensure your own safety, but also obtain justice for your two friends. I will do all that is possible to protect you and bring this person to book."

Lady Lawson nodded sombrely. Having sat for a few moments in silence, she now reached for her reticule. "I may be able to assist you in your endeavour. My husband, Sir Thomas, inherited a major shareholding in several of London's newspapers and, as such, has some sway in matters editorial. I will give this some thought and speak to him this evening."

Holmes was also clearly delighted but then held up a finger in a note of caution. "Might I suggest, Lady Lawson, that you seek immediate protection – don't see strangers, don't go anywhere, except to join your husband at some other location rather than here, so that the man who seeks you cannot find you. And might we visit you and your husband there this evening, as I have to make arrangements for your debut?"

Lady Lawson immediately understood the reason for Holmes's caution. "Yes, I shall book a suite at The Langham. Would seven o'clock be acceptable? I'll spend some little time with my diary and invite some of my more gregarious friends for *canapés*."

Holmes rose and nodded. "I look forward to it. Thank you, Lady Lawson." With a slight bow, Holmes turned and made his way from the room, leaving me to smile and nod our good-byes to our bemused hostess.

Finding a cab and returning to Baker Street, Holmes spent the rest of the day busily sending telegrams and answering their replies. I made sure that, despite the flurry of activity, we both sat and enjoyed a respectable late luncheon of scotch eggs, sliced gammon, pickles, and freshly baked bread, followed by a slice of curd tart.

By early evening, Holmes seemed satisfied with his preparations and, after dressing for the evening, we made our way down the stairs to summon a cab to take us to The Langham.

Within but a few minutes, the impressive, somewhat Romanesque, buff-brick hotel was before us. Opened a little over twenty years before, The Langham was still an imposing structure, and I marvelled as our cab drew up in the colonnaded, Portland stone entrance.

Climbing the few short steps to the marbled vestibule, I noticed a small, untidy knot of four gentlemen who appeared to be waiting a little impatiently. Upon our appearance, they seemed to coalesce around us, following Holmes towards the front desk of the hotel and then on towards one of the grand hydraulic lifts that served the upper floors.

"Who are these people?" I asked.

He seemed quite flippant, casually waving a hand in their direction, answering, "These are gentlemen of the press, Watson, who have been invited to the *soirée*. They are the ones who will expose to the masses the fashion of tattoo that is currently the preserve of the upper classes and nobility."

Reaching our floor, Holmes stepped out and confidently led the way to an elegant doorway to a suite which displayed the name "*Cavendish*" in a cursive script on a discreet name plate. Holmes leant forward, gently knocking upon the door which was opened by Lady Lawson, who welcomed our little band.

On entering, I immediately marvelled at the opulence of the furnishings, the clearly French chandelier and the rich, ornate fabrics of this most elegant room. To one end, a group of four ladies were standing together in discussion, whilst sipping champagne and laughing politely.

With the door now firmly closed, the four reporters were directed to a small group of chairs towards the centre of the room. To one side of the ladies, I noticed a solitary, handsome gentleman of some forty years, whom I took to be Sir Thomas Lawson.

Once settled, Lady Lawson, with her group of ladies standing a little behind her, stood and faced the journalists.

"Good evening, gentlemen. If I am unknown to you, I am Lady Amelia Lawson, and we are gathered here for a purpose that is of some great interest to me. What I am about to reveal to you gentlemen of the press is information that might, until now, have been thought to be too delicate a matter to discuss. It is something of which you may well be unaware, but my friends and I wish to make it public."

Lady Lawson paused and reached out for a glass of champagne from the tray of a waiter standing close by. Taking a sip, she continued, "The art of tattoo is a most ancient one, but in recent years it has become most popular with ladies of the upper classes – and, indeed, of royalty." Holding forth her arm in the direction of her friends, she exclaimed, "The first day of summer is almost upon us! In response, these ladies and I, all of whom have embraced the art of the tattoo, are not only willing but proud to display our tattoos to the world and be named as the vanguards of fashionable London."

On saying this, a murmur of conversation passed amongst the reporters as they reached for their notebooks. Lady Lawson smiled, saying, "Gentlemen, may I introduce to you Lady Agatha Spears, Lady Alice Todd, Miss Julia Montague, and Lady Violet Forbes." On hearing her name, each lady took a step forward, smiled, and then turned her back to the reporters.

My hand went to my mouth as I saw that each lady had chosen a gown which had a neckline that dipped markedly at the rear. Every one was without the modesty of a delicate chemise and revealed its wearer's back to the level of her mid shoulder blade. In doing so, any tattoo above that level was clearly on display and some, I might add, appeared to continue out of sight! The reporters, I noticed, were initially transfixed, but then were to be seen scribbling furiously. At this point, Lady Lawson, herself, turned to reveal the delicate rose tattooed on her shoulder.

It was then that Sir Thomas stepped forward and gravely frowned. "This venture, you will have gathered, is something of a crusade of my wife's. As a major shareholder in each of your newspapers, and to indulge my wife, I have arranged for photographs of my wife's and these ladies' tattoos to be delivered to your editors. I expect and require these to be published in tomorrow's edition of your newspapers."

As Sir Thomas said this, such was his tone that it was as if a brief Arctic chill had passed through the room. I shivered, as did the gentlemen of the press. Seeing that his words had had the desired effect, Sir Thomas then guided the reporters to the door.

For the next half-hour or so, we stayed with our hosts and we were introduced to Lady Lawson's friends. I chuckled as, uncomfortably for Holmes, each lady was more than willing to openly display a variety of colourful and interesting placed tattoos.

Finally, Sir Thomas, with Lady Lawson beside him, took us to one side, asking, "Do you believe that we have done enough, Holmes?"

Holmes frowned. "I believe there is little more that we could have done, Sir Thomas. Had we chosen simply to try and protect Lady Lawson, she might well have had to go into hiding. Consequently, she would have been looking over her shoulder, in fear, for the rest of her days." Holmes frowned, deep in thought for a moment. "No, it had to be done this way, publicly, to avoid suspicion. Please pass on my grateful thanks to your courageous friends, Lady Lawson. I thought your introductory speech was, indeed, perfect. But might I suggest, your Ladyship, that you remain here at The Langham for, perhaps, a few days?" On saying this, Sir Thomas slowly nodded his agreement and we then made our way to the door.

It was as we entered the front door of 221b that Mrs. Hudson appeared, clutching a large, manila envelope. This she proffered to Holmes, saying, "A constable delivered this whilst you were out, Mr. Holmes." Holmes smiled and nodded a thank you before hurrying up the stairs. I followed at a more leisurely pace and, on entering the sitting room, found Holmes, glass in hand, poring over a half-foolscap photograph.

With the photograph balanced on his knee, he began to fill his pipe. His notebook and silver pencil were, I noticed, already arranged on the arm of his leather armchair. Holmes struck a vesta on the fender and then passed me the photograph. I must admit it did not make pleasant viewing. It portrayed the exposed shoulder of Abigail Carter with its rose tattoo, but also a savage, curved knife stroke to her back and a vicious, no doubt fatal, puncture wound.

I studied the photograph with some distaste before saying, "It would appear that the killer slashed her dress to gain access to the tattoo. I trust that this was done after dealing the fatal wound to her back, for it is a most fearful incision."

Holmes nodded. "We can only hope for that mercy, for this man is as callous as he is brazen." Sitting back, he drew deeply on his pipe before saying, almost to himself, "But we now have all three elements within our grasp, and he shall be ours."

I took out my pipe and began to fill it whilst asking, "What was revealed within her tattoo?"

Holmes frowned. "There were three numbers – *5*, *8*, and *0* – which, I believe, provide us with the means to identify a specific box within the bank's vault."

Nodding slowly, I lit my pipe, drew on it, and asked, "How then are we to trap this fellow, for we cannot set up camp in the vault?"

Holmes pursed his lips. "That is true. Also, we can't be sure of the contents of the box itself." He now drew up his knees to his chest and half closed his eyes. "We have some little time in the morning to introduce ourselves at The London and Provincial Bank and to make, perhaps, an early withdrawal."

I looked quizzically at my friend, wanting to question him further, but he had withdrawn from the world and would say no more.

It was barely eight o'clock the following morning when a sharp rap upon my door and a shout of "Come along, Watson – and bring your service revolver!" was sufficient to hurry me through my ablutions. Holmes, it seemed, had already breakfasted and a cup of coffee and pile of buttered toast had appeared, as if by magic, in my place at the breakfast table. I sat and ate, but was acutely aware that every single mouthful might be seen as a moment wasted. After finishing my coffee and having consumed barely a solitary slice of toast, I felt that I could delay Holmes no longer and rose from the table.

It was as if, by doing so, someone had fired a pistol to start a race as Holmes moved towards the sitting room door and then down the stairs. I followed at my own pace and, on arrival in the street below, climbed into the waiting cab.

"How do you intend to proceed at the bank?" I asked.

Holmes smiled grimly. "The world of banking is still one of secrecy and discretion. As long as the person requiring access to a safety deposit box has the necessary means to open it, then the bank will not ask for any particulars of the person, nor ask their identity." I frowned but waited for him to continue. "Whilst you slumbered, I sent a telegram to Lestrade asking him, in turn, to inform the bank of our imminent arrival. I only trust that he is an earlier bird than yourself!"

I was about to argue the point but the cab jolted to a halt in front of The London and Provincial Bank's Mayfair branch. Stepping out and tossing the cabbie a florin, Holmes strode up the pink granite steps of this most impressive building. This banking emporium was full of elegant turned-Mahogany balustrades and counters, each topped with frosted glass windows. Holmes looked around and headed directly towards a teller's window above which, in fine, gold lettering, were the words "*Securities and Deposits*".

Holmes's gloved hand came down sharply on the silver circular bell before him and within moments, a smartly dressed clerk stood in attendance. Holmes produced his card, saying simply, "Please be so kind as to hand this to the manager." The clerk disappeared and, within half-a-minute, we were being ushered into a side office.

Standing before us was a short, balding, rather portly gentleman in a morning suit. "Mr. Holmes? I am Stephen Holt, the manager of this branch, and I have received a telegram from an Inspector Lestrade of Scotland Yard. He asks that I assist you as fully as possible." Mr. Holt waited for Holmes to respond but, as nothing seemed to be forthcoming, he continued, "With the involvement of Scotland Yard, I trust there has been no misconduct on the part of the bank or its employees?"

Holmes smiled. "Not at all, Mr. Holt, although, unwittingly, you may be the custodians of an item of stolen property. It is that that I need to establish."

On hearing this, Holt reached out to desk beside him for some support. "I . . . I trust that is not so, for the bank would never knowingly allow – "

Holmes held up his hand. "No, no, Mr. Holt. No blame can be attached to the bank, but it is necessary to verify the contents of a certain safety deposit box. Also, we need to remain within the bank, as I believe that the person responsible for the theft will attempt to remove the stolen property this very day."

Holt now took from his pocket a large white handkerchief and blotted his forehead and bald pate. "Of course, but I cannot open a safety deposit box. Only the bearer of the combination is able to do that."

Holmes smiled and tapped his waistcoat pocket, answering, "All is to hand, Mr. Holt. If you would be so kind and lead the way, time is pressing."

With no further ado, we were taken towards a large, iron-grilled doorway before a steep, downward staircase. A uniformed bank officer opened this at a single wave of a finger from Holt. Descending, we arrived before a large, vault door. This again was opened swiftly and without question, due to the mere presence of the manager and then closed securely behind us.

Looking about me, in the glare of modern, electric lights, a truly cavernous room was revealed. It appeared to be filled from floor to ceiling with green painted, metal boxes, attached securely to the walls. Ahead of me, I observed that a large letter "*N*" in gold paint hung above that bank of boxes. Realising its significance, I watched as Holmes turned right, ninety degrees, and strode towards a similar bank of boxes above which hung a similarly gilded, letter "*E*".

Taking a piece of paper from his waistcoat pocket, Holmes verified the number of the box he sought. As I looked, I realised that the boxes were not all of the same size. Those beginning with the figure "*5*" had doors which were quite large, some twelve inches by, perhaps, twenty-four inches, whilst the boxes beginning with a figure "*1*" were slim, perhaps only four inches by nine inches.

Holmes paused before Box 580. Holt, I noticed had stayed at Holmes's elbow and now waited to ensure that Holmes could, indeed, open the box which was secured by a brass, four-barrel, combination padlock. Leaning forward, Holmes grasped the lock securely and quickly arranged the tumblers to *1952* which then released the hasp. Seeing that the lock had been opened correctly, Holt now withdrew to a discreet distance.

Holmes removed the lock and proceeded to open the door to the box. The contents within were in a sliding metal tray and, upon withdrawing it, Holt now led us to a small, lit, curtained cubicle where we could examine the contents with a degree of privacy.

Surveying the contents of the tray, I could immediately discern several loose and boxed items of fine diamond jewellery and a leather bag which, on opening, revealed a variety of gold coins. However, it was a velvet-wrapped item that stood on end that I was eager to have sight of. With care, Holmes laid the item beside the tray and unfolded the velvet cover.

Before us, in a swept, gilded frame, was the work of a Flemish master. The scene was of a rustic kitchen with a classic, black-and-white tiled floor. At one side, a figure, in the distinctive attire of a Flemish woman, was holding forth a tray of roasted apples which she had removed from the open oven, seen in the background.

Peering at the picture, I ventured, "It seems that there is no mistaking the provenance of this painting."

Holmes nodded. Swiftly, he re-wrapped the painting and then moved to replace the tray within the safety deposit box and to secure it with the padlock. He then randomly turned the tumblers on the lock and then led Holt to one side for a private conversation to which I was not a party. I saw, however, Holt suddenly stop, stock still, before slowly nodding. At this, Holmes patted him on the shoulder, although of what had been discussed, I was none the wiser.

After a few moments, Holmes returned to my side. "Watson, I have something of an onerous task to ask of you. Would you be willing to keep watch here, in the vault, concealed within this cubicle? I will be on hand above, but should I be called away by Lady Lawson, I need a trusted friend to observe on my behalf."

Without a moment's hesitation I nodded, saying, "Of course, Holmes." With a smile and a nod, Holmes disappeared with Holt, and I settled down in a comfortable chair within the cubicle that had been provided for clients whilst viewing the contents of their boxes.

It was, perhaps, some fifteen minutes later that I heard the vault door open once more and footsteps approaching my position. I had already extinguished the light and, from my darkened eyrie, I observed a muscular, heavily built figure holding a leather briefcase being escorted by an elderly, uniformed officer of the bank towards the east wall of the vault. Peering through a gap in the curtain, I observed the two men standing with their backs to me, not ten feet away.

The bank officer touched his peaked cap, announcing, in a light voice that seemed to reflect his age and posture, "Here you are sir, Box 580, east wall. I will just wait until you have unlocked it." The muscular fellow simply grunted as he manipulated the lock.

With a click, the hasp fell open and the fellow reached out a hand to open the box. Looking up, he again grunted, saying, "On your way, I have no further need of you."

The elderly bank officer nodded and began to walk away, but then turned and said in a clear voice that I instantly recognised, "Oh, but I think you do, Mr. Gardner!"

The man's head shot up on hearing his name and his hand flew to the waistband of his trousers, returning with a wicked looking blade that he held before him. "How do you know my name? Tell me, quick!"

Holmes had a thin smile upon his face as he removed the peaked cap and stood more upright. "I know a great many things, Mr. Gardner. For instance, I know that you were once employed as a farrier at Bath House and, after the fire, you stole the Flemish painting and lodged it for safe keeping with Percy Small. Small vanished but you tracked him down and, on torturing him, you discovered the coded secret held within the three tattoos." Holmes paused, adding, "This knowledge is, I fear, the burden I bear for being Sherlock Holmes."

Gardner took a step towards Holmes and I drew my service revolver from my jacket pocket. "So, Mr. Holmes, the clever detective, how are you going to stop me from slicing you?"

Holmes again smiled, answering, "I am not, but my good friend, Doctor Watson, who is standing behind you with a pistol aimed directly at your head, might well."

I heard a coarse laugh from the man. "Do you think that I am foolish enough to believe you, Holmes?"

At that, the sound of the hammer of my revolver being cocked and the cylinder rotating was clearly audible, seemingly magnified by the hard walls of the vault. My arm was extended and rock steady as the incredulous man slowly turned to face me. My voice was completely calm as I spoke. "Have no doubt, Mr. Gardner, I will shoot you, without a shred of remorse, should you not drop the knife."

I stood, my face empty of all emotion. Gardner's expression was defiant – for a moment – before the knife fell from his hand.

At this, Holmes reached into his waistcoat pocket and took from it his police whistle and blew two sharp blasts upon it. Almost immediately, two constables appeared at the entrance to the vault with truncheons drawn. I kept my revolver trained on Gardner as the man was swiftly handcuffed and then led away.

Holmes's face showed a good deal of relief, but he then frowned as he bent down to cautiously retrieve Gardner's blade from the floor of the vault. He nodded to himself before wrapping the knife in his handkerchief and then stowing it safely in his jacket pocket.

With Holmes now changed back into his own clothes and the contents of safety deposit box under lock and key, we returned to Baker Street in time to enjoy a well-deserved luncheon. It was as we sat and smoked, replete, that I began to turn over the facts of the case in my mind.

"I must say, you played the part of the bank official well, but I'm intrigued to know how you knew the name of the killer?"

Holmes, now seated, gave a mock bow and sat back, drawing strongly on his pipe. "In order for the painting to have been removed from Bath House, the thief must have had access. It was simple enough to obtain a list of the household at the time of the robbery and to request that Lestrade cast his eye over it. A name that sprang out at him was one Henry Gardner, a fellow who had come to the attention of the Metropolitan Police for theft and suspected of several brutal assaults."

Holmes paused and reached into his jacket pocket. Opening his handkerchief, he leant forward to display Gardner's knife, asking, "What do you notice about this knife, Watson?"

I looked closely at the weapon, observing that it had a riveted wooden handle and a short, curved blade. "The blade appears to be somewhat out of the ordinary, Holmes. What was its original purpose?"

Holmes nodded. "You will recall that I told Gardner that I knew he was employed as a farrier. When I saw the wound to Small's back and the curved slash to Abigail Carter, the shape of the killer's blade became most significant."

I suddenly understood, stating, "Gardner was a farrier, and they use knives with curved blades to trim the horse's hooves. He must have retained his knife from his previous employment."

A thin smile crossed Holmes's face. "Quite so. A sentimental attachment that will undoubtedly send him on his way to the gallows."

Still thinking of the case, I asked, "Tell me – once the ladies had been tattooed, there was no need for Small to memorise nor write down the details to retrieve the painting at a later date." Holmes nodded whilst I continued to formulate my question. "How then, in the future, was he to have sight of the code again?"

Holmes drew on his pipe, before replying, "In your profession, Watson, you are acutely aware of the possibility of infection once the protection afforded by the skin has been breached. However, this happens, by necessity, during the process of tattooing."

I nodded and encouraged him to continue.

"I found, tucked in the back of Small's ledger, a *pro-forma* letter advising clients that, as part of his service, he would return after some period of time, to examine his work and to assure his clients that their tattoo was free of infection. I believe that this also gave him a chance to offer his services for further tattoos, but in the case of the three ladies, to gather the coded information that he required." On hearing this, I sat back in wonder at the guile of Percy Small and also at his commercial prowess.

I was pleased to hear Holmes's explanation and we smoked on, each with our own thoughts.

At some point in the weeks that followed, I recall that we received a letter from Lord Ashburton thanking us for the return of his painting and enclosing, in gratitude, a cheque for some two-hundred guineas. However, we were to learn, sometime later, that it had again become "lost" and has, to this day, not been recovered.

Lady Lawson, I discovered by way of the social pages, has become something of a celebrity. I was required to provide but the briefest of details of this to Holmes, as he refused to read of it himself!

Henry Gardner was tried at the Old Bailey for both the initial theft of the painting and also the murders of Percy Small and Abigail Carter. On conviction, was duly hanged. Enquiring further, although not reported, the death of Mrs. Heath was not considered at the trial. This, I believe, was done to avoid undue distress to the family. The original coroner's verdict was left, unchanged, as that of "accidental death".

The Problem at Pentonville Prison
by David Friend

A doctor's week can be hectic and should always end with a glass of sherry. Such restoratives are especially welcome during those long winter months in which most every denizen of our distinguished capital clumps dejectedly through the doors and demands immediate attention and the mightiest medicament. During the particular October of which I write, soon after the attempted robbery at the Capital and Counties Bank, there was not only a fierce and indefatigable illness floating upon the bitter wind, but a secretary at Barts, Mrs. Agnew, was one of the fallen, and I was forced into attempting to comprehend her frustratingly obscure filing system. This alone could have sent a hale and hearty man to his bed, though I was content to return to Baker Street and sit beside a smouldering hearth with a book on my lap and a drink at my side. Even the way the pale straw-yellow liquid burbled out of the bottle was enough to soften my sinews and I savoured the prospect of a peaceful evening alone.

I had recently become quite fascinated with naval engineering, and was a fair few chapters into William Henry Davenport Adams's *Famous Ships of the British Navy*, reading of the loss of *Royal George*, when the door sprung open and in swept a vicar.

I jolted upright in both alarm and disbelief.

Here stood an intruder unlike any other. Balding and bespectacled, with a Bible in his bony hands, a crucifix loose around his neck, and a grimace hidden within a Van Dyke beard. Stepping widely towards me, the figure took away my glass and splashed what little that was left into the fire. It hissed indignantly and, though still startled, I felt much the same way.

"What – ?" I jabbered. "Who – ?"

The clergyman cast off his collar and dropped onto the sofa. "*Wine is a mocker, strong drink is raging, and whosoever is deceived thereby is not wise.*" He lifted the Bible pointedly before tossing it to his side.

"You've deceived a few yourself, I see."

"All for the good, Watson. I was at St James's in disguise. Usually the Seal of Confession prohibits a priest from revealing anything disclosed to him during the Sacrament of Penance."

"But you're not a priest," I frowned.

"Precisely. 'Arsenic' Archie is presently enjoying such a theological discussion with Inspector Forbes."

It took but a moment for my friend to strip off his false beard and reveal his hair from under a rubber cap so expertly fixed with spirit gum.

This wasn't the first time that Holmes had disguised himself as a clergyman – it wasn't even the first time that year – and I wondered if he enjoyed being a man of the cloth. Such a person, after all, typically possesses the sort of stubborn certainty with which he searched for in his own endeavours, while both of them put significant stock in the sanctity of truth. Though I cannot recall at the present moment whether I ever confronted my friend on spiritual matters, I knew he was intimately familiar with Catholicism from quite a young age, and that he would go on to undertake some particularly sensitive matters on behalf of the Vatican, but whether these efforts had any basis in his own beliefs was never made clear to me. In any case, I had reason to avoid the subject. My mother had been a fervent follower of the Third Order of St. Francis and, as such, a lifelong pacifist, which meant that our association was severed immediately upon my decision to fight in Afghanistan. The Church, therefore, did not deliver to me solace, but rather sorrow.

Holmes slipped into his silk dressing gown and settled into his armchair with all the expectation of an audience at the Haymarket. Something, clearly, was due to occur, and it didn't bode well for my reading.

"I take it that we have a client arriving?"

"Mrs. Hudson arranged it while I was saying mass," he said.

I snapped my book shut with frustration.

It was not, in truth, too much of a surprise. Holmes had been remarkably productive of late and we hadn't gone a week without a client visiting our rooms and presenting a fresh problem for him to unravel in his inimitable way. That month alone, he had quite literally clashed swords with the notorious pirate Captain Dashwood over the Puzzle Ring of Lizard Point, recovered an ancient Rosicrucian document, and correctly identified Junius, the pseudonymous polemicist so famously critical of King George III's government more than a century earlier. The inexorable march of clients into Baker Street was, I believed, beginning to take its toll on his physical health. Throughout my career as a physician, I had seen the tell-tale signs of exhaustion countless times in my patients – weight loss, dark shadows under the eyes, and the pallid colouration of the skin – and Holmes, to my alarm, possessed every one. He was, of course, nothing if not obstinate, and though sometimes canvassed my opinions on medical matters in regards to a case, he dismissed them altogether whenever his own well-being was brought into question. Such matters would only prevent him from pursuing an investigation. The next of which, I realised, was about to begin, as the peeling bell announced a new arrival and I gave up all plans of an evening to myself.

Moments later, Mrs. Hudson was hovering over the threshold and introducing our guest. He was a stout man with grey hair, a broad, delicately putted face and a lugubrious moustache. Though a crisp autumn wind fairly brushed the streets without, he wore no coat and carried only a small book in the pocket of his tweeds. At my friend's invitation, he lowered himself heavily into the chair opposite, tight lines of tumult creasing his brow. Holmes, of course, had a way of calming nervous clients, chiefly achieved with his own easy manner and by pressing his fingers into a contemplative steeple. It wasn't just respect which he exhibited in such moments – despite his occasional abrasiveness and pithy ripostes at my expense, Holmes was usually polite to strangers. There was also a certain eager excitement, like a child about to be read a bedtime story. Fittingly, almost as though he were aware of his corresponding role, our visitor bowed his head, focussed intensely on the floor, and began to explain just what had brought him to our door.

"Mr. Holmes," he said in a husky voice, "I come to you with a matter most urgent. My name is Jebediah Fallow, a prison governor at – "

"So I perceive," interrupted Holmes and, brushing a speck of something invisible from his lap, crossed his legs neatly.

I choked back a gasp. On many previous occasions, my astonishment at these dazzling feats of deduction had been clear for anyone to see. By this point, however, I was self-consciously concerned that such a reaction would make me seem a little too credulous and simple-minded for someone who was supposed to be familiar with the man and his gifts. And so it was in a dull and disinterested voice that I attempted to display my own acute observations.

"The gentleman possesses a somewhat military bearing," I explained, "and men of authority are often enlisted from the army into the prison service. He carries with him the whiff of those places and, just visibly, has pocketed a copy of Frederic Hill's *Crime, its Amount, Causes, and Remedies*. I recognize it from our shelf."

For once, I was able to enjoy the same dignified air that had surrounded Holmes for so many years and examined my fingernails with just the right amount of cursory indifference.

"Watson," said Holmes gently, "I heard Mr. Fallow speak to the Prison Commission last year."

Our visitor, meanwhile, looked somewhere between flummoxed and offended. "What 'whiff'?" he demanded.

"You must forgive my friend," said Holmes with wry amusement. "As a doctor, he focusses more on the body than the mind, which is usually my area. Perhaps, now, you can speak of your own."

"Thank you, Mr. Holmes. I did, indeed, serve in the British Army, though was invalided out during the re-occupation of the Shwedagon Pagoda. Soon after, I graced the position of Governor at Coldbath Fields and, subsequently, Pentonville, where I have remained for almost twenty years. There have been challenges in that time, of course, but none were so difficult as the one in which I am currently faced."

Mr. Jebediah Fallow stared at Holmes with something which I had seen so often before in clients who had come to my friend for counsel. It was a sort of weak plea – a boiling torment which had curdled into cool resignation. He would, no doubt, be glad to press his problem into the hands of someone else. Holmes understood that this was part of his service, and though it interested him the least, I believe that he was pleased with whatever help he could provide, even if it did lean more towards the heart than the mind. In return, of course, he was gifted with a puzzle – a treat for him like a piece of meat to a dog – and the one in which we heard that evening seized his attention from the first.

"You see, Mr. Holmes . . . ." said our guest, wavering slightly, but then his face tightened with determination, and he spilt out the words in a hasty breath. "There has been a murder at the prison!"

Nowhere else in London would such an assertion be so commonplace, and my friend's stare remained coolly impassive. "I dare say the suspects shall be numerous."

"That is why I have come to you," said our visitor anxiously. "There are over five-hundred men at Pentonville. As we operate under the so-called separate system, they are forbidden to speak to each other and remain isolated in a cell of their own. Even when out in the exercise yard, their faces are covered in brown cloth masks – called 'peaks' – while they walk in so many silent circles. Each man, therefore, is utterly unknown to the other. Such was the scene on Tuesday last. One prisoner, however, was missing. As you can imagine, this led to a most frantic search, until they found him in a nearby storeroom. His throat had been slit with a letter-knife." Mr. Jebediah Fallow winced resignedly and I felt quite sorry for the man. He might well have lost his job over the matter. "It is inexplicable, Mr. Holmes! How could any killer harbour such hatred towards someone to whom he hasn't even spoken and whose face he has never seen? For that matter, how the devil could he identify his target? It'd be easier picking out a sheep in a flock of hundreds."

Holmes, of course, had the stubborn heart of a bloodhound and would not give up so easily. "I think," he said, brisk and buoyant, "that you should tell us about this prisoner."

This seemed to focus Mr. Fallow's mind. "His name was Albert Winch. A travelling basket-maker from Morpeth until his conviction for house-breaking resulted in a five-year sentence. He was short and reedy, almost made for slipping through windows and ducking out of view, with receding black hair and narrow, flinty eyes. His death came as quite a shock, not least because he had visited my office only a few days previously, claiming to possess information of a break-out."

It was probably imprudent of me, but I felt in my breast a stir of boyish excitement. Such an audacious act had always caught my imagination, posing most particularly an intellectual problem of a sort which Holmes himself would relish. Being dumped in a dungeon with nothing but lice and a challenge to escape was his idea of a birthday present.

"He had my attention immediately. For a working man, he turned out to be quite remarkably shrewd. Work was so mundane, he said, that he had taken to devising ways in which he might escape. He even claimed responsibility for a tunnel that was dug under the oakum shed! At first, I thought this was so much hot air, of course, but the details were so precise, and his logic so sound, that I began to feel his words might be at least partly credible. Frustratingly, however, he refused to say any more unless I first afforded him a week that was free of the treadwheel!"

"And did you?" I asked eagerly.

"Not a bit of it," said Mr. Fallow and his moustache twitched assertively. "I couldn't let anyone miss so much work, nor would I believe a petty boast unless he revealed more to me." Our visitor might have seemed hopeless just then, but I could imagine him to be quite firm when the occasion demanded it. "And so, after much prompting and the promise of a full meal, he explained all. It was, needless to say, an education. He spoke of times in which he had slipped from his cell and raided the kitchens to spending nights beneath the stars in the exercise yard. For all I know, Mr. Holmes, he could have been mounting our wall like a set of stairs!"

I turned to share my shock with Holmes. His head was tilted back, eyes closed contemplatively, fingers pressed into a steeple. At such times, he preferred nothing more than cold concentration.

"Finally, after a minute or so of blather, Winch got to the point. Somebody, he said, had asked him to work up a plan for another such escape. Something about skipping chapel and hiding in the stables during a visit from a relative and – "

" – Incapacitating the driver before taking his place in the cab," finished Holmes with a thoughtful nod. "Yes, I dare say that was a suggestion."

But our guest had not quite finished. "Of more concern, Mr. Holmes, was the man who had asked for his help." Our guest paused and seemed unable to continue. I couldn't discern at first the reason for this reticence, but then he swallowed dryly and I saw that he was scared. "Mr. Paris."

"Mr. Paris?" I repeated innocently. "Does he not have a first name?"

"Oh, I wouldn't dare speak of it! Anyone who is even vaguely disrespectful suffers some suspicious misfortune."

I glanced curiously to my side. "Have you heard of this chap before?"

To any casual observer, Sherlock Holmes was asleep. A tight smile, however, curved across his lips and he let out a loose chuckle. "Always," he said with some respect, and the grey eyes swooped open once again. "Not for nothing do they call him 'The Prince of Pentonville'. His activities over the last three years alone could fill my scrapbooks from front to back, and he's been in there for seven! Such pages remain bare, however, as he delegates all duties to the scores outside the prison who make up his organization." There was admiration in his voice, and I was reminded again that my friend's view of criminals wasn't always coloured by the morality of my own. "However, according to whispers," he revealed, "such a long imprisonment has inspired a mutiny among his men on the outside. It isn't surprising, therefore, to hear how he wants to return to them and reassert his authority."

"That's unlikely to happen now, surely?" I said. "Winch may have conceived a way of breaking out, but he's traded it in for some good food at last."

"Understandable, but foolish," reflected Mr. Fallow.

"Certainly it was," I agreed, "as Paris seems to have found out and killed him!"

The governor tensed visibly, his hoarse voice gripped with panic. "The Home Secretary is already restless. If something doesn't happen soon – "

"Pshaw!" said Holmes, lifting a conciliatory hand. "It's just a question of acquiring evidence. Dr. Watson and I shall visit Pentonville immediately."

Appreciation softened our visitor's face. After what must have been some sleepless nights, his problem was being examined by an expert. "You are most kind, Mr. Holmes. As I have reports to write tonight, perhaps tomorrow would suffice?"

Holmes agreed, though I was not so pleased. His curiosity had been piqued and he would no doubt spend the rest of the evening soaring away on his Stradivarius. I was tired enough without having my sleep disturbed and dearly wished that our guest would say something to sate him. As it was, Mr. Fallow merely thanked my friend and, with hope upon his heart, bade us both goodnight.

"Sounds promising, does it not, Watson? A case utterly without motive."

"Yet one with more suspects than any human mind can comprehend."

After such a trying day, I couldn't evince enthusiasm for anything other than rest and refused to ponder the matter any further. Holmes, unfortunately, took up his familiar stance over the hearth rug.

"Don't go on too long," I begged, but he was already at one with the music and could hear nothing else – selective deafness which, at that moment, I would have paid good money to possess.

Holmes must have been one of the finest amateur violinists in the West End. – he would sometimes join the busker who played outside St. George's Hall – yet mainly he did it to help him think, even if it stopped everyone else from doing so themselves.

Retiring to my chambers, I spent hours staring into blackness and trying to ignore the scratching of strings. My weary mind turned to Pentonville Prison and how, in that den of depravity and decay, some unsuspecting inmate had been ruthlessly impaled. I knew not the geography of the place, but my imagination made up for it, conjuring scenes of secret night-time excursions through twisting, cavernous corridors and into damp cells with sleeping men who would never awake. And somehow, foolishly, I found myself in a long, dark corridor, the walls around me stretching upwards until they were towers touching an impenetrable sky. And then, a scuffle of footsteps, an unexpected whoop, and the sudden spurt of sangria red. Finally, as an unseen violin plucked out a ponderous tune, I lay on the floor, weak as a whisper. But also, strangely, relieved.

The next morning, a shy autumn sun peeking through the curtains found me in a tangled heap on the edge of the bed and in danger of dropping out. It has often been thus. For some inexplicable reason, all the men in my bloodline were restless sleepers and seem to have spent much of history fidgeting fitfully in total darkness, hitting headboards and rolling randomly into their wives. There were no bruises in this instance, which meant the day had started well already, and I lay there lethargically, savouring the silence. Holmes had played on into the night, but now the absence of such discordance was music in itself. I imagined him inert on the sofa, cradling the violin, finally exhausted after hours of thought and inspiriting strains. On the window ledge, a bird began to chirp and I listened appreciatively, trying to identify the breed. And then, just as its song had come to a close, a loud whine sprang from the sitting room. Holmes, incredibly, was swinging his elbow still, and I almost threw myself despairingly beneath the bedclothes. There were times in which I considered moving into rooms of my own, and just then the idea seemed particularly appealing. The only way to distract my friend was to remind him of breakfast, and so, a few minutes later, I watched with satisfaction as he lay his instrument aside and picked up a knife and fork.

"This Winch fellow sounds like quite a clever sort," I observed whilst buttering my toast. "Stands to reason, I suppose. He spent years breaking into buildings and then he had to break out of one."

Holmes carved open a sausage. "Most comical," he muttered caustically.

I was hoping to hear some theories but recognized the beginnings of a moody silence. Though these were few and far between, they were liable to last some hours. "Do you still believe that Mr. Paris is the culprit?"

Sherlock Holmes looked up vaguely. "It certainly appears so," he allowed. "Naturally, in speaking of the escape, Winch would have angered him. But evidence has always been elusive where Paris is concerned."

"But he must have been caught somehow," I pointed out. "Of which crime was he convicted?"

All of a sudden abandoning breakfast, Holmes leant back in his chair and stretched as though his night had been one of deep and revivifying rest. "Tax evasion," he said with amusement. "Even Sir Augustus, the Treasury Solicitor, knew they couldn't collar him for anything else. Mark my words, Watson, we have set ourselves a most ambitious task."

Prisons always remind me of medieval castles with vigilant bowmen guarding their king from behind the battlements. Of course, they are actually quite the opposite, designed to keep people within its walls and not out of them, and those few that stand in the city may seem markedly less alarming than the gothic, dangerously remote fortresses one can find in Dartmoor and Bodmin. Such appearances, as Holmes has often shown, can be deceptive. There may only have been a flagged courtyard and an old iron railing to separate Pentonville Prison from polite society, but it was this proximity which reminded us how easily we could be sent there ourselves.

It was similarly disconcerting to see the grated windows and barred doors and know that I would soon be on the other side of them. The jangle of keys signalled as such and we turned to find a stout porter amble unhurriedly towards the gate. Of more concern, however, was the pair of bullmastiffs snapping their way across the yard at a rate of knots. Lightning cracked across my chest and I felt an instinctive urge to run, but

Holmes gripped my arm preventively. There was no escaping Pentonville, even if we were still on the outside. With a yowl of his own, the porter threw up his hands and the dogs fell into a reluctant bundle. Their glares, though, were just as fierce.

"Who are you?" the man demanded. "These two don't like strangers."

"Yes, they certainly seem shy," said Sherlock Holmes, "but perhaps they can make an exception. We have an appointment with the governor."

Mr. Jebediah Fallow met us in his office. It was a cramped, musty room with Lincrusta walls which seemed to lean claustrophobically across the grey carpet. I had the notion that everyone was a prisoner in this building, and not just those who had been convicted of a crime. The only colour came from the flowers in the Rachel Ruysch painting hung above a black Kilkenny marble fireplace, while a pot of tea was placed invitingly on an old oak desk in front of it.

Holmes, to my discomfiture, wouldn't be seated and instead browsed the corner bookshelves with a spirited interest. Every few moments, he would pull out a thick volume and glance at its contents before slipping it back and searching again.

Not for the first time, all social graces were left to me to uphold, and my ensuing conversation with the governor turned to prison life and how inmates spent their time. I learned that the bell rang each morning at a quarter-to-six and the door would be unlocked so that the prisoner could empty his chamber pot and attend chapel. Breakfasts were no luxury either, with just ten ounces of bread and three-quarters of a pint of cocoa, while all the men were afforded for dinner was half-a-pint of soup, five ounces of bread, and a pound of potatoes. Supper, finally, included a pint of pitiless gruel. It was little wonder that Albert Winch had bargained for something better. That was the least of it, of course. The hard labour was merciless, while the discipline was even more pedantic than I had experienced in the army.

To my surprise and his great merit, Mr. Fallow disagreed with the moral philosophies of our penal system. Indeed, he seemed to possess a goodly amount of sense and innovation, explaining that such tedious jobs were needlessly punitive and that they did nothing but frustrate and exhaust the prisoners. The most detested of these was the treadwheel. This was a revolving staircase of twenty-four steps, attached to an enormous paddle wheel, and the men would climb it every day for fifteen quarter-hour sessions – the equivalent of eighteen thousand steps – as the gears crushed grain or pumped water. Less exhausting, but just as repetitive, was oakum picking, which involved pulling apart tarred rope into its bare fibres so that they could be used again (though at least this has afforded us the phrase "money for old rope"). Our visit to Pentonville, moreover, occurred at a time well before the breaking of rocks and the recent decision to have such men make fishing nets or sew coal sacks and mail bags, but even then Mr. Jebediah Fallow was contemplating the future of criminal confinement.

"You seem to have a most intuitive understanding of these offenders," said I.

"Moral philosophy has always been an interest of mine. You see, involvement in criminal justice makes it necessary to understand the lawless and, more particularly, how they cope with incarceration. It is the only way in which any means of order can be permanently sustained."

My friend's movements had become too distracting. "Holmes," I said with some exasperation, "why don't you sit down? You must forgive his restlessness, Mr. Fallow. He doesn't often see where criminals end up, though he's usually the one who sends them here."

Before Holmes could pry any further – on present form, he may well have begun rifling through the governor's desk – there came a knock at the door.

"Ah, Mr. Stubbs. Gentlemen, this is our chief warder."

In stepped a middle-aged man with iron-grey hair, bushy brows, and a stern, suspicious face. I had known many such fellows in the army and could tell on sight that he had also fought. His manner, certainly, was militaristic, and he stood stiffly to attention as though he had been summoned before his commanding officer for stealing someone else's meat ration.

Finally Holmes turned to our side of the room and, in particular, the new arrival. He stared intensely, like a painter who had just espied the perfect subject for a portrait, his lips flickering into a whimsical smile.

Stubbs was clearly uncomfortable under such bright-eyed scrutiny and didn't know Holmes from Adam. In those days, photographic etchings in newspapers were mainly reserved for figures of particular import, and few people were therefore able to recognize the detective, despite several of his most prominent cases being pushed into the public discourse.

"This is Mr. Sherlock Holmes and Dr. Watson. They are here to investigate . . . our difficulty."

With effort, Stubbs unhooked himself from Holmes's still gaze and looked querulously at the governor. "Sir, dare I say it, but there is little reason to call upon outside assistance." He spoke in a Cumbrian accent and, though his words were polite, they carried with them an edge of wounded pride. Most certainly he had intended to settle the matter himself and may even have relished the opportunity. It was, after all, quite a departure from the dull routine of a warder's daily duties, and success could well have resulted in a promotion. Instead, in what must have been a humiliating slight, he was being overlooked in favour of someone who did not work in the prison service or, even more egregiously, for the police.

Mr. Fallow, however, was without hesitation. "Mr. Holmes is experienced in matters of a delicate nature, most particularly the criminal kind."

"But sir – "

"I've already said everything I intend to say on the topic." His voice, too, certainly made it plain. "Now, please, show our visitors were Mr. Winch was unfortunately found."

A few minutes later, the chief warder was leading us through a corridor so long and inky black that I half-expected to be murdered there myself. A glimmer of daylight shimmered in the distance, but we weren't venturing out to the exercise yard. Only the storeroom interested us. It was a small room with just a couple of brooms and a bucket, but its position at the corner made it perfect for an ambush. Any warder standing on each end of the corridor wouldn't have seen Winch getting snatched.

"The killer was in there waiting," said Stubbs. "Opened the door, pulled him inside, and plunged the letter-opener into his throat. Obviously someone knew what they were doing, which could honestly describe almost everybody in the building."

I was already confused. "But how did the killer know which man was Winch? All of the prisoners wear those silly masks. Furthermore, this corridor is far too dark. I can barely recognize you, Holmes, and you're not even disguised."

"There's only one explanation," said Holmes. "The murderer must have been able to see in the dark and through masks."

This was hardly a satisfactory conclusion. "Whatever happened to eliminating the impossible?" I asked.

"Ah, yes, my favourite philosophy. Well, Watson, it's simple. I decided to eliminate that instead." He turned to Stubbs. "I assume that the Yard was called?"

The chief warder nodded moodily. "They made little sense of it. I'd rather handle the matter myself."

"Oh yes?" said Holmes with an impish interest. "Have you investigated a murder before?"

Stubbs had not expected such a question, but whatever blankness crossed his face was gone in a second and replaced with something smug and airily indifferent. "I've seen a fair measure in my time," he boasted. "Things get very bleak."

"I dare say," said Holmes. His mind, however, had already turned to something else. "Did Mr. Winch send correspondence to his relatives?"

Stubbs shook his head. "Each prisoner is allowed to receive one letter every six months, but he never claimed it."

"Maybe," I suggested, "he and his family were not on good terms?"

Holmes murmured something doubtful. It was sometimes an irritation to see some of my more reasonable ideas being so arbitrarily rebuffed, but I knew that he meant no malice and would just as ruthlessly disregard his own. To him, considering a possible motive was much like trying on a trilby at the tailors. It had to fit the width of the head and feel right to the eye. Anything else was uncomfortable and wrong.

"I'd rather like to meet Mr. Paris," he said at last.

Like so many of my friend's remarks, whatever their purport, it was the most innocuous and indifferently delivered which caused commotion. Stubbs, reliably, loosed a leery jaw. "No! None of the prisoners is allowed to have their work interrupted."

"Nonsense!" scoffed Holmes. "Why must we hinder ourselves with rules? For that matter, why are bureaucrats so obsessed with them?" He tapped his temple dubiously. "There are certainly walls in this prison, Mr. Stubbs, but the ones which matter are in the mind."

The chief warder stared at him with wide-eyed bewilderment. His view of the world was suddenly obscure, like a cloud across the sun. Hastily, he searched for any excuse which could justify the prison's injudicious policy. This involved some anxious blinking and a long and empty pause. Finally, before the sweat of effort could sluice his brow, he found something which might resemble reason. "Mr. Paris is a most religious man, practising long periods of Christian meditation – and, really, might be praying even now!"

Holmes smiled whimsically. "He must have heard that I'm here."

I expected Paris to reside in a cell just as cold and claustrophobic as the one which had appeared so disturbingly in my dream of the previous night. It was, therefore, a surprise to be faced with one so flippantly dismissive of institutional standards. Walls of at least three other cells had been knocked down to accommodate what could only otherwise be considered a luxury hotel suite. A Louis XV limestone fireplace stood grandly before a sleeping Cavalier King Charles Spaniel, flanked by bookcases lined with leather-bound editions of Romantic poetry, while landscape paintings from the Hudson River School hung over scrolling foliage of William Morris wallpaper. A half-tester bed sat upon an expensive Ziegler carpet, and a budgerigar chirped cheerily from its cage in the corner. To be sure, this opulence seemed limited to just one prisoner, but even that was too much. A crime must never pay, after all, and despite my somewhat liberal regard for convicted criminals, having such men maintain a standard of living even higher than that of the magistrate who had sentenced them was inequitable. There was even a cup of Cadbury's Cocoa Essence on the nightstand!

For some minutes, Holmes and I waited on the sofa while a sickly little fellow went to fetch the occupant. The idea of a prisoner this powerful sent a cold prickle up my spine. It seemed so incongruous in a place where lawfulness was supposed to preside. Clearly the staff were aware of Paris's true character, but weren't brave enough to enforce any discipline. Even Stubbs – to all appearances a formidable man who was presumably used to dangerous criminals – had refused to introduce us to him. Fear reigned supreme and people preferred to buckle under instead of choosing to challenge it.

There was nothing else to do but stare rather incredulously at the furnishings and speculate as to which of them were forgeries. Holmes had a working knowledge of such matters after the Parmigianino discovery and asserted that each piece of the art around us was authentic. Of course, I could sometimes be a bit gullible, which was something my friend would ruthlessly exploit for his own mordant amusement, so he might well have been fibbing. Finally, just as I was scrutinizing a Frederic Edwin Church for a signature, and wondering vaguely if its rainbow was supposed to be coloured, a shadow fell across the doorway and we were no longer alone.

A short, dandyish man was standing before us. His hair was silver and sleek as a seal above a pale and cherubic face, while the eyes were a wistful, watery blue. A silk dressing gown of red-and-white polka-dots hung loosely around a pair of weak shoulders and a tousled cravat, and a long cigarette-holder was lifted limply to his lips. He was every inch the Oxford aesthete and seemed to have been summoned directly from a red brick Mayfair townhouse. A plume of smoke slipped out serenely and when it settled we could see that he was smirking.

"Mr. Sherlock Holmes," he intoned nasally and with perfect diction.

My friend stood up in what seemed like an almost deferential gesture. "Mr. Paris."

"Please, call me Desmond," said our host hospitably. "A thousand apologies for my tardiness. I was attending to my rose garden."

"I didn't realise that prisoners practised horticulture here."

Mr. Desmond Paris frowned as though he had just noticed a crease in his trousers. "They don't, conventionally, but Jebediah simply insists that I continue my hobbies. Every Sunday, he has one of the warders take me to Queen's Park so I can dab a watercolour or two in the sunshine."

"An advantageous arrangement," said Holmes dryly. "Do you go to see Adelina Patti sing as well?"

"No, of course not," said Paris with a flutter of the head. "She usually comes to me." He crossed to an armchair and seated himself primly with one leg over the other. "I have heard of you, naturally, Mr. Holmes, and though I welcome this visit, I cannot help but ponder its provenance."

Holmes stared back at him evenly. A battle of wits had begun.

"An inmate has been murdered," said Holmes in the sort of casual manner in which one might report a change in the weather. "Mr. Albert Winch from the floor below. I'm sure you're aware. He was a house-breaker serving five years, just as many others in this prison. Unlike them, however, his term was interrupted by a knife to the throat."

A pained look of pity leapt onto the other man's face. "Indeed. Tragic. Unfortunately, Mr. Holmes, not all of Her Majesty's guests understand the importance of etiquette. It's partly why I prefer to stay here. I have my paintings, you see, and if I stare long enough into the burnished blue of the distant tropics – well, it's almost as if I were there, as I someday hope to be. At other times, if I'm feeling particularly tired . . . ." He gestured to the bookcases which tottered over the rest of the room like stolen slabs of Stonehenge. "Neville will read something to me." His eyes dimmed and he began to intone reverently, '*How do I love thee? Let me count the ways. I love thee to the depth and breadth and height* . . . .' Delicious, isn't it?"

Such an appeal to romance left Holmes cold. "Who's Neville?" he asked bluntly.

"Mr. Stubbs," the other man answered, and I spent the next few moments trying to wrench the image from my mind.

Despite these efforts to distract him, Holmes remained focussed and calm. This was something which had always ensured my respect. There were men at Scotland Yard who could become uncomfortably vehement when questioning a criminal and end up spitting out threats and demands for a confession. Holmes, on the other hand, was almost laughably lackadaisical. He could lounge back in a chair, legs long and loose, and chat pleasantly and persuasively, but with an incisive eye and a secret steel. He remained so then and spoke with the serenity of the spaniel still snoozing in front of the fireplace.

"Albert Winch had devised a means to escape. According to him, you put him up to it. Is that true?"

The prisoner's lips stretched into a lazy smile. "Never have I heard anything quite like it, Mr. Holmes! But then . . . I would say that, wouldn't I?"

"Indeed," agreed Holmes. "It'd hardly be surprising, of course, if you *were* intending to leave – as it were – unofficially. After all, you must have broken almost every rule in this institution."

The eyes of our host blazed with indignation. "Trust me when I say, Mr. Holmes, that I have broken *every* rule." He blew out a plume of smoke, casual again. "One can get tired of constant acquiescence. In the evenings, lying by the fire with my wine and cheese, reading Keats while Old Wally Cartwright from B-Wing gently plays me his harp . . . well, I wonder if it's punishment or paradise."

"You're being refreshingly candid," I observed.

Paris must have noticed my sour expression. "Why not?" he said easily. "We're all men of the world. Surely, Doctor, you aren't naïve enough to expect *justice*?"

I felt an inward twist of embarrassment. Justice was something to value and I had personally seen it upheld throughout the previous years of accompanying Holmes on his cases. But maybe, I wondered, this had caused my expectations to become somewhat skewed.

Holmes had already started talking again. "Winch told the governor of your little arrangement. You will have been most angry."

It was a testament to the cordial atmosphere that I half-expected Paris to agree. Instead, he shook his head sorrowfully, as though he felt bad for Holmes. "My dear chap, allow me to be honest. A personal courtesy, you understand, in tribute to your eminent abilities and most illustrious record."

"I feel honoured," said Holmes with wry derision.

Paris smiled so widely that his eyes squeezed shut. "Your suspicions are misplaced. My sentence shall be finished in a year. The last thing I want is another prosecution. I'd have to stay here even longer instead of going there." He pointed to a painting of a river between two islands at dusk. "A Norton Bush," he explained appreciatively. "I intend to see it for myself. Do you travel, Mr. Holmes?"

"When cases warrant it, yes, although such work usually confines me to London."

"Oh, what shame! But then I suppose your little practice doesn't pay much. You should step over to my side of the divide and live like a king. The cruises are beyond compare."

I was suddenly stricken with defiance. Talk of the tropics and his intentions to retire there had loosed something inside my mind. If Desmond Paris was the murderer – and, despite his paltry protests, this certainly seemed to be the case – then he would have to be shown what justice truly meant.

"Could you tell us where you were when Winch died?" I asked.

Paris turned to me with quizzical condescension. "This one's getting rather above himself, don't you think, Mr. Holmes? He thinks he runs the business."

It would have been loyal for Holmes to disagree, but he didn't even turn a hair. Perhaps he found the man's rudeness amusing.

"You didn't answer the question," I pursued, but it just made me sound like a petulant child.

Paris seemed to lose interest in our little battle and sighed wearily. "There's a guard on the landing, Doctor. I'm not quite as free as you may imagine."

Foolishly, I almost accepted this answer but managed to remember something just in time. "You have been able to visit your rose garden."

Holmes smiled with what might have been pride. Paris, for his part, seemed to grimace slightly and this urged me to take an even harder line.

"You also boasted about the leniency of the staff," I went on wilfully. "Perhaps you sent the guard away on an errand. That would have given you time to go downstairs and hide in the storeroom."

Desmond Paris sucked on his cigarette thoughtfully. "Now you mention it, Doctor, I *did* ask for a pot of tea. Which also, of course, leaves me without a faithful alibi. Your hypothesis is therefore perfectly feasible."

He blew out another curl of smoke. Like so many arrogant, intellectual men, he obviously found it entertaining to see someone try to thwart him, and that made me want to win even more.

I demonstrated this determination by standing up as though I were about to cart him to the courts. "Do you own a letter-knife, Mr. Paris?" I asked, but he could only shake his head. "I didn't think so," I said, and left.

The second-floor landing was a circus of noise. Bolts rumbled, chains clanked, and distant bells rang out metallically. Hauntingly, however, there were no voices, though knowing the reason hardly helped. I was, at once, both disgusted and fascinated, staring awkwardly across the landing like a stranger in a foreign land. The radial design of the prison seemed somewhat influenced by Jeremy Bentham's unrealised panopticon theory of constant surveillance. Although warders could stand in the central position and view each of its five wings, they were unable to see into any individual cell without walking up to it and looking through the peephole. Such isolation must have been intolerable for the inmates, and it was no wonder so many of them were driven insane.

Originally, the idea of solitary penitence was based on the assumption that criminals acquired their habits from each other and it was therefore best to keep them silent and segregated until they learned virtue from the Bible. Hard work was also taught in the twist of the Crank, and hands became calloused and cramped over the many thousands of gruelling revolutions – a set number of which had to be reached if the prisoner was to receive food or even rest. Warders heartlessly would tighten the large handle to make it even more difficult to turn, and this earned them the damning nickname "screws" that is still in use today.

"It's terrible," I concluded, though even that word was hardly savage enough.

Previously in an effort to detail an account of a case, I would sometimes be permitted to visit Pentonville and speak to the culprit in an officer's room. Never, though, had I cause to observe the full, frightening extent of its nightmare cage. Gone by this point was the optimistic belief that righteousness could be achieved through religion and reflection. The government had obviously decided that such men were habitual lawbreakers and should be punished for no better reason than revenge. The silence was now supposed to break their will and steal their self-respect, while names were abandoned and replaced with the number of their cell, engraved on a brass badge which hung from a chain around their jackets.

Holmes didn't seem to have noticed anything remiss. For all his observational skills, he could sometimes be oblivious to the most obvious things – unless, of course, he had seen them squarely and was simply unconcerned. Indeed, he was silent and strangely sullen as we made our way past the cells and I spoke determinedly of ways in which we might prove Desmond Paris's guilt. Perhaps my manner had exceeded simple resolve and developed into irritating hubris. Certainly I was getting carried away – my little melodrama in his cell had made that perfectly plain – but this only reflected the extent to which the Prince of Pentonville had angered me with his supercilious sneering and naked boasts. He considered himself invincible and it was time somebody demonstrated otherwise.

Winch's cell was around thirteen feet long and seven-foot wide. A table and a cobbler's bench stood in the middle. The corner was filled with a broom, bucket, and an empty pot of wheat paste, while a shelf contained a pewter mug and dish, a bar of soap, and a towel. A hammock, most noticeably, was stretched between the walls and a gas bracket hung from the ceiling.

"Did the other prisoners hear anything?" asked Holmes.

The chief warder smiled in a way which suggested this had been a foolish question. "The partitions are eighteen inches thick and worked with close joints," he said smugly. "It's to stop the men from communicating."

Holmes wandered over to the wall and knocked his knuckles against it curiously. "All the same, I'd like to meet the man next door."

Another prisoner was presently prodded through the doorway. Bert Skinner had a hangdog face and a bushy Nietzsche moustache, while his bright ginger hair could have doubled as a candle if the gas had gone out. The rest of him was just as withered, almost as though he had died and nobody had bothered to mention it. Stubbs was behind him, head hung back haughtily. For once, however, such displays of power went unnoticed. It was Holmes who held sway and the other man was looking at him with obedient expectation.

"How do you do, Mr. Skinner? I'm investigating the death of Albert Winch. Had you met him at all?"

It is sometimes forgotten, I fancy, how respectfully my friend could treat people, and he was certainly so just then. Without a doubt, Holmes didn't suffer fools gladly and disliked imprecision, generalities, and prevarication, but when he believed someone possessed crucial information and was also willing to impart it, he was the epitome of ease and appreciation. The prisoner facing him, however, seemed surprised at such. Perhaps the criminal classes are so used to being treated with suspicion that they are therefore shocked when somebody affords them any measure of the common courtesy to which even the most downtrodden of us may deserve. Holmes was certainly of this mind and equally aware of its benefits.

"I never meet anyone," said the man. "My own mother could live on this landing and I wouldn't know about it."

"Presumably, therefore, you didn't know Mr. Winch?"

Bert Skinner shook his narrow-featured face. "Never. Usually we only leave our cells for exercise and chapel, and they keep us separated. We weren't even allowed to see each other when we decorated Mr. Paris's cell."

This took me quite aback. "When did this happen?"

"A couple of months back," he said. "All of us on this landing did it. Individually, like. One man a day."

Holmes paused for what felt like a full minute. "Did any of you contemplate a break-out?" he asked at last.

"Nah, 'course not. We're ain't no Jack Sheppard. I doubt anybody thought about it."

At this, Holmes seemed satisfied and let the man go, and then began searching the cell intensely.

"It seems Winch helped decorate Paris's cell," I said. "That must have been how they met."

"More significantly," said Holmes, "that's how they would have discussed the escape."

He was now sifting through a small pile of clothes, all grey but for the recognisable red line of criminal convicts.

"What *are* you looking for?"

Clearly, Holmes had recaptured his earlier enthusiasm. "All escapes need a plan."

"Agreed."

"And from the little we've learned, it involves the stables."

"Quite."

"Which means we're looking for a map of the prison. If we can just find it . . . ." He took hold of the plank bed before dropping it with a clatter. "Shame there isn't a mattress, as something's always hidden inside it. A bed is where people feel the safest, so they think that their valuables will be safe there too."

Our search, it seemed, was unsuccessful and Stubbs celebrated with a malicious smile. "There doesn't appear to be anything concealed," he said, all smugness back and bold.

With a flush of frustration, I cast around for something else and my gaze fell once more on the pot of dried wheat paste. "He must have brought this back with him after papering Paris's cell," I said casually. But then I paused. For some reason, something in me had stirred. I spun around with all the exuberance of Herbert Campbell at Drury Lane and looked at the walls.

"What is it, Watson?" asked Holmes with a sudden eagerness.

I was glancing furiously about me. Indeed, I must have seemed quite mad. And then my eyes trailed upwards and there came a wave of giddy delight.

"The map!" I said. "It's been pasted to the ceiling."

Throwing my head back, I scrutinized every inch. Neither of us had been looking there, but we may well have missed it just the same. Reaching up, I cut into the plaster with a fork. A moment later and I was peeling away a sheet of paper. The map was on the other side. It contained a detailed drawing of the premises, perfectly annotated, with a list of directions which Desmond Paris – explicitly named – was to follow. We had found our proof.

Holmes held the map at arm's length as though he were thinking of having it framed and nailed to the wall. "This certainly corroborates what the governor told us," he said. "And it makes clear so much else."

Mr. Jebediah Fallow was still in his office and seemed even more beleaguered than before. His grey head was hunkered over a pile of paperwork and he squinted harshly through his spectacles. He was pleased to see us and eager for any news which might conclude the case. Already, he said, it had caused a most unholy amount of paperwork, and he was set to spend the rest of the day penning letters to Scotland Yard and the Home Office.

"Rest assured," said Holmes, "the matter has come to a head." With a theatrical flap of his coattails, he dropped into a chair. "We have met Mr. Paris."

"And we know how he did it," I added somewhat unnecessarily.

"You give him much latitude. All that talk of religion is perfect rot, you know."

Mr. Fallow lifted a finger and began stroking his moustache. "Maybe so, Mr. Holmes, but I prefer pragmatism over piety. That need not embarrass anyone. It would be unwise to humiliate the man with hard labour. He has a vengeful spirit and many servants on the outside. Keeping him happy and allowing a few home comforts mean that my staff and I remain safe."

Holmes stared back and smiled. Then, slowly, a chuckle rumbled from behind it. Finally, he threw back his head with a bark of laughter. It echoed against the walls and Mr. Fallow stared across at him confoundedly. In an effort to explain my friend's disquieting deportment, I handed over the map.

"We found this in Winch's cell," I reported.

The governor examined it with fascination. "He's even named! Really, Mr. Holmes, you have outdone yourself!"

"It was so absurdly simple," said Holmes modestly. "Desmond Paris wanted his cell to be redecorated by the other prisoners, which happened to include Arthur Winch, who immediately began boasting about the ways in which he could escape. Paris wanted to get out himself, so asked the young man to find a way. Winch, of course, turned coat and told you about it all for the sake of a proper meal. Paris found out and killed him."

Mr. Fallow pushed away his paperwork with triumphant relief. "Yes, I can see why you would believe that, Mr. Holmes," he said, and pulled out a pair of sherry glasses to celebrate.

"And I can see that's what you wanted, Mr. Fallow."

Confusion creased the other man's features. "Perhaps you can explain yourself, Mr. Holmes."

With that, my friend's laugh rumbled back. "You are most shrewd," he said approvingly. "I shall give you that."

"In what way?" I asked, equally confused.

Holmes closed his eyes quite dreamily, as though he were picturing springtime. "You fascinate me, Mr. Fallow," he said, relishing the moment. Then, all of a sudden, his eyes flickered open and focussed on the governor sympathetically. "You are the authority here, with the title and the office and the suit, but it is *he* who rules the roost. Rich, reverential Mr. Desmond Paris."

The old man blinked. Holmes had touched a raw nerve.

"From your point of view, it must have seemed hardly fair. You have spent years abiding the law, serving your country, and keeping society safe. He, on the other hand, has lived a life of crime and corruption, yet commands no end of influence and reward, even here. Now his sentence is ending and he hopes to spend the rest of his days in South America. You find this injustice appalling and wanted to stop him. The last straw, I dare say, was a preposterous demand for his cell to be redecorated, but at least that posed an opportunity. Already your mind had turned to murder, but you didn't have the nerve to kill a leader of dangerous criminals. Your intention, instead, was to frame Paris for something which would spoil his plans and keep him here."

Mr. Fallow smiled incredulously. "This is nonsense, all of it, but please continue, Mr. Holmes. You're far more entertaining in person."

I had no time to wonder what he meant by this remark as Holmes adroitly continued. "The victim didn't matter. And, really, for me, that was the key to the whole business. All along, I'd been tormented by the arbitrary murder of Albert Winch. Who could hate him? Who could even recognise him? Once I'd disregarded such concerns, things began to crystallise."

Now it was the governor's turn to roar with laughter. "More!" he cried delightedly. "More!"

This was a man utterly without the creeping tension which often characterised such summations. He seemed so confident, moreover, that I began to wonder whether Holmes was on the right path at all.

"A few minutes before the men were due to enter the exercise yard," said Holmes, "you slipped into the storeroom and waited for them to pass through the corridor, one at a time. You had the letter-knife ready – stolen from Paris so that he would suspiciously be without one – and you waited. Finally there came the sound of footsteps. You flew the door open, grabbed whichever prisoner happened to be standing there and pulled him back inside. You had no idea it was Winch. Why would you care? That's why you didn't pull off his peak. It was only when he was identified that you even bothered to learn the man's name. All talk of his genius was nonsense. He was just a desperate petty crook who got caught. Illiterate, too, which is why he never bothered with letters from relatives and was too proud to let anyone read them to him. He certainly couldn't have made a map with all those little written details. You did that – and you pasted it on his ceiling for us to find so we could claim it as evidence against Paris."

"And do you happen to have any evidence against *me*?" asked Mr. Fallow with a sneer.

He was still holding the map and Holmes gestured to it with an open palm. "Well, there's the handwriting, for a start, though you never imagined it would be compared to yours."

"And what aroused your suspicions?"

"Well," said Holmes cordially, "at first, I only ventured to doubt. It was your transparency which made me curious. You wanted to appear kind and considerate to your men, and you were so keen to convince me of this that you even brought along a book on prison reform! Yet, as I mentioned at the time, I'd heard you speak to the Prison Commission. I recall you being quite callous, Mr. Fallow, and not at all interested in improving the living conditions of prisoners. In your office, of course, I searched your bookshelves, but there was no other literature concerning such liberal philosophies, whereas a genuine reformer would have owned stacks! Your only honesty, in fact, was the look on your face when I mentioned the mutiny in Paris's empire. This was a shock, as it is something which shall make the man destitute. Your efforts to manipulate me, therefore, in the hope that I should think him guilty of murder and recommend his arrest to the Yard, has been wholly unnecessary."

I threw the governor a questioning glance. The smile had dropped away, his mouth now pinched bitterly, and his eyes had lost their lustre.

"Shall I cable Seymour Street, sir?" asked Stubbs. He had stiffened respectfully and was looking at Holmes.

"Yes, please," said Holmes. "But don't leave him alone. As you can see from that piece of paper, he's already devised a means of escape."

I had seen quite enough of Pentonville Prison with its freezing cold cells and inhuman hard labour and wanted to rid my mind of the callous authorities which made it so possible. Before we left, however, Holmes wanted to meet one of its convicts for the last time.

"I believe this is goodbye, Mr. Holmes," said Mr. Desmond Paris.

"It has been interesting to make your acquaintance after so many years," said my friend. "You were always quite fiendishly elusive."

Mr. Desmond Paris gave another of his broad smiles and his eyes shrivelled to gimlets again. "I'm certainly not anymore. That is one of prison's more obvious disadvantages."

"And what of your dreams of the tropics?"

The old man's face crinkled wistfully. "They shall remain so, Mr. Holmes. My businesses are no more, as I discovered some little time ago, and the money went with them. I was too proud to admit it openly – even to you, foolishly, though our conversation put me briefly in my prime again. Instead, I shall serve out the rest of my sentence, patiently and without profit, and then retire to the East End. I was born there, after all." He said this as though he had only just remembered and I must have evinced some measure of surprise as he chuckled dryly. "Oh yes, my upper-class comportment is utterly fabricated," he confessed, though even as he said it, his words were still refined.

“And so, Watson,” said Holmes, as the prison gates clanked shut behind us. “The criminal was innocent, while the jailer was guilty.”

“There’s a moral in there somewhere,” I said good-humouredly. “But let’s not look for it now. Being holed up in there all day has rather made me appreciate my freedom.”

“Oh yes? And where would you like to go?”

“Simpson’s?” I suggested without even needing to think.

Holmes smiled. “Roast rib of Scottish beef?”

“Anything,” I said, “so long as it isn’t gruel!”

The Nautch Night Case
by Brenda Seabrooke

The sound of the drum beating attack brought terror to my heart. I burrowed into my blankets. The men wouldn't need me yet, not until the attack fully commenced with both sides engaged. I waited. The drumbeats sounded again, ripping across the night. Single shots. Cannonade or gun volleys would follow, but until they did, I could sleep a little longer. I might not get another chance for some time.

"Dr. Watson?"

A woman's voice. A nurse? Not here. Not on the line so far from civilization. Too dangerous.

"Dr. Watson? There's a messenger from Scotland Yard for you."

I swam toward the voice. Mrs. Hudson in her dark blue robe and ruffled night cap held a candle high as she leaned from the doorway into the darkness of my room and called my name.

"Scotland Yard? For me? Don't you mean for Holmes?"

"No, I questioned him too. He insisted the message is for you."

I gave up on sleep. "Very well. Tell him I'll be down in a few minutes."

"I think he wants you to accompany him," she said as I reached for my robe at the foot of the bed. "He came in a police vehicle."

"I may not want to accompany him."

I'm a stubborn Scot, but if this was so urgent that Scotland Yard sent a man here in the middle of the night – I glanced at the clock beside my bed. Half-one. – I might as well save time by dressing to go out. I was sure that Mrs. Hudson was right, and that the messenger would want me to accompany him.

"What is so urgent at this hour that it can't wait until morning?" I grumbled as I entered the sitting room of the flat I shared with Sherlock Holmes. A young police constable named Cord sat on the edge of a straight-backed chair in the middle of the room, twisting his hands. The banked fire gave off a warm glow in the otherwise chill room. He leaped up when he saw me.

The door to Holmes's room opened and he strode in, fully dressed as well. "Yes, Constable, what is so imperative at this hour?"

"Beg pardon, sir, my message is for Dr. Watson, here."

"Come, come, out with it," Holmes said with a flicker of impatience.

"There's been a death, sir," he said turning to me. "The Yard doctor is in Scotland for a funeral. His second is down with quinsy. The other doctors are out with patients or sick themselves. Inspector Lestrade needs Dr. Watson to act as coroner."

"Lestrade, eh?" Holmes was already at the door donning his scarf and Macintosh.

"Sir, he only asked for Dr. Watson. No need for you to interrupt your night."

"When has Lestrade ever refused my services? I've not retired for the night, so nothing is being interrupted."

The truth of it was Holmes could never resist a case, be it a missing clock or a suspicious death. He had been idle all Saturday with foul weather keeping even the most heinous of criminals at home.

"Where are we going?" I asked the constable.

"To the DeBurres Club, sir."

"Ah yes. Hardly a block from Boodle's, and looked down-upon because the chef puts chocolate in the orange fool."

"Oh, I would like to have that receipt, Mr. Holmes," Mrs. Hudson said as her candle lit our way down the stairs.

"I'll see what I can do," Holmes said, "but at this hour it is unlikely the chef will be on the premises."

"It was just a thought," Mrs. Hudson said.

The snow-covered street was lighter than the hour warranted giving more visibility than usual. It spangled the top of the police vehicle and the normally dark blanket over the back of the horse was pale blue with a dusting of flakes. We climbed aboard and the driver lifted the reins.

Before we reached our destination, the snow thickened considerably, reducing visibility to the length of the horse, but the driver seemed to know the streets well. One more turn and we were at the DeBurres Club door with its second-floor Palladian window taller than the one at Boodle's Gentlemen's Club, and its entrance portico directly beneath the window instead of on the left side.

"Here we are," the driver said.

"This way, sir," Constable Cord said to me. He glanced uncertainly at Holmes.

We followed him into the club's impressive entrance. There was a statue of a Greek god in a niche between the pair of stairs we climbed to the first floor. The large dining room on the front of the building took advantage of the light from the great window, but at night in this thick snow did not suffice. The ceiling was hung with an explosion of diaphanous curtains in colors reminiscent of India – pink, rose, red, orange, saffron, violet – that did much to warm the room. Each of the multitude of round tables of varying sizes bore a tiny flickering lantern that lent an enchantment to the scene. In spite of the death, the tables continued to be occupied by club members in various stages of annoyance, fear, perplexity, anger, and indifference as they watched our arrival. A few appeared to be sleeping, one white-haired gentleman with his hair askew leaned back on his chair, snores issuing from behind a walrus moustache.

"The stage setting for Nautch Night," Holmes murmured, "and for a murder."

"Surely not," I said.

The constable led us to a table against the wall, in the far corner away from the great window. A man lay across the table, his head buried in his arms, flung across the jumble of silver and gold-rimmed china laid across a red cloth. A pot of tea and an empty teacup stood just out of reach on the small table sized for two, but apparently only meant for one tonight.

Lestrade stood talking to a man in an impeccable black evening suit who looked to be a club employee. He broke off his conversation as we approached. "This is the club steward, Martin Johnson. Dr. Watson. Good of you to come. Mr. Holmes, did you come along for the ride? Nothing for you to do here. Cause of death will be something natural in these premises. You can mark my words."

Holmes inclined his head, smiling slightly. "Lestrade. It was a boring evening. A ride through falling snow stimulates the brain."

Lestrade snorted. "Nothing stimulating here. This man imbibed too much or ate too much or was over-stimulated by the dancing – maybe all three."

"Why did you need my services?" I asked.

"As to that, Dr. Miller is in Scotland, Preston is ill, and the others on call are out of reach with this weather. You were the closest and the one that came to mind. I need a physician to sign off on the death before we can move the body. Regulations and all that. Please stand in for them."

"Gladly." I opened my bag and got to work, but there was little for me to do at this juncture. The man was dead. I examined the position he had fallen into and searched my thoughts for what could have caused it. "Stroke and heart attack are natural possibilities," I said. "I have observed the victim *in situ*. If we could turn him over so I can examine him more fully."

Constable Cord and another summoned by Lestrade lifted the man's torso and sat him back in his chair. Holmes, who had been at the periphery of the circle around the victim, now stepped forward for a closer look as I stared at what was most likely a murder. Holmes glanced at me. No word passed between us but we were of like mind. It was almost time for him to take over, but first I had to inform Lestrade. I bent and sniffed to make sure. The scent of garlic was unmistakable. His dark bumpy complexion told the story.

I examined the man's face. It was long with wide-open brown eyes that normally would have been somewhat slitted between puffy lids. His longish hair flopped to one side and was a chestnut-brown color, as was his moustache, which consisted of two accent marks above his thin lips. His skin was a bright red against the black of his evening suit. A greenish vomit escaped from his flaccid lips.

"An autopsy should confirm my opinion, but I believe this man was poisoned with arsenic – a heavy dose. I base this on the scent of garlic, the redness of his face, and the vomit." I indicated the damp spot that had been under the man's mouth as he lay face down.

"The devil you say!" Lestrade's visions of getting some sleep tonight disappeared. "Blimey," he said under his breath, and then he glanced at the roomful of men watching us. "The club has a membership of three-hundred. Most of them are here tonight. At least two-hundred-and-forty or more, all prominent men – not to mention the staff, the hired servers, the dancers, and musicians."

I didn't blame him. It was now after two in the morning. There would be no sleep for Scotland Yard tonight, nor here at DeBurres. Not the aristocracy, but perhaps toffs and nabobs, these club members were the business elite of London. Many had served in India with the mercantile companies. They liked to feel less restrained at the Nautch Nights, named for the dancers from India. Somewhere on the premises the women would be waiting to find out what would happen to them.

"Mr. Johnson, can you identify this man?" Lestrade asked.

"Certainly. He is – or was Mr. Rembert DeHayes, an official with The West Indies Company. He is a widower. No children, I believe."

No family members to want him deceased, then.

Lestrade sent his constables to make a seating chart of the room with the names of the members and their guests, and others to collect information about the staff and the dancers.

"How long has he been dead?" Lestrade asked me.

"*Rigor mortis* hasn't set in, but the warmth of the room for the dancers may have affected it. I would say anywhere from four hours but most likely two."

"That may depend on how the poison was administered," Holmes pointed out. "If through food or drink, it could have been in place longer. The arsenic could have been on the table for a half-hour or longer before he drank or ate it." He bent to sniff the teacup, straightened and nodded. "A highly spiced blend of teas with undertones of garlic. You'll need to test the cup and the teapot."

Lestrade grimaced. Holmes's observation complicated his work. "I hope that you can narrow down the suspects for me," he said.

He then left to organize the investigation by confiscating a room in which to interview the club members, staff, and dancers. He started with the latter because they were the least likely to have known the victim or had any kind of grudge against him.

The constables removed the body on a stretcher similar to the ones used by the army when I was in India. A sheet had been procured to cover the victim, but the contour was obvious. Several members averted their gazes as the procession left the room and headed for the stairs to the street. A few, however, gave the body a hard look. The membership must know by now who the victim was, and they let their feelings show. I saw Holmes watching their reactions.

"Not the most popular member," he murmured.

We joined Lestrade at his invitation in the library where he would conduct the interviews. The room was as cozy as our sitting room. An ample fire burned cheerily in the grate, the leaping flames sending flashes of light onto the dark-red Moroccan leather-bound volumes on the shelves and the polished mahogany desk behind which Lestrade sat. In the fire's glow he looked less sallow than usual, his eyes dark in his thin face. He often reminded me of a ferret, especially when he showed his teeth in a rare smile.

A multi-branched rubber tree in a large Chinese celadon jardinière stood between two dark, green leather sofas, affording privacy to any occupants sitting on them. Holmes sat on one of these. I took the other.

"What do you know about these dancers?" was Lestrade's first question as we waited for one of them to arrive from the room where they had been kept.

"*Nautch* comes from the anglicizing of *nac*," Holmes said, "which means dance or dancing in several northern India languages including Urdu, Hindi, and Sanskrit, through several derivations such as *natya* and *nachcha*. They perform to please men with their entrancing skills. Do you concur, Watson?"

"I do. They danced in the rajah's courts in India, and for the nabobs, and the British in positions of prominence."

"That all they do? Dance?" Lestrade asked.

'Yes," I said. "It's an art form"

"You ever see any when you were in the army there?" he asked.

"No. I was but a busy army surgeon in the battlefield, where no one had time for dancing."

I did not care to remember those times any more than I had to. Just talking about it brought back the dust, the heavy spice smells, the blood, the danger, and the heat, though the latter could have simply been from the fire in the grate.

"Johnson told me that the club does this Nautch Night thing in the middle of January," Lestrade said. "To cheer up the members after the holidays are over and when the weather turns bad. A lot of the members spend the night here and the revels go on until morning, But no consorting with the dancers. They dance and nothing else."

The first dancer was called Mina Sands. She wrapped the voluminous draperies of her green-and-gold saree about her and sat gracefully in the chair on the other side of the desk from Lestrade. She was the organizer of the Nautch Night dancers and their spokeswoman. She was married to an Englishman.

"Do you just perform here at DeBurres's," Lestrade asked, "or are you engaged at other venues?"

"We perform at other clubs and affairs – weddings, christenings, social events, and small Nautch parties, as well as DeBurres's Nautch Night. We are a close group, some by kinship. Several of us are married to brothers and cousins of others. Some of the men play for us to dance. We have been together for years."

She was calm and well-spoken, as if she had grown up speaking English. Perhaps she had. She may have been born in England.

"How many?" Lestrade asked.

"Five years. Our company is made up of seven dancers and five musicians, though not all of us play or dance at the same time. That way we can perform continuously. Mr. Johnson, the steward can attest that we have all been performing here for that many years."

"I'll check that," Lestrade said. "Do any of you have any knowledge of the deceased?"

"No. We do not have occasion to speak with the customers, and the placement of the draperies prevents our seeing them clearly."

After a few more questions, Lestrade dismissed her after checking with the steward and arranging for a list of names and addresses to be left with Constable Cord. "I can't see any reason for any of them to poison Mr. DeHayes."

"Nor can I," I said.

"Reason there might be," Holmes said, "but the dancers do not mingle with the guests. Whomever did this would undoubtedly have served the poison personally in order to be certain it went to the intended victim." Lestrade concurred.

Next he turned to the tea servers or waitresses, twenty of them, five to a section of the room. Lestrade narrowed down the list. "We need only interview those five assigned to the victim's quarter."

The tea servers varied in age: Two were in their twenties, the others older. Their persons didn't have to be as comely as the dancers, and they weren't from what we could see of them. They wore voluminous clothing. Their hair was covered, and their faces were obscured by veils from the nose down. Three of them had brought tea to the victim but all were adamant it was well before midnight. "He didn't ask for any after about half-ten," one named Greta Hopkins said. Her hair was still covered, but she had removed her half-veil and looked like any middle-aged English woman.

"I was born in India," she said. "My father was stationed there with the railroad. My husband also. When my father retired, my husband and I moved back to England with him, as my mother was deceased. I'm familiar with Nautch, so I earn a little extra money serving tea at clubs that use them."

"Did he drink his last cup of tea?" Lestrade asked.

"He probably did, but we don't check on those that we serve. It is enough to keep up with their calls for drink."

"I take it some of the tea is sometimes stronger?"

"I don't know, sir. We take the small pots from the tea stand to the tables. We don't question the contents, or the bottles and glasses brought by waiters."

"What tea did he request?" Lestrade asked.

"The club only serves an Assam black tea with the spicy foods on Nautch Nights."

Holmes had asked no questions and didn't comment. Was he miffed at the dismissal from Lestrade when he arrived? He wasn't normally thin-skinned, but could upon occasion get his back up. He sat staring at the rubber tree's thick glossy leaves.

"So any server could have added something to the individual pots?" Lestrade asked.

"I suppose so. The pots are filled and wait for a server to take them to a table. No one knows which table. Sometimes when taking a pot to Mr. Jones, Mr. Smith stops us before we have reached destination. We surrender the pot and return to the stand for another. Then Mr. Jones complains when he has to wait longer for his pot." She rolled her eyes at the childishness of men.

Holmes broke in. "Could anyone else have served the members besides the waiters and tea servers?"

"I suppose it's possible," she said turning to him, "but I didn't see any. We are so busy we don't have time to observe what others are doing."

The other tea servers confirmed her testimony. Lestrade allowed them all to return home after leaving their information with the constables. They had taken the names and addresses of members whose tables were not in the victim's sector and asked if any had spoken with the victim or observed anything. The constables reported the consensus was that none of them admitted to noticing the victim. He sat alone and didn't join others at their tables

"Seems not to 'ave been a likeable chap," Constable Cord added.

"So none of them talked to him or observed him?" Lestrade asked. A note of desperation crept into his tone.

"Seems not, sir."

Lestrade waved his hand. "I need some information. Bring me somebody who knew the victim beyond a casual acquaintance at the club. Somebody from his company – the West Indies. And don't allow anybody else to leave."

Lestrade passed a hand across his face in an effort to revive himself for the next few hours.

All of the ladies had been allowed to leave, as well as some of the older club members, with the exception of the ones in the section in which DeHayes was seated. The waiters and kitchen staff remained to serve the members if they suddenly had a hunger pang. These clubs existed to please their members, and please they did. No request went unfulfilled. A roast beef sandwich at this hour would be procured immediately and impeccably prepared. The same with any drinks. A strict protocol was maintained. The tea servers could only serve tea. They could not touch alcohol or food.

The first five club members seated near DeHayes said that they saw him but didn't talk to him. They didn't work at the same company and knew him only to speak in passing. The next three said that they exchanged what passed for pleasantries with him.

"What do you mean 'what passes for pleasantries'?"

"You know – casual phrases. 'Rum night out.' 'Glad we're inside.' 'Hate to be a cabbie on this night. Or a horse.'"

The next man proved to be an employee of The West Indies Company. Mr. Phillip Harp was a middle-aged average-sized man with merely a hint of a moustache on his pale-complexioned face. He entered leaning heavily on a stout cane that may or may not have concealed a blade. He seated himself laboriously across from Lestrade and brushed a speck of dirt from the trousers of his evening suit. He rested his hands on his cane.

"Not been in the weather lately," I remarked.

He looked at me. "No, I have not. I was laid up with a pesky grippe during Christmas and New Year's. Stayed by the fire drinking gallons of hot tea. Followed that with a touch of lumbago." He raised the cane with his left hand. "And whom do I have the pleasure of addressing?"

"This is Dr. Watson, standing in for the coroner tonight," Lestrade said. I noticed that he didn't introduce Holmes, and Harp didn't make the connection to the tall man sitting half in the shadow of the rubber tree.

Lestrade got to the point. "Where was your table in relation to the deceased's?"

"I was seated diagonally across from his table, but one or two others were between us and some of the draperies, so I didn't have a clear view. I assume you're asking if I saw anything. I did not. The few times I caught sight of him, he was sitting with his chin sunk down as if in deep contemplation. Apparently someone once told him that particular stance made him appear intelligent, as if analyzing something or thinking deeply about something else. The truth is he was probably thinking of whom he could try to ruin next."

Lestrade perked up as he was, no doubt, meant to. "Ruin, sir? Do you have knowledge that he ruined anyone?"

"I do indeed. You know, of course, that the firm where I'm employed, The West Indies Company deals in commodities from that part of the world."

"I surmised as much," Lestrade said. "Are you an owner?"

"I own a small share," he said dropping his eyes with modesty.

I have always thought such mannerisms to be disingenuous, but Harp appeared sincere, and what he next told us confirmed that he was being truthful with the inspector.

"It was about twelve years ago when DeHayes – he being an older shareholder of the company – took an interest in me, a junior clerk, at the time employed only a little over three years. He took me to lunch here at this club and sponsored me for membership. This was a big event in my life. I'm descended from a long line of country parsons. Orphaned at an early age, it was left to me to make my way in the world on my wits. About a year later, DeHayes had news to impart to me, but it was confidential – if I wanted to make use of it, I must not connect him with it. Naturally, I was excited. It would have to do with financial gain.

"I was engaged at the time to a delightful young lady and would be able to marry her with just such a windfall. The news was about an almost-destitute company whose shares were going cheap. DeHayes had information that West Indies was planning to acquire it and I would make a lot of money selling to them. I bought as many shares as I could afford – and some that I couldn't – borrowing money from my fiancée's uncle. I suppose I don't need to tell you that the company collapsed, West Indies didn't buy it, and I lost everything. It took me years to pay back the money that I'd borrowed. My fiancée's family turned against me though she did not, but she listened to them and married another chap. Eventually, I married another lady, but she died in childbirth some years ago. I was too disheartened to seek the company of another. So if you're looking for someone who hated Rembert DeHayes, you need look no further."

"I take it you're not confessing," Lestrade said with almost a hint of a smile.

"I am not. I'm delighted the man is dead, but I would not risk swinging for such a worm."

"I should hope not,' Lestrade said.

"And I hope that the chap who did will not be caught."

"I see your reason," Lestrade said. "What else can you tell me about him?"

"As far as I know, he'd never been married. Lived by himself in a house about sixty years old in a good neighborhood. If he had any friends of any persuasion, I don't know about it. I've tried to warn new employees about him, but I don't know if I succeeded in spoiling his pleasure. I certainly hope so. I wouldn't like to see anyone's life changed in the way mine was."

Lestrade dismissed him, reminding him to leave his address with the constable. Harp listed to port as he limped to the door. Lestrade followed him to make sure that he made it without mishap. At the door, he told the constable to send in the next club member. When he'd gone, Holmes held up his hand.

"Just a moment – indulge me if you please." He stood and took a sheet of paper from a drawer in the writing desk. He bent and with the paper scooped up a speck from the seat of the chair. "I kept my eye on that speck from the time he brushed it off." He folded the paper and put it in his coat pocket.

"Continue," he said as the constable entered the room alone.

"Sir, we are snowed in. Mr. Johnson says they cannot open the door without snow piling into the hall."

We all trooped to the Palladian window to behold a monochromatic panorama in which nothing moved except the falling snow. The city lay before us cloaked in deep white silence. Only St. Paul's iced dome beside the river was recognizable as it rose two-hundred-and-sixty-five feet above the city.

As others exclaimed over the snow, Holmes smiled slightly and I knew he was thinking the same thing that I was. We were likely snowed in with Scotland Yard – and also with a murderer.

The next club member also worked for The West Indies Company. Alan Deakin was a few years younger than Mr. Harp. Florid-faced, plump, and an inch or two shorter as well, he looked like he needed to eschew rich foods or bear the consequences. I wasn't his consulting physician so I kept my opinion to myself. Most people know when they should change their ways but are often adept at finding a multitude of reasons not to, even when their doctors admonish them to forego quantities of rich food and drink. This man seemed to be of that ilk. His evening suit was a little tighter than it should have been. I thought perhaps that he had no wife to bring it to his attention, but he proved to be a happily married man.

"Did you ever consider falling in with the schemes of the deceased?" Lestrade came right out with it.

"With a wife and five children? Hardly. Every shilling is spoken for until next year." He laughed. "Besides, I had been warned by Harp and several others not to let him get his hooks into me. Not like young Freddy Wilson. The company found out that he had traded on some inside information and he was terminated just last week. He was despondent and didn't want to come tonight, but several of us persuaded him to join us. He needed cheering up."

"How can he come to the club if he's without a position?" Lestrade asked.

"DeBurres isn't directly connected to the businesses, even though the members for the most part are. Freddy's club dues are paid for the year, but it's unlikely he'll be able to continue his membership unless a bit of luck falls his way soon. It's a sad case. He's about to lose his house. He has a young wife in the family way. I lent him a fiver to buy food for the week."

"Kind of you. Why was he taken in by DeHayes?"

"Freddy studied the deal and thought that it was fool-proof. He was told by DeHayes not to mention it to the others because they were jealous that he hadn't let them in. DeHayes could be persuasive. Freddy didn't have any ready money so he put his house up as collateral. The deal fell through as most of DeHayes's deals are designed to do. I don't know what he got out of it, but I'm sure something went under the table, if you know what I mean. I can't imagine anyone going to such elaborate lengths just to ruin others."

"Possibly a bit of both," I said. "I've known chaps that amused themselves getting others into trouble."

Holmes stirred at this. He was thinking about those shares I almost bought once. Luckily my letter was posted too late and I was saved the loss of a lot of money I could ill-afford to lose. "I suspect that the deceased also sold non-existent shares to fictitious companies, informed the victim the company had folded, and kept the proceeds. Maybe he had multiple victims for each swindle and not just in his company or the club."

"Astute of you, Watson," Holmes said.

The next club member was an older man, Percy Farnsworth. He was as thin as Deakin was plump, a luxuriant white moustache covered his upper lip. Intelligent blue eyes under thick white brows took in the room. He nodded at us. "Mr. Holmes. Dr. Watson. Inspector."

"You recognize us from – ?"

"You were in the auction room when Wyndhurst Manor was auctioned," Mr. Farnsworth said with a small smile behind that moustache.

I was sure I would have recognized the moustache. He must have grown it since then, perhaps to compensate for his thinning white hair.

Lestrade went through the usual questions. Mr. Farnsworth was married with grown children, financially solvent, and counted many years with The West Indies Company years. "I started out as a clerk in Barbados and worked my way up to shareholder."

"What do you know of DeHayes?"

"I've heard rumors from time to time, but he kept his side business away from the company's eyes."

Lestrade frowned. Holmes steepled his fingers and stared at the fire. The inspector let out a sigh. "Can you be specific?"

"I cannot."

He wouldn't say anything that might reflect badly on the company. I'd seen these company men in India. I couldn't say that I blamed them, not the ones who made their way in the world by their wits as Mr. Farnsworth appeared to have done.

I looked up after Lestrade dismissed him. Holmes was watching me. He nodded, and I wondered if he knew what I was thinking.

"Rock solid company man," he said. Lestrade agreed.

Munro Manning was another young man who worked for The West Indies Company. Unmarried, living at the club, a handsome, slender, clean-shaven man with dark hair and eyes, he was just starting on his way up the company ladder.

"How well do you know the deceased?"

"Not well at all. I knew him when I saw him at the club, but almost never at the offices."

Lestrade got right to the point. "Have you had any dealings with DeHayes? Anything outside the office?"

"He surprised me by approaching me in the hall last November to buy some railroad shares near Ballarat, but I was short myself and Christmas was coming."

Ballarat. I met Holmes's eyes. That was the location of the railroad in which had I almost invested.

"How did that turn out?" Lestrade asked.

“Not well. I heard rumors the company folded. Something about a fire.”

“So you never invested with him?”

“I did not.”

When he’d gone, Lestrade ordered coffee sent in. After it was served, he said to the constable, “Let’s have Frederick Wilson in.”

Holmes leaned back and looked up at the ornately carved ceiling as if to empty his mind for important information.

Frederick Wilson was a fair-haired clean-shaven young man of medium height in his mid-twenties. Lestrade asked him the usual questions, even those to which he knew the answer. He came from Yorkshire but didn’t have family there now. “My mother died when I was ten, my father a few years later. I was raised by my uncle but he, too, is deceased. I used my small inheritance to buy a house and was able to marry.”

He gripped the arms of the chair and looked away.

Lestrade said nothing, allowing the young man to get control of himself. When he turned back, Lestrade said, “And now?”

He sighed deeply. “I’ve lost my house. I don’t know where we will go. My wife – ” He broke off.

Lestrade waited.

“My wife will soon give birth. I had to borrow from a friend for food this week.”

I wanted to ask him why he invested in a perilous scheme but I thought that I knew the answer. He had a family to take care of. He thought he had found a safe way to increase his assets.

“How long have you been with The West Indies Company?” Lestrade asked.

“A little over a year.”

“Not long enough to have heard about DeHayes’s swindles?” Lestrade said.

“No, the opposite. I heard he was a good man to help younger men get ahead.”

“Do you remember who told you that?”

“No. I heard it from several people. It was just the talk of the office. We younger employees talked amongst ourselves.”

“Did any of them fall for the latest swindle?”

“Not that I know of. None of them had any spare funds. I had a little because of my inheritance, and borrowed more on my house.”

“Where did you borrow the funds?”

“From a friend.”

“Is he pressing you for repayment?”

"Not exactly."

Lestrade let that go. "Where were you sitting tonight in relation to Mr. DeHayes?"

"I was sitting three tables away."

"Did you see anything that might have contributed to his death? Anyone approach him?"

"I made it a point not to look at him. He was partly obscured by violet draperies."

"The draperies are sheer. You could see through them."

"Nevertheless, I watched the dancers and tried to take my mind off my troubles."

No matter how he phrased his questions, Lestrade couldn't get him change his story. Reluctantly, he let the man leave the room. "My money is on him," he said.

During the questioning, Lestrade's constables engaged in a search of the club, despite Mr. Johnson's objections. "This is a murder inquiry," he reminded the steward.

The last room to be searched was the gentlemen's cloak room, and it was there the first evidence in the case was found. Constable Cord burst in with the news. "Sir, sir, we've found it!"

"Well come on man, out with it. What did you find?"

"We found a man's overcoat with a dancer's costume in its deep pockets. We didn't take it out, sir. We know how you like to see things the way they are."

"Precisely," Holmes said. He stood up as I did and we followed Lestrade to the cloakroom.

Silky garments in dusky shades of blue spilled from the pockets of a black overcoat. Lestrade pulled them out. They weren't a dancer's costume, but instead were like those worn by the tea servers.

"The color is more likely to blend into the shadows," Holmes said.

"Whose coat is this?" Lestrade said, with a new note of energy in his voice. The case was close to solution.

The constable opened the coat to the inside and there we saw the embroidered name: Frederick Wilson.

I felt a slight disappointment. "I didn't take him for a murderer," I said.

"Nor I," Holmes said.

"Bring Wilson back to the library," Lestrade told another constable.

We returned to the library with the coat over the Constable Cord's arm. His face was straight but wore a faint flush of pleasure with his find.

Lestrade got to the point when two constables marched Wilson in and stood beside the chair where he sat.

"What do you have to say about these?" Lestrade spread the coat and garments over the desk.

"All right. I admit I took them. I thought somebody had discarded them and wouldn't care if I took them."

Lestrade looked confused. "You took them? From where?"

"They were behind that sofa." Wilson pointed to the one upon which I sat.

"What were you doing in here?" Holmes asked.

"I needed to get away for a few minutes. Edwards was going on and on about the club and all the future events. I suddenly realized I wouldn't be here and I had no idea where I would be."

"You can find another position," I said.

"Not bloody likely. Nobody wants a financial failure in a company. I would give it a bad name."

"So you dressed up like a tea server and poisoned the man who ruined you," Lestrade said.

His mouth dropped open. "Me? No I – I didn't. Why do you think that?"

"You confessed to it," Lestrade said.

"He said he took the costume he found behind the sofa," Holmes reminded him.

"That was the first time I touched that costume," Wilson said. "I swear."

"Well, then you would, wouldn't you?" Lestrade said.

"Why did you take the costume?" Holmes said.

"I thought I could sell it so we would have money for food next week."

"A likely story," Lestrade scoffed. "You dressed up and served the poisoned tea to DeHayes to get even for your ruin. We have the evidence."

"Maybe not." Holmes stood up and went behind the rubber tree. He rummaged in the jardiniere. "Quickly! A newspaper, Watson."

I procured one from the reading rack, an earlier edition.

"Hold it for me." Holmes pulled first one shoe and then another of the kind worn by the tea servers. He shook them over the newspaper. Loose dirt rained down.

Lestrade was adamant. "This changes nothing. He removed the tea server's costume in the library, dressing himself in his own clothes hidden behind the sofa and hid the shoes. When somebody came in, he put the costume under his coat and walked casually to the cloakroom to transfer them to his deep overcoat pockets, when the attendant took a break, most likely."

Mr. Wilson looked dumbfounded. His mouth dropped open as if he wanted to speak but didn't know what to say. He jumped up and gained control of himself. "That's not what happened. I came in here and found the costume on the floor. I thought it had been discarded for some reason and concealed it under my coat. I didn't even know the shoes were there or I would have taken them too. They might have brought another week of food. I hurried to the cloak room and stuffed the garments in my coat pockets and returned to my table."

Lestrade didn't look convinced.

"Did you see the victim then?" Holmes asked.

"I did. I passed in front of the draperies and saw him. He was lying face down on the table. I thought that he was drunk or asleep."

"Here, Mr. Holmes, you can't take over my case. This is the murderer. He was caught with the goods. What did you do with the poison?"

"I did nothing with it because I never saw it. I did not poison that despicable man. If I had, I think I would be proud of it."

"Proud to swing for it?" Lestrade said.

"No, not that proud," he said with a touch of humor.

"That is what will happen. You will hang for it. Revenge is a dish best served cold. Frederick Wilson, I charge – "

"Hold on, Lestrade," said Holmes. "Let's not get ahead of things. There's still the matter of these shoes. Let's see him put them on."

Wilson took a step back. He didn't like this turn of events. If the shoes fit him, he would be charged with murder. "No."

"I'm afraid that you must," Holmes said. "For better or worse. Come, come. It is for the best."

Constable Cord gave Wilson a shove and he fell back into a chair. The constable bent to remove his shoe but Wilson brushed his hands aside. "I'll do it."

He took his right shoe off. Holmes handed the right tea server's shoe to him. He leaned over and shoved it onto his foot. The shoe went part way and stuck. "It doesn't fit," he said in a shaky voice.

"Constable," Lestrade said.

Constable Cord pulled the shoe off and fitted it again onto Wilson's foot. The shoe stuck about halfway there. He tried again. And again.

"Sorry, sir. It doesn't fit."

"Well, Lestrade," Holmes said raising an eyebrow. "This Cinderella won't be going to the ball. He'll be going home to his wife."

Wilson collapsed back into his chair.

Lestrade stared at the shoe. I thought for a moment that he would try to cram the shoe on Wilson's foot himself but he didn't. "How did you know?"

"I noticed immediately he had large feet for his size."

"You can go," Lestrade said, "but don't leave the club."

"I can't even if I wanted to – which I do – but we're snowed in."

"We are." Lestrade seemed encouraged. Maybe he thought that he still had time to catch the murderer.

"May I take the costume?" Wilson asked.

"No," Lestrade said. "It will be needed for the trial."

"Trial?" Wilson said.

"Not yours," Lestrade snapped.

Wilson hurriedly put his shoe on and almost ran from the room.

Lestrade called for more coffee. It came with a plate of sandwiches and biscuits. I tore into one feeling as if I had just fought the Battle at Maiwand. Holmes drank the coffee but he only ate half a sandwich – roast beef with proper English mustard. Colman's from Norwich.

"I don't know about you, but I feel rejuvenated by this repast," I said.

"We'll have to start over with the interviewing," Lestrade said, looking less refreshed than I felt. "I'm sorry now that I let the tea servers and dancers go. With more information, I have different questions to ask. What do you think, Mr. Holmes?"

"Are you asking me who the murderer is?"

"Do you know?"

"I have a good idea."

"Out with it, man. Let's get this case finished."

Holmes walked over to the desk with the newspaper spread over it, the dirty tea server's shoes on top. He pulled a piece of folded paper out of his pocket.

"Remember when Mr. Harp sat down?"

"Yes," Lestrade said, no doubt wondering what he had missed.

"He sat there and fiddled with his fingers on his cane and flicked something off his trouser leg. After he left the room, I slid this piece of paper under it and folded it for safe-keeping."

"Is that how you knew the shoes were in the plant pot?" Lestrade wore a perplexed look.

"No. As I sat looking at the rubber tree, I noticed the dirt was raised in the back. That's how I discovered the shoes. Now if you look at this speck of dirt from Mr. Harp's trouser leg and the dirt on the newspaper, you will see it is alike."

Lestrade slid his eyes toward Holmes and raised a doubting eyebrow. "We can prove that?"

"It can be proved under a microscope. What we can't prove is when Harp got the dirt on his hands. He may even have some under his nails, though I suspect he has scrubbed them in the washroom by now."

"What about the shoes?" I said.

Lestrade perked up and sent a constable to bring him in.

"Gentlemen," Harp said as he entered. He remained standing by the door as his eyes took in the shoes, the dirt, the costume. "I presume you have made some progress in the case."

"You presume correctly, sir. Sit and remove your shoes."

Harp remained standing, as did Holmes and I, along with the inspector and the constable.

"Remove my shoes? I think not, Inspector." He stepped back from the door and closed it quietly, leaving us and the constable on the other side.

"Who is out there, Cord?" Lestrade said.

"No one, sir."

"Try the door."

The constable turned the handle and pushed but the door didn't move. "It must be locked, sir or jammed."

Lestrade, Cord, and I pounded on the door and tried to break it open, while Holmes stood back, his arms crossed, with a wry smile upon his face. The door did not move.

"Where can he go?" Lestrade said. "The snow is deep outside. If he leaves here, we will be able to follow him easily."

"Don't count on it," Holmes said.

After a time one of the constables noticed the chair tilted under the door handle in the hall, entrapping us within. On its removal, we erupted out, Lestrade to organize an inch-by-inch search of the club, and Holmes and me to follow on our own search. "Though it will do no good," Holmes said. "Harp planned his revenge carefully and he served it frigidly. He couldn't have known the weather would be so spectacularly helpful to his plans, but surely he planned for any eventuality."

"Helpful? He can't escape. Nobody can get through all that heavy snow out there," I said.

"Oh come now, Watson. How many times have you had to slog your way through deep snow?"

"Not as often as you might think," I said, "but as one who has spent time in Scotland, I've been caught in it a time or two. I was soaking wet by the time I escaped into a warm house, but I managed."

"And this man Harp will. Lestrade won't find him. I suspect that he's gained access into the next building, no doubt with a stash of warm, disguising clothing, and is already far away. He is a master of disguise if he was able to pass himself off as a tea server long enough to serve the poisoned tea, dispose of the costume, and return to his table unmissed by anybody who, if they noticed him missing, would assume that he'd visited the washroom."

Holmes was correct. Within the hour, evidence of Harp's presence next door had been found. None of his clothing was found left behind.

"He would have put his evening suit in the bag in which his disguise rested. Workman's togs would be my supposition. Ironic."

"Ironic? Togs?"

"From *togeman*, meaning thief or ragman. Later cloak or coat. In this use the word has returned to its original meaning donned by a murderer who stole a life, so in that sense a thief."

A path was found out of the empty adjacent building and then his tracks disappeared in the welter of others. "He would have passage booked out of the country. I think we'll find that he removed funds from his bank and prepared for the eventuality of his escape if he was close to being caught. He'll probably reappear someday with another name, another profession in some country with a hot climate."

"You sound as if you admire him," Lestrade said.

"I don't admire the taking of a life, but in this case I suspect there is a measure of justice. The money lost by Frederick Wilson will be returned to him if he seeks redress. The Company will see to it to protect its name. He will be hired back to his position. He won't lose his house, and he won't need to borrow money or sell a tea server's costume for food. He can continue his happy life with his young wife and coming baby."

"Holmes," I said, "you sound benevolent – almost avuncular."

He raised his eyebrows. "Perhaps I should tell fortunes."

I laughed. "Perhaps you should."

Everything Holmes predicted happened as he said it would, except we didn't know Harp's new name, profession, or country.

"In time," Holmes said, "those blanks will be filled."

On our return to our lodgings, Holmes took a folded sheet of paper from his pocket and propped it on the teapot on the table. "I think Mrs. Hudson will be pleased to find this in the morning."

"What is it?"

"Something that she asked for. I didn't forget."

On Sunday after an excellent joint, I found out what was on the paper when Mrs. Hudson served the DeBurres chef's recipe for orange fool with chocolate, and I don't think that Boodle's could be half so good.

The following spring Frederick Wilson called on us. "I came to think you for the silver rattle," Freddy said. "Little Freddy Holmes Wilson amuses himself with it hourly."

He thanked us as well for discovering the murderer and saving him from hanging.

"I think Harp wouldn't have let you be executed," Holmes said. "He would have escaped, leaving behind letters confessing to the crime to be opened at a certain time."

"But what prompted him to kill DeHayes?" Freddy asked. "It was years since he had lost his savings to that swindler."

"No doubt he had put it aside, though it might have festered there benignly until something happened to bring it to the forefront of his thoughts, where it burgeoned until he had to act. He had seen others swindled but they managed. Your case was an especially brutal one. You were losing your house, your inheritance, your money. You couldn't even afford food for yourself and your wife, and you had a baby on the way. He lost his first love and then his wife and baby. Those feelings of loss overwhelmed him. He had no real ties to keep him in England. I suspect that he had enough put aside to retire in a less-expensive country. He made his move.

"He acted as an *avenger* more than a *revenger*, no matter how cold the dish."

After Freddy left I said, "And the world is a better place."

"Indeed it is. The mills of the gods are said to grind slow, but they are also known to grind exceedingly fine, as Rembert DeHayes learned."

NOTE

DeBurres Orange Fool

INGREDIENTS

- Slices of white or yellow cake
- Grand Marnier
- Grated rind and juice from 2 navel oranges
- Grated rind and juice from 1 lemon
- 1 cup shaved or grated chocolate
- ¼ plus 1/8 cup of powdered sugar
- 10 ounces of whipping cream
- Gooseberries

DIRECTIONS

- Line a glass bowl with cake slices
- Sprinkle them lightly with Grand Marnier
- Whip the cream
- Mix grated orange and lemon rind with the whipped cream
- Whisk the powdered sugar into the orange juice
- Add orange and lemon juice to the cream, whisking it thoroughly
- Fold in one cup of shaved or grated chocolate
- Spoon over cake slices and chill
- Decorate the top with Mandarin orange slices arranged in a flowerhead round with gooseberries cut into two leaf shapes

The Disappearing Prisoner
by Arthur Hall

An unseasonably fine March morning can hardly be anything but pleasant, yet I felt that the day had begun strangely. To my surprise, I discovered my friend Mr. Sherlock Holmes in high spirits at breakfast, a state of affairs so unusual that I felt compelled to remark upon it.

"I would think from your pleasant expression, Holmes, that you've solved the Merriton Bank fraud case that Lestrade was so concerned about."

He looked up as I took the chair at the opposite side of the table. "Indeed, I was at last able to obtain the evidence that I've been seeking since the arrests. Hoffnan and his group had no defence against it, and will doubtless spend the remainder of their active years in prison."

As I began my breakfast, he proceeded to relate the details of the succession of deductions which had led to such a satisfactory conclusion. These I would record at the first opportunity, for possible future publication. I finished the last of my toast and drank my coffee as I looked out into Baker Street to see that the early spring sky was still an unclouded blue. A cold but bright sun shone down as passers-by huddled into their thick coats, wearing mufflers and gloves.

"Yes, Watson," he said, as if had read my thoughts. "It is indeed a beautiful day for the time of year and, to anticipate your question, I would be amenable to a brisk walk in Hyde Park or St. James Park or anywhere else that appeals to you. I have no new case to distract me at the moment, although I await the results of several enquiries. So what do you say? Shall we take the air for an hour or so?"

But it was not to be. We had left our lodgings behind by no more than fifty paces when a police coach swerved to the kerb ahead of us.

"It's Lestrade," Holmes observed at once. "I very much regret that our walk is likely to be postponed."

The little detective fairly dashed from the coach, coming to rest breathlessly as he accosted Holmes and myself.

"Good morning, gentlemen," he began. "I regret this intrusion, but I thought you would like to hear what I have to say, Mr. Holmes, especially as you helped the Yard to put Cutter behind bars."

"Cutter?" Holmes retorted. "Ephraim Cutter?"

"He is to hang at the end of the week," I recalled.

"Indeed he was, Doctor," Lestrade confirmed. "But he disappeared from his cell in Newgate during the early hours of this morning."

Holmes gave the Scotland Yard man an incredulous look. "Come now, Lestrade. What sort of foolishness is this? Men cannot pass through solid walls, and I would wager that there are few more solid than those of a condemned cell. Have you visited Newgate and examined the walls and surroundings? There is surely some trickery here and I cannot say that I'm surprised – Cutter showed himself to be an imaginative and cunning adversary during the investigation."

Lestrade nodded his bulldog-like head. "Very true, Mr. Holmes, and I have seldom encountered a man who deserved his fate more. At the Yard, we have discovered six victims, at the last count. His method never varied. He would kidnap the child of a wealthy family, extract money from them, and then return a strangled body. I believe he considered this safer than leaving a child alive who could possibly identify him."

"I am familiar with the case, Inspector. I conclude from your avoidance of my question that you haven't yet visited the prison. How then did this notion of a miraculous escape come to be?"

"We will discover that when we meet the Reverend Arnold Chester, the prison chaplain. That is, of course, if you gentlemen will consent to accompany me."

He indicated the coach and Holmes glanced at me. I nodded my assent because, although I was disappointed at the postponement of our walk, I found myself intrigued by Lestrade's narrative.

Little was said during the journey. Holmes sat with his head upon his chest and the inspector wore a distant look – doubtlessly wondering as to the outcome of this strange situation. As for me, I had been this way with Holmes before, and my past impressions of the drab confines of the prison returned to my mind.

The coach came to a halt and Inspector Lestrade approached the gate to speak to the guard within. After a moment we were admitted, to be met by a heavily-built man of perhaps forty years.

"Good morning, gentlemen," he said as we alighted. "We were advised of your coming. My name is Gramwell. I am Head Guard of the condemned cell block, and the governor has instructed me to accompany you there and provide any information or assistance you may need."

Lestrade acknowledged the man and requested him to lead us to Cutter's cell, whereupon we were taken to a small building that was set apart from the main structure. On entering, I experienced again the claustrophobic and depressed feeling that I remembered from my previous visit. The inspector too appeared uncomfortable as he regarded the stone walls and tiny cells which had been the last residence of many evil souls. Only Holmes seemed unaffected.

Gramwell led us around a corner into a short corridor and stopped abruptly. A thin and nervous-looking uniformed guard stood talking to a man wearing the dark clothes of a priest, outside a cell with its door wide open.

"Gentlemen, allow me to introduce you to the Reverend Arnold Chester, our prison chaplain, and Andrew Bellows, who had special responsibility for the condemned man, Ephraim Cutter." Gramwell's disapproving tone made it clear that he blamed Bellows for Cutter's disappearance, although how this could be when the nature of this strange event was as yet unknown was difficult to comprehend.

Lestrade introduced Holmes and myself, before Gramwell announced that he would leave us to conduct our interviews unimpeded – although he would be close at hand if needed.

There was silence for a moment, during which Holmes's gaze took in the dull surroundings before returning to the two men before him. The Reverend Chester was the first to speak.

"Mr. Holmes, I confess to being confounded by all this. Mr. Cutter's conversion was remarkable, a true miracle, but I couldn't have imagined that he was to be taken literally."

My friend regarded him thoughtfully. "I am as yet unfamiliar with the recent situation here. Pray relate, in your own words, what has occurred."

"I visited Mr. Cutter soon after his arrival at Newgate." The priest averted his eyes, as if he found the memory an embarrassment. "I found him to be an evil man, given to curses and blasphemy. He boasted of his crimes and showed no remorse. During subsequent visits, however, I noticed a gradual change. The man's resistance softened. He began to listen when I quoted the Bible about God's arrangement for atonement and forgiveness, and a new hope dawned in his eyes when I explained that to Him, no man is beyond redemption."

"Could this have been a subterfuge?" I asked.

"With what object? I was convinced of his sincerity simply because his fate was sealed. He was about to face the hangman – nothing could change that. He would gain nothing by pretence."

"He would be far from the first to undergo such a change, with the prospect of approaching death," Holmes observed. "Did his new-found faith increase in response to your instruction?"

"Very much so. In fact he began to tell me of visions that he had begun to experience as he slept. This went on for several weeks, until he revealed that he believed God was about to set him free. I explained to him that he must not take this to mean that he would be released. The message, if indeed it was genuine, surely meant that forgiveness for his crimes was possible. This did not satisfy him, and on one occasion he shouted his belief that he was soon to regain his freedom so loudly and adamantly that the guards had to be called to quieten him."

Holmes looked up sharply. "When did this occur?"

"The evening before last. He kept repeating that God was about to come for him."

"And then, a little more than one day later, he disappeared from his cell?"

"So it would appear." The reverend shook his head. "I have never heard or experienced such an event. Frankly, I don't know what to believe."

A faint smile crossed Holmes's features. "We shall see what is revealed by looking into the matter." He turned to Lestrade. "Have you any questions for the Reverend, Inspector?"

Lestrade, who had remained silent until now, looked mildly uncomfortable. "Not as yet, Mr. Holmes."

"Then perhaps we can continue with whatever Mr. Bellows can tell us."

The guard who had been assigned especially to watch Cutter, possibly to prevent him from cheating the hangman by ending his own life, shrank visibly. "I can tell you nothing that I haven't already explained to Mr. Gramwell and the governor," he stammered. "I began my duty, the early shift, and found this cell empty. There was no sign of the prisoner, nor any indication as to where he might have gone."

"Do you believe that he was removed by the Hand of God?"

Bellows looked at the stone-flagged floor uncertainly. "I could not say, sir. The prisoner once told me that he expected the Almighty to come for him in a blaze of glory."

Holmes nodded, slowly. "And do you see any sign that this has occurred?"

"None, sir."

My friend walked around the cell. "Not even these substantial burn marks on the floor here, and on the lower walls? Come now, Bellows, you must have noticed these despite the poor visibility in here, and having done so must have formed some sort of explanation. Why, I can still smell traces of smoke in the air."

Lestrade peered into the semi-darkness. "I see them, Mr. Holmes, but cannot understand how there could have been fire without kindling."

"Perhaps, then, it *was* God's work," said Bellows.

Holmes moistened a finger with saliva and brushed it across the discoloured stonework. It came away coated with a deep crimson hue.

"Not unless our Creator announces Himself with a blaze of permanganate of potash, mixed with a little glycerine. The effect of that combination is much like a miniature volcano, with much fire and smoke. I am surprised that the fire brigade wasn't summoned at once." He paused, I thought for effect. "But of course, as Cutter was the only occupant of the condemned block, no one else would have noticed – except for you, Bellows. What have you to say to that?"

The guard could maintain the deception no longer.

"I had to do it, sirs. They have my family. The prisoner Cutter said that my wife would be found floating in the Thames and my children would be returned to me hacked to pieces over the next few weeks. I didn't want to betray the trust that had been placed in me, but what else could I do?"

"Most of Cutter's gang escaped the police net because there was no evidence against them," Holmes recalled. "Some were his relatives. They would have easily been capable of organising such a scheme to set him free. I don't doubt that they would have carried out their threat – or indeed, may yet do so." He turned to the now-weeping guard. "Have your family been returned to you, Bellows?"

His answer was a distraught shake of the head.

"So, we have disproved any divine intervention in this matter. Now we must ascertain how Cutter left the prison. How did you assist him?"

The young man sat in a corner of the cell with his head in his hands. He looked up at us with shamed and fearful eyes. "I gave him my spare uniform."

Holmes nodded. "Are the guards and visitors required to sign out when they leave the premises?"

"They are required to sign both in and out as necessary."

"Pray find Mr. Gramwell in the corridor, and request him to bring the attendance ledger here. Tell him it is of the utmost importance that I examine it."

Bellows left quickly and without a word. He returned within five minutes with a large leather-bound volume.

"Mr. Gramwell apologises for the delay, but he had to obtain the governor's permission."

"Very well." Holmes took the ledger and ran his finger along the entries for the early shift change-over. "How many guards work in this part of the prison?"

"There are five of us, to accommodate the various meal breaks and reliefs."

Lestrade and I peered over Holmes's shoulder, as he identified every entry. "As I expected, over the course of an hour or so six men signed out. Again, there is no mystery regarding Cutter's exit."

"I will have every constable in London on the lookout for him." Lestrade assured us.

"A wise move, Inspector, but it occurs to me that I may be able to narrow down his likely whereabouts on consulting my index. Watson and I will now return to Baker Street, and you no doubt will be anxious to get back to the Yard." He fixed his gaze on the wretched form of Bellows, who was still visibly shaking and pale. "As for you, there can be no doubt that you are guilty of a serious dereliction of duty. Nevertheless, I cannot find it in myself to condemn you entirely." I saw a look of surprise enter Lestrade's face at this. "Because I've asked myself how I would have acted in your place and found no different answer, I will intercede on your behalf with the prison governor. I cannot say what your fate will be, but I'll endeavour to reduce the harshness of it. I am certain that Reverend Chester will also assist with this."

The priest assented, placing an arm around Bellows' shoulders as we left. In the corridor we confronted Gramwell, who was eager to learn what had transpired. Holmes evasively told him that all would be explained when we returned, probably the following day, for a meeting with the governor. He asked the head guard to arrange an appointment and confirm this by telegram to Baker Street. The man looked taken aback at this, but nodded his assent when Lestrade voiced his agreement.

"Don't assume yet that the hangman won't be needed at the appointed time," were Holmes's parting words to the dismayed head guard.

The police coach delivered us back to our lodgings. As we alighted, Holmes informed the inspector that he would communicate with him by telegram the moment that he was able to confirm his suspicions. "A glance through my index should suffice, Lestrade. I cannot quite recall the date, but I am certain that Cutter's likely whereabouts were mentioned in an article published in *The Standard.* On receipt of my message, your attendance in the company of, say, six armed constables would be as well. I recall that his associates, including his immediate family, are in every way as villainous as he, though nothing as yet has been proven against them."

The inspector nodded. "In addition, I'll ensure that every man on the beat is aware that Cutter is again at large."

The official vehicle rattled off and Holmes and I were back in our rooms in minutes. Mrs. Hudson appeared to inform us that the luncheon hour had approached, only to be waved away by my friend who was on his knees racing through page after page of his index. I, being fully conscious of increasing hunger pangs, gratefully accepted a portion of veal-and-ham pie and the stewed apple that followed.

I had hardly put down my coffee cup when Holmes stood up with a triumphant shout.

"I have it, Watson! I have it!"

"You have discovered Cutter's hiding-place?"

"I'm certain of it, sufficiently so to inform Lestrade. A recent newspaper cutting mentions, here in the small print, that Cutter's sister and her husband are the owners of the steam launch *Erica*, moored in the Port of London near The Tower. I would wager that Cutter has taken refuge there."

"Would they not have sailed by now?" I ventured.

"I would have expected so, but perhaps the tides were against it, or it was necessary to gather supplies for what is undoubtedly intended to be a long voyage. At any rate, there is no mention of such a departure in the sailing lists of any newspaper. I imagine their intention is to conceal themselves among the network of English rivers until they feel that police interest in them is waning. By then, Cutter will have had sufficient time to change his appearance, as he has done before."

The glitter in Holmes's eyes meant, I knew of old, that the game was again afoot. I handed him his hat and coat and hurriedly put on my own, and we stood in Baker Street awaiting a cab moments later. We interrupted our journey to the Port of London but once, for him to vanish into a Post Office to send the promised telegram to Lestrade. Soon the sinister shape of The Tower was evident, before we left the hansom. We descended and walked cautiously along a narrow footpath, noting the name of each tethered vessel as we passed. The river curved slightly, and we saw on the opposite bank several open barges which appeared to be deserted. A number of dormant steam launches rode the water unsteadily, disturbed by the wake of a craft heaped with coal. I saw that for a good two-hundred yards ahead nothing else was berthed.

"There!" Holmes exclaimed suddenly, indicating a half-rusted tub moored near a group of overhanging trees. "I can just make out the name of the vessel. It is the *Erica*."

"She appears to be deserted."

"Which is precisely what Cutter would have us believe, is it not, until an opportune time to set sail arrives. Are you armed, Watson?"

"My hand rests upon my service weapon."

"Excellent. I also am prepared. We have no means of knowing how many opponents are concealed in there, so I think that we'll await Lestrade and his men before making an approach. It would be best to avoid any shooting if that is possible, for to the best of our knowledge the wife and children of our friend Mr. Bellows remain captive. Let us hope they haven't been harmed, or that the *Erica* doesn't leave her berth within the next half-hour."

We stood in the shadow of a tall stack of crates, listening to the movement of the Thames and the passing of its shipping, but never once averting our eyes from the *Erica*, before we heard the heavy tread of the approach of the official force.

Lestrade demonstrated uncharacteristic caution in keeping his men concealed, for they remained some way off as he responded to Holmes's signal and joined us.

"You discovered their hiding-place quickly, Mr. Holmes."

"A quick search of my index was all that was necessary. I knew that I had seen a reference to Cutter or his family quite recently."

Lestrade nodded. "According to our files at the Yard, Cutter alone has been convicted of a crime, although most members of his family have been suspected of robbery at one time or another. Unless the others break the law today, he is the only one we can arrest."

Holmes looked at Lestrade and beamed. "Inspector, I was considering a number of approaches to accomplish this, whilst preserving Bellows' family unharmed. I do believe that you have just supplied the answer for which I was searching. If we are successful, you will truly deserve all credit for the outcome."

Lestrade's expression was blank, and I saw that he hadn't understood my friend any more than I had myself. We waited for Holmes to disclose his plan.

"Lestrade," he said at length. "I would be obliged if you would order your men to form a line along the bank, in full view of the *Erica*. I assume that every man is armed?"

"All six constables have been issued firearms, Mr. Holmes, as you requested in your message."

"Capital! If you will leave it to me to converse with Cutter, I believe that I can resolve the situation."

Lestrade was silent for a moment, and appeared as puzzled as before, but he didn't dispute Holmes's intentions. "Very well."

We remained in concealment while the constables took up their positions. They stood in a line near the wide wooden plank that bridged the gap between the shore and the *Erica*'s deck. Each man brandished his weapon, presenting a formidable barrier to escape.

Without a word, Holmes strode out to stand where he was easily visible from the boat. After watching the vessel for a short time, he cupped his hands to his mouth and hailed those within.

"Halloa, the *Erica*! Ephraim Cutter, you are hopelessly outnumbered. Surrender yourself now, and much bloodshed can be avoided."

The faint echo of his words died away, without any discernible effect.

I believe he was preparing to repeat his message when the cabin door was slammed open violently. Two men stood on the threshold. I recognised Cutter from his trial, which I had attended with Holmes, but his companion was unknown to me.

"Jake Quintly," Lestrade said, anticipating my question. "A cousin of Cutter, not known to be on good terms with him, usually. He's slipped through our fingers many times because he intimidates witnesses, but his day will come."

"I'm sure it will," I replied, observing the large bearded man with a long scar above his left eye.

Even from this distance I could see the blank stare, that of the wild beast, that Cutter had invariably worn in the courtroom. He reached behind him, into the shadows of the cabin doorway, and dragged forth a young woman who cried piteously as he placed her in front of him with his arm about her neck.

"See here, Mr. Sherlock Holmes, and all you coppers!" he cried in a hoarse voice. "If you try to stop this boat from leaving here, you'll all be sorry. I'll slit this tart's throat and then both her brats, and you'll see them float down the river behind us. What do you say to that?"

As his words died away, I heard sounds from some of the constables that indicated their horror and revulsion. Even they, accustomed as they were to the dark aspects of life in the capital, were affected by the pitiless cruelty of this man. Never more, I told myself, was a man more justly condemned.

"That would be foolish in the extreme, don't you think, Cutter?" Holmes replied after a moment. "It cannot have escaped your notice that Mrs. Bellows and her children are the shield that prevents these officers from opening fire. Kill them, and what protection for you remains?"

Cutter hesitated, and Quintly gave him an uncertain look.

"We have guns too. We'll take some of you with us. I will never face the hangman."

"That may be. That is how it could turn out. But how many of your family are in there? How many will die needlessly in the battle?" Holmes paused to let Quintly, not Cutter if his intention was as I suspected, take this in. "I must tell you that you alone are wanted by the law. Inspector Lestrade assures me that none of your family have ever been convicted. This means that, provided Mrs. Bellows and her children are returned to us unharmed, all that is required for them to sail away unmolested is your return to custody."

In the short silenced that followed, I saw Quintly's expression harden. Lestrade had mentioned that the two were rarely on friendly terms, despite their family connection. Cutter turned to Quintly and spoke quickly, apparently voicing a curse or oath, before they both retreated back into the cabin with Mrs. Bellows sobbing loudly.

"I don't think that you've convinced him, Mr. Holmes," said the inspector. "You can't appeal to the better nature of a man like Cutter. If nothing happens within the next ten minutes, I'll give the order to open fire."

"Lestrade!" I protested. "Remember the woman and children in there!"

"It is not my choice nor my wish, Doctor, but I am under orders not to let Cutter escape. How many more children might die if he is allowed to resume his activities?"

"Let us be patient," said Holmes, "while they consider the situation." But the words were hardly out of his mouth when the cabin door was flung open again momentarily and Mrs. Bellows and a small boy and girl pushed roughly onto the deck. At a sign from Lestrade, one of the constables laid down his weapon and stepped aboard the *Erica* to assist them onto the bank. They were hurriedly removed from the scene as sounds and cries of much violence erupted from within the vessel. We looked on as the door opened for a final time, and a bruised and bloody Cutter staggered onto the deck.

At once the constables' guns were raised, but there was no need. Cutter appeared ready to make his escape into the river but Holmes, seeing that he was unarmed, boarded the boat with a single leap and restrained his adversary with the grip of steel that I had seen him apply before. Both men had regained the bank and Lestrade fastened police handcuffs on Cutter's wrists, before a man I hadn't seen before appeared in the wheelhouse and a heavily-built woman freed the line. Clouds of steam appeared as the engines burst into life and the craft shuddered. The vessel left the bank slowly, then more quickly as the current took her and swept her out of our sight.

"We have, I think, won the day on this occasion," Holmes observed.

Lestrade walked back along the bank with us. "Mrs. Bellows and her children are safe, Mr. Holmes, and Cutter will hang as was arranged previously. But the others on that boat could have been charged with kidnapping and assisting a convicted escaped prisoner. I can't help but feel little satisfaction, for we have achieved only a partial victory."

"I concur of course, Lestrade," Holmes said a little disappointedly, "but on occasion one has to take the view that in life, by its very nature, things often don't turn out exactly as we would have them. As it is, you will undoubtedly have further opportunities to apprehend other members of Cutter's family for future misdeeds, and I've already stated that full credit for this encounter is justly to be yours. As for the immediate future, I suggest that you instruct your men to convey Cutter to Scotland Yard, to await your arrival after you've shared the excellent dinner that I know Mrs. Hudson has prepared for us in Baker Street."

The Case of the Missing Pipe
by James Moffett

I need aid. Hurry Watson! – Holmes

These were the dreadful words that greeted me one early morning as I sat down for breakfast. The message, written in my companion's unmistakable handwriting, shook my nerves and conjured alarming thoughts as to my friend's serious predicament.

At the table, Holmes's chair was out of place, and a rumpled newspaper had been thrown carelessly upon the ashtray. A folded telegram, slightly shrivelled at one corner, lay protruding from underneath that mass of papers.

The message, which had been handed to me by young Wiggins – the spokesman of the Baker Street Irregulars – was written hastily and with an unsteady hand. The messenger had scampered fervently up the stairs and burst into our lodgings, waving the note with particular urgency.

"Where is he?" I cried, having read those words and staggered up from the chair. "Quick boy! Quick!"

I grabbed my coat and followed the lad out into Baker Street. The bustle outside was at its usual pace – pedestrians flitting by, rowdy hawkers consuming the air with their shrill cries, the clattering of wooden crates, exclamations of disgust at the smell of burnt coal, and an unending stream of carriages and hansoms rattling by.

Clambering out of the front door, I hailed a cab that had just halted a few yards away.

"No – over here!" cried the squeaky voice of Wiggins as he waved from the other side of the street. Out of breath, I abandoned the cab and weaved through the treacherous traffic to rejoin my guide. We strode briskly past several houses before stopping in front of an entry that was half-open, some sixty yards from 221. Its wooden door had a lavish coat of dark yellow paint, with an undecorated brass knob at its centre.

The façade of the building into which it led was of an equally exquisite outlook, with an assortment of fresh carnations, daisies, and tulips adorning each bottom ledge of the two windows just above the door. It was indeed a splendid house, contending with the rather bleak and urban sights that occupied the rest of Baker Street.

"In there!" cried Wiggins, pointing inside, but then running off in the other direction on some other urgent errand.

I was left upon the doorstep, distracted by horrible thoughts and the worst fears imaginable, before hurrying inside.

The narrow corridor, with its pristine surroundings, led into a parlour from which a grunting noise gradually emerged. I took a few furtive steps forward into an opulent room adorned with fine furniture, richly-dressed sofas, and a splendidly ornate chandelier hanging from the ceiling which cast off a dazzling display of light through its myriad of crystal prisms.

The parlour was warm and stifling, evidenced by the large roaring fireplace. On the ground, upon the most magnificent specimen of decorated Turkish carpet, lay the frame of a man, wearing a familiar ulster and a pair of dark trousers. He was face down, with both hands splayed to each side of his head.

"Good heavens, Holmes!" I cried, rushing forward in alarm.

"Not another step Doctor," interrupted my companion's quiet but firm voice. He had merely raised his right hand from the carpet, but kept the left side of his face onto the ground, gazing at the fireplace.

"Whatever is the matter?" I declared breathlessly. "Are you unable to stand?"

"I'm merely on the verge of affirming a hypothesis," he puffed.

Upon closer inspection, on the patch of wooden flooring between the edge of the carpet and the fireplace, a small pool of water was visible – most of it by then absorbed into the wooden flooring.

"And the aid you requested in your note?" I insisted, with a rising tone to my voice, whilst trying to understand Holmes's eccentric behaviour.

"Tobacco, Watson. I need fuel for the mind. It has been a rather agitated morning."

He lay there, looking at the puddle – or the crackling fire – immovable.

I stood there in silence for minutes.

"Have you found your clue yet?" I finally added with annoyance. "Is the evidence clear as day before your eyes?"

"It is incandescent," replied Holmes calmly. He raised himself up, brushing off his trousers, and rearranging his coat before looking at me with a grin that gave off the satisfied look of being proven right.

"I seem to have misplaced my pipe." His face shifted into a disgruntled look, as he checked his coat pockets. He took a deep breath and sighed, sniffing in the musty air of the room.

"Back home?" he suggested. Before I had uttered a reply, he walked out of the room and through the corridor.

"I'll convey the details of the case via telegram, Inspector." Holmes called, his voice traveling back through the house. Then he stepped out into the busy street and I joined my friend.

We walked back in silence to 221b, where Sherlock Holmes demonstrated his unique ability at being privy to the most obscure of details when on a case, yet be completely oblivious to human emotions directly in front of him.

I was vexed, my tone sour, and I came off as rather curt in my actions following the events of that morning. Yet all this made no influence upon my companion as we settled back into our lodgings.

My unfinished breakfast no longer looked appealing, and the tea had turned cold. Feeling somewhat dejected, I let myself slump carelessly upon the sofa, whilst Holmes busied himself in his room.

I pulled out a copy of Gissing's *Workers in the Dawn* from the bookshelf and settled in for a quiet read. But alas, as much as I tried to muse over the words before me, I couldn't keep my mind off the rustling and thudding noises emerging from behind his bedroom door.

Holmes was exhibiting another episode of the outlandish behaviour which so often took over his unquiet spirit – not least following the conclusion of a case.

"What is the matter?" I asked as he stomped in front of the fireplace.

"My elixir," he replied, looking through the piled-up papers and books on the mantelpiece. "My sustenance, my cure for a racing mind."

He turned to face me, and must have read my blank expression.

"My pipe, Watson! I cannot find it."

"Have you looked through the usual places?" I turned another page, more out of indifference than for any particular interest in the book.

"Thoroughly," said Holmes. His tall, lean figure was bent as he scoured every nook and crevice of the sitting room. My eyes followed each movement with subtlety and interest.

"Perhaps you've simply misplaced it," I suggested.

"Unheard of."

"Locked in a drawer?"

"Unthinkable."

"Maybe you left it at the house when you lay down upon the floor."

"Improbable," he muttered, pausing in front of me with an irksome disposition.

I smiled at the comment and inhaled with satisfaction. "Once you have eliminated the impossible . . . ."

"Exemplary, my dear Doctor," he interjected with a forced grin. "You have made your point, and given us a fine demonstration of your excellent skills of memory retention."

He sighed and placed his hands in his trouser pockets. "Lamentably, the mystery still persists."

From the comfort of the sofa, I gazed at my friend with renewed curiosity. He stood there, frowning, his eyes fixed upon the floor carpet, yet his mind drifted far away.

He gave one final glance around the sitting room before he darted out onto the landing. I smiled again and, for what seemed like the first time, I felt as if I had the upper hand.

It was a truly rare occasion for Holmes's brilliance to find itself overthrown by so simple a matter.

For so it was.

And at that moment, I thought I would play my little game and attempt, feeble as it might have been, to apply the same whimsical treatment of deduction and explanation as employed by London's finest criminal detective upon his clients.

"Holmes." My voice echoed through the room. I closed the book and waited for my companion to reappear, his face bearing an even more thoughtful expression than before.

"Let's take the events in order, shall we?" I proclaimed, standing up and in turn inviting my friend to sit down. He did so with a mixture of reluctance and intrigue. Having settled himself in his armchair, I clasped my hands behind my back, all the while aware of the intense scrutiny in Sherlock Holmes's stare.

I cleared my throat and took a deep breath. "You claim that you had your pipe with you this morning." I paced back and forth with a gentle but confident stride.

"Just this very morning," he affirmed conclusively, his gaze fixed upon me.

"And you are certain you left these lodgings without it?"

"That is an incontrovertible truth."

I paused and thought for a moment. I glanced at the breakfast table with its litter of half-eaten food until finally I turned to observe the figure of Sherlock Holmes, sitting in silence with legs crossed and hands clasped under his chin.

"If we had to begin our chain of analysis," I continued, echoing my friend's all too familiar style of reasoning, "we can safely assume that you sat down for breakfast with the pipe in hand."

Holmes nodded quietly.

"But this morning," I resumed, "this very particular morning, something else broke that practice." I strode towards the table where I had left my unfinished breakfast.

I crouched down to the level of its surface on Holmes's side.

The crumbled newspaper lay there still. I picked up the folded telegram and, upon closer inspection, noticed that one corner of the paper had been scorched. I took another look at the table and stood up.

"A case, it would seem." Turning round to face my companion, I held up the telegram in hand as evidence of my statement.

"The fact that you were smoking during breakfast is manifest in the slight smudge of tobacco staining one side of this newspaper where you held it up between your thumb and forefinger. Furthermore, the other side of the paper has been lightly scorched, undoubtedly caused by the close proximity of the burning pipe to the telegram when you held both in the same hand." I paused for a moment to gain my breath. "Upon reading the contents of the note and the realisation that it was another case, you left these lodgings in a hurry."

A wave of euphoria surged within me as I spun my hypothesis, and analysed data after data. Holmes sat in silence. Reticent, unmoving, steadfast in his chair.

"There is a faint trail of ash that sweeps along this side of the table," I continued, pointing at the fragments of burnt tobacco. "It lies thickest on this side where you had been sitting reading the newspaper, which then gradually thins out across the surface until it stops abruptly."

I looked at my friend and, for the first time during my discourse, noticed that his eyebrows were raised. His glance was questioning and curious, almost as if Holmes himself was imploring me to reveal how I had come to so successful a conclusion.

"Ah yes! The newspaper." I understood then how he must have felt every time he began to unravel the many cases we had been on together, the sheer sense of satisfaction at having his listeners in awe at the deductions and reasonings he forged. I too felt the same way then, and I made it clearly known I was enjoying the moment – perhaps a little too enthusiastically.

"If we took the gathered data of the tobacco stains and the singed edges on the note, and we were to conclude that you had indeed grabbed the telegram with the same hand as the pipe, it is a confident possibility that you held something else in your other." I took a step back towards the table. "The newspaper perhaps?" I asked, pointing at the rumpled mass of papers.

"So you had been reading and smoking when the note arrived. The urgency of the call forced you to drop down both pipe and telegram on the table, then followed by the newspaper on top, evidenced by the sudden end of the ash trail."

I swept off some of the tobacco ash with the palm of my hand, letting the course texture of the dust to slither through my fingers.

"Presumably you then grabbed your coat and went downstairs to investigate the case." Behind that cold stare, I could see Holmes delighted by my deductions. He uncrossed his legs and leaned forward, eyeing me with a sharp look.

"All this leads me to the irrefutable conclusion that the pipe lies here," I remarked, as I picked up the bundled newspaper from the table. "Under your very nose . . . ." My words trailed off into silence.

There, upon the wooden surface, lay the pipe, untouched since that morning. At least, that is what my mind had conjured up, after having fashioned so clear and precise, and unassailable chain of reasoning.

The bitter truth, however, was that the pipe was not there.

Above the sense of sheer disappointment and shame at my boisterous claims, a clapping sound arose as Holmes congratulated me on my attempt.

"Well done, Watson!" He came over and patted me gently on the back. "A commendable effort, no doubt, but rather amiss." He gave a faint chuckle and gestured towards the sofa. Utterly defeated, I took his muted advice and fell down, letting my arms fall carelessly upon the cushions.

"Your argument was strong, but nonetheless flawed," he began. Instinctively, he clasped his hands behind his back. Then – looking at me with some wariness – he thought better of it and placed them inside his trouser pockets instead. He could not help, however, pacing back and forth, replicating my behaviour only a few minutes before.

"All facts brought forward by your good self, until the acquisition of the telegram, were correct," he continued. "What threw your reasoning off balance was your failure in noticing the *second* trail of tobacco ash."

He bent down and pointed at the floor, before extracting a small lens from his waistcoat pocket.

"There," he said. "A few ashes have fallen upon the carpet and left a rather unusual and unnatural pattern."

I stood up, intrigued by the revelation of new data unearthed by my companion. Crouching down beside him, I noticed the faintest of outlines formed by the grainy speckles. Looking through the lens in turn, it became evident that the pattern laid out was that of a footprint.

"The pipe was, as you correctly identified, underneath the newspaper before being picked up and taken off the table."

We both stood up and took a few steps back. Holmes rubbed his chin, his eyebrows frowning in thought.

"Mrs. Hudson has clearly not been upstairs since laying out breakfast this morning. You, Watson, would have had no reason to take the pipe. I myself was not present at the time of the disappearance."

Holmes continued reasoning out loud.

"That would eliminate all suspects down to one."

"Wiggins . . . ." I muttered.

"Young Wiggins was here to deliver my message to you," agreed my friend. "He gave you the note and slipped the pipe in his pocket before leaving."

"Why on earth would he do that?" I exclaimed.

"I would say his rather impish sense of humour, rather than any other sinister motive," concluded Holmes, and placing the lens back in his pocket.

"I remain in awe at your unparalleled sense of observation, Holmes."

The sun had risen higher and I had just retaken my place upon the sofa. An hour after the revelation of the thief, we had waited until Holmes's other messengers had found Wiggins and summoned him back to 221b.

The pipe was returned unharmed along with the child's confession, which concluded with Holmes placing a few coins in the boy's dirty hands. With Wiggins having left in a hurry, my friend walked over and sat back down in his armchair. He had refilled his pipe with a new supply of tobacco before lighting the contents and sending off a thick pungent plume of white smoke.

"There is no secret to what I do," he said, playing with the pipe and testing out the stem. "You know my methods, Watson." He puffed several times until he was satisfied that the hollow space between the lip of the pipe had been cleared of any fragments. "Now, would you feel inclined to a succinct rendition of this morning's case, and why you found me face-down upon that floor?"

"It would be most welcome," I replied, having forgotten all about the charming house further down the street, the roaring fireplace, and the mysterious puddle of water. I leaned forward and listened with utmost attention to a rather remarkable and sensational story which, should time and skill give me the opportunity of doing so, I shall relate to my readers in the near future.

The Whitehaven Ransom

by Robert Stapleton

"Remind me, Watson," said my friend Sherlock Holmes as he looked forlornly up at the lowering sky and around at the cold, gray water. "What exactly are we doing here?"

The exhausting train journey from Euston, via Penrith, had brought us eventually to the small Cumberland market town of Keswick. From there, we had transferred to an open steam launch at the lakeside landing stages, for a journey of only a couple of miles along that most delightful member of the family of English Lakes known as Derwentwater.

"You have had a demanding few months," I replied. "Your work has taken its toll upon your health, and it is my decided opinion that you need time away from the big city. So when the opportunity arose of spending a few days here among the English Lakes, it seemed too good a chance to dismiss."

"And we are to spend a week with your friend, Bushy Barnswick, I believe," added Holmes, without much enthusiasm.

"That is indeed the intention," I replied. "And he's not such a bad chap, in spite of his appearance. As I told you, I know this fellow through my club. He told me he had recently acquired a small property on the shores of Derwentwater. He is unattached, with no family to worry about, or indeed to help him enjoy his good fortune. As a result, he has been kind enough to invite us both to join him here. I know that your list of appointments will allow for a brief absence from Baker Street, and I also have been fortunate enough to free myself from the demands and duties of daily life – at least for a short time."

I was aware that Holmes, as a student of crime, would be lost without a mystery to solve, but I also realized that we both needed a holiday.

I spread my hands to encompass the lake and its surrounding countryside. "A few days in a place of such magnificence can only bring much needed peace to the frayed human soul – both yours and mine."

The man at the wheel, who had remained quiet until now, removed the pipe from his mouth and pointed the stem toward the hills. "You can see Skiddaw towering behind us. He's got his hat on today. Cloud-cover. So we can expect rain before the night's out."

I looked round at the mountain, whilst Holmes seemed to pay little attention.

"Beyond that island ahead of us, you can see Borrowdale," our guide continued. "A green valley, stretching out into the hills. But we're heading to Cat Bells."

Rolling hills rose up in front of us.

"Popular walking country," said the boatman.

"In the right weather," I added.

The man chuckled, and again drew deeply on his pipe. "You'll not have much longer to wait, gentlemen," he added, as he turned the bows of the launch a few degrees to starboard. "Badger's Piece is coming up presently."

As I watched, I noticed the gray slate roof and whitewashed walls of a small but stately building gradually appear above the trees bordering the lakeside now directly ahead of us. I also noticed a small wooden landing-stage, lying below a narrow opening amongst the foliage. I also recognized a familiar figure standing on this quayside. Although dressed now in tweeds and a floppy hat, rather than the more usual bowler-hat and dark suit, Archibald Barnswick, known to his friends and creditors alike as "Bushy" in view of his splendid beard, was unmistakable in appearance.

Bushy Barnswick waved and called out his greeting as we approached. The moment the launch touched land, he helped us to disembark, together with our various items of baggage.

"Thank you, Frank," said our host, passing our helmsman a handful of coins.

"No extra for the commentary on the way," added Frank with a chuckle, before he turned the launch around and headed back toward Keswick. And civilization.

Our host seemed delighted to receive us. "Greetings, gentlemen. Welcome to Badger's Piece. I only took possession of the property a couple of weeks ago, so the place is all quite new to me. I bought the house and land from an elderly local man who, unfortunately, had allowed the place to deteriorate somewhat. At the same time, I also acquired an additional parcel of land farther along the lakeside. Nobody else wanted that land, so I picked it up for a mere pittance."

"You are indeed a fortunate man," I replied.

"As I said, the whole place needs renovating, but you are very welcome to join me here for a few days. You are in fact my very first visitors."

Holmes and I followed Bushy through the foliage, which threatened to block our way, and up a slight slope, until we found ourselves standing outside the modestly sized building I had seen earlier, constructed on rising ground.

As we bundled into the entrance hall, we were met by a large woman with an imposing presence. She looked us over for a moment.

"This is Mrs. Henderson, the housekeeper," Bushy explained.

"Good afternoon, gentlemen," said she, with a nod. It seemed that we had been accepted. "I hope you will enjoy your stay here. If there's anything you need, then please let me know."

"We also have a first rate cook, and an efficient kitchen-*cum*-house maid, who helps with many of the chores around the place."

The door opened, and a man stepped in. He was of medium height, thin in build, with a ruddy face and strong, wiry arms.

"This is Wilbert," said Bushy. "Our estate manager."

"Also general workhorse and slave," said Wilbert with a good hearted chuckle. "As Mrs. Henderson says, let her know whatever you want doing, and she'll get me to do it." So saying, he picked up our luggage and led the way upstairs.

"I've given you the two front rooms," said Bushy. "You'll find a jug of hot water in both of them, so refresh yourselves and join me down here again for supper."

After the evening meal, we sat talking as the soft summer shades of evening fell across the property and the lake.

"Mrs. Henderson tells me we are due for a soaking tonight," said Bushy. "A storm is brewing out in the hills."

The rattling of rain on roof and window-pane kept me awake during the small hours of the night, but I emerged the following morning remarkably refreshed from my first night at Badger's Piece. On my way, I passed the maid in the corridor who was carrying a dustpan and brush.

The girl stopped. "I hope you'll excuse me for saying so, sir."

"Yes, Libby?"

"If you're thinking of going down to the lake in search of that old boathouse, please be very careful."

"Why do you say that?"

"Well, it's a dangerous part of the lakeside. Mrs. Henderson tells everyone that bad things happen to people who go down there. And I wouldn't want any harm to come to you, Dr. Watson."

"Neither would I," I replied. "And thank you for the warning, Libby. But have no fear. I shall be extremely careful."

With her face still displaying acute anxiety, the girl looked back over her shoulder, as though expecting danger, and hurried on her way

A moment later, I stepped outside and made my way down to the lakeside. From the landing stage, I could see the effects of the morning breeze as it whisked away a thin mist that had settled upon the lake following the storm. Then I noticed something emerging through the filaments of haze. A small gaff-rigged sailboat, her brown sails filling with the zephyr. The early morning sun, now glinting on the water, lent an almost magical touch to the entire scene

"He is watching us," came a voice from somewhere behind me.

I turned and found Sherlock Holmes, sitting on a fallen tree trunk, smoking his pre-breakfast pipe. His gaunt face and piercing eyes had regained some of their normal lustre.

"The man in that boat has been tacking backwards and forwards across the lake for the last half-hour. He is definitely keeping his eye on this place."

"But who is he?"

"I have no idea, but we shall find out before we leave. Anyway, we must assume that he means us no harm."

Together we made our way back to the house, where we found that the cook had already prepared our breakfast

Bushy appeared as we were finishing off our second jug of breakfast coffee.

"Gentlemen," he declared. "As I told you yesterday, I've come into possession of an additional stretch of land down beside the lake. I'm in need of a boathouse, and this parcel of land possesses one. At least, it's marked so on the map that came with the ownership documents. Would you care to accompany me as I go to investigate?"

We told him that we would be delighted to do so.

Less delighted was Wilbert, the estate manager. When asked to accompany us, he turned extremely awkward.

"I'm not sure I would like to come with you, sir," he declared. "That additional plot of land you acquired lies under a curse."

"A curse? Don't be ridiculous, man. Whatever makes you say that?"

"It's just a local legend, sir."

"Nothing but hearsay."

"Perhaps, sir. But people believe it."

"Yes, mostly ignorant and superstitious people."

"That's as may be, sir, but I'm prepared to bet you acquired that land at a remarkably low price."

"True enough."

"And did you ever ask yourself why that was?"

"Indeed I did, and I told myself that its generous price was down to its isolated location on the shore of the lake. If the low sale price is the result of gossip by those loose-lipped and small-brained old men who frequent that public house in Grange, then I for one will not complain about obtaining a bargain. But I would like you to come along with us this morning, Wilbert."

Still muttering his reluctance, and with a face like thunder, Wilbert joined us as Bushy led the way down to the lakeside, and then continued south along the shoreline. Here we found the foliage growing more densely, and the going becoming more difficult. Overhead foliage blocked out much of the sunlight, and cast the place into a deep gloom. Both Holmes and I were glad that we had brought our stout walking sticks as we forced our way between tangled weeds and overhanging branches.

"Wilbert."

"Yes, Mr. Barnswick?"

"I should like you to organize a gang of men to work on thinning out the foliage along here. Cut back some of the trees, and allow plenty of light to penetrate this dark hole."

"That might not be easy, sir."

"The local lead mines are mostly worked out now, so there must be men in the area who would value a job like this."

"I shall make enquiries, sir."

"I suppose they will all be frightened of the curse, as well."

"There is no denying that, Mr. Barnswick."

Holmes, who had been strangely silent until now, cut in, "When did those stories of the curse begin?"

Wilbert pursed his lips. "Difficult to tell, Mr. Holmes. Perhaps some thirty-odd years ago now, as far as I recall."

"And news of the curse became current at the same time as the disappearance of a local man."

"Why, yes. I seem to remember it was, sir. But however did you know that?"

"It seemed a reasonable deduction to make. Somebody goes missing, for no discernible reason, and people put it down to a curse. Such gossip is always rich breeding ground for idle speculation. There may even be those who wish to benefit from such fears."

By now we had reached the remains of some small building. With a few worked stone blocks lying in a tumble-down fashion around a small inlet of stagnant water, the place looked to have been neglected for very many years.

Bushy stopped, pulled his map from his pocket, and consulted it carefully. "This must be the remains of the old boathouse," he declared, nodding toward the ruins.

The estate manager shrugged. "Must be, sir."

I followed Holmes as he stepped closer to the dilapidated building.

“The roof fell in a long time ago,” he declared, examining the surrounding rubble, “and the wooden part of the walls has mostly rotted away. But those stone blocks could provide a stable foundation for it to be rebuilt.”

“Then it can indeed by repaired?” asked Bushy.

Wilbert gave an embarrassed cough. “If you want a gang of men to work on this, you’re going to have to pay them danger money, Mr. Barnswick.”

Before our host could think of a suitable repost, Holmes crouched down and reached his hand into the water that still remained in the basin of the silted-up boathouse. “I can feel something down there,” he said grimly, as he laid aside his hat and cape. “A boat of some sort. Old and waterlogged. And I think there is something still inside the boat.”

Bushy leaned closer, whilst Wilbert and I watched with deep and growing fascination.

As Holmes and Bushy together pulled on the gunnels which lay just below the surface of the water, we saw the boat begin to rise from the murky depths. “This is far too heavy for us to lift on our own,” declared Holmes. “The boat is full of silt, making it feel as heavy as a concrete block.”

“And the harder you pull, the more likely it is for the boat to fall apart,” cautioned Wilbert. “Then you’ll lose whatever is in there.”

“The far end of the boathouse has a slope,” observed Holmes. “Perhaps the boat might survive being dragged up there.”

The estate manager and I added our own strength, and soon we had the boat pulled up the gradient, where it lay above the level of the water.

“Now we need to clear away the silt,” said Holmes.

“I know you don’t like this place, Wilbert,” said Bushy Barnswick. “But we need a bucket. See what you can find back at the house.”

With the use of a zinc bucket and water from the lake, we cleared away much of the silt that had built up over the years inside the boat.

I was holding the bucket when I noticed something white in the subdued daylight filtering through the undergrowth.

Bushy gasped, whilst Wilbert gave a groan that came from deep within him.

I stood dumbfounded.

“A skeleton,” declared Holmes. “I can hardly say that I’m surprised.”

“You thought we might find a body here?” asked Bushy.

“A disused boathouse, the story of a curse, and a missing man. The possibility of a body did seem a reasonable conclusion to make.”

As I continued to pour on water, and clear away the surrounding silt, I could see more and more the skull, its white sheen stained by the passage of time and the minerals in the water.

"Leave it, gentlemen," said Bushy, as he stood back and surveyed the gruesome scene. "This has now become a police matter. And they will need to call in the Police Surgeon to see this."

"Certainly," said Holmes. "But first, allow us to make any initial conclusions we can from what is evident."

"But what is evident?"

"Watson, what can you make of our skeleton?"

I stooped to my task and examined the remains. "The skeleton is definitely that of a man. Perhaps in his mid-twenties, judging by the good condition of the teeth. Tall. Nearly six foot in height. Well-built, without being obviously obese. No sign of disease. A good specimen of a man. But I can find no injury that might account for his death."

Holmes now stooped down to examine the remains. "As you say, Watson, there is no sign of anything that might account for his death. But what can we find beneath the bones?" He reached into the silt still covering the bottom of the boat, pulled back his hand, and opened it to reveal four coins. "Two pennies, one farthing, and a florin. They must have fallen out of his pockets when he was placed here. The man was therefore clearly not killed in the course of a robbery. Also, these aren't the coins one might expect to find in the pocket of a working man. Very little remains of his clothing, so it must all have rotted away over the years, but what remains of his boots suggests that they must have cost him a pretty penny."

"He must have been here for at least thirty years," I opined.

"Let us take a closer look at these coins," suggested Holmes. "The three copper coins are dated to the 1840's, but the florin looks new and is dated 1856. We can reasonably conclude that he died shortly after that date."

Holmes thrust his hand once more beneath the silt, directly under the center of the skeleton. This time, he pulled out a small, silver object, which glinted even in this subdued daylight.

"Another coin?"

"No. A small key." Holmes took out his lens, and examined it. "Interesting."

"What is?"

Holmes passed me the key and his lens. I looked carefully. On one side it had a number: "*24*", whilst on the reverse it showed a crest that I didn't recognize.

I handed them back to Holmes.

"Now to work, gentlemen," said he. "Mr. Barnswick, as you said, you need to contact the police in Keswick and arrange for a Police Surgeon to visit."

"That I can easily do," replied Bushy. "Wilbert, please organize a gang to clear away this undergrowth and begin work on repairing the boathouse as soon as the Police Surgeon gives permission for us to move the body. And you, Mr. Holmes – what will you do?"

"Watson and I must try to identify this man. We know that he was tall, reasonably well off, probably not a working man, and disappeared some thirty years ago. Somebody in Keswick must know something about him. They might even furnish us with a name."

"Very well, Mr. Holmes," said Bushy. "Until we can rebuild the boathouse and acquire our own form of water transport, we have no choice but to travel into town by road."

The undulating journey along the western shore of Derwentwater made me realize the value of water transport in that rough and rugged terrain.

From Keswick market square, Holmes led the way to the bar of one of the hotels located in the center of town and asked the barman for permission to make an announcement to those present.

Given permission, and from his place standing at the bar, Holmes looked around at the people who occupied the room. "Gentlemen," he began. "We are trying to identify somebody who went missing some thirty years ago. A man standing six foot in height. Not a working man, but rugged and in good health. Can anyone here help us identify this man?"

"Thirty years ago?" came a voice from the far end.

"Or thereabouts."

"Why? Have you discovered a body?"

"Just a few remains."

"I remember somebody going missing back then," said the same man.

Holmes ordered the man a drink and we joined him at his place beside the empty hearth. "Can you tell us anything more?"

The old man rubbed his chin and screwed up his eyes. "A medical man – a doctor, I think he was. Aye, that's right. He was here working with a medical practice in those days."

"Where was the practice based?"

"A big house at the far end of Market Street." The man chuckled. "But after thirty years, the doctor in charge will be long gone from there now."

Another voice added, "That was in the days when Dr. Letherholm was in charge of the practice. He retired years ago. The last I heard, he had gone to live in a nursing home, but I couldn't tell you which one."

The current secretary at the doctor's surgery pointed us in the right direction, and by early afternoon we found ourselves at a nursing home for elderly patients, situated on the edge of the town.

One of the nurses took us to a residents' lounge where we found a frail and aging man, sitting on a wicker chair, looking out at the garden.

"Dr. Letherholm?" asked Holmes.

"Indeed, sir," replied the elderly man as he looked up.

"My name is Sherlock Holmes. I am a consulting detective."

"Then you're a little out of your territory here, Mr. Holmes."

"I am in the area for a few days' holiday, together with my friend here, Dr. John Watson. We are staying at Badger's Piece, along Derwentwater."

"In that case, welcome, gentlemen. How may I help you?"

"We would like to talk to you about a former colleague of yours."

"Really? Please take a seat, both of you. Now, which one of my colleagues do you have in mind?"

"We understand that this man worked with you some thirty years ago. He was tall, and in his mid-to-late-twenties. He disappeared, apparently for no clear reason, but so far we haven't been able to discover the man's name."

The elderly doctor's face clouded over with concentration, and then lit up again. "You must mean Mortimer Chadwickson. Yes, I remember Mort. And it's true – he disappeared without giving anyone any reason. The gossips believed that he'd run away."

"Why might he do that?"

"In those days, a family known as the Harnecues terrorized the area. They were quite a rough load of villains. Amongst many other things, they had been involved in smuggling operations between the west coast and the towns and villages of north Cumberland."

"And you think Dr. Chadwickson was intimidated by them?"

Dr. Letherholm looked out of the window, but his gaze was far away, in another time.

"Mort joined me as a junior partner in the mid-1850s. He was a good and steady worker, and grew to be well respected by the people we served. Then a medical practice along the coast, at Whitehaven, asked us to help out. Their doctor had been taken ill. Anyway, I agreed to allow Mort Chadwickson to go there as *locum*, until things had settled down again. He returned after a couple of weeks a changed man. He had a hunted look in his eyes, and seemed to be on the lookout for somebody following him.

He told me he was terrified of the Harnecues catching up with him. And with him being such a notable figure, there was every chance that they would do just that. I asked him what had occurred in Whitehaven, but he had little inclination to tell me, except that he had been called to the bedside of a dying woman."

"Can you tell us the name of this woman?"

Dr. Letherholm shook his head. "If he told me, then I cannot remember after all these years. But I do remember him saying that it was a most unusual visit."

"We would be most grateful if you could tell us more," said Holmes, quietly but firmly.

"I seem to remember that the lady, who was lying on her deathbed, informed Chadwickson that the town had entrusted her mother with something valuable. The dying woman muttered something about a ransom, and that it was hidden behind a loose brick in her kitchen chimney. She was fearful that, after her death, some local rogues might get their hands on this treasure, and she wanted him to take it from its hiding place and keep it somewhere secure."

"And did he do that?"

"Oh, I think so. But I'm sure that, if he did take the treasure, Chadwickson would never have kept it for himself, let alone run away with it. He wasn't that sort of man. But shortly after that, he vanished altogether."

"We are a long way from solving the mystery, Dr. Letherholm," replied Holmes, "but we have discovered some human remains which are of a man such as I described. And now, thanks to your help, we might have a name."

"We reported Chadwickson's disappearance to the police," said the doctor, "but they could find no trace of him. It was a mystery, Mr. Holmes, and has remained so until this day. But now you're suggesting that my former colleague somehow came to a tragic end. It seems to me that here is a case to be solved, by a detective such as yourself. It also seems upon reflection that the mention of a 'ransom' has to be central to the solving of this mystery.

"I feel sure that's you're right, Doctor," said Holmes, standing up to take his leave. "In the meantime, we must bid you farewell. My colleague and I have much to attend to. And be assured, we shall certainly let you know the outcome of our investigations."

Holmes and I returned to the market square, wondering how we would make our way back to Badger's Piece, but we had no need for concern on that score, as we spotted the animated figure of Bushy Barnswick bowling towards us at speed.

"I am extremely glad to have found you, gentlemen," he told us. "The Police Surgeon from Carlisle has arrived, together with an Inspector Armadale of the county police. A sergeant from the local force is arranging for Frank to take us all back in his steam launch. As you have already discovered, the boat is more comfortable than the trackway, so I can let Wilbert take the carriage back by road, whilst we go by water."

It was difficult at first to determine which was the surgeon and which the detective, since the former was a robust, alert-looking man, whilst the policeman was short in stature and round in figure. In the presence of these two heavyweights, the local sergeant kept a low profile, speaking only in mono-syllables when replying to the occasional question put to him by his superiors.

During the short boat journey down the lake, we discussed our observations, together with the day's conclusions.

"Dr. Mortimer Chadwickson?" muttered Inspector Armadale, rubbing his chin in thoughtful contemplation. "It doesn't ring a bell with me. And, after all, you have no conclusive evidence that this is the man you discovered, do you, Mr. Holmes?"

"That is quite correct, Inspector," returned Holmes, "but it seems highly likely to be the man.

"And the cause of death," continued the Police Surgeon. "You say you could determine no sign of violence or other injury that might account for the man's death."

"That is correct, Doctor. But we did manage to discover some coins associated with the body, and found that they dated the death to no earlier than 1856."

"But again, that is inconclusive."

"Quite."

"In that case, we will have to make our separate examination of the body and arrive at our own opinions. We require facts, Mr. Holmes, not speculation."

"I would hope that the two would complement each other."

We arrived at the landing stage directly below the house at Badger's Piece, and Bushy led the way through the foliage toward the remains of the old boathouse. Whilst the sergeant remained with us in the background, the surgeon and the detective began their examination of the skeleton and the scene adjacent to it.

"We have presented the bones as clearly as possible," said Bushy, "without moving them in any way."

The Police Surgeon grunted as he continued his painstaking examination. "An adult male, approximately six feet in height, who appears to have enjoyed a healthy life. As you told us before, Mr. Holmes, there is no evidence of foul play. But the bones have clearly been here for many years."

"I would concur with the dating," added the inspector, juggling the coins we had left piled on the stonework. "Approximately thirty years or so. Again, as Mr. Holmes has already so helpfully ascertained."

"Plenty of time for the bones to have been stripped bare," added the Police Surgeon.

"But there is no way of identifying the unfortunate man," said the inspector.

The two men finished their examination of the bones and stood back to confer, before announcing their conclusions.

The Police Surgeon stood to his full height and gave his decision. "Since I can find no obvious cause of death in this case, I'm obliged to consider it a suspicious death, and I must therefore refer the matter to the Coroner. In due time, he will contact the family and arrange for them to receive the body."

"This is clearly an old case, gentlemen," said the inspector. "But no less important for that fact. It therefore requires dogged and persistent police work." He turned to the sergeant. "I think we can safely leave the matter in the hands of the local police to trace the family and arrange for a proper disposal of the remains. This might be Dr. Chadwickson, or maybe not. We can only judge by the evidence presented to us."

The police sergeant nodded. "Right you are, sir. We'll get on to it straightaway."

Holmes stepped forward, holding up the key. "One more thing, Inspector. We did come across this small key, hidden among the silt at the bottom of the boat."

The police inspector took the key and examined it. "What makes you think it has anything to do with the deceased?"

"Merely the location."

"And what kind of lock might this key fit?"

"I have no idea, Inspector. I was hoping you might be able to enlighten us on that matter."

The inspector shook his head and chuckled. "Scotland Yard tells me that you are a man who enjoys looking into a puzzle, Mr. Holmes. Detective work is for professionals, not amateurs. But if you would like to entertain yourself by looking in the significance, if any, of this key, then you are very welcome to waste your time trying."

The inspector handed back the key and then joined his two colleagues as they returned to the steam launch and set off on their return journey back up to the northern end of the lake.

The following day dawned bright, mild and dry, and a gang of workmen arrived at an early hour to begin the work of clearing the area around the boathouse, and with the further intention of restoring the old building to its rightful use. The body had been removed, and Wilbert took both his qualms and his workmen in hand. Before long, the sound of sawing and digging filled the air.

Holmes announced that he had a great deal to think over. He needed to be on his own, free from distraction, so that he could concentrate his attention more fully upon the matter in hand. Giving no indication when he intended to return, he took his pipe and pouch of tobacco and headed onto the slopes of Cat Bells.

I knew my friend well enough to leave him strictly to his own devices, and instead turned my attention to the various jobs that needed doing around the house of Badger's Piece.

After our midday meal, at which Holmes was conspicuous by his absence, Wilbert announced that he'd arranged a fishing trip for us on the lake.

"A man I know at Grange has promised to take us out in his boat this very afternoon," Wilbert explained. "He has even promised to supply us with the rods, nets, and all the bait we shall need."

As promised, the boat met us at the landing stage and took us out a couple of hundred yards from shore. There we sat down to our battle of wits with the fishes of Derwentwater. For the first hour, our piscatorial adversaries proved to be the victors in the struggle.

Even though the sun wasn't shining, the air was clear, and we all had a perfect view of the lake and its surroundings. With the fishing-line floats bobbing idly amidst the ripples of the surface water, I looked around.

Then I noticed him. "I can see a man over there, on the shoreline."

"Where?" asked Bushy.

"Toward the southern end of the lake."

"Yes, I see him."

"He's been there for at least the last half-hour, and he's been watching us through a telescope. I can occasionally see light reflecting from the lens."

Bushy screwed up his eyes. "Are you sure?"

"Oh, yes. There is no doubt about it."

Our consideration of the watcher was interrupted by a sharp tug on my fishing line, as the float disappeared below the surface and the rod bent in an arc.

"You've caught yourself something big, Watson!" exclaimed Bushy as everyone in the boat gathered round to offer their assistance.

As I reeled in the fish from its home in the depths of the lake, the boat's owner brought a landing net to bear and soon had the fish on board, where he dispatched it with a fisherman's priest.

"Ugly looking brute," I told Bushy. "I don't like the look of those teeth."

"That, Dr. Watson, is because you have caught yourself a pike," said the boat's owner.

That proved to be my one and only success of the day, but my companions managed to secure a couple of brown trout.

On our return to Badger's Piece, the trout went straight to the kitchen, whilst my pike was dispatched to the taxidermist, and now hangs above the lounge fireplace in Bushy Barnswick's new home. I consider it my thankful offering for his kind hospitality.

I found Holmes, who was in a surprisingly good mood. "How was your day, Watson?

"We have been fishing," I replied. "But a man, standing on the shoreline, was watching us for the whole of our time out on the water."

"Now that is hardly surprising," Holmes replied, with an infuriatingly enigmatic smile.

"And how went your day?"

"I fell into conversation this morning with a fellow walker of the fells," he informed me. "A reverend gentleman, who expressed an interest in limiting the amount of industrial pollution in the area, and in improving the quality of road signs in the county. In return, I impressed upon him the importance of maintaining more generally the quality of the countryside environment, and of safeguarding the beauty of the area for the enjoyment of visitors, the delight of weary souls, and the refreshing of distracted minds. He told me he would give the matter his closest attention."

After supper, Holmes sat back, smiling. "The game is afoot, Watson," said he. "Tomorrow morning, we shall take the train to Whitehaven. The answer to our many questions inevitably lies in that coastal town."

In the middle of the following morning, we alighted from the railway carriage onto the station platform at Whitehaven. We found ourselves in a busy industrial town of elegant Georgian buildings, with the sound and smell of the sea mingling with the scent of coal-dust and the sounds of heavy industry.

"I see that he has come along with us," said Holmes.

"Who?"

"Presumably the same man who was watching you yesterday."

I looked back along the platform and, sure enough, there amongst the crowd was a man who resembled the figure I'd seen on the lakeside.

"Whatever does he want?"

"We shall no doubt find out in due time."

Holmes and I made our way to the center of Whitehaven, and looked around at an unfamiliar townscape.

"What are we looking for?" I asked.

"Oh, do wake up, Watson. A bank, of course."

"In that case, there appears to be one farther along this road."

"Well spotted."

Holmes lingered for a moment in front of the main entrance. "Now do you see it?"

"See what?"

"The crest above the front door."

"Of course. It's the same design we saw on that key. That was a lucky guess on your part."

"Watson!" exclaimed Holmes. "I am disappointed in you. You know better than anyone that I never make guesses."

"Of course. You must have ventured into Keswick yesterday. Doubtless making inquiries."

"All opportunities must be investigated." Holmes smiled indulgently, and led the way inside. "Having found the right place, we now need to speak to the manager."

The bank manager appeared – tall, formally dressed, and sporting a neat mustache.

"Good morning," said my companion. "I am Sherlock Holmes, and this is my friend and colleague, Dr. John Watson."

"And I am Mr. Sheldrake, the manager here. Please come into my office, gentlemen."

"Congratulations on your recent appointment," said Holmes.

"Oh?" The manager raised an eyebrow in surprise. "Thank you, Mr. Holmes."

"The new brass nameplate on your door, and the wood shaving beneath it," explained Holmes.

"Of course."

"Your new responsibility has caused disruption to your family's morning routine," continued Holmes, "forcing you to leave home in a hurry. You were harassed, and were nearly late in arriving today."

Again, an expression of amazement. "All true, but how can you tell?"

"The dog-hair on your coat, and the toast-crumb still on your tie, which neither your wife nor you had time to brush off."

The manager gave an embarrassed cough, brushed his tie, and looked up at us again. "How may I help you, gentlemen?"

"First, Mr. Sheldrake," began Holmes, "could you please tell me if you recognize the man standing across the street, watching this building?"

The manager looked outside and heaved a sigh. "Oh yes. He's one of the Harnecue family. They have been involved in all kinds of illegal activities over the years. Has he been bothering you?"

"Not at all, but it is good to have him identified. Now to business. I have two questions to put to you."

"Pray continue," said Sheldrake.

Holmes removed Chadwickson's key from his pocket, and passed it across the mahogany desk to the bank manager. "I believe this is the key to a bank deposit box."

The bank manager examined the key, and nodded.

"Furthermore, I believe it fits a box currently residing in the vaults of this bank, and that the holder of the key, whomever it is, is allowed to open that box."

"Again, you are quite correct, Mr. Holmes." Mr. Sheldrake stood up, searched through the contents of a bookshelf, and returned with an old leather ledger. This he opened, and laid out upon his desk. "Yes. The number on that key corresponds to a deposit made here in 1858, by a man called Chadwickson."

"Dr. Chadwickson."

"That was before my time, but our records show that the box hasn't been opened even once during these last thirty years."

"Then I should be obliged if we might rectify that situation," declared Holmes.

"We can certainly do that. But first, you have another question for me."

"Indeed." Holmes sat back and riveted the bank manager with his stare. "Can you tell us anything about 'The Ransom'?"

"This might take some time to explain," the bank manager replied. "Would either of you gentlemen care to partake of refreshments? Tea, perhaps?"

I accepted. Holmes declined.

After his secretary had brought in my tea, the manager sat down and steepled his fingers contemplatively. "In reply to your question, Mr. Holmes, I must first submit you both to a history lesson."

We both settled into our seats.

"You have no doubt heard of the American naval commander, Captain John Paul Jones."

We both nodded.

"Although Scottish by birth, John Paul, who later adopted the name Jones, began his maritime career from this port of Whitehaven. Later, in command of a fleet of enemy ships during the American War of Independence, he wrought havoc amongst the commercial shipping around the shores of Great Britain, culminating in an attack on Whitehaven."

Here was a period of history that I had neglected in my studies.

"On April 17th in the year 1778, John Paul Jones and his squadron appeared out at sea. The Americans were determined to cause devastation in Whitehaven, and to set alight the fleet of more than two-hundred merchant ships in our harbor. If successful, such an act would have caused untold damage to the economy of our town. Even today, the ships in our harbor are mostly constructed of timber, and are vulnerable to fire."

"What cargoes do your ships typically carry?" asked Holmes.

"The town's economy depends mainly upon the export of coal to other areas of industrial activity. The town is built on a coalfield. We even have one colliery designed to resemble a castle, complete with turrets and towers. You can see it standing above the docks. Our industrialists and merchants have a great deal invested in this trade, and in this town."

"As do the people, no doubt."

"True."

Sheldrake looked down at the notes lying upon his desk. "On that particular day, when the people of the town feared the loss of their homes as well as their wealth, the wind came to their rescue, and blew the American fleet right across the Irish Sea, leaving them to cause havoc there instead."

"A fortunate escape," said I.

"Serendipitous, Dr. Watson. But the leaders of the town knew that John Paul Jones and his ships would return as soon as the winds moderated in their favor. Not knowing how long they had to prepare themselves, the merchants decided to organize a ransom to offer the Americans on behalf of the town. They gathered together all the wealth they could muster at such short notice, from poor as well as from rich. This amounted to several thousands of pounds sterling, and they managed to convert this money into cut and polished diamonds. I have no idea how they managed it, or where they found so many gems at such short notice in such a remote area of the country, but, within five days, they had their ransom ready – which was just in time because, in the early hours of April 23rd, John Paul Jones and his men returned to menace Whitehaven."

I sipped my Earl Grey and continued to listen to this tale with rapt attention.

"This time," continued Mr. Sheldrake, "they landed under cover of darkness and began to rampage through the town. But they were badly organized and inexpertly led by Jones's lieutenants. The result was that, before Whitehaven's merchants could arrange to offer the Americans the ransom that they had collected, the people of the town sent the entire landing party packing. True, the invaders did manage to set fire to one of the ships in the harbor, but that was rapidly extinguished."

"The town had another narrow escape," I concluded.

"But I have not yet finished my tale," said the bank manager, now very much into his stride. "The town's people had no guarantee that the American fleet would not return, and with even greater numbers next time. It was decided to keep the ransom intact, just in case they needed it in the future. They considered keeping it in the vaults of a bank. But, as you can well imagine, the vulnerability of such a scheme lies in securing ownership of the key. Believe me, gentlemen, there were, and still are, plenty of people who have longed to get their hands on those diamonds – thieves, pirates, and smugglers."

"Such as the Harnecues."

"Amongst others."

Holmes leaned forward. "So the solution was to entrust the ransom to a member of the public who could be relied upon to keep those diamonds secure."

"That's quite correct. The wife of one of our most respected citizens was asked to keep hold of the bag containing the jewels, until further notice." The bank manager once more consulted his notes. "The lady's name was Doris Ferrybridge, and she dwelt in an ordinary house not far from the docks. This lady was well known for her honesty, her compassion, and her philanthropy."

"But the ransom money was never needed," concluded Holmes, "and the bag remained in the care of Mrs. Ferrybridge until the day she died."

"And beyond. With her husband long gone, Doris entrusted the care of the bag to her daughter, until she also died. With no other family to inherit the property, the house was finally demolished. Despite a careful and thorough search of the building, I have to tell you, gentlemen, those diamonds were never found."

"Unless we conclude that somebody moved them beforehand," I interrupted.

"My thoughts exactly, Dr. Watson," said Mr. Sheldrake. "Unless somebody relocated the gems to the safety deposit box here in the vaults of my bank."

"Where they have remained undisturbed for the past thirty years."

"There is only one way to be certain of the matter, Mr. Sheldrake," said Holmes. "We need to go down to the vaults and open that box."

"But remember, Mr. Holmes," Mr. Sheldrake cautioned him. "Those diamonds belong to the people of this town."

"The ownership of whatever we discover in that box would have to be determined by a court of law, Mr. Sheldrake."

The bank manager stood up. "Of course you're right, Mr. Holmes. But I hope that it will be used to benefit the people of this town. Now, gentlemen, please follow me."

Holmes and I followed the bank manager down into the vaults of the bank. The subterranean room smelt musty and felt oppressive, but I soon forgot my discomfort as our attention was directed to the rows of metal boxes which lined the vault. Mr. Sheldrake drew one out and placed it on the table in the middle of the room.

"Number twenty-four."

Holmes nodded. "That is the number on the key. We can only assume that it fits this lock."

"Then I shall leave you in peace, gentlemen," said the bank manager. "Call me if you come across any problem, or when you have finished in here."

As the bank manager closed the door, Holmes approached the box on the table, inserted the key, and turned the lock without difficulty. The lid groaned slightly as he lifted it, and then we were able to examine the contents of the deposit box. All that I could see was a black leather bag, sewn securely shut across the top by a row of leather stitches. Holmes lifted the bag, and felt its weight. Then he slipped it into his pocket.

"Hmm."

"Is that all you can say, Holmes? Aren't you going to open it up and check the contents?"

"There is absolutely no need, my dear fellow. I know exactly what this bag contains."

"But I should like to see."

"Patience, Watson."

"I don't mind acting as your cab service," said Frank as we alighted from his steam launch at Bushy Barnswick's landing stage. "It's always a pleasure doing business with friends of Mr. Barnswick – at least until he gets his own boat.

As we stood on the landing stage at Badger's Piece, watching his launch puff its way slowly back up the lake, we heard the sound of another steam launch, coming from the other direction.

Assuming that this was not meant for us, we both turned, intending to make our way back to the house and prepare for supper. Then we noticed the man, with arms crossed and face displaying dark intent, blocking the pathway.

"Well, Watson, it seems we are to remain here. Perhaps this launch is for us after all."

When the approaching steam launch drew closer to where we were standing, the man on board jumped onto the landing stage, holding the bow line. Here was a man we recognized, the man who had been following us for the last few days.

The other man still blocking our way to Badger's Piece stepped closer.

"Now," he said in a no-nonsense tone. "Would you two gentlemen kindly step aboard?"

We did as requested, although he presented no weapon, and the launch immediately set off on its return journey toward the southeastern end of the lake.

In silence, Holmes and I surveyed the scenery as it passed, and the hills as they emerged from behind closer undulations in the landscape. The air on the lake was calm and mild, but the atmosphere in the boat felt to me as cold as winter.

The steam launch gradually drew toward another landing stage, behind which stood a building constructed of gray Cumberland slate, with white-painted frames giving even greater contrast to the darkness of the windows. Here was a building that had to be at least two-hundred years old.

The engine chugged mysteriously to itself as the launch pulled up at the landing stage and the lines were secured to the mooring posts. Beside the launch lay a small sailboat, with its brown sails furled.

Holmes saw it too and nodded.

Our escorts ushered us off the boat, along the approach path, and into the house by way of the front door.

I could sense the ghosts of history haunting this place, and the very idea made me shudder. I felt that much had taken place in these premises over the centuries. I am not usually a timid man, but it was with a certain amount of trepidation that I accompanied Holmes as we were ushered into the front reception room.

In the middle of the room stood a large chair in which sat an elderly lady, dressed entirely in black. In this respect, if in no other, she reminded me of our dear Queen in her mourning attire.

The woman looked up as we entered, whilst the two men who had brought us here took their places behind the woman's chair, reminding me of guardsmen on formal duty.

Holmes removed his hat. "Mrs. Harnecue, I presume."

The lady raised an eyebrow in surprise. "You know who I am?"

"The matter is no great secret. Your son here has been shadowing us for the past few days, and now you wish to learn what we have discovered in our search for the Whitehaven Ransom."

"That is not the reason I had my sons bring you here, Mr. Holmes."

"No?"

"Certainly not. I am aware that you discovered the key to the bank deposit box when you examined the boathouse. I am also aware that you travelled to Whitehaven to retrieve the goods from the bank."

"Your sons and their informers do you credit, ma'am. Is Mrs. Henderson perhaps the source of your intelligence?"

"Do not think badly of her, Mr. Holmes. She is a local woman, and also a cousin of mine."

"That might explain a few things."

"I have brought you here, Mr. Holmes, because I wish to clear up certain matters in your mind."

It was Holmes's turn to look surprised. "In that case, pray continue."

"You have already ascertained that the skeleton you discovered in Mr. Barnswick's boathouse is that of Dr. Chadwickson."

Holmes nodded.

"The occasion of his death took place some thirty years ago."

"That fact has already been ascertained."

"The truth of the matter is that my husband's family have had a somewhat shady past – smuggling, extortion, and anything underhanded. Over a hundred years ago, when they heard news of the ransom raised to pay off John Paul Jones, and the fact that the money had not been paid over, they were determined to lay their own hands on those diamonds. In fact, Mr. Holmes, it became an unhealthy obsession in this family. They scoured the town of Whitehaven, from one end to the other, but no trace could they find of those gems. The secret of their whereabouts had been kept safe and sound by all involved in the scheme. But as the years went by, the search remained a tradition in the family, handed down from one generation to another. Then, in 1858, the family heard about Dr. Chadwickson's discovery of the Ransom, and learned that he had deposited the jewels in the vault of the town bank in Whitehaven. They realized that, if they were to lay their hands on those jewels, they would have to locate that key. My husband, Jack, together with his two brothers, decided to confront Dr. Chadwickson, and coerce him into handing the key over to them."

"To which end they contrived a meeting down at the boathouse," said Holmes.

"It was relatively secluded, and away from prying eyes, so that is indeed where they met. Whatever was said during that meeting we can only conjecture, but the good doctor refused to hand over the key. Instead, he placed it in the most secure place he could imagine at that moment. He swallowed it. Jack and his brothers decided that the only way for them to obtain that key was to make the doctor regurgitate the contents of his stomach. This they undertook to do, but, in the process, the poor doctor choked on his own vomit and died as a result."

"You are saying his death was a matter of misfortune rather than murder."

"They always insisted upon that. The family may have been rogues, Mr. Holmes, but they were never murderers."

"But why did they leave the body in that sunken boat? And for so many years?"

"At first, they attempted to find the key. They cut the body open, and examined the contents of his stomach. But they could find no trace of the key in there. But it had to be there. Somewhere. The fools ought to have cut open his throat, and searched his gullet and windpipe. That key might even have been the object that choked Dr Chadwickson to death. Anyway, they knew that if they dropped the body into the lake, it would rise to the surface and be discovered. Even cutting it up into smaller pieces – their act of butchery might well have been discovered. Instead, they decided to allow the body to decompose, so that they could eventually locate the key, and deposit the bones in the deepest part of the lake."

"That sounds extremely cold-hearted," I told her.

The woman gave a shrug. "I am merely telling you what happened, Dr. Watson. But they never had the chance to execute their plan. Within a few months of this incident, my husband Jack died, and his brothers had been arrested for various transgressions and sent to prison. The affair of Dr. Chadwickson and the key was forgotten, or at least the memory buried beneath the many other demands of life."

"And now you want us to hand the Ransom over to you," said Holmes.

"No, Mr. Holmes," asserted Mrs. Harnecue, leaning forward and riveting him with her cold gaze. "This is the lake of Saints and Sinners. The saints had the islands, and we were among the sinners. Smugglers and crooks. But we are a decent, law-abiding family nowadays. Our lawless years are over. It is merely our reputation that remains a distasteful memory for many, but that is all humbug. As a family, we are agreed that we must do whatever is the right thing. As far as I am concerned, Mr. Holmes, you must decide what happens to those diamonds. You may decide to donate them to the town of Whitehaven, or you may give the money to Mr. Barnswick. That is now your concern, not mine."

We took our leave of Mrs. Harnecue, assured that she would be kept well informed of our movements over the coming days.

At supper that evening, Holmes gave the appearance of a man at peace with the world. As the evening progressed, all eyes became fixed upon him, and a tense silence descended upon our gathering.

Finally, I could contain my curiosity no longer. "Come now, Holmes," I cried. "Let us see those diamonds. Open the bag, and show us the contents."

"Oh, the Whitehaven Ransom?"

"Of course the Whitehaven Ransom. That is what this business has been all about, is it not?"

Sherlock Holmes merely smiled, cleared the supper plates to one side, pulled the leather bag from inside his jacket, and laid it upon the table.

There it lay – a bag of black leather, hardened by the passage of time and the smoke from innumerable domestic fires.

Holmes took a knife from his inner pocket, and slowly cut the stitching that sealed the end of the bag. Then, with exaggerated drama, he pulled apart the leather opening and drew out a second bag. This one was made of fine silk, and had survived the years in much better condition.

Holmes now opened the silk bag, and poured out the contents onto the table.

We all gaped, amazed at what we saw fall from its opening.

I looked up at Holmes in astonishment.

"Pebbles," he explained. "From the seashore."

"But, whatever happened to the diamonds?"

"Long gone."

"And you knew that all along."

He shrugged. "It seemed obvious enough. A conclusion confirmed by the stones you now see before you."

"Please explain."

"Use your imagination, Watson. Old Doris Ferrybridge was entrusted with the care of a handful of diamonds worth thousands of pounds."

"Correct."

"Mr. Sheldrake told us that she was a kind-hearted person, known for her compassion and her philanthropy. Can you honestly imagine that she would leave those diamonds concealed in her chimney, apparently forgotten by the world, whilst people around her starved? A man lost at sea leaves his wife and family destitute. What does Mrs. Ferrybridge do? She takes a diamond from that bag and gives it to the family. All is then well. Perhaps a man is injured during an accident at the colliery, and is unable to earn his weekly wage. He and his family will starve. So, what happens? Mrs. Ferrybridge takes a diamond, and gives it to him. The family is saved. An elderly couple fall upon hard times, and face starvation. So Mrs. Ferrybridge gives them a diamond, which will serve them for the rest of their lives. You can be certain that some local jewelry store enjoyed superb business during her lifetime. That good lady was entrusted with those diamonds intended for the benefit of the people of the town. How better could she use that wealth than to provide for the poor and needy? I for one heartily applaud what she did."

"As do I," I responded. "But was that not theft on her part?"

"Hardly. The theft lay in failing to return the money to the people."

"So, when she died, she left her daughter to care for a bag of pebbles. Did the daughter know?"

"Probably not, since she gave Dr. Chadwickson to understand that the bag contained the Ransom itself."

"And did Dr. Chadwickson believe the bag contained diamonds?"

"He believed it contained something of value, though maybe not diamonds. As a man of integrity, entrusted with the care of the leather bag, he took it directly to that bank in Whitehaven, where he left it in a safety deposit box."

"So, the bag had been opened many times since it was entrusted to that lady."

"Certainly. You can see along the opening of the bag that many more holes are present than are needed to thread its present leather cord through and keep it secure. We can only guess at the number of hands that have opened and re-threaded that leather bag."

By the time we were ready to depart Badger's Piece a few days later, Sherlock Holmes was looking a great deal healthier than he had been when we arrived. Bushy Barnswick had enjoyed our visit, and would have much to tell his friends during the winter months, about Sherlock Holmes and the Whitehaven Ransom – to say nothing of my pike.

As our host stood beside us on the railway station in Keswick, he handed Holmes a small wooden box.

On opening it, my companion reached inside and drew out a tie-pin. On top of the pin was mounted a small pebble, ground smooth over many years by the action of the ocean waves.

"I was determined that something of value should result from this affair," said Bushy. "To which end, I had one of the smaller pebbles from the bag cleaned and mounted, so that you might be reminded daily of your time here, and the service you rendered to our community in solving this mystery."

The bright morning sunshine made the translucent pebble appear to glow with some inner light.

"I am honored," replied Sherlock Holmes with a look of obvious delight upon his face, "to share in a legacy from an American hero like John Paul Jones – even if it is mine by default."

The Enlightenment of Newton
by Dick Gillman

In late March 1889, as I sat at ease one evening having the last pipe of the day, the doorbell in the hallway below rang with a tumultuous clamour. Holmes had been away from our rooms in Baker Street for two nights, having been called away to Yorkshire at short notice.

Rising from my chair, I listened intently, trying to garner some fragment of conversation from the maelstrom of raised voices that I heard below. Suddenly there was the sound of rapid footsteps upon the stairs before the door to our sitting room burst open and a panting figure lurched towards me, bent almost double from his exertions.

"Doc . . . Doctor Watson?" the fellow was able to gasp. I nodded, and my visitor held out a beckoning hand in a gesture that clearly was meant to encourage me to follow him. "Please, sir, if you will, my employer is in grave need of you. I fear that he may have been poisoned!"

On hearing this, I hurried to collect my bag and coat before quickly following this strange messenger down the stairs, and then hurriedly bundling into a waiting four-wheeler whose door, I noticed, carried the crest of some noble family that, in the gloom, I didn't recognise.

The horses were already well-lathered, and once I was ensconced and the door swiftly closed behind me, we set off at a fearsome pace. Looking at the fellow opposite me, I observed that he was a man of perhaps some thirty years, dark-haired and clean-shaven. It was clear that he was gravely concerned by his employer's illness, as he sat wringing his hands and appeared to be wishing the streets to pass ever more quickly as we hurried on.

I leant forward, asking, "Tell me, how are you employed, and when was your master taken ill?"

The young man turned quickly towards me. "My employer is Sir George Stringer, and I am Edward Price, his secretary. Sir George fell ill a little after dinner this evening. He rang for me with some urgency and, on entering the room, I was gravely concerned." Price dabbed his brow with a handkerchief before continuing, "I found him prostrate on the couch, clutching at his chest and struggling with his neck-tie. I rushed to him and quickly loosened it. As I did so, I noticed a strange smell about his breath as he ordered me to find you at your address in Baker Street, and also Mr. Holmes."

I was indeed puzzled at being requested by name and that Holmes had also been summoned.

"Surely Sir George would have his own physician and, if distance precluded his attendance, there would be, no doubt, a doctor closer to his home than I?"

Edward Price nodded, saying "Indeed, sir, but he would have none of it and, although racked with pain, he insisted that I fetch you."

I frowned, as I didn't recall the name Stringer, but seeing Price's distress, I now pressed the young fellow for any further symptoms. Price held his forehead as he thought for a moment before answering, "Sir George was sweating profusely and was clearly in great pain. His complexion was, I noticed, pale and somewhat waxy." I considered his observations and, from the description, they did, indeed, suggest poisoning.

I was about to question him further when the carriage suddenly lurched and then ground to a shuddering halt. Throwing open the door, Price leapt out and held out his arm as a support for me to descend to the pavement. With a cry of "This way, Doctor!" he hurried forward towards the front door of an elegant Georgian townhouse. Where we were in London, I was unsure, but from the surroundings, it was clearly a neighbourhood of some considerable wealth.

Price hammered upon the door and pushed his way in as soon as a liveried footman had opened it by merely a crack. Sprinting along an elegant, panelled hallway, he led me to a room off to one side that was clearly his master's study.

My attention was immediately drawn to a figure lying full length upon a buttoned, velvet couch. As I approached, he cried out in agony. His knees were suddenly drawn up towards his chest as his body convulsed. I hurried to kneel by his side and after a brief examination, I determined that Sir George had, most probably, been poisoned by ingesting arsenic.

Reaching into my bag, I took from it a small bottle and tried to administer a little laudanum to ease his pain but, in truth, there was little I could do for the fellow. Turning to Price, I hurriedly instructed him to summon the servants to carry Sir George to his carriage to convey him, with all haste, to the nearest hospital so that charcoal might be administered.

On hearing this, Sir George became further distressed and cried out, "No! There is no time. Holmes? Is he here?"

I leant forward, placing a firm hand on the man's chest, trying to restrain my patient as he tried to rise to look around the room. "No, Sir George. Holmes is not in London. I am Doctor John Watson."

On hearing this, his arm reached out and he roughly grasped my jacket, pulling me forcefully towards him. With my ear now barely an inch from his lips, he whispered, "Tell . . . tell Holmes that the answer lies in the gift from Alberich. The . . . the Golden Lion . . . Look beyond Newton – it holds the key!" On saying this, he fumbled as he pushed a small, folded piece of paper into my waistcoat pocket. This done, his grip on my jacket relaxed and his hand fell away. Sir George then slumped backward onto the couch. I placed two fingers against his neck, searching for a pulse in his carotid artery but, regrettably, he was now no longer of this world.

I didn't understand Sir George's message to Holmes, but I took my pocket-watch from my waistcoat and then recorded the time of death in my notebook. At the same time, I carefully wrote down his final words whilst they were fresh in my memory.

Price moved forward and gazed, wide-eyed, in disbelief that his employer had passed. His voice wavered as he enquired, "Has . . . has he truly gone, Doctor?" I nodded slowly as Price then asked, "What were his last words? I couldn't hear."

Not wanting to reveal fully what had been said, I looked towards Price and answered, "It was unclear. He was barely audible, but he mentioned a 'golden lion'. Does this make any sense to you?"

Price shook his head, replying, "I fear not, Doctor."

On hearing this, I frowned and pursed my lips as I noted that the knowing expression on the man's face did not match the words that he had just uttered.

Closing my bag, I rose and turned to face Price. "You must immediately call the police. I will remain until they arrive, and nothing must be removed from this room. Indeed, it must be locked. Do you have the key?"

At this, Price pulled a key from his jacket pocket, saying, "There is but one other. Sir George kept it on his person at all times. He judged his research to be invaluable, and all is contained within this room. He guarded his work most jealously."

I nodded and moved to Sir George's body. Carefully, I patted his jacket and, in the left-hand pocket, found a key which, on comparison, was identical to that that I had obtained from Price. Ushering Price from the room, I closed the door firmly and duly locked it, retaining both keys.

With the room now secured, Price summoned one of the servants who was dispatched, post-haste, to the local police station and, within fifteen minutes or so, a constable appeared.

Given the hour, I briefly explained my presence before showing him the body and informing him of my suspicion. The room was then re-locked and I handed over both of the keys. Only then was I allowed to leave for

Baker Street, with the understanding that I would return the following morning with a report of the evenings events.

Leaving the house, I nodded "Goodnight" to Price, and was fortunate enough to obtain a cab from a stand some small distance away. Looking around me, I quickly realized that I had been at an address not far removed from Grosvenor Square.

My return to Baker Street was uneventful. During the journey, I pondered what had occurred and, upon opening the front door to 221b, I wearily climbed the steps to our rooms. As I did so, the mournful sound of a violin as I approached our door announced Holmes's return.

As I entered, he was standing with his back to me, dressed in his mouse-coloured dressing gown. Aware of my presence, he paused in his bowing, asking, "I trust that your patient paid handsomely for your attendance, Watson, for from your gait, you seem to be somewhat fatigued by your exertions."

I frowned and pursed my lips before replying, "Hardly, for the gentleman in question is no longer with us. I believe he has been poisoned, and you might note that your presence had been explicitly requested before he died."

On hearing this, Holmes turned, his brows drawn. Replacing his violin within its case, he retired to his armchair before asking, "Indeed? Who was this unfortunate?"

I removed my coat, dropped my bag, and slowly made my way to my own chair before replying, "My patient was Sir George Stringer, and his secretary had been dispatched to bring us both to his residence near Grosvenor Square." I then related the events, including the odd words uttered by the dying man.

As I turned to face Holmes, I observed that his frown had deepened further. He rose and walked to his small library where he searched for, and then selected, a weighty tome, which he then consulted before placing a forefinger against his lips. "I find this something of a conundrum, for I have never had any dealings with the gentleman. Did his secretary ask for me by name when he called here?"

I began to nod, but then paused. "Actually, no! It was only as I questioned him in the carriage on the way to Sir George's residence that he revealed that he was to bring both me and you to his master. Sir George was greatly concerned when I informed him that you weren't present as I attended him. Given my suspicions as to the manner of his passing, I'm to return to his residence in the morning with my observations for the authorities."

Holmes had a distant look in his eyes as he considered this and then asked, "Might I accompany you to Grosvenor Square? This matter intrigues me?"

Wearily rising from my chair in readiness to retire, I nodded, saying. "Of course. Your presence would be most welcome."

The following morning, I found Holmes to be in an excellent mood and ensconced in his armchair, consulting his copy of *The Times*. The "battlefield" of our damask-covered breakfast table, bearing smears of strawberry jam and discarded cutlery scattered across its surface, indicated that Holmes had already eaten. I reached for the bell to advise Mrs. Hudson that I too was ready for breakfast, and it was as I did so that Holmes's voice behind the raised broadsheet announced, "It appears that the late Sir George was an eminent geologist and had, of late, been retained by Her Majesty's government in relation to matters in Africa."

I raised my eyebrows at this, but then recalled that as I examined Sir George, I noticed that his complexion, whilst paled by the poison, had a modicum of colour due to exposure to the sun in warmer climes.

It was as my breakfast arrived that Holmes folded his newspaper and asked, "Is the protruding piece of paper tucked into your waistcoat pocket of some relevance to your late patient, Watson? I only ask this as you are usually most particular in your appearance."

I had my cutlery raised in readiness to devour my plate of eggs and bacon, but then looked down to my waistcoat. It was only then that I recalled that, in his last moments, Sir George had pushed something into my pocket. Putting down my knife, I reached for the edge of the folded paper peeping out from its nesting place and handed it to the already advancing Holmes, explaining how it was placed there. I continued with my breakfast whilst he took out his glass and studied the item before sitting back, deep in thought.

Wiping my mouth with a fine linen napkin, I readied myself for toast topped with butter and a generous amount of coarsely-cut Seville marmalade. "Was the content of the paper instructive?" I asked, as I poured myself a cup of Darjeeling.

Holmes tapped his forefinger against his lip before replying, "In isolation, no. Tell me again what Sir George said before he died."

Delving into my jacket pocket, I retrieved my notebook and read from it the last words that he had spoken before his passing.

Holmes was silent for some minutes before saying, quietly, "I must gather more data. There are pieces of this puzzle that are missing. Come along. Grosvenor Square awaits!"

With that, Holmes gathered his coat, muffler, and hat before departing from the room. I barely had time to take a last swallow of tea before gathering my own winter garments and following my friend out onto Baker Street.

Within a minute or so, Holmes had summoned a cab and we were making our way south. Little was said during our brief journey and, as we approached Grosvenor Square, I looked about me, taking my bearings from the nearby cab stand. "There!" I cried, throwing out my arm, forefinger outstretched, whilst hammering on the cab roof with my cane.

Responding to my signal, the cabbie reined in his horse, causing the cab to slew to a halt. Holmes tossed him a shilling before inclining his head slightly. "It appears that Sir George's death has provoked some official interest." I frowned, although the presence of a constable at the front door of the Stringer residence was not unexpected, I would hardly think it worthy of comment.

It was as we walked toward the front door that a figure in the window facing us peered in our direction. It was this movement that caught my eye and the thin, almost pinched, features of Inspector Lestrade were unmistakable as he beckoned us inside.

As we reached the pillared porch-way, the constable on duty saluted smartly and, as the door opened, a familiar voice called out, "It didn't take you long to sniff this one out, Mr. Holmes. I'd heard from the lads in Sheffield that you was up there!"

Holmes entered and nodded towards the advancing inspector. "Thankfully, Lestrade, I have returned, with some little success, from those colder climes. Watson informs me that it is his opinion that Sir George may have been the victim of arsenical poisoning. Do you concur?"

On hearing this, Lestrade's lips were drawn downwards as he thoughtfully rubbed his chin. "It might well be. It has all the hallmarks of a poisoning from what Mr. Price has told us. The body has been removed and taken to the local mortuary, and we'll know what happened by this afternoon."

Looking over Lestrade's shoulder, I could see along the panelled hallway that the door to Sir George's study stood open. I felt Holmes gently nudge my elbow and, taking this as my cue, I asked, "As Sir George was my patient, Inspector, might I show Holmes where I found him?"

Lestrade gave a thin, knowing smile as he replied, "Well, if you like, Doctor. My lads have had a good look around and there is nothing much to see." On hearing this, I heard Holmes groan softly. Lestrade continued, "If it was poison, we think it might have been in his wine glass. There were some odd bits of sediment in there. Anyway, we are having strong words with the butler as yesterday evening he served the wine." Lestrade paused and then added, somewhat distastefully, "Shifty looking cove, he is . . . *A foreigner*!"

I nodded politely before leading Holmes toward the study. As we approached, raised voices could be heard coming from further within the house and Holmes was to be seen slowly shaking his head.

This contretemps must have masked the sound of our entrance to the study, as Edward Price was visibly startled when he suddenly became aware of our presence. His eyes opened wide and he seemed to instinctively clutch a cardboard folder, emblazoned with a golden lion motif, tightly to his chest.

"I . . . I was just tidying away some papers. Good morning, Doctor Watson."

I nodded in return and turned towards Holmes, saying, by way of introduction, "This is my friend, Holmes. He returned whilst I was tending to Sir George."

As I watched, a look of disbelief crossed the face of Price. He looked at Holmes and then again at me before stammering, "But this is not . . . Forgive me, Doctor, for I am confused." With that, Price hurried from the room, still clutching the folder.

I frowned, unable to comprehend what had just occurred and looked towards Holmes who, in turn, now looked troubled. In a low voice, he uttered, "There are but two explanations for this, Watson. I am hopeful for the first and fearful of the second." I could make nothing of this and watched as Holmes began to survey the study.

The previous evening I had taken little note of the room's furnishings, as all my attention had been given to my patient. Looking around me now, I noticed that one wall of the room had been given over to a large, mahogany bookcase which was completely filled with what appeared to be either neatly tied, cardboard folders or works of reference. Beneath the bookcase was a set of slender drawers of the type usually used to contain large, linen-backed maps.

Holmes, I noticed, was examining Sir George's desk. Upon its tooled, green-leather surface was an onyx desk set with pens and an ornate, brass-topped inkwell, standing beside a small pile of papers and other sundry items. Holmes let his expert eye rove across the desktop before he reached out and examined each of the pens in turn. His face bore a questioning look as he slowly replaced the pens. Having done this, he drew his hand over the surface of the desk. As I watched, he raised an eyebrow while examining what had adhered to his fingertips.

The desk was set close against the wall and opposite the large window with its internal, full-length, vertical shutters. The arrangement of the desk within the room was, I thought, both unusual and, indeed, impractical. As I watched, Holmes unfolded and then re-folded each of the two window shutters before moving toward a curious piece of furniture that seemed to be more than a little incongruous. Its appearance seemed to be part-display cabinet and also part sturdy, practical workbench.

Arranged upon the shelves, within the glazed case, were various samples of minerals which were identified by a date, their geological name and, seemingly, their origin. As to the workbench, it reminded me strongly of Holmes's own collection of reagents and glassware at Baker Street. Indeed, Holmes appeared to be quite at home as he examined all before him, seemingly particularly interested in a large brass pestle-and-mortar which, to me, looked very ordinary.

Taking a small envelope from his jacket pocket, Holmes used his penknife to remove a small sample of white powder from the mortar, placing it in the envelope before sealing it. With a final glance and a nod in my direction, he left without a single word.

I followed him down the passageway towards the front door, and it was as we prepared to leave that I remembered that I hadn't yet given the inspector my observations and suspicions regarding the death of Sir George. Holmes went out in search of a cab whilst I briefly sought out Lestrade who, I saw, was now in conversation with Price. On handing him my notes, I was surprised as he reached into his own jacket pocket and held out an envelope in return. "Fair exchange is no robbery, as they say, Doctor. We found this beneath that triangular glass paperweight on Sir George's desk. It's addressed to Mr. Holmes, and I'd be obliged if you would hand it to him." Lestrade paused and then inclined his head slightly, adding, "If there is anything that might be of interest, Doctor . . . ."

I nodded, saying, "Of course. Thank you, Inspector." As I took the envelope, I was aware that Price now stood, transfixed. His gaze seemingly riveted on the envelope that I now held. With a nod, I turned and hurried after my friend, who was now beckoning to me to join him in a waiting cab. Climbing aboard, Holmes then struck the roof of the cab with his cane and we were off.

Seeing the envelope in my hand, Holmes gave me a querying look. "Ah, this is apparently for you. Lestrade's men found it beneath the paperweight in Sir George's study, and it appeared to be of some great interest to Price."

On hearing this, Holmes swiftly plucked the envelope from my grasp and began to examine it as closely as he could, given the motion of the cab. Seeming satisfied, he then slid a slender finger beneath the flap, breaking the wax seal as he did so. Sitting back, he read the contents of the document contained within and his expression changed from one of curiosity to one that would have befitted Mr. Carroll's Cheshire cat!

"Well, well! It is as I had hoped, and the case becomes ever more curious." I gave my friend a stern look, but he would say no more.

It was only after he had spoken briefly to Mrs. Hudson on our arrival in Baker Street, and as we sat at our ease with pipes of tobacco, that Holmes deigned to explain.

Blowing out a thin stream of smoke towards our already almond-coloured ceiling, He began thus. “Let us consider what we know: A dying man sends his secretary to summon both you and, notionally, me, to his death bed. There, he whispers a cryptic message and passes you a piece of paper. But why?”

I replied, rather testily, “Well, if I’d had sight of the contents of the paper he gave me, I might well be better equipped to provide you with an answer!”

Holmes laughed out loud and slapped the arm of his armchair before reaching into his waistcoat pocket and tossing a small, folded piece of paper towards me.

“Trust, Watson, Trust! This is what it all hangs upon. Why did he not openly say what he wanted to convey? There were but two people present: Yourself and Price.”

I considered this. “You are of the opinion that Price, his own secretary, wasn’t fully in Sir George’s confidence? I must admit, Holmes, last night there was something amiss in the man’s demeanour, and he showed more than a good measure of interest in the envelope that Lestrade handed to me.”

Holmes raised an eyebrow and nodded before then waving the stem of his pipe towards me by way of encouragement to open the message. On doing so, I read aloud, “*Katanga*”. Throwing my hands up into the air, I cried, “More riddles! The man was clearly paranoid.”

Holmes now looked a little stern, asking, “Why would he write this single word and entrust it to you? Perhaps it was his own *aide memoir*, or something most private that he didn’t wish to say aloud?” Holmes now fell silent, his forefinger placed close against his lips. “Did you notice Price’s expression and his comment when you introduced me to him?”

I thought for a moment before replying. “Yes. He seemed strangely confused.”

Holmes nodded. “Quite so, for I wasn’t the Holmes that he was expecting! He had obviously been introduced previously to a very different Mr. Holmes. When I questioned Mrs. Hudson about Price’s visit here, she had informed him that whilst you were in residence, Mr. Holmes was not!”

“Mycroft!” I cried. “Price assumed that Mycroft lived here!” I was silent for a moment before continuing, “Then the letter that I was given by Lestrade, whilst addressed to ‘*Mr. Holmes*’ was meant . . . .” My voice trailed away and then I looked expectantly towards my friend.

Holmes's face had a wolfish expression as he said, "Indeed! It was meant for *Mycroft*! I suspected it to be so, although I feel no deceit in reading its content, as it was clearly addressed to '*Mr. Holmes*', so I was happy to oblige – and it makes interesting reading!" Taking the envelope from his inside jacket pocket, he handed it to me and I eagerly opened it.

Within the envelope was a small, folded map, marked with grid squares, but other than that, it seemed almost featureless. This was accompanied by a single sheet of writing paper. On opening it, I read:

> *My dear Holmes,*
>
> *I have given the information you provided some thought. As a result of my own observations and my visit to the region, it is as we feared. The Golden Lion seeks its share. The minerals present are in abundant quantities.*

I paused, wondering at the relevance of The Golden Lion before continuing.

> *I have marked the purity and locations from whence I took the samples upon the map, but with some caution. I have enclosed a copy and will reveal their detail to you when we next meet.*
> *I remain*
>
> *Her Majesty's most obedient servant,*
> *George Stringer*

It was as I reflected on this that I suddenly cried out, "Price! He held a folder marked with a golden lion emblem, and was most protective of it. But what is its significance?"

Holmes drew strongly on his briar before asking, "If I were to ask you which country would you associate with a Fleur-de-Lys, what would be your answer?"

I laughed, saying in response, "France. But the golden lion emblem is unfamiliar to me."

Holmes's eyes twinkled as he continued, "I would suggest that you might look to a neighbouring country for your answer."

I thought for a moment, trying to recall my schoolboy knowledge of European geography before tentatively suggesting, "Belgium?"

Holmes slapped his palm down loudly upon the arm of his chair, shouting, "Bravo, Watson! Yes, the Belgians are indeed most active in their quest to acquire the riches to be found in Central Africa. His Majesty,

King Leopold II himself, is the driving force behind his country's expansion and exploitation of the continent." Holmes paused, his expression now stony as he explained, "The methods employed by many European nations are questionable at best and often brutal in the extreme."

He sat back, his brow furrowed. "I must inform Mycroft of events and ascertain what Her Majesty's government's position is in this matter. I believe a carefully crafted telegram to Mycroft will provide the necessary impetus to flesh out our knowledge of African affairs." Gathering up a telegram pad, Holmes stood for several moments, deep in thought, before dashing something off, no doubt of an incendiary nature, to his brother before ringing the bell vigorously for the page.

Nothing was heard that evening, and it was as we sat at our ease the next day, some little time after breakfast, that the sound of a cab drawing to halt in the street below, followed closely by a familiar tread upon the stairs, announced the arrival of Mycroft Holmes.

He burst through our sitting room door and then proceeded to fling off his winter garb as though he were a full-bodied Emperor moth bursting forth from its chrysalis. Striding forward, he threw himself onto our settee, glaring at his brother, and growling, "What do you know of the death of Sir George, Sherlock, and, particularly, of Katanga? This is a most delicate affair, given that the man has been poisoned, and it is one not to be bandied around in public!"

Holmes raised a single eyebrow, replying, "Then I suggest that if you wish to preserve some element of confidentiality, Mycroft, that you refrain from shouting from the rooftops to all and sundry. Watson and I are most grateful that you have confirmed the cause of death. My telegram to you was discreet, but was formed in such a manner as to provoke the response I required – to wit, your presence."

I hadn't had sight of the telegram sent by Holmes and began to move forward in my seat to ask as to its content. Mycroft pre-empted my question by handing me a somewhat crumpled envelope in. Opening it, I read, "'*The late Sir George entrusted Katanga's secrets to Watson.*'"

On reading this, I blurted out, rather angrily, "More of a riddle than any secrets, Holmes, and . . . and I am still unsure as to why I became involved in the first place!"

Mycroft was still angered, but then calmed a little as he turned to me, saying, "Ah, that may well be my doing, Doctor. I mentioned your name and address in passing as a trustworthy member of your profession and as a friend of my brother."

Somewhat placated by this, I was then asked to recount, in full, all that had occurred. This I did, to the best of my ability and, over cups of tea, we sat for some time considering its import. For my part, I was still unclear as to Sir George's role in this matter and asked Mycroft to explain further.

Now no longer puce, Mycroft took out his cigar case and then offered us both a fine Havana. This I took to be something of an olive branch. With his cigar now toasted and lit, he proceeded thus. "In light of his reputation as an eminent geologist, I met Sir George and his secretary some six months ago at his residence near Grosvenor Square. As a result of this meeting, he was retained by Her Majesty's Government, ostensibly, to carry out some rudimentary mapping of the Katanga region. In practice, he was to report back on the activities of other European nations, particularly the Belgians, and also to take mineral samples whilst on safari."

I nodded and drew on my cigar before asking, "What is the history to this pan-European incursion into the Dark Continent?"

Mycroft sat back. "The Berlin conference of five years ago was called by the Portuguese and hosted by Bismarck. Its aim was, in some part, to prevent colonial wars between the European nations, and it also provided an excuse for open expansion into the continent. Several European states embarked on a scramble for both territory and wealth whilst proclaiming it to be a humanitarian act for the benefit of the native population."

Pausing, Mycroft then drew strongly upon his Havana. "King Leopold II of Belgium secretly sent Henry Stanley to the Congo to make treaties with native chiefs in order to gain territory. This gradual increase in land area by the Belgians prompted the formation of the Congo Free State. Indeed, King Leopold II claimed this new region as his own personal kingdom, where his administration is particularly noteworthy for its draconian rule and brutality towards the native peoples."

Holmes interrupted, saying, "Quite so. These squalid enterprises are as harsh as they are profitable. It is estimated that half – half mind you! – of the total native population has died through forced labour, brutal subrogation, or disease."

I nodded, as I now understood the grim human cost of these ventures, asking, "And what of Katanga?"

Pausing once more to draw on his cigar, Mycroft then continued, "It is the highly profitable trade in ivory, rubber, and the rumour of gold in the territory of the Msiri that has caused other nations, notably the French and Portuguese, to send their own expeditions further into Africa. Katanga borders an area where the territories of these different nations meet, and it is rumoured to be particularly rich in minerals. As such, it's an area of interest for our own government. Sir George was despatched, and he was to prepare a report for me shortly after his return to Britain."

It was at this point that Holmes reached into his jacket pocket and produced an envelope. "This then might be what you seek, Mycroft. It was handed to Watson, in error, by Lestrade, as he believed that I was meant to be the recipient. Given that I seemed to be the addressee, I opened it."

Taking the envelope, Mycroft frowned briefly, giving his brother a guarded look. Upon opening the envelope, he consulted the letter before then examining the enclosed map. Seemingly unimpressed by its lack of detail, he then held it up against the light from our sitting room window, but nothing further was revealed.

Leaning back, Mycroft was silent for perhaps a minute before asking, "Do you have any knowledge as to these locations that Sir George refers to, Sherlock? I see nothing here but a simple relief map of the region with a standard grid."

I looked towards my friend, who now appeared to be gazing at some point in the far distance. Holmes drew slowly upon his cigar before answering. It was as if he, too, was now some distance away. "I believe that Sir George's last words are, indeed, the key to this affair. I should be grateful, Mycroft, if you would entrust the map into my care, and I'll examine it further. I assure you that it will come to no harm."

Mycroft considered his brother's request for a moment before handing back the map, asking, "Am I correct in assuming that you suspect Price to be the one responsible for Sir George's death?"

Holmes nodded. "Undoubtedly, but I'm unsure whether it was intentional. Watson's account of Price's distress as he requested his presence appears to be quite genuine. He was greatly concerned by his master's condition – but, on the other hand, he was most eager to gain information from the dying man." Holmes paused for a moment before continuing, cryptically, "I think it may well be in our interest to delay placing a hand upon Price's shoulder, for he may be the conduit to another master."

Mycroft raised an eyebrow as he considered this and then gave a single nod, adding, "Yes, I concur. I'll arrange for a watch to be placed upon him. He will only be taken if he attempts to flee the country."

After making his farewells, Mycroft gathered his coat, muffler, and hat before leaving our rooms at a much more sedate pace than the one in which he had arrived. Sitting back, Holmes now began to fill his pipe, saying, "I'm intrigued by Sir George's final words. I take it that your knowledge of German folk-tales is somewhat limited?"

I considered this for a moment and then blew out my cheeks before replying, "I must admit that, other than 'Hansel and Gretel' from the Brothers Grimm, that is my only exposure to them."

Holmes slapped the arm of his chair and laughed heartily before then wagging his pipe stem in my direction. "I must not tease you, for the tales of which I speak have origins in stories from the ancient Greeks, the Welsh, and more recently from storytellers in Germany." Holmes nodded as he drew on his pipe before continuing. "Your mention of the Brothers Grimm was apt, for what I'm seeking is mentioned, indirectly, by them. However, the reference by Sir George of 'Alberich' relates to a German folk-tale from the thirteenth century. The gift of which he spoke was that of invisibility. In the story, Siegfried obtains a cloak of invisibility from the dwarf Alberich."

Holmes sat for a few moments, deep in thought before rising from his chair and then searching amongst his array of glassware for a particular reagent and an empty, small flask. Reaching into his jacket pocket, he took out the small envelope which he had used in Sir George's study. From it, he carefully removed a sample of white powder, which he then dissolved in acid before neutralizing the resulting liquid.

I watched, engrossed, as he took a pen and a sheet of paper from his desk and proceeded to write, using a little of the solution that he'd prepared as the ink.

Seeming satisfied, he returned to his armchair whilst waiting for his endeavour to dry. I was now curious and made my way to his workbench to examine his handy-work. However, before me there appeared to be simply a blank sheet of foolscap paper. Whatever he had written was nowhere to be seen.

With my curiosity piqued, I lifted the small flask of colourless liquid. "Tell me," I asked, "what is this concoction that you've prepared?"

Holmes's eyes sparkled as he replied, "It is a liquid which has hidden properties – an age-old method of concealment."

In a flash I understood. "Sir George has used some form of invisible ink to hide the information that Mycroft seeks."

Holmes nodded slowly. "It was as I examined Sir George's desk that I noticed a slight dusting of white powder upon its surface and, on examining the mortar, I was able to obtain a small sample from it. This is, I believe, the source of the ink. The problem now is to determine how to reveal what has been written with it."

I sat back and considered once more the final words of Sir George, asking, "What do you imagine to be the relevance of his words 'Look beyond Newton, he holds the key'?"

Holmes took his pipe from his mouth. "No, his precise words were 'it' holds the key. I believe the words relate not to the man himself, but to the science that followed on from his work. But what? Newton's fields of work included mathematics, astronomy, theology. The man had such vision – "

It was as Holmes said these words that he cried out, "Vision! The shutters, the desk, the prism!" Rushing to his own desk, he rummaged amongst his drawer of tools until he held aloft in triumph a small gimlet. Clutching this, he turned to the window and gazed outward before closing and then piercing the left shutter with the gimlet. Satisfied, he returned to his desk and began to ransack it as he again searched for some item.

"Holmes!" I cried. "For pity's sake, man, have a care!"

Holmes looked around. "I must find my prism, for it is indeed the key."

Whilst Holmes continued to search, I took the liberty of ringing for Mrs. Hudson. Whilst she stood with her hand pressed to her mouth as she regarded Holmes's frantic searching, I asked her if she had seen Holmes's triangular, glass paperweight. To my question she nodded and led me, avoiding the rain of items emanating from Holmes, to the sideboard that contained our drinking glasses. "I put it safe here, Doctor, with the other glassware, as I was forever dusting it."

Thanking her and then guiding her to the door, I called, "Holmes! I have it!"

His head shot up before he took the item from my grasp. Setting the prism on our dining table, he then proceeded to close the right-hand window shutter, plunging our sitting room into darkness, except for a single, thin beam of light from the gimlet hole in the left hand shutter. I heard, rather than saw, Holmes make his way towards our dining table where a seemingly dismembered hand reached out and adjusted the position of the prism. Suddenly, a wondrous rainbow of seven colours appeared in our room, illuminating a clearly elated Holmes, who now reached for his flask of "ink".

I stood and watched as he slowly passed the flask through the whole spectrum, the colourless liquid being illuminated by each colour in turn, but without effect. I must admit that I was somewhat dismayed, for I had expected more. However, as Holmes moved the flask away from the region of violet light and into darkness, a strange glow appeared within the liquid – seemingly for no apparent reason as I could see no visible light falling upon it.

I marvelled at this and heard a sigh of satisfaction from across the room. Holmes must then have picked up the sheet of paper that he had prepared for suddenly, a ghostly, single word glowed before me, "*Katanga*".

On opening the shutters, I was unsure as to what I had observed and sat back into my chair, quite bemused. I began to fill my pipe as I asked,

"Explain to me. What have I just witnessed, for it appears to be almost magical."

Holmes smiled and took up his pipe once more. "It is just as Sir George conveyed in his dying breath. The key was, indeed, just beyond Newton, for beyond violet, in the visible spectrum that we can see, lies a region invisible to us, named 'ultra-violet'."

Holmes drew on his briar and then blew out a thin stream of blue smoke towards the ceiling before he continued. "It is a known property of some minerals, notably Feldspar, that they will glow when illuminated with ultra-violet light. Sir George, an expert geologist, would be well aware of this property." Holmes again paused and looked wistful. "I suspect that the powder I collected from the mortar is from a specimen in Sir George's display cabinet, obtained from Katanga."

I nodded, now understanding why Sir George had placed the paper with its single word into my waistcoat pocket. Thinking about his study brought back a memory. "I thought it quite peculiar that his desk had been placed against the wall, away from the light from the window. The prism on his desk I took to be simply a paper weight."

Holmes nodded. "Yes, the incongruous arrangement of furniture in the room hadn't escaped me, but I hadn't attached any relevance to it. However, I was intrigued by what I took to be simply a carpenter's mishap in the window shutter. It was only as I then considered Newton's achievements, specifically in optics, that I was able to weave together the disparate strands to formulate a solution."

For my part, I was now eager to discover what secrets Sir George's map might reveal, once illuminated with ultra-violet light. Looking up from the map, I asked, "Are you not intrigued to discover more, Holmes?"

Rising from his chair, Holmes plucked the map from my lap and cried, "Indeed I am, but first I must undertake a small errand in Bow." I looked on in puzzlement as Holmes rapidly disappeared from view and was then to be heard descending the stairs.

It was some two hours later that he returned and, from his expression, was in excellent spirits. I sat, eyes wide, as Holmes suddenly produced from his jacket pocket not one but two maps that appeared to be identical in all respects. Peering towards him, I blinked. "I'm confused, as I believed there to be only one map in Sir George's envelope."

Holmes smiled and threw himself into his armchair, chuckling. "Ah, there is but one map. My visit to Bow was to re-acquaint myself with a certain Mr. Percival Dodds, a master forger whom I saved from the gallows by way of my testimony."

I pursed my lips on hearing this, as I didn't recall Holmes ever having mentioned the gentleman. I knew that he had, on occasion, intervened on behalf of various members of the criminal classes, saving them from miscarriages of justice. As a result, he was grudgingly respected by many and was owed various favours in return for his timely intervention. "This Mr. Dodds – he has prepared a duplicate map?"

Holmes nodded. "Indeed, to which I will add my own meagre scrawl, in good time, but first we must uncover the secrets held within the original."

Closing the shutters once more, Holmes now held the original map in the region of the spectrum to the right of the band of violet light. As he manipulated the map, glowing groups of numbers and symbols appeared at various points on the map.

On seeing this, Holmes addressed me. "Watson, be so kind as to bring my music stand so that I might be allowed to copy the information now made visible." Knowing its approximate location in our sitting room, I stumbled my way around, in almost total darkness, to retrieve the item and place it before him.

It took Holmes perhaps a quarter-of-an-hour to accurately transcribe the data from the map, with the associated grid references, onto a piece of foolscap. Once completed, he sat back and drew up his knees tightly to his chest. Holding his right forefinger to his lips, he now retreated from the world, remaining so for several minutes before then rising from his chair and reaching for the telegram pad.

Holmes's voice now became most serious. "I believe that the information we have gleaned today to be most valuable to our nation. Retrieving Sir George's data was paramount. However, with our duplicate map, we have the opportunity to mislead those who would wish to steal his work from us." Holmes paused, deep in thought. "Mycroft has the resources to provide plausible, alternative data that I might add to the duplicate map. This, then, could innocently find its way to the Continent."

I frowned, asking, "To the Belgians, by way of Price?"

Holmes nodded. "I deem it to be most likely. Once completed, I intend to return the envelope and its contents to Price – explaining, with a little flattery, that as Sir George's secretary, the map may be of use to him."

Having made the request to Mycroft, there was little to do but wait, a task which Holmes often found particularly taxing. It was not until early evening that a government messenger brought the intelligence from Mycroft.

Whilst I had enjoyed a delightful dinner of roast gammon with baked potatoes and winter vegetables, Holmes had made little attempt to eat. I was most concerned, as he had begun to pace like a caged wild beast.

The sound of our bell in the hallway below was, indeed, a most welcome relief and caused him to charge down the stairs. Hardly had he disappeared before he then returned, waving a wax-sealed, buff envelope before him.

Without a single word to me, he rang the bell for Mrs. Hudson and, when she appeared, he requested a glass of white wine. I frowned at this request and then consulted my pocket-watch, finding the hour to be what I would judge inappropriate for such refreshment.

With the glass of wine grasped firmly in one hand and Mycroft's envelope in the other, Holmes closeted himself in his bedroom for the next half-hour. Finally, the door was flung open and he emerged with a broad grin and what I presumed to be the "new" map clutched in his hand.

I raised an eyebrow, asking, "I trust that Mycroft was able to supply what was required?"

Holmes nodded. "Indeed, he did! I believe that anyone using Mycroft's data will find scant reward on the ground, and be sorely troubled by the terrain, as Sleeping Sickness is endemic."

I smiled, pleased with the outcome, but the request for the glass of wine still troubled me. "Tell me – What was the purpose of the wine? If needed as refreshment, then its timing surprises me, given your exacting palette as an Oenophile."

Holmes laughed, mockingly. "Ah, I am grateful for your confidence, Watson. Whilst the use of vinegar, urine or any acidic fruit as an 'invisible ink' may be common knowledge, white wine is, perhaps, not, and it is less detectable by its nose. However, it too can be made to re-appear when warmed."

Holmes now consulted his pocket watch, saying, "Given the hour, I believe it to be best to deliver the envelope to Grosvenor Square in the morning. I bid you a good night." With that, he turned on his heel and withdrew to his bedroom without a further word.

The following morning, Holmes sent a further telegram and, having breakfasted, we were soon on our way towards Grosvenor Square to begin the grand deception. As we travelled, I recalled the agonizing death of Sir George and felt some unease that Price, the man believed to be responsible, was still a free man. Turning to Holmes, I asked, "What do you imagine is to happen to Price? I trust that he won't benefit from his actions."

Holmes face was grim and he slowly shook his head. "Indeed not. Mycroft has him on a short leash. When we have handed the map to him, he will be followed, most closely, to determine who his masters are. Once we're sure that the information has been passed, he will, most certainly, be taken. His arrest, in itself, will work in our favour, for it will only serve to emphasise to his masters the value we place on the material he has passed on."

On hearing this, I was a little more at ease, but I didn't relish meeting the man again. Holmes, sensing my continued disquiet, grasped my forearm, saying earnestly, "It is imperative, Watson, that all should appear as one would expect. Should Price become suspicious of our motives, all will be lost. He will lose his freedom, but our nation will not fully benefit from the intelligence gathered by Sir George at such great personal cost."

I pursed my lips and nodded. "Have no fear, for I will play my part."

As I said this, the cab pulled up close to the kerb. Holmes tossed the driver a florin, asking him to wait for our return. As calmly as we could, we made our way towards Sir George's residence. At the front door, Holmes tapped briefly upon it with his cane and, within moments, we were admitted. Almost immediately, Price appeared in the doorway of Sir George's study and looked a little ill at ease to see us.

Nodding briefly towards us, he greeted us, saying, "Good morning, gentlemen. Are you here at the request of Inspector Lestrade?"

Holmes smiled broadly as we approached. "Indeed not, Mr. Price, I come to return an envelope that was given to me, in error, by the inspector. Might I have use of Sir George's desk, as the document contains a map?"

At this, Price fairly bounded into the study, making way for Holmes and me to enter. Holmes reached into his jacket pocket and retrieved the envelope. Opening it, he removed the letter and the duplicate map which he then took pains to spread out upon the leather surface of the desk.

I looked towards Price, who stood as close to the desk as he might, in order, I believe, to examine the detail on the map.

Holmes smiled once more, saying, "My brother called upon me yesterday and had the opportunity to examine the map. It seems, from the enclosed letter, that Sir George had intended to annotate the map further at their next meeting. Sadly, that was not to be. Consequently, the details he mentions are, unfortunately, missing." Holmes paused and then pointed to a brown area on one corner of the map. "There appears to be some little detail here. I was concerned as I thought I had scorched it as I sat beside the fire, yesterday evening."

As I watched, Price's eyes widened slightly. Holmes too, I believe, had noticed this most subtle change and now continued, "As Sir George's trusted secretary, I feel it only right that we return the map to you so that, perhaps, you might then benefit from it."

Price nodded. "That is most kind, Mr. Holmes. I will study it further and then add it to the archive." Turning now to me, he asked, "Is there any news from the inspector regarding the cause of death, Doctor?"

I pursed my lips before replying, truthfully, “I fear not. I’ve heard nothing from him.”

Taking the map and the letter from the desk, Price now said, “I’m most grateful for your visit and the return of the document, gentlemen. Is there anything further that I might offer by way of assistance?”

Holmes held up his hand, saying, “Thank you, no. Watson and I must be on our way, for we have a cab waiting. But might I ask a small favour? On our previous visit I noticed that Sir George had some most interesting mineral samples in his display cabinet. Might I be allowed to look once more before we leave?”

Price smiled and led the way before opening the cabinet. “Please feel free, Mr. Holmes. Sir George added to his collection after each of his expeditions.”

Holmes nodded in gratitude before peering diligently at the shelves of samples. Now and then, he carefully picked up the odd one before returning it to sit beside its label. “Wonderful, Mr. Price! I’m grateful and most envious! Come, Watson.”

With that, Holmes tipped his hat and made his way swiftly back to our waiting cab.

Once on our way to Baker Street, I turned to my friend, saying, in disgust, “The fellow did everything but dance at the prospect of obtaining the map.”

Holmes nodded, his face showing no expression. “It will do him, and his masters, little good. Sir George’s collection of minerals was, indeed, informative. Amongst them was a new addition, a piece of Feldspar which had been carefully dated ‘*January 1889*’, and labelled ‘*Katanga*’.”

On hearing this, my head jolted upright. Holmes then continued. “I took extraordinary care not to draw attention to it by picking it up, but I noticed that a small sample had been recently taken from it.”

I nodded thoughtfully, “The ink. But what of Price?”

Holmes’s face was now grim. “I believe the fellow has placed his head further into the noose. My telegram this morning was to advise Mycroft of our intentions and, as a consequence, Price might then act.”

Little further was said, and it was some little time after dinner when a soft knock on our sitting room door announced an aproned Mrs. Hudson. She approached, holding before a tray, upon which sat a telegram. “This has just arrived for you, Mr. Holmes. Will it disturb you if I clear the table?”

Holmes rose, taking the telegram from her and adding, “Your ministrations will never disturb us, Mrs. Hudson.” Almost blushing, Mrs. Hudson then beamed as she continued with her task.

Opening the telegram, Holmes face was impassive as he announced, "It seems that Price *was* in the pay of the Belgians. He was followed to a coffee shop in Piccadilly, where he was seen to hand over the envelope to a member of the Belgian consulate. Lestrade was summoned and Price is now in our hands." I nodded in acknowledgement but found myself unable to reply.

It was, perhaps, two months before we heard anything further of the case. Holmes was sitting in his armchair with his copy of *The Times* when he announced, "The trial of Edward Price has concluded and, as expected, he has been found guilty. It would appear that he claimed to have been given a drug to administer to Sir George which, he had been told, was laudanum, so that he might then search for the information he required."

I snorted in disgust. "It is of no consequence, Holmes, for he is still a poisoner."

Holmes nodded. "It is an opinion that you share with the Lord Chief Justice, for Price has an appointment in Newgate in three weeks' time – one from which he will not return." Holmes paused, adding, "I must confess that I have no feelings of sadness on hearing the sentence, and the news from Africa underlines Sir George's sacrifice."

I frowned on hearing this. "What news might that be," I asked, "for I have read nothing." Picking up my own copy of the newspaper, I waited expectantly.

Holmes held his forefinger aloft and wagged it in my direction. "You will not read of it in *The Times*, Watson, for instead I've been sent a small package by Mycroft. Included within it was a news item taken from the Belgian newspaper, *L'Etoile Belge*. This recounts how a sizeable expedition returning to Bunkaya had been all but decimated after attempting to survey a region to the east, on the banks of the Luopula River."

Holmes now paused before reaching into his jacket pocket and then tossing a jagged, glittering object the size of a cricket ball towards me. Fielding the catch, it took me barely a moment to understand its significance. "From Grosvenor Square?" I enquired. Holmes gave a single nod and I knew that it would now simply become another memento.

The Impaled Man
by Andrew Bryant

The boy's shout came up through the open window. The hammering on the door reverberated up the stairs.

"Mr. Holmes! Mr. Holmes!"

It was too early to be disturbed. The papers not yet read, the tea not finished. But we were now disturbed none the less.

Downstairs, Mrs. Hudson hushing the boy before she reached the door to open it. "The Devil's own racket," she said.

The boy's voice louder now the door had been opened. "Where's Mr. Holmes?"

"Do you have an appointment?" Mrs. Hudson asked.

"I have a message for Mr. Holmes."

"You may give it to me, and I will give – "

Footsteps pounded up the stairs.

Holmes smiled faintly to himself.

I believe that the one thing he liked above all else regarding his regiment of street informers was their complete disregard for authority and their absolute insouciance.

"If boys like this one," Holmes said, pointing to the stairs, "ever have the opportunity for an education, they will rule the world within a generation, and will likely do a much better job of it than those who rule the world now."

"It might be some time before that happens, in spite of the Ragged Schools. There seem to be as many of them on the street as there ever were."

"That is because you can't make a living if you are in school."

The boy burst into the sitting room, with Mrs. Hudson hard on his heels.

"Mr. Holmes," the boy said.

"At your service," Holmes replied.

"You are needed in Fenchurch Street."

"And why am I needed?"

"Someone's been stabbed."

"If I attended every stabbing in London, I would have precious little time for anything else."

"This one is different."

"Different?"

The boy had an uncharacteristic wild look on his face for one of his perpetually cool-headed ilk. As one running the streets for a living, he had already seen, in his meagre time, a lifetime's worth of hardship and degradation.

"He's *speared*!" the boy said.

"Speared?"

"To a door."

"Speared with what?" I asked.

"A spear."

"A man in Fenchurch Street speared with a spear to a door. Who was this man?"

"A toff. Suit, tie, hat, and cane. Not a toff no more."

Holmes smiled that hard little smile, more wicked than pleasant. "And to what door was he speared?"

"Number Three, Fenchurch. The Hudson's Bay Company offices."

"Not your typical London stabbing." Holmes jumped to his feet. "Shall we cab over there, Watson?"

"What about him?" Mrs. Hudson said, indicating the boy.

"Give him a stipend for his information, and feed him as much as he wants to eat."

"There'll be nothing left for the rest of us."

"That is what household budgets and shops are for."

Holmes brushed passed the boy. I gave the urchin a disdainful look as I passed, not wanting him to think that he had somehow got the better of us.

Holmes waved from the pavement, and a hansom pulled up. Holmes gave the driver the address. We didn't go far until we were stopped at Marylebone Road while a virtual parade of cabs and carriages and wagons crossed in front of us.

"It takes forever to get anywhere in this city," I said. "We'd be quicker to walk."

"Possibly, but the journey is always an interesting one. So many different faces, customs, and motivations to examine. Lives to unravel."

"I would rather just get where I am going."

"Anticipation is the journey. Oftentimes the arrival is the disappointment."

"I think that today the destination will be more intriguing than the journey."

"Perhaps. We'll find out when we get there."

The cab moved in fits and starts and, eventually, we stopped in Fenchurch Street where, ahead of us, a crowd of people blocked the pavement and half of the street.

We made our way through the crowd to the police line. Inspector Lestrade stood beside the impaled body of a man. He, Lestrade, had the look of someone who was unsure of how to proceed.

"Good morning, Inspector," Holmes said.

"I suppose it was only a matter of time before one of your scurrying rats brought this to your attention."

"I have a network that keeps me informed of unusual occurrences, and this appears to be unusual."

A man wearing a black suit, white shirt, his cane and hat at his feet now, body upright, pressed back, fixed, against the door. A long spear of unusual design holding him to the door, the spear piercing the heart. He would have bled to death in a minute or two. The blood loss was obvious on his shirt, dripping from the waistcoat and trouser cuffs. His dying expression one of horror and surprise, as would befit such an end.

"It would take a man of great strength and experience to attach someone so definitely in this position. Any witnesses?" Holmes said.

"None who will talk to us."

Holmes examined one side of the spear, ducked under it and studied the other side, running his hand along the shaft, feeling the slight edge of the blade that was exposed in the wound. He walked away from the victim to the point where the hurler of the spear may have stood, the crowd moving back as he did.

"May I have the spear, Inspector?"

"I suppose. But I'll need it back."

"Of course. I need to determine its construction, heft, and origin."

"Better you than me."

"Yes."

"Set to it, men," the Inspector said.

Two of the policemen took hold of the shaft and tried to pull the spear straight out. It didn't move. They worked the spear up and down, enlarging the wound and causing the victim to twitch against the door. At last, with one heaving movement, the spear pulled loose. The victim slid down the door into a sitting position, much to the horror – or amusement – of the varied spectators.

"This is a major thoroughfare. There must have been witnesses," Holmes said.

A young boy of undeterminable age – it was always difficult to judge how old these wretches were – stepped up to Holmes.

"I saw them," the boy said.

"Them?"

"Him," pointing to the victim. "And the one who threw it."

"Why didn't you tell us?" Lestrade shouted.

"You don't believe what anyone says, and you don't pay."

"I am not going to waste the City's money paying for lies."

"Continue, boy," Holmes said.

"The one who threw it wore a hide coat, an animal skin."

"Fur?"

"No, just the bare hide. And an odd belt."

"What was odd about it?"

"It had a tassel, like a sash. Red and green, and some blue and some white in it."

"And what did the man look like?"

"He didn't look like a man at all."

"Why didn't he look like a man?"

"Because he was a woman."

"A woman did this?" Lestrade indicated the victim. "I warned you of their lies, Mr. Holmes."

"Why would the boy lie about the sex of the killer? He has nothing to gain from lying."

"Making us look the fool is the only gain they desire."

"Most do not need others to make themselves appear the fool," Holmes said.

"She called him by name," the boy said.

"And what name was that?"

The boy held out his hand. Holmes dropped a few coins into the palm.

"She said 'MacDonald' as he was about to open the door. He stopped and turned, and that was when she threw it."

"Which way did she make her escape?"

The boy held out his hand again, and Holmes put a coin into it.

"Down Mark Lane," he pointed. "She walked down there."

"Walked? She did not run?"

"Walked."

"Her appearance?"

"Light weight, less than tall. Long black hair."

"Thank you."

The boy looked at the money in his hand, smiled, and ran off.

"Do you know how many of those rodents we find beaten to death because some generous soul gave them money?" asked Lestrade. "The older boys find them and try to take their money, and when the rats resist the older boys kill them. There is no benefit for them. You cannot be considerate of that lot. They are what they are and there's no changing it."

"Then you have no hope for the future, Inspector?"

"They have no future."

Holmes took the spear.

"Once you find out just who this MacDonald is, send someone around to inform me."

We walked to the waiting cab and made our way back to Baker Street. In the sitting room, he examined the spear more closely. The shaft was five feet of thin dark wood, and the head was a two-foot length of carved bone not much wider than the shaft, sharpened to a near knife edge and fit into a hole at the end of the shaft, where the two were bound together with gut.

"Not African, nor Asian," I said.

"No. The head is whalebone, of a style used by the Saami of Northern Europe. And, by the Aleut. Generally, the circumpolar peoples. But the person we are looking for is likely a resident of Rupert's Land, or Manitoba, on the Western shore of Hudson's Bay."

"The spear tells you that?"

"No."

I waited.

"Anyone can own a spear," Holmes continued. "You and I both have artifacts from numerous other societies in our possession, but that doesn't make us members of that culture. We are not what we possess."

"What then?"

"The clothes. Especially the belt, or sash."

Holmes lifted the spear and shifted it in his grasp until he looked comfortable with it. Then, in a flurry, drew his arm back as if to hurl the weapon, but restrained himself before releasing it.

"Perfectly weighted," Holmes said. "The head heavier than the shaft so, once in motion, having tremendous momentum. Good for both throwing and thrusting, as there are no barbs to hinder its withdrawal. Also good for killing seals on the ice as needed, or polar bears when necessary, or gentlemen on Fenchurch Street when required."

"Required?"

"No one commits a public murder like this, with a weapon like this, unless they are trying to send a definite and unmistakable message."

At that moment a knocking on the outer door. Shortly, Mrs. Hudson surmounted the stairs and passed a telegram to Holmes. He tore it open.

"It seems the departed was a man of some colonial note."

"Who was he?"

"Joseph MacDonald."

"I am at a loss," I said.

"A second cousin of Sir John A. MacDonald, the Prime Minister of Canada."

"What was he doing at the Hudson's Bay Company?"

"A message was found in his pocket requesting his presence at an early morning meeting. What say we return the spear to Lestrade, visit the Hudson's Bay offices, and then take a walk down Mark Lane."

Holmes picked up the spear and then we set off to see Lestrade.

"And what did the spear tell you?" the inspector asked.

"Its origin is circumpolar."

"And what does that tell us?"

"Nothing."

"And . . . ?"

"And the investigation continues."

We left the Scotland Yard and made our way down to Fenchurch Street. We didn't have an appointment, but Holmes's name and reputation got us in to see Director Meyer. "Horrific business this morning," he said.

"Indeed, but men of notable lineage are bound to have enemies, yes?"

"Yes. Someone, somewhere, always feels wronged, justifiably or not."

"To your knowledge, did Mr. MacDonald have enemies?"

"I have no idea Mr. Holmes. I had never met the man, never heard of him, never had any communication with him of any kind. In fact, I was surprised to get the message that a member of the MacDonald family was requesting an appointment."

"Why surprised?"

"Sir John MacDonald is no friend of the Hudson's Bay Company. Even though the Canadian government paid us three-hundred-thousand pounds for Rupert's Land, there are many of us, both here and in Canada, who believed that it was a forced sale. We either say 'yes' to the offer, or our land would be taken from us to fulfill the elder MacDonald's dream of colonial expansion in order to increase his own power and influence in the country, and in the world. Meanwhile, the Metis people already living in Rupert's Land were led to believe by the government that once the Hudson's Bay Company was out of the way, they would be given the territory for a Metis homeland.

"When MacDonald's white settlers started moving in from the East, the Metis fought back. We at the company knew, of course, that no British-based government is going to basically steal land in order to give it away to a nomadic people of French and Native origin. The company ended up with a bit of money, the Metis people ended up with no homeland, and MacDonald and his government ended up with one-and-one-half million square miles of territory to add to the burgeoning country."

"But the younger MacDonald wouldn't have been of age to have anything to do with that," I said.

"No, this was back in 1870. He would been a mere boy."

"Then what was the intended purpose of the cousin's visit?" Holmes asked.

"I received a note yesterday evening stating that Mr. MacDonald wanted an immediate meeting, but the purpose wasn't disclosed. I agreed to meet him first thing this morning out of curiosity, and in deference to his pedigree, like it or not."

Holmes and I stood. "Thank you for your time," Holmes said. "We may need to come and see you again as our investigation proceeds."

"I am at your service."

We went out into Fenchurch Street, and then south along Mark Lane.

"The killing was political?" I offered.

"If it was, why choose that locale? If there was no connection between the victim and the Hudson's Bay Company, why stage a deliberate murder literally on their doorstep?"

"Most politicians and men of business do far more harm than they realize," I said. "Every decision is going to benefit some and be detrimental to others. Long standing grudges exist while the focus of the grudge knows nothing of it. Decisions long forgotten by the powerful remain fresh in the minds of the wronged, and the families of the wronged."

"Sir John MacDonald himself would be a near impossible target, as an ailing man likely doesn't have much time left naturally in this world. In the mind of the perpetrator, I suspect the cousin was a suitable symbolic representation of the enemy."

"Rather cowardly, isn't it? Taking revenge against someone who had nothing to do with the initial grievance."

"Revenge is not renowned for its logic or its generosity of spirit. Revenge is nothing if not innately irrational."

We stopped at Great Tower Street. "The best way to make an escape from here?" I said.

"What would attract a woman who comes from a land of rivers?"

"How do you know where she comes from?"

"The case is almost solved, Watson. We just need a few confirmations."

I couldn't see how the case was even remotely solved, but not being in the mood for a lecture on observation and methodology, I chose not to question the remark.

We crossed over the street and, at a jetty beside the Custom House, found an old salt, or tar, at rest on a chair near a tethered rowboat.

"Excuse me, sir," Holmes said.

He looked at Holmes with an undisguised degree of awe, not because he recognized him, but because Holmes had called him "Sir" – probably the first time in his life this had been said to him, and even more surprising for him that the title came from someone who was so obviously a gentleman. I half-expected the salt to say, "I didn't do it," but it didn't come to that.

"Have you ferried anyone, or seen anyone ferried, early this morning. Notably, a dark-haired woman in a hide coat?"

"What trouble is involved?"

"None for you, no matter what your answer."

"My first customer. Though she ferried me."

"She ferried you?"

"I rowed too slow for her, so she took over and had us at her ship in no time. She was a bricky rib o' man."

"You didn't mind this?"

"Not a bit. I've had a lifetime of hard work, from the Navy to this. If a customer wants to pay me and then do the work for which they're paying me, I am not one to protest it."

"And her ship?"

"*La Recompense*."

"Could you transport us there now?" Holmes said.

"Would you like to row?"

"No, thank you," Holmes said.

"You sir?"

"No, thank you," I said.

We three went downriver at a leisurely pace, under the new bridge construction, passing the thickets of masts and through the smell of coal and the indestructible odor of the river itself. Sailors' voices were shouting over the clamour of the hulls, drubbing into each other so closely were they anchored.

Finally we came to Limehouse Pier, where the rowboat set in and Holmes and I disembarked.

Holmes paid the man. "No need to wait," he said. "We'll cab the return."

"I'll just row back then," the tar said.

The gangplank was down from the ship while the crew loaded barrels and crates as we approached. The captain was on deck at the head of the gangplank.

"Permission to come aboard?" Holmes called out.

"State your names and business."

"Sherlock Holmes and Doctor John Watson, seeking information on the death of Mr. Joseph MacDonald."

"Come aboard."

We went up the plank to the deck.

"Captain Leroux," he introduced himself.

We shook hands while the ship's activity continued around us under the keen observation of the captain.

"Where are you in from?" I asked.

"Montreal."

"You didn't seem surprised or disturbed by either the name, or the demise of Mr. MacDonald."

"And why would I be surprised or disturbed to hear of someone and something of which I already know?"

"The death just happened this morning."

"When a ship's passenger dies, especially in such unusual circumstances, news travels."

"Mr. MacDonald was your passenger?"

"He was."

"How did he come to be your passenger?"

"He walked up the gangplank in Montreal."

"Paying passenger?"

"No."

"What then?"

"The owner of this ship, on hearing of MacDonald's need of passage, and knowing the name and the history of his family, offered him free passage."

"And what was his reason for the voyage?"

"Very benign. He planned to travel from London to Scotland and visit family – in Glasgow I believe."

"As a passenger, I assume he dined with you every night."

"He did."

"And the conversation?"

"Dull. He spoke mainly of himself and of his famous old cousin. He talked as if the actions of the well-known cousin were somehow transferrable to the unknown cousin."

"Politics?" I asked.

"In spite of his cousin being a Scot, and him being Canada-born, he was very much enamoured with the British Empire."

"Were you surprised by this attitude?"

"More disappointed than surprised."

"Canada is a British country," I said.

"Only in the eyes of the British."

"And what national allegiance would you ascribe to your country?"

"Cree, Iroquois, French, Mohawk, and all combinations thereof."

"Combinations including the Metis?"

"Of course."

"And British?"

"Only in government. Only in dictatorial landowners. Only in land thieves. Only in a repressive class system."

"You don't believe the Old World belongs in the New?"

"Your Empire will fall, gentlemen," the captain said. "Your Empire will fall."

"As all Empires must," said Holmes. "But in the meantime, we are looking for the murderer of Mr. MacDonald."

"And what help can I be?"

"Would you describe yourself as a plain-talker, Captain?"

"Most men of the sea are."

"Did you have a woman passenger on the journey over?"

"A woman passenger? No."

"Dark hair, a strong woman both in physique and nerve? Not a large woman, but strong."

"There were no woman passengers."

"Women crewmembers?"

"There is not a woman crewmember anywhere on the Seven Seas that I am aware of Mr. Holmes."

"Stowaway?"

"None found. Now if you will excuse me – ships' business and all."

"You are in a hurry to depart?"

"The ship's owner conducts all business by letter months in advance. Our customers know our incoming cargo, and our vendors know our outgoing needs, so no cause to linger."

"And the crew?"

"They prefer their shore leave at home, not here."

"And what was your incoming cargo?"

"Pelts. Wolf, beaver, muskrat, fox."

"And outgoing?"

"Linens, crockery, firearms, and a few kegs of drinkable whiskey."

"Well then," Holmes said, "we won't be the reason for your lingering."

"The faster the turnaround time, the faster we return to the real world."

"The real world?"

"The New World."

"Thank you, Captain," Holmes said.

"The sea is calm tonight," the captain replied. "The tide is full, the moon lies fair."

We disembarked, found a cab, and made our way into traffic. "Number 3, Fenchurch Street," Holmes called up to the driver.

We moved at a decent pace.

"What do you make of that encounter, Watson?"

"If she was on board – "

"She was."

"Very well, she was on board. But not a passenger and not a crewmember and not a stowaway. What would that make her? The Captain's wife?"

"Perhaps."

"Why didn't you pursue that line?"

"We want to find out who she is, not chase her away. Since Mr. MacDonald hadn't yet boarded a train for Scotland, we must assume that the ship has only recently docked, and yet it is already loading for departure. The woman went to the ship after committing the murder, so either she is using it solely as a means of escape and is paying for speed and silence, or she sailed here on that ship and the captain knows more than he says, is understanding of her cause, and anxious to set sail because of it."

"The reason for the 'plain-talking' question?"

"Yes, I believe everything that the Captain has told us so far. He just hasn't told it all to us."

"Was his quotation from Matthew Arnold a challenge or a message?"

"A bit of both."

"'Catch me if you can'?"

"I believe so," Holmes said. "I believe so."

"Now to find out her cause at the Hudson's Bay Company."

"It's unlikely that we'll find her cause there, but we may find more fingers pointing in the direction of it."

The cab made its way along Commercial Street to Whitechapel, the traffic worsening the closer we got to the City proper.

"It's to be expected," said Holmes, "in a city of six million people."

"But where are they all going?" I said. "Don't they have anything better to do?"

"And what do you think they are saying about us, Watson?"

We rode the rest of the way without conversation. At Fenchurch Street we went straight in for another interview with Director Meyer. Holmes wasted no time.

"Does the ship *La Recompense* mean anything to you?"

"Yes, sailing out of Montreal. Captain's name is Leroux."

"Is it one of your ships?"

"Quite the opposite. The ship's owner, the Captain, and the crew are no friends of the Company. They are independent. They trap on our land – "

"Your land no more," Holmes interjected.

"As I said earlier, many of us still consider it our land."

"But you took the money," Holmes said.

"Why are they not friends of the Company?" I asked. "Is there not room enough in a vast country for all?"

"The Hudson's Bay Company is like a government. We have been in power since 1670, and once that power has been effectively challenged, and its enemies are aware of the challenge, control and respect become nearly impossible to maintain."

"But you took the money," Holmes repeated. "It's no longer your land to control."

"And who are these independents?" I asked.

"For the most part, disgruntled Metis trappers, descendants of the Courier de Bois, the voyageurs. As we discussed earlier, and to phrase it indelicately, the Canadian government lied to them, so now they do as they will."

"And the Prime Minister, Sir John MacDonald, or 'Cousin John' as our victim would know him, was one of the architects of this lie?"

"In my opinion, *the* architect," Director Meyer said.

On our return to Baker Street, Mrs. Hudson brought us tea and biscuits.

"Shouldn't we be informing Lestrade that *La Recompense* is nearly ready to sail," I said.

"Why? It isn't illegal for a ship to sail."

"But if a murderess is on board – "

"There is no 'if', Watson. She is on board."

"Then why wait?"

"My certainty does not amount to evidence."

"It often has in the past. And the boy on the street was an eyewitness."

"The Queen's Bench will give no credence to the evidence of some boy whom they will perceive on sight to be an idler and a waster. Such is the modern world that too often those that speak the truth will not be listened to while those who spout the most venal rhetoric are quoted in *The Times* daily."

"But if the ship sails, the guilty will go free."

"Right to the nub, Watson. But they must finish their provisioning and wait for a favourable tide. And I have a few more questions before we inform the inspector that the case is solved."

"I have a question. If our *femme fatale* and our victim sailed here on the same ship, then why did she and the captain not just throw Mr. MacDonald overboard mid-Atlantic? There would be no evidence, and water-tight alibis all round."

"Is that a pun, Watson?"

"No," I replied.

"Then I suppose that our suspect must be the very model of restraint."

"At least until the ship made landfall," I said.

"There are some remaining questions. Why did she need to cover the killing with symbolism? And why did she feel so morally correct in her actions that she had no need to run away from the bloody scene?"

I got up to leave. "If you'll excuse me, our early disruption, the sojourn on the river, and the abominable traffic has done me in. This has been enough of a roundabout for one day."

"Be back here, early," Holmes said.

In the morning I went around early to Baker Street. Holmes wasn't there.

"He went to the British Museum," Mrs. Hudson said.

"Is it open at this hour?"

"I don't believe so. Tea? Toast?"

"Yes, please."

I passed the time waiting for Holmes's return by reading *The Book of the Sword* by Sir Richard Burton. I'd read it before, of course, and like all Burton's extensive works, it was founded on personal experience and impeccable insight, written by one the most anti-colonial adventurers that the Empire has ever birthed. Burton, like our Captain Leroux, had no time for the self-interest and bureaucracy of political dynasties.

I had just started in on Chapter 4: "The Proto-Chalcitic or Copper Age of Weapons", when Holmes arrived, calling up the stairs. "There's a cab waiting. I'll explain on the way."

Down the stairs I went.

"The Custom's House," Holmes shouted to the driver.

"The Custom's House?" I said.

"Actually, the jetty beside it."

"Not the rowboat again."

"The river is less congested then the street."

"And the reason for this excursion?" I asked.

"Once we're on the river, I'll explain. It's a more conducive venue for our story."

I understood as we passed through the raucous street, with shouts of pedestrians and drivers, demands of right-of-way, and vehemence when ones' own interests weren't held above the interests of all others.

We arrived at our destination and Holmes paid the driver. We went down to the jetty. "Is your boat available?" Holmes asked the salt.

"It's you again."

"Yes, it is. I'll row."

"Then it's available."

The three of us piled into the boat and Holmes took up the oars and rowed, never flagging. I had learned early on that he was a man who never grew tired, either physically or mentally, sometimes a result of his natural propensities and sometimes the result of cocaine. We ploughed downriver.

"I spent a few hours this morning with Edward Maunde Thompson, Director of the British Museum," Holmes said.

"Are they open this early?"

"No, I sent a boy around to roust Mr. Thompson at home and suggest that he meet me there. He is a man with a curious mind, as you would have to be to fulfill his duties at the Museum, so he agreed without hesitation. He was able to fill in the empty spaces in our narrative. He is a noted historian, antiquarian, and, although nothing to do with this case, a dedicated palaeographer, as I'm sure you already know."

"Of course."

"I asked him first about the coloured sash, *un ceinture fleche*, or arrowed belt, which he explained is not just Metis regalia, and is not just an ornamentation. The weaving of the sash is a representation of the history of the people. Red is for the blood spilled in defending their rights. Green for the natural fertility of their country. Blue for their limitless depth of spirit. And white for their relationship with the Creator.

"The hide coat is, of course, common enough wear in Canada and its territories, and the spear, as already discussed, could have come from any traveller's collection. The sash was always the guide to the resolution of this."

"But why would this Metis woman want to kill Mr. MacDonald?"

"When the Canadian government paid off the Hudson's Bay Company and started to move non-Metis settlers onto the land, the Metis knew that the intention was to take their long sought-after homeland away from them. This led to the Red River Rebellion of 1869 and the emergence of Louis Riel as the leader of the resistance. He was hero to his own people, but a treasonous outlaw to the Canadian Government – although the logic that someone could be committing an act of treason while fighting for their own rights in their own country is beyond my comprehension. But, logic aside, Canadian and British troops were sent in and the Metis provisional government fled west out of their forsaken homeland, which had now become the new province of Manitoba. After years of wandering and fighting for his people, Riel finally surrendered to the Canadian militia, and was promptly charged with treason. He was hanged in 1885."

"I suppose these are the necessary machinations of Empire," I said.

"Necessary?"

"I believe in the validity of Empire," I said.

"And do you believe in the false promises, broken treaties, and the deceptions that are constantly deployed to keep that Empire intact?"

"Necessary machinations," I said. "Like them or not."

As we approached the Limehouse Pier, the old salt piped up. "She is on the move."

La Recompense drifted from the pier, sails not yet deployed, but last hawsers thrown aboard and crew jumping from the pier to the deck.

Our craft ground against the steps and we leapt from the rowboat and ran. The dock was peopled with the usual spectators of a ship's departure: Retired seafarers who can never get enough of the anticipated adventure of leaving harbour, the children hoping for last minute hand-outs, and the incurable romantics to whom the sea is a rolling and roiling dream that they themselves will never experience, and yet they dream all the same. The ship had drifted just out of reach, and, standing at the rail, a dark-haired woman in a hide coat and sash. The sash was tied about her waist, with the ends of it, the knotted tassels, hanging from her left hip.

Captain Leroux stood beside her.

"Not a passenger, Captain?" Holmes called out.

"Nor a crewmember or stowaway," the captain replied.

"Captain's wife?"

"Not that."

"Owner of the ship, then?" Holmes said with a smile that was a twitch. "In the future, I will remember that the New World is more liberal and democratic than the Old World that gave birth to it."

"The Old World gave us nothing, Mr. Holmes, except the desire to rid ourselves of it. We gave birth to ourselves out of the rivers and the rock and the animals that surround us. The land is our Mother and Father."

"And you, Mademoiselle . . . ?" Holmes called.

"I was there on November 16th, 1885, when the elder MacDonald had Louis Riel hanged. I attended his body on the journey to St. Boniface for burial. And I vowed on that day that at some time in the future, justice would be served," the woman said.

"Justice or revenge?"

"That depends on which end of the spear you are on," she replied.

The ship drifted slowly downstream.

The captain called for sail. Canvas dropped, caught the breeze, and took the ship out towards mid-river quickly.

"Your name, Mademoiselle?" Holmes shouted.

"My name is not yours to have, and it will never be yours to have."

"Are you related to Monsieur Riel?"

"All Metis people are related to Louis Riel," she said.

The ship moved apace now, we could do nothing but stand and watch her depart. She would be at the river mouth and out to sea in a few hours.

"We need to send a message to Lestrade," I said. "He can still catch her with a cutter and a favourable wind."

"Boy," Holmes called out to one of the lads watching. "How fast can you run?"

"Like the wind if I'm inclined to."

"Will this give you the speed of Hermes?" Holmes proferred a hand full of coin.

"Faster than him."

"Find the nearest policeman and alert him to the fact that a murderess escapes on *La Recompense* as we speak. Inspector Lestrade must be informed, and the fastest boat and crew of men ready for a fight needs to dispatch immediately down the river."

"I'm your man," the boy said.

"If I find out you do this in record time, come round to 221b Baker Street and that sum will be doubled."

"I'm off!" the lad said, and ran full tilt away from the pier.

Holmes turned towards the rowboat. "Shall we depart?"

"Are you going to row?" the salt asked.

"No."

"I will procure a cab for you," the salt offered.

"Nothing of the sort. It's a perfect day to be on the water."

We three climbed into the boat that was rowed slowly and unenthusiastically upriver.

"What do you think of her, Watson? A nameless woman as cold and merciless as any man. Reticent, furious, anonymous, and resolute?"

"Beneficial character traits in some circumstances, and the worst of character traits in different circumstances."

"Yes. Circumstance. Circumstance is always both creator and destroyer of worlds."

"One question," I said.

"One answer," Holmes replied.

"Why did our departing suspect choose the Hudson's Bay Company offices, and how did she know that MacDonald was going to be there at that exact time?"

"Two questions, two answers," Holmes said. "I suspect that she was the one who made the appointments. She sent a message to Director Meyer stating the urgency of an appointment at a requested time, and then sent a simultaneous message to Mr. MacDonald informing him that Director Meyer wished an interview with him at that same hour. She played both sides to ensure that MacDonald was exactly where, and when, she wanted him to be."

"But why there? There was no love lost between the MacDonalds and the Hudson's Bay Company."

"Therein lies the symbolic brilliance of the plan. Our potential escapee hated the company because they were given her homeland by British interests without a moment's thought for her people who had lived and worked there for generations. MacDonald's older cousin bought the land from the company with a vague political promise of returning it to the Metis. He reneged on that promise and instead kept the land for Canada, and actively encouraged settlement by outsiders."

"She had three demons to skewer?"

"Precisely. And with this plan she was able to murder a relative of the politician who betrayed her people on the doorstep of the Company that was arbitrarily given her homeland, and she could do it all on British soil."

"And now she sails away."

"Yes, she does," Holmes said.

I looked back and saw the ship round the bend at the Isle of Dogs.

Holmes put his feet up on the gunwales, completely at his ease. He was quiet now, watching the ragged edges of his city pass beyond the heaving and cluttered bedlam of the riverbank.

The Mystery of the Elusive Li Shen
by Will Murray

Over the course of laying before the public selected cases involving my good friend, Mr. Sherlock Holmes, I have of necessity devised certain rules which I invariably observe as I chronicle his singular exploits. Chief of these is that I recount these tales in strict chronological order. That is to say, I relate each individual case in the precise way that I experienced it, since I've had the good fortune to be present for most of Holmes's adventures.

It should go without saying that one must start a story at the beginning. This I have invariably done. It is also true that one is equally obliged to withhold certain facts from the reader until revealing them during the climax of the matter at hand. For it would do no good, and in fact undermine the narrative value of these records, to begin a tale with the name of the thief or murderer, as it were, announced to the public at large on the first page.

Otherwise, I go to great pains to withhold all salient facts until it is necessary to divulge them.

With this particular account, I fear that I must withhold one significant detail. My reasons for doing so will become apparent at the end of this narrative, but I feel compelled to mention this undisclosed element at the beginning, neither to absolve myself nor unnecessarily confound the public, but to prepare the reader for the unexpected while preserving my cherished role as an honest raconteur.

That duty out of the way, I will begin my story from the point at which Sherlock Holmes received an unexpected letter dated 3rd August, 1890.

It came in the afternoon post, accompanied by the usual trifles.

I was absorbed in *The Times*' agony column as Holmes slipped it open and perused the contents. He soon proffered this to me, asking, "What do you make of this, Watson?"

Upon reading it, I replied, "I make no more of it than what is written in plain English. No doubt you have some penetrating insight, dear fellow."

"This letter was written by an earnest but rather dull chap. Somewhat like yourself, I would imagine."

I started. "What brings you to that questionable conclusion?"

"Nothing specific. Just a general sense based upon the man's selection of words and the fact that he chooses to remain anonymous when there doesn't seem to be any compelling reason to do so."

"As you know, a great many individuals write anonymous letters to *The Times* and other newspapers."

"A great many cranks do as well," Holmes said diffidently.

I couldn't contain my skepticism. "Do you jump to the conclusion that this fellow is a crank?"

"Not at all," replied my friend. "I was merely observing that, among the ranks of anonymous public letter writers, the crank is a significant participant in that rather peculiar game. Read it again, Watson, I beg of you. Tell me if in your opinion the writer is a crank."

Here I made my first mistake. "I don't need to read it again. The person who wrote that letter appears to me to be of sound mind, perhaps merely one who simply values his privacy."

"You detect no ulterior motive?"

"There are many Londoners who would style themselves as concerned citizens. I see nothing out of the ordinary about that. As for the subject of the letter, it remains to be seen if there is such a person as the one named."

"I have never heard of anyone going by that fanciful name," mused Holmes. "On the other hand, I'm not on intimate acquaintance with the Chinese element currently inhabiting Limehouse. Oh, I have of course certain acquaintances, and even spies, in that sometimes-disreputable quarter, but by no means am I widely known there, nor welcome beyond certain of its exotic portals."

"You refer, of course, to the infamous opium dens."

"Which I have visited in my younger days – purely for the experience and the knowledge to be gained therefrom. All that is behind me though, along with my solution of cocaine."

"And if I may dare say so, Holmes, you are the better man for all that."

"Hmm. That remains to be seen. Not that I doubt your professional opinion. Only that it remains unproven, and I suspect always will be."

Taking up the letter again, Holmes read the missive aloud. I didn't understand why he did so. At least, not at that time. His prior habit was to read something twice to commit it to memory. But now he spoke every word from salutation to signature, pronouncing the words slowly and carefully, as if somehow tasting them with his mental tongue.

My Dear Holmes, (he began)

I am penning this letter as a concerned citizen.

There is a mysterious criminal operating in Limehouse who goes by the name of Li Shen, or some similar spelling. This bounder is importing and distributing opium in large quantities, which is flooding the distressed neighborhood. As time goes by, his foul merchandize will contaminate Greater London itself. Li Shen must be stopped before that occurs.

Find Li Shen and see that he is tried and convicted of his crimes, which result will no doubt end this spreading scourge.

Respectfully Yours,
A. C. Citizen

"Yes," said Holmes, reverting to his normal speaking voice. "The author of this note is an ordinary man of sound, if unimaginative, mind. I would stake my reputation upon it. That being the case, I think that we'll investigate this mysterious individual going by the name of Li Shen."

"Where do you propose we begin?" I inquired.

"I wish that our correspondent had provided a sounder starting point than a mere name and a general location. But if one wishes to locate a specific spot in a map, all that is required are the two imaginary lines known as longitude and latitude. Thus, Li Shen and Limehouse must serve as our substitutes."

Before dusk was quite upon us, we were ensconced in a hansom cab, wheeling in the direction of Limehouse Reach.

"What do you make of the name, 'Li Shen'?" I asked as we bumped along the cobblestones.

"Very little. Li is a common last name among the Chinese people, who as you know place the paternal name before the Christian one, as it were. And Shen is no more distinctive. I imagine that there are hundreds, if not thousands, of individuals so named in faraway China. In Limehouse proper, there may be only seven or eight."

"In other words," I observed, "we are searching for the proverbial needle in the haystack."

"Or a phantom, Watson. For I am not yet convinced that there is any such a personage."

"Yet you're willing to undertake such a search?"

"I'm convinced that the writer of the letter is as substantial as are you."

"I'm beginning to suspect that you are correct in your deduction, if it is in fact that."

Sherlock Holmes and I were soon walking along Limehouse Causeway, overwhelmed by the gaudy sights and sounds of the dockside district. Odors of frying fish predominated amid the noisome conglomeration of smells, which also included the River Thames at low tide and the aroma of tea and sundries from distant China and India as they were being unloaded by the grimy stevedores.

I couldn't imagine what Holmes expected to discover by such a casual investigation, but I was more than happy to accompany him. Often, I only learned of his more strenuous activities after the fact.

It was a pleasant summer evening, with the heat of the day already abating. As we strolled along the Chinese quarter, past the quaint shops with their slashing and cryptic window signs, I noted the increasing number of foreign faces among the local dock labourers and wherrymen. Owing to its convenient proximity to the bustling wharves, Limehouse was a marvel of cosmopolitan citizenry. Chinese made up the greater numbers of its inhabitants, most but not all of them distinguished by their skullcaps and long pigtails.

"With more arriving every week," Holmes murmured, as if reading my thoughts.

Here and there, I recognized the odd Malay or Arab, as well as the occasional lascar from India. Most had the look of seafaring men, for Limehouse was a sailor's town of long standing. There were almost no women going about.

"I imagine virtually every Asian nation is now represented in these confines," I remarked.

"I haven't yet seen a Pacific Islander, nor any of the recent arrivals from Siam, Annam, and Tonkin, who are fleeing French oppression," Holmes noted.

"I wouldn't know a man from Siam if I encountered him."

Spying up ahead a thick-bearded man wearing a white turban, I recognized him as a Sikh, a growing sight in a city where Hindu turbans might be observed in increasing numbers. I didn't obtain a closer look at the tall fellow, for he disappeared down one of the byways until he was lost from my sight, yet another of the cast of characters comprising this peculiar Asiatic quarter of greater London.

"Most of these Chinese hail from Shanghai," remarked Holmes, "but others call Canton and various South China ports home. I shall not bore you with the details which enable me to distinguish one from another, but their exotic dress and ornamentation tell me much."

"Would that Dickens was still among the living," I remarked. "He would be enthralled."

"I do not doubt it," murmured my friend.

"What do you expect to see during our promenade?" I pressed.

"Oh, I don't expect to see anything in particular. I merely observe. I have spoken to you about the power of observation many times. Observation by itself enables one to glean many things. For example, the man approaching us is an habitual user of opium. I can see this in his dreamy, rather vacant countenance. As I'm sure you can as well, Watson."

"I'm familiar with the slack expression, clinically speaking."

"He appears to be smoking a new variety of *chandu* that I haven't before encountered."

I knew that "*chandu*" was a term used by some Asiatics to describe opium, but I couldn't imagine how Holmes could determine from the man's face what variety he was addicted to, so I put it to him.

"How the devil can you tell that?"

"By the stains upon his fingertips. The discoloration is commonly seen among opium addicts who burn beads of opium paste over a spirit lamp before rolling it by hand and loading into their smoking pipes. The golden hue I spy is slightly different from the usual Chinese stuff. No doubt this man is a client – if I may employ so noble a term – of the individual we are seeking."

"Do you mean to follow him?"

"Discreetly, Watson, discreetly."

We did so. The vacant fellow walked along the Causeway, turned corners, and strolled up Pekin Street in the direction of Pennyfields. There, he entered a storefront which posted a sign in two languages, the English version reading: *Asiatic Aid Society*.

I frowned. "We can hardly follow him in without arousing suspicion."

"Agreed. So we will mark this establishment for a future visit. Let us continue on our way, for I've already learned something of interest, possibly vitally so."

"There you have the better of me."

"And not for the first time," replied my friend in a jocular manner.

I took no offense. Sherlock Holmes's superior mind always appeared to be a jump ahead of me, whose brain didn't tend towards jumps, but steady plodding in commonplace directions. I wasn't sure how Holmes could have gotten anything new from observing the man, but I left the point alone, confident that it would come out in due course.

Walking along, we found ourselves in the heart of Pennyfields. Here the sights were vastly more impressive than along the docks, although that might have been the result of being outnumbered by Oriental passersby.

No doubt many were law abiding citizens, but the strangeness of the cast of their faces the oddness of their costumes, combined with their difficult language, made us feel like outsiders in this remote part of London.

“What ho!” Holmes said suddenly.

“Tell me, for I don’t see what you are perceiving.”

“Nothing new there, eh Watson? If you direct your attention beyond that quaint inn marked by a yellow lantern, you will see our good friend Lestrade attempting to be inconspicuous, and failing rather magnificently.”

Holmes declined to point the man out, not wishing to draw attention to himself, or to Lestrade. So it took me a moment to pick him out of the crowd.

Lestrade was dressed in a rather slovenly manner, one ill-befitting his position in life. He wore a bowler hat that was rather battered and which resided upon his head at a disreputable angle, inclined truculently forward as if the narrow brim could somehow enshadow his features.

As a disguise, it was a monumental failure to anyone who knew the inspector, but among the inhabitants of this maritime district, he might pass for a common Londoner with no particular occupation or direction in life.

Holmes crossed the street and I followed. We were soon walking close behind Lestrade.

Overtaking him, Holmes whispered, “A word with you, Lestrade. If you will.”

The inspector smothered his impulse to start and took advantage of the first alley he came upon to stop and light a cigarette. He made a pretense of not being able to strike his match alight, so Holmes drew close and did him the kindness of producing a match from his own pocket.

I joined them. Our conversation was pitched low.

“What are you doing here, Mr. Holmes?”

“Possibly seeking the same man as you, Inspector.”

“Name the fellow.”

“Li Shen.”

Lestrade started. “Then we *are* on the same scent. What makes this your business?”

“We received a letter from a concerned citizen, inviting me to take up the chase. We haven’t been at it for long.”

“I wish that I could say the same, for this is my third week seeking the rather elusive gentleman, and I’m beginning to wonder if I could ever pick him out.”

“Have you any leads?” asked Holmes.

"I followed a man that I thought was the suspect one evening last week. I couldn't see his face from behind, and he entered a curio shop, then disappeared into the back. Rushing past the proprietor who didn't seem to speak English, I sought him out. In the poor light, I caught only a glimpse of his furtive face, and that briefly. I daresay that I could pick him out in a crowd, for his facial configurations possessed a rare distinction."

"And what is that?"

"He appeared to have no nose."

"None at all?"

"Only a black void where his nose should have been."

"No nostrils?"

"None that I could see."

"And how did he elude your clutches?"

"The suspect dodged out the back way before I could reach him, and when I emerged into the gaslight, he was nowhere to be found. I searched high and low, Mr. Holmes, but he might as well have vanished."

"Curious," mused Holmes. "A man with no nose."

"The proprietor claimed through a translator not to know the man, but they all say that, the whole lot of them. It is as if they have their own rules and ways, and the police are an inconvenience. Except, of course, when they need our assistance – which they rarely do."

"The Azure Phoenix Tong keeps the peace in Chinatown, I understand."

Lestrade glowered in annoyance. "I wish that were still true. They keep the peace between the Chinese, but not necessarily among their rivals. As you know, there is a fresh wave of immigrants from Cochin China and nearby countries. They have their own ways, and these newcomers are encroaching upon Chinese territory. There have been running battles, hatchet men, and all that rot. I fear that these troubles will escalate. And at the heart of it all is this human enigma, Li Shen. He is bringing in his own brand of opium, and stealing business from the Chinese. They are out to get him. And so am I."

"As am I," responded Holmes. "Now that I have been apprised of the situation."

I spoke up at this point, remarking, "It seems to me that a man with no nose would be very conspicuous."

"He would," admitted Lestrade, "if he had the decency to walk the streets in broad daylight, but some of these criminals sleep during the day and come out of their warrens and garrets only in the dark of night. And even that, rarely."

"Well, Lestrade," Holmes offered, "I wish you good fortune in your search, and I trust that you cheerfully return the sentiment."

"After three weeks of fruitless trudging," the inspector replied glumly, "I would be happy if you dragged Li Shen, wherever he came from, bodily into Scotland Yard without our help. Of course, I would prefer to capture him myself."

"You believe the man to hail from other than China proper?"

"It is my suspicion, given what my narks tell me," Lestrade stated. "The growing unrest between the Chinese and these interlopers into their way of life points to the new immigrants. Since they come from many spots, I cannot say for certain who is this Li Shen is. His name sounds Chinese, which confuses matters."

"It may be an alias."

"Quite possibly. If so, he is taking an alias that is the equivalent to 'John Smith', or there are many men in Limehouse named Li Shen. And so far, I have discovered none who lacks a nose."

"Good hunting to you, Inspector," said Holmes abruptly.

"The same to you, gentlemen."

We left Lestrade smoking in the alley, which he seemed loathe to abandon – at least as long as his cigarette continued to burn.

As we walked along, Holmes grew ruminative. "This is an interesting development," he said after a period of silence.

"Lestrade's unexpected appearance?"

"No, I would have expected it, given the spreading scourge of opium. But a man with no visible nose is a man who would be known to many, if not all, of those who inhabit such a narrow confine as Limehouse and its immediate environs. I think that a check of the immigration office might be in order, as well as the Asiatic Aid Society. I believe that we'll start there, Watson."

Retracing our steps to Pennyfields, we came to the place and entered.

It was staffed by a Chinese man owning a very round face and a pleasant if expressionless countenance. I took an immediate liking to him. While his smile of welcome was tentative, he grew quite warm as we spoke.

"I am Sherlock Holmes. Conceivably you have heard of me."

"Yes, yes," said the man. "Very pleased to make your acquaintance, Mr. Holmes. I am called Wing Fu. How might I help?"

"I have a client who would prefer that his name not to be known," replied Holmes. "He has asked me to locate an Oriental man who lives in Limehouse and may be a recent arrival. This man is remarkable because he appears to have no nose."

The Chinese man's rather smooth features acquired a troubled look.

"I know of such no such man, not of recent arrival. Certainly not in the last seven years, which is as long as I have held this position."

"The name he goes by is Li Shen."

"Ah. I know many men named Li Shen. Five, perhaps six in all. They all possess perfectly good noses."

"Perhaps this man has lost his nose since you encountered him last."

"Tidings in Chinatown travel on whispering wings. I hear much. I would have heard of such a man who had lost his nose." He shook his head resolutely. "I do not think there is such a man. I may be mistaken. It is always possible. But I do not think such a man exists."

"Is Li Shen a Chinese name?"

"Yes, of course."

"It is thought that this man might be from another country, such as Siam or Cochin China."

"Men from those countries are not so called. Li Shen is Chinese name. There is no mistake in this."

"I'm given to understand that this Li Shen is the source of much trouble among the sons of the Flowery Kingdom."

"I hear the same," Wing Fu said cautiously, lowering his voice to a whisper. "But the men of the tong will settle him. Or so I understand. I can say no more."

"I thank you for your time," said Sherlock Holmes graciously. "It may be that you are correct in all of your statements."

The fellow's round face beamed. "I am pleased to have been of service to the illustrious Sherlock Holmes. Do not hesitate to ask if you have other questions, the answers to which I might truthfully know."

We stepped out into the gathering dusk. As Sherlock Holmes led the way back toward Limehouse Causeway, he remarked, "Wing Fu strikes me as an honest soul. I do believe he was telling us the truth, at least as he comprehended it."

"But I don't see how a man with no nose can escape notice in Limehouse," I commented, "his nationality notwithstanding."

"Perhaps it's because the man with no nose in fact owns a proper nose."

"Lestrade doesn't seem to think so."

"Lestrade doesn't know what I know. But I now have several facts in hand which, when combined, point me in the direction of a sound solution to the mystery."

"Now you outpace me, Holmes. If your quarry does in fact possesses a nose, then you have nothing more to go on other than that he is an Oriental, might or might not be Chinese, and may or may not be named Li Shen."

"And yet out of this confusion, a picture forms in my mind. Let us see if we can ferret out this figure of mystery."

"How do you propose to do that?"

"First, by sending you back to the comforts of your home while I prowl the byways and alleyways of Limehouse by myself. Unless, Watson, you would be interested in visiting an opium den?"

"I would not!" I said sharply. "And I strongly advise you not to do the same."

Holmes smiled pleasantly. "Do not fear for old habits creeping back and seizing my spirit. I am an old hand at navigating dens of inequity. I will do what is necessary, but no more. Good night to you. I am sure you can find your way home from here."

That I did, but as I jounced along in a cab, I feared for Sherlock Holmes. Of all the precincts of London, only Limehouse made me fret for his safety, since no disguise could conceal his British nature.

The next morning's paper bought word of a calamity in Limehouse. From Limehouse Causeway to Shadwell and places in between, there had been an astounding succession of murders. Pistols were not employed. Knives and hatchets were the weapons of choice.

Scotland Yard was beside itself. There had been seven casualties, all told. The newspapers spoke of a war between the Azure Phoenix Tong and unknown rivals who were presumed not to be of Chinese extraction.

The incidents were centered around two competing opium dens, one in Newcourt, Victoria Street, and the other in the heart of Limehouse, above a gambling den on Narrow Street. The Chinese establishment has been burned to the ground in the first skirmish. Thereupon, the other establishment was assaulted, the attackers beaten off handily.

Among the casualties, one report had it, was a man without a nose.

I immediately rang up Holmes, but Mrs. Hudson answered, saying that he hadn't returned last evening.

"Good heavens!" I exclaimed. "I must see Lestrade at once."

I rang him as well, but the inspector wasn't available to come to the telephone. I hurried down to Scotland Yard in search of him, for I naturally feared for Holmes's life, as he might well have been caught up in the conflagration.

To my utter astonishment, I found Holmes conferring with Lestrade in the latter's office, to which they had repaired.

"Holmes!" I cried out. "I had feared the worst."

"And I have lived through the worst, as I was just explaining to Lestrade. No doubt you've read the morning news reports."

"I have. And I feared that you had perished in the Newcourt fire."

"Not at all, not at all. I was oblivious to that event whilst it was transpiring. I was safely ensconced in a rookery in a rival establishment, which was soon overrun by angry Chinese. I've never before made a mental connection between the Red Indian of America in the yellow warriors of China, but both seem to have a preference for employing hatchets to settle their differences. I, however, escaped in the course of events – but not without a prize."

"I hope it was worthy of the risk involved," I said more calmly.

Lestrade offered, "Mr. Holmes may have found our man."

Holmes countered, "I rather doubt it. But he should represent a lead of sorts."

"See here, Mr. Holmes," snapped Lestrade. "We have been seeking a man without a nose. Can you or can you not produce a man without a nose?"

"Yes, I can, but this man appears to have lost his nose last night, and your supposed noseless man was without proboscis a week ago. A man cannot lose his nose twice over."

At times I've been accused by Holmes of being slow of wit, but immediately I perceived my friend's point and couldn't understand the Lestrade's failure to do so.

The inspector said in exasperation, "Then why did you bring this man in?"

"Because he was a victim of the melee and I believe that once the hospital surgeon is done with him, he will have a tale to tell us."

"We've captured many Orientals who have tales to tell."

"The mere fact that this worthy has been deprived of his nose makes me think that his tale will stand out from the rest."

Lestrade frowned. "Go on."

Holmes obliged, "Last night, I was placidly listening from my curtained smoking compartment to all that I could hear, and it was an interesting way to pass the evening, for I learned much."

"I didn't know that you understood the Chinese tongue so well," I noted. "Will wonders ever cease?"

"They may or may not cease, Watson, but they do not begin with me. The language I was eavesdropping upon was not Chinese, but *French*."

"French!" exploded Lestrade.

"Yes, the language spoken by many in the French colony of Cochin China. Of course, they have their own tongue, but I'm no more a master of it than I am of Chinese. In any event, I was absorbing all that I could, and learning much, when the noisome establishment was invaded by pigtailed men brandishing hatchets, along with the disposition to do as much harm as possible. I didn't understand what it was all about, but I didn't need to. Seeking to escape injury, I witnessed a remarkable sight, a man being deprived of his nose by the crude instrument of a tong hatchet.

He was about to have his head split open when I trained my revolver on the hatchet wielder, who promptly fled for his life. Taking the injured man outside, I blew on my police whistle – not that it was necessary – for constables were swarming, summoned by the screams and the screeches of the combatants milling all about us.

"I admit that I contributed to the quelling of the riot by firing shots into the air, followed by a judicious bullet into one intractable soul, one whose hatchet arm is quite useless at present. But my aim was accomplished, and I regret nothing. I took the noseless man in a cab to the nearest hospital, where I stood watch over him until Lestrade could be summoned to fetch him. That is why I am here, Inspector. To fetch you."

"My word!" I exclaimed. "Holmes, you got more than you bargained for!"

"More than I bargained for, yet also as much as I dared to accomplish. I think that a visit to the noseless man is in order, for by now he should be awakened to the day."

We all three went around to the hospital and paid a visit to the unfortunate individual.

The man lay in a bed, the remnant root of his nose bandaged, breathing through his mouth. He was a pitiful sight, pale of visage and crusty of eye. His English proved to be broken, but it was sufficient for a preliminary interrogation.

Lestrade opened this up.

"What is your name?"

"Wong."

"What are you doing at the opium shop last night?"

"Defending my brother."

"And who is your brother?"

The man was reluctant to respond, and gave a mixture of English and Chinese, apparently calculated to confuse us. Lestrade pressed him and got from only that he was part of the attacking party who were avenging a wrong done to them. What "wrong" wasn't made explicit.

Lestrade said to us, "This man is obviously a member of the Azure Phoenix Tong. The attack was doubtless meant to avenge the burning of the Chinese-owned opium den."

Holmes interjected, "With your permission Lestrade, I have a few questions."

"See what you can do with him," he said huffily.

"Mr. Wong, I am Sherlock Holmes. It doesn't matter if you know my name or not. I witnessed the attack upon you. Your assailant was not Chinese. He made an absolute point of removing your nose. Why is that?"

"Wong not say. Private matter. Matter of honor."

"I preserved your life from a second blow, one calculated to split open your skull. A man intent upon cold-blooded murder by that means doesn't bother with removing a nose prior to slaying his victim. There was significance to the removal of your nose. I would like to know what it is."

Wong remained reluctant to speak. Holmes's penetrating gaze did not leave his bandaged face. It bored into him.

At length, the man relented. Reluctance threaded his voice. "We came for the other man's nose."

"Whose nose?"

"He goes by many names. We call him Gou. Enemies call him Cho."

"Does he also go by the name of Li Shen?'

"Li Shen is another name he uses. But that is not his name. No one knows his true name. But we call him Gou."

"This man is from Tonkin?"

"Yes. From Hanoi. But no one knows his name. Few have seen his face. He has smuggled in his own *chandu* to compete with Chinese. Takes away customers. Angers the Azure Phoenix Tong. Tong seek revenge."

"But why remove Gou's nose?" pressed Holmes.

"I will not say. Private matter. Private matter between Li Shen and Azure Phoenix Tong. To be settled by them and no other."

"He is a stubborn one," remarked Lestrade. "I'm surprised you got that much out of him."

"It is sufficient."

Lestrade raised an eyebrow in Holmes's direction and his mouth fell open. I don't think he knew what to say to that, so I asked the obvious question in his stead.

"Holmes, I don't see how you have advanced your investigation in the least. This business of noses makes no sense to me. If we're looking for a man without a nose, what is this business about other people losing *their* noses?"

Instead of replying directly to my question, Holmes addressed the inspector. "Lestrade, I imagine that your gaols are full of suspects collected during the course of the evening's activities."

"We have over twenty-five Asiatics in custody. We have them packed two and three to a cell. I understand that there have been a number of scuffles, since my men haven't the skill to separate the Chinese from some of the other nationalities, some of whom are apparently their rivals."

"I believe that an examination of these prisoners is in order. Allow me to propose an identity parade."

"If you think that it would accomplish anything useful."

"It's possible that our quarry is among this group. That is, if your men were thorough in apprehending the combatants – particularly those defending the opium den where French is spoken. If not, we should learn additional facts that would enable us to run the man at the heart of all the trouble to earth at last."

"Insofar as I am apprised of the situation," muttered Lestrade, "my men picked up no suspects possessing facial deformities of any kind. I particularly instructed them to look for absent noses."

Holmes smiled diffidently. "Humor me, Inspector. I promise that you will not regret it one jot."

Back to Scotland Yard we went. There, Lestrade ordered the Chinese prisoners brought out before us.

There was a spacious hall used for this purpose, and the men were assembled as if upon the theater stage. Guards were posted at the doors and all around the stage. When all was at last in order, we entered.

These fellows made a forlorn picture. Standing elbow to elbow, cheek to jowl, crammed onto the stage, often two abreast, with those more guilty loitering in the rear of the line. Some had long queues, while others sported close-shaven polls. Many bore facial contusions and other marks of the night's battles. All were attired in the shirtings and cotton trousers preferred by the Chinese race.

Holmes paced before the group, which stood in two ragged rows, and scrutinized each man's features as he came to them. As he conducted his examination, he began a recitation of his tentative conclusions that was as astounding as any I've heard in my capacity as his good friend and confidant.

"Several clues conspired to paint a picture which, while fanciful, seemed inevitable to me, even though I had to strain my imagination to its a fullest in order to resolve it in my mind.

"Let's begin with the fact that the names by which we know this man, although apparently aliases, taking together point in a single direction. The Chinese called him '*Gou*', which in their language means '*Dog*'. Among his own people, the mysterious fellow is known as '*Cho*', a word that I suspect also has a canine connotation. I'm confident in this last deduction because early on, I received an inkling that the first name by which we became aware of him, Li Shen, was not his real name. Our investigation suggested that he came from French Indochina, which would make him Annamese, not Chinese."

"Chinese also live in French Indochina," Lestrade pointed out.

"Certainly, they do. But for the moment it was simpler to assume that a man from Hanoi would be a native of that country."

Holmes ceased his pacing and directed the guards to move the men standing in the back row forward, many of whom were so short of stature that only the tops of their heads, and perhaps their eyes, could be seen between the heads of those arrayed in the front.

As these individuals were brought into the gaslit glare, Holmes continued. "If the Chinese element were unified against him, it stood to reason that our quarry would not be Chinese. Otherwise, he would be absorbed into the local population. He was not. He stood apart. So when I selected an opium den to frequent last night, I chose one where Chinese was not the dominant language. This proved to be fortunate, because as I've previously stated, I was able to understand much of what I overheard, since the common language was French."

Additional suspects were hauled forward, some of them reluctantly.

"In our first encounter, Lestrade," Holmes continued, "I was struck by the fact that you pursued a man without a nose. I didn't think that a noseless man would lack nostrils, given that without the nose, the human nasal cavities are rather in the nature of open wounds. I didn't think such gaps could be covered up successfully. Therefore, I considered the possibility that the man was not absent a nose, but that some other physical deformity was present, one that concealed his nose from view in poor light."

Holmes continued studying the new faces that were being thrust forward when there came a commotion, during which a man noisily refused to be brought into the light.

Police guards converged on him. Pulling him by the collar, they manhandled the reluctant one until he stood before us, head bowed, barking and snarling sulphurously in what I assumed was his native tongue.

"Lift his head so that I may see his features," requested Holmes.

A constable seized the man by his dark hair and brought his face into the sputtering gaslight.

Lestrade gasped. I was too shocked to emit such a human sound.

For the Oriental man who snapped so vociferously at us, possessed a perfectly whole nose, except that it was flat and as black as a piece of coal. This gave him a peculiarity of countenance, upon which Lestrade remarked excitedly.

"Jove! He looks like a human dog!"

"More like a low cur," remarked Holmes dryly. "Here is your culprit, Lestrade. Li Shen is not a Chinese name. It is not his name at all. Rather, it is a French term, which has been the official language of Tonkin and all of Indochina since the Treaty of Tientsin. His name is actually '*Le Chien*', otherwise '*The Dog*'. No doubt it was a name that he acquired as a result of his unfortunate birthmark, which appears confined to the vicinity of his rather truncated nose. I imagine the fact that the scoundrel speaks in barks and snaps as he is doing now contributed to the cognomen."

Staring at the fellow, I quickly realized the truth.

"That is a massive liver spot!" I exclaimed. "I have never seen one quite like it!"

A stream of invective erupted from the culprit. I understood none of it.

Lestrade ordered, "Take this man and confine him to a cell of his own."

Snapping and snarling in the Annamese tongue, with occasional outbursts of vituperative French, the elusive Li Shen was dragged away and out of our sight.

Lestrade turned and said graciously, "Mr. Holmes, it is as if you have spun an orderly web out of gossamer moonbeams, with every strand in its proper place. I would never have thought that the disparate threads you fell heir to could lead to such a sound conclusion."

"I have already admitted, Lestrade, that imagination played a larger role in my deductions than is usually the case. But a man either owns a nose or he does not. When I considered that fact, as well as the sound of the name *Li Shen*, it all came together in my mind. The rest was, if you will pardon the expression, dogged determination."

"And some luck as well? Had you chosen a different opium den, you might have burned up in that hellish conflagration."

"The clues I had already accumulated led me to the correct den of inequity, Lestrade. No luck was involved. Only sound brain work."

"No matter how the pudding was prepared, we are in your debt again."

"Consider it my contribution as a concerned citizen," remarked Holmes, looking toward me for some obscure reason.

Sometime later, Holmes and I were discussing a newspaper account that was as unexpected as it was grisly.

"It seems that our opium dealer of many aliases had an unfortunate encounter with one of his rivals while in prison," my friend related dryly. "An altercation led to the abrupt removal of the man's dark and distinctive nose."

"How was this accomplished under such well-guarded circumstances?" I demanded.

"The Chinese perpetrator employed his natural teeth to effect the amputation."

"How poetic – in a ghastly way," I remarked.

"It seems that Li Shen's unusual physiognomy marked him among other recent non-Chinese arrivals to Limehouse, and inspired from the start a desire to remove his nose as a way of teaching him a lesson. Perhaps threats were made on that order. Hence the vicious and calculated maiming of the tong man who lost his nose, who remained reluctant to give us the full story, owing to the vows of his secret society. Now Mr. Wong's tragic disfigurement has been avenged and Li Shen has been traded, if reluctantly, one facial deformity for another."

"But how did he escape notice all that time?"

"A man cannot conceal the fact that he lacks a nose, which was another consideration in my thinking at the time. And a black-hued nose is almost as problematic. But Asian women have their own brand of facial powder. A man could easily avail himself of a supply and powder his nose in such a way that it might pass inspection by night, if not scrutinized too closely."

"So we might have passed him on the street, never noticing his powdered proboscis?"

"Precisely."

"Well, that wraps up the matter rather tidily, even if the details make one pale."

"Not quite, Watson. There still remains the mystery of the man who wrote the intriguing letter signed, '*A Concerned Citizen*'."

"In the scheme of things," I said dismissively, "I consider that to be a trifle, unworthy of further consideration."

"On the contrary. I think it highly significant. And I formed a theory at the first, which I will now share with you."

I confess that I blanched at this point. But I held my tongue. My expression was all that Sherlock Holmes needed to read.

His gaze transfixing me, Holmes stated, "I propose that the author of that letter is no less than the distinguished Dr. John H. Watson of London."

"This is the limit, Holmes," I returned hotly. "The absolute limit!"

"You deny it?"

"What would be the point?" I said in exasperation. "But however did you deduce this?"

"You have certain cadences in your speech, my dear Watson, which are reproduced in your written work. I recited the letter aloud, if you will recall, which further cemented my first impression. And since you're in the habit of writing me letters from time to time, I've always noted your stubborn insistence upon capitalizing the word '*Yours*' in your customary closing, '*Faithfully Yours*'. While you possessed sufficient guile to replace this with '*Respectfully Yours*', you repeated the error, rather like a schoolchild carrying over a mistake in mathematical computation."

“You have me. I do not deny it.”

“Then pray explain what motivated you to take such a roundabout method to arouse my interest in the matter?”

“That much is simple,” I explained. “This new type of opium has been leaking out of Limehouse and into the West End and the general population. I have had no less than three patients who appealed to me for succor. This is unheard-of in my long practice. Questioning my patients, I learned rumors of this *Li Shen* – or should I say, *Le Chien*. I contrived to bring the matter to your attention, but knowing well your ever-changing moods, feared that you might reject it as having insufficient mysterious elements to attract your interest. So I fell upon the ruse of writing you an anonymous letter.”

“And I’m very glad that you did, for not only did you hand me an ingenious riddle to unravel, one the nature of which you did not at the time suspect, but I had the distinct pleasure of a secondary mystery, which proved to be the easiest to resolve.”

“I don’t know what to say. I composed that letter very carefully, limiting my words, thinking you would never suspect the truth.”

“I suspect everything, Watson. You should know that by now.”

“I have learned my lesson. You cannot be beaten.”

“Kindly refrain from including that erroneous point in one of your stories about me. I have been beaten. More than once, in fact. And I imagine that I’ll be beaten yet again one day. But today, I sit triumphant and quite satisfied with the results of my efforts.”

“As am I,” I admitted reluctantly. “For I have had no recent opium addicts coming to my practice in need of weaning from the poppy’s tyranny. And for that I am very grateful to you, my good friend.”

The Mahmudabad Result
by Andrew Bryant

I stood at the window of the sitting room looking out at the venal day, the telegram still clasped in my hand. The rain fell harder now and the winds seemed to come from all directions, not from just one fixed origin. Swirling, then finding an outlet between the barriers of the city blocks, and channelling the rain straight along Baker Street. The rain horizontal, so that even as I stood in the upper reaches of the place it hit the window directly in front of me, and the rolling drops blew away before they reached the bottom of the panes.

Holmes was silent in the chair behind me. I hadn't yet shown him the telegram. My reaction on reading it had been to rise from my chair and go to the window to look outside, so as not to have to look inward.

"What can I do, old friend?" Holmes asked.

Before me I was faced with a naturally demoralizing day, a demoralization only matched by the message on the crumpled paper I held.

"What can I do?" Holmes repeated.

I flattened out the paper and handed it to him.

He read it aloud:

> *Office of Origin: Ilfracombe.*
> *To: Doctor John Watson (In Care of Mr. Sherlock Holmes)*
> *221b Baker Street, London*
>
> *Major Charles Longhurst dead. Murdered. Can you come to Ilfracombe?*
>
> *Mary Longhurst*
> *Royal Clarence Hotel*

How quickly do the hoped-for buried memories leap to the forefront when an uncalled for and unwanted stimulus rouses them?

"An old military colleague?" Holmes said.

"Maiwand."

"Were you close?"

"He was an officer in the 66th Foot when my regiment, the Fifth Northumberland Fusiliers, was sub-joined to it. So we weren't close by friendship, but only through shared experience."

"And Mary Longhurst is his daughter, of course."

"Yes, but why *of course*?"

"A widow or a sister would be unlikely to use the man's rank when calling him by name. Any man with the self-discipline and personal authority needed to earn the rank of Major would undoubtedly run a strict household, and only the daughter raised in that household would be inclined to address her own father by his military rank."

"Correct."

"I remember him as a member of the Nonpareil Club," Holmes said.

"Yes, the Major was an acquaintance of Colonel Upwood, but wasn't implicated in any way in the Colonel's scandalous behaviour. The Major was a difficult man, but one of strict morality dedicated to duty and the standards of his profession, and of the Crown. The Major never spoke to, or of, Upwood ever again."

"You have met the daughter?"

"Yes, we are acquainted. I've attended a few functions with the Regiment where she was present."

"Ilfracombe is a holiday destination for them?"

"I assume so."

"Why do you think she has called upon you for assistance when you have only met her a few times?"

"My guess would be that she has read some of our adventures and is hoping that if I answered her request, there was a good chance that you would accompany me."

"Guesswork and chance? Neither! If you weren't personally close to the Major, then the only motive behind this telegram is to have us both attend the scene of the crime. Not that I am averse to that. A few days at the seashore would be a welcome respite from the drear we are currently experiencing. But if you weren't close to the Major, why did you appear so stricken when you read the telegram?"

"I wasn't thinking so much of him, but more of the campaign itself, and the other men in it."

I didn't care to elaborate on this, and Holmes, recognizing and respecting my rights of memory, didn't press me on it.

"I'll send Miss Longhurst a telegram confirming that we will be there as soon as we can," I said.

"I can be on the morning train."

"I'll meet you at Paddington," I said, and put on my coat and raised my collar against the day.

We met on the platform, with the steam and smoke hanging low in the heavy morning atmosphere. Stowing our luggage in the carriage, we sat opposing each other at the window as the train pulled out. Holmes liked to arrive just as a train was leaving so as not to waste any time with waiting. We moved out into the drizzle, falling as the remnant of yesterday's storm.

It was a two-hundred-mile journey, with a change of train in Barnstaple for the final leg to Ilfracombe.

Holmes had been silent so far, occasionally glancing at me, but mostly concentrating on *The Times* or on the scenery.

I drew a breath and began.

"The dust is the worst part of the country. The geography is striking – stark, but as striking as any on earth. The soil, a clay loam, turns to dust in summer with every footfall, with every hoof, and with every wheel turning. It wasn't unusual to walk through dust ankle deep in June when the daytime temperature could easily reach one-hundred degrees. We wore khakis, and the name well suited us as we were the same colour as the dust. We marched through these choking clouds from Kandahar to Maiwand to meet and defeat the Ayub Khan's army. That was how self- righteous we were. We weren't just marching out to meet the Khan's army. We were marching out to *defeat* his army. We had no doubt in our moral superiority, or our technical superiority. And the Major was the most confident of all. We were the British Empire – how could we be defeated? As it turned out, the Khan had an army estimated to be twenty-five-thousand strong with both infantry and cavalry and several batteries of artillery. We advanced across a dry ditch and confronted the enemy. Almost immediately the tide was seen to turn and within hours we were retreating back the way we came. A thousand of us were killed that afternoon. My souvenir was an Afghan round in the shoulder, which, as you know, pains me to this day. Both the soldiers of the Khan and the geography were our enemies. The dust was like something that their God stirred up to choke us, strangle us, and defeat us."

I stopped there, and after a moment, Holmes said, "There is only one God for all of us, Watson."

"I know there is only one God. But sometimes, in some circumstances, it seems that there is more than one. There is the one who is your saviour, and there is the one who applauds your destruction."

"Nonetheless, there is only one."

I wasn't in the frame of mind to continue, and instead I looked out the window at the green pastoral countryside we rolled through. And I thanked God that I was here, in spite of my wound, I thanked God that I was here and not back there.

Holmes remained silent, thinking whatever whirligig thoughts his mind threw at him. Possibly he wasn't even thinking of what I had just said, but was already planning ahead to the meeting with Mary Longhurst and the case ahead of us.

I cannot say that Holmes was a sympathetic person. He knew when a line had been drawn, but oftentimes I wondered if he stopped at the line only to observe what was happening on the other side of it. Did he care what happened at the Battle of Maiwand, or was it simply part of the investigation? Such was my distracted mind that I would question the motives of my friend. But memories such as those aroused by this case weren't easily quelled. The past is an irrational dictator, and however much you might fight against it, at your weaker moments it assails you anew – it assails you as if you were there still, living in it still, smelling the gun smoke, breathing the dust, still hearing the butchery on both sides, still feeling the bullet's entry into your body. Still feeling your younger self lying in that dust, incapacitated and useless as the battle rages around you.

Holmes, like so many others, could never understand this. In spite of all the speeches and sympathies, all the pleasantries and the patriotic jargon, they could never understand this.

We took a cab from the station to High Street and the Royal Clarence Hotel. Miss Longhurst was waiting in the lobby. "My dear Doctor, thank you for coming. It means the world to me."

She held my hand for longer than would normally seem appropriate.

"This is a terrible tragedy," I said.

She turned away from me.

"This is Mr. Sherlock Holmes," I said.

She took Holmes's hand in both of hers. "I can't tell you what it means to me that you are here."

"Quite," Holmes replied.

"Do the police have any new leads?" I asked.

"No."

"Witnesses?"

"Only me."

"You?" I exclaimed.

"Yes, I am the only witness. The major and I were walking along the quay, taking one of our several daily constitutionals. We have always walked out any time of day and in any weather when visiting here. The Major had a habit of quoting from the classics before we set out, usually a line extolling the virtues of fresh air and the natural morality of being out and about. On that day, which was only the day before yesterday, though it feels a lifetime ago, he said as we left, '*Let them henceforth do me good or evil, all their actions are indifferent to me, and whatever they may do, my contemporaries will always be as nothing in my eyes*'."

"Rousseau," Holmes said. "A man after my own heart – or is it after my own soul."

"One and the same I would hope," Miss Longhurst said.

"In some, but not all."

"We walked the length of the esplanade. It was a cold miserable afternoon, the sea rough, and with a misty rain falling. We hadn't seen another person out – "

"How were you dressed?" Holmes asked.

"We were dressed for the weather, of course. A wardrobe suited to all climes is needed here. I was in my woolen three-quarter length and hat, and the Major in his greatcoat but no hat. Some people say that all the heat from your body escapes through the top of your head, but the Major called that 'fishwife's stuff and nonsense'. He always went out without a hat, which is unusual for a man, but he believed that the more your head, your brain, your mind, was exposed to the elements, the more astute that you became. As I said, we hadn't seen another person when a man appeared walking toward us. He was an older man, but walked with the vigour and directness of a younger man."

"Why did you think he was an older man?"

"His hair was quite grey, and his face weathered. As he approached, he looked from me to the Major and said 'Good evening' to us as he passed. And we responded in kind."

"And then?"

"And then I heard footsteps running at us from behind. I turned to see the man coming back at us at full tilt, his face full of rage. He shouted 'Major!', and lifted him bodily off the ground and towards the sea wall. As he did this he uttered a strange word, something foreign, but I couldn't understand it then, and still haven't been able to decipher it."

"What was the word?"

"It sounded like '*myhoodbad*'."

"My hood bad," Holmes repeated.

"And did the Major react to this word?" I asked.

"He looked shocked when he heard it, but that may also have been because of the ferocity of the man's assault and his obvious intent to harm."

"And then?"

"The Major went over the seawall and down. The tide was only half in, so the rocks below were still mostly above water. The Major struck the rocks and went into the water."

"And what did you do?"

"Not very much, I'm afraid. I was too shocked by it all."

"And the assailant?"

"He looked at me, seeming appalled at himself for what he had just done. He looked as if he himself could not believe that he had done it. Then he ran from the quay into a side street and was gone."

"And the Major?"

"The Major was in the water, his head bleeding. His mouth just above water, but the sea was rough and, even as he fought against it, he sank, looking up at me as he did."

"You didn't attempt to rescue him?"

"I don't swim," she said matter-of-factly.

"Then what did you do?"

"I went from the quay to find help, but by the time I returned with some men, the Major was nowhere to be seen."

"Once his coat was saturated and his boots and pockets full of water," Holmes said, "the weight of his clothing alone would have pulled him under. His injury, his age, and the cold water made the outcome inevitable. There was nothing you could have done, Miss Longhurst, swimmer or not."

"Thank you for those words Mr. Holmes. I've been feeling as if I was somehow negligent."

"And his body hasn't been recovered?"

"Not yet. The police have men looking along the coast, and have notified everyone from Morte Point to Combe Martin to have a watch-out.

"The police questioned all the hotel staff and circulated a description of the attacker?"

"Yes, but to no avail. They had men at the station watching every outgoing passenger, and also questioned all carriage and wagon owners. So far, nothing."

"If no hotel recognized him," Holmes said, "it's likely that he was a day tripper. He would have left cross-country, and will be long gone by now,"

"What about enemies?" I said.

"He was a man of rank . . . ."

"And a strict man," Holmes interrupted.

"Yes, a strict man," Miss Longhurst said. "As strict as was necessary for his rank."

"Would you call him harsh?" Holmes asked.

"I suppose I would," she replied, immediately upset that she had admitted such a thing about her own father.

"How would you describe the assailant's physique?"

"About six feet in height – strong, as if he might be a labourer."

"Age?"

"Older, as I said. Perhaps nearing fifty years."

"But he moved quickly for a man of his age?"

"Yes, he was strong and quick."

"An older man, then," said Holmes, "who keeps himself active. Not letting himself go to seed as so many aging gentlemen do. A military man perhaps, used to the discipline and standards of army life."

"An acquaintance of the Major?" she asked. "A former comrade?"

"Or else a madman," I said.

"Perhaps a little of both," added Holmes.

Miss Longhurst was visibly tired. The experience and the re-telling of it obviously sapping her.

"You look exhausted," I said. "We'll leave you to recuperate. We will be in our rooms if needed."

"Or possibly out walking," Holmes said.

She left us and went to the stairs.

"No love lost between daughter and father," Holmes said.

"As she admitted, the Major was a harsh man."

"Harsh is a word with numerous connotations, depending on the experience of the one using the word. I believe that she called on us because she wants this crime solved so she can bury her father and her demons at the same time. She wants to do right by him, not just out of filial responsibility, but also so she can lay him to rest, both in the ground and in her soul."

"She deserves peace."

"As do we all, but some of us will never attain it. Tell me, Watson – in your experience of the Major, does the word *harsh* fully convey the man?"

I paused before answering, thinking of one of my fellows at the Battle of Maiwand, dragged begging for mercy back to the edge of the dry ditch during the retreat. I thought of the bullet fired there. I hadn't mentioned it yet to Holmes, but the murderer's blurted foreign word *myhoodbad* could have been *Mahoudbad*, the hamlet on the far side of the ditch.

"I would describe the Major as having a harshness bordering on fanaticism, which is a personality flaw that inevitably leads to cruelty," I said.

"And this fanaticism was applied across the board, at home and in the field?"

"I can only comment on actions in the field, but the fanaticism was expressed to foe and fellow equally."

We dined that evening in the hotel with Miss Longhurst, now rested and in better, if subdued, spirits.

"Does the prospect of being fatherless distress you?" Holmes asked her.

She paused. "The Major wasn't a man who would raise weak children. I wouldn't have his respect if I fell to pieces at his death. And even though his body hasn't been recovered, I am reconciled to the fact of his demise."

"He made you strong."

"Yes, I suppose he did. I wasn't one of his soldiers, but I learned early the benefits of discipline, and more importantly the benefits of self-discipline."

"Your mother?" Holmes inquired.

"She died when I was quite young. The Major admitted afterwards that some men should only be married to their careers, and that their only children should be their career successes. Some men marry solely because it is expected of them – it's the social norm, and it is unfortunate that some men don't ignore the social norm and remain unwed. It is better for them that way, and also better for their wives and children."

"I couldn't agree more," Holmes said. "I'm a committed bachelor. I enjoy my distractions, but only when they take me away from home, not when they bind me to it."

"You have made the choice that's best for you and for everyone around you."

"Yes, I have."

After dinner, Miss Longhurst retired to her room.

Holmes and I took a walk along the quay. We were quite alone. Not another soul wandered out in the near dark. I heard the waves below, sliding against the stones quietly, with barely a breath of wind and the sea calm.

"Could our murderer still wait in shadow?" I said.

"He wouldn't find you and me such easy targets as the Major."

"I wouldn't describe the Major as an easy target. He was aging, yes, but I am sure he would still have been a formidable opponent had he not been surprised by his killer."

"I meant more that he believed himself to be above such an attack. He believed that his reputation and his rank gave him an aura of invincibility. His arrogance was his self-protection. After years of giving orders and having them obeyed without question, it would have been unthinkable to him that one of his subordinates could possibly turn on him. I'm sure that the Major's look of shock on being assaulted was as much to do with the personal insult of the attack as with the strange word spoken."

"Then you believe that he recognized the attacker as one of his former comrades?"

"Without a doubt. But I use the word 'subordinate', not 'comrade', and I would use the '*belonging to a lower order*' definition of subordinate. Even you, Watson, seem to disbelieve that this seeming-immortal could have been killed by a mere mortal."

"He was someone that seemed could never die."

"An illusion of his own creation."

I stopped at the seawall, looking out at the black expanse. Holmes stopped beside me.

"On 27 July, 1880," I said. "Private William Andrews refused to fire on the enemy. He threw his rifle down in the dust and ran from the Ayub Khan's army. He was caught by his own men at the ditch across from the cluster of houses that made up Mahmudabad. The Major, who became his judge, his jury, and his God, gave the immediate verdict of cowardice to young William. He was a boy not suited to war, a boy who didn't want to kill, a boy with no hatred, no vehemence, or prejudice in his heart. He joined the army just to escape where he came from and would have been quite happy preaching his 'Live and let live' motto to both sides. That attitude is, of course, unacceptable on a battlefield. The Major ordered young William to kneel down and make peace with his Maker, which he did, praying for the redemption of his soul. Mid-prayer, the Major shot William through the head and let his body fall back into the ditch.

"The Major's official charge was '*Shamefully casting away arms in the presence of the enemy.*' An offence punishable by death.

"We never had the chance to retrieve the body. The Khan's army closed on us, and we began our desperate retreat to Kandahar. Between the British and our Indian allies, we lost one-thousand men, nearly half our force. Two Victoria crosses were awarded on that day, but of course the name of Private Andrews has been forgotten by all except his comrades who saw him fall into the ditch."

"This Private Andrews was well-liked?"

"Yes. He was quiet, but well liked. He had friends in the Regiment. I half-expected the Major to fall in the ensuing conflict. But he didn't – he lived to return home and prosper."

"Why would you expect him to fall?"

"I can assure you, Holmes, that the heroic deaths of many officers were actually at the hands of their own men. A bullet on a battlefield can come from any direction, and whether the bullet is from an Afghan Jezail musket or from a British Martini-Henry rifle, no one is the wiser when the officer falls. Officially, officers fall leading their men, or defending their flag, or protecting the honour of the regiment. But everyone knows that this happens, and no investigations are ever undertaken to confirm from which side the bullet came."

"And after the execution of Private Andrews, you assumed that one his friends would do the same to the Major?"

"It was on everyone's mind, but due to lack of opportunity or failure of nerve, it didn't happen to the Major on that day."

"But perhaps the opportunity presented itself here, a decade on. Someone from the Regiment was finally able to exact revenge."

"You're quite certain that it was a member of the Regiment?"

"How else would he know?"

"Know?"

"The Major was dressed in civilian clothes, yet the murderer addressed him by his rank. How did he know? How did the murderer know the obscure place name Mahmudabad? It wasn't a planned killing. It wasn't a clever murder. It was impulsive. I believe the assailant came across the Major and Miss Longhurst strictly by chance. Sometimes impulsive murders are more difficult to solve. When passion, whether it be love or hate, is the sole motive, there is only a tenuous connection to logic. But at least we now have what appears to be the motive."

In the morning, Holmes and I were awakened by Miss Longhurst knocking on our doors.

"Doctor Watson, Mr. Holmes – The Major has been found! The Major has been found!"

I answered the door, embarrassed to be seen by her in my night clothes, dressing gown, and slippers, but of course my visitor couldn't be put off at such a time.

Holmes was completely at ease, seated barefoot in his dressing gown, one leg draped over the other, waiting for the details.

"He was found, just before light, by a policeman patrolling the beach near Watermouth. His body is on the way here now, and then to Barnstaple and on to London. I must pack."

She ran down the hallway to her room.

"We must also pack," Holmes said.

"But surely the investigation isn't complete."

"The Ilfracombe aspect of it is. The London aspect now begins."

Miss Longhurst made the trip to London seated in the baggage car beside the casket of her father. She chose this as a sign of respect and devotion, and impressed everyone at the station with her stoicism.

"We won't see him at the funeral," Holmes said. "But we must look for him on the outskirts of it."

The countryside jostled passed us, but now under a blue and uncluttered sky.

"Miss Longhurst's description could fit many men."

"Yes. He won't be in the church, as he knows that she can identify him, but he'll be watching. We need to be on the lookout for a furtive and reclusive visitor. He may be wearing his old uniform, as a token of respect to the memory of Private Andrews. But he will be there to watch the funereal show, as it were, and he'll want to see what result his action has generated. He won't be able to rest until he's satisfied."

"He'll return to the consequences of his crime, if not the actual scene of it?"

"As a man who has lived his life by strict confines of rank and class, our killer will feel guilt, but he will believe that he did the right thing and, like you, he may not believe that the icon is actually dead, and so will need to see the ceremony with his own eyes.

"Remember the classics, Watson. '*Methought I heard a voice cry "Sleep no more! Macbeth does murder sleep."*' Our assailant has done the same to himself."

Holmes read *The Times* obituary aloud:

Major Charles Longhurst

Death, which comes to claim us all, has come for the body, but not the soul, of an heroic representative of the Empire. 'The Major", as he was known, was taken from the nation in a vile act of cowardice by a perpetrator as yet unknown. The Major will always be remembered as a gentleman in the true sense of the term, that being a man of grace and bold demeanour, and coming from a class which naturally begets the heroism shown at the famous Battle of Maiwand where, after leading a spirited attack upon the enemy, he fought a bitter strategic retreat that has entered the annals of English fortitude. His passing comes as a blow to the men who loved and respected him in times of war and peace, and to his only remaining family, daughter Mary.

No man better represented the anonymous words dedicated to defense of Empire:

. . . so he bore his spear
forth to the fight. He had good intentions
so long as he could hold with his hands

a shield and broad sword – he would validate his vow
when the time came to fight before his Lord.

"That should be a small *L* in Lord, but, no matter, it is an impressive departure all the same."

"Justice done," I said, "or revenge fulfilled?"

"One and the same, depending on the point of view you bring to it. Our killer had his revenge against a perceived injustice, and now justice will be done in return."

"Only poor Andrews never saw justice done."

"A commanding officer has the right to execute a soldier in the field. Section 4 (2) of the Army Act states just that."

"The Army Act is just words on a piece of paper. Those words don't consider personality or temperament or suitability to the task. The words don't consider the heat, the volleys of gunfire, the dust, or an enemies' relentless charge."

"Precisely why the Act must be adhered to. If every man was considered on his individual merits or failings, the structure and discipline would fall to pieces and the result would be anarchy. That is why there are officers, and why there are subordinates."

"You have never been in a war, Holmes. You have faced grave personal danger many times, but you have never been in a situation of such colossal chaos that you knew, without a doubt, that you were going to die and had accepted that physical and moral certainty, and then, by some extraordinary circumstance, you don't die. You live, and then must learn to live."

"No, Watson, I have never been in that situation. And I hope I never am. I will freely admit that I would make a terrible soldier."

"Yes, you would," I said.

The service was held on the high ground in the chapel of the Nunhead Cemetery of All Saints on the south side of the Thames. Holmes and I were near the doors in order to observe the mourners.

Miss Longhurst sat, veiled, in the front row, a few relatives from her mother's side around her.

The service was heavily attended. Officers and men of the 66th Foot, a few government officials, some members of the Nonpareil Club who had made the effort to come south of the river, and a raft of friends, acquaintances, and curious civilians filling the remaining pews to overflow.

The Minister read from *The Book of Psalms*: "*Blessed be the Lord, my rock, who trains my arms for battle, who prepares my hands for war.*

He is my love, my fortress: He is my stronghold, my saviour, my shield, my place of refuge."

And *Ecclesiastes*: "*Wisdom is better than weapons of war, but one sinner destroys much good.*"

"Onward Christian Soldiers" was sung with gusto: "*Onward Christian soldiers marching as to war, with the cross of Jesus going on before . . . .*"

I stood for the hymn, but didn't sing it.

When the service was done, the casket was carried out the doors by six young members of the Regiment. The Major's final resting place was a low stone sarcophagus into which the pallbearers lowered the casket. Miss Longhurst bowed her head as she stood beside the tomb but, with the veil, it wasn't possible to tell if she was weeping or not. The lid was slid on, grating stone on stone. The Major's name, rank, dates of birth and death, and the Regiment's badge, laurel leaves closing on a crown, had been chiselled into the lid.

Holmes and I dawdled outside the chapel and alongside the grave, looking up into the trees and around the older stones. The mourners chatted, wept, offered solace, and then gradually dispersed. I didn't recognize any of the soldiers present, most of them younger men of the Regiment. The few older men were officers who wouldn't have associated with me a decade ago.

Holmes and I remained after all others had departed. We were alone outside the Chapel.

"What now?" I asked.

"He will come, Watson. I apply the same analytical approach to crime as Doctor Freud applies to the mind. Sometimes the vagaries of an individual case will throw the theories into temporary disarray, but ultimately the result is irrevocable. Behaviour can be predicted. He will come."

"But we can't know when."

"It will be soon. He will wait for the anonymity of darkness. He needs to know that all debts have been settled."

"And our next move?"

"Tonight will be clear, with a three-quarter moon."

"And?"

"And now to Baker Street, for pistols, and apparel suited to a night in a cemetery."

The dark had just fallen and the moon slightly risen when we returned to the Nunhead Chapel. We both wore heavy overcoats and gloves in the cool evening, and we each had loaded pistols in our pockets. The rising moonlight gave a blued-ivory atmosphere to everything around us. Away from the thrum of the city, the quiet was enthralling.

"Sequester yourself in the shadow of the Chapel, Watson. I'll be concealed on the hill above the Major's grave. We'll have a bit of a wait, at least until the night has completely come on and the moon is fully risen."

Holmes moved quickly up the hill and disappeared into the maze of trees and graves.

I hunkered down in the gloom beside the Chapel and kept my hand on the pistol, as much a panacea against the environment in which I loitered as a defence against our quarry. This three-quarter moonlight looked the same everywhere in the world, a spectral illumination that has kept mankind awake with fear since we became sensate – since the primitive soul in us began to fear the things that walk abroad in the ashen light.

Everywhere that I had been in the world, I had looked up at the night sky to find Ursa Major and the seven stars in it that make up The Plough. The finding of it always reassured me that everyone, everywhere, could look up and see what I was seeing.

I leaned back against the wall, wondering if there was really a purpose for us being here, almost hoping that there was no purpose, almost hoping that our villain was going to go against type and not show himself, almost hoping that he wouldn't show himself and be revealed as a former comrade.

I may have slept briefly, leaning there in my shadow, but I came around at the sound of footsteps and braced myself against the wall. He came walking into the openness before the chapel, out of the obscurity of the lane, stopping to survey the scene before moving off in the direction of the Majors' grave. He carried an unlit lantern in his hand.

I followed the shape, walking only when he walked to disguise the sound of my own footfalls with his. When he went into the darkness of the trees, he stopped and lit his lantern and carried on with it swaying in and out of the stones until it stopped at the Major's tomb. His description and demeanour matched Miss Longhurst's account, and I believed, but wasn't certain, that he wore a khaki tunic. He put the lantern down and withdrew something from his coat, I saw the silver line of moonlight on a dagger blade as his hand danced and scratched and dug at the stone.

I waited for Holmes's lead.

I didn't see him stand up, but suddenly Holmes was there, standing above the grave, pistol in hand, shouting, "Stand down!"

The dagger clattered on the stone and in its place the glint of a revolver. A shot was fired, the flash brief but the report echoing around us. I drew out my pistol and ran at him, Holmes returned fire and then our prey was off running deeper into the graveyard. Holmes was fast behind him, with me trailing both. As Miss Longhurst had described him, he ran quickly over the uneven terrain, agile, a dark figure in the shade but sometimes briefly lit by the moon in the clearings.

Our objective ran into a larger glade where he was fully visible for a moment.

Holmes stopped.

"Stand down!" he shouted again.

The runner continued on as Holmes raised his pistol, aimed, and fired. The suspect fell, and when I entered the space Holmes stood over him, each with their pistols pointed at the other. I cocked my revolver and aimed it at the man on the ground.

"I don't want to shoot either of you – especially you, Doctor. But feel free to shoot me. It will be in self-defence."

"Who are you?" I demanded.

"Briggs, Archibald. Private."

"Archie Briggs?"

"We aren't going to shoot you, Mr. Briggs," Holmes said. "And if you aren't going to shoot us, then we might as well all disarm,"

Holmes and I pocketed our weapons, and Briggs dropped his arm. I knelt and felt for the wound.

"Why didn't you just kill me, Mr. Holmes?"

"You intentionally fired wide when you shot at me, Mr. Briggs."

"And you likewise on your first shot."

"But not on my second."

"No, a leg wound to stop me, but not to kill me."

"A dead suspect is no suspect at all."

The bullet had gone through the back of the leg just above the knee, breaking the femur. There was some blood but not an excessive amount, indicating that neither the femoral artery nor saphenous vein had been severed.

"Come on, Watson, let's take an arm each and get Mr. Briggs somewhere better suited to medical attention."

We got Briggs on his feet and struggled with him back towards the lantern and the Chapel.

"You attended the service today, Mr. Briggs," Holmes said.

"Yes, I was on the hill watching. Did you see me?"

"No."

"Then how did you know?"

"You knew where the grave was."

Briggs gave a short laugh. "And do you know why I did it? Do you know why I killed him?"

"Watson told me about Private Andrews. He was a good friend?"

"Best mates. The Major had no right to do what he did."

"Legally he did," Holmes said.

"Many things are legal, Mr. Holmes, but that doesn't make them just."

When we reached the Majors' sarcophagus, we sat Briggs down on it. Holmes picked up the dagger and put it in his pocket.

"I'll find us a means of transport," Holmes said, and walked off towards the lane.

Briggs took a flask from his tunic. The tunic smelled stale, as if it had been hanging up unwashed in a wardrobe for years. He took a swig and passed it to me.

"Brandy."

I took a drink and passed it back. "You might want another swig," I said.

I forced my handkerchief into the bullet hole to stop whatever blood I could.

Briggs grimaced and laughed.

"A return to field medicine?" he said.

"Do you have a handkerchief?"

He passed me his and I tied it as a tourniquet above the wound.

"If your leg goes cold let me know and I'll ease it."

He had another drink and so did I. I picked up the lantern and shone it on the lid. Scratched into it was the word *MURDERER* under the Major's name.

"How did you know he would be in Ilfracombe that day?" I said.

"I didn't. I work and live at Trimstone Manor, three miles from there. Whenever I want to get my sea air, I ride to Ilfracombe for the day. That was how I was able to escape. My horse was tethered nearby."

"Holmes surmised that it wasn't a planned assault."

"He was correct. I passed the Major and his daughter walking. I was cordial with them in passing, but then realized who it was I'd just encountered. I was overcome with rage to such an extent that I wasn't in Ilfracombe anymore, I was beside that ditch where we saw William fall down dead. God knows what happened to his body. He had no burial, no service, no memorial. No one saluted the dust he lay in, while the Major came home and carried on as if nothing had happened. Poor Andrews never got this much respect in his whole life." He slapped his hand down on the stone.

"If you tell the court your story, they may have compassion. You may not hang."

"And I'll spend the rest of my life in Dartmoor Prison. No, I'll not excuse or explain what I did. Better to die and go to Hell than to go to Dartmoor and live in Hell."

I sat down beside him.

"You should have shot me," he said.

"I would never have done that."

"What if I would have shot Mr. Holmes?"

"Then I would have shot you."

He laughed, and we shared another drink.

"You always were a loyal one," he said.

"How well did you know Briggs?" Holmes asked.

We were in the sitting room at Baker Street.

"An acquaintance only. Always quick to anger, a hot-head. Intelligent enough, but his personality would never let him rise above the rank of private."

"I've arranged with a stone mason to grind out the offending word from the Major's grave."

"Thankfully Miss Longhurst won't have to see it."

"Do you believe the word is true?"

Briggs was awaiting trial, the outcome already known to all. Mary Longhurst would be a stalwart witness, her testimony easily putting Briggs at the end of a rope – even easier when Briggs planned on offering no defence. A common soldier cannot kill an officer, no matter the reason. The Empire would rise and fall on matters of imperial protocol – or so it seemed to all the powers involved.

"How would it be described?" I asked. "True, but with just cause? True, but unacceptable because of an archaic hierarchy? True, but the alternative would condemn us all to Bedlam?"

Holmes stared at me.

"I already knew the details of the Battle of Maiwand before you told me," he said. "When I first met you, I researched the battle with the help of an acquaintance in the War Office. I wanted to be sure of the man with whom I would be rooming."

"Why didn't you say?"

"I was waiting for the time when you were ready to tell me. Please don't think that I was being deceptive . . . but I had to wait until you were ready to tell me."

The Adventure of the Matched Set

by Peter Coe Verbica

Chapter I – A Question of Honour

The bustling on London's cobbled streets enlivens and lulls during differing parts of a day with a pocket watch's recurrent predictability. This observation came to me most keenly when I first returned in post-convalescence from the vestiges of an intestinal fever and bullet wound, which I've described previously in more detail. Upon homecoming, a man quickly acclimates and the change in tempo fades from perception, despite its continued ebb and flow as the tide. In the early hours, activity awakens. Servants in their eight-button jackets re-stoke the stoves with coal. Grooms in tweed caps bridle, brush, and saddle the mares and geldings, drivers wearing bowlers hitch their wagons and drays, city dwellers open shutters to summon sunlight off of the Thames into their homes, sobering laborers wearing open vests queue to the docks, mills, and factories. Domestics with their white bows, bonnets, and brown wicker baskets migrate to the produce markets. In contrast, at the edge of dusk, sand settles to the bottom of the day's hourglass and the din tempers. Lamplighters climb their wobbly ladders with quick agility. Ladies ring silver-plate dinner bells and families gather in anticipation of their soup and supper. Gentlemen retire to their cigars, velvet jackets, weeklies, and shilling shockers.

The trees lining the lane upon which I walked were illuminated with yellow, red, and orange leaves. It was the cusp of early evening, before the final ebbing of natural light, and I found myself preoccupied with thoughts of a difficult medical case. Contributing to my challenge was my patient's faith in antiquated treatments and quackery, which modern medicine and science were debunking with rapidity. But superstitions die hard. My attempts to dissuade my stubborn patient the benefits of brain salts, toxic elixirs, and mesmerisms were faring poorly. I wondered if I would have a chance to treat her maladies, or whether her attraction to dubious cures – like a proverbial moth to a flame – would deny me of every reasonable opportunity. I mentally wrestled with the best method to deal with my convalescent, as the metronome of my cane struck time upon the sidewalk.

A ruckus directly ahead interrupted my deliberations. A full-bearded man of approximately six feet in height, wearing a short coat and bowler hat, was speaking roughly to a distraught woman. As I approached, I discerned that he had a bulbous nose and was yelling at her with a rural accent and abused grammar which would cause even the modestly educated to wince. The red-faced woman wore a cocked white bonnet, a bleached blouse, and coal-black dress. She held her arms about her head, as if ready to fend off blows. I stepped into the quarrel and found myself squaring off with an agile rogue. The maid quickly seized the opportunity to take her leave. Her antagonist exposed a wild mane as he removed his hat and shook his fist at me. His brows pulled downwards, and he sported a distorted grin. "You meater! You coward!" he rasped. "How dare you muck about in my business!" The man proceeded to toss the bowler, remove a hunting dagger with a bone grip from a sheath beneath his jacket, and move about me in a clockwise motion.

"If you're interested in robbery, I'm a poor candidate," I told him, looking to orient myself and gauge his threat. I raised my cane and held it crosswise, so that I could strike a quick blow with either end. I moved in unison with him, facing his solar plexus.

"Robbery! I have no need to take a farthing! You've knocked at my honour, not once, but now twice!"

"If you understand honour, sir," I invited, "then you can understand why I interrupted your argument with the lady. I saw an imbalanced pairing of adversaries. Let me take your leave so that I will no longer affront your evening's enjoyment."

"I will show you unequal!" the scalawag countered, crouching and looking at me with wild eyes as if I were atop a carving tray.

He stepped forward and I stepped back, unsheathing the blade from my swordstick, now having both the sheath with which to parry and the blade to strike.

"The equities favor me at present, sir," I said amiably. "Why don't we depart as gentlemen, rather than dispute further?"

The man looked at his dagger and slipped it deftly back into its hidden scabbard.

"Very well, Watson. If you insist."

With a magician-like sleight-of-hand, the wild hair was removed, along with the prosthetic nose. The entire comportment and countenance of the person before me changed. Regality replaced roguishness.

"Holmes? For God's sake, why on earth would you put a man through such subterfuge?"

"Re-sheath your weapon, Watson. Let us make our way to Baker Street, where I will explain the reason for my guile."

Chapter II – A Steady Aim

We headed in that familiar direction, and I worked at calming my pulse from its previously heightened state. Holmes thrived on intrigue and adventure – not so much for the emotional amplitudes, but rather for the puzzles he was invariably solving. The weather was neither chilly nor balmy, perhaps a calm akin to what a ship's captain experiences before a storm.

"Watson, I've been researching duels – their histories and the provoked state of mind of the contestants. From legends, such as Hercules versus Antaeus and Achilles versus Hector, to dead poets, such as Pushkin, unfortunate statesmen, such as Hamilton, and gamblers, such as the one felled by Wild Bill Hickock in 1865. Provoked honour does strange things to a man's sensibilities. While out and about in this disguise, I was conferring with an acquaintance when I saw your approach, and decided to try an experiment. The lady was willing to play along. I hope that you'll forgive me. Your measured response was most unusual, and a tribute to your character as a gentleman."

Having returned to metabolic normality, I responded. "To what end, Holmes? Such idiocy has virtually vanished from Great Britain."

"Vanished from the public's view, but bring forth a slight, contested affections of a damsel, common misconceptions regarding honour, or lust for revenge, and you have the ready-laid foundation for a duel. All that's needed are lethal weapons, compliant witnesses, and ground to provide equal footing. I've been wrestling with the mental machinations of the aggrieved and their foils, so pardon my previous play-acting. I commend your calm while being challenged. We may have laid the practice publicly to rest, but the Slavs, those from hot-blooded countries, and certain rustic segments of the Americas have been reluctant to let go of this deadly tradition."

I nodded in agreement, uncertain of the conversation's direction.

"What do you know of the traditions of dueling, Watson?"

"Like most, I've read Alexander Dumas' accounts of his brash musketeer, D'Artagnan . . . . Of course, there's David and Goliath in the *Book of Samuel*. In short, relatively little, I confess."

"I've been reading a concise treatise, *The Code of Honor or Principals and Seconds in Duelling*, written by the late John Lyde Wilson and published in 1858. Wilson served as governor of South Carolina and as an officer of the American courts. He ardently advocates that an individual has a right, no different than a nation, to correct material grievances with martial force. He draws analogy from nature and cites self-preservation as paramount, no different than a rosebush fighting off a noxious weed or a tree being choked by a vine. He heralds '*uniform urbanity of manners*', and holds a skeptical opinion of '*Christian forbearance*'. Composure, coupled with force, I believe, is the formula which Wilson envisions fending off the evils of anarchy and savagery."

"All well and good if one has a steady aim and can fire with alacrity, I suppose," I responded.

Holmes turned to me and his facial features, though not stern, bore the look of a man seriously weighing his thoughts and measuring his words.

"Two qualities, Watson, which notable gunsmiths, such as Wogdon and Barton, sought in the manufacture of their weapons! Curved stocks and use of bronze at the muzzle ends were believed to enhance balance. Dueling pistols could include 'set' or 'hair' triggers, which, when cocked forward, had a trigger pull of two pounds, rather than ten or twelve."

"Barbaric," I replied.

"Not completely. Pistols were often designed without rifling or sights to lower their accuracy and increase the chance of opponents missing their intended targets."

"Poor insurance upon which to bet one's life," I retorted.

"Governor Wilson argues that the fatal consequences of a duel provide a check and balance. Its spectre, especially for those who spuriously accuse others, are ill-tempered or habitually uncivil, inspires men to better self-governance. A stern truce, of sorts, with the more beastly aspects of mankind being domesticated by the threat of force for the overall benefit of overall society."

I could see the recognizable Georgian terraces of Baker Street as we rounded a corner. In front of Holmes's door, I observed a black, enameled brougham with red piping. Its sides eerily reflected the last light of the day, as a flat, glassy lake might reflect the moon. Two broad-shouldered horses were hitched to the front and the driver sat at attention. His top hat and black frock accentuated an already tall stature.

Holmes let one of the bays smell his hand and patted its neck. A brass plate of heraldry glinted from the animal's hitch: A thin cross with arms of nearly equal lengths, rounded ends, dotted with a single bird in the center of each of its four quadrants. He looked up at the driver, poised with a buggy whip.

"You've been here awhile, I deduce, by the temperature of this horse," Holmes offered. "Your passenger must have a keen desire to converse with me."

As Holmes spoke, one of the brougham's doors opened and a well-dressed gentleman who reminded me of a fox promptly exited the carriage. He had a triangular, pale face with a neatly groomed mustache, short beard, small nose, concave cheeks, and trimmed head of grey hair which he promptly covered with a shiny top hat. He wore a dark cravat, black full-length coat, charcoal vest adorned with a gold watch chain, and two-tone weaved leather shoes. Facing us, I could see that he was neither of heavy build nor light. Though he was of medium height, his assured bearing portrayed him as a man who was accustomed to giving instructions and having them followed. His eyes, though partially concealed by the hat brim and the dusk which befell us, glistened with a sharp alertness.

Extending his hand, Holmes greeted the gentleman, "*Cruce spes mea.*"

The handshake which occurred after the pronouncement was reactive, and the man was momentarily taken aback. "Not many know our family motto, Mr. Holmes," he replied with an American Southern accent.

"'*My hope is in the Cross*' would be the rough translation, would it not, Mr. Byrd?" Holmes asked rhetorically, then touched an index finger to his own temple. "One of your illustrious family's feudal seats is in Cheshire."

"True, Mr. Holmes. Home to Little Moreton Hall no less . . . ."

Holmes motioned to the door in front of us. "Your letter outlining your son's predicament gave me a head start into your family's history – and more to the point, the practice of dueling in general. Why don't we retreat to the privacy of my flat and we can discuss your quandary further, shall we?"

Chapter III –The Prodigal

We removed our topcoats and Holmes lit two additional gas lamps, bringing a warm light into the room. He produced a small Bavarian wood box with protruding wooden claws at each corner. Its top was adorned with a handle made of two stylized birds. The container's front had a metal locking mechanism with a small key. Lifting the lid, Holmes unveiled four neat rows of previously concealed cigars which he presented first to our visitor and then to me. We each took one from the humidor. I pressed a box of matches onto Mr. Byrd. After he had lit his cigar to his satisfaction, he passed the matches back to me and I followed suit. Holmes dug a briar pipe into a Persian slipper, filled the bowl, and then pushed the mound down firmly with his thumb. Holding the pipe upside down over a gaslight for a couple of seconds, he extracted it deftly and puffed until a mushroom of blue clouds obscured his noble profile.

"Before we discuss your prodigal son, Mr. Byrd, do you prefer Jamaican or Barbadian rum?"

"I would be equally blessed by either," the man responded, as he looked about the flat, including phials in their holders, a brass microscope, patterned burgundy wallpaper, stacks of books, and my etching of Chinese Gordon wearing a fez which still hung upon the wall. Though he did his best to remain composed, certain quick movements of his head and arms revealed an inner agitation.

"I presume, then, that you're aware of the recent articles regarding Richard . . . ." the guest mused.

"Reading about crimes and misadventures in the papers is an admitted pastime of mine," Holmes responded. "The story of the wayward son usually draws the reader's sympathy to the abject state and contrition of the spendthrift, but it is as much a lesson regarding a father's unconditional forgiveness. And, I suppose my sentiments also go to the steadfast brother, who must scratch his head in bewilderment as he witnesses his father forget the transgressions of his wayward sibling. Even if the good son bridles his jealousy, he must at least be allowed a strong measure of bemusement."

"Holmes, my rebellious boy has been a trial ever since his mother decided to leave with him and the midwife shortly after his birth. Her family lived in Texas and were involved in a well-run cattle and timber operation. Her grandfather had participated in the Westward migration and fought in the Battle of San Jacinto. He made his money running a country store – no easy feat in that rough-and-tumble part of the world. I met him before he passed and he declared that he owed his modest success to three principles: One, he was never more than arm's length from a fully loaded revolver. Two, though he priced his goods fairly, he refused to extend credit to patrons, many of whom were transients. And three, he spoke Spanish fluently, treating all cash-carrying customers with equality.

"He took his profits and bought land, which one needs in some quantity there to raise livestock, given the harshness of the terrain. I have great fondness for the memories of our conversations and respect him for his hardscrabble industry. His first two children died at an early age, so he spoiled my former wife when she was growing up – with fancy dresses, perfumes, fine horses, and costly jewelry. Unfortunately, his young princess grew up to be delightfully endowed, but also demanding and spoiled. I was too smitten by her beauty to notice her flaws during our initial courtship."

Mr. Byrd sipped his rum with poise, set the glass on a table, and pulled gently at one of his cuffs, straightening wrinkles in his sleeve. I was struck by the Southerner's civility and, while compatriots of mine would prejudice their appraisal of this man's intellect because of his drawl, it was clear to me that this would be in error. Though I had never met him before,

I knew of the family: One of the most landed, and an avid exporter. Here was a man who, despite his successes, remarked on the accomplishments of others rather than his own. He struck me as a person of depth, and the impeccable polish of his shoes was but one reflection of his attention to detail.

"My former wife's beauty was only eclipsed by her pride," he continued. "Heredity, as you know, is still the calling card in much of our society, no matter which continent, and though she was married to me, I speculate in hindsight that she found it difficult to achieve the social preeminence for which she strove because of her family's humble beginnings. She felt tolerated rather than venerated by the aristocracy."

The gentleman took a sip from his tumbler and discreetly cleared his throat. "I was abroad for an extended time on business when the boy was born. (Our family's enterprises are chiefly in Virginia, but textile manufacturing and an importing business draw me to spend time in England as well.) It was only after her flight that I was able to negotiate Richard's return with a governess in exchange for an annual stipend of some significance to his mother. By then, the boy was two, and, I'm afraid, imprinted with his mother's impetuousness. Oddly, in his late teens, I found that there were months when he would apply himself with zealous industry and quiet diligence, and other periods where he would exhibit an amoral disdain and maddening sloth. It was as if once he built upon his successes, some inner force would possess him. Richard would become his worst saboteur and tear the edifice down.

"Over the years, I've had to bail him out of numerous scrapes with the law, and the gravity of each offense seems to increase. First, he broke a chambermaid's broach. Then, he broke a classmate's nose. Later, he racked up gambling debts. Confounding to me, of course, are the instances when Richard's moral compass pivots from debauchery to prudence, such as helping a neighbor retrieve an errant horse or assisting a driver repair a wheel. It is as if he harbours two distinct minds."

"Watson, what do you think? I've read of the work of Dr. Emil Kraepelin and mental deformities, but this seems more under your purview than mine."

"Premature dementia, Holmes? I would need to examine the subject. It does remind one of our Scotsman's novella, *Dr. Jekyll and Mr. Hyde*, doesn't it? Did your son suffer a head trauma of any kind in his youth?"

"Not of which I'm aware, Doctor. Now, to the matter of his current predicament . . . My son is a seductively handsome lad and, when it suits him, he can charm and cajole, especially when it comes to the affections of affluent and, more unfortunately, married women. In this instance, his aptitudes and appetites have put him at odds with a particularly jealous husband, Sir James Thaddich, formerly of the Royal Engineers. Sir James was awarded the Victoria Cross in the defence of Rorke's Drift and is a marksman with few parallels. I've heard him described as righteous at best and a dangerously inflexible at worst. Thaddich's wife enjoys an age significantly younger than her husband's. Her naturally pale skin, ample bosom, love of occasional spirits, and impressionable demeanor attracts harmless flirtations. But Richard progressed beyond flattery and found himself entangled. My son was challenged to a duel and fled for a period. He apparently has gained newfound courage and has solicited Thaddich to name a time and place. Richard cares nothing for a second, or a surgeon, which brings me to meet in desperation with the both of you."

The distraught father distractedly smoothed his pant legs. Holmes eyed him and then turned his attention to me. "What say you, Doctor?"

"Well, at close range, if either opponent strikes center mass, the wound will damage internal organs. If he doesn't perish immediately, sepsis will condemn him shortly thereafter."

"A grim predicament, Mr. Byrd. No persuading your son to offer his *mea culpa* to the offended party?"

"I've tried, Mr. Holmes, but I'm afraid Richard has made up his mind – unless, by some miracle, you and Dr. Watson can persuade him otherwise. While I would never tender this sentiment regarding military duty, when it comes to a petty squabble such as this, I'm not too proud to say that I would prefer to be the father of an enduring chicken rather than a departed lion."

"Well, Watson, will you assist me in this deadly game of honour?" Holmes asked.

"It appears the occasion necessitates it," I responded with reluctance, as I knew that dueling would fall under homicide laws.

Mr. Byrd stood and faced us squarely with his shoulders back.

"Gentlemen, I am much obliged," he said. "I will notify Richard that Mr. Holmes will serve as his second and, you, Dr. Watson as his surgeon." He firmly shook Holmes's hand, and then mine. "Knowing that you two will be at Richard's side provides me a small sense of relief." He presented the shadow of a smile and took leave.

Chapter IV – Whitechapel

A few days later, I had agreed to meet Holmes in Whitechapel, made famous by its gruesome prostitute murders. No self-respecting Londoner enjoys descending into the seedier parts of the East End, which teems with gamblers, harlots, thugs, grifters, and murderers. I imagined Hippocrates looking down at me with disdain from his lofty cloud for I had, as a medical man, sworn his "do no harm" oath. I left my revolver at home, but my martial training did inspire me to pack a stout but compact lead-tipped cosh for my defence. The baton's handle was constructed of black rattan, and the weighted ends were held with sewn leather: A wrist strap helped prevent losing the weapon while in combat. Holmes had mastered a variety of fighting styles which lent confidence for excursions such as these. I, however, lacked his finesse. I leveraged my elementary boxing skills with an implement against the possibility that we found ourselves outnumbered. What would a surgeon be without his tools? I wondered. Adding to the cosh's personal appeal was that it was an arbitrary gift from Holmes, who had seized it during a fight with an Irish sailor. As the proverb advises, "*Hope for the best, but prepare for the worst*."

I stood under a sign front which read "*Hickinbotham*", next to a boarding house with rooms for rent by the hour. The stalwart British constitution is built upon withstanding the odors of horse urine, manure, basement cesspools, and the stink of coal fires and the Thames, but, in poorer districts where the cleaning of streets occurs with less frequency, the difference is noticeable. I was grateful for a slight dampness in the air which distracted one from the stench. A cacophony of sounds increased my uneasiness: Wheels slogging through the mud, shopkeepers' dogs barking, wagon drivers yelling at pedestrians to stand clear of their way. I moved against the building's brick wall to prevent getting surprised from behind by a pickpocket – or worse. While I did my best to look nonchalant and blend in, my washed face and matched clothing gave me away as someone who didn't belong. I hung a frown on my face to ward off solicitations or confrontations. Nonetheless, a tall, agile gentleman wearing a working man's cap, with a hawk-like nose, grey eyes, and thin face appeared before me. After a momentary lapse, I quickly realized that it was Holmes, looking more akin to a laborer than a detective.

"Watson, you look as if you're steadying yourself for an ambush," Holmes said, patting me on the shoulder.

"I suppose I am," I answered truthfully.

"I've been researching the haunts of our wayward Master Richard. Shall we get a glass in hopes of learning more?" he asked, smiling slightly. He pointed to a pub a half-block down on our same side of the street. On the thick front window frames, "*Wines, Ports, and Sherries*" had been painted in large black letters. Higher up, under a row of cubed wooden filigree, a sign read, "*Bonder of Foreign Wines*".

A group of men stood outside wearing caps and bowlers, staring at us. They had either stepped out to get some air, or perhaps more likely, had exhausted their meager grubstakes, despite its being late morning. They ranged in age from twenty to sixty, but looked uniformly haggard.

We entered one of the main doors and a small bell hanging from the inside handle announced our entrance. As my eyes adjusted to the darkened room, I could see rows of empty wine bottles lining the walls, each a small trophy to time which had been squandered. The gas lamps were turned low. A bartender in a black smock hunched behind a long cherrywood buttress. He absentmindedly wiped a glass with a white towel, squinted in our direction, and then turned his attention briefly to another figure who sat by himself at a cloth-less table. Holmes walked to the bar, scooped up a couple of worn leather dice cups, and walked over to the lone patron.

"Best of three for a round?" Holmes asked cheerily.

"Not fair if I have to pay for both of you," the man turned to us and answered. His voice was course-grit sandpaper being run over a piece of timber. His eyes were rheumy, and he had the broken nose and abused ears of a boxer. His hands were disproportionately large, the joints gnarled and swollen.

"I'll even the stakes. If I lose, I'll pay for two," Holmes responded, placing the cups on the table.

They shook for three rounds and it was clear from the calls that Holmes was going to be underwriting the man's next two drinks.

"You're a cocky one, Mister."

"Sherlock Holmes and Dr. John Watson," Holmes responded, lifting his arm to signal the bartender. "Quiet this morning."

"Still early," the man replied.

"Not much passes by you, I imagine, Mr. Barkley." Holmes said.

"How do you know my name, Mr. Sherlock?"

"You trained with Jem Mace, as I recall."

"He wasn't in his prime and I was much younger – and smugger – then."

"Speaking of smug, may I ask you if you know a Richard Byrd? He's got himself in a bit of trouble and I've been asked to be of some assistance."

"Always being bailed out by his father, that one . . . ." Mr. Barkley responded, rubbing his chin distractedly.

"What's he like? Dr. Watson and I would appreciate your measure of him."

"Brash loud-mouth, I'd say. Waves his arms about to make his point. I popped him in the gut once to shut him up."

"A hot-head?" Holmes asked.

"Like a coal furnace. He can barely contain himself. He's going to cross the wrong man and wind up in a country ditch."

The bartender stood sullenly at our table, as if he resented leaving his post at the bar. He listed forward, like someone with the wind to his back.

The old boxer held up two curled fingers. “Two of the usual for me, George, on this chap here.”

“Watson? What elixir for you this fine morning?”

“Tea for me.”

Holmes looked up at the bartender and said, “I’ll have whatever Barkley’s having. If it’s good enough for him, it’s good enough for me!”

The bartender shuffled off. The light filtering through the window slats changed slightly, igniting dust motes which flecked in the air with tiny pinpoints.

“How does Richard Byrd dress? Is he casual or formal?” Holmes asked.

Barkley took a nip from his drink and set the glass in front of him. Though he appeared hulking, there was a priestly reverence to the manner in which he studied his beverage.

“Like a fool dandy, I’d say,” he replied, clipping his sentence with scorn. “He always looked like he was ready to attend the King’s Ball. Shiny shoes. Waltzed rather than walked. Soft hands of someone unaccustomed to work. Held his arm behind his back as if he thought he was much more important than the rest of us.”

“Any accent or odd manner of speech?” Holmes asked.

“Not that I could tell,” Barkley replied. “He sounded like one of us,”

The bartender returned with our drinks. There was no cream for my tea, but I offered no comment or complaint.

Barkley looked up after a few moments more of chat and turned to Holmes. “If you see that scoundrel, tell him he owes me money. Worse dice player than you, Mister.”

Holmes tipped back his glass, stood, and we shook the man’s hand. “Heck of a left hook against Renwright,” Holmes said. Barkley weaved a bit in his seat and delivered a mock blow to the empty air in front of him.

“I’d set them up with a cross beforehand,” he said to us with a smile. “It’s always the punch that they don’t see that knocks ‘em out.”

We exited the front doors into the grey light. A woman with an ashen-faced child sat on the sidewalk against the building. I could see scraps of paper and playbills on the cobbled street. While police never came to this part of town except in force, and though it was peppered with shouts and the clip of horses’ hooves, the district exuded an odd tranquility at this time of day. I was mesmerized as if in front of a cobra. The pace hadn’t changed, but I had acclimated to the surroundings.

But my calmness fled to alarm as we stepped through a narrow alley. A group of five unsavory men abruptly walked upon us with clenched fists and stern faces. They clearly had lain in wait, and fanned into a half-circle before us. One brandished an ominous dagger approximately a half-foot in length. Though I knew Holmes could be effective and formidable in situations such as these, I wasn't looking forward to a potentially fatal encounter. The reputation of men from these parts was that they cared little for limb or life. I pulled out my lead-shot bludgeon and took a defensive stance. To my surprise the rogues' eyes widened and they turned on their heels, retreating as quickly as they had approached. I tapped my weapon against my open palm, inwardly congratulating myself at my evidently fearsome impression.

"We seemed to have given them a bit of a scare, Holmes," I said, relieved as I repacked the leather-and-blackwood cosh inside my coat. I shivered involuntarily and looked over to Holmes. It was then that I noticed he was wielding a top-lever sawn-off coach gun. The barrels had been shortened nearly to the brass shotshells. I had never seen one so compact. He slipped the weapon into a discreet holster and it disappeared under his coat, demonstrating yet again his manual dexterity in conjuring.

"Goodness," I said as we hailed a cab. "You are a man of relentless surprises,"

"I'm just glad I had no need to discharge it. Whenever I fire it, the shock sprains my wrists for a week. It does provide an introduction more effectively than a calling card in this unfriendly part of London. Those scoundrels had been eyeing us since we first stepped into the bar."

"Ten-gauge?" I asked.

"Any lower gauge is a bit unwieldy," Holmes answered with a straight face.

"Unwieldy, indeed," was all that I could muster as St. Mary Matfelon's vestry tower and steeple receded in the back window of our hansom.

Chapter V – On the Level

I traipsed up the stairs of 221b and found Holmes peering over a lighted candle, a mold of some sort, a pile of fine powder, and an array of small bottles of paints and brushes. For a man whose thoughts could be supremely focused, he also was a person comfortable with performing tasks in parallel. He reminded me of the grand-master chess player who easily engages multiple players at once. I couldn't imagine what he was up to – perhaps mimicking the royal seal of an important document.

"Watson, join me for an excursion to the countryside," he said. "We are going to meet the steward of the dueling pistols and inspect the site of the upcoming confrontation as well.

Once again, I deferred some minor duties related to my practice, which were more research-related than immediate. I could review the historical medical cases in a day or two, but I asked myself how often does a doctor become engaged in the drama of a duel? Reviewing the dueling pistols and the walking the level ground for the encounter are but two of the responsibilities of a "second", I learned through Holmes.

Holmes scrutinized me briefly. "Spat with Mrs. Watson?"

"A minor difference of opinions. What would inspire you to make such a remark?"

"The subtle wrinkle in your collar and small discoloration of an iron burn on your left cuff. Your wife's pressing your shirt wouldn't have left such abnormalities. Therefore, I surmise that you pressed it yourself. I know of no absence planned by your spouse, which you would have mentioned to me in small talk. Therefore, I deduce that she is teaching you a lesson of some sort."

"As are you, I suppose, with your indiscreet observations," I responded.

"With your grace, I would like us to stop so that you may retrieve your medical bag. There might be an interest by the parties to inspect your surgical tools. And I hope that you will bring some anesthetic for the day of potentially mortal combat."

I nodded my assent and we began our sojourn. Later exiting the train, we secured a weathered-faced driver dressed in black. He took us down several country lanes, past criss-crossed lean-to fences of the sort hunter-jumpers love to clear in pursuit of foxes. We arrived at a remote copse dappled with leopard lighting and a clearing in its centre. A charcoal-coloured phaeton with a bonnet and oversized wheels stood next to its tied horses.

I discerned two men standing beside it. The older one propped himself with a walking stick and wore gloves. He was in his late sixties, pear-shaped, and his pink-face framed by mutton-chop sideburns which draped down the sides of his jowls like lamb's ears. I presumed him to be the barrister of the court who was the pistol set's steward. Because of the risk to his profession, I've employed a pseudonym to avoid making his name known. The man's trustworthiness, according to Holmes, was without question.

The "second" was reportedly a retired cavalry officer, younger than his companion. Gaunt in stature, he wore a tightly clipped mustache and pointed beard, accenting his flat cheekbones. The man would, if necessary, step in for Sir James. The former officer displayed professional bearing but appeared civil rather than officious in comportment. Neither Sir James nor Richard Byrd deemed their presence necessary. Nor had Sir James bothered to request another surgeon, such was his level of confidence that the upcoming duel would tip easily in his favor.

"Gentlemen!" the older and more portly man with the cane exclaimed with an oddly warm resonance. "What a strange set of circumstances to facilitate our meeting, eh? Mr. Sherlock Holmes and Dr. Watson, allow me to introduce Colonel Brownfield. I'm Lord Kinyon."

We shook hands firmly all around. The colonel cleared his throat quietly and then cleared it again twice, apparently a nervous habit.

Holmes' preoccupations turned to the mottled ground. He stood on a concave spot, stepped back, and looked at his own imprints.

"I see that Sir James has been here yesterday," he said.

"Yes, that's perceptive of you, Mr. Holmes," Colonel Brownfield offered, hacking recurrently. "Have you been shadowing him? I've read of your exploits as a detective."

"I've met him in the past," Holmes responded. "Thanks to the voles and their mounds, I can see impressions in the soil which are of a size dissimilar to both you and Lord Kinyon. I just tested the dirt with my own weight. The fresh, square-toed imprints are of a taller man than the both of you, and thirteen to fourteen stones in weight, I'd estimate. The width of the strides is of someone walking briskly – one might even say with confidence. Thus, my reasonable speculation."

"Easy to understand once you explain it," Lord Kinyon said.

"Most observations are," Holmes replied. "Perhaps I might examine the weapons and you both can see what Dr. Watson plans to bring in case of a medical emergency."

Holmes removed a bone-clad pocketknife and flicked the blade open.

"I'd like to mark each round with an '*X*' after I review them to help ensure that they remain untampered-with beforehand. Are all amenable to that request?"

"I think it's reasonable," Colonel Brownfield responded.

We walked to their lightweight carriage and the barrister set a locking burlwood box on an unfolded stand. He opened the handsome display case, revealing a matched set of percussion weapons fitted between green velvet dividers, along with a brass gunpowder flask, an assortment of bullets, and other loading, casting, and cleaning paraphernalia. Holmes surveyed the weapons, pointing out their hair-trigger and the absence of gunsights. Then, after ensuring they were unloaded, he held each up independently and inspected the barrels.

"No rifling – at least that's visible," Holmes reported. "As I would expect."

"Dr. Watson, perhaps you can show these gentlemen your surgical kit while I mark each of these rounds with a small '*X*'"

"Certainly, Holmes."

I walked to our coach, removed my medical bag, and returned. From the satchel, I removed the wooden box which housed my surgical set. It included a small bone saw, an array of high-grade steel knives, and a pair of sharp clippers. I had purchased it second-hand, but it was made by Arnold and Sons and of superior quality. The expressions on the faces of the colonel and Kinyon were somber. Both men instinctively pulled their lips inward as they pondered the grim prospects of my having to use the tools. I closed the box and showed them a syringe set, stethoscope, and anesthesia phials.

Holmes handed the closed pistol case back to Lord Kinyon. "One more thing, gentlemen," he said to Brownsfield and the barrister. "Let's flip to see which of the seconds load the weapons."

Holmes showed the two men a silver trade dollar, including the heads of Britannia holding her trident and shield, and tails of the coin displaying a scrolled border and large Chinese character in its center.

"Call it in the air, Colonel," Holmes invited with a reedy enthusiasm in his voice, launching the coin into the air.

"Heads!" Brownfield responded, with his hat at his hip, as he stared closely at the rise and fall of the piece of silver.

Holmes caught the spinning coin and slapped it on the back of his hand. He slowly lifted his long fingers and showed Lord Kinyon the image.

"Tails it is," the barrister announced, putting a hand to his own chin as if studying a legal brief. "Mr. Holmes, you have the honor of loading the pistols."

"We shall return in two days unless the contestants come to their senses," Holmes said. "I'm satisfied that there is plenty of room to pace off and that the footing is equitable. The time is such that the sun should be directly overhead, so neither man will have an advantage."

Holmes turned to the two men. "Lord Kinyon and Colonel Brownsfield, with your grace, we take your leave."

"Of course, of course, Mr. Holmes," the flush-faced Lord Kinyon responded. The colonel somberly saluted us both and clearing his throat like a muffled bullfrog. Holmes tipped his hat and I reflexively saluted back.

Chapter VI – A Stranger at the Window

Upon our return to London, rather than stopping at Holmes's flat, we proceeded to the Byrd estate. From the exterior, the home was unimposing, despite its gothic architecture. It appeared pressed onto the lot. The masonry was predominantly rows of earth-coloured bricks. Every six feet or so, the monotony of the pattern was broken with a band of burgundy blocks. The woodwork of the window frames and gables was painted in white, and thin spires rose from the end peaks of its roof. The subtle scent of herbs at the side entrance drew my attention to a large, well-groomed rosemary bush. The discreet door was marked with the family's heraldry of a thin cross with arms of nearly equal lengths, rounded ends, and surrounded by a single bird in each of its four quadrants, similar to the Byrd coach. A small porch screened the entrance to protect it from the elements and insects. Mr. Byrd, rather than a butler, greeted us and beckoned that we should enter as he held open the door. His eyes appeared sunken and weary from the strain of his son's poor choices.

Once we entered, I took in the wood panels which were a warm honey colour. A large painting of a pastoral scene ornamented one of the walls and a large-paned, double-hung window allowed light from the garden to fall upon the detailed parquet floor. In the main salon, a fire blazed and faced a sizeable carpet with a pattern of large diamonds. On each side of the hearth, utensils with decorative cut-outs in their scoops served as sentries. A silver frame propped prominently on the mantel housed a black-and-white photograph of a man in his twenties wearing a cocked hat, a self-assured grin, and a flower in his lapel. Behind the framed photograph of the bright-eyed youth, etchings with hand-painted Egyptian hieroglyphs of dog-headed deities and other half-human and half-animal dominated the decorations across a plastered wall.

"The boy's mother hated them," Mr. Byrd stated when he noticed my curiosity about the exotic art.

"I recognize *Sefkhet-Abwy* by the animal skin she wears," Holmes said.

"The goddess of scribes," our host replied.

"Perhaps she can be of assistance when you write of our adventures, Watson," Holmes jibed.

"I hope your retelling of this one has a suitable ending, given that my son's life is at stake," Mr. Byrd re-joined. "Please, gentlemen, have a seat while I pour you a cup of tea."

"You live without many domestics?" I asked after thanking our host.

"Dr. Watson, it's said that those great at amassing fortunes aren't always good at spending them. I suffer from this vice. To pay someone to wash a dish which I could easily wash myself seems nonsensical."

"I've yet to meet your son, but from your photograph of him on the mantel, I can see how he could get in trouble with the fairer sex," Holmes said as we followed our host's instruction and sat on upholstered chairs which were decorated with vines and pastel flowers.

"The lothario's moved in and is staying with me at present," he said as he served us. "We've spoken very little. He's been uncharacteristically subdued."

"As one would expect with the Sword of Damocles hanging over his head," I said.

"May we survey the room in which he's staying?" Holmes asked.

"Normally, I would guard my son's privacy," Mr. Byrd answered, "but under these troubling circumstances, I will honor your request."

"I don't need to touch or move any of the contents, Mr. Byrd, so you needn't feel compromised."

We walked down a narrow, high-ceilinged hallway, and up a set of servant's steps to an Arabesque, spade-shaped bedroom door. Mr. Byrd knocked sharply and receiving no response, pushed down on the bronze handle.

One at a time, we entered the dim, medium-size room. Dark wood beams ruled a plaster ceiling. Light from narrow, opaque leaded windows outlined each of us with an ethereal, ghostly aura. Mr. Byrd struck a match and lit a kerosene lantern wick, giving a brief sensation of sulphur and fuel to our nostrils. A set of clothes neatly lined the closet, and toiletries sat in organized rank upon the dresser. A bed was located against an opposing wall. Its gray and blue wool blankets were squared precisely. Wine-red cased pillows had been placed equidistant from the bed's sides. Rustic scenes of what appeared to be Herefordshire farms in gilded frames from the panels captivated my eyes. A recessed bookcase stowed a myriad of leather-bound classics. A volume on Cassini had been pulled from a shelf and lay open on an Italianate secretary with spindled legs and stenciled floral paintings.

A sharp click at a partially open window alerted us, and Holmes raised an index finger to his lips, motioning for us to stay quiet. Another click against the window sounded as if a pebble had struck the glass. Someone was trying to summon Richard Byrd from below. We remained motionless. Then, we heard a man whispering up to the room's window in strange foreign language. Holmes opened the window slightly and it could be heard with more clarity. Whoever it was attempted to project his voice without alerting other members of the household. I failed to recognize the odd dialect.

Mr. Byrd and I stood behind Holmes as he pushed open the window. We could see an intruder below covering his face with a cape.

Mr. Byrd, provoked by someone trespassing on his grounds, and yelled, "What ho! Who's there?"

The dark figure spun quickly and zig-zagged his way through the garden foliage. In an instant, he had disappeared.

"Are we going down to see if any prints have been left below?" I inquired.

"No, Watson. I have a good idea as to whom the visitor was. I've been pursuing a particular theory, and my suspicions are proving correct."

I wasn't surprised that Holmes was making progress, but I felt the whole matter was progressing to a less than agreeable conclusion. Instead, all I could envision was a culmination with the death of Richard Byrd should he show himself at the appointed hour. I also had some misgiving as to what consequences might befall Holmes and myself for our complicity in this affair.

We exited the room and retraced our steps, following Mr. Byrd to the main door, through which we had originally entered.

"Will you be joining us in the outskirts of London day after tomorrow?" I asked the gentleman.

"Though my son may be a petulant fool who has managed to entangle himself in an impossible predicament, he is my offspring. I have no interest in watching him shot down, Doctor. He faces a renowned marksman, and unless Mr. Holmes can engender a solution, I'm afraid that his doom is sealed."

"I'm not a purveyor of false hopes, Mr. Byrd, but I believe that this much anticipated event will end favorably for your son."

"Let us hope so, Mr. Holmes. At noon, I will be on my knees at the Temple Church requesting divine intervention."

We left Mr. Byrd's home and, on the ride back to Baker Street, Holmes seemed to be in a calculating but light-hearted mood.

"Well, Watson," he said, "our actions may not be judged 'divine' when we're finished, but I do anticipate them being effective."

Chapter VII – The Report of Duelists' Pistols

A low cloud cover draped London as I greeted Holmes in the early morning cold with my medical bag. I felt an abundance of misgivings but kept them private. Holmes, to the contrary, appeared fresh-faced, shaven, and determined. He had donned a country cloak and woolen scarf. His grey eyes made a quick assessment of our surroundings and we set off towards the train station, and then to the copse we had visited days prior. I looked out the railcar window along the way and observed an icy light piercing the leaves. The chill on my clothes seemed to linger. The stress of the impending duel and the cool temperature agitated my old war wound, bringing a dull, persistent pain to the forefront of my consciousness. I hoped that Richard Byrd would be so lucky, and that he should see additional days, even with such discomfort. But probable death was the unforgiving consequence of his youthful recklessness.

We arrived early and I set my case at the base of a nearby tree. A dark brougham arrived after we finished a breakfast cigar, and soon thereafter, another carriage followed, which I recognized as Byrd's. The drivers pulled their carriages up some distance from each other's and from ours. The hues of the trees changed slowly with the rising sun, the greys becoming greener. For some reason, I noticed birds chirping, though I'm certain they had been stirring earlier. Before the passengers exited, Holmes leaned to me.

"Watson, I'm afraid that I'm going to ask for your assistance in restraining Master Byrd when I instruct you."

"Well, if it means averting a death, then of course I'll oblige you."

"And, no matter how harrowing things seem to get for me, there's no need for you to step forward. Do you understand?" Holmes asked rhetorically.

I nodded my assent and hoped that I wouldn't regret it later. I recognized Lord Kinyon, who looked like a pin from a bowling green, but for his fluffy grey sideburns. He carried the pistol case and used a cane to steady himself. The thin Colonel Brownfield with his pointed beard followed. Another stout man in his late forties with squared shoulders, a forceful jaw, pugnacious nose, and somber, brass-buttoned clothing and square-toed boots marched behind them as if he was using the other men to flush quarry. I surmised him to be, by his military bearing, Sir James Thaddich, the wronged husband and keen marksman who had instigated this duel.

"Mr. Holmes and Dr. Watson," Lord Kinyon stated, extending his hand. Colonel Brownfield followed suit and we waited for an introduction to Sir James.

"Well, let's get along with it," Sir James said perfunctorily, skipping any pleasantries and tightening his lips over his teeth with a grimace. He removed his coat and handed it to Mr. Brownfield, as one might a butler. The duelist's shoulders jutted from his vest, giving him an ursine appearance.

"Sir James, would you like to inspect the field?" Holmes asked.

"That won't be necessary," he responded. "I can see it plainly from here."

From the Byrd carriage emerged a handsome, beardless young man in his early twenties, approximately five-feet eight-inches in height and of medium build. He walked towards us with purpose and absent of hurry, wearing a grave expression. He wore a student's coat, white shirt, raised collar, black cravat, grey pants, and cap-toed Oxford boots. I recognized his triangular face and large dark eyes from the photograph on the mantel. He walked toward us, looking more like a boy than an adult. Richard Byrd had arrived to face his fate.

"Good morning, Master Byrd," said Holmes. "It is my greatest regret that I haven't had an opportunity to urge you in person to reassess your decision to enter this folly. Did you receive the letter which I wrote you, urging you to reconsider?"

"Yes, Mr. Holmes," the young man replied evenly. "I received your letter and appreciate your efforts. But we are a proud family, with strong bonds."

"Very well. As your father undoubtedly informed you, I'm your second, and Dr. Watson is willing to serve as your surgeon. And, this is Sir James Thaddich," Holmes proffered, turning instead to Colonel Brownfield.

The young man shook our hands firmly. He turned to Sir James' second and acknowledged him with a nod. I stood close, awaiting Holmes's signal.

"Mr. Holmes," Colonel Brownfield responded, "perhaps this occasion has arrested some of your faculties. I'm Colonel Brownfield, as Mr. Byrd certainly knows."

Richard Byrd had turned his attention to the grassy interior area inside the grove and seemed to pay slight heed to our conversation.

"Fifty feet distance satisfactory?" Holmes asked the young man.

"Twenty paces will be fine," Byrd responded, absentmindedly.

Sir Kinyon presented the pistol case in front of us. "Mr. Holmes, you won the toss, so please load the pistols."

"As you wish," the detective replied. Holmes showed two of the bullets to Kinyon and Brownfield. "My '*X*'s' are still present, so all is in order," Holmes said, stepping back from the neatly arranged weapons.

Holmes then looked briefly at Richard Byrd's scuffed Oxfords and said, "I see that you're casting about a six-inch shadow, which would put the angle of the sun tangent, or six inches over five feet eight inches." Holmes clapped his hands and finished, "We'll be starting shortly."

"You've identified opposite over adjacent, or 'tangent', correctly, Mr. Holmes," the young man commented, "but, it's five-feet eight-inches over six inches . . . ."

"Seize this imposter, Watson!" Holmes shouted. Byrd was taken aback by Holmes's outburst.

I quickly put the young man in a chokehold. When he attempted to free my restraint, I applied pressure to his Adam's apple. He thrashed about a bit more, and then realized that I had the advantage of weight and leverage.

"What's the meaning of this?" the fledgling duelist managed to gasp.

Holmes looked at me, the young man and then turned to the three others nearby. "This isn't Richard Byrd, but his twin, Gabriel, who was raised primarily in America. Richard can't keep count of his losses in a card game, according to Barkley at the bar, but his brother reads the works of astronomers and mathematicians. Gabriel also understands the principles of trigonometry."

"How did you know?" Gabriel Byrd replied, his head slumped in dejection.

"Myriad reasons, but with your present confession, you are clearly ineligible for this combat."

"This is one scrape from which I can no longer help my brother escape," said the young man quietly. "He's morally frail, but we share both flesh and blood."

"That may well be true," interjected Sir James with baritone officiousness. "But I have been wronged, and am entitled to a duel to defend my honour!" He shook his fist for emphasis.

"Very well, Sir James," Holmes answered. "I've committed myself to be second and I shall stand forward on behalf of Richard."

"So be it, Mr. Holmes," the burly man responded. "Though this is highly irregular, I accept your substitution."

Lord Kinyon still held the burled pistol case, propping himself up with his walking stick. "Well, gentlemen, this is most confounding, but under the circumstances, I imagine, since the parties seem to agree, that we can proceed. Colonel Brownfield, will you help me open this case so that these two men can pick their pistols?"

"*These are the times*," an author on the other side of an ocean wrote, "*that try men's souls*." I deliberated with great remorse my promise to Holmes. I continued to restrain the young man at Holmes's request. The fight in him had subsided, but I kept my arm around his throat in case he changed his mind. Still, I felt an inner torment which would be difficult to articulate. Every fibre in my body wanted to stop the altercation. Holmes's steely expression of sheer calm checked my emotions. I knew his skill with a pistol was impressive, but Sir James, with his downturned lips, clenched teeth, and furrowed brow, was not a man not to be underestimated.

Holmes removed his jacket. He wore a dark green paisley shirt under a brown vest. It appeared absurdly informal under the circumstances, but I knew Holmes rarely acted without reason. I realized that in the mottled light of the copse, it acted as an effective camouflage.

"Would you or your second like to select your pistol first, Sir James?" Holmes asked.

The former officer extended an open hand to the pistol case, inviting Holmes to choose first. Holmes deftly removed a firearm and Thaddich did the same. Colonel Brownfield escorted both men to the center of the grove's clearing. The duelists turned their backs to each other. My body temperature had risen, and I brushed perspiration from my eyes with the back of my free hand. I could feel Gabriel Byrd inhaling and exhaling with alarm. I felt a morbid sense of helplessness as I watched the scene unfold in front of me.

"Gentlemen!" Lord Kinyon announced, his voice reverberating. "Proceed twenty paces each, turn, face each other, and on my signal, fire!"

My senses grew more acute. I watched the two proceed through their paces. I could hear the protests of leaves beneath the soles of their feet, and other sounds interstitial: My breathing and that of my restrained charge. Brownfield's intermittent throat-clearing and various birds, and a haunting breeze through the foliage. I stood motionless, and in my strained state, I imagined the ticking of my pocket watch in my vest, each second hovering like a deadly spider. The clarity of these horrific moments reminded me of when I was thrown from a horse as a boy: I knew that I had become dislodged from the saddle, but during my trajectory time seemed to slow, as if I'd been suspended in an ethereal gel, trapped in some heretofore unknown dimension. *Should I yell?* I wondered now. *What benefit would that be, and would such a futile gesture distract Holmes?*

Such were my thoughts when I heard Lord Kinyon bellow, "Fire!" followed in near tandem by the report of the duelists' pistols and the dramatic sight of orange-red sparks and clouds of smoke blasting from their barrels. I released Gabriel Byrd, instinctively grabbed my surgical bag and moved forward, watching the two clouds of smoke began to dissipate. One of the men was screaming on his knees, holding his hands to his forehead. He dropped to the ground and began writhing, cursing loudly. I ascertained that it was Sir James. Brownfield also was approaching the injured man. In the corner of my eye, I could see Holmes standing motionless and erect, appearing taller than his six feet. Under the circumstances, the chiaroscuro of his outline appeared heroic, near mythical.

"Are you hurt, Holmes?" I yelled.

"In one piece, Watson!" I heard him reply.

Thaddich's second, Brownfield, reached his felled companion first and bent over him. "I've been shot in the head!" the wounded man barked.

"Brownfield! Move so I may examine the man!" I yelled, strong-arming the thin man from my path.

Thaddich's eyes were wild and wide, the pupils enlarged and his face reddened. He breathed rapidly, and his hands and forehead were covered with blood. I dressed the wound with antiseptic and pressed a clean cotton cloth firmly against the man's skull. He yelled but accepted my assistance. I checked the back of his head with my free hand. No bullet had exited. I then examined the bullet's entry on his forehead. To my surprise, the skin exhibited a surface perforation, but the bone hadn't been breached. At first, I thought perhaps the bullet had grazed him, but the mark was just above his eyes, upon the center of his forehead rather than across his scalp.

"Sir James, you appear to have been graced with an extraordinarily thick skull!" I said in amazement.

I could see the four men surrounding me as I knelt and recognized one as Holmes. Their figures partially blotted out the overhead sun.

"Or graced by a bullet I constructed of sand and wax," Holmes said perfunctorily.

"You rogue!" Sir James bellowed at the detective.

"Irregular, indeed!" Colonel Brownfield remarked, his voice dripping with indignation.

When Holmes had urged me to refrain from interrupting the duel earlier, I realized that he had orchestrated the outcome far in advance.

"Gentlemen, I'm happy to report this matter to Inspector Lestrade of Scotland Yard, should you wish. Why don't we chalk all of this up to an invigorating experience? Lord Kinyon, you wish to see your reputation marred? But for a probable scar, Sir James, you will live to see another day, and honour has been satisfied by the exchange of shots."

"Colonel Brownfield, take off your coat and place it beneath his head won't you?" I instructed.

Sir James' second followed my instruction. The wounded man laid down fully. I pulled a small flask of brandy and administered it to his lips. I stayed with him for a few minutes until his breathing evened off and was marked by regular intervals.

Holmes and I escorted Master Byrd, packed our things, and took to our respective carriages. We left the slender Colonel Brownfield and pudgy Lord Kinyon standing over Sir James' hulk as he rested upon the leaves in an uneasy peace.

Chapter VIII – A Secret Language

A day later at the Baker Street flat, after a light supper, I sat in a comfortable chair with a cigar and waited for Holmes to unravel details from this odd and exhilarating adventure. Dull pangs in my shoulder from my old war wound were a reminder that restraining Gabriel Byrd during the duel had a price which I was currently paying.

"Please enlighten me. Twins? My gracious. I guess that's an old ruse. I dimly remember some Gnostics even attributing the miracle of Christ's resurrection to a twin. But, your revelation isn't one easily apparent to me. What gave you to suspect that there were two Byrd brothers, working in concert?"

Holmes took a pair of tongs and carefully lit his briar pipe with a hot coal. He flicked the glowing ember back into the hearth and rehung the tarnished brass tool. I watched him puff until he was cloaked in a healthy halo of pungent smoke. He placed one of his elbows on the mantel and nonchalantly began his explanation.

"Quite simple, Watson. The behavior of the young Byrd staying at his father's home mismatched everything I had heard prior. Barkley the boxer described Richard as a hot-head dandy who was poor with numbers. Yet, at the father's house, we find a young man curious about Italian astronomers and of measured, organized countenance. What would cause such a marked difference in behavior? I began to suspect that the boy's mother gave birth to more than a single child when the father was absent. One stayed to be raised by her and the other child was returned to be raised by the father. As they grew older, they surreptitiously would change households with the father being none the wiser. The mother continued to receive a substantial stipend from her former spouse and enjoyed the company of her young sons, though not at the same time."

"And you tested the brother at the grove, I take it?"

"Indeed! And, in multiple ways. Firstly, he made no correction of my reversing Brownfield and Thaddich's names. Secondly, the young man quickly calculated the conversion of feet into paces, as well as catching my trigonometry error. Third, unlike his dandy brother, his shoes were un-shined and scuffed. Fourthly, his gait was measured as opposed to his brother's, described by Barkley as waltz-like. Finally, when the boy spoke, he was nearly inanimate, despite Richard Byrd's reputation for showmanship."

"You were sure of your conclusions."

"Watson, it was the *idioglossia* we overheard at the Byrd estate which convinced me. I had just read an article on the topic which appeared in the North-West London Clinical Society's *The Clinical Journal*."

"Please feel welcome to remind me what this involves, if you would?" I asked, trying my best to avoid underscoring my ignorance about a medical matter.

"After the stones were thrown at the bedroom window, we overheard a language which you deduced as foreign. Though the sample was brief, I knew it to have no connection to any languages which I have studied over the years. A *secret language*, Watson. Usually spoken amongst very few people – along the lines of the baby talk a nursemaid may engage in with a toddler. Or, Watson, in this instance, *twins*. Both were in Britain because of Richard's predicament."

"And your calm during the duel? Due to your substitution of the *faux* waxen bullets for the real ones. Your marking them with an '*X*' was just a theatrical distraction, I take it."

"Now, you've managed to injury my sensibilities," he winked. "I thought that you would attribute it to my confidence in my shooting skills."

"Well," I replied, "that was an excellent shot. I take it you didn't aim for the torso, the surer shot, because you knew that both of you were using *faux* bullets. You still could have put out one of his eyes. Wax bullet or not, Sir James didn't appear pleased."

"I abhor dueling. And, unlike Hamilton, I wasn't going to fire in the air and be a target for my opponent. While Sir James has been tricked out of revenge for his dishonor, the use of wax bullets spared his life. I would hope that he's learned there are other ways to settle a dispute, no matter how grievous."

"He did seem chastened," I nodded.

Holmes drew a puff from his pipe and exhaled slowly. "To your point about my aim. True, Watson, I took more liberty and sport in drawing my bead than if it had been real lead. As for Thaddich's wound, dueling isn't without its dangers. I did draw a bit of blood, didn't I?" Holmes replied, part of his lip moving into a subtle smile.

"I have further questions. How did you know you would win the coin toss? If the Colonel had loaded the pistols, he would have noticed the fake bullet's lighter weight and their softness."

Holmes dug into his pocket and placed his fist in front of me. "Watson, I see that you will allow this magician no peace unless I answer your riddle."

He opened his hand to display three coins and passed them to me. I turned them over in my palm. One exhibited heads on both sides, another tails, and still the other, both heads and tails on its obverse. I returned them after my brief inspection.

"I see, as usual, you were prepared for all contingencies."

"Ideally. Most make the mistake of using a double-headed trick coin for the flip. I flip the real coin and quickly replace it before the coin is caught. It takes speed and practice."

"I'm still surprised by one thing. Thaddich was reported to be an excellent marksman, and yet, you remained unscathed."

Holmes raised his eyebrow and removed his smoking jacket. He rolled up his cuff and showed me a black and blue welt on his bicep the size of a small saucer.

"It wasn't a killing blow, Watson, but it stung like the dickens. When it struck, I wanted to curse with some bit of passion!" Holmes rolled down his sleeve and slipped back into his jacket.

Placing a hand upon my shoulder as if for dramatic emphasis, he confided with a quiet voice, "But Watson, I just couldn't give Thaddich the satisfaction."

When the Prince First Dined at the Diogenes Club

by Sean M. Wright

A Tale Inspired by Chef Joseph Schmidt

From the Journals of Mycroft Holmes

I might be starting this tale end-first, but the warmed-over roast beef was exceptional. Not that I had anticipated dining on warmed-over roast beef at midnight, mind you.

Best you draw up a chair while I explain.

A lowering sky threatened rain that late Friday afternoon in October in the Year of Grace, 1890. The chill made for a brisk walk to Pall Mall and the Diogenes Club.

A new chef had been installed in the club the day before, but my introduction to his cuisine had been delayed by a singularly obtuse functionary in the Exchequer unable to comprehend how a half-penny rise in the tax on French claret would affect the price of American cotton. The Congress would feel compelled to raise the rate of an already highly protectionist tariff, a move the Commons sought to prevent.

Having been thus foiled the day before, today I was all the more keen to sample the newly-retained chef's fare.

Two months earlier, having mentioned the club's need for a chef, my indefatigable secretary, Sylvanus Griffin, began making enquiries. Before long he brought word of Yosep Schmidt's dissatisfaction with the Habsburg princeling employing him.

"My wife's brother's friend had a letter from his cousin, Bessie," Griffin soon informed me. "She is employed as a chambermaid at the country estate of the royal family of Luxembourg.

"Grand Duke William is devastated, Bessie wrote, having overheard the chamberlain lamenting his failure to lure Herr Schmidt into the Duke's employ. To grace the ducal kitchens in Luxembourg, the chamberlain sobbed, Herr Schmidt would have been offered his weight in gold. Vehemently refusing the offer, Herr Schmidt made known his desire to find a berth far from the interminable intrigues of the Viennese court."

"Yes, Herr Schmidt refused the Grand Duke, having had his fill of personal backbiting and political backstabbing. With this in mind," I continued, jotting down a final entry in my journal, "the Committee assured him that he would have a free hand in the kitchen. This condition, coupled to his being informed of the club's rule of absolute silence, decided him. The Grand Duke never had a chance."

"It's understandable, sir," Griffin replied. "Since the fall of Louis Napoleon, the Luxembourg House of Orange-Nassau outdoes the Habsburgs when it comes to palace conspiracies." Glancing up from the file he added, "Did you hear, sir, how Jules Grévy had become involved for a brief time, hoping to entice Herr Schmidt to Paris?"

"Working for the president of the ferociously anticlerical French government?" I chuckled. "Impossible, Griffin. Herr Schmidt is a Servo-Austrian and, from all accounts, robustly Roman Catholic. His appointment might have touched off a constitutional crisis. You know how prickly French diplomats have become since the *Boulanger* catastrophe last year." [1]

I paused, staring at nothing particularly.

"Yosep Schmidt is but thirty years of age, Griffin. Yet, employed by the President of France, it could be conjectured that he might cause the downfall of the Third Republic.

"With all these intrigues circling around Herr Schmidt, the Committee acted with the utmost circumspection. Should Luxembourg's Grand Duke William III realize how his nose had been tweaked by a private club in London and complain to Wilhelm, the new Kaiser, or to Franz Josef, the old Emperor, a chill would descend on British relations with both Germany and Austria-Hungary. It would never do for Herr Schmidt to begin his career at the Diogenes by plunging the British Empire into a state of animosity with Central and Eastern Europe.

"Behold the power of the man!" I exclaimed, laying down my pen. "And he's not even a Bonaparte."

Griffin allowed himself a smile.

"The word from the chef at Old King Lud's," he remarked, now at my desk gathering a few stray letters for the last post, "is that young Schmidt's *canard à l'orange* is second to none."

"Thank you, Griffin, but I believe I'm up to something more substantial than fowl this evening. Duck tomorrow, eh?"

Now, strolling to Pall Mall from Whitehall, I became aware that my appetite, so carefully cultivated all the day, had fled. Most unusual.

Entering the Diogenes Club, I ensconced myself in the reading room as the dinner hour approached. I settled my bulk more deeply into the soft leather armchair and ordered a medicinal whisky poured over a slice of lemon. As if to underscore the distress I felt at my loss of appetite, the late newspapers were devoid of any stories of interest.

Members arrived, dined, and took their leave – more than a few with a scowl, I observed. Surely this was not indicative of the cuisine. Were the attendants at fault? Perhaps an ill-closed window was creating a draft.

Club members residing outside London left early to reach home before the storm broke. The lingering few, such as myself, were those living close by. Not a trace of conversation transpired among us, of course. To this day, silence in the club remains a paramount concern.

I struck a match. Perhaps a good cigar would settle my system. Within a few minutes its fine aroma decided me that my judgment was sound.

Discreetly peeking 'round the barren newspaper, I saw no more than a dozen members remaining. We were a peculiar sort, but then, the Diogenes Club had been established for such as we: Misanthropes and recluses, the antisocial, nonsocial, and unsocial, who yet enjoy an atmosphere of quiet lassitude, accompanied by first-rate meals, fine liquor, and a good smoke.

Some members were painfully shy, like Brookhurst the scholar. Cox of the wandering eye sympathized with the Irish rebels. Kipinger Lowry was quite another sort – a hard-headed Scot, he was an *attaché* of no little competence in the Foreign Office. Capable of immense charm, he nonetheless had his peculiarities. Sylvanus Griffin, ever alert to special moments in the lives of office personnel, brought Lowry to my notice the week before. He'd taken time off this Friday morning to be married. Returning from Gretna Green, his young bride in tow, the tall Scot left her at home. [2] Settled in the barrel chair opposite, Lowry was reading a magazine as if he had not another blessed thing to do. With cigar and port at hand, he left his bride to her own devices while taking his ease in the Diogenes.

The clock struck ten. The number of diners thinned. Eleven o'clock sounded. And, just before the first quarter sounded, the rain began rapping on the windowpanes and my appetite returned. The chef was on call until midnight I reflected cheerfully. Finally, I would discover the culinary artistry of Yosep Schmidt.

At precisely this juncture His Royal Highness, Albert Edward, Prince of Wales, noisily, and quite unexpectedly, materialized in the club's entry, accompanied by three cronies of the Marlborough set. It became clear that it was somebody's birthday. Albert Edward and his companions, clearly in a celebratory mood, were looking for a late supper.

"You should see the Temperancers," one of the Prince's friends loudly proclaimed to no one in particular. "They've fanned out across the city. Been marchin' all evenin', beatin' drums and shakin' tambourines. They've been frightnin' one publican after another into signing pledges to shut up early. Bunch o'Grapes and the Raspberry Mitre closed their doors promptly at nine, and others a' been followin' suit."

The silence shattered, outraged members slammed down their newspapers and stared fiercely at the speaker. With respectful speed, attendants materialized, escorting the royal party into the now-vacant dining room, sliding the heavy oaken doors shut before the raucousness caused further disturbance.

The aforementioned three members, with myself, were members of the Committee. At my signal we hastily repaired to the cloakroom to consider a course of action. Whispering feverishly, we first of all unanimously refused to relax the rule forbidding speech outside the Stranger's Room, the tradition being so long established.

Lowry confessed to being at a loss. Cox furiously stroked at his long, scraggly hair. After a time, Brookhurst hesitantly moved that we dub the dining room a Stranger's Room for the duration of the Prince's visit. Speech being allowed in the Stranger's Room, the rule enforcing silence would suffer no breach. Cox lost no time seconding the Solomonic proposal. The motion passed without objection.

In the dining room, I announced the decision to our visitors. Created a member some years earlier, the Prince protested good-naturedly, demanding he be silenced like any other member. His friends chortled.

Kipinger Lowry drew on his Scottish eloquence. "Your Royal Highness, it was properly moved, seconded, and voted by competent authority that it would be utterly monstrous – indeed, a churlish slight – were we to silence the heir to the throne of mighty England within – ah – this room.

"Monstrous," repeated Cox, jabbing Brookhurst in the ribs.

"Oh, yes," the round, little man added timorously. "Utterly churlish."

"The dining room is now a temporary adjunct to the Stranger's Room," Lowry continued. "There is no more to be said," he concluded, sweeping his hand with graceful inclusivity. "Your Highness." He nodded to the Prince. "Gentlemen." He nodded to the others. "Please continue your conversation."

"Hear, hear!" one of the Prince's friends cried out blearily while another applauded, "Hey, Bertie, that's a bit o'all right, ain't it?" The third companion simply sat, smiling blissfully. At the time, I was unsure about the Prince, but the others were most certainly the worse for whisky.

"Gentlemen, my thanks," the Prince smiled, winking at our clearly contrived decision, "Now, temperance marchers be damned. From Balmoral to Berlin, the news has spread. Yosep Schmidt is *chef de cuisine* at the Diogenes Club. I would take supper nowhere else this evening. It is my friend's birthday and this is my gift. And, may I add, in the face of so powerful a protestation of loyalty, I would be remiss not to invite you gentlemen to join our repast."

A satisfied Lowry drew up a chair while Cox took his seat with unaccustomed aplomb. Brookhurst's pudgy face positively beamed. I was grateful that we had avoided a *contretemps*.

The unanticipated appearance of royalty seeking a meal a mere forty minutes before service ended might have daunted a lesser man, especially a chef in possession of his kitchen for but a second day. This was my first instance of finding in Yosep Schmidt a man who refused to retreat from a challenge.

Advised of the Prince's desire to sup, Herr Schmidt swept into the room, clad in white, his toque worn as grandly as a monarch wears a crown. Waving the attendants aside with an imperious gesture, it was as an equal that Yosep Schmidt, *chef de cuisine,* made a courtly bow to Albert Edward, Prince of Wales, and asked his pleasure.

"Your fame precedes you, Herr Schmidt," his always gracious Highness replied. "Aware of the lateness of the hour, I put my friends' palettes in your capable hands. Whatever you have at hand, be it mutton or grouse, pork or roast beef, such will do for Wales and his friends tonight."

"Roast beef!" The first of the Prince's companions exclaimed. He rose to sing: "*Oh, the roast beef of old England, and all the old English roast beef!*" He fell back into his chair, winded. His arms thrown behind him, he resembled a deflated bagpipe

The refrain ended, Herr Schmidt stated determinedly, "It is Friday, Your Royal Highness. I am a Catholic – whether mutton or beef, grouse or pork, I serve no flesh meat tonight."

This speech explained the frowns of the early evening.

"Well, hang it, man," the Prince responded genially, "I'm not a Roman!"

"Such is not my fault, Your Highness. That you must take up with your ancestor, *le Roi* Henri."

Before the incipient dispute could advance I interposed, "Herr Schmidt, the prohibition regarding the eating of flesh meat on Friday ends at midnight, I believe."

"That is true, sir."

"Until that time, Herr Schmidt," I replied, purposefully consulting my watch, "might we partake of other fare?"

The chef's eyes brightened. His thick, dark moustache bristled with delight as the problem's solution dawned. "Ah, but of course." Yosep Schmidt drew himself square. "I shall not disappoint Your Highness," he said simply. "I trust you will find the quality of my cookery fit for your celebration."

Clicking his heels he bowed again, retiring in splendor to the kitchen, a monarch in progress to his own domain.

Albert Edward nodded amiably. "A very diplomatic solution, Mr. Holmes."

There soon appeared before us a thoroughly enjoyable lobster bisque. Before the next course could be served, however, an attendant brought me a folded scrap of paper on his salver, a situation not without precedent.

"Your Highness, gentlemen, I must beg your indulgence. My brother Sherlock awaits me in the – ah – principal Stranger's Room."

"Your brother?" enquired the Prince. "Is this the Sherlock Holmes I've read about in the public prints? The indefatigable detective?"

"The same, Your Highness, The lateness of the hour suggests an urgent affair. If you and your friends will excuse me?" The Prince gave leave and I made for the steps off the entry leading to the Stranger's Room.

"Forgive the intrusion, Mycroft," Sherlock drawled with seeming unconcern as I entered. Aware of his moods, I knew his outward calm masked an inner agitation. Having doffed his hat and gloves, his walking stick leaning against an end-table, my brother had not removed his dark, heavy ulster. It was evident that he had been pacing the room, a whisky-and-soda already in hand.

"I understand you're entertaining royalty," he continued. "I regret the interruption, but my problem is particularly vexatious."

Voices singing "The Roast Beef of England" wafted up the staircase.

"I'll not be missed," I remarked dryly.

Sherlock responded with a weary smile. "You'll have a devil of a time explaining the situation to the Committee."

"A select sub-committee made the dining room a temporary Stranger's Room for the duration of the Prince's stay. That decision will have to satisfy the others. Now, Sherlock, how may I be of assistance?"

He sat in his rain-spattered overcoat as I took the armchair opposite. He leaned forward, about to lay out the details of the case, when a clatter of footsteps was heard on the staircase and the Prince of Wales entered, a bottle of Scotch whisky and two glasses in hand. He quickly gestured for us to remain seated.

"Do pardon my intrusion, gentlemen." He set down the glasses and bottle, drawing up a wing chair. "I've left the others to enjoy their meal, instructing the attendants to continue serving, and that I would return presently."

I introduced my brother. The Prince took his hand and shook it vigorously.

"I've read in the newspapers, Mr. Holmes, how, by use of deductive logic, you solve cases the police cannot. I was determined to see how it's done. I surmised," the Prince added, arching his brow, "your brother left us without taking refreshment for himself. The barman told me you had a glass already, so . . . ." He held up the bottle. "May I stay?"

He presented a rather endearing sight. Save for the grey in moustache and beard, he might have been a little boy begging his parents' leave to stay up another hour. Unstopping the bottle, he poured a generous dollop into my glass, followed by a substantial libation for himself. "Well, sirs?"

"I don't believe it would betray a confidence if Your Highness sat in." Sherlock smiled. "A piece of the puzzle has escaped me. I'm hoping that my brother can help me sort it out. If not, Your Highness may have come on a fool's errand."

The Prince met my brother's gaze. "I'll take the chance. Should you find no satisfactory conclusion, you have my word to keep it to myself." He raised his glass conspiratorially. "To a satisfactory conclusion, gentlemen."

We answered his toast and all drank deeply.

"You're in time to hear me lay out the particulars, Your Highness," Sherlock began, sitting back and steepling his fingers. "I am recently arrived from the Church of St. Giles, Cripplegate. Last Sunday the rector, a Dr. Barker, set out on display part of the regalia of one of his predecessors, Lancelot Andrewes."

"Ah, one of the esteemed translators of the venerable English Bible," the Prince mused, "authorized by King James."

"Later Bishop of Winchester," Sherlock nodded. "The display consisted of a first edition of the Authorized Version, and several handwritten pages from one of the bishop's sermons, set in an extended frame under glass. Along with these were several episcopal vestments worn by Andrewes.

"Laid out on a long table in the North Chapel, [3] about three feet behind the chancel rail, were Andrewes' heavy, silver episcopal signet ring, a crosier, a pair of liturgical gloves of knit silk, a jeweled mitre and cope, along with a finely wrought, bejeweled gold pectoral cross and chain. The display was to end this coming Sunday after Evensong.

"Today, while the acolyte lit candles on either side of the altar, Dr. Barker laid out the items in the sanctuary as he had done each morning preceding the first prayers after sunrise. [4]

"My visit tonight showed that, apart from the cross and candles of the central altar, the only other features of note are the large stained glass window forming the wall behind the central altar, and an imposing dark oak chancel arch of Gothic design laid into the white plaster above. Altars in the North and South Chapels flanking the central altar have similar appointments.

"The vestry is situated behind the South Chapel. The central aisle has a series of arches and pillars on either side, terminating at the tower and choir loft. Busts of John Bunyan, Daniel Defoe, John Milton, and Oliver Cromwell sit in a recessed gallery in front of the choir loft."

"I have been to St. Giles, Cripplegate" I interposed. "I dare say you have as well, Sherlock, the parish being so close to Barts. [5]

"I attended Barts to study anatomy, not architecture, brother," Sherlock replied crisply.

"Nonetheless, I know that half the candles lit for ceremonies surrounding the prayers of Prime, Matins, Lauds, and so forth would be behind the location of this display as you described it. And, if I recall aright, in addition to the central nave, there are parallel aisles, north and south, leading to the side-chapels. The door in the rear of the north aisle fronts Fore Street. Another door, diagonal to it, heads the south aisle, opening into the parish garden across which is the rector's manse."

"Your memory serves you well, Mycroft. Following the early service, worshippers customarily leave by the north door leading to Fore Street. This morning, Dr. Barker stood there to share a smile or a few words with worshippers taking their leave, after which the rector made for his manse to breakfast.

"Crossing the transept, he glanced at the table. To his horror, the ring and pectoral cross had vanished. Standing riveted in confusion, the parish verger, Donald Paulson, stormed into the church from the garden door, dragging the acolyte, George Cartwright, by the arm. In his other hand Paulson held high the missing ring, loudly accusing the boy of attempting to steal it and the pectoral cross.

"Dr. Barker, a kindly man, was shocked, but bade the verger leave off his accusations, loath to think ill of the obviously scared, rail-thin, blonde-haired lad. Gently, he asked the boy how came he by the ring.

"'After morning prayers,' the boy told the rector. 'As I extinguished the candles, I caught sight of the ring lying on the floor of the chancel, close by the altar steps. I thought it odd, that the ring should be so far from the display, so I picked it up and slipped it into my pocket, thinking to give it to you after completing my task.'

"Returning to the vestry," Sherlock continued, "the boy hung up his robes and retrieved the ring from his pocket to present Dr. Barker. He stood in the vestry, gazing at it when Mr. Paulson entered from the rear door. Snatching the ring from his hand, Paulson grabbed the boy's arm and dragged Cartwright out of the vestry, through the garden, and into the church, accusing him of pinching the ring and pectoral cross.

"Hearing the lad's story, the rector asked if anyone had dawdled near the table. The boy had seen no one. 'And the pectoral cross?' asked Dr. Barker. Cartwright shrugged. He hadn't seen it, and had no idea it was missing until Paulson mentioned it."

Albert Edward frowned. "The lad's story seems rather thin, wouldn't you say?"

"The verger was of the same mind, Your Highness," said Sherlock. "While Dr. Barker interrogated the boy, Paulson officiously ran down the street and dashed off a telegram to Scotland Yard."

"Why would young Cartwright pocket the ring before removing his robes if he meant to return it to the rector?" the Prince mused.

"Other circumstances yet to be heard might exonerate him, Your Highness," I suggested.

"Ah, yes," replied Albert Edward, "'It is a capital mistake to theorize in advance of the evidence,' I seem recall Dr. Watson writing."

"My friend will be gratified to learn of your interest in his published accounts," Sherlock replied. "In this present difficulty, the lad explained that he had to be to work by half-past-seven. Since it was nearing seven and he takes the Underground to Regent Street, he thought it best to finish his duties, hang up his cassock and surplice, and then bring the ring to the rector who was standing at the Fore Street door. From there he could easily dash to the train. Otherwise, he'd lose time crossing back to the vestry to hang up his robes."

"Well, now," the Prince slapped his knee soundly, "the lad's plan is entirely sensible."

"Glancing 'round the church, Dr. Barker noticed the sexton. The man had entered after services and was high up a ladder leaning against the sanctuary wall adjoining the South Chapel, between the large stained glass window forming part of the wall behind the altar and the chancel arch. Since he had his back to the display, the rector had small hope that he could be of assistance. Still, at young Cartwright's urging, he bade the man, whose name is Cosgrove, to come down.

"When asked if he had seen anyone lingering near the display following services, Cosgrove rubbed his chin. He hadn't paid much attention, being intent on washing the window. He thought he saw the acolyte pass the table carrying a long candle extinguisher, an incident Cartwright readily admitted, having to extinguish the candles on that side of the sanctuary. The rector thanked him and Cosgrove returned to his duties."

The Prince's brow knitted. "The sexton's statement, while putting young Cartwright at the scene of the theft, is hardly decisive. What followed?"

"Paulson returned and demanded that the boy remain until a Scotland Yard investigator arrived. Cartwright was in some distress at his being late to work, but Paulson held firm. Dr. Barker acquiesced but took pity on the lad. Stepping across the garden to his manse, he returned with some toast and jelly on a plate with a glass of milk.

"As luck would have it, my old friend, Inspector Lestrade, was on morning detail and appeared in Cripplegate near eight-thirty."

Sherlock paused for a healthy swallow of whisky. The Prince poured another draught into his glass and then into his own, remarking, "When I was that age, I can tell you the presence of a police official would be enough for me to admit to any wrongdoing. My father was very strict with us. Honesty, integrity, the honor of the family, was everything to him."

Into the silence that befell I ventured to say, "At the age of fourteen, I was employed as a messenger for the Foreign Office. Still green about the gills, anxious not to offend, I was given some briefs and dispatches in a file one morning to deliver to the office of the Home Secretary. Turning a corner in Westminster, I grew inattentive and careened head-on into the Home Secretary and his companion. The file fell from my hands and papers flew everywhere.

"Mortified, I rushed about, gathering them, not daring to look at either man. The Secretary began a tongue-lashing but, before getting properly underway, he was rebuked by his companion. I heard a Germanic voice asking the Secretary if he had never made a mistake, adding that he should make himself useful and help pick up the papers.

"Thankful for his kind words, I glanced up to find your father, the Prince Consort himself, stooping over, lightheartedly picking up sheets of foolscap. The Home Secretary ceased his railing, saw the sense of it, and helped gather what must have been forty pages of information strewn about the hall.

"Putting the file back into shape, I glanced back and forth at the two of them, not knowing what to say. Swallowing hard, I offered the file to the Home Secretary, stammering, 'Thank you, sir. Mr. Springthorpe of the Admiralty asked me to deliver this to you, sir.'

"My remark and accompanying action took them by surprise. Your father gaped at me momentarily then burst into such hearty laughter. The Home Secretary could scarce keep from joining in. I continued presenting the file but neither took it, they were laughing so hard. I understood the humor of the situation but was too terrified to join in the merriment. I only knew that, thanks to your father, my blunder would not prove fatal to my position.

"Presently, his laughter subsiding, your father said. 'Deliver it you did, young man! You'd best get back to the Foreign Office or Mr. Springthorpe will be after you next!' He took the file and handed it to the Home Secretary. Then he playfully punched my right shoulder saying, 'I wager you'll be more careful next time you are called upon to make a delivery, eh, young man?' The memory of his graciousness is always before me when I need patience with subordinates – especially other awkward, untried youths."

The Prince swirled the Scotch in his glass. Bitterness tinged his words. "My father could be quite charming and understanding – outside the family."

Sherlock and I exchanged a glance. The life of a royal is more constrained than most people realize.

Sherlock resumed his tale. "Regarding young Cartwright: His family is not well off. His father ekes out a living in a foundry. Three of the four children hold small positions at various businesses close by. Dr. Barker told me that George Cartwright has been an acolyte at St. Giles since the age of eight, known to be devout and conscientious in his duties – the last person the rector believed would steal anything.

"He is also well-regarded at the district messenger service in Regent Street where he has been employed for five years. I've spoken to the owner, a man named Wilson. He has no information regarding young Cartwright's family, nor has he any complaints about the boy's work. Apart from this one difficulty, no one has a word to say against the boy."

"And Lestrade's impression?" I asked.

"Well, this dyspeptic fellow, Paulson, continued agitating against Cartwright, fairly dancing around the lad with accusations and remonstrations until Lestrade, quite exasperated with his antic behavior, asked the verger to keep quiet. Paulson's behavior made the inspector rather more sympathetic to the lad.

"Still, Lestrade immediately put together a clever premise, suggesting that the young acolyte had formed a rather unrealistic scheme to sneak the items out of the church, take them to a pawnbroker for ready cash to help make ends meet at home, with the boy then inventing a story about how, through some good fortune, he had come across the cash.

I shook my head. "One should never advance a theory before all the data are in hand."

"So I've heard, Mycroft," my brother remarked dryly. "Dr. Barker made another attempt to get the lad to confess, promising to take no further action if he would but return the cross. The rector allowed that young people can sometimes give in to temptation, convincing themselves that, through their sin, they might still be a source of goodness for others."

"This Dr. Barker seems actually to have read the Gospel and taken it to heart, unlike most clergymen I've had the misfortune to meet," Albert Edward said caustically.

"Yes, Your Highness. Yet Cartwright indignantly denied taking cross or ring. He became resentful that no one believed him, even turning out his pockets to show them empty."

"Did Cosgrove the sexton make a statement to the Scotland Yarder?" the Prince asked.

"Yes, but he had nothing more to add to what he told the rector, intent on his work and barely noticing the lad. For all he knew, another parishioner might have leaned over the chancel rail, absconding with the ring and pectoral cross.

"Having given his statement, the sexton asked if he might put his cleaning paraphernalia away. Lestrade gave him leave. He turned to Dr. Barker to say he found no evidence to hold Cartwright and that he should be let go."

"A question, Sherlock. Did Lestrade have the presence of mind to check Cosgrove's bucket?"

"Ah, Mycroft, I knew that detail would not get by you." Sherlock sipped his drink. "Cosgrove, a tall, lanky man with a large towel slung over his shoulder, began to gather up his equipment. Lestrade offered to carry the pail of water and sponge. The sexton demurred, saying it was no bother. Lestrade replied that, at least he could help carry the long ladder. He asked Cartwright to lend a hand on the other end, promising to take the boy to work by hansom cab and explain his tardiness as part of an investigation.

The Prince chuckled with me. "Lestrade must have thought himself quite cunning," I said. "I take it he found nothing in the bucket but dirty water?"

"Indeed. Yet a pail with dirty water would be a perfectly reasonable means of carrying both cross and ring out of the church unobserved," Sherlock agreed. "Lestrade even held the sponge while Cosgrove emptied the water into the flowerbed. Give the devil his due, Lestrade did not overlook the obvious."

"Holding the sponge is obvious?" A moment passed before he grasp the implication. "Oh, of course. The sexton, if he were guilty, might have deposited the ring and even the pectoral cross into a hole made into a large enough sponge, with no one the wiser. I'm impressed that this Inspector Lestrade was intelligent enough to think of the sponge."

"Intelligent to be sure," Sherlock agreed, "but he lacks imagination."

The Prince looked at him uncomprehending. "What do you mean?"

"A man of imagination would have felt for a deep slit even in the empty sponge while in his grasp. Finding one, he could hold the man or boy on suspicion. Lestrade did not. In compensation for imagination, Lestrade possesses a dogged determination in pursuing his quarry," Sherlock admitted. "The inspector has assigned a constable to remain on the grounds of the church to nose about, just in case the boy did not take the pectoral cross."

I shrugged. "That was, at least, constructive."

"But why did this inspector allow Cartwright to leave? No evidence implicated the sexton so, in my estimation, the lad now seems to be the only possible suspect."

"Inspector Lestrade is acting on the same theory, Your Highness," Sherlock said. "I have no doubt that he had an officer shadow Cartwright during his messenger duties. I believe that Lestrade has reasoned that Cartwright is working in league with another."

"Ah!" said the Prince. "So, having no evidence against them, the inspector brought the matter to your attention."

Sherlock smiled ruefully. "Forgive me for misleading you, Your Highness. Inspector Lestrade has not brought this case to me for consultation – although I expect to see him in this connexion before long." The thought amused him as he rummaged through his pocket for a tobacco pouch and a battered briar-root pipe which he began to fill.

"But – but if Lestrade did not bring the case to your attention," His Royal Highness stammered, "how did you get so thorough an overview of the problem? Did Dr. Barker or Mr. Paulson come round to see you?"

"The lad, this Cartwright, has consulted my brother," I said softly.

"The lad?" exclaimed the Prince.

"Who else could give so full a report?" I inquired.

As Sherlock tamped down a load of tobacco in the bowl of the pipe, I offered the Prince one of my cigars and lit it for him, his face a study.

"I've known Cartwright for some time," my brother said at last, testing the draw on his pipe. "He has acted intelligently and most diligently for me on more than one occasion. [6] Working for a messenger service allows him entry to places otherwise denied to me. People rarely pay attention to the commonplace of youngsters – or adults for that matter – in uniform. For that reason messengers, commissionaires, and the like, make excellent agents for my enterprise.

"Lestrade let Cartwright go, I believe, with the notion of setting a thief to catch a thief." Lighting his pipe, an ironic expression crossed Sherlock's features. "I would have enjoyed seeing the inspector's face upon discovering that Cartwright sped directly to Baker Street after completing his duties."

The end of his cigar glowed brightly as the Prince of Wales puffed away on it. "Very well. The sexton is exonerated," he said, "as is the lad. If they are not guilty of the theft, who is? Where is the pectoral cross, if no parishioner, nor sexton, nor acolyte has taken it? Where are we now in this matter, gentlemen?"

"Your Highness is a trifle imprecise in your summation," said Sherlock. "but you now comprehend the dilemma facing me, the reason I came to my brother. I hope he can guide me along the correct path to find the missing treasure."

The Prince turned to me. "Have you learned the answer from what your brother related?"

I regarded my cigar a moment before answering.

"I have, Your Highness."

"Well, good Lord, man! Don't leave us hanging. Who is the thief?"

"Oh, I dare say my brother already knows who the culprits are, Your Highness."

"Culprits?" Albert Edward's chin sagged, "More than one culprit?" He hastily grabbed his cigar before it fell.

"Oh yes, Your Highness. That was evident early on," said Sherlock. "The present location of the pectoral cross is all that eludes me. Only after finding it can I proceed against them. Such was my purpose for consulting my brother."

Now it was Sherlock who took the bottle of whisky to pour some out for the astonished prince. By now I, too, was in need of refreshing my drink, after which I sat back in the armchair.

"The sexton, Cosgrove, laden with his cleaning implements, is the first of our rascals," I began. "With the towel over his shoulder, sponge and pail in one hand, the ladder in the other, he entered the church from the garden door. Setting down his equipment, he opened the gate of the chancel rail. He then retrieved his load but, nearing the display table, surreptitiously cast the sponge toward it, giving him a reason to set down the ladder and bucket again. He crossed to the North Chapel to recover the sponge. At the same time he swept the display table with his towel, allowing himself the opportunity to pick up the ring and pectoral cross without creating the least bit of attention."

"But Cartwright was right there, extinguishing the candles."

"Certainly, Your Highness – but Cartwright, intent upon his task, his back to Cosgrove, would give scarce notice to the sexton on so ordinary a mission as retrieving a sponge. With Cosgrove's towel covering the objects, especially the chain dangling from the pectoral cross, no one would make the connection. A neat trick, to be sure."

"Neat, but obvious."

"Obvious, but nonetheless effective, brother."

Sherlock snorted

"A moment, gentlemen," the Prince interposed. "Supposing Cosgrove actually did drop the sponge, aside from the business with the towel, his actions, as you've described them, seem perfectly natural."

"Well, not out of the ordinary," Sherlock said, "but hardly natural. Loaded down with cleaning gear, he would more naturally call to the acolyte a few steps away to bring him the fallen sponge, saving him the bother of setting down and retrieving his load yet again. The boy, seeing the sexton so encumbered, would readily oblige."

The Prince took a long pull from his glass. "That does seem the more likely course."

I took up the narrative. "Cosgrove returned to his gear. With the towel concealing the objects, he released his grip, allowing them to drop into the water. The ring, however, fell to the stone floor. He never saw it roll several feet away, not far from the altar steps on the opposite side of the chancel – exactly where Cartwright said he discovered it."

The Prince raised a peremptory forefinger. "Surely Cosgrove would have heard a heavy silver ring fall on a stone floor."

"One would think," I said. "Yet a heavy metal heavy silver ring striking the floor would produce only a soft thud.

"Not realizing that the ring was gone, Cosgrove carried his load more deeply into the sanctuary. Setting up his ladder against the south wall, he began cleaning dust and soot with his sponge in order to quickly blacken the water. This is when Cosgrove learned the ring was gone. It is also where he gave himself away."

I turned to my brother. "Sherlock, you said that Cosgrove told Dr. Barker he was cleaning the stained glass windows."

"Yes, indeed, Mycroft. Cartwright mentioned it twice."

"My dear Sherlock, the stained glass in St. Giles, Cripplegate dates to the thirteenth century. A properly instructed sexton would never wash the window from inside the sanctuary. Since Cosgrove carried a towel, I understand the confusion."

"But why not, Mr. Holmes?"

"The staining of glass is accomplished with vitreous paint, a colored solution made with glass particles suspended in a liquid binder. Vitreous paint is applied to the exterior of the glass to face the interior of the church. When fired, the glass particles in the paint fuse into the surface on which it was painted – hence the name 'stained' glass."

"My dear Mycroft," Sherlock replied peckishly, "that's basic procedure for any artist in stained glass. There's nothing unusual about it."

"True," I answered. "The difference I allude to concerns a technique used for painting details *onto* the interior surface of the glass. Artists in better studios attain a calligraphic precision, applying the paint with specially pointed brushes.

"You see, details created in surface paint on older examples of stained glass fade greatly with repeated washing. During the fifteenth century, stained glass artists here and on the Continent developed a paint that could not be washed away. At university I had occasion to write of this phenomenon for Professor Weisberg, my instructor in medieval history.

"Properly trained sextons are aware of this distinction and would never apply soap, water, and sponge to the stained glass windows inside a church as old as St. Giles for fear of losing the details painted thereon. The exterior surface of the glass can be washed, but a sexton would only lightly dust the interior surface with a soft towel or a feather duster."

"Great Scott, Holmes!" exclaimed the Prince, "You've just convicted Cosgrove. That kind of evidence would be devastating in open court." His brow furrowed. "But who is the other culprit?"

"Why, Your Highness, the other felon is Paulson the verger," said Sherlock. "Even Cartwright, once he had had time to consider the events of the day, realized that there was something decidedly queer about the fact that Paulson accused him of stealing the pectoral cross before anyone else spoke of its disappearance.

"Paulson entered the vestry moments after the rector discovered that both ring and pectoral cross were missing. Yet when he saw the boy examining the ring alone, Paulson accused him of stealing the cross as well. He had no way of knowing both objects had been taken unless he had conspiring to steal both. I confirmed this detail with Dr. Barker and put him on alert. He has asked the constable assigned to stay on until I can discover where Cosgrove secreted the cross."

"That is the next step," I said. "You were at the church earlier today, Sherlock. Did you notice the busts?"

"Yes, Mycroft, I mentioned them earlier – Bunyan, Milton, Cromwell, and Defoe, all recent additions in the gallery below the choir loft at the far end of the nave. Cosgrove, by all accounts entered the church from the garden by the side door, not from the tower entry in the rear."

"An excellent point, Sherlock. You remind me to be more precise. You mentioned the Gothic chancel arch crafted of dark oak. Did you notice the busts in *bas relief* at either end, specifically the one closer to Cosgrove and his ladder?"

Sherlock grew agitated. "I saw no busts there. Darkness had fallen by the time I arrived. I was without a dark lantern. Damn! I should have asked the constable for his." He calmed himself. "Well, there it is."

"There it is, indeed. If I recall aright, a bust is carved into each terminus of the chancel arch. On the north side of the arch is the explorer, Martin Frobisher." I drew in some smoke from my cigar and expelled it before adding, "On the south side is a bust of the bishop, Lancelot Andrewes."

The revelation galvanized Sherlock. Rising, he swiftly collected his affects. "Of course!" he barked, pulling on a glove. "How easy is a bush supposed a bear – if only one sees the bush! [7] Lestrade's presence denied Cosgrove the use of bucket or sponge. What better place to deposit his largesse until he could again take advantage of the ladder to dust some out-of-the-way corner? If he's still in residence, that is. What a fool I've been!"

Albert Edward and I stood up. "I disagree with your assessment of your talents, Mr. Holmes, although I fear Cosgrove and Paulson know that the game is up."

Sherlock nodded, still out of humor, "I'll send a telegram to the Yard to have the boat train watched and to alert the port authorities at Dover and Plymouth."

I grasped his shoulder. "It was the darkness that hindered your investigation, Sherlock. Your deductions were sound. Tomorrow you would have seen the busts and found the cross."

"Certainly," the Prince agreed. "Come daylight you would certainly find the pectoral cross dangling from Andrewes' bust."

My brother shook his head. "Possibly. Still, the two thieves would be long gone. Besides, Cosgrove would never be so precipitate as to leave the cross dangling."

"But what more natural than to place a pectoral cross about a bishop's neck?" asked the Prince. "Did not the French investigator, Dupin, find a letter which eluded discovery because it was in plain sight?"

"Dupin." Sherlock repeated the name, his teeth on edge. "Your Highness has not considered that the chancel arch is illuminated by an entire wall of stained glass open to the eastern sky. At daybreak and for the next five hours, the gold and jewels of the pectoral cross would glisten and sparkle as stray sunbeams stream through the prismatic irregularities of the glass. In the darkness, the hiding place is ingenious. I doubt Cosgrove would overplay his hand by risking the sunlight or," he grimaced, "a consulting detective armed with a dark lantern."

"Ah, of course," said the Prince. He took my right hand followed by that of my brother. "I want to thank you, gentlemen, for a thoroughly entertaining twenty minutes. I have but one request."

Sherlock paused. "Your Highness has but to ask."

"Should I ever have need of you," said Albert Edward, "I hope you will not refuse me."

Sherlock inclined his head. "My brother and I are ever at the service of the Crown." [8]

With that he was gone.

We had missed two courses, but the Prince and I returned in time for the entrée. Our plates were heaped with mashed potatoes in which was mixed finely-sliced caramelized onions, thyme, and slivers of fresh Montrachet goat cheese *gratin*. Peas and pearl onions sat alongside piles of wafer-thin slices of warmed-over roast beef crowned with diced shallots and sliced mushrooms, cloaked by a delicate Béarnaise sauce – served two minutes past the hour of midnight. As I pointed out at the start of this memoir, it was quite delectable.

After the Prince of Wales' late night meal, a Saturday midnight tradition was born at the club and *Boeuf Royale à la Diogenes,* as it was dubbed by its creator, became one of Herr Schmidt's most popular specialities.

A few words will suffice for the epilogue.

Sherlock returned to St. Giles where, using the sexton's ladder, he astonished Dr. Barker by locating the missing pectoral cross and chain sitting on the back of the oaken ruff carved around the neck of the bust depicting Lancelot Andrewes at the southern terminus of the chancel arch.

Cosgrove and Paulson had vanished. Sherlock's telegram arrived in time for the port authorities to apprehend the two criminals in Dover before they could cross the Channel. Under their real names, Farrell and Brent, the pair were known to Scotland Yard as notorious art thieves sought by police in seven nations. Confronted by a mountain of evidence, the criminals confessed to the successful execution of over fifty thefts from museums, galleries, and churches in various cities of Europe during the past decade.

Farrell and Brent admitted to planning the Cripplegate theft for some months, ingratiating themselves into Dr. Barker's employ with forged credentials. The Lancelot Andrewes display had been suggested by Farrell in his guise as Paulson.

After further investigation, my brother broke the back of an international ring of art thieves headed by one Reggie LeBorg, an Anglo-French felon of no mean skill, headquartered in Cherbourg.

Young Cartwright was fully exonerated. Indeed, Sherlock explained to the police, that it was due to the lad's initiative that the true felons were captured. He arranged for Cartwright to receive several rewards that had been offered for the capture of Brent and Farrell.

The Prince of Wales took the opportunity to present the parish of St. Giles, Cripplegate, with a large display case for its treasures, graced by wide glass panes, and secured with a sturdy lock.

The press on both sides of the Channel heaped fresh laurels on his brow, but my brother was diffident to the adulation.

"LeBorg escaped his lair, three steps ahead of the police," he said some days later while dining with me at the Café Royal. "I doubt that he'll be captured. I find it difficult to get a firm grasp on the tentacles of Continental crime," he continued while attacking a thick, sizzling beefsteak.

"See here, Mycroft, you deduced the location of the pectoral cross. The praise rightly belongs to you."

"Nonsense, Sherlock. I serve the Crown in my own way, preferring a life of anonymity. I am well enough known to my own set. Anyone I might aid knows where to find me."

One of those places would be the Diogenes Club, where Herr Yosep Schmidt remained *chef de cuisine* for the following forty-four years. His meals were savoured thereafter in a most satisfactory silence.

And where only seafood and omelets were served for dinner on Friday evenings.

NOTES

1 – Following Prussia's victory over France (1870), a reactionary French general, Georges Marie Boulanger, advocated revenge on Germany, while revising the Constitution to allow the return of the Bourbon monarchy. After he won a seat in the Chamber of Deputies in January 1889, the government panicked. In April a warrant for his arrest was issued, citing conspiracy to commit treason. Boulanger fled to Brussels. His movement collapsed by the end of the year.

2 – From 1753, English law held that if one or both parties to a marriage were not at least twenty-one years of age, parental consent was required. This law had no force in Scotland, so eloping couples would often take the train to Gretna Green, the village closest to the border. Scottish law required only the presence of two witnesses to make a marriage valid.

3 – In these days of liturgical change and confusion, it should be pointed out that these altars were set against the wall, so the North Chapel of St. Giles would be on the left side of the altar, the South Chapel on the right as one faces them.

4 – This would have been the canonical hour of Prime in the Anglican breviary, celebrated at six o'clock. Some parishes in London make the Divine Office (now called "*The Liturgy of the Hours*") part of public worship. Evensong is a combination of Vespers and Compline, sung at nightfall.

5 – "Barts" refers to St. Bartholomew's Hospital, adjoining the Priory Church of St. Bartholomew the Great, a parish church of Smithfield, London. Rahere, jester to Henry I, was stricken by a malarial fever on pilgrimage to Rome. He vowed to God he'd build a hospital in London if he were cured. When this occurred, King Henry granted Rahere a parcel of land in Smithfield where he founded the church and hospital as an Augustinian priory in 1123, He left off jesting, joined the Augustinian order, serving as first prior until his death in 1144. Barts escaped destruction by Henry VIII and survived the Great Fire of 1666. It is one of the oldest churches in London. Rahere's tomb is in the Lady Chapel behind the main altar.

Rahere is the name of a poem by Rudyard Kipling, beginning:

> *Rahere, King Henry's Jester, feared by all the Norman Lords*
> *For his eye that pierced their bosoms, for his tongue that shamed their swords,*
> *Feed and flattered by the Churchmen – well they knew how deep he stood*
> *In dark Henry's crooked counsels – fell upon an evil mood.*

In 1881, Barts was where young Stamford took his friend, John Watson, an army doctor newly returned from a tour of duty in Afghanistan, to meet Sherlock Holmes, a rather odd student. Gazing at the plaque commemorating the event set up by the Norwegian Explorers, a scion society of the Baker Street Irregulars, has become the goal of Holmesian pilgrimages.

6 – Although he makes reference to utilizing the boy's services more than once *The Hound of the Baskervilles* is the only case in which Cartwright is seen in the employ of Sherlock Holmes, searching hotel waste baskets for the cut out pages of a newspaper, and then delivering Holmes's supplies and messages upon the moor.

7 – Sherlock's ironic remark is inspired by a speech of Theseus to Hippolyta: "*Or in the night, imagining some fear, How easy is a bush supposed a bear!*" *A Midsummer Night's Dream,* Act 5, Scene 1.

8 – Although Sherlock Holmes later refused a knighthood, he did aid the Prince, later King Edward VII, after he approached Holmes to save Violet de Merville from becoming an entry in Baron Adelbert Gruner's "lust diary", as noted in a case Dr. Watson entitled "The Adventure of the Illustrious Client", found in *The Casebook of Sherlock Holmes.*

The Sweetenbury Safe Affair
by Tim Gambrell

I am not often taken to poetic tendencies, but there is something about Hyde Park in October that forces one to consider the autumnal caresses of Mother Nature with more than the usual shade of lyricism. The variegated oranges, the greens turning to browns, dressed against a backdrop of London grey, all seen through steamy breath. I was contemplating thus when Sherlock Holmes joined me at our pre-arranged time.

"You take objection to the trees, Watson?" he said, as he appeared at my shoulder, causing me to start.

"Quite the opposite," I told him, recovering with a self-conscious laugh. I turned and shook him warmly by the hand. It hadn't struck me until that moment just how much I'd missed seeing him every day.

"I recommend you don't stand there apparently talking to them, then," Holmes replied with a gentle smirk.

We moved off, following the pathway, it being too cold a day for sitting on the benches. Holmes was clearly in high spirits.

"How long a leash has Mary permitted you today, my friend?"

I laughed. My wife was attending to some social appointments thereabouts. I had taken the opportunity to arrange to see Holmes, and it was in fact Mary's suggestion that we meet in Hyde Park and not at Baker Street, in order to simplify us coming together afterwards and sharing a cab home.

Our route led us to the shores of the Serpentine. The sound of the lapping water on such a quiet day was soothing – a far cry from the frenzied heights of summer. We smoked as we walked. I spoke of the pleasantries of married life, but I could tell that Holmes wasn't particularly interested in that subject, beyond common courtesy. This was understandable, since he'd never shown an affinity for affections of the heart. I quickly turned the conversation over to him and his cases. He energetically regaled me with details of some of his wondrous adventures overseas. It pleased me greatly that he had kept himself busy in the lonelier station to which my marriage to Mary, and my return to practicing medicine, had unfortunately left him. I cannot, however, deny the considerable pleasure I took in knowing that he hadn't replaced me in his life, or even sought to do so.

I had begun to venture the suggestion that I attend him over several days and attempt to commit these international cases to paper, when we were both distracted by a heavy splash and a considerable thrashing in the water near the opposite shore. There being no one discernible nearby to attend, except some ladies who appeared perturbed, Holmes and I immediately set off as fast as we could run around the perimeter of the lake, in the hope of being able to assist the poor victim before he drowned.

As we drew nearer, it was clear that the figure in the water was losing the struggle. I removed my overcoat, top hat, jacket and waistcoat as I ran, and cast aside my walking stick before diving in off the bank. The water was freezing cold and my muscles immediately went into spasm. I surfaced, gasping for breath, near enough to reach the floundering figure. It was an aging man. I trod water for a time as I held his head above the surface and allowed him to take the desperate breaths he needed. He was wearing a long, heavy overcoat, which seemed to be the main cause of his problems. Slowly, I managed to swim closer to the shore, where a number of stout fellows had formed a chain and were waiting with Holmes to assist us.

Water poured from the old man's coat and clothing as he was dragged up onto land. A cry from Holmes alerted me to the man's other major problem – his left leg ended above the knee. I turned immediately and, freed from the encumbrance of the old man, I swam and dived for several minutes to try to locate the missing wooden leg on the bed of the lake, but the water was too cloudy from all the thrashing, and it was entirely possible that my rescue efforts had encouraged the leg to float away and lie further afield. It became clear, after several minutes, that I was on a fruitless endeavour. I returned to the shore, apologising to Holmes for my failure.

"Good God, man!" Holmes cried as he helped me, dripping, onto land. "That can wait for another time. We must ensure neither of you die of the cold first. Here."

He directed me to the nearest bench seat, where my various discarded affairs had been gathered and left. My overcoat was immediately wrapped around me and I indicated one of the side pockets. Holmes delved in and produced my hip flask.

"Brandy," I muttered, through chattering teeth. He gave me a good swig, after which I indicated, with a nod to the one-legged man who was lying, shivering on the ground, surrounded by a crowd of onlookers. No one appeared to be showing any concern, and clearly they were only there for the spectacle and gossip. It doesn't take a cynic to realise that if the half-drowned man had appeared to be affluent, they would have been falling over themselves to assist. As it was, his clothes betrayed him as a beggar or vagrant, and so they stood back to see if he would resuscitate by his own means, or simply expire there and then.

The liquor did much to revive me. Unwilling to see anyone left to die like that in a crowd, I staggered over, venting my spleen as I did. I administered to the poor fellow, checking that he was still breathing before rolling him on to his side. After a severe bout of coughing, he seemed to be out of immediate risk, save catching a chill from being drenched on a cold day – as I was too.

Holmes appeared and caused the crowd to disperse. I hadn't acknowledged his absence until then. He brought a constable with him, and a cab. The driver was clearly not happy to take us in our sodden condition, but Holmes promised a handsome reward, and I assured the fellow that we would sit on the hard floor, not the seats. With the driver's acceptance begrudgingly given, Holmes and I carried the poor one-legged man to the cab, and I joined him on the floor. Holmes took a seat, along with my hat, jacket, stick, and waistcoat – which thankfully retained my silver pocket watch in full working order. As we trundled along, the unfortunate man and I finished what remained in my hip flask. By the time we reached Baker Street, he and I had both revived a little more.

Old habits die hard, as they say, and I think this was why it didn't even occur to me that the cab wouldn't be taking us to 221b Baker Street. It meant that I would somehow need to get a message to Mary to inform her that my circumstances had changed unexpectedly. But that could wait until a little later. First, dear Mrs. Hudson was on hand with a charitable flourish to wrap our new acquaintance and me in towels. Hot drinks and more brandy were provided, while Holmes set a raging fire in the hearth. Mrs. Hudson drew us both a hot bath, laced with fragrant decongestant oil to help clear our lungs and aid our breathing.

The one-legged beggar, for we were still unaware of the chap's name, insisted that I take the bathwater first, while he huddled by the fire. This was clearly a matter of concern to him, and I saw little point in objecting. As it was, I was quickly done, and Mrs. Hudson produced some clothes which I had either been prudent in leaving behind when I married, or careless to have overlooked. The reasoning behind the beggar's insistence was clear once he'd bathed, for the water was so murky and foul that I doubt he'd bathed for many years – and this after a good thrash around in the Serpentine. Dried, combed, shaven, and dressed in some other of my apparently unwanted clothes, his humble expression belied a certain poise and dignity with which the smarter attire blessed him. Common to many vagrants, his face was ruddy and pitted, and his eyes spoke of deep sadness. Holmes had furnished him with a crutch which had been left in a corner after an old injury.

At my gesture, the man took a seat with us before the fire where some lunch had been laid out on the occasional table. Quail, a little cold roast beef, some bread, cheese, and a lovely rich fruit cake. There was a pot of tea and another of coffee. To avoid his further inconvenience, I plated up a selection for him before looking to my own. The man ate voraciously, like one who feared his food may be stolen at any moment. I turned with my plate full to find he already had nothing left.

"More?" I asked, offering him my plate.

He nodded and took it, then looked crestfallen. "I am sorry. In this walk of life with which God has blessed me, there is never any time for the application of manners."

The man spoke with an uncommonly fine tongue. I didn't need my friend to point out that this apparent beggar was, in fact, a man of breeding. Evidently he could read the confusion on my face. He continued.

"I can see that the discrepancy between my station and my voice is not lost on you. Alas, gentlemen, I have not always been as you find me, but that is a story which need not concern us now."

"Many people fall upon hard times," said Holmes sagely. He had declined to eat.

"Indeed, they do."

I had no wish to cause the man further pain or shame, so I changed the subject. "I hope that we have been able to do enough to stop either of us from contracting a chill, at the very least."

"Thank you both, indeed, Doctor Watson, Mr. Holmes. It has been many years since I've felt as clean, warm, and comfortable as I do now. I cannot repay you for the clothes, or the hospitality."

Holmes raised an eyebrow. "You have us at a disadvantage, I perceive?"

The man inclined his head. "You are both figures of some notoriety, in all walks of life, Mr. Holmes. As, indeed, is this address."

"Speaking of walks," I said, rather needlessly indicating his stump. "I assume the missing part of your leg was wooden?"

"It was."

"I searched in the Serpentine, but was unable to locate it, I'm afraid."

The man drank the last of his tea. "Very kind of you, Doctor, but I think it became detached when I was set upon by ruffians on the shore."

"Good grief!"

"Indeed. It was they who threw me into the water afterwards – in the hope, I believe, that I would drown."

"As you surely would have done, I have no doubt, if my reckless friend here hadn't jumped in after you."

I gave Holmes a glance and a smile, in thanks for his compliment.

"Certainly, as none of the other onlookers were prepared to help," I added. "Why did the ruffians attack you?"

The man paused, clearly considering his response. "I believe they thought that I had some information from which they could take advantage. I was a close friend of someone back in my army days, and so . . . ." His voice drifted off. "Do you know Lady Sweetenbury, by any chance?"

"Only by repute," Holmes answered, steepling his fingers to his mouth.

"I knew her son. We served together."

I sat up at this. "Lady Sweetenbury doesn't have a son."

"He died in the Crimea." The man indicated his own missing leg, leaving us in no doubt as to where he obtained that injury. "I wonder if I could ask you gentlemen to pass on a message to her – if you'd be so kind? For the memory of her loving son."

Holmes inclined his head the merest fraction, which was taken as sufficient assurance by our guest.

"Please tell her simply this: '*Tonight*'."

I looked at my friend to see what he had made of such an enigmatic pronouncement.

"Tonight," he repeated, matter-of-factly.

"Yes. Tonight," the man confirmed. Then he raised himself up on his crutch. "And now, if it is not considered ill-mannered, I must be on my way. I shall head back to Hyde Park, to see if my missing leg has been left in the bushes where I was attacked."

I was struck by a sudden thought. "Are you likely to be attacked again?"

The man turned his gaze to me, ponderously. "In my walk of life, one is always vulnerable," he replied. "But specifically, with reference to today's earlier events, Doctor Watson, I sincerely hope not. That is the best I can hope for. Thank you both again for your charity. I shall never forget this, as long as I may live."

And with that, he left.

I turned to Holmes. "Did the fellow give you his name?"

Holmes shook his head. "I realised early on that he had to be a man of class and breeding fallen upon hard times. Often, they are unwilling to give their name, even to discreet persons such as ourselves – it's too strong a reminder of their fall. I asked once, while you were in the bath, but he did not respond, and I chose not to press him for it." He rose. "Are you able to accompany me to Lady Sweetenbury's, or have I already preyed too greatly upon your time?"

I couldn't help the broad smile that stretched across my face.

"I think that perhaps, on this occasion, Holmes, you'll be the one accompanying *me*! Her Ladyship happens to be a patient of mine."

"My dear Watson, of *course* she is. That much was obvious."

My spirits sank immediately. "It was?"

"Don't be disheartened, my friend. It was a simple deduction, revealed by your reaction to the news that Lady Sweetenbury had a son. You're not the type for common social gossip, so she was clearly someone with whom you had a pre-existing relationship. I'm not aware that you mix at that level socially, nor have you ever sought to. *Ergo*, it was a professional relationship and you are her physician."

I had to hand it to Holmes. I had plainly given myself away. But at least my familiarity would assist us in passing on the mysterious message. However, I needed to organise my own message first to Mary. I was sure that she wouldn't be in the least surprised to find that I had become embroiled in another mystery during what was supposed to be a purely social occasion.

A messenger was easily obtained out in the street for the price of a shilling, and very soon Holmes and I were heading off in a cab towards Mayfair. I had applied some of Mrs. Hudson's decongestant oil to my handkerchief and periodically sniffed at it to ensure my nose didn't begin to fill with catarrh. After a few such sniffs, I gathered by Holmes's reaction that the decongestant's aroma was distasteful to him.

A number of police constables greeted us upon our arrival at Lady Sweetenbury's address, and I immediately feared the worst for her Ladyship, who was of advanced years.

"Wouldn't have thought it was worth botherin' you with any of this, Mr. 'Olmes," an aging constable called after us as we strode up the steps to the front door. Holmes didn't respond. I did my best to keep at his heels. Hedges, the housekeeper, saw me from the door and raised her hands in a gesture of praise.

"Thank the Lord you're here, Doctor. There's been ever such a to-do."

I introduced Sherlock Holmes to her. She paused briefly to curtsey before continuing at pace.

"Masked ruffians it was. Broke in through the gardens at the back and caused a terrible fright."

"In broad daylight?" I was stunned.

"Indeed, sir. They attacked my Phyllis and young Gordon and knocked poor Harper unconscious."

"The butler," I informed Holmes, quickly. "What of her Ladyship?"

"Oh, mercy me for being a chatterbox. You must attend to her immediately. She heard the commotion and fainted dead away in her chamber."

I was off up the stairs without further notice. Holmes and Hedges followed on, and I could hear the housekeeper continuing to fuss and fluster to my poor friend.

"It will be the end for poor ma'am, I'm sure of it. Oh, to think it's all come to this. And what with his Lordship not yet buried two years."

I paused at the top of the stairs to allow Hedges to pass.

"Please, announce me with all haste."

She knocked quietly and opened the door. Lady Sweetenbury's maid appeared and quickly ushered me in. I found her Ladyship in bed, certainly having had a shock, but also clearly not on death's door by any means. She was well known as a formidable woman – it would take a lot to shake her to her foundations.

"Thank you for attending so quickly," she said, grasping my forearm fondly. I declined to apprise her of the misconception – fortune, on this occasion, had served us well.

I hadn't brought my bag with me, of course, but I was able to undertake a rudimentary assessment which sufficiently assured me that there was no danger to her health. She remained, as always, hale and hearty for a woman of advanced years. I prescribed a minor restorative mixture, easily prepared by the household, more for appearance's sake than anything.

"Nothing that a good rest and some quiet won't cure," I told her. She was more concerned about Harper, who had been knocked senseless in the attack. I promised her that I would attend to him next.

As Holmes wasn't waiting outside her Ladyship's chamber for me, I assumed that he was investigating the intruders. Therefore, I continued with my ministrations. I quickly located Harper, laid out in the servants' quarters, with a cold compress to his head and jaw. He was in a predictably foul mood, given what he'd been through, but also just as concerned for his mistress as she had been about him. I quickly reassured him that Lady Sweetenbury was as strong as an ox and would be back on her feet in no time. This calmed him somewhat. I diagnosed a slight concussion and a bruised jaw, prescribing for him plenty of rest, to which he stubbornly made objections. We finally reached a compromise with him accepting an early night, along with a good dinner and a tot of medicinal brandy – which he administered immediately from a hip flask, much to my amusement.

No sooner had this happened than Mrs. Hedges appeared, along with a pair of constables who began to question the poor bruised butler. I stood back, but remained, since I was also interested to learn the details of the incursion. More than once I struggled to contain my mirth as Hedges answered all of the constables' questions for Harper, including confirming his name. I have felt, at times, that Holmes was a little unfair in his assessment of the quality of the Metropolitan Police Force, but this was a witless pair and no mistake. Without a second thought they noted down the housekeeper's responses to the questions they posed to the butler, staring at his non-moving lips the whole time.

I was disappointed to find there was little to learn besides that which I'd already been told by Hedges, although I noted that it was three felons who broke in. They apparently scaled the garden wall at the rear of the property, both on the way in and then back out again once they fled. Poor Phyllis was attacked as she hung out the laundry. I also found it interesting that the three men hadn't ransacked the house, but had sought one room in particular: The bedroom of Lady Sweetenbury's long-dead son, Henry. It was still being examined, one of the constables claimed. Assuming that this was where I was most likely to find Holmes, I entreated Hedges to escort me there.

I was correct in my assumption. Holmes was standing in the middle of the room, deep in concentration. All around him was what looked to be petty devastation – broken drawers, spilt clothes, trampled knick-knacks. A maid was doing her best to tidy and bring things to order, accompanied by another of the police constables. The maid stood and curtseyed as I entered. Hedges suppressed a moan of grief at my shoulder.

"Holmes?"

He turned to us. "Ah, Watson. How is everyone? Do not worry, Mrs. Hedges, everything will be in order before we're finished. Molly, here, has been doing a sterling job and the constable is noting anything known to be missing."

"Is there much?" I asked.

"Nothing so far," he replied. "Merely damage."

"'Pon my soul," uttered the housekeeper, with a sob. "This will surely finish her Ladyship."

Holmes held up a hand. "No need to inform her of anything untoward as yet." He turned to the maid and the constable. "Thank you, Molly, my dear, but if you could leave us for now, I'll advise you when the work can continue. You too, Pitman. No doubt you could do with a tea break."

The constable gave a sniff. "I'll need to let the inspector know."

"Do," replied Holmes, brusquely. "He knows where to find me if he takes umbrage."

Hedges, Molly, and Constable Pitman left us, and I gently closed the door.

"Such wanton destruction," I said with a shake of my head.

"And all for nothing, it would seem."

"So far. They're bound to find something missing, though."

"I doubt it."

I'd worked with Holmes for years and was well aware of his brilliance, yet I couldn't help but scoff at this.

"You can't possibly know that for sure."

He fixed me with those penetrating eyes of his and wafted a hand around the room.

"Window dressing, that's all this is, Watson. Window dressing. I've studied the room at length, and I believe I've already found what the intruders" intentions were. The devastation is too thorough to be caused by anyone looking for something. It was done to distract, to deceive."

I urged him to continue.

"The maid was very forthcoming. She often came in here to dust. It seems Lord and Lady Sweetenbury had only one child – the son that the beggar mentioned. Henry. He went off to fight in the Crimea and died in action. Her Ladyship kept this room exactly as Henry left it, a shrine to his memory. And there he is, you see?"

Holmes pointed to a large portrait, hanging above the fireplace which hadn't been lit for over thirty years. Henry Sweetenbury, in full regimental regalia. It was somehow odd to find the portrait in place and untouched, when the poor deceased soldier's other affairs had been strewn all over the floor.

"It's a fine portrait. Seems a shame to have it shut away in here."

"Indeed."

"Was it disturbed at all?"

"Splendid, Watson. It was."

I noted from the back of the room how it was hanging squarely. Presumably it had been corrected by the maid.

"That was the first thing I asked when I entered," confirmed Holmes. "Neither the maid nor the constable had touched it."

"Then – ?"

"Take a close look around the edge."

I did. There was a darker fringe of wall around part of the frame towards the bottom edge of the painting. I looked at Holmes and he nodded.

"It had been hung very slightly off-centre for years." He joined me. "Help me lift it off."

We very carefully removed the painting. Behind it was a small metal safe, built into a cavity within the chimney breast. I had seen the type before, with a small circular dial in the middle of the door. Holmes tried the door. It was locked.

"This, Watson, this was what our villains were looking for." He rapped on the safe with his knuckles.

"Good job they didn't find it, then," I said.

"Oh, but they did. That's why the painting was put back incorrectly."

We replaced the painting ourselves. As we did so, I pondered what Holmes had said and tried to trace in my head some of the leaps of logic he'd made.

"They found the safe," I said, thinking aloud.

"Yes."

"And they couldn't open it."

"Yes."

"Because they didn't have the combination to release the lock."

Holmes sucked his teeth. "I suspect that they wouldn't have bothered if they didn't. But the number that they had was incorrect."

"Right. So, they put the picture back to make it look like they hadn't found the safe."

"Precisely. But they did too good a job and put it back too neatly, not how it had previously been hanging. Hence the slight fringe of darker wall."

"Then they messed up the room to make it look like an ordinary burglary."

"And arguably did too thorough a job there, too. No skilled burglar worth their salt would turn a room over as thoroughly as this."

He was right. We had seen a great number of burglaries in our time, and indeed, been on the receiving end of several. I looked for a means of escape. The sash window was unfastened and led down to the rear.

"And what, then, does all of this mean?" Holmes asked.

"They'll be back to try again, of course!" I pronounced, with some jubilation.

"Oh!" Holmes raised his hands ecstatically. "My dear Watson, how I have missed you!"

I rubbed my chin. "It still leaves one mystery."

"How they knew that the safe was here?" Holmes gave me a calculating grin. "I have a theory about that. I'd like to speak again with our one-legged beggar."

I almost slapped myself. The message for Lady Sweetenbury had completely slipped my mind in all the consternation.

"I'm not sure that's relevant anymore," Holmes muttered, as he returned to studying the portrait of Henry Sweetenbury. "I think what the fellow expected to happen tonight happened before we arrived here, instead."

There was a knock on the door. Before either of us could comment, Inspector Lestrade entered, Constable Pitman just behind him. Lestrade stared acerbically at us as we stood before the portrait.

"Admiring the artwork, gentlemen? You could have done that while my constable finished his task, surely?"

Holmes gave Lestrade his nearest approximation of a warm smile and gestured for them to enter. Constable Pitman and Molly, the maid, meekly returned to their tasks.

"Wonderful timing, Inspector, of course. Tell me, do you happen to know the whereabouts of Mrs. Hedges?"

We found the housekeeper in the kitchen, fussing over Harper and issuing a stream of concerns. At our request, she willingly joined the three of us in the drawing room, much to the obvious relief of the poor butler.

"What can I do for you, sirs?"

"The safe in Master Henry's room – " Holmes began.

"What safe?" burst Lestrade. Holmes held up a cautionary hand.

"Oh la!" said Hedges. "Has it been forced?"

"No, no," Holmes confirmed. "It's perfectly secure. But supposing the police inspector here wished to check the contents against an inventory. Could you assist him?"

"Alas, sir, I could not. The young master took the code with him to his grave."

"Really?" I found that somewhat difficult to comprehend. "Does her Ladyship not know it?"

"No, sir. His Lordship neither, when he was with us. They even had specialists in to look at it, but it was no good. Without the code, no one can unlock the safe, and the secret's long gone. Many's the evening they've lamented it."

"Are the contents of the safe known at all?" I asked.

Hedges shook her head. "The young master used to tease us all about what he'd put in there. Some says it was unrequited love letters. Others, a small fortune in jewels, a gift from Lord Sweetenbury's mother to her favourite grandson. In truth, there could be nothing."

"I see," said Holmes quietly. He nodded to himself, deep in thought.

"You can't have been housekeeper at the time of the young man's death, though, surely?" asked Lestrade.

Mrs. Hedges emitted a rather squeaky laugh, like a bicycle passing by in need of oil.

“Thank you, Inspector. No, I was but a maid here at the time. My mother, God rest her soul, was housekeeper before me. I took over from her near on twenty year ago, now.”

“Thank you, Mrs. Hedges,” said Holmes, suddenly dismissing her. “You’ve been most helpful.”

She rose, curtseyed and left.

Lestrade watched her go. “What safe is this, then, Mr. Holmes?”

“The one behind the portrait in the bedroom, of course.”

“Of course,” Lestrade said, wearily. “Anything else you’re concealing from the police, while we’re at it?”

“My good man, I’m not concealing anything. It’s all there to see, if only your constables looked properly.”

Lestrade stood. “Fine. I’ve got to get on. Once Pitman’s finished upstairs, that’s us done.”

We watched him march from the room, and then I turned to Holmes.

“What next?”

“We don’t have much time, now. We need to find our one-legged vagrant.”

“Back to Hyde Park?” The thought filled me with trepidation. This was going to be an awfully large venture for just the two of us. “Inspector Lestrade!”

It is somewhat disconcerting when one asks for a carriage to Hyde Park, only to find oneself being driven to Millbank Street instead. This was our situation at present. I had caught up with Lestrade on the stairs and hastily explained our relationship with the vagrant. I described him as best I could, also stating where we had left him and to where he claimed to be heading at the time. Holmes joined us and Lestrade was already on the move before I finished my story, barking out orders to a sergeant as to what the remaining police should do once Pitman had finished his inventory of Henry’s bedroom. When we reached the police carriage outside, the inspector immediately instructed the driver to take us to the old mortuary at Millbank Street.

“A detour?” I asked, as we trundled along.

“Actually, Doctor Watson, I have a hunch that I can save you gentlemen a lot of fruitless searching.”

The implication worried me.

Holmes cleared his throat. “Not that I don’t have a regard for your perceptiveness, Inspector – ”

“Of course not, Mr. Holmes,” Lestrade replied, drily.

“But perhaps you could explain your reasoning?”

"Just before I returned to Mayfair, I heard mention at the Yard of a one-legged beggar being found dead on Albion Street, just off the Bayswater Road."

"That is near to Hyde Park, I'll admit," I observed.

"But not firm proof of the man we're looking for," said Holmes. "There must be plenty of one-legged beggars on the streets of London."

Lestrade nodded. "But this chap was found clean and naked – or as near as, anyway, and with no crutch or obvious means of support."

"You're certain he was a beggar?"

"Face and hands, Mr. Holmes. They tell us plenty."

Holmes smiled. "A capital piece of deduction, Inspector. And why would anyone want to steal the clothes of a beggar – ?"

I finished the thought for him. "Unless they were particularly clean and of fine quality."

"Exactly, Watson."

I felt sickened to the pit of my stomach. "We thought we were doing the fellow a service. Instead we sent him back into the world under a death sentence."

"Don't upset yourself unduly, my friend," said Holmes, shaking his head. "I believe the man already had the death sentence hanging over him anyway."

Regardless, I wasn't convinced, and we finished the journey in brooding silence.

This day had really not turned out as I had expected. I'd looked forward to spending a pleasant few hours with my old friend, then to return home with Mary and attend to some overdue administrative chores at my practice. Here we were instead, nearing the end of the afternoon with daylight beginning to fade, and already a little intrigue had turned into murder.

Millbank Street was as familiar to me as many of the London hospitals – a fact which did nothing to ease my apprehension. My scented handkerchief was a boon, but the dank aroma of viscera was only part of the mortuary's charm. The ancient whitewashed walls were in need of urgent attention, and the gutters for channelling away the fluids were overdue a thorough sluicing. Very little ever seemed to shake Holmes from his focus, but I could certainly see Lestrade blanching from time to time as we made our way to the one-legged man on the slab.

Although he was hideously bruised and swollen, I could tell at a glance that this was our vagrant. Holmes agreed. The hairline, the set of the shoulders (slightly stooped), and the shape of the jaw in particular. And the same leg was missing – his right one. As Lestrade had indicated in the carriage, the skin of his face and hands readily showed the rigours of a life on the road.

The inspector grabbed the label tied to the man's only big toe. "Do you have his name?"

"He didn't give it," I said.

"That's helpful."

"Any particular cause of death?" Holmes asked.

I checked the label to see if anything had been noted. *Cranial haemorrhage*, it said. But his whole upper torso was a mass of bruises and lesions.

Lestrade tutted and shook his head. "Beaten to death with his own crutch, I'd say."

"Not with these injuries, Inspector," I said, remembering the crutch that Holmes had given the man.

"Indubitably, Watson. The crutch would have snapped and broken long before sustained injuries like this could have been inflicted. However, what if the man's wooden leg was used as a club?"

"Very probably, assuming a solid, hardwood limb." I paused as the full horror sank in. "So, either he found his missing leg, as he aimed to, or – " I couldn't go on.

"Or, the ruffians who attacked him earlier at the Serpentine actually stole his wooden leg. Either way, they used it to kill him when they found him again. After having broken into Lady Sweetenbury's house in Mayfair, of course."

"Is there anything else?" the inspector asked. He was clearly eager to leave.

"Only this." Holmes leaned forward and grabbed the dead man's left ear. We all peered closer and I felt a shiver run through Lestrade, next to me. "See it?"

There was a pink blotch covering the man's left earlobe.

"Strawberry birthmark," I noted.

"Or where you've just pinched him," Lestrade muttered.

"Not at all," I said. "This long after death, and with so much blood loss, the skin wouldn't blotch like that. Is it important, Holmes?"

"We'll see when we get back to Lady Sweetenbury's," he replied, enigmatically. "I have a hunch."

Lestrade pointed to the dead man. "So did this fellow."

"Gallows humour does not become you, Inspector," I told him, before turning on my heel and leaving. I'd had more than enough of that place.

It was fully dark when I stepped outside, although I was washed by the warm glow from the streetlamp above. Despite the heavy traffic, the air seemed like ambrosia and I gulped down breath after breath before Holmes and Lestrade finally joined me. The Inspector immediately left us and I turned to my friend.

"I'd like to go home, Holmes," I told him. "If you don't mind."

He nodded. "Of course, my dear fellow. I know how unpleasant this has become for you. Go home, see Mary – of course, with my regards. Have dinner. But I would appreciate it if you'd do me the honour of assisting me with one further aspect of this case."

Although I was feeling guilt over the savage death of the poor one-legged man, I remained eager to see justice done. I asked what else would be required of me.

Holmes was returning to Lady Sweetenbury's at Mayfair. He was convinced that the villains would make another attempt on the safe that night, and he wanted me to join him in his vigil.

"Surely that's ill-advised, though, to burgle the same place twice in one day?"

"By the same token, Watson, wouldn't it also be precisely the *best* time – when everyone else least expects it? You said yourself you expect them to try again. Besides, it's my view that these men are too eager and careless to wait, hence their earlier attempt in daylight."

I acquiesced and promised to join him as soon after dinner as I could make it.

Mary was surprised and overjoyed to see me. She had assumed, from my hasty message, that I would be gone for the remainder of the day. As it was, we spent a pleasant evening together and enjoyed a relaxing dinner before I told her that I'd promised Holmes that I'd return to assist him. I expected her to be angry at this, and the fact that I'd not warned her before, but I often underestimated Mary's perspicacity, and my guilty admission was met with a laugh, and a kiss and the full understanding of how I felt beholden to my old friend.

I changed my clothes and removed my revolver from the bottom drawer, where I kept it carefully wrapped. It had been a while since I'd held the weapon, and it took me a few minutes before I was sufficiently comfortable with it to holster it safely away under my jacket. I've never lost the apprehension of carrying a gun, although it had been put to good service on many occasions. I promised my wife that I would return home again as soon as I could, to which she assured me that she would be perfectly all right with her needlework and the maid for company. Before I knew it, I was being ushered out through my own front door and back into the bosom of the night.

I brought my medical bag to Mayfair this time, so that I could at least give Lady Sweetenbury and Harper, the butler, a further check-up upon my arrival. I was also able to examine Mrs. Hedges' daughter, young Phyllis. She had thankfully been merely handled a little roughly earlier and thrown to the ground. Apart from some superficial bruising and a little damaged pride, she was fine. Indeed, she offered to give the ruffians a taste of their own medicine should they try her again. Hedges reminded Phyllis that such behaviour was not becoming of a lady's maid and so she settled instead for promising to trip them down the stairs if the opportunity arose.

Harper was still sore and in a frosty mood, although he would shortly be retiring to take the early night which I had prescribed for him. Lady Sweetenbury had remained abed all day and had enjoyed her restorative posset so much that she'd had Hedges make up a batch for the whole household. Her Ladyship was on her third jorum by the time I attended her, and I was obliged to warn her that drinking it so late in the evening might prevent her from sleeping. She tapped the side of her nose and assured me that all was prepared. I suspected Holmes's hand in this, so I bid her goodnight and headed to Henry's chamber.

All was darkness within, so I closed the door behind me before turning and waiting for my eyes to adjust. Order had been restored as much as possible, and Henry's affairs tidied away. A shaft of moonlight through the window drew a silver line across the room.

"I have a seat for you here," hissed a disembodied voice. Holmes, of course.

I headed for the darkened corner, past the window, shaded by the wardrobe. From this vantage point we could see perfectly the door and the portrait on the chimney breast, whilst remaining hidden by the shadows. With only a few words of courtesy passing between us, we settled down to wait.

I knew not what hour it was, or if indeed I'd drifted off to sleep, but I sat bolt upright as the distant sound of breaking glass reached us from downstairs. My heartrate quickened and a thrill coursed through me, the like of which I'd not felt for some time. It must have been obvious, as Holmes placed a hand of caution on my arm. There was no further noise. I wondered, briefly, if I'd imagined it, since there was no sound of the house rousing itself.

"Hold fast, Watson," Holmes whispered. "I specifically instructed the house not to react if they heard an incursion."

"What of her Ladyship?"

"The same. She is protected."

I nodded, which I appreciate was pointless in the dark, then drew my revolver and waited.

It wasn't long – maybe a minute or so – before the bedroom door was eased open. Three shadowy figures entered, wordlessly. The last of them, briefly silhouetted by one of the electric wall lamps left alight on the landing, was brandishing a club of some kind. The door closed again. The moonlight shining through the open curtains now perfectly framed the portrait of Henry Sweetenbury on the chimney breast. The first two entrants carefully removed the painting and leaned it against the fireplace, while the third held up the club against the moonlight, as if he was trying to read it. Six whispered numbers reached us – the combination! The figure in the middle reached up and attempted to open the safe.

We watched from the shadows, barely even risking a breath. On the final turn of the dial there was an audible click, but the safe door remained resolutely closed. The middle figure tugged on it, cursed, then thumped it with his clenched fist, causing it to echo a dull chime.

"Christ, McCulloch," hissed the man holding the club. "Do that again and I'll smash you down where you stand."

"It's not working, Jackson. The code is wrong."

"Just stay calm," said the third figure. "Take your time. Go through it again."

The man with the club, Jackson, took a long look at the portrait, then hissed angrily at the others.

"We've waited thirty years for our reward. And it's there, behind that door. Now let's get this done and be out of here before someone wakes up. All right?"

"Gimme the numbers again." The middle figure, McCulloch, wiped his palms on his hips.

Jackson held up his club to the moonlight and squinted. As he whispered the digits, he was quickly interrupted by the third man.

"Five? You sure? You said it was a six, last time."

"Did I?" He seemed unsure.

"Can't we put a light on?"

"A light on? During a burglary? I'm amazed you've lived this long, Jolliffe." Jackson wiped his mouth with his hand. "Try five. It didn't open last time."

McCulloch finished his job. Again, the mechanism clicked, and again the door remained shut fast.

"He *definitely* gave us the wrong code – again!" bleated McCulloch.

Jackson virtually roared with frustration. "He *can't* have! He swore his life on it."

"He *lost* his life on it, Jackson," hissed Jolliffe. "He's had us. We can't ask him a third time."

"Now, Watson," Holmes hissed, and we both stood, stepping quickly out of the shadows to block the window. "Remain still, gentlemen," Holmes barked. "We are armed."

"Peelers!"

"How the blazes – ?" yelled Jackson, who immediately came at us, swinging his club. McCulloch and Jolliffe seemed to freeze to the spot in front of the portrait. I backed away into a chest of drawers, unable to fire a shot safely. Holmes dodged and ducked, before popping up and catching the fellow a firm punch on the nose. Undeterred, he staggered around, swinging wildly in panic and this time catching Jolliffe across the head, felling him instantly. In the momentary distraction, I dived low and managed to rugby tackle McCulloch to the floor.

"Lestrade!" yelled Holmes, and seconds later the door was flung open, the electric light was switched on, and the room instantly filled with police. They crowded around the bloodied Jackson, preventing him from swinging his club. Holmes moved in and wrestled the weapon from the ruffian's hands.

"I'll take that, thank you, Mr. Jackson."

He passed it to me as I stood up: A wooden leg, as we suspected. The three interlopers were vagrants, each around fifty years old, if I were to hazard a guess. Lestrade's men quickly had Jackson and McCulloch restrained. Jolliffe was out cold.

The inspector looked at the men with undisguised contempt.

"Scum! he spat. "Breaking and entering, criminal damage, and murder. If you see the light of day again, it'll be on the way to the gallows."

"We were only claiming our due!" Jackson retorted. He looked past Lestrade, directly at me. "We was promised a reward for helping him!"

We watched in silence as the police led them away. I heard one of the vagrants stumble on the stairs, and I wondered if young Phyllis had exacted her revenge.

We were alone. Holmes turned to me.

"Thank you, my friend. I know that was a risky endeavour, and I'd have hated to face them on my own. But I wanted to do it my way."

"As always," I replied, smiling. "I wonder what Jackson meant by *promised a reward*. And *for helping him* – helping who?"

"Lieutenant Henry Sweetenbury, of course. I suspect they assisted him, possibly saved his life, when he lost his leg."

"Lost his – ? Good grief, Holmes. How do you know that?"

He beckoned me to the portrait, still leaning against the hearth.

"Observe the face – or more specifically, the left ear."

I did. It showed a subtle, but definite strawberry birthmark on the left earlobe. It matched the one we'd seen on the one-legged corpse.

"Good God." I held my head in my hand. The vagrant I'd saved in the park was Henry, Lord Sweetenbury. No wonder he had avoided giving us his name.

"He's dead, now, isn't he?"

The voice caught us both by surprise. Lady Sweetenbury had entered the room on the arm of her maid. She turned to look back through the still open door.

"Hedges, my dear, can I leave you to arrange clearing up downstairs? Then back to bed for everyone, I think."

Hedges curtseyed, said "Yes, ma'am," and departed.

Lady Sweetenberry gave a sigh and glanced at her maid. "Off to bed with you now, too, Nancy. I will speak with these gentlemen, then retire again myself."

"But, milady – ?"

"No buts, child. My doctor is here, after all. Now, off you go."

With a curtsey, Nancy left us.

Holmes quickly brought forward one of the chairs that we'd used and assisted the lady to be seated.

"I'm so terribly sorry, your Ladyship," said Holmes. I knew that if he'd been aware that she was listening, he'd never have revealed the death in such a way.

She brushed his concerns aside. "Never mind, Mr. Holmes. The truth will out, like it or not. I think there is much you can tell me. And I suspect there is plenty that I can tell you also."

"Please," said Holmes, "tell us about your son." He sounded genuinely concerned.

Henry had been an only child. Difficulty with the birth had led Lady Sweetenbury's physician at the time to discourage her from having further children at the risk of her own life. Henry had been an attentive, studious, and loving son, but also awkward, clumsy, and accident prone. Lord Sweetenbury decreed that Henry should join the army. In his view, a military life would cure his son of these tendencies and turn him into a fitting and honourable heir. Thus, Henry purchased a Lieutenant's commission in the Buffs and immediately found himself at the siege of Sebastopol.

"A hard-bitten endeavour, by all accounts," I said during a lull in her Ladyship's story.

She nodded and continued.

"He returned, but with only one leg. He told us he'd lost it in action. Of course, I was heartbroken, but overjoyed to have my only child back safely with me. My husband also seemed to thaw in his disapproval of Henry. Walking with crutches made him much more careful and nowhere near as clumsy. To try to help with his self-confidence, we had an ornate wooden leg specially made for him – "

Her Ladyship's voice caught in her throat as she noticed the leg in question, lying at my feet. I glanced at Holmes, unsure whether to say anything or not, but after a moment she continued.

"The hope was that Henry could perhaps enjoy more mobility that way. Lord Sweetenbury was also eager to secure Henry a good marriage. We lived, somewhat secluded, for several weeks, while Henry got used to his new situation and learned to walk again.

"Then, one day, three soldiers turned up at the door. They were presented to his Lordship, who spoke with them at length, alone in the drawing room. I knew not the subject of the discussion at the time, but immediately after he had them thrown out, down the steps. When they caused a scene in the street, he went out with the footmen and thrashed the three men to within an inch of their lives. It was all incredibly distressing.

"Henry was by now aware of what was going on and came down from his room as fast as he could. When my husband saw him, he grabbed Henry and threw him out, as well, accusing him of being an imposter and trying to sully the memory of a fine young man.

"I can hear Lord Sweetenbury's words as if it was yesterday," her Ladyship said, holding back a tear. "'I have no son!' he roared. 'My son is dead!'"

"I wept for days. I begged my husband to change his mind, but he would not hear my pleas. He told the staff that the man who had returned as our son was known to be an imposter. Henry had died in the Crimea, a proud and brave lieutenant and a promising leader of men. His memory would forever be honoured.

"But I knew my son. It *was* Henry who had returned, who had been thrown out on to the street like a common beggar. I kept his room as he left it, here, as a shrine to his memory. I would look out through the drawing room window to see if he passed by, but he never did.

"We continued with our lives, as one does. I didn't know what it was about Henry, or the soldiers, that had angered Lord Sweetenbury so much, and he wouldn't tell. After a while I stopped asking.

"As you know, I'm sure, my husband died July last. On his deathbed, somewhat out of the blue, he finally confided in me about that fateful day. Henry *had* lost his leg in the Crimea, as he said when first he arrived home. But he hadn't lost it in action. He'd been overseeing some land clearance after a battle and had lost his footing on the uneven ground. It caused him to fall into an animal trap, which snapped shut around one of his legs, shattering it from the knee downwards. Three soldiers were nearby, and they rescued him, effectively saving his life. They took him back to the British camp, where his leg was quickly amputated to avoid further pain or infection. Henry had initially told the men they would be handsomely rewarded for saving his life. But later, he appeared to exhibit regret and embarrassment over the whole situation. The three soldiers quickly found themselves reassigned to a different regiment.

"The three men who had come to the house were those same three soldiers from the Crimea. They told my husband what had happened and demanded the reward which Henry had originally promised them. That's when they were thrown out. Lord Sweetenbury was angered at the soldiers, but also humiliated by the shameful way Henry's clumsiness had led to the loss of his leg. On top of that was the dishonourable way he had treated the three soldiers who had saved his life. This was too much for his Lordship at the time, which was why he threw poor Henry out and claimed him as an imposter. By the time my husband had calmed down, it was too late. Henry had gone and Lord Sweetenbury was not a man who would go back on his word, even though he knew that he was in the wrong. He carried that guilt for all those years. I looked in my heart, and I was saddened, gentlemen, to discover that truly I could not forgive him for his actions."

"A highly lamentable situation, Lady Sweetenbury," said Holmes. "Innumerable wrongs have been committed in the light of human rigidity. I completely sympathise with you."

"There is just one further thing, Mr. Holmes, and I'm getting to the last part of the story. After my husband's death, I was advised that a one-legged beggar had endeavoured to gain entry to the house, but he'd been repelled by Harper. He'd claimed to have a message for me –a warning that three men – three vagrants – were still seeking their reward. I instructed the staff that should this happen again, they must let me know, but he never came back. I know now that I missed my final chance to hold my dearest boy to my bosom once again, and tell him how sorry I was for how he'd been treated by those who loved him."

Here, Lady Sweetenbury found she could contain her grief no more and gave full vent to the pent-up anguish which she had carried with her for over thirty years. It felt to me like a token gesture, but I sat with her and held her hand, which seemed to help. As the tears gradually subsided, Holmes took the floor.

"The story you have related and the confidences you have revealed to us, Lady Sweetenbury, have proven invaluable. I believe now that I can fill in some of the gaps leading up to tonight, if you would care for me to expound?"

She nodded and he continued.

"I suspect that what the three soldiers got up to in the intervening years between your husband tossing them out on the street and them encountering your son once again in the vagrants' community in Hyde Park is largely immaterial. Without a doubt, the three men detained tonight are those same three soldiers. I suspect that they walked a different path to Henry until recently. If the four of them had stayed together for all those years, it's likely that further attempts would have been made on the house, or frustration would have come to the fore and they would have done for your son a long time ago.

"I doubt Henry ever went far. You may not have seen him, but I'm confident that he will have seen you often but kept himself hidden as best he could. His hands and face showed only too clearly that he'd lived the hard life of an itinerant beggar here in London. That will be how he knew of his father's death, and why he attempted an approach.

"Somehow, though, Henry met with Jackson, McCulloch, and Jolliffe, within the community of London vagrants – and relatively recently, too. Clearly, despite Henry's circumstances, something convinced the three ex-soldiers that they could still get their promised reward. And that's where this fascinating article comes into play."

Here Holmes hefted the wooden leg into his arms.

"There's an intricate design etched into its surface. It covers much of the veneered surface, but it appears to be unfinished. I assume, then, that this was an endeavour to which Henry applied himself from time to time over the years." He approached me and held out the false limb. "This area here is particularly interesting, Watson, don't you think?"

I looked. It appeared to be a series of interlocking geometric shapes. I ventured as much.

Holmes nodded. "Ii is, yes. But then again, if you hold the limb thusly," he rotated it and held it to my leg, as if I was wearing it. "See?"

Suddenly the seemingly random shapes took on an order and formed a clear image. The whole design was an optical illusion. "It's a plan, isn't it? Or a map."

"A plan of this very house, in fact. Including the location of the safe."

It was obvious once I knew. And a careless word here or there would no doubt have been enough to give it away. Next to the diagram, six numbers had been inelegantly scratched into the veneer with the tip of a blade. These were the ones that Jackson had read out earlier. I couldn't tell if there was a five or a six either, just as Jackson had been confused.

"So," I said. "The three soldiers, down on their luck, had bumped into Henry living out on the street. They found out that his leg showed a map of this house, and Henry's safe, with the promise of riches therein."

"Exactly. When it became clear that Henry wouldn't be a party to burgling his own family home, they attacked him in Hyde Park, stole his leg, forced him to give them the code to unlock the safe (which turned out to be wrong), and then threw him in the Serpentine. And that was where we came in. We rescued him, cleaned him up, and sent him back out in smart clothes, with a crutch. Meanwhile the three men had broken in here, found the code to be incorrect, and got out again before we arrived to warn the house. They located Henry easily enough in his new garb. They threatened, or more likely tortured, another code from him which he'll have promised them was the truth on his life. Then, either through frustration or simply being unable to hold back anymore, they set about Henry with his wooden leg and beat him to death."

Lady Sweetenbury gave a sigh.

"What about his clothes?" I asked.

"Almost certainly removed later by other street dwellers. The three soldiers wouldn't be careless enough to obviously parade what they'd done."

"And what of the safe? Perhaps he'd legitimately forgotten the code after all those years?"

"Ah yes, these numbers scratched into the leg. Lady Sweetenbury, you claim that no one except Henry knew the code to open the safe."

"That's right, Mr. Holmes," she replied. "He had it installed himself. It was built specially, and he set the code."

"Well, we know that these numbers don't work, either with a five or a six. But I can guarantee that the correct code is on that wooden leg, somewhere."

I looked it over but could see nothing.

Holmes pointed to a small mark near the ankle. "What's that?"

I looked more closely. There was a design and a serial number beneath it.

"Manufacturer's mark," I said. "Such things are common."

"On a bespoke wooden leg? This isn't an off-the-shelf item, Watson. That's supposed to *look* like a manufacturer's mark, but if you read me the serial number, I think you'll find it's six digits long and we'll see what happens."

The print was very small, and Holmes leant me his magnifying glass.

"*Two, seven, nine, one, three, five*," I read, before placing the leg on the floor.

Holmes carefully adjusted the dial on the front of the safe. There was another click and this time the small metal door swung open. We both peered up to look.

The safe was empty.

My stomach felt hollow. "After all that."

Holmes closed the safe again and we carefully hung the portrait back on the chimney breast. As we turned, we found Lady Sweetenbury cradling the wooden leg, like a baby.

"My boy. My beautiful darling boy . . . ."

"Come," said Holmes. "I think it's time we made our way."

It had been refreshing to dip back into the life I had previously enjoyed with Sherlock Holmes, I'll admit, but I'd had my fill again for now. I pondered over the day's events in the cab, what Holmes had uncovered, what Lady Sweetenbury had been through – not to mention her poor son – and what I'd learned myself. Lies, deceit, stubbornness, and murder had made for a long and emotional day, and years of pain and suffering for the Sweetenbury family. This case had shown the very worst aspects of humanity at times, and all for nothing as it turned out.

The cab pulled up and there I was, outside my house once again. Mary's face was pressed against the window, the very best of humanity. I knew that this was where I now firmly belonged: *Home*.

About the Contributors

The following contributors appear in this volume:

The MX Book of New Sherlock Holmes Stories
Part XIX – 2020 Annual (1882-1890)

Ian Ableson is an ecologist by training and a writer by choice. When not reading or writing, he can reliably be found scowling at a clipboard while ankle-deep in a marsh somewhere in Michigan. His love for the stories of Arthur Conan Doyle started when his grandfather gave him a copy of *The Original Illustrated Sherlock Holmes* when he was in high school, and he's proud to have been able to contribute to the continuation of the tales of Sherlock Holmes and Dr. Watson.

Brian Belanger is a publisher and editor, but is best known for his freelance illustration and cover design work. His distinctive style can be seen on several MX Publishing covers, including *Silent Meridian* by Elizabeth Crowen, *Sherlock Holmes and the Menacing Melbournian* by Allan Mitchell, *Sherlock Holmes and A Quantity of Debt* by David Marcum, *Welcome to Undershaw* by Luke Benjamen Kuhns, and many more. Brian is the co-founder of Belanger Books LLC, where he illustrates the popular *MacDougall Twins with Sherlock Holmes* young reader series (#1 bestsellers on Amazon.com UK). A prolific creator, he also designs t-shirts, mugs, stickers, and other merchandise on his personal art site: *www.redbubble.com/people/zhahadun.*

Andrew Bryant was born in Bridgend, Wales, and now lives in Burlington, Ontario. His previous publications include *Poetry Toronto*, *Prism International*, *Existere*, *On Spec*, *The Dalhousie Review*, and *The Toronto Star*. His first Holmes story was published in *The MX Book of New Sherlock Holmes Stories - Part XIII*, with the second in *Part XVI*. The two stories in this collection are the third and fourth. Andrew's interest in Holmes stems from watching the Basil Rathbone and Nigel Bruce films as a child, followed by collecting The Canon, and a fascinating visit to 221B Baker Street.

Lizzy Butler has been the Fundraising, Community, and Events Manager at the Stepping Stones School, located in Hyndhead, Surrey, since early 2019.

Nick Cardillo has been a devotee of Sherlock Holmes since the age of six. His first published short story, "The Adventure of the Traveling Corpse" appeared in *The MX Book of New Sherlock Holmes Stories – Part VI: 2017 Annual*, and he has written subsequent stories for both MX Publishing and Belanger Books. In 2018, Nick completed his first anthology of new Sherlock Holmes adventures entitled *The Feats of Sherlock Holmes*. Nick is a fan of The Golden Age of Detective Fiction, Hammer Horror, and Doctor Who. He writes film reviews and analyses at *Sacred-Celluloid.blogspot.com.* He is a student at Susquehanna University in Selinsgrove, PA.

Chris Chan is a writer, educator, and historian. He works as a researcher and "International Goodwill Ambassador" for Agatha Christie Ltd. His true crime articles, reviews, and short fiction have appeared (or will soon appear) in *The Strand*, *The Wisconsin Magazine of History*, *Mystery Weekly*, *Gilbert!*, *Nerd HQ*, Akashic Books' *Mondays are Murder* web series, *The Baker Street Journal*, and *Sherlock Holmes Mystery Magazine*.

Craig Stephen Copland confesses that he discovered Sherlock Holmes when, sometime in the muddled early 1960's, he pinched his older brother's copy of the immortal stories and was forever afterward thoroughly hooked. He is very grateful to his high school English teachers in Toronto who inculcated in him a love of literature and writing, and even inspired him to be an English major at the University of Toronto. There he was blessed to sit at the feet of both Northrup Frye and Marshall McLuhan, and other great literary professors, who led him to believe that he was called to be a high school English teacher. It was his good fortune to come to his pecuniary senses, abandon that goal, and pursue a varied professional career that took him to over one-hundred countries and endless adventures. He considers himself to have been and to continue to be one of the luckiest men on God's good earth. A few years back he took a step in the direction of Sherlockian studies and joined the *Sherlock Holmes Society of Canada* – also known as *The Toronto Bootmakers*. In May of 2014, this esteemed group of scholars announced a contest for the writing of a new Sherlock Holmes mystery. Although he had never tried his hand at fiction before, Craig entered and was pleasantly surprised to be selected as one of the winners. Having enjoyed the experience, he decided to write more of the same, and is now on a mission to write a new Sherlock Holmes mystery that is related to and inspired by each of the sixty stories in the original Canon. He currently lives and writes in Toronto and Dubai, and looks forward to finally settling down when he turns ninety.

Sir Arthur Conan Doyle (1859-1930) *Holmes Chronicler Emeritus*. If not for him, this anthology would not exist. Author, physician, patriot, sportsman, spiritualist, husband and father, and advocate for the oppressed. He is remembered and honored for the purposes of this collection by being the man who introduced Sherlock Holmes to the world. Through fifty-six Holmes short stories, four novels, and additional Apocryphal entries, Doyle revolutionized mystery stories and also greatly influenced and improved police forensic methods and techniques for the betterment of all. *Steel True Blade Straight.*

Steve Emecz's main field is technology, in which he has been working for about twenty years. Steve is a regular trade show speaker on the subject of eCommerce, and his tech career has taken him to more than fifty countries – so he's no stranger to planes and airports. He wrote two novels (one a bestseller) in the 1990's, and a screenplay in 2001. Shortly after, he set up MX Publishing, specialising in NLP books. In 2008, MX published its first Sherlock Holmes book, and MX has gone on to become the largest specialist Holmes publisher in the world. MX is a social enterprise and supports three main causes. The first is Happy Life, a children's rescue project in Nairobi, Kenya, where he and his wife, Sharon, spend every Christmas at the rescue centre in Kasarani. In 2014, they wrote a short book about the project, *The Happy Life Story*. The second is the Stepping Stones School, of which Steve is a patron. Stepping Stones is located at Undershaw, Sir Arthur Conan Doyle's former home. Steve has been a mentor for the World Food Programme for the last several years, supporting their innovation bootcamps and giving 1-2-1 mentoring to several projects.

David Friend lives in Wales, Great Britain, where he divides his time between watching old detective films and thinking about old detective films. Now thirty, he's been scribbling out stories for twenty years and hopes, some day, to write something half-decent. Most of what he pens is set in an old-timey world of non-stop adventure with debonair sleuths, kick-ass damsels, criminal masterminds, and narrow escapes, and he wishes he could live there.

Mark A. Gagen BSI is co-founder of Wessex Press, sponsor of the popular *From Gillette to Brett* conferences, and publisher of *The Sherlock Holmes Reference Library* and many other fine Sherlockian titles. A life-long Holmes enthusiast, he is a member of *The Baker Street Irregulars* and *The Illustrious Clients of Indianapolis*. A graphic artist by profession, his work is often seen on the covers of *The Baker Street Journal* and various BSI books.

Tim Gambrell lives in Exeter, Devon, with his wife, two young sons, three cats, and now only four chickens. He has previously contributed two stories to *The MX Book of New Sherlock Holmes Stories*: "The Yellow Star of Cairo" in Vol. XIII, and "The Haunting of Bottomly's Grandmother" in Vol. XVI. He also contributed a story to *Sherlock Holmes and Dr Watson: The Early Adventures*, Vol. III, from Belanger Books, and has a further tale in Vol. II of the forthcoming collection *Sherlock Holmes and The Occult Detectives*, also from Belanger Books. Outside of the world of Holmes, Tim has written extensively for Doctor Who spin-off ranges. His books include two linked novels from Candy Jar Books: *Lethbridge-Stewart: The Laughing Gnome – Lucy Wilson & The Bledoe Cadets*, and *The Lucy Wilson Mysteries: The Brigadier and The Bledoe Cadets* (both 2019), and *Lethbridge-Stewart: Bloodlines – An Ordinary Man* (Candy Jar, 2020, written with Andy Frankham-Allen). He's also written a novella, *The Way of The Bry'hunee* (2019) for the Erimem range from Thebes Publishing. Tim's short fiction includes stories in *Lethbridge-Stewart: The HAVOC Files 3* (Candy Jar, 2017, revised edition 2020), *Bernice Summerfield: True Stories* (Big Finish, 2017) and *Relics . . . An Anthology* (Red Ted Books, 2018), plus a number of charity anthologies.

Dick Gillman is an English writer and acrylic artist living in Brittany, France with his wife Alex, Truffle, their Black Labrador, and Jean-Claude, their Breton cat. During his retirement from teaching, he has written over twenty Sherlock Holmes short stories which are published as both e-books and paperbacks. His contribution to the superb MX Sherlock Holmes collection, published in October 2015, was entitled "The Man on Westminster Bridge" and had the privilege of being chosen as the anchor story in *The MX Book of New Sherlock Holmes Stories – Part II (1890-1895).* (Dick also has a story in Part XXI.)

John Atkinson Grimshaw (1836-1893) was born in Leeds, England. His amazing paintings, usually featuring twilight or night scenes illuminated by gas-lamps or moonlight, are easily recognizable, and are often used on the covers of books about The Great Detective to set the mood, as shadowy figures move in the distance through misty mysterious settings and over rain-slicked streets.

Arthur Hall was born in Aston, Birmingham, UK, in 1944. He discovered his interest in writing during his schooldays, along with a love of fictional adventure and suspense. His first novel, *Sole Contact,* was an espionage story about an ultra-secret government department known as "Sector Three", and was followed, to date, by three sequels. Other works include five Sherlock Holmes novels, *The Demon of the Dusk*, *The One Hundred Percent Society*, *The Secret Assassin*, *The Phantom Killer*, and *In Pursuit of the Dead*, as well as a collection of short stories, and a modern detective novel. He lives in the West Midlands, United Kingdom. (Arthur also has a stories in Parts XX and XXI.)

Christopher James was born in 1975 in Paisley, Scotland. Educated at Newcastle and UEA, he was a winner of the UK's National Poetry Competition in 2008. He has written two full length Sherlock Holmes novels, *The Adventure of the Ruby Elephant* and *The Jeweller of Florence*, both published by MX, and is working on a third.

Roger Johnson BSI, ASH is a retired librarian, now working as a volunteer assistant at the Essex Police Museum. In his spare time, he is commissioning editor of *The Sherlock Holmes Journal*, an occasional lecturer, and a frequent contributor to The *Writings about the Writings*. His sole work of Holmesian pastiche was published in 1997 in Mike Ashley's anthology *The Mammoth Book of New Sherlock Holmes Adventures*, and he has the greatest respect for the many authors who have contributed new tales to the present mighty trilogy. Like his wife, Jean Upton, he is a member of both *The Baker Street Irregulars* and *The Adventuresses of Sherlock Holmes.*

John Lescroart is a New York Times bestselling author known for his series of legal and crime thriller novels featuring the characters Dismas Hardy, Abe Glitsky, and Wyatt Hunt. His novels have sold more than ten-million copies, have been translated into twenty-two languages in more than seventy-five countries, and eighteen of his books have been on *The New York Times* bestseller list. Libraries Unlimited has included him in its publication "The 100 Most Popular Thriller and Suspense Authors". Lescroart was born in Houston, Texas, and graduated from Junípero Serra High School in San Mateo, California (Class of 1966). He earned a B.A. in English with Honors at UC Berkeley in 1970. Before becoming a full-time writer in 1994, Lescroart was a self-described "Jack of all trades", who worked as a word processor for law firms as well as a bartender, moving man, house painter, editor, advertising director, computer programmer, and fundraising executive. Through his twenties, he was also a full-time singer-songwriter-guitarist, and performed under the name Johnny Capo, with Johnny Capo and his Real Good Band. In addition to nearly thirty novels, Lescroart has written several screenplays, and he is an original founding member of the group *International Thriller Writers*. John's blog at *JohnLescroart.com* is updated regularly with writing tips, insights on his books, recipes, recommendations, book give-aways, and more! Please also find John on Twitter and Facebook.

David Marcum plays *The Game* with deadly seriousness. He first discovered Sherlock Holmes in 1975 at the age of ten, and since that time, he has collected, read, and chronologicized literally thousands of traditional Holmes pastiches in the form of novels, short stories, radio and television episodes, movies and scripts, comics, fan-fiction, and unpublished manuscripts. He is the author of over sixty Sherlockian pastiches, some published in anthologies and magazines such as *The Strand*, and others collected in his own books, *The Papers of Sherlock Holmes*, *Sherlock Holmes and A Quantity of Debt*, and *Sherlock Holmes – Tangled Skeins*. He has edited fifty books, including several dozen traditional Sherlockian anthologies, such as the ongoing series *The MX Book of New Sherlock Holmes Stories*, which he created in 2015. This collection is now up to 21 volumes, with several more in preparation. He was responsible for bringing back August Derleth's Solar Pons for a new generation, first with his collection of authorized Pons stories, *The Papers of Solar Pons*, and then by editing the reissued authorized versions of the original Pons books. He is now doing the same for the adventures of Dr. Thorndyke. He has contributed numerous essays to various publications, and is a member of a number of Sherlockian groups and Scions. He is a licensed Civil Engineer, living in Tennessee with his wife and son. His irregular Sherlockian blog, *A Seventeen Step Program*, addresses various topics related to his favorite book friends (as his son used to call them when he was small), and can be found at *http://17stepprogram.blogspot.com/* Since the age of nineteen, he has worn a deerstalker as his regular-and-only hat. In 2013, he and his deerstalker were finally able make his first trip-of-a-lifetime Holmes Pilgrimage to England, with return Pilgrimages in 2015 and 2016, where you may have spotted him. If you ever run into him and his deerstalker out and about, feel free to say hello!

James Moffett is a Masters graduate in Professional Writing, with a specialisation in novel and non-fiction writing. He also has an extensive background in media studies. James began developing a passion for writing when contributing to his University's student magazine. His interest in the literary character of Sherlock Holmes was deep-rooted in his youth. He released his first publication of eight interconnected short stories titled *The Trials of Sherlock Holmes* in 2017, along with previous contributions to *The MX Book of New Sherlock Holmes Stories.*

Will Murray is the author of over seventy novels, including forty *Destroyer* novels and seven posthumous *Doc Savage* collaborations with Lester Dent, under the name Kenneth Robeson, for Bantam Books in the 1990's. Since 2011, he has written a number of additional Doc Savage adventures for Altus Press, two of which co-starred The Shadow, as well as a solo Pat Savage novel. His 2015 Tarzan novel, *Return to Pal-Ul-Don*, was followed by *King Kong vs. Tarzan* in 2016. Murray has written short stories featuring such classic characters as Batman, Superman, Wonder Woman, Spider-Man, Ant-Man, the Hulk, Honey West, the Spider, the Avenger, the Green Hornet, the Phantom, and Cthulhu. A previous Murray Sherlock Holmes story appeared in Moonstone's *Sherlock Holmes*: *The Crossovers Casebook*, and another in *Sherlock Holmes and Doctor Was Not*, involving H. P. Lovecraft's Dr. Herbert West. Additionally, his Sherlock Holmes stories have appeared in *The MX Book of New Sherlock Holmes Stories.* His most recent book is *Tarzan, Conqueror of Mars.*

Sidney Paget (1860-1908), a few of whose illustrations are used within this anthology, was born in London, and like his two older brothers, became a famed illustrator and painter. He completed over three-hundred-and-fifty drawings for the Sherlock Holmes stories that were first published in *The Strand* magazine, defining Holmes's image forever after in the public mind.

Roger Riccard of Los Angeles, California, U.S.A., is a descendant of the Roses of Kilravock in Highland Scotland. He is the author of two previous Sherlock Holmes novels, *The Case of the Poisoned Lilly* and *The Case of the Twain Papers*, a series of short stories in two volumes, *Sherlock Holmes: Adventures for the Twelve Days of Christmas* and *Further Adventures for the Twelve Days of Christmas*, and the new series *A Sherlock Holmes Alphabet of Cases,* all of which are published by Baker Street Studios. He has another novel and a non-fiction Holmes reference work in various stages of completion. He became a Sherlock Holmes enthusiast as a teenager (many, many years ago), and, like all fans of The Great Detective, yearned for more stories after reading The Canon over and over. It was the Granada Television performances of Jeremy Brett and Edward Hardwicke, and the encouragement of his wife, Rosilyn, that at last inspired him to write his own Holmes adventures, using the Granada actor portrayals as his guide. He has been called "The best pastiche writer since Val Andrews" by the *Sherlockian E-Times.*

Brenda Seabrooke's stories have been published in sixteen reviews, journals, and anthologies. She has received grants from the National Endowment for the Arts and Emerson College's Robbie Macauley Award. She is the author of twenty-three books for young readers including *Scones and Bones on Baker Street: Sherlock's (maybe!) Dog and the Dirt Dilemma*, and *The Rascal in the Castle: Sherlock's (possible!) Dog and the Queen's Revenge.* Brenda states: "It was fun to write from Dr. Watson's point of view and not have to worry about fleas, smelly pits, ralphing, or scratching at inopportune times."

Matthew Simmonds hails from Bedford, in the South East of England, and has been a confirmed devotee of Sir Arthur Conan Doyle's most famous creation since first watching Jeremy Brett's incomparable portrayal of the world's first consulting detective, on a Tuesday evening in April, 1984, while curled up on the sofa with his father. He has written numerous short stories, and his first novel, *Sherlock Holmes: The Adventure of The Pigtail Twist*, was published in 2018. A sequel is nearly complete, which he hopes to publish in the near future. Matthew currently co-owns Harrison & Simmonds, the fifth-generation family business, a renowned County tobacconist, pipe, and gift shop on Bedford High Street.

Robert V. Stapleton was born and brought up in Leeds, Yorkshire, England, and studied at Durham University. After working in various parts of the country as an Anglican parish priest, he is now retired and lives with his wife in North Yorkshire. As a member of his local writing group, he now has time to develop his other life as a writer of adventure stories. He has recently had a number of short stories published, and he is hoping to have a couple of completed novels published at some time in the future.

Vincent Starrett (1886–1974) was a Canadian-born American writer, newspaperman, and bibliophile. Born in Canada, his father moved the family to Chicago in 1889. In 1907, he began working for the *Chicago Daily News* as reporter, feature writer, and columnist. In 1920, he wrote the Sherlock Holmes pastiche "The Adventure of the Unique 'Hamlet'", and his most famous work, *The Private Life of Sherlock Holmes*, was published in 1933. He wrote the book column, "Books Alive", for *The Chicago Tribune*, which ran for twenty-five years before retiring it in 1967. Starrett was one of the founders of *The Hounds of the Baskerville* (*sic*), a Chicago scion of *The Baker Street Irregulars*.

Kevin P. Thornton is a seven-time Arthur Ellis Award Nominee. He is a former director of the local Heritage Society and Library, and he has been a soldier in Africa, a contractor for the Canadian Military in Afghanistan, a newspaper and magazine columnist, a Director of both the *Crime Writers of Canada* and the *Writers' Guild of Alberta*, a founding member of *Northword Literary Magazine*, and is either a current or former member of *The Mystery Writers of America*, *The Crime Writers Association*, *The Calgary Crime Writers*, *The International Thriller Writers*, *The International Association of Crime Writers*, *The Keys* – a Catholic Writers group founded by Monsignor Knox and G.K. Chesterton – as well as, somewhat inexplicably, *The Mesdames of Mayhem* and *Sisters in Crime*. If you ask, he will join. Born in Kenya, Kevin has lived or worked in South Africa, Dubai, England, Afghanistan, New Zealand, Ontario, and now Northern Alberta. He lives on his wits and his wit, and is doing better than expected. He is not one to willingly split infinitives, and while never pedantic, is on occasion known to be ever so slightly punctilious.

Thomas A. (Tom) Turley was born in Virginia, grew up in Tennessee, and lives now in Montgomery, Alabama. He and his wife Paula have two grown children and one beautiful granddaughter. Although Tom has a Ph.D. in British history, he spent most of his career as an archivist with the State of Alabama. Approaching retirement, he returned to a youthful hobby: Writing fiction. Tom's first story, "The Devil's Claw", appeared in *The Book of Villains*, a 2011 Main Street Rag anthology. His pastiche "Sherlock Holmes and the Adventure of the Tainted Canister" (2014) is available as an e-book and an audiobook from MX Publishing. It was also published in *The Art of Sherlock Holmes – USA Edition 1* (2019), in company with a painting by artist Angela Fegan. Three of Tom's stories, "A Scandal in Serbia", "A Ghost from Christmas Past", and "The Solitary Violinist" have appeared in MX Publishing's ongoing anthology of traditional pastiches (Parts VI, VII, and XVIII). The latter two were praised by *Publishers Weekly* in its reviews of the relevant MX volumes. "Ghost" was also included in *The Art of Sherlock Holmes, West Palm Beach Edition* (2019), paired with a painting by artist Nune Asatryan. Tom's latest short story, "A Game of Skittles", appears in MX Publishing' spring 2020 anthology, *Part XIX*. Later this year, Tom should complete a collection of historical pastiches entitled *Sherlock Holmes and the Crowned Heads of Europe*. The first story chronologically, "Sherlock Holmes and the Case of the Dying Emperor", is already available from MX Publishing as an e-book. Set in Berlin in 1888, during the brief reign of Emperor Frederick III (son-in-law of Queen Victoria and father of the notorious "Kaiser Bill"), it inaugurates Sherlock Holmes's espionage campaign against the German Empire, which ended only in August 1914 with "His Last Bow". When completed, *Sherlock Holmes and the Crowned Heads of Europe* will also include "A Scandal in Serbia" and two new stories on the last dynastic tragedies that befell the House of Habsburg. Tom's non-literary interests include hiking, ship modeling, classical music, and University of Tennessee athletics (not a popular pursuit in Alabama!). Interested readers can contact him through MX Publishing or his Goodreads and Amazon author's pages.

Peter Coe Verbica grew up on a commercial cattle ranch in Northern California, where he learned the value of a strong work ethic. He works for the Wealth Management Group of a global investment bank, and is an Adjunct Professor in the Economics Department at SJSU. He is the author of numerous books, including *Left at the Gate and Other Poems, Hard-Won Cowboy Wisdom (Not Necessarily in Order of Importance), A Key to the Grove and Other Poems,* and *The Missing Tales of Sherlock Holmes (as Compiled by Peter Coe Verbica, JD).* Mr. Verbica obtained a JD from Santa Clara University School of Law, an MS from Massachusetts Institute of Technology, and a BA in English from Santa Clara University. He is the co-inventor on a number of patents, has served as a Managing Member of three venture capital firms, and the CFO of one of the portfolio companies. He is an unabashed advocate of cowboy culture and enjoys creative writing, hiking, and tennis. He is married with four daughters. For more information, or to contact the author, please go to *www.hardwoncowboywisdom.com.* (Peter also has a story in Part XXI)

Sean Wright BSI makes his home in Santa Clarita, a charming city at the entrance of the high desert in Southern California. For sixteen years, features and articles under his byline appeared in *The Tidings* – now *The Angelus News* – publications of the Roman Catholic Archdiocese of Los Angeles. Continuing his education in 2007, Mr. Wright graduated *summa cum laude* from Grand Canyon University, attaining a Bachelor of Arts degree in Christian Studies. He then attained a Master of Arts degree, also in Christian Studies. Once active in the entertainment industry, in an abortive attempt to revive dramatic radio in 1976 with his beloved mentor the late Daws Butler directing, Mr. Wright co-produced and wrote the syndicated *New Radio Adventures of Sherlock Holmes* starring the late Edward Mulhare as the Great Detective. Mr. Wright has written for several television quiz shows and remains proud of his work for *The Quiz Kid's Challenge* and the popular TV quiz show *Jeopardy!* for which The Academy of Television Arts and Sciences honored him in 1985 with an Emmy nomination in the field of writing. Honored with membership in *The Baker Street Irregulars* as "The Manor House Case" after founding *The Non-Canonical Calabashes, The Sherlock Holmes Society of Los Angeles* in 1970, Mr. Wright has written for *The Baker Street Journal* and *Mystery Magazine*. Since 1971, he has conducted lectures on Sherlock Holmes's influence on literature and cinema for libraries, colleges, and private organizations, including MENSA. Mr. Wright's whimsical *Sherlock Holmes Cookbook* (Drake) created with John Farrell BSI, was published in 1976 and a mystery novel, *Enter the Lion: a Posthumous Memoir of Mycroft Holmes* (Hawthorne), "edited" with Michael

Hodel BSI, followed in 1979. As director general of The Plot Thickens Mystery Company, Mr. Wright originated hosting "mystery parties" in homes, restaurants, and offices, as well as producing and directing the very first "Mystery Train" tours on Amtrak beginning in 1982.

Matthew White is an up-and-coming author from Richmond, Virginia in the USA. He has been a passionate devotee of Sherlock Holmes since childhood. He can be reached at *matthewwhite.writer@gmail.com.*

The following contributors appear
in the companion volumes:

The MX Book of New Sherlock Holmes Stories
Part XX – 2020 Annual (1891-1897)
Part XXI – 2020 Annual (1898-1923)

Hugh Ashton was born in the U.K., and moved to Japan in 1988, where he remained until 2016, living with his wife Yoshiko in the historic city of Kamakura, a little to the south of Yokohama. He and Yoshiko have now moved to Lichfield, a small cathedral city in the Midlands of the U.K., the birthplace of Samuel Johnson, and one-time home of Erasmus Darwin. In the past, he has worked in the technology and financial services industries, which have provided him with material for some of his books set in the 21st century. He currently works as a writer: Novelist, freelance editor, and copywriter, (his work for large Japanese corporations has appeared in international business journals), and journalist, as well as producing industry reports on various aspects of the financial services industry. Recently, however, his lifelong interest in Sherlock Holmes has developed into an acclaimed series of adventures featuring the world's most famous detective, written in the style of the originals. In addition to these, he has also published historical and alternate historical novels, short stories, and thrillers. Together with artist Andy Boerger, he has produced the *Sherlock Ferret* series of stories for children, featuring the world's cutest detective.

Deanna Baran lives in a remote part of Texas where cowboys may still be seen in their natural habitat. A librarian and former museum curator, she writes in between cups of tea, playing *Go*, and trading postcards with people around the world.

Derrick Belanger is an educator and also the author of the #1 bestselling book in its category, *Sherlock Holmes: The Adventure of the Peculiar Provenance*, which was in the top 200 bestselling books on Amazon. He also is the author of *The MacDougall Twins with Sherlock Holmes* books, and he edited the Sir Arthur Conan Doyle horror anthology *A Study in Terror: Sir Arthur Conan Doyle's Revolutionary Stories of Fear and the Supernatural*. Mr. Belanger co-owns the publishing company Belanger Books, which released the Sherlock Holmes anthologies *Beyond Watson*, *Holmes Away From Home: Adventures from the Great Hiatus* Volumes 1 and 2, *Sherlock Holmes: Before Baker Street*, and *Sherlock Holmes: Adventures in the Realms of H.G. Wells* Volumes I and 2. Derrick resides in Colorado and continues compiling unpublished works by Dr. John H. Watson.

S.F. Bennett has, at various times, been an actor, a lecturer, a journalist, a historian, an author and a potter. Whilst some of those things still apply, she has always been an avid collector, concentrating mainly on ephemera and other related items concerning Sherlock Holmes and British science-fiction of the 1970's. To date, she has written articles on aspects of The Canon for *The Baker Street Journal*, *The Sherlock Holmes Journal*, and *The Torr*, the journal of *The Sherlock Holmes Society of the West Country*. When not collecting, she can be found writing science-fiction and mystery stories, and has contributed to several anthologies of new Sherlock Holmes pastiches. Her first novel was *The Secret Diary of Mycroft Holmes: The Thoughts and Reminiscences of Sherlock Holmes's Elder Brother, 1880-1888* (2017). She is also the author of *A Study in Postcards: Sherlock Holmes in the Golden Age of the Picture Postcard* (*Sherlock Holmes Society of London*, 2019).

Thomas A. Burns, Jr. is the author of the *Natalie McMasters Mysteries*. He was born and grew up in New Jersey, attended Xavier High School in Manhattan, earned B.S degrees in Zoology and Microbiology at Michigan State University, and a M.S. in Microbiology at North Carolina State University. He currently resides in Wendell, North Carolina. As a kid, Tom started reading mysteries with The Hardy Boys, Ken Holt and Rick Brant, and graduated to the classic stories by authors such as A. Conan Doyle, Dorothy Sayers, John Dickson Carr, Erle Stanley Gardner, and Rex Stout, to name a few. Tom has written fiction as a hobby all of his life, starting with The Man from U.N.C.L.E. stories in marble-backed copybooks in grade school. He built a career as technical, science, and medical writer and editor for nearly thirty years in industry and government. Now that he's truly on his own as a novelist, he's excited to publish his own mystery series, as well as to contribute stories about his second-most-favorite detective, Sherlock Holmes, to *The MX anthology of New Sherlock Holmes Stories.*

Bob Byrne was a columnist for *Sherlock Magazine* and has contributed to *Sherlock Holmes Mystery Magazine* and the Sherlock Holmes short story collection *Curious Incidents*. He publishes two free online newsletters: *Baker Street Essays* and *The Solar Pons Gazette*, both of which can be found at *www.SolarPons.com*, the only website dedicated to August Derleth's successor to the Great Detective. Bob's column, *The Public Life of Sherlock Holmes*, appears every Monday morning at *www.BlackGate.com* and explores Holmes, hard boiled, and other mystery matters, and whatever other topics come to mind by the deadline. His mystery-themed blog is *Almost Holmes*.

Leslie Charteris was born in Singapore on May 12th, 1907. With his mother and brother, he moved to England in 1919 and attended Rossall School in Lancashire before moving on to Cambridge University to study law. His studies there came to a halt when a publisher accepted his first novel. His third one, entitled *Meet the Tiger*, was written when he was twenty years old and published in September 1928. It introduced the world to Simon Templar, *aka* The Saint. He continued to write about The Saint until 1983 when the last book, *Salvage for The Saint*, was published. The books, which have been translated into over thirty languages, number nearly a hundred and have sold over forty-million copies around the world. They've inspired, to date, fifteen feature films, three television series, ten radio series, and a comic strip that was written by Charteris and syndicated around the world for over a decade. He enjoyed travelling, but settled for long periods in Hollywood, Florida, and finally in Surrey, England. He was awarded the Cartier Diamond Dagger by the *Crime Writers' Association* in 1992, in recognition of a lifetime of achievement. He died the following year.

Harry DeMaio is a *nom de plume* of Harry B. DeMaio, successful author of several books on Information Security and Business Networks, as well as the twelve-volume *Casebooks of Octavius Bear.* He is also a published author for Belanger Books and *The MX Sherlock Holmes* series edited by David Marcum. A retired business executive, former consultant, information security specialist, pilot, disk jockey, and graduate school adjunct professor, he whiles away his time traveling and writing preposterous books, articles, and stories. He has appeared on many radio and TV shows and is an accomplished, frequent public speaker. Former New York City natives, he and his extremely patient and helpful wife, Virginia, and their Bichon Frisé, Woof, live in Cincinnati (and several other parallel universes.) They have two sons living in Scottsdale, Arizona and Cortlandt Manor, New York, both of whom are quite successful and quite normal, thus putting the lie to the theory that insanity is hereditary. His e-mail is *hdemaio@zoomtown.com* You can also find him on Facebook. His website is *www.octaviusbearslair.com* His books are available on Amazon, Barnes and Noble, directly from MX Publishing, and at other fine bookstores.

Ian Dickerson was just nine years old when he discovered The Saint. Shortly after that, he discovered Sherlock Holmes. The Saint won, for a while anyway. He struck up a friendship with The Saint's creator, Leslie Charteris, and his family. With their permission, he spent six weeks studying the Leslie Charteris collection at Boston University and went on to write, direct, and produce documentaries on the making of *The Saint* and *Return of The Saint,* which have been released on DVD. He oversaw the recent reprints of almost fifty of the original Saint books in both the US and UK, and was a co-producer on the 2017 TV movie of *The Saint*. When he discovered that Charteris had written Sherlock Holmes stories as well – well, there was the excuse he needed to revisit The Canon. He's consequently written and edited three books on Holmes' radio adventures. For the sake of what little sanity he has, Ian has also written about a wide range of subjects, none of which come with a halo, including talking mashed potatoes, Lord Grade, and satellite links. Ian lives in Hampshire with his wife and two children. And an awful lot of books by Leslie Charteris. Not quite so many by Conan Doyle, though.

Anna Elliott is an author of historical fiction and fantasy. Her first series, *The Twilight of Avalon* trilogy, is a retelling of the Trystan and Isolde legend. She wrote her second series, *The Pride and Prejudice Chronicles*, chiefly to satisfy her own curiosity about what might have happened to Elizabeth Bennet, Mr. Darcy, and all the other wonderful cast of characters after the official end of Jane Austen's classic work. She enjoys stories about strong women, and loves exploring the multitude of ways women can find their unique strengths. She was delighted to lend a hand with the "Sherlock and Lucy" series, and this story, firstly because she loves Sherlock Holmes as much as her father, co-author Charles Veley, does, and second because it almost never happens that someone with a dilemma shouts, "Quick, we need an author of historical fiction!" Anna lives in the Washington, D.C .area with her husband and three children.

Matthew J. Elliott is the author of *Big Trouble in Mother Russia* (2016), the official sequel to the cult movie *Big Trouble in Little China, Lost in Time and Space: An Unofficial Guide to the Uncharted Journeys of Doctor Who* (2014), *Sherlock Holmes on the Air* (2012), *Sherlock Holmes in Pursuit* (2013), *The Immortals: An Unauthorized Guide to* Sherlock *and* Elementary (2013), and *The Throne Eternal* (2014). His articles, fiction, and reviews have appeared in the magazines *Scarlet Street*, *Total DVD*, *SHERLOCK*, and *Sherlock Holmes Mystery Magazine*, and the collections *The Game's Afoot*, *Curious Incidents 2*, *Gaslight Grimoire*, *The Mammoth Book of Best British Crime 8*, and *The MX Book of New Sherlock Holmes Stories – Part III: 1896-1929.* He has scripted over 260 radio plays, including episodes of *Doctor Who*, *The Further Adventures of Sherlock Holmes*, *The Twilight Zone*, *The New Adventures of Mickey Spillane's Mike Hammer*, *Fangoria's Dreadtime Stories*, and award-winning adaptations of *The Hound of the Baskervilles* and *The War of the Worlds*. He is the only radio dramatist to adapt all sixty original stories from The Canon for the series *The Classic Adventures of Sherlock*

Holmes. Matthew is a writer and performer on *RiffTrax.com*, the online comedy experience from the creators of cult sci-fi TV series *Mystery Science Theater 3000* (*MST3K* to the initiated). He's also written a few comic books.

Sonia Fetherston BSI is a member of the illustrious *Baker Street Irregulars*. For almost thirty years, she's been a frequent contributor to Sherlockian anthologies, including Calabash Press's acclaimed *Case Files* series, and Wildside Press's *About* series. Sonia's byline often appears in the pages of *The Baker Street Journal*, *The Journal* of the *Sherlock Holmes Society of London*, *Canadian Holmes*, and the Sydney Passengers' *Log*. Her work earned her the coveted Morley-Montgomery Award from the *Baker Street Irregulars*, and the Derek Murdoch Memorial Award from *The Bootmakers of Toronto*. Sonia is author of *Prince of the Realm: The Most Irregular James Bliss Austin* (BSI Press, 2014). She's at work on another biography for the BSI, this time about Julian Wolff.

Jayantika Ganguly BSI is the General Secretary and Editor of the *Sherlock Holmes Society of India*, a member of the *Sherlock Holmes Society of London*, and the *Czech Sherlock Holmes Society*. She is the author of *The Holmes Sutra* (MX 2014). She is a corporate lawyer working with one of the Big Six law firms.

Dick Gillman – *In addition to stories in this volume, Dick also has a story in Part XXI*

Denis Green was born in London, England in April 1905. He grew up mostly in London's Savoy Theatre where his father, Richard Green, was a principal in many Gilbert and Sullivan productions, A Flying Officer with RAF until 1924, he then spent four years managing a tea estate in North India before making his stage debut in *Hamlet* with Leslie Howard in 1928. He made his first visit to America in 1931 and established a respectable stage career before appearing in films – including minor roles in the first two Rathbone and Bruce Holmes films – and developing a career in front of and behind the microphone during the golden age of radio. Green and Leslie Charteris met in 1938 and struck up a lifelong friendship. Always busy, be it on stage, radio, film or television, Green passed away at the age of fifty in New York.

Arthur Hall – *In addition to a story in this volume, Arthur also has stories in Parts XX and XXI*

Paula Hammond has written over sixty fiction and non-fiction books, as well as short stories, comics, poetry, and scripts for educational DVD's. When not glued to the keyboard, she can usually be found prowling round second-hand books shops or hunkered down in a hide, soaking up the joys of the natural world.

Stephen Herczeg is an IT Geek, writer, actor, and film-maker based in Canberra Australia. He has been writing for over twenty years and has completed a couple of dodgy novels, sixteen feature-length screenplays, and numerous short stories and scripts. Stephen was very successful in 2017's International Horror Hotel screenplay competition, with his scripts *TITAN* winning the Sci-Fi category and *Dark are the Woods* placing second in the horror category. His work has featured in *Sproutlings – A Compendium of Little Fictions* from Hunter Anthologies, the *Hells Bells* Christmas horror anthology published by the Australasian Horror Writers Association, and the *Below the Stairs*, *Trickster's Treats*, *Shades of Santa*, *Behind the Mask*, and *Beyond the Infinite* anthologies from *OzHorror.Con*, *The Body Horror Book*, *Anemone Enemy*, and *Petrified Punks* from

Oscillate Wildly Press, and *Sherlock Holmes In the Realms of H.G. Wells* and *Sherlock Holmes: Adventures Beyond the Canon* from Belanger Books.

Steven Philip Jones has written over sixty graphic novels and comic books including the horror series *Lovecraftian, Curious Cases of Sherlock Holmes*, the original series *Nightlinger, Street Heroes 2005*, adaptations of *Dracula*, several H. P. Lovecraft stories, and the 1985 film *Re-animator*. Steven is also the author of several novels and nonfiction books including *The Clive Cussler Adventures: A Critical Review, Comics Writing: Communicating With Comic Book , King of Harlem, Bushwackers, The House With the Witch's Hat, Talisman: The Knightmare Knife*, and *Henrietta Hex: Shadows From the Past.* Steven's other writing credits include a number of scripts for radio dramas that have been broadcast internationally. A graduate of the University of Iowa, Steven has a Bachelor of Arts in Journalism and Religion, and was accepted into Iowa's Writer's Workshop – M.F.A. program.

Susan Knight's most recent collection of short stories, *Mrs Hudson Investigates*, was issued by MX Publishing in November 2019. She is the author of two other non-Sherlockian, story collections, as well as three novels, a book of non-fiction, and several plays. She lives in Dublin where she teaches Creative Writing. She is currently working on a new Mrs Hudson novel set in Ireland.

John Lawrence served for thirty-eight years as a staff member in the U.S. House of Representatives, the last eight as Chief of Staff to Speaker Nancy Pelosi (2005-2013). He has been a Visiting Professor at the University of California's Washington Center since 2013. He is the author of *The Class of '74: Congress After Watergate and the Roots of Partisanship* (2018), and has a Ph.D. in history from the University of California (Berkeley).

David L. Leal PhD is Professor of Government and Mexican American Studies at the University of Texas at Austin. He is also an Associate Member of Nuffield College at the University of Oxford and a Senior Fellow of the Hoover Institution at Stanford University. His research interests include the political implications of demographic change in the United States, and he has published dozens of academic journal articles and edited nine books on these and other topics. He has taught classes on Immigration Politics, Latino Politics, Politics and Religion, Mexican American Public Policy Studies, and Introduction to American Government. In the spring of 2019, he taught British Politics and Government, which had the good fortune (if that is the right word) of taking place parallel with so many Brexit developments. He is also the author of three articles in *The Baker Street Journal* as well as letters to the editor of the *TLS: The Times Literary Supplement, Sherlock Holmes Journal*, and *The Baker Street Journal*. As a member of the British Studies Program at UT-Austin, he has given several talks on Sherlockian and Wodehousian topics. He most recently wrote a chapter, "Arthur Conan Doyle and Spiritualism," for the program's latest book in its *Adventures with Britannia* series (Harry Ransom Center/IB Tauris/Bloomsbury). He is the founder and Warden of "MA, PhD, Etc," the BSI professional scion society for higher education, and he is a member of *The Fourth Garrideb, The Sherlock Holmes Society of London, The Clients of Adrian Mulliner*, and *His Last Bow (Tie)*.

Michael Mallory is the Derringer-winning author of the "Amelia Watson" (The Second Mrs. Watson) series and "Dave Beauchamp" mystery series, and more than one-hundred-twenty-five short stories. An entertainment journalist by day, he has written eight nonfiction books on pop culture and more than six-hundred newspaper and magazine articles. Based in Los Angeles, Mike is also an occasional actor on television.

David Marcum – *In addition to a story in this volume, David also has stories in Parts XX and XXI*

Steve Mason has been the Third Mate (President) of *The Crew of the Barque* Lone Star scion society in Dallas/Fort Worth for over seven years. He is also the Chair of the Communications Committee for *The Beacon Society*, a national educational scion society. With Joe Fay and Rusty Mason, he produces the *Baker Street Elementary* comic strip each week, the first adventures of Sherlock Holmes and John Watson.

Jacquelynn Morris, ASH, BSI, JHWS, is a member of several Sherlock Holmes societies in the Mid-Atlantic area of the U.S.A., but her home group is Watson's Tin Box in Maryland. She is the founder of *A Scintillation of Scions*, an annual Sherlock Holmes symposium. She has been published in the BSI Manuscript Series, *The Wrong Passage*, as well as in *About Sixty* and *About Being a Sherlockian* (Wildside Press). Jacquelynn was the U.S. liaison for the Undershaw Preservation Trust for several years, until Undershaw was purchased to become part of Stepping Stones School.

Mark Mower is a member of the *Crime Writers' Association*, *The Sherlock Holmes Society of London*, and *The Solar Pons Society of London*. He writes true crime stories and fictional mysteries. His first two volumes of Holmes pastiches were entitled *A Farewell to Baker Street* and *Sherlock Holmes: The Baker Street Case-Files* (both with MX Publishing) and, to date, he has contributed chapters to six parts of the ongoing *The MX Book of New Sherlock Holmes Stories*. He has also had stories in two anthologies by Belanger Books: *Holmes Away From Home: Adventures from the Great Hiatus – Volume II – 1893-1894* (2016) and *Sherlock Holmes: Before Baker Street* (2017). More are bound to follow. Mark's non-fiction works include *Bloody British History: Norwich* (The History Press, 2014), *Suffolk Murders* (The History Press, 2011) and *Zeppelin Over Suffolk* (Pen & Sword Books, 2008).

Will Murray – *In addition to a story in this volume, Will also has a story in Part XX*

Robert Perret is a writer, librarian, and devout Sherlockian living on the Palouse. His Sherlockian publications include "The Canaries of Clee Hills Mine" in *An Improbable Truth: The Paranormal Adventures of Sherlock Holmes*, "For King and Country" in *The Science of Deduction*, and "How Hope Learned the Trick" in *NonBinary Review*. He considers himself to be a pan-Sherlockian and a one-man Scion out on the lonely moors of Idaho. Robert has recently authored a yet-unpublished scholarly article tentatively entitled "A Study in Scholarship: The Case of the *Baker Street Journal*'. His is the author of *Dead ringers: Sherlock Holmes Stories* (2019). More information is available at *www.robertperret.com*

Gayle Lange Puhl has been a Sherlockian since Christmas of 1965. She has had articles published in *The Devon County Chronicle*, *The Baker Street Journal*, and *The Serpentine Muse*, plus her local newspaper. She has created Sherlockian jewelry, a 2006 calendar entitled "If Watson Wrote For TV", and has painted a limited series of Holmes-related nesting dolls. She co-founded the scion *Friends of the Great Grimpen Mire* and the Janesville, Wisconsin-based *The Original Tree Worshipers*. In January 2016, she was awarded the "Outstanding Creative Writer" award by the Janesville Art Alliance for her first book *Sherlock Holmes and the Folk Tale Mysteries*. She is semi-retired and lives in Evansville, Wisconsin. Ms. Puhl has one daughter, Gayla, and four grandchildren.

Richard K. Radek, the author of *The Sequestered Adventures of Sherlock Holmes* series, is a native of Evanston, Illinois (USA), and a graduate of Northern Illinois University. He is a prominent arbitrator, certified educator, and author of many legal articles and awards. A long time student of The Canon, Mr. Radek writes traditional, period-authentic Holmes adventures, faithful to the style and chronology of the original Doyle tales. One hallmark of his work is the accuracy of the historical detail Mr. Radek instills in the plots, persona, and settings of his Holmes stories. Another is the wit and wry humor woven in and interspersed. The result is a body of work that can be appreciated by the entire spectrum of Holmes aficionados, from the novice only just learning about Sherlock who wants an entertaining story, to the most discriminating experts who can appreciate the many, sometimes subtle, Holmesian insights Mr. Radek hides in the stories. In the main, Mr. Radek's tales are great fun to read.

Tracy J. Revels, a Sherlockian from the age of eleven, is a professor of history at Wofford College in Spartanburg, South Carolina. She is a member of *The Survivors of the Gloria Scott* and *The Studious Scarlets Society*, and is a past recipient of the Beacon Society Award. Almost every semester, she teaches a class that covers The Canon, either to college students or to senior citizens. She is also the author of three supernatural Sherlockian pastiches with MX (*Shadowfall*, *Shadowblood*, and *Shadowwraith*), and a regular contributor to her scion's newsletter. She also has some notoriety as an author of very silly skits: For proof, see "The Adventure of the Adversarial Adventuress" and "Occupy Baker Street" on YouTube. When not studying Sherlock, she can be found researching the history of her native state, and has written books on Florida in the Civil War and on the development of Florida's tourism industry.

Jane Rubino is the author of A Jersey Shore mystery series, featuring a Jane Austen-loving amateur sleuth and a Sherlock Holmes-quoting detective, *Knight Errant*, *Lady Vernon and Her Daughter*, (a novel-length adaptation of Jane Austen's novella *Lady Susan*, co-authored with her daughter Caitlen Rubino-Bradway, *What Would Austen Do?*, also co-authored with her daughter, a short story in the anthology *Jane Austen Made Me Do It*, *The Rucastles' Pawn, The Copper Beeches from Violet Turner's POV*, and, of course, there's the Sherlockian novel in the drawer – who doesn't have one? Jane lives on a barrier island at the New Jersey shore.

Geri Schear is a novelist and short story writer. Her work has been published in literary journals in the U.S. and Ireland. Her first novel, *A Biased Judgement: The Diaries of Sherlock Holmes 1897* was released to critical acclaim in 2014. The sequel, *Sherlock Holmes and the Other Woman* was published in 2015, and *Return to Reichenbach* in 2016. She lives in Kells, Ireland.

Joseph W. Svec III is retired from Oceanography, Satellite Test Engineering, and college teaching. He has lived on a forty-foot cruising sailboat, on a ranch in the Sierra Nevada Foothills, in a country rose-garden cottage, and currently lives in the shadow of a castle with his childhood sweetheart and several long coated German shepherds. He enjoys writing, gardening, creating dioramas, world travel, and enjoying time with his sweetheart.

Kevin P, Thornton – *In addition to a story in this volume, Kevin also has a story in Part XX*

Christopher Todd has been a nurse for four decades, was a radio production director and copywriter for twenty years, and has been an ordained Episcopal priest for eighteen years, as well as an interim Lutheran pastor and jail chaplain for eight years. He has been a Sherlockian since he was twelve, was a member of *The Noble Bachelors of St. Louis*, has been published in *The Baker Street Journal* and cited three times in *The World Bibliography of Sherlock Holmes and Dr. Watson*. His numerous careers and widespread interests color his blog at *preacherofthenight.blogspot.com*. He lives in the Florida Keys with his wife and is indoctrinating his grandkids in his faith and in Sherlock Holmes, possibly in that order.

D.J. Tyrer is the person behind Atlantean Publishing, was placed second in the Writing Magazine "Local Reporter" competition, and has been widely published in anthologies and magazines around the world, such as *Disturbance* (Laurel Highlands), *Mysteries of Suspense* (Zimbell House), *History and Mystery, Oh My!* (Mystery & Horror LLC), and *Love 'Em, Shoot 'Em* (Wolfsinger), and issues of *Awesome Tales*, and in addition, has a novella available in paperback and on the Kindle, *The Yellow House* (Dunhams Manor) and a comic horror e-novelette, *A Trip to the Middle of the World*, available from Alban Lake through Infinite Realms Bookstore.
His website is: *https://djtyrer.blogspot.co.uk/*
The Atlantean Publishing website is at *https://atlanteanpublishing.wordpress.com/*

Charles Veley has loved Sherlock Holmes since boyhood. As a father, he read the entire Canon to his then-ten-year-old daughter at evening story time. Now, this very same daughter, grown up to become acclaimed historical novelist Anna Elliott, has worked with him to develop new adventures in the *Sherlock Holmes and Lucy James Mystery Series*. Charles is also a fan of Gilbert & Sullivan, and wrote *The Pirates of Finance*, a new musical in the G&S tradition that won an award at the New York Musical Theatre Festival in 2013. Other than the Sherlock and Lucy series, all of the books on his Amazon Author Page were written when he was a full-time author during the late Seventies and early Eighties. He currently works for United Technologies Corporation, where his main focus is on creating sustainability and value for the company's large real estate development projects.

Peter Coe Verbica – *In addition to a story in this volume, Peter also has a story in Part XXI*

I.A. Watson is a novelist and jobbing writer from Yorkshire who cut his teeth on writing Sherlock Holmes stories and has even won an award for one. His works include *Holmes and Houdini*, *Labours of Hercules*, *St. George and the Dragon* Volumes 1 and 2, and *Women of Myth*, and the non-fiction essay book *Where Stories Dwell*. He pens short detective stories as a means of avoiding writing things that pay better. A full list of his sixty-plus published works appears at:
http://www.chillwater.org.uk/writing/iawatsonhome.htm

The MX Book of New Sherlock Holmes Stories
Edited by David Marcum
(MX Publishing, 2015-   )

"This is the finest volume of Sherlockian fiction I have ever read, and I have read, literally, thousands." – Philip K. Jones

"Beyond Impressive . . . This is a splendid venture for a great cause!
– Roger Johnson, Editor, *The Sherlock Holmes Journal,*
The Sherlock Holmes Society of London

Part I: 1881-1889
Part II: 1890-1895
Part III: 1896-1929
Part IV: 2016 Annual
Part V: Christmas Adventures
Part VI: 2017 Annual
Part VII: Eliminate the Impossible (1880-1891)
Part VIII – Eliminate the Impossible (1892-1905)
Part IX – 2018 Annual (1879-1895)
Part X – 2018 Annual (1896-1916)
Part XI – Some Untold Cases (1880-1891)
Part XII – Some Untold Cases (1894-1902)
Part XIII – 2019 Annual (1881-1890)
Part XIV – 2019 Annual (1891-1897)
Part XV – 2019 Annual (1898-1917)
Part XVI – Whatever Remains . . . Must be the Truth (1881-1890)
Part XVII – Whatever Remains . . . Must be the Truth (1891-1898)
Part XVIII – Whatever Remains . . . Must be the Truth (1898-1925)
Part XIX – 2020 Annual (1882-1890)
Part XX – 2020 Annual (1891-1897)
Part XXI – 2020 Annual (1898-1923)

In Preparation
Part XXII – Some More Untold Cases

. . . and more to come!

The MX Book of New Sherlock Holmes Stories
Edited by David Marcum
(MX Publishing, 2015-   )

Publishers Weekly says:

Part VI: *The traditional pastiche is alive and well . . . .*

Part VII: *Sherlockians eager for faithful-to-the-canon plots and characters will be delighted.*

Part VIII: *The imagination of the contributors in coming up with variations on the volume's theme is matched by their ingenious resolutions.*

Part IX: *The 18 stories . . . will satisfy fans of Conan Doyle's originals. Sherlockians will rejoice that more volumes are on the way.*

Part X: *. . . new Sherlock Holmes adventures of consistently high quality.*

Part XI: *. . . an essential volume for Sherlock Holmes fans.*

Part XII: *. . . continues to amaze with the number of high-quality pastiches . . .*

Part XIII: *. . . Amazingly, Marcum has found 22 superb pastiches . . . This is more catnip for fans of stories faithful to Conan Doyle's original*

Part XIV: *. . . this standout anthology of 21 short stories written in the spirit of Conan Doyle's originals.*

Part XV: *Stories pitting Sherlock Holmes against seemingly supernatural phenomena highlight Marcum's 15th anthology of superior short pastiches.*

Part XVI: *Marcum has once again done fans of Conan Doyle's originals a service.*

Part XVII: *This is yet another impressive array of new but traditional Holmes stories.*

Part XVIII: *Sherlockians will again be grateful to Marcum and MX for high-quality new Holmes tales.*

The MX Book of New Sherlock Holmes Stories

Edited by David Marcum

(MX Publishing, 2015-)

MX Publishing is the world's largest specialist Sherlock Holmes publisher, with several hundred titles and over a hundred authors creating the latest in Sherlock Holmes fiction and non-fiction.

From traditional short stories and novels to travel guides and quiz books, MX Publishing caters to all Holmes fans.

The collection includes leading titles such as *Benedict Cumberbatch In Transition* and *The Norwood Author*, which won the 2011 *Tony Howlett Award* (Sherlock Holmes Book of the Year).

MX Publishing also has one of the largest communities of Holmes fans on *Facebook*, with regular contributions from dozens of authors.

www.mxpublishing.co.uk (UK) and *www.mxpublishing.com* (USA)

Lightning Source UK Ltd.
Milton Keynes UK
UKHW011431290520
364087UK00001B/3